EX LIBRIS

HINC IN ALTIORA

THE HALL
HAMPSTEAD

Pennington

K M PEYTON

Pennington
A Trilogy

CONTAINING

Pennington's Seventeenth Summer
The Beethoven Medal
Pennington's Heir

OXFORD UNIVERSITY PRESS
Oxford London Melbourne

Oxford University Press, Walton Street, Oxford OX2 6DP

Oxford London
New York Toronto Melbourne Auckland
Kuala Lumpur Singapore Hong Kong Tokyo
Delhi Bombay Calcutta Madras Karachi
Nairobi Dar es Salaam Cape Town
and associated companies in
Beirut Berlin Ibadan Mexico City Nicosia
Oxford is a trade mark of Oxford University Press

Pennington's Seventeenth Summer first published 1970
The Beethoven Medal first published 1971
Pennington's Heir first published 1973
The edition first published in one volume 1985

British Library Cataloguing in Publication Data
Peyton, K.M.
Pennington: a trilogy.
I. Title
823'.914[J]   PZ7

ISBN 0-19-271492-9

Printed and bound in Great Britain by
Biddles Ltd, Guildford and King's Lynn

Pennington's Seventeenth Summer

Chapter 1

Penn read slowly down his report. Apart from games— 'Excellent'—the remarks were the usual, brief and unenthusiastic: 'Poor', 'Fair', 'Could do better'. Under Mathematics it said, 'Idle and destructive in class, in spite of innate ability', and under the heading 'Extras: Music' a crabbed hand had written angrily, 'May God forgive this boy for abusing so unusual a talent.' Penn pondered this remark, scowling. Then he yawned, and passed the document to his friend, Bates.

Bates read it and said, 'Only Dotty Crocker makes any effort at all. He gave you a good one last term. How did it go?'

' "This boy plays the piano as befits the captain of the first eleven." '

'Yes. That was good.'

'A plus,' Penn agreed.

'What's Soggy said?'

Penn turned the report over to 'Character and Obedience'.

' "Unsatisfactory in the extreme. It is imperative that Pennington cultivates a sense of responsibility in keeping with his position in the school",' he read.

'Old enough to have more sense,' Bates translated.

'Old enough to leave,' Penn said heavily.

He certainly looked old enough to leave, a fourteen-stone hulk of a boy, with shoulders on him like an all-in wrestler, and long reddish-brown hair curling over his collar. He would, in fact, have left the year before if he had had his way, but his mother had browbeaten all the formidable male opposition— Penn himself, his father, and almost all the staff at the Beehive Secondary Modern—into subjection. She hadn't been educated herself and she wanted her boy educated, and if the inefficient

1

bunch at the Beehive that called themselves teachers couldn't achieve it in the fifteen years prescribed by law she was quite prepared to give them another year. All the very sincere protestations by the Beehive staff that another year wouldn't make any significant difference in the level of Penn's attainment, because the boy himself did not choose to be educated, had not persuaded her to change her mind. Only the games master had shown any joy, Penn's presence at the Beehive being the prime reason why the school held the county shields for both soccer and swimming. The eccentric music master, Mr. Crocker, had kept his thoughts to himself: they were complicated thoughts of despair and frustration, lifted on occasion by moments of acute joy when Pennington chose to show what he was capable of. Mr. Crocker was not prepared to discuss with anyone how Pennington caused him to suffer. All the rest of the staff would discuss the fact only too readily.

'Another year of him!' Even the headmaster, a cautious man, uttered the heresy. 'The only subject he has anything to show for in the way of attainment is music. Oh, and I believe he scraped a pass in R.K. A strange pair of passes,' he added cryptically to Penn's form master, Marsh, 'for a boy who, let's face it, is essentially a thug.'

'I've been facing it for two years now,' said Mr. Marsh. And Penn was committed for another year. ('Committed' was his own word.)

On the back seat of the bus Penn's arch-enemy, Smeeton, was lighting his report with the cigarette he was smoking. He held it up, flaming, to the admiration of all around him. Even Penn, against his will, was impressed.

'Ruddy show-off,' he said to Bates.

'He wrote a letter to his mother, two years ago, saying that reports had been abolished, and put Stacker's signature on it,' Bates said.

'Oh, he's bright,' Penn said disparagingly. Penn had broken into a sweet shop with Smeeton two years previously and stolen four Easter eggs and ten cigarettes, and he had been put on probation; no one had known about Smeeton. Penn had never forgiven Smeeton for this superior crooksmanship. Smeeton was slight, sharp-witted, greasy, and mean.

As the bus lurched into the village they piled down the stairs, Penn managing nicely to thump Smeeton off balance so that he landed heavily on top of the conductor, who swore at him very satisfactorily. The shopping women glared and said, 'It's time someone taught you yobs some manners!' They always said that. They complained to Stacker about the boys' behaviour, and their hair, and their swearing, and Stacker was very charming to them, and gave them a cup of tea, and said he'd give the boys something to remember, but when the door had closed behind the women he just went back to what he was doing before they interrupted him.

'You coming down to the boat tonight?' Penn asked Bates, before they parted. He raised his voice so that Smeeton would hear him.

'Yep. If you're going.'

'I'm going.'

'Okay. See you.'

'Funny thing,' Smeeton said to Penn. 'Gerry and I thought of taking the boat out tonight. His brother'll most likely come, too.'

'Amazing!' said Penn.

Satisfied by the reaction, he turned on his heel and walked home. The evening showed promise, in that short exchange. The prospect of mashing Smeeton was never less than entrancing. Penn's physical superiority was a source of constant satisfaction, for Smeeton had to collect at least three friends before he would risk a fight with Penn, and Smeeton did not come by friends easily. Penn grinned to himself, turning in at the gate of his house. The boat, an ancient fishing-smack rotting quietly away by itself on the river, provided perennial fight potential, both boys claiming ownership. Its former owner, in a confused dotage, had promised it to both boys when he died. At the time of the promise Penn and Smeeton had been on amicable terms, but the old boy had taken a long time in dying. The two boys could easily have shared ownership if they wished, neither of them particularly wanting to use it until he knew the other did, but it was a useful source of grievance, a convenient excuse for argument. Anything, Penn thought, to relieve the boredom.

Going in the back door, he remembered his report, and the gloom settled again. He dropped the battered kitbag containing

3

his filthy soccer gear, running shoes, smelly socks and two blood-stained handkerchiefs on the floor, and made for the television set.

'Your tea's ready.' His mother waylaid him before he got out of the kitchen. 'Sit down with your father. I'm not going to stand at the cooker all night. That blazer'll have to go to the cleaner's this holidays. I don't know what you do with your clothes half the time.'

'I just wear them.'

'You got something fixed up for the holidays?' his father asked. He was sitting at the kitchen table, mopping up the remains of his dinner with a slice of bread. He had just got up, being on nights for the next three months. Penn had forgotten about the switch-round, and glowered at his father.

'There's no jobs going round here.'

'Not if you haven't asked, I dare say,' his father said sarcastically. 'What's wrong with the chicken factory?'

'I'll find something.'

'Pick this rubbish up,' his mother said. 'You got a report, or are you hiding it?'

'No.' Penn pulled the crumpled letter out of his pocket and dropped it on the table, slumping into his place opposite his father. 'It's nothing to get excited about.'

'That'll be the day,' said his father.

But Penn knew that his father boasted about his playing centre-half for the county schools eleven, and preferred this prowess to high scores for English literature. It was not the 'poors' and 'fairs' that were going to get him into trouble, but old Dotty Crocker's broadside.

His mother put his dinner down, poured herself a cup of tea, and opened up the document. She read down it, frowning.

Penn watched her, apprehensive. His mother was Irish, with an Irish temper, a flinty, unlovable mother. She worked in a trousers factory in Northend and spent most of her wages in the betting-shop. She was voluble, argumentative, and unpredictable, treating Penn according to her mood with indulgence, indifference, or gross injustice, so that in sixteen years he had never known where he stood with her. His father was easier to understand, although no easier to live with, settling all arguments by means of a good thumping. Penn's own predisposition to settle arguments by the same means was merely imitative, not a psychological Freudian aggression to be treated by the Child Guidance Clinic, as some of the more nervous pedagogues at the Beehive suggested. 'Pennington is only what his parents have made him,' suggested Mr. Crocker, but nobody listened to him, and Penn had to take the blame for his nature himself.

'What's this, of Mr. Crocker's?' his mother asked. 'What's he mean?'

Penn shrugged, shovelling in food.

'What's he mean? "Abusing—"? I never can understand this man.'

'I was in the bog playing my harmonica, and he heard me and waited, and when I came out he blasted off about if I spent as much time practising Bach and Co. as I did playing rubbish on a rubbishy instrument I'd be Paderewski or somebody by now. Well, that's what he meant. He didn't say it exactly.'

'Your hair's long enough,' said his father.

'We're paying good money for your lessons,' his mother said. 'They're not on the rates, like the rest of your education. You'll be sorry later on you wasted time monkeying about.'

The reaction was milder than Penn had expected. He heaved a sigh of relief and said, 'I'm going down the river.'

'You're practising first.'

'Afterwards.'

'Now. Let your dinner get down.'

Penn sighed, heavily. He pushed his plate back and wiped his mouth.

'You can see about a job, too,' his father said. 'Purvis might take you.'

'I've asked him.'

Penn escaped. He didn't want to tell his father what Purvis had said. The Easter eggs and the ten cigarettes had branded Penn, and people in the village still threw it up in his face, as if it was murder. Penn didn't care much, except when it was inconvenient, like losing him a job off old Purvis, who kept the boatyard. 'I can't afford to lose gear,' Purvis had said. Young Jim Purvis had said, 'Oh, come off it, Dad. Pat wouldn't touch anything here.' 'I'm not employing Patrick Pennington,' old Purvis had reiterated.

Penn went upstairs and changed into jeans and a denim shirt. He dropped his school clothes in a heap on the floor, combed his hair carefully, and examined the one or two spots on his face in the mirror. He put the harmonica that lay on the chest of drawers into his back pocket, and went downstairs to the front room, where the piano was.

'Mrs. Jones, here I come,' he muttered, and played a chord that shook everything in the room. Mrs. Jones lived next door, and had hammered on the wall so often that Penn thought she would soon be right through. He sat slumped, looking down at his hands, thinking about a job. The boatyard would have been all right. A bit of humping gear and slapping on the old paint. His hands were enormous, the nails broken and grimy, an old soccer scar across the knuckles. But from the wide, thick palms the fingers tapered, long and agile, altogether out of keeping with the rest of his bulk. These were the fingers that old Crocker drove and nagged at and kept flickering up and down the keys in obedience to knotty exercises devised by Czerny and Clementi, the fingers that lapsed, as soon as his back was turned, into the current number one on the charts, or Penn's personal jazz rendering of 'Down by the Riverside'.

'Extraordinary technical brilliance, yes,' said Mr. Marsh to Mr. Crocker. 'Intellect to give it meaning, no.'

'I know the boy is in the C stream,' Crocker said. 'But not because he's dim. He's by no means dim—'

'He's in the C stream because he's infernally lazy, lacks any kind of responsibility or self-discipline and is bloody-minded into the bargain,' said Marsh—whom the boys called Soggy.

'Given those parents, hardly to be wondered at,' Matthews, the games master, put in quietly.

6

'A born troublemaker,' Soggy said.

'Phenomenal hands,' Crocker said. 'Stretch a tenth without trying, strongest fingers I've ever come across. I never cease to wonder at such talent coming from such a background.'

'Well, how come?' queried Matthews. 'I thought pianists had to start at the age of three, or something?'

'But he did, that's the amazing thing. That ghastly mother of his, give her her due, started him on the piano—God knows why—I suppose she has some fiddling Irish ancestors back in the Sligo bog somewhere and considers herself musical—found he was a natural, and actually kept him at it. Got an old dragon of a church harmonium player to teach him. I looked this dragon up once, out of curiosity. She said he was a sweet little boy—get that, Marsh—but by the age of about ten he was getting out of hand fast, and she gave him up because he was—well, the Pennington we know, I suppose. I know how she felt, because I've given him up a dozen times myself. But it's a wicked waste, enough to make a man weep.'

'Pennington,' said Soggy finally, 'will never—I repeat, never —get any sympathy from me.'

Quite aware of, but indifferent to, the opinions of his teachers, parents, neighbours, and passing acquaintances, Penn played the piano when compelled to, but not otherwise. He now pursued a fluent but joyless path through the three movements of a Mozart sonata, a Chopin Polonaise, and a piece by Prokofiev, then started on a rave number, which set Mrs. Jones off with her poker. Glad of an excuse to give up, Penn ducked out through the kitchen, ignoring his mother's rebukes, framing silent, suitable words for her under his breath.

Once in the open, away from his natural enemies, he felt better. He tossed back his hair and started to whistle 'The Butcher Boy'. Good for old Smeeton, he thought, game for a bit of turbulence . . . although, with Smeeton, one was never sure there mightn't be a broken bottle or a bicycle chain. Not yet there hadn't, but Penn thought he might graduate before long. Penn dribbled a stone along the road, not altering course when a car hooted behind him. The road was a 'No Through Road' down to the river, and Penn reckoned he owned it. The car, a white Jaguar, edged him over, the driver glaring. Penn

thumped its back wing for good measure and thought of some
good adjectives for the driver.

'She went upstairs and the door he broke,
'He found her hanging from a rope,' he sang.

Penn's voice was nothing special, but he knew verse after
verse of the songs he sang, and the songs were neither in Mr.
Crocker's repertoire nor in the pop charts. It was Bates who had
the voice. Bates who could sing: 'Oh, dig my grave long, wide,
and deep', and wring your heart. Penn shot his stone straight
and true into the flank of one of Mr. Turner's heifers, regarding
him through the barbed wire, and had the satisfaction of seeing
it put up its tail and cavort away towards the sea-wall. Bates's
father was Mr. Turner's cowman. Bates had no trouble finding
a holiday job; he just worked on the farm. Bates's father
wouldn't have Penn. Penn didn't hold it against him.

He came down to Purvis's boatyard, climbed the sea-wall
and surveyed the river, and the marshes beyond. His smack, or
Smeeton's, was on a mooring in mid-stream, a sad, faded thing
with swinging halyards. Purvis said it would fall to bits under

them unless they did something to it, but they had no cash to spend on it, and nobody cared. It was rotten, but they only pottered on the river, when they could get its engine to go, or took it fishing up Fiddler's Creek. They had never taken it out to sea, save in calm weather. Penn had messed about on the river ever since he could remember. Old Purvis had taught him to sail years ago, and lent him a sailing dinghy which he had raced occasionally with Jim. He didn't rave about it, but it was quite a satisfactory way of passing time, and the old smack was a valuable hide-out. He and Bates used it quite often. They had a crate of beer in the forepeak, along with the fishing-lines. Penn looked at the old boat, *Mathilda*, with affection.

'You haven't been long,' Bates said, appearing at his elbow.

Penn grunted. They stood together, looking out over the water. The sun was still well above the wall and it was warm enough to send the gnats spiralling. 'Warm enough to swim,' Penn said. 'Warm enough for *you*,' Bates quali-
fied it. Bates couldn't swim, although he had
played on the river all his life.

They fetched Jim's old dinghy and rowed out
to *Mathilda*. It was Friday night, and some of the
yachtsmen were down, fitting out. Purvis's yard
boasted a line of yachts on moorings, very
smart beside *Mathilda*. The man in the Jaguar
was carrying an inflatable down the hard.
Penn's eyes narrowed as he watched him.

'Think they own the place, some of these
yachty blokes.'

Bates went below and stretched himself out
on one of the bunks in the dark, cramped saloon.
Penn followed him down, his bulk blotting out
the light. Penn slouched along most of the time,
looking shapeless and slack, but when he moved
into action he was remarkably light on his feet.
What looked like fat, when he was in his
normal indolent posture, hands in pockets,
shoulders rounded, was, in fact, all muscle.
Beside him, Bates was a weedy specimen, a self-
effacing, spotty-faced henchman. They were
called Laurel and Hardy at school, out of

9

Penn's hearing. Nobody knew what Penn saw in Bates.

Bates opened two cans of beer out of the cardboard box on the floor, and Penn hunched himself on the other bunk, elbows on knees, and started to play his harmonica.

'Keep an eye out for Smeeton,' he said, and played, very softly, 'Blowing in the Wind'.

'That old crap,' Bates groaned.

Penn knew that Bates needed the beer before he would mellow, the whole pint before he would sing, and two pints before he started singing well. Penn didn't mind the time lag, running through the tunes that came to mind, and trying out some train noises that might fit in with Bates's 'Freight Train'. All the songs Bates sang had to do with death. He only sang of executions, drownings, heartbreak, and suicide. The happier he got in his singing, the more melancholy were the things he sang about, so that when he sang 'Take me to the graveyard and lay the sod o'er me', Penn knew that he was really away. After that he would sing 'The Butcher Boy'.

'That sound like a train?'

'Ten-thirty out of Liverpool Street,' Bates said.

Penn, searching with his tongue for the American coyote call of the legendary prairie train, would have cursed him if he could. He snored into the harmonica, trying to find the right evocative rhythm, making it throb through the opening and closing of his hands.

'Sounds like the sea,' Bates said.

Penn listened to it, switching his mind from trains.

'Like under a groyne or something,' Bates said.

Penn tried it softer, lower down, less urgently. He saw what Bates meant.

'What could we use it for? Who gets drowned in your repertoire?'

Bates sat up suddenly. 'Smeeton,' he said.

Penn grinned. 'I wish he did.' He flung the harmonica down and looked out of the hatch.

'Yeah. Smeeton and Co. They've got Gerry's dinghy.'

Bates lay back on the bunk again. 'I'm not fighting,' he said.

Penn went up on deck. A low sun flooded the river with a golden evening light, and gilded the undersides of a drifting cumulus with a generosity that turned the prosaic river scene into a page out of a 'Beautiful Britain' calendar. In the cockpit of a shapely yawl on the next mooring, the London yachtsman, joined by a friend, admired the scene, a glass of gin in his hand, the red glow of a cigarette pricking his lips. Penn leaned against *Mathilda*'s shrouds, squinting into the brightness, working out a plan of campaign, his face eager and excited. Smeeton was rowing out from the hard, his friends trimming the small dinghy rather anxiously. The tide was running hard, and Smeeton was having difficulty keeping the dinghy up against it.

'I say, Bates! Come and watch this! What did you say about drowning Smeeton?'

Bates put his head out and found Penn stripping off his clothes, capering about on one foot with the other stuck in his jeans.

'I didn't say anything,' Bates said.

'I'm going to sink him.'

Bates smiled. 'Watch he doesn't lay you under with an oar.' He folded his arms on the hatch, impressed with Penn's idea.

'I don't want to get mashed,' Penn said. 'I can't hold off four.'

Stripped down to resplendent red underpants, he cupped his hands to his mouth and bellowed, 'Smeeton, you basket! Start praying *now*!'

Bates laughed. Penn did a racing dive off the stern of the smack and struck out for the plodding dinghy with his powerful splashy stroke. Bates, coming up on deck to get a good view, sensed immediate paralysis strike the dinghy as the significance of Penn's move sunk in. Smeeton stopped rowing, drawing in his oars, and the dinghy started to move off sideways on the tide. It was well out from the bank and Penn was moving too fast to make retreat a likely possibility, but Smeeton, recovering from his first shock, had the sense to start rowing again with the tide, straight down the river, to make as much speed as possible. Penn, seeing his manoeuvre, quickened his pace, and started to overhaul the dinghy.

Smeeton stopped rowing.

'Stow it, Pennington, you lousy creep!'

'Warm as toast!' Penn shouted. 'You'll love it!'

Smeeton pulled in one oar and lifted the other out of its rowlock. He had to move very carefully, for there was only about six inches of freeboard on the dinghy. His friends, two in the stern and one in the bows, sat tensely, muttering advice. The dinghy was now opposite the yawl, *Escape*, and the two men in the cockpit were watching the drama as closely as Bates.

Penn knew that Smeeton was a sitting duck. He flung back his hair and laughed. He swam in close, watching Smeeton carefully. Smeeton lifted up his oar, but Penn, fractionally out of range, rolled under the water and disappeared.

'Sit still!' Smeeton hissed. He waved the oar, narrowly missing the head of the boy in the stern who was watching the trail of bubbles that ran on the tide. The dinghy drifted, serene as a swan, crabwise on the water. All four boys gripped the gunwales, eyes flicking the water.

'*Yaaaaah!*' Penn surfaced so close and with such energy that Smeeton thought he had come on board. He was the opposite side from where they had all been expecting him. Everyone in the dinghy swung round. Smeeton lashed out with his oar, dropped it in his eagerness and lunged forward to retrieve it. The dinghy dropped one corner of its transom under, and immediately the water poured in all over one side. Smeeton stood and leapt, instantly, straight for Pennington's grinning face. They submerged together, Smeeton's epithets dissolved in another flurry of bubbles. Penn, the water roaring in his ears, was enjoying himself. He knew Smeeton did not fight fair, and was not prepared to give him a chance, either under water or on top. When he eventually came up for breath, he had his hand firmly on Smeeton's face, holding it under.

'I say!' The shout, in cultured accents, rasped across the water. 'I say, you boys!'

The two yachtsmen had launched their rubber dinghy and were rowing out. Penn, feeling Smeeton failing beneath him, took his hand off his face and pulled him up by his hair.

'You lousy—stinking—' Smeeton was almost sobbing with rage.

'Leave that poor boy alone, you young hooligan!'

Penn, submerging Smeeton once more, looked up into the face of *Escape*'s skipper. He saw a little military moustache fairly bristling with military rage, outraged eyes like glass chips.

'You young thug! I'll get the police to you!'

Penn swam free of Smeeton, leaving him to his own devices,

and turned and faced the yachtsmen in their smart white caps. He flung his hair back, deliberately, so that it sent a shower of water across the frosty expressions. He then started to swim towards them, submerging after two strokes. The glass chips glazed momentarily.

Penn swam underneath the rubber dinghy, his back rubbing the bulges that were the two yachtsmen's seats. He rolled over and rocked the dinghy, quite gently, feeling its smooth surface against him like some friendly whale. He felt the bulges betray alarm in a most satisfactory manner. He laughed, belching up a roaring froth of air. He rocked the dinghy until his breath ran out, then he kicked away and swam out, making for *Mathilda* without looking back.

The new constable rode down to Purvis's yard at dusk, conscientiously familiarizing himself with his area. He was very keen, and liked to think he was working hard, but in fact it was pleasant enough, chatting up the locals, seeing the caution in their eyes. A big Jaguar was parked on the edge of the lane, which he noted. He got off his bike and pushed it up the gravel incline to the top of the sea-wall, where he stood silhouetted, an unmistakable figure of authority.

Purvis, locking up his shed for the night, said to Jim, 'Here's trouble.'

He shifted the cap on his forehead, and put the key in his pocket.

'Evening, constable,' he said.

'Lovely spot,' said the constable matily.

'So they say.'

'I'm new to this area. Mitchell's my name. Just having a look round, getting to know what's where, so to speak.'

'You're instead of P.C. Perkins, then? Helping Sergeant West, like?'

'That's right.'

'I'm Purvis. Run the yard here. This is my son, Jim.'

They stood in a row, looking out over the darkening water. The wind was light and the water was quiet, near the end of the ebb, so that banks of glistening mud lay uncovered, plopping and trickling here and there, the occasional curlew twittering uneasily. From the big white yawl lights glowed through the ports, very cosy. The glow from *Mathilda* was subdued by comparison, a faint flush in the open hatchway. But a sound came with it, very plaintive and soft on the damp spring air, a voice singing, accompanied by a reedy descant on the harmonica, full of sorrow and longing. The three men could not help but listen, the lament coming and going with the breathing of the wind, laced with the curlew's flitterings, and the water running through the outfalls from Mr. Turner's pasture. The last note was held, very pure and free, clearly carried by the wind. There was a silence of a few seconds, then a raucous laugh and the sound of an empty tin being flung overboard, some thumping and cursing, and a few bars of 'Nellie Dean', sung very coarsely.

Jim Purvis cleared his throat. 'You coming, Dad?'

'Aye.'

'You lose any gear, a place like this . . . valuable stuff lying around?' the constable asked.

'We've lost a couple of echo-sounders, the odd pair of oars and suchlike. Nothing big, as yet.'

Jim fidgeted with the money in his pocket. There was a silence again, and into it the sound of oars plugging into the ebb. The constable peered down the causeway.

'That'll be Major Harmsworth, off the yawl,' Purvis told him. 'He'll be going up to the Crown for the evening.'

'That his Jag?'

'That's right. He's from London.'

They waited until the Major and his friend came up the hard. The Major had a reefer jacket on and gum boots with white edges.

'Evening, Purvis,' he said.

'Evening, sir.'

The Major looked at the constable and said, 'You should have been here a bit earlier. Who's the lout on the smack, Purvis—got hair like a girl?'

'That'll be young Pennington, sir. Lives in the village.'

'He's a danger to the community, the way he carries on. Ought to be locked up. He sank a dinghy with four young lads aboard, just now. Might have drowned the lot of them. He damned nearly sank us, too.'

Jim grinned, turning away, but old Purvis said, 'Really, sir?' his expression not changing.

14

'You heard of him?' the Major asked the constable.

'I'm brand-new around here, sir. Just been telling Mr. Purvis here, I'm making acquaintance of my area.'

'Well, you keep an eye on him. It'll pay you.'

'Sergeant West knows all about him,' Purvis said.

'He's got a record, no doubt?' barked the Major.

Purvis did not reply. 'You locked the other shed?' he asked Jim. Jim nodded. 'We'll be getting along now, then. Good night, sir. Good night, Mr. Mitchell.'

They all went their separate ways, by bicycle and by Jaguar. The river settled into silence again, until the tide turned, and the boats on the moorings started to swing, snubbing gently on their chains. The harmonica wailed, its natural stridency gentled by pure skill into a strange, plaintive beauty. With it Bates's voice came once more, its hesitancy forgotten, mellifluous with beer and confidence, spilling into the night.

Long after Major Harmsworth and his friend had returned to their boat and gone to sleep, Penn and Bates rowed ashore and pulled Jim's boat up above the watermark. They moved rather unsteadily, and laughed a good deal, lapsing into, 'I say, I say, boy! Look what you're doing!' at every blunder. Bates stood on top of the sea-wall, swaying slightly.

'What you going to do when you leave, Penn?' he said.

'Leave where?'

'School, you fool.'

'I'm going to enjoy myself.'

'No. Really.'

'Oh, don't make me miserable! What a subject!'

'I want to sing,' said Bates, earnestly. 'Sing properly, on the telly.'

'It'll cost you a fortune in beer,' Penn said. He was standing beside Bates, contemplating the gleaming Jaguar below him.

'I mean it, though.'

'You! You don't open your beak except on the boat where you think no one can hear you! Why didn't you sing in the school concert when you were asked? You, on the *telly*—' His voice grated with scorn.

Bates was silent.

'I'll tell you what,' Penn said. He slithered down the wall on to the grass and stood beside the Jaguar. 'What I feel like, I mean. What would give me the greatest pleasure in the whole wide world—'

'What, Penn?'

Bates staggered down the wall. He saw Penn stoop down beside the Jaguar's back wheel, and heard the explosive hiss of air escaping from the valve. The Jaguar sank gradually to an askew angle, looking rather quaint. Penn went round and treated the opposite wheel in the same fashion and then to the front. The Jaguar squatted, pathetic in the thin starlight.

Bates giggled.

'I say, I say, boy, you shouldn't have done that!' He kept repeating it all the way home.

Chapter 2

'Pat! For heaven's sake!'

Penn was awoken by his mother shaking him violently by the shoulder.

'What you been up to? Jim Purvis is at the door, and says his father wants to see you, no messing. He's raving, he says.'

'Let him rave,' Penn grunted.

'Get out, you lazy oaf. It's gone eight.' She threw back the blankets and stared in exasperation at the great bare shoulders hunched against her. 'God, Pat, your hair! When you going to the barber's, for heaven's sake? Get out now, and come down and see what Jim wants. It's no joke from the look of him.'

'Oh, lay off!' Penn muttered.

'Come on! I know trouble when I see it. You won't get a second chance. I've told you before. You put a finger wrong again and they'll have you in one of those places where you do everything at the double. And good luck to you, I say. You won't be able to lie in bed—'

'For cripes' sake!' Penn surfaced into reality, baited into consciousness. He heaved himself from the bed, thudding on to the floor. 'Stop laying into me, this time o' the morning! I've got to sleep, haven't I? A growing boy—we get it at school. They *tell* us we've got to get eight hours, and here's you—'

'Growing! You grow any more and you can go in a circus for a freak! Pity your brain isn't a match for your brawn! If I hadn't had my own way you'd have been out of that school on your ear by now, and working for your living! You've got me to thank—'

'Thank!' Penn sat on the side of the bed, feeling himself shake with desolation and nausea. 'Cripes, I've got nothing to

17

thank you for! If I was working for a living I could leave home
—I might get some peace.'

'That's a fine way to show your gratitude!'

'Gratitude! For God's sake, you only had me because you
weren't blooming clever enough—what have I got to be grateful
for?'

Penn swore at his mother. When she started laying into him
he felt he would like to strangle her. When she was in one of her
raves, which was often.

'Get out!' he said. 'I want to get dressed. I thought you
wanted me to hurry or something.'

The door slammed. Penn groaned. He started to dress, trying
to dredge up out of the blankness in his head the thing that was
making Purvis rage. He remembered Smeeton. He wasn't in
trouble over that, surely? He thudded downstairs, combing his
hair as he went.

'What's up, Jim?'

Jim was in the kitchen, looking agitated, for him. Jim was a
slow-moving, imperturbable young man of few words, but
today he was crisp.

'You'd better come, Pat. It's no good thinking you can get
away with it. Dad sent me to fetch you.'

Penn shrugged.

'I'll just have my breakfast and—'

'He said at once.'

Penn shrugged again. His father wasn't home yet, luckily.
He got his jacket and fetched his bicycle out of the shed. Old
Purvis's rage seemed to have rubbed off on Jim, for Jim was
cold and short. They cycled down the lane in silence, while
Penn searched back in his mind to the evening before. Apart
from the highly satisfying Smeeton episode, one other thing had
given him great comfort. For some minutes he couldn't remember what it was. Then when they came to the part of the lane
where the car had overtaken him the day before, he said to
Jim, 'It's not to do with that Jag, is it?'

'Oh, Pat, you're a ruddy fool,' Jim said. 'I tried to stick up
for you, but—' He sighed.

They came down to the yard, Penn not caring terribly. It
was only the valves, after all. Jim was acting as if he'd carved
the tyres with a knife. It was only a bit of fun.

Old Purvis was standing beside the flattened Jaguar. Penn rode up to him, not very enthusiastically, and as he came alongside the car the reason for the peculiar Purvis emotion was made plain. Painted with tar in crude black letters all along the car's side was an unmentionable four-letter word.

Penn's face went tight, in a way Soggy would have recognized. Smeeton's crafty face swam before his vision and was mangled out of recognition by all the things Penn wished on it. One look at Purvis's expression, and Penn felt the injustices of the whole wide world belting him in the empty stomach regions; all the cries that welled through his indignation were those of a child: 'It's not fair! I didn't do it!' But he said nothing. The shock, with its wild emotions, flared and died. It was almost, for a moment, as if—because they all expected these things of him— he could easily have done it, almost wished he had. The situation was not new to Penn.

'Well?' Purvis barked.

'I didn't do it,' Penn said.

'You're standing there, large as life, and telling me you never touched this car?'

'Yes, I ruddy well am,' Penn said.

'You said, up the lane, was it to do with the Jag?' Jim put in stolidly.

'Yes, it was the tyres I meant.'

'You let the tyres down?' Purvis said.

'Yes, I let the tyres down, but I didn't write that stuff. You won't believe me, will you? Well, I'm not wasting my breath saying anything else.'

'No, you can use it on the Major when he comes ashore,' Purvis said shortly. 'And if you didn't do it, you're going to carry the can for whoever did, my boy. You lads are all as bad as one another round here. I let you keep that wreck on a mooring out there, and all I get from you is trouble. You start bothering my customers and that's my livelihood. So I'm telling you, I've had enough. You can explain to the Major when he comes ashore, and while you're waiting you can start trying to clean it up. We've got a foot-pump you can start on the tyres with. I doubt you'll get the tar off, but you can try. I reckon it'll need a respray when it's off, and the bill will go to your father. Now get moving!'

Penn, seeing when he was beaten, got moving. He pumped the tyres up, which, with Purvis's inadequate pump, took a long time. Far longer than it had taken to let them down.

'Lucky you're fit,' Jim said.

Penn scowled. 'I'm not doing anything to the message, seeing as I didn't write it.'

Jim said, 'I would. Dad was all for getting the police in, but I managed to cool him down. If you play him up now, he'll tell West what's happened.'

Choked by the injustice, Penn looked down at the sticky can of dissolvent Jim produced. He was ravenously hungry. Jim brought him a cup of tea at eleven and squatted down beside him, surveying Penn's work.

'It's taking the ruddy cellulose off as well,' Penn said. 'It's going to need a respray.'

'Just as well the Major's gone sailing. He should be in a good mood when he gets back.'

'Not for long he won't be,' Penn commented. He was fed up with the amusement of the visitors to the boatyard, seeing what had happened to the Major's Jaguar. Saturday morning was busy. He had received plenty of advice, all of it facetious. He felt like writing the same message six foot high all along the side of Purvis's shed. When he had finished at one o'clock the message could be read, not in tar, but in the matt trail worked by the dissolvent over the otherwise glossy surface.

'It *is* going to need a respray.' Jim's statement of the obvious did nothing to improve Penn's spirits. He could not bring himself to say anything. He viciously booted the can he had been using into Purvis's tip and turned away to get his bike. The job his father had been urging him to get for the holidays seemed suddenly very desirable. Something, he thought, where he wouldn't have people on his back all the time, niggling, nagging . . . 'Get your hair cut' . . . 'Take your hands out of your pockets . . .' The teachers at school—with two possible exceptions, to be fair—were all counting the hours till he left. Several of them, under provocation, had told him so. But no employers were lining up for his services either. His mother was pleased when he went out and disapproving when he came in. Penn rarely thought of all these underlying grievances, but the thought of his father being presented with a bill for the Jaguar's respray was prompting an instinctive scrub round for a line of defence. Not that his father was going to hear anything about the story from him . . .

'What was it all about, then?' his mother asked him. 'Your dinner's half cold. I turned the oven out an hour ago.'

'Oh, nothing.'

'You going out this afternoon?'

'Yeah.' He would make sure he was out around the time Major Harmsworth was likely to return from his sail.

'If you go down Moorham you can get your hair cut.'

Penn did not reply.

He went upstairs and washed and shaved and put a clean shirt on and went to call on Bates. Bates was watching soccer on the television, but came out when he saw that Penn had something to tell him.

'I'll get my bike.'

Picking morosely at the privet hedge, Penn told the tale of the Jaguar while Bates disentangled his bike from a clutter of gardening-tools and gum boots. Bates was duly appalled.

'What'll your father do when he gets that bill, then?'

Penn shrugged.

'No one'll believe I didn't do it, not after I was fool enough to say I did the tyres. They all know we were down there till gone midnight. Smeeton knew what he was doing all right. I'll corpse him next time I lay eyes on him.'

They cycled abreast down the lane signposted to Moorham, scowling into the grey, damp afternoon. Moorham, a mile down the river from Fiddler's End, the village they lived in, was a small unlively town, given over to a desultory boat-building industry. It was three miles from the sea, and boasted one or two fishing-boats which unloaded occasionally at the jetty, several rows of yachts and motor launches on moorings, and a flotsam of small craft of all shapes and sizes pulled up on the mud or out on the wall. Apart from the boat-building there was no industry, other than the few cafés that fed the week-end influx. The children that passed out from the local primary school went, along with the Fiddler's End children, to the Beehive Secondary Modern in the nearest big town, twelve miles away by school bus. Penn and Bates went to Moorham at week-ends to get a coke and ten cigarettes, and eye the birds that walked along the quay; perhaps, if they were lucky, take over the ferryman's job for an hour while he went for a drink (because George knew that whatever else Penn's failings, the boy knew how to use a boat in the strong tide and could bring the launch into the quay without smashing anything). Apart from that, there was the odd scuffle with the local opposition, a scrounge down on the shore to see if there was anything to pick up or a barracking of the local soccer talent on the playing-field, all of which passed the time, if nothing else.

They went into the café on the quay and sat staring out of the steamy windows. Bates offered Penn a cigarette, but said nothing, recognizing the heavy despair in Penn's face. Even when cheerful, Penn's face had an aggressive cast. Scowling, the heavy jaw pushed forward, lower lip thrusting, small blue-grey eyes bitterly reflective, his looks cast him to perfection into the role of thug, a word he heard too often. He had no illusions as to his looks, but was proud of his physique, which he perversely disguised by his slouching posture. He was also proud of his hair, and it pleased him that its length annoyed his parents, and was beginning to worry Soggy. Nobody at school had got away with hair as long as his, yet. The future in this direction

promised interest. Meanwhile, the immediate future promised only trouble of a less subtle nature.

'There's Dotty,' Bates said, scrubbing a hole in the steam on the windows.

Dotty was often to be seen in Moorham, for he was a devout fisherman. He went out to sea in a tiny outboard dinghy, and sat anchored for hours off the sand banks watching his line. Music and fishing were the only interests in his life, each as holy as the other. Penn sensed that Dotty, out fishing, recharged his batteries during long hours of solitude so that he was capable of coping with life at the Beehive. A gentle man by nature, Dotty was forced to act in his job with a severity that came to him uneasily, not instinctively—as it did to Soggy and a few more Penn could quickly name. This mixture of nature and assumption caused Dotty to act eccentrically, getting carried away equally by the beauty of music and the unbeauty of the Beehive boys, so that he steered an erratic course through lessons between tender, all-loving enthusiasm and demoniacal fury. Penn was quite fond of him, in an unthinking way. He also liked the games master, a young, bullet-headed man called Matthews. All the other teachers he either despised or loathed with a completeness equalled only by their similar feelings towards him.

'Nut-case,' Bates muttered, watching Dotty crouching over

his outboard, trying to get it to start. The tide was out, and was already carrying Dotty's boat down towards a line of moored yachts. The boys knew that when he hit one Dotty would raise his cap to the owner if he happened to be on board and say, 'I beg your pardon.' Dotty was well known in Moorham.

Penn, his glance bored with Dotty, brought it idly back to the quayside. Bates saw him stiffen.

'Oh, Bates!' he whispered. He stubbed his cigarette out in the ash-tray and stood up.

Bates looked through the hole in the steam and saw Smeeton coming along the quay with Gerry and Gary Green, and a red-haired, very thin boy called Fletcher. His eyes swivelled quickly up to Penn's.

'You ought to be careful, Penn.'

It was a bit different, he was thinking, attacking in the centre of Moorham on a Saturday afternoon, compared with out on the deserted shore at Fiddler's End. But Penn was already away. Bates finished his coke, and followed him reluctantly.

Penn waited in the doorway of the café until Smeeton, un-aware, came abreast of him. The quayside was about twenty feet wide, and on the far side there was a wall, and a drop down to the low-tide mud some twelve feet below. Opposite the café the wall gave on to the wooden jetty where the fishing-boats un-loaded. Penn stepped out, leading with his shoulder in such a way that Smeeton was pushed right across the quay and on to the jetty before he knew what had hit him. Penn knew he could only put Smeeton where he wanted him by working fast. Fletcher and the Green brothers were no mean fighters, not pacifists like Bates.

Smeeton went sprawling, shouting with pure funk. Penn stooped down and dragged him bodily to the edge of the jetty by one leg, and got him half over the edge before Smeeton's re-inforcements moved in. Penn braced himself, stamped hard on Smeeton's clutching fingers, and had the satisfaction of seeing him go before Gary Green's head hit him in the diaphragm. Penn's diaphragm was up to plenty of weight. Penn swung round and barged Green while he was still in momentum from his own attack, and Green sailed over the end of the jetty like a diver at high water. Penn had a momentary regret that Smeeton hadn't gone with the same velocity, but then recognized immediately that he was going to be hard put to stay on top himself. Fletcher brought him down while he was still off balance, and they rolled viciously together, over and over, across the width of the jetty. Fletcher was inspired by the dangerous knowledge that he might have bitten off more than he could chew, and was glad to see Gerry Green hovering, waiting to bring his boot into the right man's ribs.

Penn was strong and furious enough to be almost a match for the two boys together, and the three bodies, flailing across the wooden jetty, proved an irresistible attraction to what seemed to Bates a very fair proportion of the population of Moorham. Bates stood, like a referee, watching Penn, and sizing up the gathering crowd. He was anxious, but not alarmed, experienced in supervising Penn in similar situations, aware that an incensed old lady brandishing an umbrella was about to inflict on him a good deal more punishment than either Fletcher or Green was so far managing.

'You wicked boys! You ought to be ashamed of yourselves!' The umbrella caught Penn smartly across the ear, so that he looked up in surprise and saw, for the first time, the size of his audience. His moment's inattention gave Fletcher the opportunity to roll clear. Like a flash he turned and dropped a knee across Penn's throat, and Gerry, for the first time, got a clear aim for his boot. He swung in with a grunt of satisfaction, but Penn got an arm up in time and jerked him off balance while the kick was still in mid-air. Green fell heavily, and Penn crashed a fist into his ear which made him shout. Fletcher, shaken off momentarily, came back with a blow that Penn was too late to duck. It made him shake his head and swear furiously, but Fletcher found himself immediately on the ground again, Penn's great hand round his neck. He threshed out wildly, and the two of them rolled dangerously to the edge of the jetty.

Bates frowned. He could not see Penn getting free of both boys in a hurry, and the crowd was now getting agitated. Some women with shopping-baskets were urging the nearest male spectators to do something.

'It's downright disgraceful, right in the middle of the town! Can't you stop them?'

The young men grinned, enjoying themselves, but an older,

respectable-looking man and the proprietor of the café pushed
their way to the front and advanced gingerly.

'I've rung the police,' the café proprietor said.

'Ruddy young hooligans,' the other man said.

'I saw who started it.'

While they were talking the old lady moved in and speared
Penn in the ribs with such force that he let out a yell. He flung
Fletcher away from him and rolled up on to his knees. Bates got
in beside him and said urgently, 'Pack it in, Penn! The coppers
are coming!' The lady with the umbrella then hit Bates so hard
across the face that he went sprawling half over the side of the
jetty.

The crowd let out a cheer. 'Go it, old girl!'

Penn grabbed Bates and heaved him up by one arm, felt
someone come up close behind him and instinctively swung
round, fist raised, aware of his precarious position. The fist was
already moving when Penn became conscious of the fact that

his new assailant was neither Fletcher nor Green. His reaction
was instant, the force behind the blow snatched away in mid-
air, but the falling knuckles brushed flesh.

'Like that, is it?' said the police-constable. 'Oh, cripes,' said
Penn very quietly. He stood still, hands hanging, and tossed back
his hair. Bates stood close behind him, refereeing still, but seeing
only total defeat.

'What's all this about, then? Who started it?'

The police-constable was brisk and very young. Penn was
puzzled by not knowing him, realizing he must be new.
Mitchell put out a hand, closing it round Penn's upper arm.

'He started it,' said the man from the café, gesturing at Penn.
'He set on two young fellows and threw them off the end of the
jetty.'

'That right?' said Mitchell to Penn.

'Yes, but—'

'The buts can wait. What's your name?'

'Pennington.'

'Oh, is it?' Mitchell looked pleased, and Penn guessed that he knew all about him, new as he was. He glanced over the jetty and said, 'These the boys you attacked?'

Penn looked round and saw Smeeton and Gary Green coming up the jetty steps. For a short, lovely moment he was happy. They were both plastered in liquid mud from head to foot. They came up to Mitchell, and Penn grinned and said to Smeeton, 'It's good for pimples. I was just doing you a favour.'

'I'll do you a favour. I'll come and visit you in Oakhall,' Smeeton said. Oakhall was a detention centre.

Mitchell started sorting things out. If it had been West, Penn thought, he would have stood a chance, but this new man was too keen. Several of the crowd were only too anxious to tell him what had happened, and the café proprietor's evidence was damning.

'I saw this boy attack the others as they were walking past. They gave him no provocation at all. He just went straight for them . . .'

Mitchell diligently took the man's name and address. Penn stood scowling, waiting. One of the women said, 'What he wants is a good hiding. A dose of the birch. It should never have been done away with.'

'Nor hanging either!'

'Too soft with 'em these days . . .'

'Never did a bully any harm, that sort of treatment.'

'Just gave him a stiff neck,' Bates muttered.

'I'll give you all the evidence you want,' said the café man to Mitchell. 'I'm tired of these yobbos. Be glad to see them get their deserts.'

Mitchell turned back to Penn.

'I'm arresting you for assault . . .'

Penn wasn't surprised. The tension went out of him, and he slumped, frowning and silent.

'You'd better come along to the station. You others can beat it.'

Penn knew his own way to the station, and headed through the crowd, glowering, his hands in his pockets. He was on his own now, and the spindly, anxious figure of the disappearing

Bates wrenched him with self-pity. He thought fleetingly of his mother and father and then, not fleetingly at all, of Oakhall. The familiar polish and disinfectant smell of the police-station closed round him.

'All right,' said Mitchell. 'Turn round. Face the wall. Put your hands up.'

Mitchell went through all Penn's pockets, dropping everything he found on the floor. Penn leaned his hands against the wall, very careful not to say anything, feeling all the excesses of hatred flushing through his body, almost surprised that Mitchell was not receiving live shocks of it through his filthy inquisitive fingers. The search finished, Penn did not move. He knew all about martinets like Mitchell.

Mitchell went to a file, rifled through, and started reading. The telephone rang and he answered it, and took down a long list of particulars about a lost dog, then went back to the file again. When he had finished he said, 'Pick up your things.'

Penn was picking them up when Sergeant West came in. West looked thoughtfully at Penn.

'What are you doing here?'

'Ask him,' Penn said bitterly, with a jerk of his head in Mitchell's direction.

'I've arrested him for assault,' Mitchell said coldly.

He explained the circumstances and West listened, watching Penn with his disappointed-father look, which Penn did not like.

'Why did you go for Smeeton?' West asked.

'Because he got me into trouble down at Purvis's—something he did and I got the blame for, and no one will believe I didn't do it—'

'To do with a Jaguar?'

'Yes.'

'Hm.'

Penn waited. West knew about the Jaguar; there were no secrets, as if the very sea-gulls scattered the scandal about the marshes, screaming it from raucous, jeering bills. No doubt Fiddler's End was already receiving intimations of the latest dust-up in Moorham.

West said to Mitchell, 'Put him in the detention-room for ten minutes.'

Mitchell opened the door for him. Penn slouched through, heard the key turn in the lock behind him. The room was small, furnished merely with filing-cabinets, a table, two chairs, and an ash-tray. Penn walked round it twice, and found that all the filing-cabinets were locked, then he sat down on one of the chairs. He knew it would be Oakhall for him this time. Oakhall and all the stories he had heard about it preoccupied him; the old familiar, scorned threat used by both his parents and, on occasion, by Soggy and Stacker, came very close and sharp, and all his thick, pent-up truculence gave way to what felt ominously like a case of the panics. He got out a cigarette, his fingers jerky, then remembered that it was Bates who had the matches. He put his arms down on the table and rested his head on his wrist and said, 'Oh cripes! Oh God, 1 don't want to go there!'

After a few minutes he became aware of a sharp, unpleasant pain in his side which puzzled him, until he remembered the old girl with the umbrella. He pulled up his shirt and found an impressive red abrasion, flecked with blood.

'The old buzzard! If Mitchell's going to charge me with assault, he's got nothing to show for it. I could charge *her* with assault, a thing like this!'

He remembered Smeeton and the mud, and smiled, then he remembered the Jaguar and old Purvis's face, and Oakhall, and he got up and walked round the room, kicking at the filing-cabinets. Outside he heard the boys going home from the playing-field, still punting the ball with hollow thuds across the road, and the sudden smell of soccer, the crushed grass and the sour leather, the sweat and salt of it on the tongue, made him suddenly feel as if he had been at it himself, out in the road. It gave him a twist of feeling that he could put no name to; it was like a pain, a great longing for something without identity; it made him feel sick for being where he was, and the thought of Oakhall. He didn't think his home was anything much, but, by God, he didn't want to be taken away and pushed around by blokes like Mitchell. It was quite silent after the boys had gone, as if the whole of Moorham had gone home to tea. He sat, and the smell of polish and the dumb evidence of the filing-cabinets, full of records of petty crime, hung in the room, a dusty smog of wretchedness.

It was a very long ten minutes.

When eventually the door opened and West came in he got nervously to his feet, but West beckoned him to sit down again. Penn slumped back, and West sat on the edge of the desk.

'You're a darned young fool, Patrick. It's high time you grew up, time you learned to think. You don't *think*, do you, Pat?'

There was no answer to that. No help to say what he thought about coppers like Mitchell. He had thoughts all right. He sat scowling, feeling himself going down. West was watching him, lips pursed.

'You leaving school in July?'

'Yes, sir.'

'Thought what you're going to do?'

'I've *thought*, but—' Penn shrugged. Back to thoughts again. It hadn't got him far.

'Anything you do at school give you an interest? You get any sort of training for a trade?'

'All we get is useless, sir. History and geography and reading old plays and things, and a load about God. Doesn't get you a job.'

'Woodwork? Metalwork? Nothing like that?'

'I made a coffee-table . . .' Penn frowned. His mother had put a trayload of cups and saucers on it and it had collapsed and two cups were broken. She had sent a letter of complaint to the woodwork master, who had given Penn a detention for shoddy work. Penn wasn't allowed in the metalwork room; the master said the equipment was too valuable to let Pennington loose on it.

'I can't even get a job for the holidays,' he said, to avoid the question. 'That's what I came to Moorham for this afternoon, to see if I could find a job.'

'You hardly went the right way about it,' West said drily.

'No, sir.'

'You've got yourself a bad reputation, Pennington. You can't afford a bad reputation in a small place like this. You're not stupid. You've done badly at school, workwise, because you're lazy and undisciplined, not because you're stupid. You go on acting this way and you'll find yourself in bad trouble once you start trying to earn money. You know all this, don't you?'

'Yes, sir.'

31

'Well, look, I'm not accepting Mitchell's charge. I know you young kids like a fight, and there's no harm in it, only *you*, of course, have to be fool enough to start it right in the middle of town. Bit daft, wasn't it? Try to use your loaf, Pennington, that's all I ask. I don't want to see you in here again—please bear it in mind.'

Penn felt himself coming up, shining and cheering, out of the deep water. The little bare room danced round him. He had a sense of freedom, of all the river and the shore and the sea and the fields lying there unchanged, and the steamy cafés to comfort, even the old Beehive familiar about him, a womb of lesser evil than the dreaded Oakhall.

West saw him to the door. Mitchell watched him, and Penn could tell that he was furious. He was another enemy now, as good as Smeeton. Penn revelled in the thought, seeing the grey evening through the door, the puddles shining in the street.

'Good-bye, Pennington. Don't come back.'

'No, sir. Thank you, sir.'

Penn ran down the street, the release of energy bursting in his heels. He went across the quay and skimmed a few stones across the water, shook back his hair and looked up at the grey wet sky. If he was Bates, he would be singing, 'Take me to the graveyard . . .' 'Oh, Bates boy! We're all right!' Penn sang, and scuffled a stone down the quay. He would fetch his bike, and go and knock up Bates. 'Cripes, I'm ravenous! Not even a cup of mouldy prison tea! That new copper's as mean as a snake.' He went past the jetty and the café to the wall where he had left his bike. It wasn't there. He looked at the blank wall, swelling with indignation.

'Some lousy creep's knocked it off!' It was a good bike. His father had got it cheap because it had already, earlier in its history, been knocked off. Penn had not thought it would happen to the same bike twice.

The wall belonged to a pub, the Green Man, which looked out over the river. As Penn stood there, kicking the wall, wondering if Bates had put it somewhere, a man came out of the side door of the pub and said, 'If you're looking for a bike, it's in my back yard.' He pushed a gate open and jerked his head to indicate that Penn could go inside. Penn nodded. The back windows of the pub showed the glow of light through from the bar. Penn could hear the Saturday-night voices, careless and cheerful, and smell the meat pies in the oven through the open kitchen door. The landlord's wife put her head out, saw her husband and said in a harassed voice, 'For heaven's sake, Arthur, get a move on! I'm run off my feet. There's a sinkful of glasses to wash. I can't do everything. What a night for Joe to pack it in!'

Penn turned to Arthur and said, 'I'll help you out.'

'Get in there, then,' Arthur said.

Penn had got himself a job.

Chapter 3

When he was washing up, Penn realized that he had only taken on the job because he was afraid to go home. His parents would know all about the incident on the quay by now: he had just had evidence of how fast news travelled in this area. He cursed himself for a fool, groping for a slice of lemon that was blocking up the plug. Washing up for a job! He must have been demented.

'How old are you?' the nagging woman asked him belligerently.

'Sixteen.'

'Don't set a foot out of this kitchen, then, or we'll have trouble. I'll bring the glasses out here, and you can see to the pies. And that sliced loaf, get it buttered. Here's the butter. Look sharp.'

She was worse than his mother.

But at eleven when the pub shut, Arthur gave him twelve and sixpence and said, 'If you're at a loose end the next fortnight, d'you fancy a job? The wife's going away and I can't do the cleaning. Can't get down on the floor, like. If you could come in, say, seven in the morning, till opening time. How old are you?'

'Sixteen.'

'Oh, I thought you was older. You look eighteen to me. Pity. I could use you in the bar if you were eighteen, while the wife's away. But if you're sixteen—' He shrugged.

Penn considered. He knew the chicken factory wouldn't take him unless he got his hair cut. Unhygienic, the foreman said. The only other alternative was to go to his father's place, labouring. Even scrubbing the pub floor would be better than

34

his father's company all day, especially after the bill for the Jaguar put in its appearance.

'I could still clean up, couldn't I? Out of hours—it'd be all right, wouldn't it?'

'If you want to do it, yes.'

Arthur was obviously a man who took an easy course in life. 'Yes, you come in if you fancy it. I might find you something to do outside, too. That yard needs tidying up. I've been saying it for the last ten years.'

Penn had noticed. He had got himself employed, for better or for worse. And as it turned out, it was a very satisfactory arrangement, for Arthur was easy; he did not nag or scold or disapprove. Arthur suffered himself, from his wife, and when his wife was away he liked Penn, who said very little. Penn cleaned up early, and when the pub opened he went and worked in the yard, cleaning out the piles of lumber and junk in the sheds, the accumulation of decades, burning all the rubbish. He worked slowly, to spin the job out for the whole holiday, but Arthur did not mind. The bill for the Jaguar came for Mr. Pennington (for the sum of ninety-six pounds eleven shillings). Penn's father gave him a pasting and threw it on the fire, and Penn took to using *Mathilda* as his pad, to keep out of the way of his father.

One lunch-time, when Penn was tending his bonfire, Mitchell saw him when he came out of the pub to use the Gents. Mitchell was off duty, but he stared at Penn and said, 'What are you doing here?'

'Working.'

Penn reckoned Mitchell was, too, by the way his eyes took everything in. When the pub was shut at two-thirty Penn went into the kitchen, where Arthur had a meat pie and a pot of tea waiting.

Arthur said, 'Why's that copper interested in you? Asking me all about you, he was.'

Penn told him.

'He's too keen,' Arthur said. 'You don't want that in a little place like this. Just makes trouble.'

Penn agreed. 'He wants me shut up.'

'You be careful,' said Arthur.

It started to lash down with rain outside. Arthur settled

down to watch horse-racing on the television, and Penn went to sweep out the bar. He leaned on his broom by the glass door of the public bar, scowling at the squally water beyond the quay. He hadn't anywhere to go, or anyone to see, and there was nothing to go home for, save nagging. Looking at the rain, he could think of nothing—not one thing in the whole wide world—that gave him one moment's stir of anticipatory pleasure. (Apart, of course, from the purely hallucinatory dreams of mashing Soggy and Mitchell and Smeeton and Stacker and setting fire to the Beehive, and the shadow of Oakhall, and Mitchell's pants, and the white Jaguar . . .) Even soccer, the best way of passing time, was packed in for this gloomy, puking, compulsory period of forced labour known as the summer term that hovered on the immediate horizon. 'If I grow my hair long enough, I'll get suspended,' Penn thought, and at once he felt better.

There was an old piano in the corner of the bar, and he opened it and tried a few chords to see if it worked. It did, and was in tune. He could hear Arthur snoring in the back, and the commentary jerking spasmodically from fence to fence, so he sat down and played one of Bates's dirges, very sad and rainy and appropriate. He didn't mind, if he could play what *he* liked, but even in this thing, which was supposed to be pleasure, it was nag, nag, nag all the way, and being told who he was supposed to like. For God's sake, how could they expect you to like their deadly stuff because they said it was good? You even had to take exams in it, this *pleasure!* What right had Dotty to say that this bluesy achy stuff was rubbish, when it was exactly how he felt, or that rave-ups were tripe? Who was *he* to say—God Almighty? Penn got more cheerful, playing for once without his mother yelling for deadliness instead of pop. He moved on to his mother's favourite loathes, and forgot about Arthur and the rain. It was as good as playing the harmonica in *Mathilda*, because he could do as he pleased. Cripes, all these years he had played, and always to order, for Dotty or his mother! 'I'm just a slave,' he thought . . . do this, do that . . . what bliss if he could leave home . . . Arthur's wife was coming back on Thursday. She was deadliness again. Penn played a few bars of Chopin's funeral march.

'Why didn't you tell me you could play that thing?' Arthur

36

said, padding out into the bar. 'We used to have music here—got the licence for it and all—till Joe packed it in. Saturday nights—it was great here. I could give you a job if you weren't under age. You're as good as Joe ever was.'

Penn scowled.

Arthur said, 'You don't look sixteen. If you hadn't told me, I'd have put you at eighteen.'

'Old West and Mitchell know how old I am.' Penn would have been quite prepared to turn himself into eighteen for Arthur's sake, if it hadn't been for the vigilance of the law. He would have fancied a job as a pub pianist, better than scrubbing.

'You come here when you're eighteen, and I'll take you on all right.'

'It's a dead easy way of earning money,' Penn said, wondering why he had never thought of it before. 'How much d'you get for playing for a night?'

'Oh, free drinks and a quid or two. Depends. Pity.' Arthur reflected a moment, and said, 'There's a crowd of weirdies used to come here for musical evenings. Folk-singing or something. They used the piano, but none of 'em played it as good as you. They had guitars as well, and a mouth-organ or two. There was a spot of trouble one night and they use the village hall now, Wednesday nights. They come round here first for a few crates of beer. You might get a job with them.'

Penn was interested.

'Wednesday nights? Old Bates might like a spot of that,' he thought. His dirges were mostly folk stuff. Penn had never found out yet where he got them from. He asked him the next time he saw him.

'I get them out of the library. Books,' Bates explained. 'They're all in books.'

Penn had never heard of anyone using the library before. Not any of his friends.

'You want to try this old thing Arthur was talking about, then? Load of geezers singing? With beer,' he added, for incentive.

'I don't mind giving it a listen.'

They went, suspicious, sullen, and leaned against the door at the back of the hall. Penn was comforted by the length of hair. There was a man who sang who could scarcely see out. Penn couldn't see that there was anything in it for him, but he liked it. It had this thing that touched him when he played for Bates, that one played and sang to relieve something, to feel good, not for the sake of mastering a tortuous conglomeration of composer's fads for old Dotty's sake. For *pleasure*, for God's sake! Penn was jolted.

The audience was thin, but enthusiastic, joining in all the choruses. The long-haired man sang unaccompanied, but two others sang and played guitars, and another man played the harmonica. Penn found that a lot of the songs were Bates's; he could have joined in quite a lot of them if he had wanted. Not that he did want. He leaned against the doorpost in the dark outpost of the hall, superior, pulled against his will into a warmth, liking it, but resisting. His inside was going with it, but his face scowled. Bates was muttering under his breath, excited.

'This is my stuff,' he said.

'Yeah, well, they're public, aren't they?' Penn said witheringly. 'You said so. They're in the library.'

'I know, but—'

The long-haired man was introducing someone else, a girl. Penn's interest quickened. She was thin and frail-looking, with enormous sad eyes and long, straight, silver-blonde hair. Her voice was very clear, almost shrill, with a sadness that went with her looks.

> 'Ten thousand miles it is too far
> To leave me here alone
> Here I may lie, lament and cry . . .'

Penn stopped scowling, transfixed by the sword-edge of the girl's voice. He had never seen a bird as perfect as this one, so utterly desirable. She was like a piece of crystal, delicate, brittle, rare. He had never seen one like it. All the girls he knew were busty and thrusty and strong, all private giggles and shrieks, nudging and daring and passing notes. They had no reticence, brash and sniggering. But this little wispy thing, like a puff of breeze, her voice full of tears . . . Penn's eyes were wide open, hypnotized. When she was finished he could not say anything. Bates looked at him and he scowled.

He could not get her out of his head.

When they went home he said to Bates, very cautious, 'That bird wasn't bad.'

'What bird?' Bates said.

'Oh, cripes,' Penn said to himself. He felt spent and shattered and not all present. He did not know what to do.

Penn duly went back to school. Having been isolated in the Green Man all the holidays, Penn's natural gloom at returning to the deadly Beehive was lifted somewhat by the sight of Smeeton, and the thought of tangling with him once more.

'Haven't seen you down the river lately, Smeeton. You scared or something?'

'I've been working, thickhead. I'll be down the boat as soon as I fancy an evening's fishing, don't you worry.'

'I'll be there to help you aboard,' Penn said kindly. 'Just you tell me what night. I'll have everything ready for you.'

'I'll surprise you one of these days, Pennington,' Smeeton said.

'You surprise me all the time, Smeeton. That anyone so disgusting can actually draw breath is a perpetual—'

'Soggy!'

They all scattered into their places. Soggy had the boys on one side of the class-room and the girls on the other, all the dullest, ugliest and spottiest specimens occupying the desks where the two sexes actually came together. The girl Penn had dated up to the end of last term, by name Rita Fairweather, occupied a desk next to the wall, and Penn had one against the window at the far side, which ranked them both, by Soggy's system, high in the sex-appeal stakes. Much biro fluid had been expended by the girls in the Beehive on little notes and decorations declaring love for 'PP', but Penn, although he talked sex a lot like all the others, had privately—till now—thought girls pretty tedious. Not that he would have admitted this to anybody, except possibly to Bates. He had not given Rita a thought the whole holiday. In fact, the holiday had been a pleasant respite from the weekly date where Rita had spent most of his pocket-money for him on her never-ending passion for crisps and coke and given nothing in return but a few salt 'n'vinegar flavoured kisses on the back seat of the last bus. Penn, doing what he had thought were the right things, had been left un-

moved. 'Give me a harmonica for company any day,' he said to
Bates. And Bates, on his second can of Double Diamond, had sung:

'I wish I was a butterfly, I'd fly to my love's breast.
I wish I was a linnet, I would sing my love to rest.
I wish I was a nightingale, I'd sit and sing so clear,
I'd sing a song for you, false love, for once I loved
    you dear.'

Penn didn't see it himself—then. But since the girl with the
voice he didn't know what he thought. Every time he recalled
her he felt weak in his stomach, as if suffering from something
physical. He could not tell even Bates about this. Sometimes he
thought the girl was just a figment of his imagination, and that
she had never existed at all, but when, for a sort of try-out, he
said to Bates, 'That bird that sang, d'you reckon she was any
good?' Bates didn't say, 'What bird?' He said, 'Yeah. She
could sing all right. Not much to look at, though.' And Penn
felt stabbed again. Bates liked hunky big girls when he thought

about them at all. Penn, who had never bothered about any of them, could not understand why the little blonde kept fluttering in his inside.

'Coming events,' Soggy intoned. 'Dates to fix in your thick heads for the summer term . . . don't bring me any excuses later, saying I didn't warn you. I'm warning you now. First and most important, upper school social event for pupils and parents Saturday, May the tenth, in aid of the Common Room extension fund. Compulsory for you lot. Parents to be dragged along if possible. Mr. Robert Tate is coming to sing for us.'

Everyone groaned, as a matter of form.

'What group's he with, sir?' someone asked.

'He sings,' Soggy explained, 'properly.'

Everyone groaned again.

'I repeat, compulsory attendance,' Soggy said. 'May the tenth, five p.m. Everyone got it?'

Penn's faint flicker of goodwill drooped and died. His last term, true to form, stretched like grey, spent chewing-gum, tasteless, useless and tedious, into the hazy horizons of his seventeenth summer. He looked out of the window and saw the glazed walls of the new buildings shining in the sunshine, the hotchpotch of roofs beyond and, through the gap between Langford's chimney and the slate roof of the Methodist church, a shimmer of soft blue that was the sea. The tiny gap of shimmer made him feel physically ill for a moment. To get out, to get shot of the lot of them . . . To what? To where? How? The dirty—

'Pennington!'

He refocused. 'Sir?'

'I'll give you two days to get your hair cut.'

Penn felt the waters rising.

In the lunch-hour, closeted with Mr. Crocker in the music-room, Penn revealed—not by saying anything, but merely through the way he played—that he had done no practising since leaving school at the end of last term. Little Mr. Crocker danced with rage. Penn felt sorry for him.

'What can I do with you? What use are you to me? To any-one? To yourself? Why do I trouble? I ask myself over and over, why do I trouble?'

Penn felt, very faintly, guilty. Mr. Crocker did trouble. He was the only one. He shifted on the stool and stared morosely at the music. Mr. Crocker slipped another sheet down over the one he was looking at, an ominous affair headed 'Andante and Rondo Capriccioso' by Felix Mendelssohn.

'Look at that.'

Penn looked at Dotty suspiciously.

'You have one more term with me, Pennington. Why should we waste it? I understand from the rest of the staff that you waste a good deal of your time here. Well, I thought, not with me he won't. I am ambitious for you, you see, Pennington.'

'But, sir—'

'There's to be a music festival here in Northend at the end of June. I've entered you for the Open Solo Pianoforte. The Andante and Rondo Capriccioso is the set piece.'

Penn stared at Dotty, aghast. 'The *Open*?'

'You are perfectly capable of playing this piece. So why not? We will work very hard this term, you and I.'

"But I don't want—'

'I'm sorry,' Dotty said. 'But to borrow a favourite word from Mr. Marsh, it's compulsory.'

He leaned on the piano. 'It was discussed at a staff meeting. Everyone agreed that it would be a very good thing, both for yourself and for the school, if you could do well in this competition. It was also

agreed that you waste a good deal of time while you are in school. So, with a little co-operation from all concerned, we drew up a time-table for you, Pennington, to make sure that you get all the practice in that you need. It's arranged so that you get at least three hours in every day. An hour at lunchtime, an hour after school, when I shall work with you, and various other periods each day—for example, Miss Harrington is generously prepared to forgo the pleasure of your company in her Religious Knowledge lessons on Tuesday and Thursday; Mr. Peach tells me you're banned from the metal-work shop, which gives you an hour and forty minutes on Wednesday afternoon, and Mr. Marsh seems to think Current Events could get along without you very well—that's Tuesday again. A splendid day, Tuesday—you will get over three and half hours.'

He expounded, at great length, every minute of this formid-able time-table, while Penn sat looking at the music, resistance setting in like arthritis, stiffening his whole body. There was no escape. It was a gigantic revenge, plotted by the gleeful, scheming staff to sabotage his indolent summer.

'All this time wasted during the winter on soccer,' Crocker went on scornfully. 'Hours tossed away! Every time I tried to get a lunch-hour Matthews had got you out on the field. And then that broken arm—six weeks gone! Well, now, you can make up for it this term. Sit up! *Sit up!* Let's get the cramp out of those fingers. Twenty minutes of this, please.' Another sheet of deadliness, close and black, slipped down before his eyes. 'With the metronome at . . .' Penn groaned out loud. Crocker brought a ruler down with a crack across his knuckles and Penn jumped. He started to play. He had a feeling that he was sliding under again, the rapid clock of the metronome count-ing his pulse as he drowned in a sea of deadliness.

'This crummy concert, with Mr. Robert Tate. We've decided to do something about it.'

They were packing up after afternoon school, and Maxwell, a prefect from 5A, banged for attention on the desk.

'We reckon we can string together an evening's entertain-ment that'll put old Tate in the shade. After all, we want this blooming Common Room extension and nobody's going to come and listen to old septuagenarian Tate bleating his hey nonny, are they? Even the parents aren't that far past it.'

Penn, seeing more work in the offing, attempted to slip nonchalantly out of the door, but Maxwell caught him by the arm.

'It's you I want, oaf.'

'I'm strictly the old Beethoven, Bach and blooming Brahms,' Penn said. 'You ask Dotty. Even farther back than Tate.'

'Look here,' Maxwell said. 'We aren't interested in that lot any more than you are. It's Bates I want to know about.'

'Bates!'

'Rumour has it he's got a repertoire of soul—'

'Why don't you ask him?' Penn was grinning.

'He'll shut up like a clam, you know that. You've got to work on him for us.'

'It's the old beer he sings for, not me.'

'How do you mean?'

'He has to get loosened up. And he won't do it in public. To make him do it in public you'll have to get him really oiled.'

Maxwell looked a little dubious. A bright boy, right-half to Penn's centre, he was a friend of Penn's. 'We can't have him drunk, you fool. There must be a happy medium in this. He just wants a little something to loosen the inhibitions?'

'That's it.'

'Well, I don't see why that shouldn't be arranged. You'd play the old harmonica for him? He wouldn't be alone, after all. Could you talk him into it, do you think?'

'I can try.'

'He's good? Worth the trouble?'

'He is a darned sight better than old Tate.'

'We'll have an audition after school next week. I'll lay the beer on. It could be all right, this affair. We don't want the parents to think we're so pathetic that we can't give Tate any competition. 5B's got a group that's not bad, and there's Finnigan's trumpet, and Midwinter's monologue, cleaned up a bit, and you on the old joanna, if it's the stuff you do in the Common Room, not Dotty's murk. I can leave Bates to you, can I? Talk him into it . . .'

Bates looked gloomy as soon as the subject was introduced. 'What, me stand up there? I can't sing, anyway.'

'Well, I'm your manager now, and you'll do what I say. I've signed you on.'

'What'll I sing, for heaven's sake?'

'What's wrong with "The Butcher Boy"? Good meaty stuff.'

Bates went crimson. 'It's a girl's song. They'd roll up, me standing up there . . . "I wish I was a maid again". . .'

Penn considered. It had never made him want to roll up, Bates's tale of the wronged girl. But, spotty old Bates . . . He looked at him thoughtfully. Of course, it was a bit daft, when you came to think of it, spotty old Bates singing:

'I wish my baby it was born
And smiling on its daddy's knee
And me, poor girl, to be dead and gone
With the long green grass growing over me.'

But he had never laughed. Penn could not understand why.

He said raspingly, 'Who wanted to sing on the telly the other night, then? Who wanted to sing for his living? Where's the old ambition? If you can't stand up and sing for a few dozy old parents you jolly well *ought* to be a crummy girl.'

Penn had already decided that he wasn't going to play the piano, not for anybody's sake, but Bates was ruddy well going to sing. Bates, who never did anything at school but sit in the corner staring out of the window all day, was going to get up on the platform and sing. He, Patrick Pennington, had made up his mind.

If it had been a concert forced on them by the staff he would have been as uncooperative as possible, but as it was one organized by Maxwell to do down Hey Nonny Tate, he was prepared to show willing.

Bates, who was sitting on *Mathilda's* bunk when this conversation took place, opened his mouth to voice another protest, but stopped in mid-word, staring at the suddenly darkened hatch.

Penn turned round just as Smeeton jumped. Smeeton, in his enthusiasm, had not stopped to balance himself and fell upon Penn in a sprawl of arms and legs, from which Penn detached himself more quickly than his attacker. But already the hatch had darkened again, and first Fletcher then Gary and Gerry

45

Green dropped through, like parachutists, Bates thought. Bates pulled his legs up on to the bunk and sat in the corner, cradling his knees in his arms, watching the rapid transformation of the small cuddy take place before his unsurprised eyes, utter chaos shattering the domestic peace like fireworks through a letter-box. Penn did most of the damage, flailing like a harpooned whale under the mass attack, so that table, beer, and paraffin lamp all went flying, wood splintering and glass shattering. Grunts, cries, and breathless invective punctuated the graver noises of destruction. Bates sighed, and felt the old smack rock as if a squall had hit her. The tea-cups chinked on their hooks, and the tins in the lockers rattled faintly; the rusty gimbals swung at the impact of a boot, the empty kettle clattered round its compound. Bates heard Penn's voice from below, muffled and *in extremis*, and gradually the heaving of limbs slackened off and Smeeton's voice could be heard, triumphant, from beneath Fletcher's posterior: 'Let me get up, Fletcher, you louse. We've done for him.' Bates peered down. He saw Penn's eyes glittering. Bates grinned. Penn started to move again, but Smeeton, quick as a stoat, picked up the lamp-glass, which was broken across the middle, and brought the jagged edges sharply up to Penn's face. Penn, already moving forward, tasted the blood on his lip.

'You scurvy—' Penn was almost weeping at his defeat, the words brimming on his tongue. The glass had stopped him. Smeeton, half alarmed by the blood, half exhilarated, sat back, nervously passing the glass from hand to hand. Penn raised himself on his elbows, feeling very ill from his treatment.

'We thought we'd go fishing,' Smeeton said, slightly uncertain. 'Didn't we?' He appealed to his henchmen, who were sitting on the bunks. 'We thought we'd go out for the evening.'

'Yeah,' they all said.

There was a pause, which seemed to emphasize Smeeton's unfamiliarity with victory, and Fletcher said, indicating Penn, 'What'll we do with him, then?'

'He won't make any more trouble, not from the look of him. You don't want any more, Pennington, do you? You've only to say.'

Penn said nothing, groping for a handkerchief.

'Come on, get the engine started, then,' Smeeton said to

Fletcher. 'Get the gear on board. You two stay down here or you'll get pasted again,' he added to Penn and Bates.

The invading party departed up the hatchway, and could be heard thumping around on deck, unloading gear out of the dinghy. Penn went on lying on the floor. Bates unwound himself and sat up, looking dubiously at Penn.

'You want a beer or something?'

Penn told him, curtly, that he didn't.

Bates shrugged. 'Fag?' Penn shook his head. In the hold the engine started up with a series of backfires, and the fumes filtered through, blue and filmy. The smack vibrated, and all the crockery started to shiver again, and the beer-cans trembled in their case. Bates started to tidy up, gathering up the bits of lamp, stepping over Penn. He heard the mooring go with a splash, and the old smack made a juddering circle and set off down the river. The engine was at full throttle, rough and strangled, coughing unhappily at frequent intervals, and the cuddy was filled with the clatter and banging of loose gear on deck, of halyards swinging on the mast and blocks tapping. Smeeton was singing. Bates looked up and saw the summer evening sky, clear and inviting, sliding past. The boat seemed to be moving very fast. He looked at Penn, whose handkerchief now looked very bloody, and said, 'Are you okay?'

'Oh, get stuffed,' Penn said.

Bates went and stood in the hatchway, leaning his elbows on the deck, watching the quays of Moorham slipping into sight, and the jetty where the battle was first joined. The houses on the quay, facing south, were bathed in a golden light, the long shadows flung behind them. Bates could smell summer, and felt perfectly content. He started to sing under the racket of the engine, watching the boat's shadow moving down the river. The tide hurried *Mathilda* seaward. The sea-walls moved back, fading against the fading sky, and the sea spread out, gold and smooth and glittering. The ease of *Mathilda*'s passage—in spite of the din—enchanted Bates . . .

> 'The salt seaweed was in her hair
> Lowlands, lowlands away . . .
> And then I knew my love was dead . . .'
>   • • • •

47

Two beer-cans, tossed away by the company at the helm, bobbed away, shooting metallic stars. Smeeton was laughing. The boat was going too fast for the fishing, but nobody cared, least of all Bates.

> 'When he was dead and laid in grave
> Her heart was struck with sorrow.
> Oh mother, mother, make my bed,
> For I shall die tomorrow.'

The engine, throwing out clouds of thick blue smoke, made a curious choking noise and stopped. In the startling silence Bates heard his own voice, and stopped as abruptly.

'Go and kick it, Fletcher,' Smeeton ordered.

'Give it some beer,' Gerry suggested.

'Go and get Penn,' Smeeton said. 'He can ruddy well work his passage. He always thinks he knows all about it.'

They came aft. Bates retreated and said to Penn, 'They want you to fix the engine.'

Penn said, 'They can—'

'Pennington, you louse, get up here,' Fletcher said, bending down to peer through the hatch. 'Get this engine going again. We don't want to get our hands dirty.'

Penn went, hunched and muttering, blinking at the sunset, swallowing blood. Bates saw them go down the aft hatch, and presently heard the familiar noises of the flywheel being turned over, and Penn arguing with Fletcher as to the reason for the failure. Bates did not care. He stood in the hatch again, squinting at the strange gold gloss that was the sea, the smack's shadow drawn long and dark across the water. She was drifting, slowly turning her bows to the outgoing tide, rolling as she came across the swell. There was no land in sight, the low sea-walls lost in the encroaching haze. The sun lay on the horizon like a huge red buoy. Bates was touched by the austere beauty, never having known such loveliness before.

'The fuel's not coming through—'

'Clean the carburettor, then.'

'. . . can't see a thing down here and you've broken the lamp.'

Fragments of altercation, muffled, did not disturb Bates's

reverie. He was looking down the bleached sweep of *Mathilda*'s decks and out to sea, where dusk was rapidly tarnishing the impossible gold. The smack had settled herself, bows into the tide, and was going away from the shore stern first. The shadow of her mast was ten miles long, to the horizon. A violet haze ate up the sun, the shadow vanished, and the sea was cold, grey and unkind, the change taking place in a matter of seconds. Bates was amazed, hurt. He went below again and lay on the bunk. 'Poor old Penn,' he thought. He started to sing.

Smeeton came down, looking annoyed, and said, 'Any candles on this old heap? Penn said there were some in a locker.'

Bates groped for them and handed them over. Smeeton retired. Flickers of light came and went, and hammering, and the hopeless noises of a goaded engine trying and failing, to an accompaniment of swearing. Half an hour later the smack hit something with a crack that sent all the gathered crockery shooting back on to the floor again. She lifted and came down with a jar that Bates felt come out of the top of his head. He went up on deck.

'We're aground,' Penn was saying. 'Ruddy fine skipper you are, Smeeton.'

'What do you mean, aground?' Smeeton said, staring over the side. Sea surrounded them to infinity on all sides, gleaming now in the first light of a half-moon.

'On the bottom, pinhead. On the sand. What are you going to do about it?'

Penn, holding on to the shrouds, was ready when the swell dropped the smack again, but the shock sent Smeeton sprawling. Penn laughed. Bates looked at him cautiously. He knew that to go aground in a smack as frail as *Mathilda*, even in a calm sea, was no joke, but Penn was laughing.

'What are you going to do?' Penn asked Smeeton again.

'Oh, I don't know,' Smeeton said crossly. The failure of the engine had destroyed his confidence.

'Anchor,' Penn said. He sat on the coaming of the hold, his elbows on his knees, and looked out over the shoal, fingering the congealing blood on his lip. The shoal was marked by a large area of breaking water in an otherwise calm sea. 'You've put this old boat in a nasty situation, Smeeton,' he said conversationally. 'You ought to do something about it.'

49

Smeeton looked at Penn and saw by the set of his shoulders that Penn was no longer to be ordered about. He said to Fletcher, 'Go and put the anchor out.' He paused until Fletcher and the Green brothers had tramped away to sort out the anchor, and said, 'What do we do, then?'

Penn said, 'I don't know about you, but I'm turning in.' And he went below and installed himself in the lee bunk, the only one that was comfortable when the old smack, drying out on the sand, lay down on her side.

Chapter 4

Bates, although he knew all about the shoals out at sea, had never met one in the flesh before. While the rest of them slept, Penn soundly and Smeeton and Co. very uncomfortably on the floor and deck, Bates went for a walk. He walked on a hard ridge of unmarked sand, virgin as arctic snow, shining like slate under the hard moonlight, with the sea all round him and waders twittering eerily on the fringes of the water. It was so strange that he could hardly believe it, although he told himself that it happened every night, and was only a few miles from home. The night was sharp, with a rising wind. Clouds started to drift over the moon and, standing beside the stranded smack, Bates could hear the noise of the wind whining in the shrouds. The loose halyards swung out in restive arcs, slapping the deck. When the water started to come back it was no longer smooth; it broke on the sand with considerable force, and Bates could see the white crests spitting in the darkness, even where the water was deep. When the tide was nearly back to the smack, he climbed on board and went below to Penn. Smeeton and Fletcher, propped uncomfortably on the tilting floor, were only dozing, and mumbled at him, but Penn was deeply asleep, sprawled out on his back.

Bates shook him. He had no faith in Smeeton.

'The water's nearly back. What are we going to do? The wind's come up as well.'

Penn grumbled into consciousness, and lay listening to the restless noises all about him. 'Ask Smeeton,' he said to Bates. 'It's his trip.'

'You're always making out you're an engineer,' Smeeton said. 'If you can't make the engine go, what can I do about it?'

'The engine won't go—you needn't worry about that any longer,' Penn said. 'She'll have to sail out, if she's going at all.'

'Sail!'

Penn shut his eyes again. 'There's sails in the forepeak.'

There was a long silence. Bates sat down on the bunk by Penn's knees, anxious. 'Penn,' he said, 'Smeeton can't sail.'

'He should have thought of that before he got us into this mess.'

'What are you going to do, Penn?' Bates insisted.

'I'm just keeping a stiff upper lip,' Penn said.

'It's no joke!'

'No, it isn't. It's true.'

'Oh, stow it, Penn. It's bad. You know it is.'

Penn did know, although he shut his eyes again and did not move. He could hear the wind through the rotted rigging, and the slap of the water on the hull, and knew that the old boat was going to take a pounding that might well open her up before she floated. They had no dinghy with them, nor flares, no life-saving equipment of any kind. He judged that they were about five miles off shore. He thought, with luck and an ingoing tide, he might swim that, but he knew none of the others could. He was sorry for Bates.

Smeeton got up without saying anything and went up on deck, where he could be heard muttering to the others and thumping about. They opened the forehatch and Penn could hear them looking for the sails, stumbling about in the dark. The smack was beginning to shudder as the force of the deepening water got under her, buffeting and shouldering the rotten timbers. Yes, thought Penn, it was bad. But he felt exhilarated more than frightened. Bates shook him again.

'Penn, you aren't going to leave it to Smeeton, are you?'

Penn was touched. 'No. I don't want to drown. But let him sweat! He deserves to.'

'It'll be all right?'

'Yes, of course, you fool.'

Penn did not move until he felt the crack as the smack's keel left the bottom and dropped for the first time. It was ominous. He rolled his feet off on to the floor and sat combing his hair. The smack was wallowing horribly from side to side, like a cow struggling in a bog. Every few seconds she bumped, and every minute or so a larger wave would lift and drop her with a sickening crack. He went up on deck, Bates following anxiously at his heels.

Gary and Gerry, who knew more about boats than Smeeton, had got the headsails on, but were now being sick over the side, while the unleashed canvas flogged and cracked dangerously across the foredeck. Smeeton and Fletcher, standing over the anchor chain, were in danger of being flailed overboard. Penn went to the mast and dropped the sails.

'Have you pulled up on that anchor?' he asked.

'Can't move it,' Smeeton muttered. In the darkness his face was a white, petrified blur. The water was slopping up over the foredeck, moving apparently in all directions with a malicious strength. The sand was marked by a white, blowing spray. Penn looked at it, and was frightened. They were alone with their crank boat and there was no one to help them. He was the only one who knew anything about it—and he didn't know much. It was cold, and he was soaked already by the spray.

He said to Fletcher, 'Go and see if you can find some sheets for those sails. They're useless without. Rope, I mean. Bring up anything you can find.' He elbowed Smeeton out of his way, and grasped the anchor chain where it came over the fairlead.

'Get behind me and pull when I pull. When she comes up, heave.' Smeeton was just a weed. Penn got his hands round the chain, bracing one leg against the bulwarks. The smack rolled and the stem lifted. 'Now!' Penn flung himself on the chain and pulled in about a fathom before it stopped him. Smeeton had the sense to get the slack round the samson-post. The smack snubbed up with a snatching, chafing motion, slewing round on her shuddering stern. The water came over with sharp thuds, the smack dropping on the hard sand, sawing at her anchor. The shocks of her pounding went up Penn's spine like explosions. He had never guessed it would be as bad as this, in spite of what he had said. Bates was crying.

'Again!' he said to Smeeton, getting hold of the anchor chain.

It came in in snatches, a foot at a time. Penn got as much as he could, until exhaustion stopped him, and Smeeton feverishly made it fast as it came, sliding the slack back down the hause-hole. Dragged forcibly towards the deep water, *Mathilda* began to ride, dropping with less force, gradually freeing her stern. Penn went below to see how much water she was making, but there was none over the floorboards, which cheered him considerably, although he could hear it swilling in the bilges. He knew her pump was useless. He rested for a moment in the hatch-

way, biting the side of his thumb, looking out into the darkness. All he could see was breaking crests, the south-westerly wind kicking into the tide, knocking the tops off the making waves, driving the smack, if it could, farther out to sea. To sail back would mean beating into it. The mouth of the river was unlit, and full of shoals, but they could not wait for daylight, because by then the tide would have turned again, and an old smack like *Mathilda* would not make against both wind and tide together, however skilfully she was sailed. They had to go now, whether they liked it or not. Penn stood a little longer, licking the blood out of his lip, which was bleeding again and stinging with the salt. 'So much for Smeeton's evening fishing-party,' he thought. He reckoned that by the time they made base, if they ever did, he'd have Smeeton crying for mercy.

The mainsail was lashed on the boom, and Penn got Gerry and Gary to shake it out and start tying down the reefs.

'It's probably full of holes. Any of you used it lately?'

They shook their heads. 'We always go on the engine,' Gerry

said. They were prepared to do anything Penn said. Gerry had reeved on some makeshift sheets to the headsails. Penn changed the knots from grannies to bowlines, and took the ends back aft and gave them to Bates.

'She's got to pay off the right way when the anchor comes out, or we'll just go back on the sand again. When I shout at you, cleat this down here, tight as you can and put the tiller over this way. Point her like this.' He pointed. He had to shout at Bates, both crouching on the deck, hunched against the spray. 'I'll come back as soon as the anchor is out. It might take some time.' He knew the theory, but not much else. 'We could do with Jim here right now,' he said to Bates.

He got Gerry and Gary to stand by the mainsail, ready to haul, and Fletcher on the staysail. 'Smeeton, you can help me with the anchor.' They were all falling over each other, flung about by the violent motion of the smack. The water kept coming over in dollops. There was no point any more in ducking to miss it; they were soaked through. Penn went to the anchor and picked up the chain again. 'Ready?' he asked Smeeton.

It took twenty minutes to get the anchor. Penn swore at Smeeton with what snatches of breath he could spare, and swore at the grating fairlead when the chain inched back, and at the water swilling through the bulwarks. Everyone but Penn was sick. When Smeeton retched up all over the sliding, clanking chain he was trying to make fast, Penn laughed.

When the anchor came out at last, and Gerry and Gary sweated up the sails, the old smack lay down and ran, more under the water than over it. The loose chain ran with a crash into the bulwarks, Smeeton frantically chasing it. Fletcher and Gary dangled on the ends of the halyards, groping for their cleats; Fletcher had lost his balance and hit the corner of the hatch with such force that he was doubled up and useless. Penn stumbled over him, shouting at Bates, 'Free off! Free off!'

'Which way?' Bates sobbed.

'For cripes' sake!' Penn clawed his way along the lee deck, knee-deep in water. It was pandemonium, the loose jib flogging with guts enough to pull the forestay out. Penn got the tiller off Bates and eased it, freeing off so that the wind was more on the beam. The smack got up, and the water poured out along her scuppers.

'Get that sheet! Pull it in! Here, let me have it!' With his thigh to the tiller, Penn hauled in the flogging jib, brute strength capturing it. Bates wound the sheet frantically round the cleat.

'Go and find a compass, for God's sake! Tell Smeeton to look out for shoal water, or buoys or something. If we go aground again—!' It would be curtains, at the rate *Mathilda* was travelling, but he didn't say so to Bates. He was shivering, although the sweat was running off him after getting the anchor. He thought he was as scared as Smeeton looked, but hadn't as much time to think about it. Thank God, Gerry and Gary had made the halyards fast. How long they would hold was another matter. Any of the gear was likely to give up at any moment, mast and hull included. Most of the crew had given up already, retching up what was left in their stomachs. Penn, tonguing his lip, was fiercely satisfied. They had hurt him last night. He wasn't used to being beaten.

The way into the river was up into the wind. The compass did not help much, without a chart, and there was no chart on board. The sea was very rough, but Penn knew that the shoals would be marked by even rougher water. They all stared for it, blinking through the spray, aware that it mattered more than anyone was prepared to admit in words. *Mathilda* shouldered through the waves, plunging into troughs with shuddering cracks that set all her seams weeping. The floorboards below were awash. Fletcher, almost out for the count, went and lay down, groaning, and the water broke over his dangling hands. swilling a sour stench of old paraffin, fish and beer through the

black cuddy. Smeeton went to look for a leadline, and was sick again. He hadn't the strength to climb back out of the cuddy, and sat on the bottom step of the companion-way, moaning softly to himself. Bates went to have a look, and the sight cheered him immensely.

'It's like one of those old emigrant ships,' he said to Penn, 'that engraving for "Botany Bay".' Botany Bay was one of his songs.

'Yes, pity it's only three miles, and not ten thousand. Go and ask Smeeton why he's not fishing.'

Bates did so. Smeeton didn't reply. Bates came back and said, 'There's enough water down there. He doesn't even have to move.'

Penn hoped privately that it wouldn't increase. A faint light behind them suggested that dawn might come in time to show them the mouth of the river. Having come so far, Penn was feeling more confident, amazed that the old ruin had held together in such conditions.

'You know,' he said to Bates, 'we ought to have tried sailing her more often. Not in this sort of weather—I mean on nice days. Just a bit of wind. I never thought she'd do this.' He wiped his hair out his eyes, squinting ahead. 'We'd better go about. I think that's shallow ahead.'

He put the tiller over. *Mathilda* was an old cow to tack, unbalanced with her reefed mainsail. He made a hash of it and had to sail again, the line of white foam unpleasantly close. The second time she hung in stays for what seemed a century, but at last, when he was beginning to feel the panic getting hold, she paid off and went away on the skirts of the white foam, heading for deep water. Penn wiped his face, shaking. He had never been scared like this before, he realized, not for anything so important—only for people sometimes, his father and Soggy and the magistrate, which was different. He was pleased that he had kept his head. It made him feel strange, that he could enjoy what was happening at the same time as feeling scared to death. Not like Smeeton, giving in, like a jelly. They'd be lucky if they made it, with *Mathilda* rotten as a wormy apple, but now he thought they would.

'What about it, Bates?' he said. 'She's not so past it, is she?'

Bates gave a green smile.

'We'll sail her again. I didn't know she would.'

If there was a nice day, he thought, they could lay off school and have a trip out.

When it got light they were off the mouth of the river, where the water was always worse than anywhere else, even in good weather. *Mathilda* rattled about, groaning and straining, long splits opening out in her staysail. She was full of water. Penn gave the tiller to Bates and went forward. Gerry and Gary were sitting on the forehatch.

'Enjoy yourselves?' Penn asked.

He put his head in the hatch and shouted down the cuddy, 'Smeeton, come up here! And Fletcher.'

'Lay off!' Smeeton muttered.

'Why should I? I'm going to court-martial you. You can get ashore up on the mud here. Bates and I are sick of your stench.'

Smeeton didn't move, until Penn started to come down the companionway, then he got up and crawled up into the air. His face was grey.

'Best cure for seasickness in the world,' Penn said, pointing to a hard mud spit that came out from the sea-wall ahead of them. 'Land. It'll do you good, Smeeton, believe me—I'm doing you a favour. We can't go too close in, mind you—just close enough for you to jump.'

If there had been any fight in them at all they could just have easily turned on him and shoved him out on the mud. But Penn's confidence smothered them, and they were sick enough to want to go. They jumped when Penn said jump, and landed

58

in four feet of dark, cold water. Penn stood at the tiller and watched them flounder up the spit. He felt marvellous. He laughed, loud enough for them to hear, and Bates sat smiling, and saying, 'That was terrific, Penn. You do have good ideas.'

Penn didn't feel so marvellous when he got home.

'Oh, so you've condescended to drop in for some breakfast?' his mother said. 'It's nice to see you when you're just passing by. Do sit down and make yourself at home.'

'I'll get washed.'

'We've hot and cold in every room in this hotel.' She flounced round from the cooker, her lips tight. Penn waited for the onslaught, weary and hating her. He took his hand away from his face and she saw his lip and her expression changed.

'How d'you get that? Fighting?'

'Smeeton had a lump of glass.'

'God in heaven, what a mess! Go and run it under the cold tap. It's just like your father had that time outside the Plough and Sail when young Billy knocked his beer over and they all went berserk. He's still got the mark now. And I reckon you'll have, too, unless you get it stitched. You'd better go down to the surgery.'

'Oh, Ma, it'll wait till tonight.'

'You'll do what I say for a change! You've missed the school bus as it is. Get a move on now! You *choose* to do these things, don't you? You choose to stay out all night and get slashed up fighting with that load of layabouts, then you take the consequences, my lad. Fat lot of good your education has done you so far! All what I fought for to get for you, and you're still as big a yob as the rest of them—'

Penn shoved his way past and out of the kitchen, slamming the door. He went upstairs, almost in tears, all his pleasant feelings of triumph over both Smeeton and the sea—especially the sea—shattered and scattered and obliterated. He locked himself in the bathroom and contemplated his lip, scowling, in the mirror. It looked awful. He cleaned himself up very slowly and got a clean white shirt out of the airing cupboard and fetched his tie. He hated his mother bitterly. When he got downstairs again he ate his breakfast with difficulty and his mother railed at him without stopping, on and on, so that he got the sour impression that the house was wired up for canned invective, like a restaurant for canned music, and if his mother had gone out it would still have gone on and on. Only he had no way of switching it off. He could only depart.

'To the doctor's,' his mother shouted after him. 'Else I'll get your father on to you.'

The surgery was full of smelly, yelling babies and stupid women, and nothing to read but *Woman's Own* and *Country Life*. He read all the problems at the back of the women's papers, until the doctor buzzed for him.

'What did you do to get this?' the doctor asked, prodding ominously.

'I met a piece of glass coming the other way.'

'Young louts, wasting our time. You deserve all you get . . .' He treated Penn with marked lack of tenderness, so that Penn squirmed and swore. Half-way through, old Miss Marble, the district nurse, came in and said, 'If you're going to school after, Patrick, I can give you a lift as far as Parkfield. I've got a confinement there.'

Penn had already decided that such treatment as he was getting warranted a day off, but the doctor said, with a sadistic smile, 'It's your day, Pat, obviously.' Penn guessed that he was referring to Miss Marble's notorious driving: many people decided that they were going in the opposite direction when Miss Marble offered them a lift. 'You're perfectly fit to go to school,' he added, reading Penn's intentions. 'I'm sorry. Don't smile, that's all.' He grinned. Penn had no intention of smiling.

He went outside and got into Miss Marble's Mini, fastening the safety belt carefully.

'What have you been doing? Fighting?' Miss Marble asked brightly. He scowled.

'If you didn't frown all the time, Patrick, you'd be quite good-looking. How's the piano playing going? I hear you're very good.'

Penn grunted, wishing he'd hitch-hiked.

'Miss Sparrow was wanting someone to play for her on Saturday mornings, for her dancing classes in the village hall. She asked me if I knew anyone. Would you fancy that? She'd pay you ten bob, I expect.'

'No,' said Penn. If the girls had been sixteen or so, he'd have said yes, but they weren't.

'I thought you'd say that. What a shame! You have so much to give, dear, with a talent like that. Really, Patrick, you ought to pull yourself together and start using your time more responsibly . . .'

The old bag, because she'd delivered them all, thought she could do the God Almighty, just like Soggy and Stacker . . . He pulled off the safety belt.

'If you put me down at the next crossing, I can get the bus,' he said.

'But I can take you on to Parkfield, dear. It will be quicker for you.' She went straight on past the turning, and overtook a lorry on a blind bend. Penn fastened the safety belt again quickly. 'I'm surprised they let you grow your hair so long at the Beehive, Patrick. I would have thought they had rules about that sort of thing . . .'

Penn shut his eyes and felt himself shrink. His outside felt hard, like shell, and his inside all churning, like the slosh through the window of a washing-machine. He remembered the sea, and the salt crusty to the tongue, the feeling of exhilaration, old *Mathilda* beating and flogging into the wind. Then he remembered the school smell of sweat and ink and dust, and the yellow keyboard of the Bechstein, all his for three and a half hours, and Soggy's eyes, cold and sarcastic.

Soggy gave him a detention for being late without a good excuse. He could see with his own eyes that Penn's explanation about going to the doctor's was true, but he chose not to accept it.

'I'm working to rule,' Soggy said. Penn knew that it was because of his hair. 'I'll give you till next Monday, Pennington,' he said. And Penn thought, 'With any luck, next Monday I'll get the sack.'

Next Monday a staff meeting was held, with Pennington's hair on the agenda. Mr. Peach, an irredeemable gambler, had run a book in the staff-room on the effect of Soggy's ultimatum to Pennington, and had made a profit of thirty bob. The sight of Pennington's hair in assembly, falling thick and shining to his shoulders as he played a Bach prelude to fill in a technical hitch (Stacker having lost his glasses), had made Mr. Peach's day. Mr.

Matthews, the games master, was the only one to be equally satisfied by the result. He had won a pound off Mr. Peach. He had not considered that his money had been in any danger at all. 'If they think Pennington's going to step down now,' he said to Peach on Friday, 'after the whole thing has been made into an issue, they don't know their Pennington. He's as pig-headed as they come. Fighting spirit and all that—why else is he so good at soccer? Because he's aggressive and dirty. He wants to blast the opposition off the field. And what do they do in this cock-eyed school? Sit him at a piano all day! Marsh has no more idea of how to handle a character like Pennington than fly in the air.'

'Well, let's face it, the piano is the only thing he's any good at, games apart.'

'Unfortunately for Pennington, yes.'

The whole school was now familiar with the strains of Mendelssohn's Rondo Capriccioso, or the old Capritch, as Penn's friends referred to it. Penn, unsupervised in a small practice-room for a good deal of his generous playing time, could not be trusted to keep on working—Crocker, calling in on him unexpectedly, had found him reading a paperback entitled *Sexual Permissiveness on the American Campus*, and had therefore insisted that Penn do his practice on the grand piano in the hall, where, if he stopped, he would be reported immediately by any one of several masters who would be teaching within earshot. This ruse was not popular with those forced to listen, many of whom found a solid hour of double octave scales a tedious background to their own voices, but it had the desired effect. Even now, the staff meeting was being conducted to the distant echoes of a Beethoven Sonata. To those members of the staff not particularly interested in Pennington's hair, the music was having a distinctly soporific effect.

'We can't go on ignoring this,' Mr. Stack said. 'Others are following suit, and there's a limit to what's acceptable. Pennington reached that some weeks ago.'

'Pennington's been the limit ever since he first came here,' someone remarked.

'Yes, but we have only another two months of Pennington,' Mr. Stack pointed out, to the accompaniment of several interjections of relief. 'We can surely handle this without actually making an issue of it?'

'An issue has been made of it already, by Mr. Marsh,' said Matthews.

'Am I supposed to accept Pennington's hair without comment, then?' Soggy asked acidly. 'If I had my way I'd cane the living daylights out of him, but as our governors—God help us—consider this unenlightened, I would be grateful for any alternative constructive suggestions anyone can make—including you, Matthews.'

'I'm not concerned,' Matthews said. 'I only know that Pennington will get sacked before he'll get his hair cut, the way he feels at present.'

'And much as we'd all quite like to see the back of him, I'm not sacking him at this stage,' said Mr. Stack. 'With parents like his it's just not worth it. They'll have it in the newspapers immediately and the school will just be a laughing-stock—quite the last thing we want. But I agree with Mr. Marsh, we can't ignore the whole business, much as we'd like to. Loss of privileges, possibly? Extra work—'

'He's already lost all his dinner-hours and an hour after school every day,' Matthews said, beginning to feel like fighting for Penn.

'But not his games,' Mr. Marsh said, his eyes gleaming. 'Not his swimming and his athletics and his P.E.—which I understand he actually enjoys. The only subject, Mr. Matthews—if you can call it a subject—which he would be unhappy to miss. I suggest, Mr. Stack, that Pennington is stopped from games until he gets his hair cut.'

Mr. Stack looked at Matthews, and dropped his eyes doubtfully. 'Well—'

'That's extremely unfair to me!' Matthews said hotly. 'And to the school, too! We've got a whole list of fixtures for the term, and he's in just about every one of them! And there's the swimming gala next month—we're all set for the cup if—'

'Well, if it's that important, it's up to you to see that he gets his hair cut,' Soggy said.

'Up to me! But *I* haven't made an issue of it, have I? I don't care if his hair is down to his backside if he wins.'

'It's a matter of principle, Matthews,' Stack said wearily.

'Sir, you know Pennington as well as I do! He won't get it cut now that it's been blown up into something on the agenda of a staff meeting, not even if you take him off games and sit him at the wretched piano all day and all night.'

'That's a good idea,' said Soggy malevolently. 'No games, and Mr. Crocker can have him for the whole of the games periods. That would please everyone.'

Mr. Crocker turned round and glared at Soggy. 'Are you turning my subject into a punishment, Marsh? Are you using it to further this ridiculous, petty nonsense about hair? I protest, Mr. Stack!'

'It's a punishment for Pennington already,' Soggy said coldly.

'How dare you!' Mr. Crocker had gone bright red, and his big hooked nostrils distended like a race-horse's. 'Matthews and I are the only people in this school who have got anywhere with Pennington at all, and you are prepared to *use* our successes merely to humiliate the boy over a point of order that is quite meaningless.'

'I agree!' said Matthews. 'Marsh is Pennington's form master, and I admit he has my sympathy in that respect, but the hair thing is his pigeon. You must have known, Marsh, when you gave the ultimatum—you know him well enough, God knows—'

'My hands are completely tied by this soft attitude of the Education Committee. I would—'

'Yes, we all know your natural inclinations,' Crocker said.

'I am afraid corporal punishment for this sort of thing is out,' Mr. Stack put in. 'But Pennington must be made to see reason and I do feel—I'm sorry, Matthews, to say this—that the only line of action that stands any hope of succeeding is, as Mr. Marsh suggested, through putting him out of all the teams until he toes the line. It will take him out of the limelight, no bad thing— deprive him of his opportunities for showing off. He might well give in.'

'And what if he doesn't? Without him we won't beat North-end Parkside in the gala, and the cup has been ours for three years running!'

'If he's that important, all the more power to the argument,' Mr. Stack said. 'I'm sure you will persuade him, Matthews.' He glanced at his watch. 'In any case, he can't swim in the gala like that. He won't be able to see where he's going. I've no more on the agenda. Has anyone else anything to say?'

· · · ·

Penn, released from the Bechstein by the clock striking five, left in mid-bar and made for the Common Room, where Maxwell and the concert party were waiting to start their audition. He met the staff trailing out of the staff-room, and was surprised to be waylaid by Matthews at the bottom of the corridor.

'They've passed the buck to me, Pennington. It's either hair and no games, or games and no hair. Think about it.'

He disappeared into the staff Gents, leaving Penn seething at the injustice. He shouldered the door into the Common Room and found the concert committee drinking beer, pouring it out of a teapot into innocuous white teacups, with saucers and teaspoons. Looking at the froth, Penn said, 'That wouldn't deceive an infant child.'

Bates was already mellow, he could see. Maxwell said, 'We want you for just about everything, Penn. Midwinter's monologue has to have dirgy stuff for the background, for atmosphere —it's about this grave opening and a corpse getting out. He says it's got music, but he can't find it; but he can sort of tell you how it goes. And the trumpet needs an accompaniment, too. Then Rees and Crombie and Burton are going to do this send-up of the Superbes—they've got the music for that. The sketch is okay, unless you can think of a way of improving it. We've gone over most of the things except Bates's. The girls are using a record for their can-can thing—look, here's the stuff for the Superbes. Let's do that. Have a cup of tea first.'

Penn told them what Matthews had passed on to him, and they were all duly appalled.

'That's stinking, passing it on the Matthews. What are you going to do?'

Penn shrugged. 'Sleep on it,' he said. 'Give Bates another cup of tea,' he added softly. He fetched himself a chair and sat down and while the others argued about what they were going to practise, he played the tune of The Red Flag, which was his personal anti-Soggy hate piece, designed to relieve feelings. He played it very loud, hoping it might even reach Soggy out in the corridor.

'Cripes, Penn, you don't half stick your neck out,' Crombie said, grinning.

At Christmas old Crocker had taught the choir to sing the

German carol 'Tannenbaum', which was sung to the same tune as 'The Red Flag'. It was a popular choice, being rousing and rhythmic, but Soggy had objected to its being chosen for the Christmas service owing to the rebel associations of the tune.

'Highly unsuitable,' he said to Mr. Crocker. 'I will prevail upon Mr. Stack to forbid you to use it.'

'It is a carol about a Christmas-tree,' Mr. Crocker said, breathing very hard. 'An innocent Christmas-tree. These children are not old enough to know anything else about it. But if you forbid it, they will find out the reason why. You have a nasty bigoted mind, and you will infect these children with your hysterical political views and make issue where no issue was intended.'

Penn, who had been playing the piano for the choir and had been sitting near enough to overhear this exchange, had been intrigued by it, and had played the tune to his mother at home and asked her what old Dotty had been talking about.

'It's the tune the Communists used to sing,' his mother said vaguely. 'In the Revolution and that. I suppose that's why he doesn't like it. He's a right old Tory from the look of him.'

This explanation had endeared the tune to Penn. He liked anything that irritated Soggy. He had played it in the Common Room the next day when Soggy had come in to collar Maxwell for a Mathematics detention, and Soggy had gone bright red, and come over to the piano, twitching dangerously.

'Why are you playing that tune?' he asked, aware that Penn had heard the exchange of the day before, and suspecting him of pure insolence.

'I'm a Communist, sir,' Penn had replied, playing on.

Soggy had twitched some more, but been uncertain of how to deal with the situation. At the end of the afternoon, when he had had time to think about it, he gave Penn a double detention for some trifling offence, and Mr. Stack informed Mr. Crocker that 'Tannenbaum' was not to be used in the Christmas service. The whole school knew what had happened, and why the choir's repertoire had been curtailed, and Penn started a Young Communist Party which the whole fifth form joined, although they didn't know a Communist from a Liberal. Ever since, one bar of Tannenbaum, whistled or hummed, had the power to send Soggy raving. Only Penn dared to bait him with it and had been caned twice for the pleasure (in spite of the Education Committee).

When he had worked off his feelings Penn obediently went through the bill, working out possibilities. It all seemed very promising. Penn refused point-blank to do a solo. 'You want me to die of overwork? They don't want to hear my stuff, and if I do anything decent old Crocker'll go off the deep end. You know him.'

'Give 'em the old Capritch. It grows on you when you hear it often enough.'

'I haven't noticed,' Penn said coldly. 'Let's get old Bates going. He's nicely away. Bates, stand up. I can't play the ruddy harmonica, thanks to Smeeton—we'll use the piano for now. What do you want, Bates? "Lowlands Away?" "Down by the Royal Albion?" ' He played a few exploratory chords. Bates took him up.

'As I was a-walking down by the Royal Albion
The night it was stormy and so was the day,
When who should I see but one of my shipmates
Wrapped up in a blanket and colder than clay.'

Bates's tenor was clear and high, and in sad songs touched a nerve that Penn realized was not peculiar to just himself—so far, Bates's only audience. He sang, when slightly drunk, with such sincerity that the stark words had a pathos that was undeniable.

'His poor head was aching, his sad heart was breaking . . .'

Penn glanced at Maxwell and saw him shut his eyes thoughtfully. Maxwell was held, and even the larking Midwinter. Penn did not play much, merely following with a few suitably poignant chords, feeling it on the harmonica, and cursing Smeeton.

'At the head of the gravestone these words shall be written . . .'

It was perfect, Penn thought, just like in *Mathilda*'s cuddy. He was warm at the thought of being Bates's manager.

67

When Bates had finished the audience was impressed.

'Fancy old Bates—!'

'Queer old stuff. Gets you.'

'Yes, but what's eating him exactly?' Crombie said.

'He's dying of V.D., you twit,' Penn said.

'Oh, very suitable for a parents' evening,' Maxwell said. 'Just the right touch! That's out for a start. Try something else.'

'They're all earthy,' Penn said.

'We can stand earth, but no subsoil,' Maxwell decided.

Penn guided Bates on to safer ground, with 'Tom's gone to Hilo' and 'Lowlands Away'. When he was well away they did 'The Butcher Boy' and, such was Bates's power, even Maxwell did not question its morality. The difficulty was to stop Bates. Penn was triumphant.

'You're blooming good, Bates. Pipe down now, and stop drinking tea, for cripes' sake. I've got to get you home.'

'The only surefire flop in this old concert,' said Maxwell, 'will be Mr. Robert Tate, for whom I am not responsible. The only baritone corpse in the south of England.'

The next day Crocker broke the news to Penn that he was going to have to accompany Mr. Tate in the concert, because Mr. Tate's usual accompanist was sick.

'Sick of old Tate, I reckon,' Maxwell said.

Crocker said, 'You must come in plenty of time, to go through his songs with him. He says he'll let me know what they are beforehand, but I doubt if he will. I know him. He's not at all considerate, to put it mildly.'

Penn was disgusted to be given a part in the programme the whole school was pledged to despise.

'He's a frightful old woman. Make sure your nails are clean for a change.' Crocker looked worried.

'Suppose *I'm* sick on Saturday?' Penn muttered to Maxwell. 'Sitting there thumping away the whole blooming concert. I was only going to blow the old harmonica for Bates.' He had been doing the Capritch the whole afternoon, while his class went swimming. He hadn't had any time to get his hair cut, even if he had decided to, the rate they were working him. He pointed this out to Matthews, whom he could see was getting depressed. In spite of liking Matthews, Penn still hadn't decided what to do. Matthews was entirely sympathetic.

'I might go Saturday morning, then,' Penn said to him, eased by the sympathy.

But on Friday afternoon Soggy, incensed by an insolent remark that Penn had thought he was too far away to hear, gave him a thousand lines to write over the week-end: 'Long-haired boys should learn to keep a civil tongue in their heads.' The punishment was so puerile and so much in keeping with Soggy's arid mentality, that Penn's resolve to go on defying him was renewed.

Chapter 5

On Saturday morning, after writing one hundred and thirty-seven illegible lines, Penn went round to Bates's. The fact that they would have to catch the three-o'clock bus back to school for the concert nullified all natural optimism at the thought of a Saturday, and Penn's face was gloomy.

'You coming down to Moorham, till lunchtime?' Penn asked.

'What for?'

Penn shrugged. 'Something to do.'

Bates said, 'You know what you were saying about trying to get some sails for *Mathilda*, so's we could try sailing her?'

'Well?'

'I saw Fletcher this morning and he said there are some smack sails that nobody wants in the old sail-loft up Fiddler's Creek. He said Smeeton was going to get them.'

'Did he now?' Penn considered, frowning. *Mathilda*'s sails were in ribbons after their eventful night out, and he had fancied sailing again. He had asked Jim if there were any sails around that anyone didn't want, but Jim couldn't think of any.

'He said they were off old *Bluebell*, and stowed away in the top loft. I was going to come round and tell you.'

'We could go and have a look,' Penn said.

'That's what I thought.'

It would be as less deadly a way to pass the morning as anything else, especially if Smeeton was hanging around up there.

70

They set off, walking, as they both had punctures which they couldn't be bothered to mend. A track led away over Turner's farm, converging with the river. Then it was along the sea-wall, and right-handed into Fiddler's Creek. The old sail-loft was derelict, a landmark for some miles around. Once, in the days of barges, the wharf had been busy, but now no one ever came there, except the occasional cranky water-colourist.

Penn wanted to see Smeeton. Smeeton, after the night at sea, had been overheard to say that he would like to kill Penn, but he had made no attempt so far to even annoy him. Penn guessed that he was awaiting his opportunity, which was the way he worked, but Penn's nature was incautious. He was not afraid of Smeeton. He despised him too much.

The tide was just about at its lowest ebb, the creek a winding snake of mud with a thread of water glistening here and there. They found Fletcher and Gerry Green sitting on the wharf throwing stones at an old can lying in the mud.

Fletcher looked round sourly. 'What you doing down here?'

'Bates said you've found some sails. We thought we'd have a look.'

'Flaming cheek. They're ours if they're any good.'

Penn grinned.

He went round the side of the sail-loft with Bates to the rickety old outside ladder that gave access to the top storey. The bottom floor was full of the local farmer's machinery, and the second floor was a mouldering junkheap of old gear off the barges. Penn went up the ladder first, followed by Bates, and then by Fletcher and Gerry. It was steep and rotten, but nothing gave, even under Penn's weight, and he came out at the top on the tiny balcony, some thirty feet high, that gave on to the door. Bates, waiting at the top of the ladder, looked down and said, 'Strewth, Penn, get a move on! This gives me the creeps.' The door was closed by massive oak bars that slotted down into iron brackets. They lifted easily and the door opened inwards. Penn went inside, followed quickly by Bates.

The loft comprised the whole of the top floor, making a room big enough to lay out a barge mainsail. It was lit by windows overlooking the river and big skylights, so that it seemed almost as if there was no roof at all. The floor was solid, worn smooth by generations of trouser knees, soft slippers and sliding sailcloth. It was also remarkably empty.

'I don't see any sails,' Penn said, lifting an old tarpaulin that seemed to be the only bit of gear around.

It was then, as the door closed, that he got the idea. He stood rigid, not saying anything. It was too late.

'What's up?' Bates said.

The bars dropped in place outside the door with heavy thumps. There was a snigger, and a shuffle, and Fletcher's voice, muffled and distant. 'See you later!'

'I don't get it,' Bates said. 'What's he playing at?'

'Oh, cripes!' said Penn. 'Don't you see?' His face went white momentarily, and a pulse flicked the corner of his mouth. He could not say anything else, choked by pure physical rage. Bates was astonished.

'What's eating you? They're only larking about.' He went over to the door and shoved it. It did not move an inch. 'Fletcher, you idiot!' he bawled.

'Save your breath,' Penn said shortly. He glanced at his watch. It was eleven o'clock. He walked across the room and stood looking down over the empty river. He was so angry at being tricked so easily that he felt almost faint with it, his stomach hollow and sick. The humiliation shook him.

'They'll come back,' Bates said, not very concerned.

'Yes, tonight,' Penn said.

'What do you mean, tonight?'

'After the concert.'

Bates stared at him. 'You don't mean—?'

Penn leaned against the window-frame, picking at the wood-worm holes, laying his forehead on the dusty glass. There was a long silence. A swallow flew in through a hole in the top pane and flew out again in a panic with a flurry of wings.

'You mean it's so that you'll miss the concert?' Bates said eventually.

'Smeeton couldn't have found a better way of getting me into trouble if he'd thought for a month.'

'I'm not sorry,' Bates said.

'*You're* not sorry! You're so ruddy chicken, Bates, you make me sick!'

Penn could have wept. He picked at the splintery wood, tearing long strips out of it. He remembered old Crocker telling him to clean his nails. He banged his forehead against the glass, staring down into the shining bed of the creek below. Bates came and stood beside him.

'Perhaps someone might come by,' he said. 'And if we shout —'

'No one comes out here.'

All they could see, thirty feet below, was a stretch of cobbled wharf, quite empty, and the creek. In the far distance, beyond the bluish flat marshes and clumps of old elm, they could see the highest buildings in Northend, some twelve miles away.

'Well, keep looking,' Penn said sourly. 'If you think we're going to have visitors.'

There was certainly no way out. The windows that gave on to the creek were all broken; they could have got out there if there had been a way down. There was also a door in the wall, which opened, but the drop below it was sheer. It had a pulley over the top and had been used to raise and lower goods up and down on a rope. But there wasn't a shred of rope in the loft. The room was painfully bare. Even the tarpaulin was shredding with rot.

'Jump,' said Bates, and shuddered.

Penn opened the door and stood looking down. After a minute or two he looked at his watch again.

'What time's high water today?'

Bates shrugged. 'Around teatime, I think.'

'Five? Half-past four? Yes, it was about midday last Sunday.' Penn leaned against the side of the door, looking down at the wharf below. It was about fifteen feet wide, and very hard, in spite of the grass growing through the cobbles. Beyond it the

creek bank sloped away, hard, smooth mud. Penn stroked the scab on his lip, scowling.

'What's up?' Bates said. He wasn't worried.

'Just wondering,' Penn said.

He went on looking. Bates got bored and wandered round the shed, kicking a chip of wood in front of him. 'What'll they do without you, Penn?' he said. 'Old Maxwell will go raving if you don't turn up.'

Penn wasn't bothered about Maxwell. He was going to turn up, because Smeeton thought he wasn't. He hadn't moved his eyes from the wharf.

'When the tide comes up, I'm going to jump,' he said.

Bates stopped kicking his bit of wood.

'You're joking?' he said.

He came and looked out of the hole, pursing up his lips. He looked shaken. 'You don't mean it?'

'When the water's up the wall by about a foot, I reckon there'll be enough to jump into without breaking my ruddy neck.'

'You'll land on the wharf.'

'Not if I take a run at it. There's the whole length of the shed. I reckon I'll land about three feet out from the bank, in about four foot of water. The longer I wait, the better it'll be, but we've got to be in Northend by five, to make it worth the trouble.'

'If high water's half-past four, it won't be up that high much before three.'

'No.'

'You won't catch the bus.'

'We'll bother about that bit when we get to it.'

'You're not really going to, are you, Penn?'

'Yes. I am.'

Penn could be moved by his instinct for revenge to extraordinary daring, as Matthews had noticed several times on the soccer pitch. Now, hate for Smeeton was far stronger than a natural disinclination to attempt the unpleasant exit he was visualizing. Unfortunately, as Penn was not slow to realize, Smeeton was going to get satisfaction of a kind, for the four hours that had to pass before the water came up promised little joy. Sitting in the window, contemplating the distance to the ground for all that length of time was not calculated to cheer.

Bates was no help.

'You'll go splat, as far as I can see,' he said. 'The wharf's too wide.'

Penn glowered. 'If you think I'm going to give Smeeton that much pleasure, you can think again.'

The prospect, of saltings, pasture, cows and the distant haze of the open sea, was serene. The sun poured into the loft and a small breeze chivvied the dust on the floor; a butterfly flew in

and sat basking on the window-ledge. Penn lay down in the sun and shut his eyes. He wished it didn't matter . . . for God's sake, he didn't give a hoot about the crummy concert, and would be more than grateful to miss the treat of playing senile accompaniment to that sour-faced mothball, Tate . . . but he was damned if he was going to sit back waiting for Smeeton to come and rescue him, and he was also damned if he was going to let Bates contract out so easily—dozy old Bates, the butt of 5C, who hardly ever uttered in school, treated by all the masters with weary cynicism . . . he had more talent under his spotty hide than any of the rest of Maxwell's line-up. Apart from which, if *he* didn't turn up . . . Penn thought he might as well never turn up again. To go splat in the attempt would be a merciful release compared with the doom which would await him at the Beehive. Penn groaned.

The water started to come back, rippled by the fresh breeze. Penn lay with his chin on his hands, watching it. Far away at at the top of the creek two little spots moved on the mud. They were digging for bait, Penn supposed. Pity they hadn't chosen the old wharf. Nothing else human appeared to exist in the world at all. The water was pushing up all the little runnels in the channel, sniffing and withdrawing, and then running up with a surge, pushing a yellow scum on its lip. It was two o'clock. Penn shut his eyes again. He should be getting changed now, scrubbing his finger-nails for the baritone corpse. He picked at them with a nail, and yawned. Bates was leaning against the far wall, apparently in a coma.

The tide came up, inexorably as always, and faster, eventually, than Penn wished. The circus act had very little appeal, now that it was so close. In spite of Bates's opinion, Penn did not think there was much risk of hitting the concrete; it was just that one's natural instinct was against launching one's all into so much space. Penn had never been keen on the top board at the best of times. He stood up, and fidgeted with the woodworm again. Bates came up beside him and peered down.

'You're not going to, are you?'

'Yes.'

'I don't mind missing the concert a bit.'

Penn thought, 'When the water covers the wall a foot—say, up to the bit of seaweed caught on one of the big stakes—I'll go into orbit.' The water came up and covered it. He took his watch off and gave it to Bates. It was twenty-five to four. He took off his shirt and dropped it on the floor.

'Look,' Bates said, 'just for a stupid concert—'

'Oh, belt up.' Penn thought there ought to be a roll of drums, but all was perfect tranquillity, the skylarks trilling off the wall, the water starting to lap, lap, lap against the wharf, pushed by the summer breeze. He thought of Smeeton's face, and walked back down the shed. The horrid word 'splat' passed through his brain as he started running, and continued with him as he flew through what felt like outer space. But it was water below, not gravestones, and he pulled up his knees to make a shallow landing, grasping them with his hands. The water hit him with a crack, and then it was all completely normal, a mere swim in the creek, his pent-up funk dissolving in a feeling of overwhelming relief. He turned over on his back, kicking against the tide, and waved at Bates's peering face.

'Piece of cake!' he yelled.

He felt more relieved than he would have admitted. He turned over and did a rapid crawl to the bank, smiting the water as if it were Smeeton, savagely triumphant. When he unbolted Bates, Bates looked green.

'I feel sick,' he said.

'Run it off,' Penn said. 'All the way home. We've got to sprint.' He pulled on his shirt, tucking it hastily into his dripping jeans. Bates gave him his watch. It was twenty to four. Half an hour to get home, ten minutes to change . . . it was still a doubtful proposition . . . barely an hour, and hitch-hiking was rotten on a Saturday afternoon. He was starving—

'Come on!'

Bates was hopeless.

'What would I have done, if you'd hit the concrete?'

'What would *I* have done, come to that? I don't see *you* had anything to worry about!'

'I don't know how you could. You've got no imagination, Penn. I feel ghastly.'

Penn said savagely, 'For cripes' sake! It's finished now. Don't be such a girl! Come on—'

He pushed him out, almost kicking him down the ladder. They started to run, but Penn, fit from soccer, went ahead judging the pace to fit the distance. He had to be there long before Bates, for Bates was last on the programme. Bates had all the time in the world. Having estimated thirty minutes Penn got to his garden gate twenty-five minutes after setting off from the sail-loft. He vaulted it, squeezed round his father's motor-bike which filled the path, and let himself quietly into the kitchen. His mother was out and his father snoring on the bed, for which Penn was profoundly thankful, not wanting to waste time arguing. He changed, combed his damp hair and grabbed the harmonica off his chest of drawers. His father was still snoring. Penn padded downstairs, got himself a hunk of bread and cheese out of the pantry, and let himself out into the garden again. The village street was absolutely deserted, save for the bedraggled figure of an exhausted Bates, weaving wearily up the turning from the farm. It was a quarter past four. Even if he got a lift immediately, he was never going to make it for five. The Beehive wasn't on the main road; there was ten minutes' walk across an estate to get to it. Penn thought of Smeeton, grinning in the audience, and touched the scab on his lip with his tongue. His eyes went to his father's motor-bike.

Bates reeled up.

'Come on,' Penn said. 'I've been waiting *hours*—' He opened the gate.

Bates groaned, the sweat trickling down on either side of his nose. Penn heaved the bike off its stand, and wheeled it through the gate. Bates stared.

'Penn, you're not!'

'It'll be all right.' He would get to the concert in time, at least. What might happen afterwards was something to face when the time came. Penn did not believe in looking too far ahead. There was only one thing that mattered just at that moment. He pushed the bike away from the house, and started it up. It was a racing 600 c.c. machine, and the din scorched the village street.

'Get on!' Penn yelled at Bates.

Bates, gibbering with dismay, scrambled on to the pillion.

'What if you meet a copper?' he yelled.

Penn said something very rude that was drowned in the acceleration as he took off down the street. It was a chance he was prepared to take in the heat of the moment. He hadn't sweated all day in that loft to be stopped in the last lap. He took the bend out of the village at forty, and opened up to sixty down the lane. He felt marvellous, completely of the moment, triumphant and fighting. Nobody could do him down. Smeeton would pass out when he arrived.

'Penn, for cripes' sake!' He did not hear Bates moaning, only his frantic hands on his trouser belt. Cripes, if he had a bike of his own—! It was glorious. He cornered on to the arterial, and went into the fast lane, overtaking a Rover 2000 and a Triumph. He didn't care then what happened afterwards: he was in a world of his own, the speedometer passing eighty, and tempted to keep on going. The side-road to the Beehive came up like a sick headache. The deceleration depressed his spirits. By the time he got off the bike in the car park he was wondering what the hell had been the point of coming back to deadliness with such fervour. Smeeton had done him a good turn, if he had but recognized it. He could be up there still, watching the butterfly.

Maxwell met him at the door, rolling his eyes. The audience was already dribbling into the hall.

'Old Dotty's raving,' he said. 'He's got a search-party out for you. He's in the music-room with the corpse. Hey, what's wrong with old Bates?'

'Nothing's wrong with old Bates,' Penn said. 'Go and find someone to swap clothes with him, and give him a nice cup of tea. With froth on it.'

'I was all right till Penn laid on the transport,' Bates said. He was as white as paper. Penn laughed.

'You won't be laughing when Dotty sees you,' Maxwell said.

Penn shrugged and pushed past, and up the stairs. He must be mad, he thought, seeing the sun coming through the landing window as it had come, warm and lazy, into the loft. That butterfly had more sense. Dotty's face was twitching with rage; he hissed at Penn, 'Are you mad, leaving it as late as this?' The baritone corpse looked him up and down as if he were a freak.

'I would have thought that normal courtesy would have entailed coming in good time,' he said.

Penn said nothing. He had all but broken his neck in the name of normal courtesy, had old Senility had the grace to inquire.

Tate was thin, vinegary, with a face like a worn boot. He thought boys should stand to attention when he spoke to them. Penn glowered. Mr. Crocker looked at his watch and said, 'We've got twenty minutes. Sit down, Pennington, and Mr. Tate will just have time to go through a few points.'

'Twenty minutes!' Penn thought. The old bike must have shifted. The lettering on the cover of the music was drawn like imitation rustic-work: Penn put it in the first decade of the century.

'I don't suppose you could transpose this into B flat?' Senility said patronizingly.

He was getting his own back. His eyes were nasty, lingering on the abundance of Penn's hair. Penn, hating his guts, transposed into B flat, playing so well that the old windbag was stunned. Crocker, seeing the way Penn was reacting, heaved a private sigh of relief. Tate stood over the piano, and nagged, because Penn wasn't the type of boy he approved of, and Penn didn't listen, ploughing through staves of Victorian codswallop, all trills and frills and melodic swoon. Tate's voice was a drone, like a bluebottle hung up in the net curtains.

'I hope the central heating will be on in the hall, Crocker. It's very sharp for May, and I have to watch my chest. And no smoking. I hope you put a notice up. People have no consideration, no understanding at all. That's marked *dolce*, boy. Use your eyes. And the tempo is too fast. I sing it ter—um, ter—um, ter—um, like that. Keep that left hand softer. Try this one. Start at the bottom of the page. I wonder you can see what you're doing with all that hair. I would have thought Mr. Stack would have something to say about these modern tendencies. Can't tell the boys from the girls these days, eh, Crocker? Play the opening bars to this one, keep it flowing . . . it's a sentimental piece, very delicate. And again, do the first six bars again. Yes. When we were young we were proud to look like men. You boys to-day—God help us all if the country depended on you.' Penn stopped playing and looked at Crocker.

'Yes,' said Crocker hastily. 'I think that's about all we have time for—'

'Fetch me a glass of water,' Tate ordered. 'I must take these tablets before we go down.'

Penn went to get it, and Tate said, 'That boy is an extraordinary pianist, but his manners are non-existent. A typical modern youth. Or teenager, as we are supposed to call them. I really think, if that's the type that is going to run the country in the next few years, the sooner I go to my grave the better.'

Penn came back in time to mutter 'Hear! hear!' to the last phrase. Crocker gave him a hard, but not entirely unsympathetic, look. While Tate was fussing with his bottle of pills, Crocker said quietly to Penn, 'The old boy's a bit deaf. He won't admit it, but you should know, in case you have to ask him something. Your native mumble will not be understood.'

'Pity the audience isn't deaf, too,' Penn said.

'Yes,' Crocker said, lapsing absent-mindedly from pedagogue to human being. 'He's on the Education Committee, you know. We just have to take it, when he offers us his favours.'

Mr. Stack and two prefects appeared at the door, smiling and unctuous.

'A very good audience for you, Mr. Tate! The hall is quite full.'

They trailed down the stairs, all suiting their pace to Mr. Tate's doddering steps. They went on to the stage, behind the velvet curtains, and the noise of the audience could be heard, in leash behind the velvet. Penn knew they were all waiting to leer at the girls' legs, and hear old Finnigan and old Midwinter and old Bates, not deadly old Tate who had to be endured first. He combed his hair; Tate glared at him, and Penn gave him a wide, polite, insolent smile. Maxwell and Crombie were standing in the wings, making messages all over their faces in Penn's direction, and pointing at Bates, who was standing beside them, swaying slightly and staring into space. Maxwell made a cross-eyed drunken face, and did the thumbs-up. Penn hoped they weren't overdoing it. Bates's borrowed clothes were slightly bizarre, the blazer being about two sizes too large, and the trousers too short, revealing almost six inches of the unsuitable sky-blue socks he had been wearing with his jeans. Mr. Tate was taking another pill, saying to one of the prefects, 'A delicate throat like mine, you can't be too careful this time of year.'

'A tight piece of string would do it the world of good,' Penn murmured.

Mr. Stack was stepping forward, making signs to Maxwell to get ready to open the curtains. Mr. Crocker and the prefects retreated and Penn sat down at the piano, his face showing nothing but infinite boredom. Mr. Crocker turned back and said, 'I'll get you someone to turn the pages.' Penn nodded.

He then saw what was going to happen. He half got up to stop it, but Maxwell was opening the curtains and the full attention of the audience was piling eagerly through the majestically parting velvet, applause and stamping bursting out to relieve the boredom of waiting. The smiling Bates was in Mr. Crocker's path, obviously doing nothing—incapable, Penn could see, of doing anything—and Mr. Crocker took him by the arm and propelled him gently on to the stage. 'Go and turn over for Pennington,' he said. Mr. Stack stepped forward to speak, and old Tate cracked his face into affability. Bates wavered out of the wings, and converged, with obvious difficulty, on the piano. He leaned his elbows on the far end of it and gazed at Penn under the lid. 'Fancy seeing you,' he said.

Penn ignored him and opened the first piece of music. Mr. Stack was intoning: ' . . . so happy today . . . our old friend . . . generously giving his valuable time . . . grateful . . .'

Bates groped his way round the piano's bulk and came and stood beside Penn, breathing heavily. 'I feel sick,' he said. 'But I'll do this little thing for you first.'

Penn looked frantically into the wings, and saw Maxwell and Crombie and Rees and Midwinter all rolling about, doubled up at what had happened. He made furious faces at them, but they just shrugged and made gibbering grimaces, and hand-clasps over their heads. Penn knew that the idea of livening up Tate's performance appealed to them enormously, and his own predicament was to be all part of the act. He groaned, indignation flooding him. He looked at Bates's green face and whispered, 'Go and get someone else!'

Bates leaned down and put his arm round Penn's shoulders. 'But I want to do it for you, Penn. You're my friend.'

Penn looked at Maxwell, and saw that he was leaning against the wings, helpless with laughter.

'For the first piece, Mr. Tate is going to give us . . .'

Tate stood well forward, his back to the piano. Penn glanced down into the audience and saw that their eyes were, as one, on Bates. They were expectant, utterly attentive. He looked at

Tate for a signal to start, and saw a little silk tab sticking up over the collar of his jacket, saying, 'Dry-cleaning is recommended for this garment.' He had a neck like a tortoise. Penn played the introduction to 'The Vagabond', Bates wavering

over his shoulder, trying to focus on the music. If anyone's jacket, Penn thought, was going to need dry-cleaning . . .

Bates said, 'What's this old crap?'

Penn twitched his shoulder to shake Bates off, but Bates leaned down, still with his arm tenderly round him, and said happily, 'Say when, just say when, and I will tu-urn the page.' His stomach rolled emptily and he said, 'I beg your pardon. I will tu-urn the page whenever you want.'

Penn turned it.

'Hey,' Bates said. 'That's my job. I want to do it for you, Penn. I'm your friend.'

He put his hand out and turned the page while Penn was still at the top of it. Penn flipped it back, snarling, 'Get off me, you creep!'

'Give the jolly heaven above
And the byway nigh me.
Bed in the bush with stars to see,
Bread I dip in the river—
There's the life for a man like me . . .'

'Bread he what?' Bates said. 'Bread he what did he say?'

'Turn over!'

Bates turned over two pages. Penn, carrying on with one hand, grabbed at the sheet and shot it back. Bates leaned over him and with both hands arranged the book, very deliberately, smoothing it down so that Penn could only see fragments of what he was supposed to be playing.

'What does he do with his bread?' Bates insisted.

'Move your great mitts, for God's sake!'

Bates turned over again. Penn turned back.

'I'm only trying to help,' Bates said.

Penn could feel the sweat breaking out. Couldn't the oafs in the wings do something? Obviously not; as one glance showed him they were all helpless, holding each other up.

Bates bent down very earnestly and said in Penn's ear, 'Did he say he dipped it in the river?'

Penn ignored him.

'That's a ruddy stupid thing to do.'

'Keep your hands off the music!' Penn stopped him just in time.

'Must be to make it pappy, for his dentures.'

Penn, playing louder to drown Bates's commentary, strained for Tate's bleat. The old vagabond, with his Rolls-Royce parked outside and his central heating and his pep-pills . . . Penn ground his teeth in fury at his lot, holding Bates at bay by playing with his left elbow well out.

When the piece was finished the applause broke out with astonishing vigour, crashing out of the body of the hall, accompanied by stamping and whistling. Penn saw that the upturned faces were all grinning, full of anticipation. 'Good old Bates!' a voice from the back called out. Everyone clapped again with huge enjoyment. Tate turned round, beaming with pleasure, and said, 'They certainly enjoyed that, didn't they?'

Penn, his hand on Bates's upper arm to stop him bowing, sent a speaking grimace towards Maxwell, appealing for help. But Maxwell was dancing about with his hands clasped over his head, mouthing, 'It's a wow! Keep it up!'

The audience was settling down for a further session, all on the edge of their seats, agog. Stacker, having taken a seat in the front row after making the introduction, had his eyes on the piano, glazed. His whole body was stiff. The sight of him, obviously prepared, like Penn himself, for disaster, gave Penn the feeling that judgement day was not far off.

Tate was wavering: '. . . that lovely old ballad . . . one of the heritages of our glorious . . .' Penn fingered the music. What lousy old ballad, for heaven's sake, out of the mildewed pile in front of him? Bates had one foot up on the piano stool, doing up his shoelace.

'These socks are all wrong for this sort of thing,' he said. 'They're sports socks. Not formal socks.'

' "Cherry Ripe" ', said Tate.

Everyone cheered and clapped. Penn winced.

'The old cherries,' Bates said. 'They're underneath "Annie Laurie". I saw them. Squashed flat by now.'

Penn flipped up the right sheet, very tattered, all trills and pencil marks.

'Ripe, I'll say it's ripe,' Bates said. 'You know, Penn, when you passed that Rover on the arterial, if he took your number you'll be in jug. There's a fifty limit on that stretch.'

Penn, just about to start, dropped his hands and hissed at Bates, 'Get off this stage, you drunken basket!'

Tate turned round, his bonhomie frozen on his face, and met Penn's eyes, incredulous. Penn took a deep breath, switched his gaze to the music and plunged into a startled introduction, drowning in the scurry of ornamentation, concentrating hard. Tate came in two bars late, still gasping, and Penn braked, finding him. Bates turned over.

85

Penn let out a yelp.

'Say when,' Bates said. 'I'm ready for you.'

'Leave it alone!'

'Cherry ripe, cherry ripe,
Ripe, I—I cry—y . . .'

'Cherry tripe, cherry tripe,' Bates intoned. 'Tri—ipe, I cry.'
He hiccuped and said, 'These old cherries give me the pip.' He
laughed. Penn snorted, seeing the big hands swoop like owls in
daylight over the music rack. He knocked one up out of the
way, and went on playing with one hand, fending Bates off.
Bates struggled with him and Penn brought his elbow up and
jabbed him sharply in the stomach. Bates let out a groan, and
Penn withdrew abruptly, remembering . . .

'All right, now!' he spat at Bates.

Bates turned with such vigour that the frail sheets came apart
and started to slide in a shower down over the keys and on to
the floor, followed in a slippery, musty-smelling stream by
"Annie Laurie", "The Rose of Tralee", "Barbara Allen".—
' "And Uncle Tom Cobbleigh and all",' Bates said loudly,
dropping down on his hands and knees. Penn swept all the
paper aside, shut his eyes, and improvised, going down fast.
Bates was underneath the piano, lumbering about on his hands
and knees. 'Cripes, Penn, I do feel ill,' he said at knee-level.

'We're nearly there,' Penn muttered. 'Hold it, for God's
sake.'

He was clammy and shaking, and did not know the tune
after 'Where my Julia's lips do smile', so went straight back to
the chorus, losing Tate *en route*. That was his bad luck. Bates put
his hand on the pedal and Penn trod on it. Tate caught up.
Bates started to retch quietly to himself. Penn brought the
melody to an abrupt close, got up from the piano stool, marched
over to the curtain pulley and pulled hard. The audience broke
into a thunderous roar of clapping, cheering, and whistling so
rapturous that Tate, pop-eyed with rage at Penn's eccentricity,
was forced to change his mind. He stepped forward, smiling,
and disappeared from view in a swoosh of velvet and dust.

Penn leaned against the wings, overcome by the experience.
He felt like sobbing. The others went to fetch Bates, so weak

with laughter that they looked as drunk as he did. Behind the curtain the audience was roaring.

'You've ruined it, Pennington,' Maxwell was moaning. 'It was ruddy marvellous, and you've finished it. Listen to them!'

The audience was shouting, 'Bates! Bates! Good old Bates!' Maxwell opened the curtains again and revealed Mr. Tate still bowing, coughing slightly, but wreathed in smiles. Penn went back to the piano, gathered up the music and sat down, to another outburst of cheering. Tate came over to him, overcome by the enthusiasm.

'How they love a good old song! Just hark at them!'

Penn looked at Stacker, and saw that he was running a finger round his neck, just inside his collar. He looked back at Penn and inclined his head slightly, once or twice. Very ominously.

'You can take a bow. Just one,' said Tate.

Penn got up and bowed to Mr. Stack. The audience roared again. Penn sat down.

' "Pale Hands I Love," ' Tate said to Penn.

'Oh, God,' thought Penn. To think, he could still have been lying in the loft, with the butterfly.

Chapter 6

In the interval Penn went to Maxwell and said, 'Where's Bates? What've you done with him?'

'We can't do anything with him, that's the trouble. You'd better see him,' Maxwell said. 'He's laid out.'

Bates was in the Common Room, moaning, his head in his hands.

'What did you give him, for heaven's sake?' Penn muttered to Maxwell. 'He only needed—' He looked at Bates in despair. The day's adventures had done for Bates. Penn, with ten minutes to get results, took charge.

'Find him something to eat. He's starving. Then a nip of the First Aid brandy just before he goes on. That should do it.'

'How are you going to get the First Aid brandy, for Pete's sake?'

'I know where the key is,' Penn said.

'You'll get killed if anyone sees you.'

'You go and get him something out of the dining-room. Buck up!'

Bates said, 'I'm not going to do it, Penn. They were laughing at me just now, and I was only turning pages. What if I get up and sing—'

'Oh, stow it. I'll be doing it with you, won't I? You know the stuff backwards.'

Bates sobbed.

'Oh, you're such a crawling twit, Bates!' Penn breathed.

There was very little time. He sprinted up to the staff-room, head down. The corridor was empty. He knocked at the door and, to his relief, there was no answer. He went in, took the appropriate key off its hook on the keyboard, and unlocked the petty-cash drawer in Soggy's desk. The flask of brandy was at the back, underneath the paperwork. He pulled it out. 'It only needs Soggy,' he thought, 'to walk in now . . .' He heard the door handle rattle, and aged ten years. Maxwell put his head round.

'Got it?'

Penn leaned against the lockers, shivering.

'It's me that needs it now,' he complained bitterly. 'Bates can't feel anything like as bad as I do, after what's happened.'

'Stacker wants to see you afterwards. He's sent someone round already so you get the message loud and clear.'

'Well, I did my best, didn't I? What else could I've done?' Stung by the bitter injustice, Penn galloped back to the Common Room. Crombie and Rees were stuffing Bates with chocolate éclairs. Bates was too weak to protest. Penn took the top off the brandy and took a few swallows. Someone was shouting for him from the wings.

'You've got to go on. It's Midwinter's monologue.' Maxwell gave him a shove.

Penn gave him the brandy bottle. 'Look, about five swallows'll do him. Time it properly.' He leaned over Bates and said, 'You can do it. You're great, Bates. You show 'em. I'll come back for you in a minute. Don't you worry.'

It was while he was playing the dirge music for Midwinter, which was the same notes nearly all the time, so that he had almost gone into a coma, that he saw a face in the audience that almost stopped him in mid-chord. It was his bird, the folk-song girl. She was in the third row, smiling, her hair hanging in whitish, shining wings down over her leather jacket. Penn felt as weak as Bates, staring, his heart pounding, all the blood rushing up into his neck. He looked away, trying to breathe slowly, trying to pretend it didn't matter. But it mattered terribly. When he came to stand up at the end he felt as if he were an elephant, engulfing the stage.

He went back to Bates, slowly, and sat down. He lay back in the old cane chair, looked at the ceiling, and took long calming breaths. Maxwell came in and said, 'What's eating you? You're on after the next.' Penn thought, 'I must talk to her afterwards. Find out where she lives.'

'Yes,' he said.

'I never knew it could get you like this,' he thought.

'Shall I dose Bates?'

'Yes.'

Ten minutes later he was standing in the wings with Bates, waiting for the girls' can-can to finish. Maxwell was looking at them dubiously. Bates was still white, looking distant, glazed and zombie-ish, and Penn was strangely subdued, as if all the fight had gone out of him. He looked nervous. Maxwell had never seen Penn nervous in the whole course of his career. Having stolen the First Aid brandy and chucked the empty bottle in the dustbin in the kitchen would have been good reason—for anyone else—to look worried, but Maxwell knew that Penn took such incidents in his stride. Whatever was on his mind, it wasn't that. Maxwell got ready to close the curtains, recognizing his cue in the Offenbach record. So far the concert had been a wow. Maxwell sent up a brief prayer for the last item to be as good as the first. At least it had the same leading man.

After the row had calmed down, Penn went on to the stage, marching Bates in front of him with a hand firmly on his elbow. He thought that Bates was in the right mood, with an other-whereness glaze in his eyes, but he wasn't sure that he might not, if the worst came to the worst, pass out altogether. Penn, taking care not to look into the audience, blew a few runs on the harmonica and launched straight into 'Lowlands Away.' They could hardly make a greater hash of the thing than they had, between them, in the first item.

Bates nearly didn't start. Penn could see him shrinking, the panic in his eyes. He played softly, willing Bates, watching him, playing the melody twice over until the moment came when Bates either had to go or retire altogether. Penn saw his mouth open. Penn shut his eyes, and drew on the sonorous D that started the verse, willing Bates with such energy that it was as if the voice came without Bates having anything to do with it.

'I dreamed a dream the other night . . .'

Penn was so relieved that his breath shook, the melody quavering. But Bates, once away, like a body of water released from a dam, started to flow as if there had never been a doubt at all, his voice in perfect control. Penn saw his expression change, relax, and the look come into his eyes that meant he was in charge. Penn could leave him, ornamenting, playing a weaving harmony high above Bates with his mind free to concentrate, the awful doom he had been anticipating put away. The scab on his lip was a curse, getting hung up occasionally with fearful pricks, but Penn remembered that he had beaten Smeeton yet again, and the sad tune went soaring and Bates was with him: they would show the lot of them what a real song was . . . Penn was happy.

The applause for 'Lowlands Away' was long, astonished, and genuine. The school had never known old Bates could do it.

'You've got to give 'em something cheerful before "The Butcher Boy",' Penn said to him urgently. 'You can't give 'em all morgue stuff.'

' "Down by the Royal Albion",' Bates said.

'Over my dead body,' Penn said.

He started on 'The Golden Vanity', which had a corpse, but a merry tune to go with it. Bates muttered something at him and did not come in, so Penn came round again, needling Bates with such a stern eye that he took off in the right place, and never looked back. Penn was breathless by the end.

Bates had no inhibitions now about singing the tale of the wronged maid. The others had been mere throat-clearing. His voice was full of self-pity, soft, and yet clear to the back of the hall. It had the direct quality that Penn could not put words to, a lack of affectation that put the story across so vividly that Penn could feel the involvement of the audience like a tangible link reaching out over Maxwell's footlights. Bates believed each word of it and his voice as an instrument carried every nuance as plainly and as perfectly as the story demanded.

> 'Oh, dig my grave long, wide and deep,
> Put a marble stone at my head and feet,
> And in the middle a turtle-dove
> That the world might know that I died for love.'

It faded, and Penn faded with it, and the shades of Mr. Tate were buried, defeated utterly by a plain skill that the old man had professed and never possessed all his singing days. There was a silence that Penn recognized as the greatest compliment accorded during the whole of the show; then the audience broke out into a roar of appreciation that made Bates look at Penn in amazement.

'Bow,' said Penn. 'Go on. Do the thing properly.'

Bates grinned. Penn laughed.

Maxwell closed the curtains. They were all rushing about and capering, the tension broken in the lovely sound of the audience all with them, and cheering like mad. Bates had to go out again and bow. Everybody clapped and stamped. Mr. Stack stood up and made the usual blah, and then the audience was filing out, making for the spread laid out in the dining-room. Penn went to the exit nearest to where his bird had been sitting, and Bates followed him as a matter of habit. They stood in the corridor outside the door, Penn craning for a glimpse of the blonde hair.

'Let's go and get something to eat,' Bates said. 'Who are you looking for?'

'That girl who sang in the hall at Moorham was here. I saw her. I want to talk to her.'

'What on earth for?'

They were pushed all ways. Penn didn't know what he was going to say anyway, only that he had to make the effort, or suffer for it. When he saw her he felt all the blood rushing again, and the embarrassment like a suffocation. He was speechless. Bates gave him a shove. Penn stared, his shoulder braced against the pushing throng. The girl turned, saw Bates, and stepped out of the crush against the wall and said, 'I think you were marvellous.'

Bates gave her an idiotic grin and nudged Penn. Penn could have strangled him. He couldn't think of anything to say, and went on staring, and the girl said to Bates, 'I've never heard that song before. I've never heard you before either. Do you sing with any of the clubs?'

Bates looked at Penn to see what was silencing him. Penn, with the effort it might have cost him to push a steam-roller into motion, said, 'Can we take you down to tea? We heard you sing at Moorham one night, a week or two back, and we thought you were pretty good, too.'

It was the greatest social breakthrough of his career.

The girl gave him a dazzling smile and said, 'Oh, thank you, yes,' and dropped her long black eyelashes in a way that made Penn's toes curl up.

'Pennington.'

The voice behind him was unmistakable. Most of the crowd had gone now, and they had tagged on to the last stragglers tailing down the corridor. Penn turned round just as Soggy drummed a forefinger on his shoulder.

'Mr. Stack wants you in his room, immediately.'

'Sir, I—'

'Go!'

Penn hesitated. Soggy's hand closed round the back of his neck and propelled him bodily across the corridor and through the archway back into the hall. Penn wrenched himself free and turned on Soggy with a look on his face that made the teacher take an involuntary step backwards. Penn saw the malice in Soggy's eyes, and knew that he had treated him like that, in front of the girl, with a perfect awareness of what it meant. It was not blundering tactlessness; it was intended, and enjoyed. Penn thought for a second that he was not going to be able to stop himself from hitting him, but the habit of the infinite, deadly number of his years at school proved effective. He was able to control himself; he closed up, shutting his face, hunching his shoulders, pushing his hands into his pockets. He stared at Soggy, and Soggy looked at him and said, 'You insolent young beggar.'

Penn went and knocked at Stacker's door. When he went in Mitchell was standing looking out the window.

'The police-constable wants a word with you, Pennington,' Stacker said. 'It's about a motor-bike.'

In that instant several points registered in Penn's mind. He knew that his face had—momentarily—betrayed alarm at the mention of the word 'motor-bike', and that Mitchell had seen it. Mitchell had been watching for it. But Mitchell's own face also betrayed rage at Stacker's slip in giving away the object of the interview. Penn, used to police procedure, recognized immediately the advantage Stacker had inadvertently given him. He did not say anything. He realized that he was in an extremely precarious situation.

'I've no doubt,' Stacker said—obviously having a great deal —'that you will be able to clear up whatever it is the constable wants to know. Meanwhile I must go down and play the host, Mitchell, if you will excuse me.'

He bowed himself out and Mitchell perched himself on the desk and said to Penn, 'Sit down.'

Penn was thinking furiously behind a truculent expression. He knew perfectly well that riding his father's bike without permission and without a certificate of insurance was an arrestable offence. Oakhall was just around the corner, unless some miracle happened. This was it, the moment he had least expected it. He waited, silent, watching Mitchell getting ready to pat him about, a cat with a mouse. He felt resigned and sick and hating Mitchell so much that he could scarcely bear to look at him. He had been expecting a domestic row about manners and alcohol, not this. He was tired, and now he was going to have to think like blazes.

But Mitchell was unexpectedly inexact in explaining his mission.

'I just want to know what you've been doing today. Where you went. Times, if you know them. Anyone who saw you.'

Penn hesitated. He knew that he was within his rights to keep quiet, but he doubted whether such outright uncooperation would improve his case. To answer wasn't difficult, but the story was unusual. Too unusual, Penn hoped, for Mitchell to feel he was making it up. Mitchell knew the sail-loft. When Penn said he had jumped out, Mitchell looked at him narrowly. He took notes of everything Penn said. Penn did not hurry, saying as little as possible, so that Mitchell had to prompt him a good deal.

'What time did you jump out?'

Penn wanted to make it earlier, so that he could give himself more leeway when it came to the time it had taken him to travel to Northend, but the time was tied to the height of the water in the creek, which could be checked. He couldn't say he jumped into a dry creek: he wouldn't be there to tell the tale. He dragged it out, saying he hadn't really noticed.

'You could show me, if we were on the spot, how high the water was when you jumped? You must have been very careful about this, surely?'

'Yes.'

'You jumped as soon as you thought it safe?'

'Yes.'

'How high is the loft?'

'About thirty feet, I suppose.'

'Risky, wasn't it?'

Penn shrugged.

'Anyone see you?'

'Only Bates.'

'Was that the boy who sang?'

So Mitchell had been in the audience, Penn noted. If Mitchell asked Bates anything, Penn knew he was doomed. Bates was a hopeless liar. Penn couldn't understand why Mitchell was bothered about the loft episode.

'What did you do when you were out?'

'Unlocked Bates. Went home.'

'Straight home?'

'Yes.'

'Anyone see you?'

'No.'

'Anyone at home? Anyone who could say what time you got in?'

Penn could feel his mouth getting dry. He could see Mitchell watching for exactly such symptoms.

'My father was in.'

'What then?'

'I changed and came here.'

'How?'

'My father ran me in on his motor-bike.'

It was a gamble. Penn could feel the sweat breaking out. He was so flaming guilty he felt as if the word was stuck in writing all over him, like the message on the Major's Jaguar.

Mitchell sat up and read through his notes, tapping his pencil against his teeth.

'Can you ride a motor-bike?' he asked.

'Yes.'

'Got a licence?'

'No.'

Penn sat very still. He could feel a bead of perspiration on his lip, and dared not wipe it away. He thought Mitchell could see it. Mitchell was looking at the notes, pursing his mouth, thoughtful.

'I'd like to see Bates,' he said. 'Where will he be? Still here?'

This time Penn knew his face gave him away. He opened his mouth and stumbled on the first word. He cleared his throat.

'In the dining-room,' he muttered.

Mitchell went to the door and out across the corridor to the staircase, where he bellowed for a boy who was on the stairs at the bottom. He gave his message and came back, knowing perfectly well that Penn had considered flight, and seen the uselessness of it. He sat on the desk again and watched Penn, and Penn looked at the floor.

'Your headmaster not say anything about your hair?' he said, after a long silence.

Penn did not reply.

Mitchell repeated his question.

'What's it got to do with it?' Penn's voice quivered.

'To do with what?' Mitchell said.

Penn was silent. He knew Mitchell was trying to break him, and he knew Mitchell was damned nearly succeeding.

'Do the girls like it?'

'I haven't asked them.'

'What's it for, then?'

'To keep me warm.'

Mitchell's eyes narrowed again.

'What did you do to your lip?'

'I cut it.'

'How?'

'Talking.'

Mitchell said, 'You're asking for it, Pennington, aren't you?'

There was another long silence, relieved eventually by the hesitant entry of Bates. He saw Penn sitting in the chair, and Mitchell on the desk, and his mouth opened.

Mitchell said, 'What time did Pennington jump out of the loft?'

Bates blinked, and said, 'Twenty to four. Why?'

Penn looked at Mitchell and saw the shock of surprise carefully covered up. He felt a stab of satisfaction.

'Why are you so sure of the time?'

'Penn gave me his watch to hold.'

Mitchell nodded, and wrote. Penn felt that Bates had thrown him, but could not understand the way the interview was going any more. He felt as if the pressure was off him, but Mitchell was still there, and the motor-bike was still down in the yard, if Mitchell chose to go and look. He did not move, avoiding looking at Bates. Bates was more dangerous than anything. Penn thought of the silver-haired girl, and shivered.

Mitchell said to Bates, 'All right. You can buzz off.'

Bates did so, with an alacrity that twisted Penn. Mitchell stood up and said, 'Come and see me to-morrow. At the station. Say three-thirty.'

'Is that all?'

'For now.'

Penn was amazed. He got up and went out of the room and downstairs and into the bog, while Mitchell got clear. Then he went out into the yard, and watched Mitchell get into his white police Mini and drive away. He went out of the main gate and towards the town centre, not stopping to look for a motor-bike on the way. Unless he had already seen it. Penn, very puzzled, went out and found the machine exactly as he had left it, behind the bike shed. He stood fingering his lip. He felt he ought to feel relieved, but he had a feeling that Mitchell was preparing a trap for him. He felt unsure of what Mitchell was getting at, wondering whether his own guilt had made him jump to conclusions when Stacker said it was about a motor-bike. Mitchell's questions had not fitted in with what Penn thought it was all about: just as they had come to the hot spot, Mitchell had lost interest.

Penn looked at the bike. The yard was completely empty. It was going dusk, and the supper party was in full swing away on the other side of the school. Penn knew that to ride home on the bike was risky, but to leave it behind was impossible. There was his father to face, besides the police. And the sooner he got home and told his father about the lie that he must substantiate if Mitchell chose to check up on it—and Penn knew that Mitchell would—the safer he would be. There was no doubt in Penn's mind that his father would stick up for him before the police; there was also little doubt that telling his father what he had done was not going to be funny.

But his father knew. Penn didn't have to say anything, only screw up enough courage to step into the kitchen, and it all broke round him, almost literally. His father had heard the bike, and came in from the television, his face distorted with his wild temper. His wife came with him, saying frantically, before anything happened, 'Leave him alone, Bill, for God's sake!'

'I'll leave him alone when I've finished with him—it won't take long!'

Penn put his arms up over his face and half-turned, hunching a shoulder, ducking his head. He would have been all right, save in the ensuing fracas, ducking neatly sideways to avoid one of his father's wilder blows, he came up sharply against the hard metal of the tin-opener fixed to the wall and nearly knocked himself out. As he went down he saw his mother pick up a frying-pan and swing it like a golf-club. It glanced off his father's shoulder and went straight into a row of glass jars full of sugar, rice and currants. Penn hit the floor and doubled up, like a jockey under Becher's, rice, sugar, and currants falling like rain. His father kicked him, twice, before his mother went at him again, and Penn heard their voices, rising and falling in torrents of blame and hate while they grappled, and—far away in the dark front room—the noise of Mrs. Jones's poker hammering on the wall.

Penn dragged himself into a sitting position, resting his head against the gas cooker. His father was puffing like a grampus; Penn knew the way of it, and listened to the invective that flowed over him, rich and familiar and inventive, so that he was almost able to admire it. The tin-opener had caught him just over the eyebrow. He felt dizzy, and starving hungry. His mother was crying.

Then Penn realized that Mrs. Jones's poker had turned into something much nearer at hand.

'Go to hell!' his father roared.

Penn staggered to his feet, urgent and scared.

'Dad, listen! It's the police—'

His father was silent, instantly. 'What have you done?' he whispered to Penn. 'Is it the bike?'

'I told them you drove me in. We left about a quarter past four.'

'What, and back?'

'I suppose so. He didn't ask. He just asked about how I got to school.'

'You—' His father swore at him. The knock came again, loud and authoritative. 'Why should I get you off, you little—' His father went off again, his words foul.

'Get on with it, you fool,' his wife choked at him.

He went out into the hall at last, shutting the door behind him.

Penn leaned against the wall, very tired and sore, but not frightened. He got out his comb and started to put his hair to rights. The voices argued at the front door, and Penn knew that there was no immediate cause for alarm.

'Thank God,' he thought, 'for a father you can trust.'

'Two blokes went out to Fiddler's Creek on a motor-bike, left it by the sea-wall and went out on to the mud to dig for bait. At two o'clock, as near as we can fix it, they heard someone start it up and drive it away. By the time they got up on to the wall to see, it had vanished. It was found, two hours later, abandoned and pretty well smashed up, on the outskirts of Northend. Patrick Pennington, by his own admission, was up at Fiddler's Creek at two o'clock. He and his friend John Bates were seen going up there by Turner's tractor-man at ten o'clock. They did not come back while the tractor-man was working, which was until two o'clock.' Mitchell mumbled away, leafing over his notes, while Sergeant West was locking up for the night.

'And what is Pennington's alibi? I've no doubt he's got a very good one?' West asked.

'Yes, he has.' Mitchell outlined it. West's eyebrows went up at the mention of the jump out of the sail-loft.

'That's hard to take. I'd like to see him do that.'

'Yes. That's what I thought. I'm going to take him up there tomorrow and see if he sticks to the story. I'm pretty sure I'll get him, because he's frightened about something. When the word motor-bike came up, he nearly jumped out of his skin. Just for a moment. And he was worried when I was questioning him. Very worried.'

'He didn't say much, if I know him.'

'Minimum. What he did say, apart from yes and no, was insolent.'

West sighed. 'I thought we might be getting somewhere with him. But with parents like he's got—what can you expect? It might not be a bad thing if he's sent away for a few months.'

'I gather that his headmaster wouldn't be sorry to see it happen. He says they can't do anything with him.'

'It's not for lack of wits. Just bloody-mindedness,' West said. 'Bad example at home, no one to guide him. Even the probation officer's had enough. He says you might as well talk to a sack of potatoes. The parents never stop hammering the lad at home, but as soon as we suggest that his behaviour isn't all it might be they do a right-about turn and make out that the boy is God's own gift to the universe. What can you do?'

'I can't work up much sympathy for him, I'm afraid.' Mitchell put his file away and locked the drawer. 'Funny thing,' he added. 'A yob like that being musical. I got stuck with watching the last half of their concert. He can play the piano as if he's not even thinking about it.'

'Probably isn't. Thinking is the one thing that comes hard to Pennington.'

'I shall be surprised if we don't get him on this.' Mitchell sounded satisfied, as West put out the lights. 'I'll swear he's lying somewhere along the line. That business about the loft— if that's the truth, I'm a Dutchman.'

Chapter 7

By the time Penn went up to Bates' the next morning he knew what Mitchell was after. His father, having repaired to the pub for refreshment after beating up his family, learned about the theft of the motor-bike from the top of Fiddler's Creek. He went home and woke Penn up, threatening him drunkenly and loudly, until Mrs. Jones pounded her shoe against the wall. But Penn knew he was in the clear, and slept more soundly after his father's visit. Everything was explained. If he was lucky, he would get out of the tangle without his own actual crime being discovered. But Bates had to be fixed.

'If he asks you how you got to school yesterday, you've got to say you hitch-hiked,' Penn told Bates. 'I told him my father drove me there and back on the bike, and my father's told him the same. But if you go and say it was you on the pillion, for heaven's sake, he'll know something's up.'

'All right,' Bates said, not very eagerly.

'Say someone picked you up and took you all the way, someone you've never set eyes on before. Don't be clever and say it was Miss Marble or somebody, else he'll check up and prove you're a liar. Say a fawn Anglia, or something, nothing conspicuous.'

'All right.'

'He probably won't bother. It's earlier on he's trying to work out. And we're cast-iron and in the clear for that, thanks to Fletcher.'

Business over, Penn hesitated before he opened the subject that was as much on his mind as the motor-bike escapade. Trying to sound as if it was just something to say, to fill in the silence, he mumbled, 'You find out that bird's name yesterday?'

'What bird?'

'The one you took down to tea, when Soggy butted in.'

'Oh, her. Yes.'

'What is it?'

'Sylvia.'

'Where does she live?'

'How should I know?'

Penn shut his eyes, strangling inclinations towards violence. A deep, bitter disappointment pulled him down. He could not keep it out of his voice.

'Cripes, Bates, you knew! You could have asked—!'

'What do we want to know for?' Bates asked indignantly. 'I got landed with buying her a cup of tea, didn't I? What else was I supposed to do? Ask her round to supper?'

'Didn't you find anything out? What she does? What club she sings with or something?'

'Oh, yes, she did natter on. Oh, yes. She invited me round to sing at the place she goes to. What do you think of that?' Bates giggled.

'What did you say?' Penn breathed.

'Not on your nelly.'

'Where is it, this place?' Penn was so patient it was making him shiver.

'It's called the Old Barge Club. Meets on a barge. In Northend somewhere—the gasworks jetty, I think. She said there's going to be a Folk Festival and they're going—it's in Tolchester next month. Would I like to go and sing "The Butcher Boy"? With my friend. That's you, Penn. It's on the nineteenth of June. There you are. What more do you want?'

Penn started picking bits of moquette out of Mrs. Bates's chair arm, where the cat had pulled them. The nineteenth of June was the date of the Andante and Rondo Capriccioso.

'Pat, stop wrecking my furniture! Clear out into the kitchen. I've got my work to do.' Mrs. Bates gave him a shove with her dustpan. 'When are you going to get your hair cut, if it's not a rude question? They think our John's courting, seeing you around.' She laughed.

Penn scowled at her.

'Cheer up, love. It might never happen.' Mrs. Bates was a lot nicer than his own mother.

'It has,' he said.

'You look like it,' she said happily.

They mooched out into the kitchen. Penn told Bates about the nineteenth of June. Bates said, 'That lets us out nicely, then. I couldn't go without you.'

'We'll go,' Penn said.

'But you can't.'

'Why can't I? There's no law I've got to play in the Northend thing, is there? It's a Saturday. Even Crocker can't force me.'

'But, Penn, what'll he say? He'll go raving. All that work you're putting in.'

'Good reason for packing it in. We'll go to this thing in Tolchester. He can say what he likes.'

The girl's face, inviting Bates, smiling at him, scoured Penn. 'We'll go to the Old Barge and you can sing. You're better than any of 'em, Bates.'

'It's just the girl you're after.'

Penn didn't say anything, thinking of her so close yesterday, and her eyes with that stuff making them look enormous, and her hair, and then Soggy talking to him like that in front of her, and putting his hand on the back of his neck and shoving him, as if he was two years old. Penn could feel the blood coming up into his face at the memory of it, and his feeling towards Soggy was so wild he was almost frightened of it. He thought he could kill him quite easily. He would enjoy it.

In the afternoon he went down to Moorham to meet Mitchell. He wasn't as worried as he had been yesterday, but he knew he had to be very careful. He could see that Mitchell had good reason for believing that he had pinched the bike, and the possibility that he might be booked for something he hadn't actually done was unnerving.

Mitchell had a Northend copper with him, another sharp-eyed youngish bloke. They told him to get in the back of the car, and drove him out to Fiddler's Creek. Mitchell parked the car on the quay, and they stood there contemplating the wharf, and the door in the sail-loft high above. It was a grey day with a fresh breeze blowing in from the sea. The water was scuffled with waves, lapping up over the mud.

'If you jumped in at twenty to four yesterday, you could do it today at twenty to five, allowing roughly an hour for the advance of high water. We want to get these times right. You jumped as soon as you thought you could get away with it?'

'Yes.'

Penn knew he was safe with his times. The tide, give or take ten minutes, was not going to play him up, unless the end of the world was at hand. The two coppers made him take them up into the sail-loft, where they opened the door that gave out over the creek and stood looking down.

'This is where you jumped from?'

'Yes.'

'You don't want to change your mind about this story?'

'No.'

Penn, looking out, too, was not surprised at Mitchell's scepticism. In the cold grey wind the prospect looked, somehow, far nastier than it had looked the day before. The ground looked much farther away, and harder, the white Mini very small below; even the water looked dangerous. He began to feel worried. Mitchell glanced at his watch.

'Four-fifteen.'

There was still mud below. Penn leaned against the wall, trying not to think of anything. He supposed Mitchell would wait till the water came up high enough, check on the time, and then they would clear off. There was nothing he could get him on. He kept thinking about the girl. Sylvia. He couldn't think of her as Sylvia, somehow.

At twenty to five the water was a good foot short of where it had been when he had jumped. Mitchell looked at it and said, 'I don't believe your story, Pennington. Anything more you'd like to say?'

Penn was outraged.

'How else did we get out, then? You see if you can open that other door when the bars are down!'

'I'm just suggesting that you tell the truth now, before it's too late.'

'I have told you the truth.'

'All along the line?'

Penn's eyes flicked. 'Yes.'

'I don't believe you. I'm warning you now, anything you say may be taken down and used—'

Penn felt the flames rise. 'You ruddy coppers! You believe

just what you want to! I'll show you I did it, if you don't believe me!'

Mitchell laughed.

Penn straightened up, and moved very fast. He saw the expression change on Mitchell's face very abruptly. He knew the wind was blowing off the marshes, into the sail-loft, and he was short of a valuable foot of water and that, this time, the circus act was extremely dangerous, but it did not stop him. It was as good a way to go under as any, and take Mitchell with him, come to that. 'Lad questioned by police throws himself to death.' Penn threw himself. The death part was an eyelash away. The fear, falling, was terrible. The wind held him back, and it was only the edge of the water below, and the big stakes and the roof of the Mini—all to stop Mitchell's scorn. Penn would have embraced Mitchell now, if there was any way Mitchell could have stopped him. He curled up and got his head down between his forearms, and the name Sylvia ran right through him, like electricity. He hit two feet of water and the bed of mud, and his ankles took the shock, and his soccer knee screamed out, but he wasn't dead. A tiny, awkward sliver of him was disappointed.

Floundering, he launched himself forward into the balm of deep water, and let it hold him while he took stock. He had no breath and coherent thought beyond amazement that he was still alive. The two policemen were staring down. Penn swam to the old jetty downstream, against the tide, wondering which of the pains were going to meet him when he got out. He was going to get out and walk away, even if it killed him. He saw that he still had his watch on, and was furious. He'd send the repair bill to Mitchell.

He got out, trying to look as if he was in no hurry, because he couldn't hurry. Besides his knee, which didn't want to hold him, he was flabby with shock. But he climbed the wall, holding on to the jetty, and stood up at the top, pushing his hair back. The wind was cold and went right through him. He saw Mitchell and his colleague come out of the shed onto the top of the ladder, so he turned his back, shoved his hands in his pockets and started to walk home along the sea-wall, willing his knee to bear up. He didn't turn round, but he heard the Mini start up and drive away towards the top end of the creek.

It was a very long way home.

His father thought the story a huge joke and laughed like mad.

'That's the way to show the beggars!' he kept saying. He got Penn some dry clothes, and rubbed his knee with wintergreen. He poured out two cans of beer, and held one up to Penn, who lay back in the armchair and turned on the television.

'Here's to us,' he said. 'Disaster to all coppers.'

Penn smiled.

'There's a load of us saw you drive in on that motor-bike,' Smeeton said to Penn. 'If any old copper starts asking, that is.'

'What did the copper want?' Crombie asked.

'He wanted to congratulate me on my performance in the concert,' Penn said.

They laughed derisively. They shouted at each other, the din in the dining-room like a pain, the big tins of rice pudding sloshing down the tables. Penn had been sounding off about having to look at Smeeton, who was sitting opposite him, for the whole fifteen minutes of eating-time. 'It's enough to put any-one off their food. Those pimples!'

Smeeton, smarting, brought up the subject of Mitchell. Fletcher said to him, 'Tell us about what goes on in Oakhall, Smeeton, what your cousin says.'

Smeeton's cousin was at Oakhall for stealing cars. Conversation concerning the privations of life at Oakhall, as related by Smeeton, had a gruesome popular appeal, and everybody except Penn liked to hear the tale.

Penn said, 'We don't want to hear about Oakhall, Smeeton.'

'Oh, yes, we do,' said Fletcher.

'You get up at five-thirty,' Smeeton said, stirring mounds into his rice pudding, smiling, watching Penn, 'have a *cold* shower and do P.E. for an hour outside, in just shorts. Even in the rain. Old-fashioned sort, press-ups and knees-bends and crippling suchlikes. Go in and have another *cold* shower, get dressed, inspection just like in the army. Baked beans for break-fast every day of the year. Get changed again. You spend all day getting changed and washing. Scrub floors all morning—'

'We don't want to hear about Oakhall, Smeeton,' Penn said.

'Stew for lunch, thin and greasy.'

'Like you, Smeeton.'

'Every day of the year, never any different. Drill after lunch, like in the army, round and round, up and down, ex-army sergeant-major.'

Penn put his spoon down. 'Shut up, Smeeton.'

'Wash and change,' said Smeeton. 'Go and dig the kitchen garden.'

Penn said to Maxwell, next to him, 'Pass the rice pudding down.'

'Pass the rice pudding down,' Maxwell said. 'Bread and marg for tea.'

The rice pudding, very full, came sploshing up the table and stopped opposite Penn.

'After tea, lessons, six till eight. Wash again.'

Penn got up, kicking back his chair. He leaned over the table and put both hands round the back of Smeeton's neck, linked his cast-iron pianist's fingers, pulled Smeeton bodily out of his chair and pressed his face down into the rice pudding. The dish served twenty-four, and Smeeton went in over the ears. Penn went on holding him, while everyone watched, goggle-eyed.

'I say, Penn—' Maxwell began.

Bates was laughing. Smeeton's flailing arms knocked over a water jug and a plate of pudding into Fletcher's lap. Fletcher jumped up and jabbed his fork into Penn's hand and Penn let go and got Fletcher by the wrist, jerking up his arm so that Fletcher went over backwards. Smeeton lifted his head, choking out rice pudding in all directions, and Penn ducked him again, until Maxwell tapped him on the arm.

Soggy had arrived, and the dining-room was silent as a tomb, save for Smeeton drowning.

'Get out, Pennington,' Soggy said, his voice shaking. 'Go up to Mr. Stack's room and wait for me there. Fletcher, get up. Take Smeeton out. Maxwell and Bates, get a cloth and clear up this mess.' His eyes flamed at Penn; Penn expected to see a forked tongue flick out. 'Never, in all my forty years of teaching, have I seen such an appalling display of irresponsibility. Get out of my sight, Pennington, *quickly*!'

Penn got out. It was worth it, whatever happened.

'He didn't!' exclaimed Peach, beaming at the thought. 'God, I wish I'd been on duty. What a lovely sight it must have been. What's Marsh going to do now?'

'God knows. What can you do with a boy like that?' Matthews was searching Soggy's desk with a worried frown between his eyes.

'Smeeton's half drowned,' he said. 'In rice pudding, of all things. What an accident to write up in the First Aid book! Look, Peach, has anyone had the First Aid brandy? I can't find it anywhere.'

'Not that I know of. It should be under the petty cash.'

'Well, it isn't. That's where I put it back, last time.'

'Who's swiped it, then?'

'It was a half-bottle, near enough full. Have I got to report a theft as well?'

'The only person I've seen under the influence around here lately is Bates,' Peach said.

'You mean we're back to Pennington again? It's just as likely to be someone on the staff. Three-quarters of us are boozers. I'd better make out it's used up. We don't want any embarrassment, do we? Miss Harrington probably. She's got a nose like a port-hand light. Smeeton can make do on sal volatile.'

'I wouldn't waste brandy on him. It's Marsh who'll need it, if he's dealing with Pennington. I reckon that boy's got Marsh beat.'

'Marsh has no idea. Pennington's obviously not going to get his ruddy hair cut in time for my swimming gala, thanks to Marsh's interference. It's enough to make a man weep. Don't say anything about the brandy, Peach. There's enough trouble in this place without our turning up any more.'

In spite of the Education Committee's distaste for corporal punishment, Penn had some difficulty in making himself comfortable on the piano stool when he eventually turned up for his music lesson.

'Where've you been? We've plenty to get through. The nineteenth isn't far away now,' fussed Crocker.

'Mr. Marsh kept me,' Penn said. 'It's not my fault.'

'That man's always interfering. What are you doing this afternoon? Are you free to play?'

'Yes. It's swimming.'

'Good. Don't you get your hair cut before the nineteenth, whatever happens, Pennington. Now, what were you doing this morning? The arpeggio exercises? You really do need to concentrate on this octave section more than anything else. It's the arm action that matters. I've told you all this. Shoulders taking the arm weight so that the whole arm is relaxed and light and you get a good free vibration right down, in and out of the keys on a good oblique angle. You can do that for half an hour when I leave you. Start fairly slowly with the metronome and step it up. I think the rest of it is coming along quite nicely, apart from the fact that you don't treat it with the delicacy it deserves. You do know what it's about, don't you, Pennington?'

'Well . . .'

'You've heard the scherzo from Mendelssohn's music to "Midsummer Night's Dream"? It must have the same fairy-like quality, Pennington. Fast and light and soft. Not bashing the ball out to Maxwell at right-half. Keep your physical beef for the closing passage.'

Penn sighed.

'I've sorted out some pieces here which I want you to begin on right away, all very light and delicate . . . this Chopin study, opus twenty-five . . . some more Mendelssohn, "The Bees' Wedding" and "The Spinning Song". Very good stuff for you. Chopin was the finest pianist of his time, yet he had no physical strength at all, Pennington. You could bear it in mind. I'm not suggesting you pretend you're dying of consumption, but you get what I'm driving at?'

'Yes, sir.'

'Less of the Polonaise in A major and the Revolutionary and a few more pieces in the nocturne style, I think. Even the Polonaise doesn't have to be played as fast and as loud as you play it.'

'I like it that way.'

'Mr. Marsh doesn't, I'm afraid. Not in the hall, at least. If you promise to work, Pennington, you can go back to playing in the practice-room, and give them all a rest.'

'I don't mind playing in the hall,' Penn said, pleased that he was driving everybody mad.

'Very well. I must say it's a much better instrument down there. You're working very well, Pennington. Working. Several people have remarked upon it. I'm not the only one to have noticed.'

Faced with periods of two or three solid hours at the keyboard, Penn had found that working was less boring than not working. He had noticed himself that he was working, and been amazed. He pretended that he wasn't impressed by his progress, but he had to admit that he had surprised himself. He had so much time now to think about it. There were times when he even thought he was enjoying it, but this heresy he would stifle the instant it stirred.

'Look, this festival thing,' he said to Crocker. 'I don't want to go in the Open. I'm doing something else that day.'

'You're joking, of course,' Crocker said, looking like a nervous horse.

'No, I'm not.'

'Pennington, I'm not giving you the choice. You're going in for it.'

'There's something else I've got to do,' Penn said.

'You can do something else another time.'

'No, I can't. It's the same day.'

'You're not doing this to me, Pennington,' Crocker said. His voice shook slightly. 'You can do it to Stack and Marsh and even Matthews, but not to me. Not now.'

Penn didn't know what else to say. Strangely, he was on Crocker's side, in a way. But he was going to the Folk Festival just the same.

'You can't do exactly what you want all your life, Pennington.'

Penn was indignant. 'But I don't! I do what other people want all the time. That's what gets me—'

'And what would you do if you could do exactly what you wanted?'

This had floored Penn before now. He had no answer. He was angry and sullen. 'I wouldn't do this, for a start.'

'No, you ignorant child, and I wouldn't do this!' Mr. Crocker's venom startled Penn. 'But we're stuck with it,

Pennington. Both of us. And we must make the best of it. And let me tell you, Pennington, that this gift God gave you, which you are too thick-headed to acknowledge, is the one and only grace you possess, or are ever likely to possess, and while I'm

stuck with my part in this ill-conceived system, I'm going to make quite sure that you're stuck with yours. So get on with it! You're wasting time, Pennington. You've only got *two hours* today, and there's a lifetime of work ahead of you—'

Penn thought, 'The old fool's bonkers,' and lifted his hands and drowned Crocker's voice in the thunderous passage that closed the Mendelssohn piece. He felt as if he was sitting on a bed of nails. 'Cripes,' he thought. 'Roll on, old age!' The next two hours, he felt, would see him there.

Chapter 8

Penn felt pretty desperate, taking stock of what was happening to him and unable to deflect the inexorable course of his fate by any means whatever.

Getting dressed the following Saturday evening to go to the folk-club meeting at the barge, he was more conscious of Mitchell than of Sylvia, his mind returning all the time to the question of how long he had before he was charged with either the offence he hadn't committed or the offence he had. He could not believe that Mitchell was so stupid that he would not find out about the ride to school on the borrowed Honda. And when he did, that meant Oakhall.

Penn stared gloomily into the mirror, combing his hair. It was true that he didn't know what he did want to do, but equally well he knew what he didn't want to do. Oakhall was top of the list there. If, by a great effort, he was able to move his thoughts from this priority, he found no cheer in the fact that, since his father had received the Jaguar bill, he had stopped paying his son any pocket-money. Penn had exactly sixpence with which to woo Sylvia.

He went downstairs and took his mother's purse out of the sideboard drawer. It had four pounds in it. Penn took one, and put it in his back pocket. His mother came in and saw him.

'Just give me that back, you thieving—' She swore at him, her high Irish colour flaring up with rage.

'No, I won't,' Penn said. 'If you want it, you can take it off me—if you can.' He stood with his back to the sideboard, glowering at her, knowing that she could not touch him, hating her.

She shouted at him, bringing in Oakhall again. Penn felt the violence rising up in him.

'It's your fault I haven't any money, isn't it? Making me stay on at school! What am I supposed to do, go to bed every night when I come home? I haven't had a penny for over a month. I haven't been out anywhere for weeks, have I? I haven't even got anything for a coffee or fags or *anything*. I might as well be in Oakhall already as go on here!'

Self-pity flooded him, listening to himself. His righteous indignation must have touched his mother, for she paled down, merely breathing hard.

'I haven't even got a decent shirt fit to go out in,' Penn said, knowing his mother, pressing hard. 'And my bike needs a new tyre—I can't use it. I've got to hitch to Northend tonight. I might as well be dead, at this rate.'

'I'll give you some money for a haircut,' his mother said.

'Well, I've told you, haven't I? I can't get it cut now. They've made a thing about it at school, that old Soggy—you know him. If I back down now it's just being chicken. He'll gloat. They're on at you all the time, I've told you, just like being in the army or something. Why should I? It's a free country, isn't it?'

'What's it got to do with them?' his mother asked. 'You mean they've told you to get it cut?'

'Yes, I'm suspended games and everything. Can't be in the swimming gala—'

'That's a flaming liberty! Who do they think they are, then?' His mother was getting all red again.

'Well, I've told you. What with them, and Dad going on at me, and you—Oakhall'd be a rest cure.'

'Oh, Pat, don't say that. Your father'll get you out of it.'

Penn knew he had won.

'Here, take another pound. I'll talk to your father about the pocket-money. And don't do anything about your hair. Not if that's the way it is.'

Penn took the money and went, without another word. He called for Bates and they walked up to the main road and got a bus. Now that his hair was so long, hitch-hiking wasn't easy any more. People looked at him and drove on. In fact, Penn found his hair a darned nuisance, what with washing it and swimming, but he knew he was stuck with it now until the end of term. He was silent and morose, and Bates let him alone. He was thinking about Sylvia, and all his nerve went. He didn't know anything about girls, or how you made them interested in you. He only knew that he just wanted to stare at her.

When they went down into the barge it was quite crowded. There were a lot of girls, as well as Sylvia, but Penn didn't notice them. Bates, not worried at all, went up to Sylvia and said, 'Look, we've come.' Penn said nothing.

'Oh, John, how nice,' Sylvia said, smiling at Bates. 'I told Colin about you. I'm glad you've come.'

Colin was the guitar-player, dashingly handsome. Penn, watching Sylvia, could have strangled Bates for the 'John' and the smile. For himself there was an uncertain half-smile, no more. Plunged in gloom, he leaned against the wall, his hands in his pockets, listening and scowling. Bates brought him a beer. There was a lot of singing and strumming, and a new song practised, Sylvia sitting beside Colin and laughing with him. She wore a very short silvery sort of dress, and her thighs were slim and brown. Penn couldn't stop watching her. He wished he were dead.

When the evening was well under way, and Penn had got more and more miserable, Sylvia came over to Bates and asked him to sing. Bates didn't seem to have any more inhibitions— Penn supposed the school concert had been good for his ego— and it was he who stood up and said to Penn, 'Come on, what's the matter with you?'

Penn took out his harmonica without a word. He felt stunned. He played with such haunting despair that 'The Butcher Boy' was a sadder story than even he remembered it. When they had finished there was a very respectful response.

'I say, that was very good indeed,' Colin said, obviously impressed. 'Are you coming to the Tolchester festival? If you can repeat that, the Old Barge Club will be able to put out a very good programme. Sylvia said you were good, but that was really something.'

'Of course they're coming,' Sylvia said. 'I told you the date, didn't I?'

'Yes, but—' said Bates.

'Yes, we're coming,' Penn said.

Sylvia looked at him for the first time. Her eyes were green like the splintered, cloudy edge of a broken beer-bottle. She said, 'What's your name?'

114

'Penn,' said Bates.

'Patrick,' said Penn.

She pushed back a wing of silver hair. Penn wondered if it was real.

'Will you play for me?' she said. '"Freight Train?" Or—no— "Will ye go, Lassie?"'

Penn nodded. He didn't know it, but wherever she went he would go, too. Colin started on the guitar and Penn waited for Sylvia, hitching his backside on a table, watching her shape under the silver dress. He had no breath for the harmonica. The melody communicated; he played with it and over it, embroidering the voice, watching the white curve of her cheek, feeling dislocated.

When it was finished, Colin said, 'You play that thing very well. You play anything else?'

'Only the piano.'

Sylvia smiled at him. Penn felt his face burning. What did

you do, he wondered? What did you say? There was nothing inside him except a painful incoherence.

'Colin, perhaps he could play with us at the festival? It goes well. How about trying "O, Waly, Waly"?'

Penn watched her again, singing, finding the sad, nebulous tune with his tongue.

> 'There is a ship that sails the sea,
> She's loaded deep as deep can be,
> But not so deep as the love I'm in,
> I know not if I sink or swim.'

Penn was sinking, and knew it.

Colin liked it, and said, 'Come down next Saturday and we'll work on it. It could be all right with the harmonica.'

Sylvia went away with Colin, giving Penn another half-smile. Another girl was singing, but Penn wasn't interested.

'Come on,' he said to Bates. 'Let's go home.'

'What's wrong with you tonight?' Bates asked.

'Nothing.'

'You didn't mean it about going to this folk thing on the nineteenth? Not with Mr. Crocker and—'

'Yes, I did mean it. I've already told Crocker.'

'He didn't wear it, surely?' Bates was incredulous.

'Well, I told him, and he can't say I didn't warn him.'

'He'll go berserk if you don't go to the piano thing.'

'Well, that's his affair.' Penn was short, thinking of Colin touching Sylvia, taking her home, easy and good-looking, and Sylvia smiling, and her cloudy green eyes and her thin, silver body. Mitchell was out of his head, a moon-shot away.

'Oh, cripes,' said Bates, understanding. 'You, of all people! Fancy *you*—!' He went ahead down the gasworks jetty, kicking a lump of coke, choked with disgust.

Bates went into the music-room where Penn was working with Crocker and waited, hopefully.

Penn was saying, 'This thing you gave me. The Chopin study, opus twenty-five, number two. I don't get it. It says two-two, but the left hand looks like six-four and the right hand looks like four-four to me. Why couldn't he write it in six-four and get rid of these silly triplets in the right hand?'

'You might not believe it, Pennington, but Chopin did know what he was doing. Difficult, granted. You have to feel the right-hand groups of triplets against the left-hand in six. Two large beats will help. You've got to feel two rhythms at once.'

'So it's really like two against three enlarged?'

'Mmm. Yes. Put your thumb here, like this, on the start of each of these groups of three. On each C. Try it. That's it.'

Bates coughed and said, 'Excuse me, sir.'

'What is it?' Crocker turned round testily.

'Mr. Marsh wants Pennington, sir. He's got to come to the swimming gala.'

'But I'm not swimming,' Penn said.

'You've got to spectate. All the fifth forms are going to spectate and he said to fetch you. The bus is waiting.'

'Oh, God,' groaned Crocker. 'What we're up against! Get along, Pennington. Go and spectate. Don't work too hard at it.'

Penn got up. Strangely enough, he was annoyed at having to leave the piano just at that moment, having got into a frame of mind to carry on for the next two hours. The fact that he was reluctant amazed him. He followed Bates, wondering whether he was getting hooked by this habit of work. The idea worried him. Just brain-washing, he thought. The uneasiness stayed, to accompany all the other uneasinesses with which his mind was filled: Mitchell and Soggy and Sylvia and not going to the competition. Worrying was new to him and he did not like it. He stared out of the bus window and Smeeton said to him, 'What are you thinking about, Pennington? As if I couldn't guess. She's blonde and flat as a pancake.'

Penn swung round and hit Smeeton, crashing his weasel face against the window so that his jaw sagged.

'*Pennington!*'

Soggy stormed out of his seat, blue with apoplexy. He reached over Bates and dragged Penn to his feet by a handful of hair.

'Get out of your seat! Go and stand up at the front by the door. You're not fit to take out in public! You're untrained, Pennington, you're not even civilized! You are activated by the brain of a Neanderthal man. You are—'

Penn had heard it all before. He lurched down the bus and stood by the driver. The driver said, jerking his head towards the tirade, 'Something biting him?'

'He can't help it,' Pennington said tolerantly.

Very softly, but just loud enough for Soggy to hear, he whistled a few bars of 'Tannenbaum'.

At the baths Penn sat at the back of the crowded spectators' gallery with Maxwell and Crombie and Bates, and they started a game with the cards Maxwell had brought. With the six Northend schools participating, the baths were frantic with excitement, but Penn, ostracized from what would have been his day of glory, was determined not to take an interest. They could all drown, as far as he was concerned. Especially Soggy, who was sitting with Mr. Stack and the other head and senior masters in a row along the bathside, near enough—Penn noticed with satisfaction—to get wet. Matthews was the starter. Penn did not look up from his cards as the first gun went.

By three-quarters of the way through the afternoon Penn had won a florin and the Beehive was ahead by two points.

'Cripes, it's hot in here!' Maxwell complained. 'Your go, Bates.'

'Northend Parkside will go ahead if Turner doesn't win this.' Bates had to yell to pierce the girls' screaming.

Matthews was looking grim. Turner came third.

'You shouldn't have played that king, you ruddy fool,' Penn said to Bates. 'You knew Crombie had the ace.'

'There's only the four hundred metres freestyle after this, and Parker'll never get that. So if Burton doesn't get this one, we've lost the cup.'

'Hearts are trumps, Bates, you ruddy idiot! Cripes, I *need* the money, Bates, even if you don't. Bates, you are activated by the brain of a Neanderthal man.'

Penn groaned, loosening his tie. The humid, chlorine-laced atmosphere shivered to the tension of the Beehive spectators scenting imminent disaster. The girls' screaming reverberated round the acoustics like the sound of a panicking parrot-house.

'Pennington, Mr. Matthews wants you downstairs.' A boy appeared at Penn's elbow, eager sweat shining. 'He says hurry.'

'You're joking,' Penn said sourly.

'No. Honest I'm not.'

'Crickey, Penn, go on!' Maxwell said, foreseeing a row of really resplendent proportions if the omens were correct.

'Hurry!' said the messenger, hopping on one foot. 'He said hurry!'

Penn went, not hurrying, but scowling hard, hands in pockets.
'He can only want him for one thing,' Maxwell said, eyes
gleaming. 'What do you bet me? Can you see Matthews? Yes,
there he is, worried as hell.'

'You mean the four hundred metres?' Bates said, aghast.
'He wouldn't!'

'If Burton wins this one, he won't. If Burton doesn't win, he
will. Matthews is starting them now. You watch. As soon as
they're off he'll go out of the swing doors to intercept Penn.'

He did. There was no sign of Penn, but Matthews's demeanour was enough to go by. He was bristling with anxiety, watching
Burton's failure with glazed, suicidal eyes. Northend Parkside
screamed and stamped until a baths attendant warned them
about the condition of the gallery. In the front row, Mr. Stack
and Mr. Marsh exchanged sporting, congratulatory smiles with
the Northend Parksides. The loudspeaker crackled with the
results, which gave Northend Parkside a lead of two points over
the Beehive.

'Only a win in the last race will give us the cup,' Maxwell
said, agog. 'Win or nothing. Poor old Penn! He's in for it!
You watch. And old Matthews will be minced, utterly minced,
by Stacker. Just watch Stacker's face when he sees Penn. And
old Soggy's! God, this is lovely. Gorgeous!'

Bates was rather more dubious. 'You don't really think—?'

Maxwell did. There was still no sign of Penn, although the
other five competitors for the last race were jogging about by the
starting-blocks.

The loudspeaker began to intone: 'Senior four hundred metre
freestyle. Competitors are as follows: Lane one, Northend
Parkside, N. G. Peterson. Lane two, Market Road Comprehensive, P. R. Stubbs . . .'

'There he is,' Maxwell said, in a tone of the deepest satisfaction.

Penn had appeared out of the doorway to the changing-rooms
on the side where he was hidden from Stacker and Soggy. He
was in swimming-trunks, biting the side of his thumbnail with
some anxiety, watching Matthews, who was standing with his
starting-gun at the ready. The other five competitors were already on their marks.

'Lane six, Beehive Secondary Modern, P. E. Pennington.'

As soon as the loudspeaker finished, Matthews raised his gun and bawled, 'On your marks!' Penn stepped forward, came to the block, and dived as the gun went off, all in one fell swoop. From the Beehive section of the gallery a shrill scream of glee went up, '*Penn*ington!' Maxwell clutched Bates in ecstasy.

'Look at Soggy! Look at Stacker! Oh, what bliss! What makings of superb, undiluted head-rolling!'

Bates looked, doubtfully. Soggy was white as a sheet, goggling at Penn as he passed by three feet away, shaking Penn's spray off him as if it were drops of blood. Stacker's face was expressionless, glazed, barricading his thoughts from the breathless gaze of the whole of his senior school in the gallery above. The delight of the gallery was ecstatic. Matthews, Bates noticed, had disappeared from sight.

'But it's not Penn's fault,' he said, looking ahead. 'He's only doing what he's told.'

'If he loses,' Maxwell said, 'he might as well drown.'

'Oh, he won't lose,' Bates said, his faith in Penn boundless.

'He's going to have a job. That's Peterson swimming for Parkside.'

Penn was swimming at a pace that suggested that his line of thought was very much in accord with Maxwell's. At the second turn he was his own length ahead of Peterson and various other lengths ahead of everyone else, swimming with little grace but extraordinary power, pushing up a bow-wave that travelled up the side of the bath with him like the Severn bore. Soggy watched him pass and repass like a snake watching a rabbit. He said something to Stacker. Bates could guess at the hiss of his voice, the familiar venom. He felt a deep, sad sympathy for Penn.

So did Crombie. 'Poor old Penn. Four hundred metres, and he only came for a game of cards.'

Peterson came up until he was riding at Penn's shoulder, his stroke very easy. At the fifth turn they were almost a length ahead of all the others. Parkside started to shout, and the Beehive, who had been shouting right from the start, raised the pitch of their noise, which echoed with painful effect through the torrid dome of the Northend Municipal Baths. Stacker got out a handkerchief and patted delicately at the sweat of rage on his brow.

'Oh, cripes,' said Maxwell, as Peterson drew level. His glee had turned to the same agony as that afflicting the rest of the Beehive spectators. Only the Beehive spectators knew exactly why Penn had to be the winner.

Peterson, on the next turn, went ahead. Bates wondered if Penn knew he was there; he surely could not see anything for hair. Bates felt almost like crying. He prayed for Penn to win, screwing his eyes up, but still looking. Penn, on the sixth turn, drew up with Peterson again, and they turned as one, twisting like otters. Peterson's stroke was now frantic, the elegance abandoned, but Penn's was no different, only more rapid. He put his head down and appeared to Bates to do the last length without another breath, drawing all the water in the bath after him, to leave all the others floundering through his triumphant wake. Peterson's head was at Penn's hips when Penn touched the bar. Bates found that he was crying, but they were all so sweaty nobody noticed.

Penn was so whacked when he finished that he stayed where he was, holding the bar, head down. He had this feeling, very strongly, that the only safe place was under the water, where it was blue and silent and unapproachable, and he did not want to come up, or climb out, or hear anything. He stayed there as long as possible, in spite of the tumult going on above him, but when everyone else had finished and climbed out, he was forced to make a move. He brought his legs under him and stood up. Soggy was standing right in front of him; Penn looked up and saw him from a new eye-level, and saw all the hairs in his nose bristling with anger, and the scraggy, drawn tendons of his neck standing out like handrails up from his tie.

'Pennington, I—'

Penn put down his head and flung back his hair with splendid effect, spraying Soggy from head to foot. Then, because the instinct was so strong, he pulled up his legs, twisted round and submerged again, and swam right down to the other end of the bath, under water. When he saw the steps at the deep end he surfaced, climbed up them, and made his exit through the nearest doorway. He found himself in the women's changing-rooms.

'Who do you think you are?' said the attendant indignantly.

But it was empty, the girls'
events having finished earlier,
and Penn refused to move,
knowing that Soggy was unlikely to pursue him into so embar-
rassing a setting.

'I'll get the manager,' said the woman.

'You can't bring him in here,' Penn said, sitting down on the
attendant's chair. He put his elbows on his knees and sat, hands
dangling, feeling curiously divorced from his actual situation, as
if he were not in trouble at all, as if he were still in the music-
room, working out the rhythmical subtleties of Chopin's Etude.

'Creatures like you,' said the attendant, eyeing the curling
tendrils of hair which dripped over his shoulders, 'make us
wonder which changing-room we're in half the time.'

Penn could think of several good replies to this and even a
demonstration, but as they were all obscene he contented himself by saying, 'Oh, get stuffed.'

'What school are you from?' she inquired frigidly.

'Northend Parkside,' Penn said.

She went away, and Penn looked out, saw that the bathside

was emptying fast, and that Stacker and Soggy had gone, and went out, padding back to the men's changing-rooms. Matthews met him at the doorway.

'We've got an appointment with Stacker when we get back to school,' he said. 'Both of us.'

'That doesn't surprise me,' Penn said.

'You swam a splendid race,' Matthews said. 'Beating Peterson is something to be proud of. I knew no one else could do it. Look, you won't get into trouble, so don't worry. Get changed and I'll wait for you. The bus has gone. I'll run you back in my car.'

Penn could see that Matthews was a worried man. He got changed and went out to the car park. Matthews didn't say anything, but gestured to Penn to get into the battered little Ford he drove. Penn got in and Matthews put the ignition key in, but did not turn it, sitting thoughtfully, staring into space. Penn waited.

'Look, Pennington,' Matthews said eventually. 'I'm sorry about this, but I want to ask you to do me a favour.'

Penn could see it coming. He, too, stared into space.

'After all, we won the cup. He can't say much, can he, if we go back, and you've had your hair cut?'

Penn was silent.

'I like my job here,' Matthews said. 'I don't want to have to move or anything. I've got a nice house on a mortgage, and the wife's having a baby next month. I'm due for a rise in responsibility pay next year, the way things are. I'm terribly sorry to ask you this.'

Penn said, 'I'm fed up with my ruddy hair, but it's Mr. Marsh. I'll have plaits before I get it cut for him.'

'Yes, I can see that. I understand, believe me. But would you, all the same?'

Penn did not say anything, fed up beyond measure. He recalled the grotesque appearance of Soggy from underneath, Soggy manhandling him in front of Sylvia, Soggy rating him in the bus.

'He came to shout me out at the end of the race, and I didn't listen. He'll think I got it cut because I'm scared. Well, I'm not scared. Not of anything they can do.'

'Look, I know that. Suppose I tell him? Would that be all right?'

'What, you go up to him and say I'm getting my hair cut because *you* asked me to? Because of your mortgage and your wife and all that? You'd tell him? Tell him, as far as he's concerned, I'd like to grow it long enough to wrap round his neck—'

'Yes, all right. I'll tell him.'

'Even the last bit?'

'If you insist.'

'Yes. All right.'

Matthews drew a happy sigh, and started the car. 'Where do you go? I'll wait for you.'

'The one on the front, next to the Odeon.'

Matthews drove down to the front and parked the car. He groped in his pocket and pulled out three florins and a few sixpences.

'There you are.'

Penn looked at the money and said, 'It's twelve and six the way I have it done.'

'God, Pennington, don't be all night.' Matthews gave him a ten-shilling piece. 'I want to get this over.'

Crocker was laughing his head off.

Peach said to him, quietly, 'Be a bit more ruddy tactful, can't you? Marsh doesn't think it's a joke.'

'I do,' said Crocker.

They went into the staff-room together, into the stale five-o'clock atmosphere of stewing tea and cigarette smoke.

'I hear we won the cup!' Crocker said breezily. 'Splendid news, Mr. Marsh. You must be feeling really bucked! I must congratulate Matthews. Where is Matthews?'

Soggy looked at Crocker with loathing.

'It's the first time I've heard you take any interest in sports results, Crocker. I wonder you knew the event was taking place.'

'I only knew because you deprived me of my pupil for a good afternoon's work, merely for the sake of spectating, as Bates put it. I hope he spectated with credit.'

'Are you being funny?' Marsh said, very tight.

'You can't deprive me of my games, Marsh, and the Education Committee doesn't approve of teachers being caned.' Crocker's voice was sharp and amused.

'My God, Crocker—'

Soggy was interrupted by Miss Harrington coming in and saying, 'I would never have believed it! I've just seen Pennington and he's had his hair cut. He looks so elegant I didn't recognize him.'

Everyone in the staff-room turned round and stared at her.

'Never!' said Peach.

Crocker's good humour stopped, like a tap being turned off, and his face fell into its more habitual lines of bitter resignation.

'No!' he said. 'Oh, no! Why has he done that? The foolish boy!'

Soggy turned round, smiling. 'I'll tell you why he's done it, Crocker. Because he knows when enough is enough. He knows how far he can go. He is frightened of the consequences of this afternoon's little escapade, and hopes to make things easier for himself. In other words, he has given in.'

Soggy's eyes glittered with triumph. He laughed, pleased with Crocker's dismay. Miss Harrington's news had erased his bad humour as completely as it had shattered Crocker's glee.

'I must speak to Stacker about this situation,' Crocker muttered, making for the door. 'I must see Matthews. I must have more of that boy's time, hair or no hair. There is so little time left, just as we are getting somewhere.'

Soggy shook his head. 'You're not deluding yourself, my dear Crocker, that you are getting anywhere with Pennington?'

'I may be deluding myself, but yes, I am getting somewhere with Pennington.'

He opened the door, having reverted to his normal image: that of a frustrated, absent-minded gnome. As he opened it, Matthews came in, looking extremely cheerful, and Crocker stepped back again. Matthews looked round at the inquiring faces, avoided Soggy's glance and said, 'Well, that wasn't so bad. I'm still on the staff.'

'You've merely held Mr. Stack's authority up to ridicule in front of the whole school and given the school's worst influence since the year dot a splendid opportunity of turning himself into the hero of the afternoon—not bad, at all,' said Soggy grimly. 'Congratulations.'

'Thank you,' said Matthews quietly. 'And while we're at it, for Pennington to beat Peterson, who has swum for England, wasn't bad either, and as he is completely guiltless, for a change, of any of the disobedience that occurred this afternoon, it wouldn't be out of place for you, his form master, to at least refrain from baiting him about it, if not to congratulate him.'

Matthews looked as astonished at his own speech as all the other people who heard it, including Soggy.

'I shall congratulate him,' Soggy said acidly. 'On his haircut.'

Matthews looked uneasy.

Soggy went on: 'His defiance is not, it seems, as absolute as it appeared, which is greater cause for congratulation to my mind then winning the four hundred metres. I shall heap congratulations on him,' Soggy promised with an edge to his voice.

'I have something to tell you, Marsh, about that haircut.' Matthews was worried, on Penn's behalf, but it was a promise. 'It wasn't his idea to get it cut, it was mine. I asked him to do it, to help smooth the situation over for me. And he agreed to it, on the condition that I told you why he was getting it cut. In other words, he insisted that you knew he wasn't getting it cut because he was frightened of you. He said—' Matthews paused, wondering whether he was doing the right thing. 'He said that, as far as you're concerned, he'd like to grow it long enough to wrap round your neck.'

There was a silence so profound that the clatter of the care-taker doing the floors two storeys down came quite clearly. Matthews looked at Soggy and sensed that, perhaps, it might have been wiser to pass off to Pennington a white lie as to what he had told Soggy. Soggy turned and went out of the door without another word, his face tight with fury, his lips twitching.

Matthews knew he had made a mistake. Pennington had helped him, but he hadn't helped Pennington.

Peach started packing his briefcase, cheerfully unconcerned. 'I do like a homely, friendly atmosphere in a staff-room, like we have here,' he said. 'I've always said—that's what I like about the Beehive, the way the staff work together with a will, always a helping hand, a cheerful smile—'

'Oh, shut up,' said Matthews.

Chapter 9

Penn went to school the next day, and suffered so much sarcasm from Soggy concerning his manly appearance that on
Friday he opted out and stayed at home. He went down to the
river and lay on the sea-wall in the sun, thinking of Sylvia. He
told himself that Soggy didn't bother him, but he just didn't
want to take any more. He had been working too hard, what
with beating Peterson and the hours he had put in at the keyboard. He felt on edge, as if things were closing in on him. They
were, in fact, and he knew it. There was a day to go before he
saw Sylvia, and then a week again to the festival at Tolchester,
but he didn't know, if Mitchell was still probing around, whether
he would still be about then. He had heard—and was pretty
sure it was true—that a Northend youth had been pinched for
the motor-bike incident at Fiddler's Creek, but he very much
doubted if, with Mitchell ill-disposed towards him and nosing
around like a stubborn bloodhound, he was going to get away
with riding the Honda.

On Saturday, in the barge, they played 'O, Waly, Waly'.
Sylvia gave him her half-smiles, but said very little to him, beyond what the practice demanded. She was friendly and easy
with Colin, and even with Bates, but towards him she was very
quiet, almost shy. He thought it was because he was such an
oaf, not knowing even how to speak to her, let alone make a
pass at her.

Just before she went, she said, 'John told me something about
you're supposed to be playing in a piano competition next
Saturday. But you said you're coming to Tolchester?' It was a
question, and Penn recognized it as one.

'Yes,' he said. 'I'm coming to Tolchester.'

'I'm glad,' she said.

What did it mean, Penn wondered? Glad to have a harmonica in the act?

'Why have you cut your hair?' she said. 'I liked it.'

He shrugged. The answer to that was too long. She touched his shoulder in passing, and he felt fires go through him, and despised his frailty so profoundly that he wished he had never set eyes on her. It was all so ruddy useless, like everything else. Getting you nowhere. He hated himself, everything about him. Particularly what he was going to do to old Crocker next Saturday. He was set on Tolchester now, because of this damned sex-urge, and he was too callous to do the right thing, yet not callous enough not to feel ashamed. He was slipping, he thought, to care, and yet he did care. Pathetic old Crocker, who had forced him like a hothouse cucumber, was going to get a cold reward.

Morose, preoccupied, he spent Sunday going over _Mathilda_'s engine, getting it to go again. Bates bought a gallon of petrol, and they patrolled the river once or twice, and Penn tried not to think about things.

He went back to school and spent most of the week in the music-room, having been handed over to Crocker almost entirely for the period before the competition. This pleased him well enough. There were hours of concentrated work when, at least, he didn't have time to think about anything else, and periods when he accompanied for choir practice or the fourth form singing, which killed time and kept him out of Soggy's way. It was the lull before the storm, he thought. Crocker brought him a Beethoven sonata which kept him occupied most of Wednesday, but on Thursday afternoon the peace was broken when the subject was broached by a direct question.

'This rubbish you were talking last week, about going somewhere else on Saturday—just put my mind at rest, Pennington. You're such a bastard you might well have been serious. Are you intending to present yourself at the Town Hall on Saturday and take part in this competition?'

'No, I'm not.'

Penn found it hard to say, and could not look at Crocker. There was long, hopeless silence. When he eventually looked at Crocker, Penn saw that the old man's eyes were full of tears. He felt so embarrassed he could not go on sitting there, but had to get up and go out to the bog. When he came back Crocker had gone.

'The old fool. As if it matters,' Penn said out loud. And he played the Andante and Rondo Capriccioso, as if it were the competition, and started work on the sonata again. An hour later Crocker came back. He looked his usual self.

'I have news for you, Pennington,' he said.

Penn looked at him, suspicious.

'Look here.' Crocker, standing at the window, gestured for Penn to join him. Penn went and looked out, and saw the white police Mini parked in the staff car park. The shock came so unexpectedly that he felt himself quiver. His stomach turned over, and everything Smeeton had said rattled round his empty brain-box, each word sharp as a dried pea, and about as invigorating.

Crocker looked quite jaunty. 'It could all be out of our hands, what you are doing on Saturday. The police-constable has just taken a statement from Mr. Marsh to the effect that he saw you riding some motor-bike on the day of the school concert, which apparently was not yours to ride. Mr. Marsh said his evidence could be used against you "with pleasure", and if he'd asked me, Pennington, I could well have used exactly the same phrase.'

Penn, choked, turned away. He could picture Soggy's satisfaction. He thought, in that moment, that if he had one more day left to him at Beehive Secondary Modern, he would get even with Soggy.

'He also questioned Bates, and seemed to get a good deal of satisfaction from the answers. More than poor Bates got in giving them. Bates is a very poor liar, although he tried. You shouldn't corrupt a good boy like Bates, Pennington.'

Penn went out of the room. He locked himself in the lavatory and stayed there until everyone had gone home, except the cleaners, then he emerged and went home himself. He thought he might just get the week-end before he was charged if he was lucky, if Mitchell had plenty of work on hand. There had been a fire in Moorham, at one of the boatyards, and that ought to keep him occupied for a day, at least.

Mitchell did not call. Penn went to school on Friday, and was caught by Soggy coming back from assembly.

'Lessons as usual for you today, Pennington. Crocker says

you can have a day off, so that you are fresh for his competition.'

So Crocker had not told anybody about the intending defection . . . Penn was not surprised. It wouldn't do his ego any good, after all the effort he had put in. Matthews, after P.E., said to Penn, 'Good luck tomorrow, Pennington, on this music lark.' 'You're just bound to win,' Maxwell said cheerfully. 'Bash 'em like you did Peterson.' 'Oh, Penn, can we come and watch?' the girls said. Only Bates did not say anything, watching Penn unhappily. He had confessed, bitterly, and wept again, because Mitchell had got the truth out of him about the motorbike.

'They had me in the staff-room, and there was him and Soggy and Matthews and Crocker came in, and then Stacker, and Soggy was a pig, almost worse than Mitchell. They got me all tied up, and I'm such a rotten liar, Penn, I can't do it like you. I'm sorry. I'm terribly sorry.'

'Oh, stuff it. It was Soggy, more than you.'

'Yes, He must have seen you. He could describe the bike and everything. And he told Mitchell that he was only too pleased you were getting your deserts at last and that you should have been passed for Borstal when you took your eleven plus, and then Matthews told him the remark was uncalled for, and they started having a row—this was when Mitchell had gone, and they had forgotten I was still there. It was quite funny really.'

'Hilarious,' said Penn.

'What are you going to do?'

'Before I get booked, I'm going to do for Soggy.'

Bates opened his eyes very wide.

Penn wanted to humiliate Soggy before the whole class, as Soggy had so often done to him. He wanted to burst his pomposity, make him weep. There was nothing bad enough really, but there was a limiting factor: it had to be something that would not interest the police, for Penn had no desire for his three months at Oakhall to be improved into two years at a Borstal. He went into a huddle with Rees and a staunch Soggyhater called Patterson. Everyone knew what was in the wind, and the class was full of a curious tension that made Miss Harrington say in the staff-room, 'Whatever's got into 5C today? They're in the strangest mood.'

'When Pennington's gone,' said Soggy, 'we might get somewhere with them.'

For his part, he was full of optimism at the way things were looking.

In the dinner-hour Penn screwed a large hook into the ceiling above the class-room door. Rees was hammering a hole into the rim round the bottom of an enormous galvanized bucket which he had taken out of the cleaners' cupboard.

'It's what they do in the *Beano*,' Bates said. 'It'll never work.'

'Oh, won't it?' Penn said grimly.

They had several run-throughs, and Penn marked a chalk cross on the floor just inside the door. And another one a foot or two farther in.

'You must stand there, Rees, to stop him coming any farther. He's got to be on this first chalk mark, or it'll miss him.'

'I've got some rope,' Patterson said. 'I asked Matthews and he gave me some.'

'Did you tell him what it was for?' Penn asked, grinning.

'I said it was for Soggy.'

'Penn, you're not really going to?' Rita Fairweather said. The girls were all pop-eyed and giggling. 'He'll kill you.'

'I don't care what he does,' Penn said recklessly.

'Maxwell and Crombie have made the mixture,' Bates came up to report. 'They've got it in the chemistry lab. Maxwell says he's just adding a smell to it. Herbs, he said, to give it a bouquet. He wants to know, before he hands it over, whether you're going to promise you're taking full responsibility, Penn. He wants it in writing.'

'Yes, if he wants it.'

'Oh, Penn, you're not—' Bates knew he was chicken, but the sight of the mixture had brought the gravity of the operation home to him. He had thought it had all been a joke at the start. But he could see now that Penn was in no mood for jokes.

'What's in it?' the girls wanted to know.

'Soot, liquid manure, oil, blood—'

'Shut up, Bates. It's a secret recipe,' Rees said. 'We don't want everyone to know it.'

Maxwell and Crombie brought it up and everyone stared at it in awe.

'I hope that ruddy hook's strong enough,' Penn said, eyeing the ceiling.

'I must come and see,' Maxwell said. 'This I cannot miss.'

'Soggy has got to walk from 3C to get back here when the last bell goes. It should just give us time to get it fixed. Put the bucket in the cupboard, Maxwell. Patterson, you're to watch for Soggy outside. It would be criminal to waste it on the wrong man. Rees and I will rig it, then I'll operate it, and Rees can stand on the second chalk cross. And everyone else can stand back and cheer.'

'Oh, cripes,' said Bates. He was already pale as a dead leaf.

Penn tested how much weight the hook was up to with a bucket of water. Then he rigged up the pulley system with some more hooks, and fixed the rope on to the bucket. By which time the bell went, and the girls went to Domestic Science, and the boys to Gardening, where they spent most of the lesson looking for the liquid manure which they all knew was in the bucket in their class-room.

Penn, Patterson and Rees got away early and sprinted back to the class-room. By the time the last bell went the bucket was in place and Penn already had his hand on the pulley rope which ran from the hole in the rim up to another hook at a suitably sharp angle, and down to Penn. The girls came in, cautiously avoiding the chalk marks, and stood in silence. Some of them were pale, and the more chicken characters packed up and went downstairs, unable to face the impending situation. Bates sat in a desk in the farthest corner of the room, looking at the wall. He was trembling, and didn't want anyone to notice.

'All set?' Patterson poked his head in from the corridor.

'Yes.'

'I hope it works after all this,' Rees said, taking up his position.

There was utter silence in the class-room. Twenty-five of them stood as if carved out of stone, watching the door. Penn picked up the rope.

Smeeton said, 'Cripes, Penn, this'll do for you.'

Rees put his head in. 'He's coming!'

It worked all right. Penn had not gone to so much trouble to muff it right at the end. He pulled the rope at exactly the moment Soggy stepped on the chalk mark, and the awful, stinking, filthy black mixture poured out of the bucket with the smooth precision of hot steel from the smelter, its exact target the top of Soggy's head, where the long grey hairs were manfully smoothed across the bald dome. It parted over his crown and ran in glutinous streams down his face and over his ears and down into the back of his collar, then in rivers over the shoulders of his suit, being absorbed, in big globs and splashes, on to his trousers, in a film over his hands and the whole of 3C's English compositions. Penn, giving the rope a final jerk, hoped the bucket would follow up, braining him, but his handiwork had been too good to provide this final satisfaction. He dropped the rope, and stood with his hands in his pockets, taking in the beautiful sight, his face quite grave, composed, and utterly calm.

There was a silence, profound as the dark inside of a tomb. Then one of the girls started to laugh. It was a hysterical laugh, but it was music in Penn's ears. Rees, standing his ground, caught Patterson's eye over Marsh's glistening shoulder, and hiccuped. He turned away. Patterson curled up, leaning against the door jamb, his shoulders heaving, and the bolder girls started to laugh with their usual spluttering and squeaking. Taking courage, even the timid spirits let out horrified giggles, and in a moment the whole room was in an uproar. Only Penn stood, faintly smiling, never taking his eyes off Soggy's plight.

To give him his due, Soggy remained commendably calm. He put his books on the floor, groped for a handkerchief and wiped his face so that he could see what was going on. When he could see, he saw Penn. When everyone saw him registering, his mind coping, the uproar died down to a silence as tense as the one that preceded it.

'Pennington?' he said, his voice silky.

'Sir?'

'You did this?'

'Yes, sir.'

Soggy turned his head to Smeeton and said, 'Fetch my cane.'

Smeeton fetched it, smiling.

'Come here, Pennington.'

Penn went. He didn't care, for the image of Soggy, dripping

with filth, would stay in his mind as a comfort for ever, until the day he died. It was the nicest thing that had ever happened to him and nothing Soggy could do now could take it away.

'Hold out your hand.'

It hurt, but Penn wasn't bothered. Soggy was up to six when Rita Fairweather said, in a strangled voice, 'But, sir! Penn's playing in this competition tomorrow!'

Nobody, least of all Penn, had remembered the significance of tomorrow. Penn involuntarily took his hand away, and everybody gasped, fascinated by the implications. Soggy paused, blinking. Penn could see the various possibilities chasing themselves through his mind. As he himself was the only one who knew that he wasn't playing in the competition tomorrow, he was more curious than horrified, and relieved, physically, that Rita had stopped Soggy.

But Soggy's reaction was unexpected.

'Hold out your other hand,' he said.

Penn did so, and got another stinging six.

Soggy then said to Rita, very smoothly, 'Pennington is old enough to know that certain courses will incur certain consequences. He is no longer a very small boy, without logic, although one would often think so from the way he behaves.' He then turned to Penn, the malice shining in his eyes, and said, 'I am sorry if you find you are unable to play in the competition tomorrow, Pennington. Very disappointing after all the work you have put in. But I think you will appreciate that I felt bound to equalize—I would not like the punishment to have been as lop-sided as your thinking. I've no doubt that what has happened will be a great disappointment to Mr. Crocker, for which you have yourself entirely to blame, not me.' He smiled, transparently delighted that the caning had had a punishment value far and away beyond the simple infliction of physical pain. 'Come and see me on Monday morning, Pennington, in Mr. Stack's office, after assembly. Mere caning is not, of course, the end of this.'

He picked up 3C's dripping exercise books and turned away, gratified by the horror with which everyone was regarding the consequences of the afternoon's work. At the door he paused.

'Pennington must learn to think,' he said softly, 'mustn't he, Pennington?' And went out.

134

In that moment Penn, his satisfaction blasted, blind hate seizing him, vowed he would win that ruddy competition if it was the last thing he ever did in his life.

Without a word to anyone he turned away, fetched his duffel-bag from his desk, and made for home. He got some food and changed his clothes and said to his mother, 'If anyone wants me, I'm out. And I'm not coming back.' He went down to the river, rowed painfully out to *Mathilda* and lay on the bunk in her cuddy, vowing damnation on everyone he could think of, from Soggy to poor chicken Bates, and Major Harmsworth— drinking his gin on the next mooring, admiring the peace of the evening.

Chapter 10

Bates came out late, hailing him from the bank. Penn ignored him for a bit and then, because of the urgency in Bates's voice, he rowed out and fetched him.

'Mitchell's been to your house. I saw him,' Bates said.

'We'll push off, then. I don't want to know till Sunday,' Penn said.

They went aboard, threw off the mooring, and motored down towards Moorham, anchoring in a lonely spot above the town in the mouth of a small creek.

'We'll have to catch the bus in Moorham to get to Tolchester,' Bates said. 'You think we'll do it without getting spotted?'

'I'm catching the bus for Northend. You can go to Tolchester on your own,' Penn said.

'What are you talking about? I can't keep up with you.'

'I've decided to play in this old festival after all.'

'Why? Because of Soggy?'

Bates understood. Penn did not answer.

Bates looked at Penn's hands doubtfully. 'What about—?'

'Oh, they're all right,' Penn said. 'It won't stop me.' He had had them in a bucket of water most of the evening, but he wasn't going to admit to Bates that Soggy had put him to this inconvenience.

'What about Sylvia?'

'Well, what's the use?' Penn said. He didn't want to think about it. He didn't want to think about anything. He rolled himself up in a blanket and went to sleep.

The morning was grey, drizzling, and in accordance with Penn's mood. He motored the smack down to Moorham and picked up a buoy amongst the fishing-boats, on the assumption that they would be less conspicuous there than anywhere else. All the smacks looked the same to a twit like Mitchell. Besides, they could not get ashore anywhere else, having left Jim's dinghy on the mooring at Fiddler's End, but where the smacks moored was close to the ferry crossing. Penn knew that George, the ferryman, would pick them up if they gave him a shout.

'Look,' he said to Bates, 'let's go ashore and get some bacon. I'm blowed if I'm going to starve. We can't sit here looking at each other all morning.'

The river and quay were virtually deserted. George picked them up on the half-hour when they waved, and they mooched up to the nearest shop, bought some eggs and bacon, and went back to the quay. They had to wait for George, and while they were waiting an elderly woman came up and stood on the quay beside them, gazing distractedly down the river.

Penn took one look at her and scrambled up hastily, kicking Bates in the bottom. It was Mrs. Crocker. Unfortunately, before he could beat a retreat, she looked at him, and recognition dawned.

'Oh, Pennington, fancy you being here! I wonder if you can help me, dear. Have you seen my husband anywhere?'

'Not down here,' Penn said shortly.

'I'm worried to death,' she said. 'He went out last night and he hasn't come back. Fishing, I mean. He's always having trouble with that outboard. And he was in a state last night—something at school, I think. He was very upset, and said if he didn't get out and find some peace and quiet he'd go raving. So I said, "Very well, dear," thinking he'd be back in a few hours. It was a lovely night early on, very calm and a big moon. I thought it would do him good. And I haven't seen him since. I must say, I'm rather worried now.'

Penn did not reply. What was he supposed to do, he would have said, if he had said anything. Hadn't she learned by now, after a hundred years of married life, that the old fool wasn't safe to be let out on his own?

'If you've got your boat down here—' She was eyeing the eggs and bacon, summing things up; she knew they had *Mathilda*, blast her—'I suppose you couldn't just go down and see where he's got to? He doesn't generally go far. If you've nothing else to do?'

She was a bit pathetic, like old Crocker himself. And they hadn't anything else to do until twelve, save sit looking at each other in the cuddy, Penn reflected gloomily. He might even have a chance to tell Crocker that he'd changed his mind, which would cheer the old fool up tremendously.

'Okay,' he said.

Mrs. Crocker's face lit up. 'Oh, thank you, dear. That's very kind of you. I should be so relieved.'

Penn, not used to having anyone thank him for anything, felt uncomfortable. He yelled at George, and George collected them. As the water widened between him and Mrs. Crocker, he felt a lot better. He told George what they were going to do.

'That old madman?' George said. 'He should have drowned ten years ago, that cranky boat he goes around in.'

'I expect his outboard's packed in.'

'I wouldn't be surprised. He runs it on marmalade, judging from the state it's in.'

They went aboard. Penn got the engine going and chucked off the mooring, and Bates started to cook breakfast on the primus. It was ten past nine. The Tolchester festival started at three, and the Northend competition at five; they had plenty of time. Penn decided he would as well be standing at the helm of *Mathilda* reverberating down the river as anything else he could think of just at that moment; perhaps the old hag had done them a good turn. He held the tiller with his thigh, and studied the palms of his hands, flexing his fingers in and out. There was no doubt that Soggy's treatment was hardly going to help when it came to the widest stretches prescribed by Felix Mendelssohn, but it would be painful more than impossible. His fingers hadn't been touched, and none of the skin was broken, although the weals showed. Penn had hardly expected to get away with less, but he was damned if Soggy was going to have the last word on the matter. He'd just show him, the old beggar. After that, Penn did not know anything. Lately, along with the habit of work, he had taken to thinking ahead, and it had given him nothing but worry and foreboding. He must get out of these bad habits, before they did for him.

'I say,' said Bates, putting his head out of the hatch, 'there's an awful lot of water sloshing about in this old boat.'

Penn shrugged. 'You got breakfast yet?'

Bates disappeared, and came up a few minutes later with a plate full of bacon, some rashers burnt and some nearly raw, and two mangled, frizzled eggs.

'You seen him yet?'

'There's a dinghy out by the Pitt Shoal. Could be him.'

The Pitt Shoal was two miles off the mouth of the river, farther than Penn really wanted to go. They could hardly turn back now, but he wasn't sure how much petrol they had left in the tank. He shovelled in his bacon and eggs. There wasn't another boat in sight anywhere; the morning was grey and drizzly and the sea heaved unpleasantly. Penn wished they hadn't come.

Bates said, 'It looks like his boat. There's an anchor out. But where is *he*?'

Penn frowned. As *Mathilda*, swilling out on the last of the ebb, rattled towards the Pitt Shoal, he could make out the dinghy quite clearly. But it appeared to be empty. There was a hump of what looked like old oilskins, nothing else.

'Looks like that could be him, in the bottom of the boat. Perhaps he can't get the outboard to go, and is having a nap till someone turns up.'

'But he always carries oars. He's not that stupid.'

'Waiting for the tide to turn, then.'

When *Mathilda* was about fifty yards off, Penn gave a shout, and another, but nothing stirred.

'She's in pretty shallow water,' Penn said, seeing the danger. He put the tiller over, but had left it too late. *Mathilda*, rising up on one of the uneasy swells, dropped with a crack and stopped abruptly. Penn put the engine in reverse, but to no avail. Thick sand churned out astern, swilling away on the tide, but the old smack merely shuddered. She was on hard, having been travelling at quite a lick. Penn swore horribly. He put the engine into neutral, but it cut out. The sudden silence was unexpected, and ominous.

'Cripes, don't say we're out of petrol!' He scrambled below for the dipstick and tested the tank. The stick came up dry. 'Oh, cripes, we're in a fine mess now!' He was furiously angry, at Crocker, himself, and everything else he could think of. *Mathilda* heaved and thumped, her old timbers groaning.

'What about him, then?' Bates said, gesturing across to the

silent, rolling dinghy. 'What do we do? Is that him, that heap?'

'How should I know? I suppose it must be. He must have died or something. If he was asleep, he must have heard us.'

'Died?' said Bates incredulously.

'Well, he takes pills when he gets all het up. Haven't you seen him? He goes all blue and white in turns. When he's cross.' Penn had good reason to know, having so often been the cause of the phenomenon. 'And Mrs. Crocker said he was upset.' No doubt himself again.

'Well, what are you going to *do*?' Bates said, his face all screwed up and tremulous.

'Me do? Cripes, why me?' Penn was indignant.

'You came out to rescue him, didn't you?'

'Well, I like that!'

Penn could see it coming, what he had to do, and the indignation welled up at the injustice of it, of doing someone a good turn and getting all tied up, of running out of petrol, of putting the old boat aground. He started to take his clothes off. He was for ever taking involuntary swimming lessons, almost every day, for some reason or other. Never because he *wanted* to. His mind raged. Bates watched him, silent and pale. Penn took off his watch, which only went sometimes anyway, thanks to its earlier ill-treatment, and gave it yet again to Bates. The wind was cold and he felt the goose-pimples rising. He did not want to go out to old Crocker very much now that he thought he was dead, and he stood naked, shifting from one foot to the other, glowering at the water.

'Go on,' Bates said.

'Why don't you go, then?' Penn snapped. 'The water's not deep. I'm not hogging it if you want to go.'

He launched himself gingerly, miserably, off the stern. Ten feet off the smack the water *was* deep, which made him even more angry, because it meant that *Mathilda* had gone on a miserable cheating little spit, not on the bank proper at all. Crocker's dinghy was anchored in deep water. Penn swam up to it slowly, and hooked his hands over the transom.

The old man was huddled in the bottom of the boat, either dead or unconscious. Penn could not tell. His face, what Penn could see of it, was a terrible colour. Penn's indignation turned into a rather sick, creepy feeling of panic. He had never seen a dead person before, let alone had to do something about it. A ridiculous fragment of knowledge came to him: that you put pennies on dead men's eyes to keep them shut, and he looked at

old Crocker's eyes, and saw the lids flicker. They opened. Penn felt the hair rising up on the back of his neck as the familiar gaze regarded him from the bottom of the boat.

'Help me, Pennington,' the blue lips mumbled, and the eyes shut again.

'*Cripes!*' Penn felt as if a ghost had just confronted him. He was trembling all over.

He handed his way round the gunwale until he came to the bows of the dinghy and heaved at the anchor warp, but without anything but the water to brace himself on, nothing happened. He had to follow the warp out and swim down, break out the anchor under water and swim back with it. 'Why me?' his mind kept exploding. He was as cold as a dead fish. He humped the anchor over into the bows of the dinghy, and then swam back to the smack, pushing the dinghy in front of him, which was hard work. The dinghy was much too cranky for him to attempt to get in. All the way his mind was raging at this thing he had got stuck with, and the scary, panicky feeling was very close underneath. Bates, staring down from the stern of the smack, looked as stricken as he felt.

'Oh, cripes, Penn,' he said uselessly.

'Take the warp, for heaven's sake, and make the dinghy fast.' Penn's teeth were chattering almost too much for him to talk. When Bates had got the dinghy he swam to the bobstay and climbed on board, with considerable difficulty. The cold wind blasted his bare flesh. He could have wept.

'Is he dead?' Bates asked.

'No. He said something.'

'What are you going to do?'

'Get dressed,' Penn said.

He dried himself on a blanket and put his clothes on again, still shivering. *Mathilda* was thumping and crashing, driving up on to the sand, the water sloshing about in her bilges. Every time she thumped, dollops of uneasy water splattered Crocker's recumbent form.

'We must go back to Moorham,' Penn said, biting his thumb-nail. 'We'll have to see if we can get the outboard working. The trouble is, if I get in, I'll sink the blasted thing.' Penn had scaled fourteen stone eight pounds at the last weigh-in and was very conscious of the fact. Bates, at a bare eight stone, didn't know

how outboards worked. Penn lay down on *Mathilda*'s deck and
leaned precariously over into the dinghy. The two craft rolled
together, going up and down independently on the swell, grinding together, and after about ten minutes of vain fiddling and
tugging at the starting-rope, Penn, head down and full of petrol
fumes, had to retreat in order to bring up Bates's queasy breakfast. Bates watched him in despair.

'Penn, what are you going to do?'

Penn groaned.

'Oh, Penn!' Bates cried out.

Penn got up and leaned against the shrouds, wishing he were
happily unconscious like old Crocker. Crocker's outboard was
about as much use as Bates's cooking.

'You'll have to row him home,' he said shortly to Bates.
'There's nothing else we can do.'

Bates looked incredulous. 'Me?'

'Yes, you.'

'Why me?'

'Because, one: if I get in that dinghy it'll have a freeboard of
about two inches, whereas if you get in it it'll have about four,
which is two more inches farther away from getting swamped.
Two: what will you do if you're left on board here? I can't see
you getting the engine started again.'

'Well, I don't see you getting it started either without any
petrol.'

'Someone's bound to come by before long and I shall shout
and get some petrol, or get a tow or something. Buck up, Bates.
It's no good saying you can't row, because you can row as well
as I can, and the tide is on the turn. You'll have it under you.
Even if you just sit there, you'll arrive eventually.'

'Oh, cripes, Penn, I can't sit there rowing a corpse.'

'He's not a corpse, idiot! Else it wouldn't matter, would it?
But he will be if you dither about much longer. He ought to be
in hospital. Get a move on!'

Penn drove Bates down into the dinghy, swearing at him
bitterly. Bates groped round for the rowlocks, and Penn leaned
over, holding the dinghy by the gunwale. Old Crocker looked
terribly uncomfortable, his head lolling about against the ribs
of the boat, but it was impossible to shift him without risking a
capsize, so Penn shoved the dinghy off bodily as soon as Bates

143

got out the oars. Bates was white and gibbering. Penn watched him go, hunching himself down on the hatch, his elbows on his knees. What a flaming mess the whole thing was! His watch showed him that it was getting on for half-past eleven. Penn knew that the day was doomed.

After a few minutes he decided he should have put the anchor out about an hour ago. *Mathilda* was just driving up on to the sand, although the tide was now flooding. He dropped it over the bows, but knew that she would go on crashing and banging and driving up the sand for some time before her scope stopped her. By then she could well have fallen apart. Exploring below, he found that the water was over the floorboards and still rising. The probability that he was going to go down with his ship did not strike him as strange at all, only a perfectly appropriate way to end this disastrous day. He went below and made himself a cup of tea to try to get warm and by the time he had finished the water was up to his knees. He was unmoved. He didn't care if he drowned.

Bates was a speck in the distance when he went up on deck again, but there was no sight of anyone else on the face of the earth. He looked at his watch again. Twelve o'clock. The sea was smooth and dreary, the sky a uniform grey. He went on sitting there, wondering what was the use of being alive anyway. The Rondo Capriccioso could have been conceived on Mars, for all the relevance it had to him in his present situation.

It was half-past twelve before he saw a boat. It was a yacht coming in from the sea, beating very slowly into the light headwind. With luck, it would come fairly close to him on its port tack. Penn watched it gloomily. It was a yawl. When it got nearer he recognized it as Major Harmsworth's *Escape*. His faint optimism, which had stirred in spite of everything, keeled over and sank without trace. The trouble was, he thought, *Mathilda* would soon follow suit.

He got to his feet and waved a white tea-towel on the foredeck as the yawl crabbed slowly towards the sand, carried on the tide. He doubted if the signal would be misunderstood, especially as *Mathilda* was now so low on her marks, but he was relieved when the yacht went about and hove-to. Major Harmsworth was looking at him through binoculars. Penn thought, 'Even after the Jaguar, he can't leave me to sink, the rat.'

The fruity voice came over the water through a loud-hailer, making Penn wince: 'We can't come in any closer and we have no dinghy. Can you swim?'

Could he swim! God in heaven, he spent half his life swimming! The old idiot had good reason to know he could swim anyway. Penn wasted no time, but dived off *Mathilda*'s stern and struck out for the yacht, watch and all. He wouldn't need his watch in Oakhall, according to Smeeton. When he got to the boat, getting on board proved extremely difficult and took about ten minutes, with Charles and Humphrey having opposing theories about what to do with bights of rope and block and tackles and carrying on a well-bred argument over his head. When he was eventually landed, sprawling and exhausted, and the problem was obsolete, he got the reception he had anticipated, cold as the grey water. He said nothing, letting Harmsworth's hostility slide over him. There was no point in explaining anything: he felt too cold to argue.

'I suppose you'd better go below and get dry,' the Major said at last. 'He can have that Aran jersey of mine, Humphrey, the one I use for painting in. And there are some slacks in the forward locker.'

Below, Humphrey was slightly more affable than the Major himself, producing a towel and the clothes, and lighting the Calor gas to make a cup of tea. He asked Penn what he was doing, alone on the sinking smack, but Penn, after the rating he had got, was not disposed to make polite conversation.

'I was just out for a look round,' he said.

He glanced at the clock on the bulkhead. It was one o'clock. There was a bus to Northend at four, and one at six, but the wind had dropped light, and the yawl was making very slow progress. Penn expected the Major to put the engine on, but the Major appeared to be in no hurry. Humphrey started to make a salad, and the Major spent a lot of time watching some stupid sea-birds through the binoculars. Penn went up on the foredeck out of the way and lay down and went to sleep. He just didn't want to think about it any more. Old Bates would have been back long ago.

The Major anchored when he got back into the river and sat with Humphrey in the cockpit admiring the beauties of nature. They were too far out to make it worth Penn's while to go ashore, and he was tired of swimming. He lay listening to the murmur of the cultured voices, knowing that everything was finished for him, that he would not even have the satisfaction of levelling scores with Soggy. Not that he cared in any other way about missing the competition, for he hated playing in competitions; he hated the sacred atmosphere and the intense women with their hair in buns and the smooth boys with their nice voices—infant Major Harmsworths—who had smooth, nice relationships with their music teachers ('Well *done*, Nigel!') and smiling, elegant mothers. He hated the way they gave him looks, because he wasn't their sort. But he had wanted to go desperately. Lying there, his hands clasped behind his head, he thought it rather odd that old Dotty was himself the reason for stopping his playing, the way things had turned out. He could not help feeling a bit sorry for the silly old beggar.

But, having plenty of time to think, he was sorrier for himself.

'You, up there! You might as well work your passage! Get up the anchor chain, will you? Young lad like you, plenty of beef—'

By the time he had got in the yawl's nine fathoms he was very conscious of his hands again, stiffening and sore. But it didn't matter any more. It was half-past five. The competition had started half an hour ago. The yawl butted her way up the river under engine, the tide having turned against her. His own watch having stopped, Penn went aft and peered at Humphrey's. As they came up to Moorham it was ten to six. Penn began to bite the side of his thumbnail.

'If you wouldn't mind—' he said, hesitantly. 'If you could go close to the fish-quay, I'll jump for it.'

'I thought you lived at Fiddler's End?'

'I'm supposed to be playing in a competition at Northend. I might just catch the six o'clock bus.'

'And what about my clothes?'

'I'll bring them back to Mr. Purvis's yard tomorrow.'

'Hmm.' But the Major put the tiller over, making for the fish-quay. His military eyes raked Penn, who stood on the side-deck, hands in pockets, scowling with the effort of being polite.

'Pity there's no military service any longer for young chaps like you. Do you the world of good,' the Major said. 'You get everything too easy these days, that's your trouble.'

Getting shot would have done the Major a world of good, Penn thought.

The yawl went into the quay, travelling fairly fast, and Penn jumped from the shrouds, catching the top of the wooden jetty with his hands and hauling himself up painfully. Once on his feet, he ran. The bus was at the clock-tower, the driver just starting the engine. Penn leapt on and ran up the stairs. God only knew how many entries there were for the competition, but the Andante and Rondo Capriccioso took six minutes to play, and he would get to the Town Hall approximately one hour and forty minutes after the start of the competition. Allowing for the interminable time the judge took to make the hieroglyphics in his little book after each performance, he would, with luck, still be operating by the time the bus arrived. Penn put his feet up on the seat and tried to pretend that he had everything under control, but he was hollow with doubt. He was also hollow with plain hunger.

The conductor came up for the fares and Penn discovered that the Major's trousers harboured no forgotten coins.

'Look, you know I've got a school pass,' Penn said urgently. 'For God's sake don't chuck me off.'

'Cripes, mate, I'm not a philanthropic society.'

Penn argued, spurred by the single-minded determination that had seized him since the Soggy incident. The bus conductor, who knew him well, got bored and said, 'Oh, well, stay on. I can't be bothered . . .' There were only two other people on the bus, both downstairs.

Penn sat with his arms clasped across his chest, hands in his armpits to keep them warm. He concentrated on the music, seeing it in his mind as it was printed on the page, humming the opening theme to himself. He took his hands out and stretched them and did silent scales all up and down the back of the seat in front of him. By the time the bus lurched into the North-end Broadway, Penn wanted to slam the Andante and Rondo Capriccioso more than anything else in the world; he had spent so many sweating hours on its cunning ways, wishing Felix Fiendish Mendelssohn frying in hellfire, writhing to his own tempo on the metronome, that the wretched piece had to be exorcised, offered up as sacrifice on the sacred Steinway belonging to the Northend Municipal Council, or else Penn felt that it would haunt him for the rest of his days. After the Mendelssohn and the thumbed pile of Bach, Mozart, Beethoven and Co. that spilled out of Crocker's cupboard entirely for his consumption, Penn thought Oakhall would be a haven of rest, in spite of anything Smeeton said. He got up and dropped heavily down the stairs as the bell rang for the Town Hall.

It was only as he went up the imposing staircase and came to the arrow pointing down the corridor to 'Open Pianoforte Competitors' that Penn became conscious of the fact that he was not exactly, in appearance, the most prepossessing of performers. The official standing outside the door of the Council Chamber, where the competition was taking place, eyed him coldly.

'What do you want?'

'I'm a competitor for the Open Pianoforte. Is it still on?'

'You can't come in here like that!' said the official, outraged. 'It started at five. The last competitor has just finished. Mr. Smythe-Potter is working out the results now.'

'But I'm entered!' Penn said. 'I couldn't help being late! There was an accident—my music-teacher's had to go to hospital—oh, look, *please*—' He put his hand on the door-knob, desperate. 'I'm sorry about my clothes, I couldn't help it! Please would you ask him?'

The official hesitated.

'It's very unorthodox. Who are you? Your name—?'

'Pennington. Patrick Pennington.'

'I'll go and see. Just step inside then, and stay by the door.'

They went inside together, into the hushed, nervous arena of hard chairs occupied by hushed, nervous pianists and their friends and relations. Penn smelt the tension, and saw the God Almighty judge sitting at his little table with a glass of water and sheets of notes, and the officials hovering, and the bored reporter of the *Northend Standard* doodling in his notebook with a biro. The municipal Steinway crouched on the raised dais, malevolently impartial. Penn leaned against the door, stretching his palms against the pains that afflicted them, willing the God Almighty to give him his chance. The official conferred, and the God Almighty's gaze reached out to Penn as he leaned against the door, and considered him, while the official went on explaining. Penn, embarrassed by Major Harmsworth's paintbespattered trousers and the highly unsuitable Aran jersey with the unravelled cuffs, straightened up and tried to look godfearing and acceptable. Everyone else in the room was staring at him.

The official beckoned. Penn padded down to Jehovah's seat, hearing the faint squelching of his wet plimsolls. Jehovah looked him up and down, cold and unwelcoming.

'Sit here,' he said, gesturing him to a chair. 'I'll hear you in a few minutes.'

Penn sat, resting his elbows on his knees, rubbing his hair back from his face. He felt drained and bleak and horribly alone. He would have given his most precious possession, his useless wet watch, to have had soppy old Bates sitting beside him in the abattoir. The watch stood at twelve fifty-two. Penn unfastened it and put it in the back pocket of Major Harmsworth's slacks. Old Crocker could well be dead now, for all he knew. Penn wished it had been Soggy. He would have swum out to the dinghy and turned it over and held the cold blue face under . . . His hands *hurt* . . . Oh, cripes, what was the use? He fixed his mind on the opening bars of the Mendelssohn piece, feeling that this time, now and tomorrow with Mitchell, he was really going down, foundering without trace. And there was nobody there even to see him go, let alone care.

'All right,' said Mr. Smythe-Potter, nodding to him. He put his pen down and sat back in his padded, alderman's chair, and put the tips of his fingers together, and watched Penn walk to the piano. Everyone else in the audience watched, disapproving, and praying for calamity. Penn could sense the hostility. It made him feel almost at home. 'Okay, Soggy,' he thought, lifting his hands, hitching himself into position on the piano stool. 'I'll show you, you murky sadistic swine . . .' He paused, scouring his mind clean of everything but the music, praying that out of this confusion and bitterness he could express the serenity of the Andante as if he had been lying on the sofa thinking of nothing but Mendelssohn's flaming fairies all afternoon. His hands started to play, very softly, smelling of Major Harmsworth's anchor chain, but responsive and obedient. Penn, enchanted by the Council's superior instrument, was immediately cut free from his anxieties, eager only to release the melody with the first stroke of his right fourth finger on the

G sharp and let it fall as sweetly as he knew how into its shapely poignant pattern on the keyboard. This was the hardest part of the whole piece for him, for he was happier when the fireworks came and the old fingers really had to move, when the subtleties of dynamic control and *tempo rubato* which old Crocker had had him slaving over for the last two months stood down before the demands of sheer fingerwork. ('Ruddy technician!' Crocker would growl at him, piling on the Chopin nocturnes and preludes. 'Think boy, feel!' and Penn would curse with as much indelicacy as the music demanded delicacy.) Somewhere in his mind Penn had all this stowed away, and he knew now that mere technicians did not win competitions, and he played to warm poor Crocker's soul and to damn Soggy and to lift the Mendelssohn melody out of the County Council piano into the cold dome of the Council Chamber to stab the alien heart of Mr. Smythe-Potter with its vigour and beauty.

Mr. Smythe-Potter, watching Penn closely, opened his eyes very wide and tapped his forefingers slowly together to convey his emotion.

Six minutes of pure sweat, Penn thought, recapitulating on the Scherzo theme, and what to show for it but words in the

Smythe-Potter notebook and the echoes fading out over the surface of the Victorian painting of 'Integrity and Labour' on the ceiling? Nothing in the hand, nothing ruddy anywhere, to show whether he had done well or failed, or even existed, yet never had he worked and felt and *thought* so hard. He came down the octaves with his tongue sharp between his teeth, his palms splitting, one or two inaccuracies proving that he was putting soul before mere perfection—or so he hoped. The mistakes stung him, but the sum total was rich and beautifully controlled. He knew he had nothing to reproach himself with at all.

As the last note faded Penn heard his empty stomach roll forlornly, and realized that he was ravenously hungry. He also, with a fierce pleasure, knew that he had never played the Andante and Rondo Capriccioso any better. He got up and went back to his seat, and Mr. Smythe-Potter went on writing on his sheets of paper in a very neat, small hand, lines and lines and lines. Penn, recalling past occasions, and the long, deadly ramblings on each competitor that had to precede the actual results, slumped back in his chair and prepared to go into a coma for the next hour. Not having heard any of his rivals, he kept a weather ear open for undue praise on Smythe-Potter's part, but for the most part let the flat, dry voice ride over him. He was extraordinarily tired. Whether he won or not was out of his hands; strangely, knowing that he had played as well as he was capable of, it did not worry him. Even Soggy had shrunk, like the desiccated, tiny-minded carcass that he was, to infinitesimal significance. Instead, Penn felt a tender concern for potty old Crocker that surprised him. 'I could go and see him in hospital,' he thought. 'And tell him I played. It might cheer him up.' If he was still alive to be cheered up. Penn, sitting and not listening, but feeling strangely contented, wondered why he was no longer worried about things: even Oakhall did not seem very important any more. He supposed he was too tired to care.

'And so to the last competitor, P. E. Pennington . . . a pupil of the Beehive Secondary Modern and the youngest person to perform today . . .'

Penn sat up, and felt a cold goose-shiver creep up between his flesh and Major Harmsworth's jersey. 'If he slates me,' he thought, 'I'll get up and mash him, the toad-voiced old beggar.'

He was thin and dry, in Soggy's blood-group . . . 'An extraordinarily accomplished performance, taken at a very ambitious tempo yet without loss of clarity . . .'

After the first shock, Penn found that the words were not registering. Praise came to him so rarely that he was incapable of understanding it for what it was. 'The old boy's playing me along,' he thought; 'he's going to bring in the crunch at the end.' But at the end Mr. Smythe-Potter said, 'I am therefore placing this competitor first . . .'

Penn looked at him, his face tight with suspicion. He felt hollow and breathless, like being winded in soccer, when mere air was so desirable, and yet apparently unattainable. Then the professorial face smiled at him, and Penn realized that this was no sarcastic liar, like Soggy, having him on, but a normal human being congratulating him on his talent. He smiled back. He felt wonderful suddenly, in a way quite new for him. 'I must go and see old Crocker,' he thought instantly. As long as Crocker knew, he didn't care a fig for Soggy.

He got up, after the other winners had been announced, and started for the door, but there were people in his way: an official telling him about the Mayoress awarding the prizes on Wednesday evening and he would be expected to attend ('But I shall be in prison on Wednesday,' he nearly said, but didn't. 'Yes,' he said), and the reporter wanting to know the story of his life, and an awful fluting woman asking if he was interested in joining her chamber group for Schubert evenings ('So refreshing, dear, if you've never played with other instruments . . . here's my address . . .'), and various fellow competitors saying congratulatory things which amazed him (quite the last thing he would have thought of saying to anyone who might have beaten *him*) . . . by the time he got to the door, the place was nearly empty.

Except for—

'Oh, cripes!' Penn said softly. 'What are you doing here?'

'I just wanted to see you,' Sylvia said.

Chapter 11

'What for?' said Penn, almost as if it were a Soggy-trap.

'What do you mean, what for?' she said. 'What do you think what for?'

It was unanswerable. She was looking at him with those consummately improved eyes, smiling and tender, like in the figments of his wildest imagination. She put out her hand, and rested it on his arm.

'You said you *only* played the piano,' she said, slightly accusing.

'Why, did you hear it? Did you come on purpose? Bates told you?'

The hand on his arm had given him courage. They walked slowly down the mosaic-floored corridor under the portraits of the past fifty-odd Mayors of Northend Corporation, and Sylvia's hand moved down and took his own. Penn felt it, cold and incredible, against the dull throbbing of Soggy's caning. He remembered that he hadn't any money.

'Yes. He said you were going to play in this competition. He was late for the Festival. I thought neither of you was coming. He had some crazy story about some old corpse he'd had to row up the river—I thought he was raving. He is a weird boy, isn't he? Then he said you'd changed your mind, and weren't coming, and one of the boys had to come back early, so I asked him for a lift and I came here to see you instead. I sang first, so nobody cared.'

'Did Bates sing?' Penn, not daring to face the implications in Sylvia's speech, in case he'd got them wrong, asked a practical question.

'Yes, he did. Colin played for him. He's wonderful isn't he?'

'Yes.' If Bates had got to the point of singing in public without himself to goad him, Penn was willing to concede this fact.

'But cracked,' she said.

'Yes.'

'But you,' she said, 'wasting time on the harmonica when you can do that. Any fool can play the harmonica.'

Cripes, she sounded just like Crocker! Penn looked at her warily. She smiled at him, no half-smile, but a sweet and tender whole smile.

'I think you're wonderful,' she said.

Cripes! Penn was afloat, drifting over the mosaic.

'I saw you at the swimming gala,' she said, 'and I cheered and cheered for you, and they were all cheering for Peterson and they pushed me under the seat and sat on me and I still cheered for you and they said they'd throw me over the gallery, but they couldn't really. I didn't care.'

'At the *swimming* gala?' What had she got to do with the swimming gala? Penn was puzzled, adrift.

'I go to Parkside.'

'To school?'

That this little, perfect, poised, painted fragile bit of what Maxwell called crumpet was still a schoolgirl astonished Penn. She had no more in common with the Rita Fairweathers of the Beehive than he had with the Major Harmsworths of the world.

'But why didn't you say, last Saturday—say—?' Penn stumbled, unable to follow the workings of the female mind. On Wednesday she had cheered him in the swimming gala to such extent that the rest of the school had sat on her, yet the following Saturday she had given him nothing but cool smiles and said she had liked his hair better the way it was before. What sort of logic was that?

'I was too shy,' she said, 'in front of Colin and them. But now it's all right. You don't think I'm awful, coming?'

Penn was in no fit state to pass comment on his own feelings. No words he knew could describe such confusion. By the time he became conscious of his surroundings again they were on the High Street, and his sexual appetite was overwhelmed by the purely practical craving for food, as the smells of hamburgers, fish and chips and coffee steamed out of the neon-lit doorways.

'Have you any money?' he asked, desperate. 'I didn't know

—I'm sorry, but I haven't a penny. I left it in the pocket of my jeans when I changed—' 'It' was a solitary florin and three sixpences, the bus-fare to Northend.

Sylvia searched in her handbag. 'One and threepence.'

Penn's heart sank to join his empty stomach.

'We'll buy a coffee and a bun,' she said, heading into a smoochy coffee-bar with a juke-box accompaniment and tables in confidential little cubicles, 'and share it.'

Penn, trying not to dwell on the fact that one and threepence worth of chips would have suited him a lot better, followed her and gave the order. While they waited she said to him, 'Why are you wearing such peculiar clothes?' and he told her the story of his strange, disjointed day.

Back on the river at Fiddler's End Major Harmsworth, twiddling the knob of his transistor in search of the Aldeburgh Festival, came upon a local news programme. 'Drama came to Moorham this afternoon when local schoolboy, John Bates, rowed up to the quay with the unconscious body of fifty-eight-year-old amateur fisherman, Mr. Edwin Crocker, lying in his boat. Mr. Crocker had suffered a heart attack while out fishing, and young Bates, passing in his own boat, saw him and went to his aid. Unable to lift the unconscious man on board his own boat, he rowed him back to Moorham. Police say he undoubtedly saved the life of Mr. Crocker, who was rushed to Northend General Hospital in a critical condition. Bates, on being congratulated on his presence of mind, said, "There was nothing else I could do." '

Major Harmsworth said to Humphrey, 'Well, I'm glad to hear some of these kids can do the decent thing. One is apt to think that they're all the same type as that yobbo we picked up this afternoon. Never so much as a thank you!'

That announcer's voice continued: 'The Open Pianoforte competition which concluded Northend's Music Festival this afternoon in the Town Hall was won by the youngest competitor, Patrick Pennington, a pupil at the Beehive Secondary Modern School, from a record entry of fifteen.'

'How very strange!' said Humphrey. 'You said that yobbo's name was Pennington—or am I getting mixed up?'

'Yes, his name is Pennington. Some relation perhaps.'

'But he said something about playing in a competition in Northend when he left us.'

'Good God, man, ping-pong or some such! Ah, this is it. The flute concerto by Leclair . . .'

Penn drank half a cup of coffee from the opposite side to the large silver lipstick marks, and ate half the dried-up bun which fell into his empty stomach like a pebble into a bucket. He did not know whether his hallucinatory state of mind was due to Sylvia or hunger.

'I could have died when I found out you were still at school,' she said. 'I thought you were nineteen or something.'

Penn, having thought Sylvia was above such Rita Fairweather-type remarks, contracted slightly, and stared into the coffee-cup.

'I didn't think you were at school either.'

'Well, I'm leaving next month. I'm going to be a hairdresser. What are you going to do?'

Cripes, that was a question and a half! Apart from going to Oakhall for three months, he had no more idea now than he had when he was in his pram. He could not understand why, with Sylvia in front of him, admiration shining from her fantastic eyes, he felt these cold areas of despair touching him again.

'Drive a lorry or something, I suppose, if I'm lucky.'

'Can you drive?'

'Yes.' There was an old car on the farm that he and Bates had learned to drive on, progressing from tractors.

'But everyone wants to drive a lorry,' he said gloomily.

And no one was going to want a lorry-driver with Oakhall on his record.

'What shall we do?' Sylvia said.

Penn could scarcely believe it, but when she said that he had a yearning to be at home, curled up in bed, out of the world. His last night, and he would even have found comfort in his parents quarrelling, and Mrs. Jones hammering on the wall, and his father slamming out to the pub. He crushed the thought.

'Shall we walk along the front?' she said. 'Or we could go home? I only live ten minutes away. Would you like that? My parents won't mind.'

A brief picture slipped through Penn's mind of a comfortable sofa, the lights dimmed for television, the parents out—or possibly the mother out in the kitchen preparing a great big meal—and Sylvia's hand in his as it had been before the interruption for coffee.

'Yes. All right,' he said.

They got up and went outside. Sylvia came up close and put her arm round him inside the Major's Aran jersey, so that it lay on the bare flesh of his midriff. Penn felt the hair rise up on the back of his neck exactly as it had when Mr. Crocker had opened his eyes in the bottom of the boat. 'Cripes,' he thought, 'what doesn't she know?' Yet she kept on walking, and chatting away, as if she thought it made no difference to him at all: the effect of her four fingers and thumb spread over his right-side bottom floating rib. It occurred to him then that she was, in fact, unaware of the feelings she aroused. She was talking about hair-dressing. He was wildly indignant, not listening, thinking of all the things they said about girls at school, and how right they were, how unfair it all was. It was always the boys that got into trouble for taking advantage, but no one ever said how the girls led you on, with their eyes looking and their dresses showing everything . . . how was a boy supposed to know what on earth they wanted? And then afterwards it was all easy for girls, too. They could get any old job, and stop as soon as they got married in a year or two, and live on somebody else's money with their feet up watching the telly, while the poor bloke was at work all day. He put his arm up and touched her, moved by this indignation, and she pulled away and said, 'Hey, who do you think you are?' Then she giggled. The injustice of it! The disturbing hand dropped and held his own and they walked on in silence. Penn was soothed. Girls spoilt everything when they talked. They had no idea. He hoped her house wasn't much farther. His damp feet were cold as clams and all shrivelled up like toad's skin.

'Here we are,' she said.

The house was smart, tarted-up Northend early Victorian, pink-washed stucco and converted pent-house looking out into the sky. Penn was put off by the smell of affluence, until Sylvia said, 'We don't own it, for heaven's sake! Just a flat. My dad's the caretaker.' She let herself in with her own key and shouted, 'Mum! I'm back! I've got a friend.'

They were watching the telly, but got up far more brightly than his own parents would have done in the same circum-stances, and switched it off. Penn was impressed by such manners, and self-conscious about Major Harmsworth's seventeen-inch trouser legs. Sylvia introduced him, and explained about the clothes, and told her parents all about the Folk Festival, only nothing about coming home early for the reason she had told Penn. Penn was invited to sit down, not on the sofa, but on a fireside chair with wooden arms. Sylvia's mother sat on the sofa next to Sylvia, and her father sat opposite Penn looking slightly gloomy and obviously wondering how the Saturday-night play had been going to finish. Sylvia's mother was a well-preserved, carefully made-up, very friendly little woman, her father the type that was used to never getting a word in edgeways, and who had opted for the line of least resistance. He looked at Penn with a cautious, faintly sympathetic expression on his face, as if sorry for him for getting involved with the same women who had defeated him long ago. Sylvia, throwing off her coat, revealed the same silvery, very short dress that had so fascinated Penn before. Seeing her now, so close and yet quite unattainable, in the presence of her parents, Penn was overcome by a sense of opportunities lost: when he could have got somewhere with her, just now, if he had been smooth and cunning, when they were alone, he had wasted all his time getting indignant and fuming away about girls having all the luck. Now, because he could not touch her, he had only to look at her to feel his desire to touch her rising up inside him, expanding like an awakening chrysalis. He pulled his eyes away and looked at her father instead.

Sylvia's mother said, 'And what do you do, Patrick?'

'He plays the piano,' Sylvia said. 'Not just like most people do, but properly, just like—like—' She hunted round to think up the name of a famous pianist, in vain, and said, 'Like Yehudi Menuhin plays the violin.'

'*Cripes!*' thought Penn, looking at the floor and going scarlet. He wanted to sink.

'He's just won the class at the festival. I went to hear him. He's absolutely marvellous. Go on, Pat, play that thing you played at the festival for Mum and Dad. Mum's ever so keen on the piano. She plays, but nothing like you do.'

'Oh, yes, dear, how lovely! Do play for us! I used to play in all the festivals when Sylvia was a little girl. My word, how I love it!'

Penn, wanting to die, looked up and saw to his horror that not only was there a piano in the room but Sylvia's mother had got to her feet and was opening it up and moving a pile of knitting off the stool. He could not believe the magnitude of his bad luck.

'You haven't got to,' Sylvia's father said.

'Oh, but of course!' Sylvia's mother contradicted. 'Why, it's years since this old piano was used properly! Although we always have the tuner in every six months, so it's quite all right. Come along, dear. Do play for me! Why, I can't imagine any way I'd rather spend an evening!'

159

Penn said, desperate, 'It's rather a noisy piece. The people upstairs—' Shades of Mrs. Jones.

'Oh, but my dear, he *can't* complain! He's a piano-teacher himself. We spend hours listening to his terrible little boys and girls, so he really can't say a word.' She laughed delightedly. 'There, you've no excuse, has he, Sylvia?'

Sylvia laughed, too. Penn set his teeth. He could never have imagined such treachery. He got up and went over to the piano without another word. He played the Andante and Rondo Capriccioso with what felt like his last remaining strength and when he thundered up and down the double octave scales at the end of the piece a photograph of a wedding-group on the mantelpiece fell flat on its face, teetered and dropped into the hearth. The glass broke, and Penn was fiendishly pleased.

'Oh, my word, but that was splendid!' said Sylvia's mother, her face glowing with admiration. 'Gracious me, but no one's ever played this old piano like that before! Oh, my dear, if only I'd kept it up . . . Get up a minute, dear. All my music is in the stool. Let's have a look at it, and perhaps you could play some of my favourites for me? What's the thing by Chopin that I used to spend so much time on, Henry? Do you remember? Look, what have we here?' She was scrummaging and rummaging, pulling out piles and piles of music which she laid all over the floor. 'Oh yes. Here, Patrick. Look, do you know this one? Oh, how I love that thing! I don't think anything more lovely has ever been written . . . Sit down, dear, and play it through for me.'

Penn sat down, taking the music with a feeling not of wanting to die, but having died. The music was an unrecognizable version of the Polonaise in A major, emasculated into beginner's fudge. He put it on the rack and started to play the real thing, and he played it with a passion that was in reality pure rage. The effect was magnificent, the best he had ever played it, even with Crocker standing over him. When he had finished the rage had died out, and an unfamiliar little quirk of elation touched him, just as when he had finished the competition and had known he had played well. He had stretched himself, and been surprised by what he could do. He was very happy and did not want to stop, and went straight on into one of the nocturnes, while Sylvia's mother was still saying, 'My word, but it never

sounded like that when I played it!' After the Chopin he played Beethoven's Pathétique Sonata and three of Mendelssohn's Songs without Words, and the first movement of the Moonlight Sonata, and two Chopin preludes, a waltz, and a Mozart study.

When he got up from the piano the room was very quiet. He stood, yawning. The fire was out, and Sylvia and her mother had gone. Henry was stretched out in his armchair, fast asleep. The hands of the clock on the mantelpiece had passed midnight. Penn closed the piano and Henry opened his eyes and said, 'You beat 'em, Patrick. They went to bed half an hour ago. Well done, boy. You can sleep on the sofa, if you want.' Penn shook his head, and went to the front door and let himself out, closing it silently behind him. The cold sea-air came to him, cooling the sweat beneath the Aran jersey, rattling the dead laburnum blossoms and the rusting lilac, blowing the sweet-papers along the gutter. Penn put his hands in Major Harmsworth's pockets and walked along, aimlessly, in the direction of the front. Then, still strung up by the music, he thought of Mr. Crocker, and turned up the next street which led to the hospital. He had to tell old Crocker, and he had forgotten all about it. He did not know what would please Crocker most, that he had won the competition or that he had played for three hours because he wanted to and not because he had been told to. His hands burned as if they were on fire, but all the rest of him shivered, and the self-pity gnawed as strongly as the hunger. His mind was full of Oakhall, but he was so hungry he kept thinking of the baked beans and the thin stew and the bread and marg, and they were so desirable that he began to wish he were already there. He felt stoned, like Henry in the armchair, washed up on the sea of noise that he had wrung from the upright Bluthner with the wrought-brass candle-holders, which had dispersed the women and broken the picture-glass. He walked warily, an eye for the prowling copper.

When he came to the hospital, he went to the Casualty door out of force of habit (having had to present himself there on various occasions on what Maxwell called their 'après-soccer evenings', after particularly hard-fought matches), and when he found out his mistake he was too tired to go away, but sat down on the nearest chair.

A brisk young nurse came out and said, 'What's wrong with you, then?' And then, 'Why, hullo, Pat. I thought the soccer season was over?'

Penn recognized a particularly nice nurse who had defended him once when a Soggy-minded sister had given him a jab for tetanus which had evoked from him a bellow that had woken up the whole slumbering ward. (The nice nurse had said the needle was blunt enough to shame a veterinary surgeon specializing in rhinoceros disease, and the sister had blasted her out for her impudence with invective worthy of Soggy himself; after that he and the nurse had become very friendly.)

'Hullo,' he said. 'I'm visiting. I'm all right.'

'Our visiting hours are two to three-thirty in the afternoon, not in the early morning,' she pointed out.

'Have you got anything to eat?' he asked. 'I'm starving.'

She went off and came back with a solitary currant bun. 'Nurse O'Brien's slimming. You're lucky. Now then, what's the trouble?'

Penn explained. 'The point is, I think he got ill because of— of things that happened, to do with me, and things I said that worried him. But now I've won this old competition it might cheer him up quite a lot. It doesn't mean much really, but it does to him. He's a bit cracked that way. I just thought he ought to know.'

'I'll ring through,' she said. 'They'll never let you see him this time of night.'

She picked up the telephone, and after a good deal of back-chat and giggling, she said to Penn, 'Now then. What was the message?'

'Just say Pennington played in the competition and won it.'

The nurse passed it on. 'For Mr. Crocker,' she said. 'There you are,' she said to Penn. 'Message delivered. He's asleep at the moment, but they'll tell him when he wakes up.'

'He's all right?'

'He's not all right, but not expected to die.'

Penn felt enormously relieved, in a way that surprised him. Almost as if everything was all right, as if he even wasn't going to Oakhall, and wasn't stranded in Northend without a penny, dying of starvation and nowhere to go.

'I'm ever so glad,' he said.

The nurse looked at him curiously. 'I thought you hated all school-teachers?'

'Nearly all. Not him. I suppose you haven't got a spare bed in here?'

'Not for healthy specimens like you. Go out and get run over, and I'll see what I can do.'

He went out and down the drive. At the bottom there was a car park with three cars in it. Penn tried the doors, and the third one, an Austin 1100, was unlocked and had the key in the ignition, as if the whole thing was meant. Penn got in and sat in the driving-seat. He thought he would drive himself as far as the Wagon and Horses, a mile and a half from home, and leave the car in the car park there, and no one would connect it with him. He wouldn't be fool enough to drive it right to Fiddler's End. Then it occurred to him that there was no particular reason why he had to drive home at all. If the car had enough petrol in it, he could drive anywhere he chose, and when Mitchell came knocking for him he wouldn't be there, and nobody in the whole wide world would know where he had got to. He switched on the ignition and started the engine, to get the petrol gauge registering. The needle went right up to Full. Penn switched off again, and went on sitting there. It was as if providence had provided. What difference would it make, he wondered, because they were putting him away anyway? A nurse walked past him down the drive, and didn't even give him a glance. Stealing a car was so easy it was criminal to take advantage of it. He sat back in the seat, fiddling with the lever to give himself more leg-room, wondering where to go. Everywhere seemed rather pointless. He knew, even then, that he wasn t going to go anywhere, because if he had meant to he wouldn't have switched the engine off after he had seen the petrol gauge so encouragingly full. He was just too hidebound, father-fixated, Mitchell-hounded, Stacker-nagged, Soggy-beaten, to have the guts left to run away. He could have cried, the way he felt.

He got out of the car and walked back up the drive to the ambulance shed, where two men were playing cards in a little room. Crombie's father was an ambulance man, and Penn asked them if they knew him, and after a bit, when they were quite friendly, he asked them if they'd let him bed down in the shed until it was light. They gave him an old stretcher that was out for repairs, and a red blanket, and he lay down and went to sleep.

Chapter 12

At eight-thirty the following morning an extremely considerate woman in Fiddler's End started labour pains, and the ambulance men gave Penn a lift home on the way to collect her. He arrived outside his own front gate at nine o'clock. A pale blue Austin Princess was parked outside, which he studied suspiciously. It did not look like a police car. Penn went in at the kitchen door, uncertain of what to expect.

His father was in the kitchen, reading the *News of the World* and drinking tea. He looked up and said, 'Oh, so you've decided to come home?'

'Who's here?' Penn asked. He could hear his mother talking to someone in the living-room.

'Some bloke asking for you. I thought it was a plain-clothes man, but it isn't. You know the coppers are looking for you?'

'Bates said.'

'I thought you'd scarpered.'

Penn shrugged.

His father said, 'It might come easier for you if you go down to the station. I'll take you down on the bike when I'm ready.'

'All right. Anything to eat?'

'I've had mine. What you wearing, for Pete's sake?'

'I got wet, I borrowed these. Who's this bloke then?'

'Search me. Go and ask him. He looks like a blooming parson.'

Penn frowned. He looked in the pantry for something to eat, in vain, took a handful of raisins out of the jar on the shelf and went upstairs. He didn't want to face any old parson in Major Harmsworth's get-up. The sooner his mother stopped yapping and cooked him some breakfast the better he'd be pleased. He washed, scrummaged in the airing-cupboard for some clothes, and went downstairs combing his hair. His mother, hearing him, came out of the living-room and said, 'Oh, Pat, wherever have you been? There's a gentleman here interested in your playing. Come and speak to him.' She looked agitated, and slightly out of her depth. Penn said, 'What playing?' undecided between soccer and the piano, and then, urgently, 'I'm starving, Mum. Can't I have some breakfast?'

His mother, ignoring him, put her head into the living-room and said, 'He's here, Mr.—er—' She took Penn by the arm and shoved him bodily into the room.

A man was standing in front of the empty hearth, wearing a weary expression which Penn guessed had been brought about by too much of his mother. The man confirmed this by saying, with a touch of asperity, 'Can I speak to him alone for a few minutes?'

'Go in the front room, then. You'll be comfortable in there.'

She opened the other door and gave Penn another shove in its direction. The man followed, and shut it behind him decisively. Penn looked at him without saying anything, his face cold. It could only be trouble. The man had an air of authority that Penn could sense instinctively: it was much stronger than any he had yet come across, and Penn was a connoisseur of people in authority. He was about forty-five, tall, well-dressed, and extremely sure of himself, with a look in his eyes that commanded respect. Penn felt distinctly uneasy.

'My name is Hampton, Professor Hampton,' he said. 'I heard you play the piano last night.'

Penn was not cheered by the news.

'At the competition?'

'No, at a house in Laburnum Avenue.' The man explained: 'I was staying with an old fellow student of mine—I've been in Northend for a few days judging the part-singing and the school choirs. This friend has a flat in Laburnum Avenue, one up from where you were giving a recital last night. We heard you through right to the end—we had no choice, in fact—flats being what they are. This morning we inquired as to your name and looked up your address in the entries for the festival.'

'I wasn't giving a recital,' Penn said, wanting to get the facts straight. 'The old girl there wanted me to play. She didn't give me any choice.

'Were you playing what she asked for?'

'I just played all the stuff I knew.'

'Who teaches you?'

'Mr. Crocker at school.'

'Crocker? Edwin Crocker?'

'Yes, I think he's Edwin.'

That's interesting. I knew him once. Used to play first flute in the Academy orchestra, very sound man. Well, isn't that strange?' He looked pleased. Penn was bored, wanting his breakfast.

Hampton said, 'You're not in a hurry, I hope?'

'I've got all day.' (Apart from an appointment at the police-station.)

'How old are you?'

'Nearly seventeen.'

'When are you leaving school?'

'Next month.'

'What are your plans? Where are you going to study?'

Penn nearly said Oakhall, but stopped in time. He looked at Hampton suspiciously. 'What do you mean, study?'

'Do, then. What are you going to do?'

'Get a job.'

'At what?'

The same old question. 'Drive a lorry or something.'

'What about your music?'

'Well, what about it?'

They stared at each other, Penn on the defensive against this unexpected probing. He wasn't at the police-station yet. When the man's gaze did not leave him, Penn looked away, worried. What was it all about?

'Look,' said the man. 'Sit down here and play me something. Whatever you're studying. Your choice.'

Penn sat down and played the Minute Waltz, the shortest piece he could think of. Hampton watched him intently. When he had finished he asked him for scales and arpeggios in several keys, and asked him to play a piece of Bach which he provided out of his briefcase, and a piece Penn had never set eyes on before, and to play a Mozart duet with him, also provided out of the briefcase. Penn's suspicions settled into a baffled resignation.

'Go and look out of the window,' Hampton said next. 'Tell me what key I'm playing in.'

Penn went. Bates was coming down the street, looking very cheerful, making for the Pennington front gate.

'B flat,' he said.

'What modulations am I making?'

'C major to B flat major . . . to E flat . . . F minor . . .' Bates saw Penn standing in the window and stood on the path making incomprehensible signs.

'What is the middle note of this chord?'

Bates mouthed, 'Did you win?'

'F sharp,' Penn said, and nodded his head at Bates.

'This one,' Hampton said.

Bates clasped his hands over his head and started prancing about until he got hooked up in a rose-bush.

'E,' said Penn.

'And this?'

'C sharp.'

'What?' mouthed Bates. He came close to the window, and peered in, flattening his nose on the glass.

'Intervals?' said the Professor.

'Fifth . . . augmented fourth . . . diminished fifth . . . major ninth . . .' Penn mouthed at Bates, 'Clear off!'

'Who's he?' Bates said, rolling his eyes towards the Prof.

'God knows,' Penn said, shrugging his shoulders.

'I beg your pardon?' said the Professor.

'Minor seventh,' Penn said.

'Very good indeed,' said the Professor. 'Come here.'

Penn put out his tongue to Bates, and went back to the piano.

'Play me the piece you played for the competition. Mendelssohn, wasn't it?'

Penn scowled. There was a smell of frying bacon creeping under the door, which made him feel faint.

'Now?' he asked mutinously.

The Professor just looked at him, without a word, and Penn sat down and played the Andante and Rondo Capriccioso. When he had finished he found his father was standing in the doorway watching him. As soon as the last chord faded his father said, 'Look, this is all very well, but if those coppers come up here, Pat, and find you monkeying about on the piano when I know they want you, I'll get into trouble as well as you.'

'It's me that's monkeying about on the piano, as you put it,' the Professor said. 'What are you talking about—coppers? What's wrong?'

'They want him,' said Mr. Pennington. 'They've been wanting him since Friday night. They're going to book him for riding a motor-bike uninsured.'

'Oh, is that bad?' Hampton said.

'Well, it is for him, seeing as they gave him his last chance the time before last, so to speak.'

'Why, does he do it often?'

'He does other things as well,' Mr. Pennington said heavily. 'It's not always that. They've got it in for him, that's all.'

Hampton looked at Penn, who felt humiliated. But he could not deny the charge.

'What's likely to happen to him? This time, I mean?'

'Don't mind me,' Penn thought. 'Just carry on talking.'

'He'll get three months.'

'How extraordinary!' said Hampton. He looked at Penn as if he were a new species. Penn didn't see his reasoning.

'Do you mind?' he said to Penn.

'Yes, of course I mind.'

'Why did you do it, then?'

'I wanted to get somewhere in a hurry.' Afterwards, when it was too late, he thought he could have added, 'To play the piano.'

The Professor looked at his watch. 'Would it help if I drove you to this police-station, wherever it is? Would you mind if I came along?'

Penn shrugged. 'I don't mind.'

'Go and put a tie on,' his father said. 'We might get you out of it if we say the right things. Yes, sir, no, sir.'

Penn went upstairs and his father followed him up, while the Professor went outside to turn his car round.

'What's he want?' Mr. Pennington asked Penn. 'Who is he, for Pete's sake, sticking his nose in?'

'Search me. You said he was the vicar,' Penn said crossly. 'Giving me a blooming examination this time of day! Aren't I going to get any breakfast? I shall die!'

'Doesn't look like it. Start dying.'

Penn groaned, and thudded downstairs again. They went out of the front door and out to the waiting Professor. Bates came round from the kitchen door and said to Penn, 'I say, I wanted to talk to you. Where you going?'

'Can't you guess?' Penn said gloomily.

'Oh, look, I say, I must talk to you before you get done. Is there room for me?'

'Yes, get in,' said the Professor.

'The more the merrier,' thought Penn. 'Take me to the graveyard and lay the sod o'er me.' He and Bates got in the back of the car, and as the Professor drove out of the village, Bates said, 'You won, you said?'

'Yes.'

'I knew you would! That was some day! Do you know, I sang, and someone asked me and Colin if we'd go and perform at some old party. For money! And there's a group in Tolchester asked if I would sing with them at some do or other next month. I mean, that was a good old day, wasn't it, you winning, and my career all starting up like that?'

'And mine,' Penn thought gloomily. 'Yes,' he said.

'Oh, and look, this thing I really want to tell you.' Bates hesitated, and looked stricken. 'I couldn't help it, Penn. I don't know what you'll say. About this old rescue thing yesterday—Mr. Crocker—'

'What about it, then?'

'Well, there was quite a fuss when I got back here. You know, quite a crowd gathered, and they asked what had happened and everything, and a man came from a newspaper, and the ambulance and—and they all made quite a fuss. Of me, I mean.' His voice dropped. 'And when I got back last night, Mum said somebody had been round saying something about me being put up for some old medal or something. Something about a Humane Society.'

Penn said nothing.

'Do you mind?' Bates said nervously.

'Why should I?' Penn said, choked.

'You know why.'

'Well, what am I supposed to do?'

'I'm sorry, Penn. I told them it wasn't me, all of it, but you know, they get it all wrong. I suppose I didn't say it properly. I could've died when Mum said about a medal. I thought if you were to come and see this bloke, whoever he is, you could say it should be you.'

Penn flamed up. 'I don't want a stinking old medal, do I? What good's it to me, where I'm going? Ruddy great medal hanging round my neck! Don't talk such stupid crap, Bates.'

'Oh, Penn, I'm terribly sorry.'

'Shut up, Bates. You make me sick.'

'Oh, listen, Penn. That bird, the one you're stuck on, did you see her last night? She asked me where you were.'

'Yes, I saw her. She took me home with her and I had to play the ruddy piano for her mother all night.'

'Well, what d'you expect? I hope it put you off her.'

'Yes, it did.'

'Good.'

The conversation had run its natural course, and they were in Moorham, coming up to the police-station. The Professor had been talking to Mr. Pennington all the way, but what about, Penn had no idea. They all got out and went inside. Bates had second thoughts as soon as he got inside the door and said, 'I must be dreaming!' He turned sharply to make a retreat, but Sergeant West had seen him and called out, 'Stay with us, Bates!' Bates groaned.

The Professor went up to West and said, 'May I have a word with you, in private?'

'Yes, sir,' West said in a tone of voice which made Penn think that he, too, recognized an air of authority when he met it. West opened the door to the interrogation-chamber and said to Mr. Pennington, 'If you'll just wait in here with the boys— I'll be right with you.'

They filed in and the door shut.

'You are a damned fool, Pat,' Pennington said to his son. 'Getting sent down for a damn-fool thing like this.'

'I've nothing else to do for the next three months,' Penn said savagely.

'Well, I don't know,' his father said. 'That bloke—what's his name?—said he'd like you to go up to London to some place or other. I've forgotten the name he said. Wouldn't cost us any-thing, he said. I said if it did, I wouldn't be interested.'

'What are you talking about? To do what?'

'To play the piano. He said you'd get a grant, a scholarship, or something.'

Penn was furious. 'Me? Are you raving? *Me*? Go to a twit house full of pianists! He never said that!'

'Who are you telling? He did say it.'

'He must be ruddy daft! I'm no good for that sort of thing. He ought to ask Crocker if I'm any good. Ask Soggy! If I am, they've been keeping it ruddy dark all this time.'

'You won that competition, didn't you?' Bates said.

'Yes, from a lot of old women. That doesn't count for anything, does it?'

'What competition?' Mr. Pennington asked.

Penn scowled, shaken to the marrow-bone. He sat down and laid his arms across the table, feeling quite weak.

'I thought it was a bit funny myself,' his father said. 'But he didn't seem to be joking. I'll ask him again afterwards, if he's still around.'

'Nosey old beggar,' Penn said. 'Interfering.'

Whatever it was the nosey old beggar had to say to West, it seemed to take some time. Penn could hear their voices without being able to distinguish what they were saying. He didn't care for being discussed, like a thing; what little command he had ever had of his own fate seemed to have crumbled away completely during the last few weeks. He was utterly exhausted, like a wet sock, and as useless. He dropped his head on his arms and shut his eyes.

West put his head round the door.

'Mr. Pennington, we want a word with you.'

His father went out, grumbling, but Penn did not move. The voices went on, with Mr. Pennington's indignation added for dramatic effect. Bates got up and stood by the door, straining his ears, but the police-station doors had been built to frustrate just such contingencies.

'They're cooking up something horrible for you, Penn. West is going to book you for driving the piano too hard.'

Penn was not amused.

'I'm sorry, Penn,' Bates said miserably. 'Really, about everything.'

He leaned against the door, watching Penn, until the door

jerked him in the shoulder-blades and West's voice hailed him crisply:

'Come on, you two, jump to it!'

He got out of the way and West, with a jerk of his head, beckoned them outside. Penn dragged himself mutinously to his feet. His father was standing outside the door, looking dazed and slightly apprehensive.

'Pat, it's all right,' he said. 'You've got off.'

West eyed Mr. Pennington sternly.

'Tell him the whole story. There are conditions.'

'Pat, listen to this. Mr. Hampton—the Professor here— wants you to go up to London somewhere and study with him. Won't cost us anything—he says you'll get a grant or a scholar- ship or something. Sergeant West says if you go, he'll let you off.'

'Oh, come, Mr. Pennington, I didn't put it quite like that. I said, "Let the boy think it over." Professor Hampton here wants to take him out for lunch, for a little chat. I said it's Mitchell that wants to arrest him, and Mitchell isn't around just at the moment, as fortune might have it. And if, over lunch, the Pro- fessor is able to talk Patrick here into doing something sensible with his life, who knows that I won't be able to talk Mitchell into dropping this nonsense about a motor-bike?'

Penn, seeing himself delivered from one academy of forced labour straight into the bosom of another, felt the indignation well up like water from a burst main. He opened his mouth to protest, but saw the room going round him in a most peculiar manner, and the words hadn't the strength to even fall, let alone explode, from his lips.

West hastily pushed him on to a chair and shoved his head down between his knees.

'Go and get a glass of water,' he said to Bates.

Mr. Pennington said angrily, 'You ruddy police! Hounding him, that's what you've been doing! No wonder the kid—'

Penn's voice came faintly from the floor. 'I don't want water. I'm ruddy starving! I want my breakfast.'

The Professor laughed.

'Breakfast! I've already made my offer. If you pull yourself together, I'll take you down to the Swan for lunch.'

'It's a good offer, Pat,' said West. 'The whole deal. Come on, you think about it.'

He waved a file of papers about under Penn's nose, and Penn got uncertainly to his feet. The Professor moved forward and took his elbow, and Penn found himself propelled smoothly out of the room, across the outer room and into the street. The wind off the river, bringing spray and ooze and mud and freedom, restored his equilibrium. He leaned against the wall for a moment, not quite sure what was happening. The Professor stood regarding him with a certain amount of sympathy.

'Don't think I'm presuming to order your life for you. I just chatted up the sergeant. I take it you don't want to be—how do they phrase it?—sent down for three months?'

'No. But I don't—' He hesitated, looking into the Professor's steely eye. 'I don't know what . . .'

The Professor worried him. He knew that the Professor had got him off, with his private word in West's ear, and that the Professor was going to manipulate him, smoothly, and cleverly. He was another of them, telling him what to do. But the Professor was more clever than any of the others. Penn sensed it, and it frightened him. He knew he could neither despise nor disobey the Professor. He walked beside him in silence. The fact that he had got out of Oakhall meant very little beside the significance of what he had got into.

'What's the matter?' the Professor said. 'Apart from your being hungry, I mean? Which we shall soon put right. Is the idea of studying music seriously completely new to you?'

'Nobody's ever suggested it before, no.'

'Mr. Crocker never suggested it?'

'No.'

'Why not? Do you know?'

'I suppose because—' Penn was not articulate enough to express what he felt. He could not explain to Hampton just what Crocker was up against, in their strange, closed world of frustrated effort; he could not tell Hampton what a pig he, Pennington, was; how he had driven Crocker nearly to death.

'I—I get into trouble. I don't work. They want me to leave. Tomorrow, if I go back, I shall get expelled for something I've done.' Even while he was speaking, he was amazed at what he was saying. As if it was a confessional or something. He must be more light-headed than he knew. The Professor opened the door of the Swan, and they went into the dining-room, and the waiter took them to a table and pulled out the chairs for them. The Professor was the sort of man waiters did not ignore. The smell of roast lamb and roast beef and roast chicken made Penn feel faint again.

'I don't like playing the piano,' he said.

'Why did you play for three hours last night, then?'

'I started because that woman made me.'

'She kept on at you, for three hours?'

'No. Just to start. When I finished they were all in bed asleep.'

'Why, then?'

Penn did not know. 'I felt like it, I suppose.'

The Professor smiled.

Penn said angrily, 'There's no *pleasure* in it.'

'I should hope not indeed. The pleasure is for the audience. For you it's pleasure sometimes, but a good deal more of the old sweat and pain. I'm having the minestrone, I think. What about you?'

Penn took the menu. He wasn't going to win, so he might as well go down eating. Sweat and pain. The old geezer could say that again.

'Oxtail,' he said. 'And roast beef.'

'It would, of course, be a crime if you were to become a lorry-driver.'

'I've got to do something.'

'I'd like to take you on, you know. You would get a scholarship without any trouble. You'd live in a room in London, with enough money to get by on. You'd have to practise four or five hours a day and you'd have to go to some lectures and concerts which you might, conceivably, find interesting. The rest of the time would be your own.'

Penn was silent. The waiter brought the soup, and they both drank it without speaking. Penn ate three bread rolls with his, and the Professor's prospect seemed less impossible than it did on an empty stomach.

Just before the beef came he said, 'People like me aren't students.'

The Professor laughed. 'Don't be so Victorian! Under-privileged backgrounds are in, these days. Parents like yours are fashionable. Horse-radish sauce, please,' he added to the waiter.

Penn was indignant, but immediately distracted by a large

plate flowing with thin red rounds of beef and steaming gravy, and mounds of roast potatoes, peas, carrots and Yorkshire pudding. He started to eat, concentrating hard. When he had finished he saw no reason at all why he shouldn't be a student. After all, he was used to about three hours a day, and even if he didn't like it, he didn't like anything else better.

'I could try it,' he said cautiously.

The Professor smiled. 'I don't ask many people to study with me,' he said, very smoothly. 'Usually they ask me, and I turn them down.'

'Take that,' thought Penn. He knew when he had met his match. Oakhall would be nothing compared to what was opening up before him. Cold showers and press-ups would be as summer zephyrs beside the relentless pressures of Bach, Beethoven, and Brahms that hove on the horizon.

'I'll have the chocolate gateau,' he said to the Professor, who was offering him the menu again, 'with fresh cream. And a large coffee.'

Another five hundred calories or so, and he would be able to face it with equanimity.

The nurse said to Mr. Crocker, 'There's a boy outside called Pennington who wants to see you. I said no, but he's very insistent.'

'I would like to see him,' Crocker said. 'He is the one person I want to speak to.'

'Only for a few minutes, then,' said the nurse.

Penn, looking very tidy and awed, appeared round the door and came slowly up to the bed.

'Hullo, Pennington.'

'I'm sorry, sir, if it was to do with me, you landing here. I had to come and say.'

'It was to do with Mr. Marsh, Pennington. What he did, after all our work . . . even if you deserved it, I didn't.'

'It's what made me go and play in the competition,' Penn said.

Mr. Crocker looked at Penn wonderingly. '*That's* what made you? But, of course, I see now! That's the way you work, Pennington. Of course! Like the long hair! Oh, my God, we must make sure he finds out, Pennington, why you won the competition! What a strange boy you are—but consistent, I'll give you that. And you won. But of course I knew you'd win!'

'And there's something else,' Penn said. 'A Professor Hampton. Do you know him?'

'Of course I know him. Everyone knows him. He's one of the finest teachers of pianoforte in the country.'

'Well, he's going to teach me.'

'He—?' Crocker could not find words. He stared. His complexion went through white, grey, blue, white, pink and bright red. Penn got up in horror, thinking he had brought on another attack, and called the nurse.

'What is it?' she said, bustling in.

'Is he all right?' Penn asked.

'Yes, I'm all right, Pennington,' Mr. Crocker said softly.

'What have you been doing?' the nurse said severely to Penn. 'He's not to have any excitement, I told you that.'

'Stop nagging,' said Mr. Crocker. 'They're just like someone we know, eh, Pennington? Always on at you.'

Penn smiled. 'Yes.'

'That's all very well, but what am I supposed to say to the doctor when he looks at your chart? Now just say good-bye, you,' the nurse said to Penn, 'and let him have some rest.'

'Are you all right, sir?'

'Yes, Pennington. I've never been more all right in all my life.'

'Well—er—' The nurse had him by the arm and was saying, 'Out.' 'Good-bye and—er—thank you and all that—'

'Thank *you*,' said Mr. Crocker.

'*Good-bye*,' said the nurse to Penn, and shut the door.

Penn, who always played the piano for assembly, finished 'Jerusalem', remembering just in time that it didn't have an amen, and, while the school sat down with a din like charging elephants and old Stacker shuffled his notes for the week's announcements, he fished out 'Jesu, Joy of Man's Desiring' ready for the dismissal. Maxwell was leaning on the lectern behind him, having read the lesson. Penn heard him yawn. He had told Maxwell and company about getting off the motorbike charge, but he hadn't told anyone about the Professor. The Professor and his plans were something Penn felt he had to

177

get used to himself before he made the news public. It was something that came strangely; to be told that he was good was so uncommon that he had to chew it over to get the flavour, to reassure himself. He didn't, in fact, know if he could do what the Professor wanted, but he was willing to give it a try. He fancied living away from home, and he fancied very much being treated like a human being, which seemed to be the Professor's way. He liked the idea of telling Sylvia that he was going to college and coming down the odd week-end to take her out (but not home), possibly looking up old Crocker to report on progress. He liked the word student, meaning hair whatever length he chose, and way-out clothes, and a room of his own in a comfortable house somewhere with no one to tell him what to do. For all this he was prepared to work quite hard.

These thoughts were going through his head while Stacker was giving out the notices. There was no point in his listening, because he knew that immediately after assembly he was going to be expelled. He had seen two of the governors arriving in their cars. He didn't care a bit. Soggy was sitting in his usual place just below the platform, no doubt looking forward to the ceremony. He knew, for the whole school knew, that Penn had won the competition, but he had said nothing, and nobody in 5C had dared mention the subject to him.

Penn, watching Soggy, was suddenly aware by Soggy's expression of what Stacker was saying. Soggy's face had tightened up, the skull pressing out, the eyes glittering.

'. . . must congratulate him on winning the Open Pianoforte Competition in the Northend Music Festival . . . a great honour indeed for the school . . .' Nothing about the twelve stripes on the palms of his hands to help him on his way. Everyone was clapping and cheering except Soggy, who sat motionless.

When the noise had died down Stacker said, 'I think it would be an appropriate moment, in view of this success, for Pennington to give us a short recital. Mr. Crocker, unfortunately, is not here to conduct the choir in their usual Monday morning —er—piece, and, in view of the fact that Pennington will *very shortly* be leaving us, I feel we should take advantage of this opportunity to hear him play a few of the pieces he has been working on.'

Penn heard Maxwell give a snort of amusement behind him.

His heart plummeted, a shot duck . . . He turned to Stacker.

'Now?' he asked angrily.

Stacker smiled sweetly. 'Yes, Pennington. Now.'

The old beggar was going to make him go out working. It was part of the punishment, the pre-expulsion aperitif, to get him sweating . . . He scowled furiously at Stacker.

'The competition piece first, and then perhaps that Chopin thing that everyone likes?' Stacker, still smiling, sat down and leaned back in his chair, adjusting to a musical-appreciation expression. There was an expectant, dead silence. Penn waited a moment, hoping for some phenomenal act of God, like a gas explosion or an aeroplane crashing, to deliver him, but nothing happened, and into the silence he was forced to deliver the Andante and Rondo Capriccioso which now, having served its purpose, was beginning to bore him to tears; everyone else sat back staring into space, glad to have their time wasted. The injustice speared him.

The applause at the end was prolonged, Penn was sure, by

the purely self-protective instinct to put off starting lessons. He sat gloomily, waiting, and Stacker came over and said: 'Very nice, Pennington. Now the Polonaise.'

Useless to say he wasn't in the mood, that he didn't want to play his favourite Polonaise for *him*. He just wanted to sit, staring into space, as he did every day between the musical items of the school assembly, letting it all go past like seaweed on the tide. But he had no alternative. He took his blazer off and dropped it on the floor. He thought, if Stacker asked him for another one after this, he would say his hands hurt too much.

He waited for a diminuendo in the school's shuffling and snuffling and coughing, rather to put off what he didn't want to do than to play the part of the concert pianist, and while he waited he decided he would play the Polonaise for Crocker, for the last time, willing it in the direction of Northend General Hospital. He would play it how Crocker liked it, not as fast and as loud as he liked it himself, and he would sustain himself by thinking that one day, if his luck held, old Stacker would have to pay to hear him play the Polonaise. He nursed this very pleasant thought until the silence was complete, and then turned his whole attention to the precise time values the piece demanded, forgetting resentment in the effort of vindicating dotty old Crocker for his absurd faith in him. It was Soggy he was showing, scorching him for his cheap sneers. He played it very well, as well as he had played it for Sylvia's mother, and the applause, when it came, was loud and enthusiastic. Penn, very satisfied, looked at the audience. He saw Soggy, sitting ten feet away, lift his hands and clap once, and put his hands down again on his knees. His face was like stone.

Stacker came over and said to Penn, 'Just one more, I think. Whatever you like.'

It was then that Penn had a quite marvellous idea.

'Yes, sir.'

Maxwell, who had been propping himself against the piano while Penn played, was surprised to see Penn smile, as if he was perfectly happy. Not a bit like when Stacker had said, 'Now the Chopin.' Penn sat waiting for the school to settle down again. He looked at Maxwell and said, softly, 'I'm going to play "Tannenbaum".'

Maxwell goggled.

'You're *not*! You wouldn't dare!'

'Want to bet?' Penn said.

Maxwell went stiff with horror, watching Penn. He thought Penn was having him on, but with Penn anything was possible. Penn sat very still, waiting for silence, then started to play.

Maxwell had heard Penn play 'Tannenbaum' several times, generally when he was in a bad temper, and he had always played it very loudly and angrily, but now—and Maxwell thought for a moment that Penn had been joking after all—the opening chords rippled off the keyboard as daintily as the Mendelssohn fairies. Maxwell watched Penn's hands, not daring to look at anything else, amazed less by their virtuosity than by their nerve. The melody, familiar to Maxwell in its honky-tonk version from the mangled bowels of the Common Room piano, swelled from the Bechstein with an authority that made it seem perfectly in order as a concert piece, very round and romantic. Penn's face was expressionless, watching the performance of his fingers as if nothing was meant. But to Maxwell the stately tune, growing gradually louder, with rebellious arpeggios starting to sing out under the left hand, was quite simply a shattering public statement of Penn's scorn for everything Soggy stood for—as explicit as speech. It was as if all the very best four-letter words were being delivered to Soggy from the platform, wrapped in exquisite form, insult through melody, denigration through apparent obedience to the whims of Mr. Stack, who still sat smiling, oblivious of the messages quivering through the atmosphere.

That the whole school was not oblivious of Penn's meaning was only too obvious. Maxwell took a white glance into the body of the hall, and saw the faces transfixed with utter, incredulous delight. The tension came to him like electricity, as if the whole school had stood up. The eyes were alight, sparkling with malicious glee, nudges and squeaks passing up and down the rows like wind through corn. Maxwell felt the hall tremble.

'Cripes, Penn!' he whispered. 'He'll kill you.'

Soggy was sitting bolt upright, his eyes fixed on Penn. Maxwell could see the threads of his rage working in little flicks and ticks round his jawbone and down his neck, his mouth twitched and the sides of his nostrils filled out and drew in with the emotion that Maxwell could see could not possibly be contained for much longer.

Penn smiled.

'He can't do anything,' he said. 'Not now.'

And the tune came up out of the Bechstein like thunder. Maxwell could see the muscles working all down Penn's arms through the white shirt, and the tendons standing out on the back of his hands like the strings up Soggy's neck. He started to grin. It was just too beautiful, impossible not to enjoy it, and the whole school started to stir, no longer able to contain the same fantastic pleasure. The beginnings of mass laughter came like the prelude to some gigantic sneeze, spitting and popping up from the floor in uncontrollable tiny explosions. Soggy got to his feet. He stepped forward and came to the platform, so that his waist was on a level with Penn's feet, hard on the pedals. The sweat stood out in beads on his forehead.

'Mr. Stack, that is enough!' he cried out. His voice was out of control, like the school. The first genuine shriek of laughter burst out behind him. He swung round, hands clenched. Maxwell thought he was going to have a fit.

Stacker stood up, goggle-eyed, unaware of what was causing the unbelievable behaviour of the whole school before his very eyes. He looked at Soggy having public hysterics and, with a promptness born of panic, roared into the hubbub, '*Dismiss!*'

Penn, in mid-bar, withdrew his hands, adjusted the music on the rack before him and immediately started to play 'Jesu, Joy of Man's Desiring'. The whole school turned as one man, drilled by sheer habit, buzzing with glee.

'Silence!' Stacker roared.

The lines started to file out, obediently silent, but buoyant with suppressed excitement. Penn played serenely, his eyes on the music, his fingers working on the gently flowing triplets in sweet legato as if nothing had occurred between this and the Chopin.

Maxwell came and stood at his shoulder, watching his hands sadly.

'I wouldn't like to be you, Penn,' he said.

'It doesn't matter,' Penn said. 'I've got myself a job. I'm going.'

He turned over a page, and played on. He was supremely

happy, and playing the Bach was as fitting a way to feel happy at that moment as any other he could think of. It was beautiful in its ordered sanity; it was unbothered, tranquil, unpetty, utterly controlled and of inspired perfection. He could not think of words to express it, but the feelings were like silk. He felt wonderful, and played with total concentration, content that this was what he was going to do. It had all come right, and the Bach was the most right thing of all.

Mr. Stack came up behind him and said, heavily, 'When you've finished, Pennington, come to my room. We have several things to discuss, I think.'

'Yes, sir.'

And Bach, as if he had known, went on and on, and Penn played him right to the end, and what was going to happen afterwards, he neither knew nor cared.

The Beethoven Medal

Chapter 1

'Tell me,' said Ted, standing at the kitchen window and craning towards the front drive, 'am I seeing things, or is Ruth actually mowing the lawn?'

'Oh, hark who's talking!' replied his mother sarcastically. 'When did you ever mow it without being asked, might I ask, when you were resident here?'

'Well, I didn't. But then nor does Ruth, as far as I know.'

'She does since the baker got a new delivery boy.'

'Ho, like that, is it?'

'She mows it regularly at about one o'clock every afternoon, when the bread's due.'

'It must be getting pretty bare by now.'

'Yes, it is.'

'Does he stop and tell her how lovely it looks?'

'As far as I know he doesn't even notice she's there. It's unrequited, this passion of hers.'

'What's set her off then? Is he gorgeously handsome? I must have a squint at him. There's a van up the lane now.'

I

'That'll be him. You tell *me* what she sees in him. I'll be interested to know. She has the weirdest taste in boys. Your father and I get worried about her at times. We worried about you once, I suppose. Well, you were bad enough, but a sixteen-year-old girl just about takes the biscuit. She was a lot easier when it was all horses.'

Ted, aware that his own disastrous marriage did not prompt his mother to view Ruth's affairs with much optimism, did not pursue the subject, but he was curious. Six years older than his sister, he had always thought of her as a scruffy kid and, looking at her thoughtfully through the window, he could see little to make him change his mind. She wore jeans with holes in the knees and a faded blouse: she was slight and thin, with no figure to speak of, all wire and sinews to Ted's way of thinking, due to too much hard riding of fast ponies. She was quiet, not a party type like his Barbara—which might even be an advantage, he thought with a slight bitterness. Who was to know what anybody saw in anybody else anyway, save themselves? What was the good his mother asking? It was just chemicals in the blood or something. He wished often that his chemicals had never got involved with Barbara, but an innate optimism kept him buoyant through the domestic trials of his own home life. All the same, he was interested in Ruth's baker.

'If you want to study him, you can tell him a large uncut,' his mother said. 'Give him a shout—he usually leaves it in the box by the gate, but I want to pay him today. These boys—they're always in too much of a hurry to stop for the money. They run you up a bill as long as your arm—they drive you mad.'

Ted thought privately that it wasn't a job he would go much on, trying to please a load of fussy women. He saw the van crashing through the pot-holes towards their front gate, and went out into the garden, smiling at Ruth's tense nonchalance at the lawn-mower.

'Ma says a large uncut and tell him to call for his money,' he told her.

'You tell him,' she said, with a quick, scared desperation.

He laughed. The colour flared up in her cheeks. Ted, remembering what it felt like, turned away and went back into the kitchen.

'I put the money on the mantelpiece,' his mother said, smoothing a sheet over her ironing-board. 'It's right. You give it him.'

'She's got it badly,' Ted said.

'Hmm!' It was more a snort than anything else. The iron went down with a bang. 'That sort! You've only got to look at him——'

Ted looked at him, tolerant towards his sister's fancy. He saw immediately that the boy was not the sort to please mothers, being offhand and long-haired and as scruffy as Ruth herself. He was tall and powerfully built, but moved with an aggressive ease; there was a scornful, belligerent air about him that suggested to Ted that he could easily get into trouble, although Ted suspected that not many would want to tangle with him. Ted recognized instantly what it was that attracted Ruth, and no doubt many other girls as well, but to his mother—too far gone—the boy was merely truculent and without charm. He did not smile, or say anything at all, ticking off the payment in the book, handing in the loaf, and retreating with the basket slung over his arm, hands in pockets, shoulders hunched.

'Loads of sex appeal,' Ted said to his mother, grinning.

She brought down the iron with a crash. 'You two!' she said. 'I don't know what I did to deserve it!'

'Poor Ruth,' Ted said, with genuine sympathy, remembering.

'Poor Ruth be bothered! Mooning about all day like a lost thing. Now she has no exams she seems to have no aim in life at all, a face as long as a fiddle—she makes the whole house miserable. She never goes out, yet there's lots of boys round here call for her, all decent, respectable boys most girls would be only too happy to go out with. That Gordon Hargreaves—he's even got his own car since he passed the test, and he's always asking after her, a really nice, well-mannered lad——'

Ted let out a terrible groan, and his mother's face closed up, anger whisking in her eyes. Ted got up to go, knowing that the abyss had opened; they were on different sides, irrevocable. Poor Ruth! Decent, wet Gordon Hargreaves . . .! Did his mother not remember even a little bit, what it felt like? Was she honestly blind, at forty, to what made the baker's boy different from good Gordon Hargreaves with his polite muff's face? Ruth, who had always taken everything so hard, starting with her first pony—quiet, vulnerable Ruth—had an implacable will, and would do, Ted knew, exactly what her stubborn inner voice directed, and would not love her mother's choice.

'I must get back to work,' he said. 'Thanks for the dinner.'

'You're welcome.'

His mother gave a short sigh.

He walked down the long rutted path to the gate. The lawn-mower stood abandoned, and Ted was surprised to see that the van was still at the bottom of the drive, obstructing his exit on the motor bike, and that Ruth was talking to the baker's boy. Aware that she would never have got into conversation with him on her own initiative, he was immediately curious, and went up to them with his usual candour.

'What's up?'

The boy turned round and said with a vehemence that surprised Ted, 'I've cut my finger on the ruddy door.' He spoke as if it were a disaster of the first order, yet to Ted it was merely a scratch, bloody but insignificant.

'The staff of life, with spots on,' he said, looking at the loaf in the basket.

The boy said something very rude about the bread, and flung the basket in the van.

'Go up to the kitchen and run it under the tap,' Ted said. 'There's some elastoplast in the cupboard. Ask Mum.'

'Yes,' said Ruth, all shining at the opportunity. 'You can't leave it like that, because of the bread.'

They all walked back up the path, Ted grinning at Ruth's luck. He couldn't get out until the van was moved, and he liked interesting situations.

'Now what?' said Mrs. Hollis, still sour from her thoughts over the ironing-board.

'A mortal wound,' Ted said. 'Blood-enriched bread . . . extra nourishment——'

'Oh, shut up!' Ruth said angrily.

'Put it under the tap,' said Mrs. Hollis. 'There's some sticking-plaster somewhere.'

She went rooting in the pantry. The boy ran the finger under the tap and studied the ragged little wound with an intent scowl. His hands were large and the fingers, flexible, square-tipped, gave an impression of uncommon strength. Good strangling hands, Ted thought, having watched a pair doing their work on the television two nights previously.

'Oh, cripes,' said the boy. 'What a flaming——' He cut off the next word in time, catching Mrs. Hollis's eye, and shrugged.

She held out a plaster strip.

'Haven't you got any disinfectant?' he asked.

The Hollis family, who by nature were not fussy about their health, all eyed him with suspicion, even Ruth. Ted sensed her disappointment, and smiled. Mrs. Hollis produced a bottle of Dettol which had been mostly used up, Ted remembered, on the cat's leg when it got bitten by a rat, and the boy bathed the finger with immense care. They all watched in silence. When it was dry again he put the dressing on, fixing it with a gravity out of all proportion to what was involved.

'I hope it won't be too painful,' Mrs. Hollis said.

Made aware by her voice of the lingering scorn in the atmosphere, he looked at her angrily, opening his mouth to say something. But whatever it was to be, he thought better of it for he turned away very abruptly, and went out of the door without a word.

'Thank *you*,' said Mrs. Hollis scathingly, when he had gone. She picked up the iron again. 'Get along with you, Ted. You'll be late.'

Ted went down the garden path again, and Ruth came with him, silent. They watched the van leap off down the lane, and Ted took his crash-helmet off the seat of his motor bike and put it on.

'He's a raving hypochondriac, Ruthie,' he said.

'Oh, he isn't!' she flared back. 'He——' But she had no defence to offer, and shrugged. 'He's a student,' she said. 'His name's Pat.'

'How do you know? You never asked him!'

'The other baker told me.'

'Student of what? Medicine?'

'Oh, shut up!'

'Pat . . . Patricia,' Ted grinned, kicking his motor bike into a strident roar.

'I hate you!' Ruth screamed at him through the din. 'You're beastly!'

She was so easy to tease, Ted could never resist it. He laughed,

5

ignoring the hint of shame put up by his better nature, let out the clutch and roared away down the lane. He had bigger problems than Ruth, but if he told her that she would never believe him.

Ruth flung herself down on the grass, not wanting to hear any of the remarks her mother was bound to make if she went back into the house. She felt cruelly cheated by the way things had turned out. The incident, full of the most lovely promise, had been turned to sour disappointment. Ted and her mother had ruined it. She could not bring herself to admit that this marvellous boy was himself the cause of her disappointment. Ruth's heroes weren't cissies; their physical courage was boundless; they were reckless and debonair and cared for no man. Pat, until today, had been full of promise; she had loved him desperately. But now . . .

Ruth plucked at a blade of the overcropped grass. She had broken her collar-bone once, in a riding fall, and finished the day out. One just did, according to her code (of course, she hadn't known it was broken until later). Her father was always laughing at her. He called her an incurable romantic, but she didn't see why. 'Come down to earth,' he said. But at least he laughed; he didn't get exasperated like her mother. Ruth groaned. Everything she did lately seemed to annoy her mother, but Ruth would not admit that any of it was her own fault. Vulnerable over Pat, Ruth would not approach her mother now; she lay flat on the grass, feeling the warm sunshine through her blouse, liking the quiet.

It was quiet where they lived, out of the village, away from the new estate, in an old cottage which her father had done up, using his own skill and ingenuity rather than money. Ruth had always loved it. In fact, she still loved it, but lately everything had got all tangled up in what she liked and what she didn't like, and sometimes she wished she lived on her own somewhere, where she could do as she pleased. She wasn't due to leave school for another year, and when she did she didn't really know yet what she wanted to do. Her mother wanted her to do typing and book-keeping. 'Something useful,' she kept saying. The only thing Ruth wanted to do was to work in a stable like her friend Thea who had gone away to take her B.H.I.

6

instructor's course, but there was great opposition to this plan both at school and at home. 'Unworthy of her intelligence,' they said. As if intelligence was completely unnecessary when it came to running a stable of valuable horses . . . Ruth, hating them all, missed Thea bitterly. She had lately decided that, if they wanted her to be an intellectual, she would stick out for art school. There had already been some preliminary skirmishes on this idea.

'But what good is it?' her mother had asked, appalled.

Ruth sometimes thought her mother never *saw* anything— only the holes in one's tights, and fluff under the bed. The night before they had been to see a film in Northend. To Ruth it was a beautiful film, touching and sensitive and visually breath-taking, and she had come out into the street in a state of ecstatic bliss.

'Oh, it was lovely! Lovely!'

And her mother had said, very sharp, 'It was disgusting! Disgusting!'

'Disgusting?' Ruth had recoiled, as if her mother had struck her. She had had to adjust, to try and see what her mother had seen, and the shock of it was like a pain.

'It's you——' she started, almost crying. 'It's——'

'Fish and chips everyone?' her father had put in rapidly. 'If we sprint we'll beat the queue. Quick, Ruth, you're the fastest!'

And she had run, the street all lights in the warm rain and the smell of the sea coming up with the traffic, and she was choked with such a maze of emotions that they ran into a great choking confusion like the lights in the wet road. She had cried, and had no idea what she was crying for, only that she wanted to be on her own somewhere and think her own thoughts and just—just *be*. She kicked at the over-mown grass.

Her mother called out of the kitchen door, 'Ruth, are you going into Northend this afternoon? You'll miss the bus if you don't go and get changed now.'

'I'm going like this,' she called back.

But she got up, brushing the grass off her front, and went slowly to the kitchen.

'You can just pop this suit of your father's into the cleaners,' her mother said.

There were only four buses a day out of the village. Ruth

combed her hair, looping it back over her ears, which did not hold it for long. Her mother was always saying it was a mess, but Ruth liked hair just as it came, long and straight. She did her eyes, changed into a pair of jeans without holes in and fetched her library books, stuffing them into the basket with the suit.

'You'll be back on the five-fifteen?' her mother asked.

'Yes. Unless anything wonderful happens.'

Once she had missed a stipulated bus because she had been offered a ride on a thoroughbred which had won six point-to-points, and beside such bliss, in those days, the times of buses lost all meaning. Now the phrase was a family habit, to cover such eventualities.

Amazingly, something wonderful happened before Ruth was five minutes away from the house. Walking up the lane, she heard the noise of an engine coming up behind her and moved over to give the vehicle room. As she did so, she knew that the engine was that of the baker's van; she recognized its particular note, having listened for it so avidly during the last couple of weeks. She also knew that the round was finished and the van was going back to Northend, and there was no time at all in which to think or rethink. She turned and put her hand up and the van came to an abrupt halt beside her. The boy looked at her coolly out of the window.

'Can you give me a lift into Northend?'

'If you like,' he said, without any joy.

She went round to the other side and he leaned over and opened the door for her. She got in and closed it, and sat looking straight ahead, her heart thudding so loudly that she felt its noise filled the whole van. The air was suffocatingly hot beneath the tin roof in spite of the open windows, and the smell of fresh dough and spiced buns, laced with engine fumes, was thick in Ruth's nose, so that she felt almost faint. She had a quick, pin-prick vision of herself falling against the hulking shoulder beside her, and him having to lift her up and carry her out into the shade and kneel beside her, smoothing her brow. This dream she hastily banished, to cool her palpitations. Her mind then went quite blank so that they drove on in silence, the van cavorting through the pot-holes at a pace a good deal too fast for its constitution.

8

Pat drove with his elbow out of the window, pushing the old van, but his reactions were quick and Ruth was not worried for her life, merely for her complete inadequacy to rise to this fantastic opportunity. Having in that impetuous moment acted out of character, she now found it impossible to follow up the suggested role of the easy, uninhibited hitch-hiker; her mouth was as dry as the last of the buns in the back of the van, her vocal chords fixed in silence, and she was forced to stare straight ahead at the undulating road like an imbecile, her inside tense with an agony she had never experienced before.

Pat was equally silent. Ruth put his silence down to pure boredom, and was mortified further. The van ground over the ridge above the river valley where the village lay, and the dual carriageway opened up before them, sweeping down under the line of pylons towards the arterial beyond. Ruth could see the new high blocks of Northend, and the glimmer of the sea; they were half-way there and neither of them had yet said a word. Pat changed back into top gear and the van sped down the white curving road, the cooling wind streaming into the van. He turned and glanced at her.

'You going shopping or something?'

'Yes.'

The word burned her throat. She stared down at the floor. She thought of Ted's easy way, his teasing, and a sharp despair prodded her.

'You—you——' She was like a fish on a quay, gasping and flapping. 'You've finished now?'

'I reckon to be off by two, yes.'

They had come to the clover-leaf which gave access to the arterial. He put the van into third and roared up the slip road, turning to watch the line of traffic he had to join. A tanker went by, and he slipped in behind it, and almost immediately pulled out to overtake.

'The rest of the day's my own,' he said, with a hint of bitterness.

'What do you do?' Ruth found she was getting back into the habit.

'Oh, I work,' he said.

'What, again?'

'Oh—it's different. I mean study.'

'You're a student?'

'Yes.'

'What of?'

He didn't say anything, pulling out to overtake again, watching in the mirror. When they were back in the inside lane he said, 'Zoology.'

Ruth's ideas had to be reshuffled to take this. She had supposed engineering or something mechanical. He wasn't the conventional university type. His manner and attitude suggested a hard upbringing, and there was no suggestion of affluence and very little of refinement in his appearance, which she supposed was why she had imagined a subject severely practical. Zoology, to her mind, was as rarified as her mother considered art to be. It meant nothing at all to her, except zoos. She could think of nothing to say on the subject at all.

'You still at school?' he asked her.

'Yes, I've got another year. Then I'm going to art school.'

He made no comment on this, possibly as thrown by art as she was by zoology. She was easy now, warmed by the fact that he had spoken to her, wishing they were going to the north of Scotland. But they were already slowing down for the roundabout and the turning into the town. He was concentrating on watching for an opening, his foot hovering over the accelerator. Ruth looked at his hands on the wheel, the finger with the sticking-plaster on held out, away from contact; his arms were very hard and muscly. She wondered if he did weight-lifting, and hoped not. She could not place him, somehow. He did not fit into any particular pigeon-hole: an uncouth student, a hypochondriac he-man, a zoologist baker's boy: it was all contradictions. It did nothing to damp her admiration for him at all. It just added to the fascination. Usually the physically attractive boys were terrible let-downs when they opened their mouths and better left unapproached on their pedestals, but this time Ruth knew that she was badly committed, and heading for a painful heartache. It was a very happy thought.

She said, because she wanted him to talk again, 'What's your name?'

'Pat.'

'Pat what?'

'Pat*rick*.'

It was a snub in a way, but offered in a perfectly agreeable tone.

'Are you Irish then?'

'My mother's Irish.'

They were threading their way rapidly into town. The time was running out.

'Where do you go to university?'

'In London.'

'But you live here?'

'Yeah—I come home in the vacations, that's all. Get a job, work—if you can call it a vacation.'

'Don't you get a grant?'

'Yes, I've got a grant, but you need more than that, for heaven's sake. Do you want to get out along here somewhere?'

'It doesn't matter where I get out,' Ruth said, wanting to go all the way. 'I'll get out where you do.'

'The bakery's round the back of the Parade. That do?'

'Yes.'

He pulled up for the traffic-lights, and sat drumming his fingers on the wheel, staring into space. Ruth wanted to ask him where he lived, but did not dare. She wanted to ask him how old he was, how many brothers and sisters he had, what he did in his spare time, whether he had a girl-friend, what his surname was, what he liked to eat, where he liked to go . . . she could feel the minutes running out, and she was struck dumb again. It was impossible to speak.

He made a patient right turn, probing a gap in the oncoming traffic as the lights turned again. The van threaded its way up a congested street and turned into a yard, to meet a brother smell of dough and spiced buns, stronger and fresher than the faded aromas of the van. Pat parked in a row of identical vans, switched off the engine, and sat back.

'That's it then.'

It was as good as saying, 'Get out.' Ruth got out. She stood beside the van, looking at the ground, holding her basket.

'Thank you very much.'

'Any time,' he said, very casual. He pulled his money-bag and the ledger out of the van, slung the bag on his shoulder, and went away towards the office. He did not look back, or say good-bye, or give even a flip of his hand in salute. Ruth wondered, for a moment, whether it was worse than the whole thing never having happened at all. She felt flattened, humiliated by her own inadequacy to prove any sort of an attraction at all.

She walked slowly out of the yard. The inadequacy—not even to be able to speak, let alone make bright, intelligent remarks—speared her. He must have thought her a complete half-wit. The glib advice of the *Marybelle* comic floated through her brain: 'Be *bright*—be *interested*! Ask him about his dreams, his fears! He is just as shy as you at heart!' Ruth doubted it somehow. In *Marybelle* he would have dated her, and they would have had a fab time. But things like that didn't happen to her. She crossed the road without seeing anything, walked on up the road and came to a halt at the traffic-lights they had passed earlier, hardly aware of which direction she had to go in.

'Hi,' a voice beside her said.

She nearly jumped out of her skin. It was Pat, on a bicycle, stopped for the red light.

'Don't spend too much,' he said.

'Oh!' The *Marybelle* things danced through her brain, even as her mouth gaped open and the colour flared up in her cheeks. She stared at him.

'Cheer up!' he said. 'You'll soon be dead.'

The red light changed to amber.

'Don't do it,' he said.

'Do what?'

He put his hand up and made a throat-slitting gesture, gave a passable imitation of a death-rattle, and cycled away through the snarled traffic. Ruth leaned against the traffic-light, utterly vanquished.

'Who told you?'

'Mrs. Pargeter.'

Ruth glowered at her mother. 'I thought you said that the thing you hated most about villages was village gossip. I thought you didn't take any notice of it.'

'No. I'd *rather* not take any notice of it. In fact, I didn't take any notice of it, until Mrs. Brown said she'd seen you in the baker's van, presumably on your way to Northend. That puts a slightly different complexion on it. In any case——' Mrs. Hollis looked up from the potatoes she was peeling and gave Ruth a long, hard look—'I'm not making an issue of it. I'm merely passing on what I was told.'

'Gossiping.'

'Be careful, Ruth.'

Ruth shook her hair back angrily. 'Well, what does it matter? People are put on probation for absolutely nothing. Just—just going over the speed limit or something. Did she say what it was for?'

'No. She just said that she had lived next door to the Probation Officer in Northend and knew that that boy—Pat whatever his name is,—was one of his—er—clients, I think was the word she used.'

'What is it anyway?' Ruth asked crossly. 'This probation thing?'

'Well, it's used if someone comes up in court for an offence not bad enough to be sent to prison. They're fined and put on probation, which means they have to report to this Probation Officer at regular intervals, and he keeps an eye on them, sort of thing—tries to stop them getting into any more trouble. Helps them really.'

'Well, it's not a bad thing then.'

'No, I didn't say it was. I wouldn't have bothered to tell you about it at all if it wasn't that you're so *interested* in the boy. I just thought you ought to know.'

'It couldn't be a bad thing else he'd never have got a job with the baker's. Handling money, I mean.'

'No.'

'She's probably got it all wrong anyway. Gossip's hardly ever right.'

'Well, she knew his name and where he lived and everything. I don't think she'd got it wrong.'

'What is his name, and where does he live?'

'I'm sure I wasn't interested enough to remember.'

'You remembered the other thing!'

'Oh, Ruth, let's not argue! We're coming very close to it . . . lay the table. Let's not talk about it any more.'

'You started it——' Ruth bit at the words, too late. She saw her mother's face. 'I'm sorry, I'm sorry! It's just that—oh, it's not fair! It's——' She stumbled, close to tears. 'Oh, it doesn't matter. I don't care.'

'Put the beetroot out, and that jar of pickles.'

Sometimes, when her mother was reasonable, it was worse than when she was just plain angry. Ruth crashed everything on to the table. None of the whole silly thing mattered anyway, not even if he was a murderer. He wasn't interested in her, and was probably madly in love with another girl. No doubt there were female zoology students with far more charm than herself, as well as the baker's office girls, and girls at home. She fell into a dream, trying to imagine his home, and him looking at things under a microscope all afternoon and making notes, and studying into the small hours. It was very difficult, with so little to go on, and not knowing where he lived, or what his parents were like, and after a little while her mind went back to the information supplied by Mrs. Pargeter, and she fell into another dream, in which he beat up a party of thugs who were annoying a lovely young girl (herself), unfortunately killing one of them so that he found himself in court on a charge of manslaughter. The judge commended him on his chivalry, but was compelled to find him guilty, and put him on probation for three years. This kept her in a trance-like state all through tea, and her mother said: 'The trouble with you is—you haven't got anything to do since that pony went away.'

'When I had him you said I spent too much time with him.'

As this was true, Mrs. Hollis made no reply, choosing to ignore the tone of voice in which it was stated. Ruth, still in her dream, wandered down the garden to the empty stable, and leaned over the door, picking at the splinters of wood, sniffing in the nice smell of old hay, of cool shadows and spiders' webs and things past, wishing she was at peace, wondering how it ever happened: the dull imperturbability of being adult. They had no feelings, no bliss, no agony. It was all the same to them; a little worry was very much the same as a little joy. Nothing they felt was the whole world as it was to her. Ruth groaned and hung over the door, her arms dangling. 'I love you, oh, I love you, Pa*trick*,' she said to the echo of the old loose-box. A few weeks back she could have said it into the mane of dear Toadhill Flax, and received a slobbery nuzzle for comfort, but Toad had cut his leg so badly in a jumping accident that he had nearly had to be

14

put down, and now he was turned out for the rest of the summer up at the McNairs', recuperating. The McNairs had owned Toad in the days of his youth, so he was at home in a sense—Ruth had no doubts for his happiness. Only her own.

'Oh, Pat*rick* . . .' she said, and it meant a thousand thousand things—half things and fragments. She didn't know what. It was all tangled up like the winter fuzz of the wild clematis that had died and still hung in one of the old pear trees; it was as insubstantial as the smell of the absent pony, the fluff of the dandelion clocks that disintegrated round her ankles as she walked through the grass. She put out her arms and shut her eyes and revolved in big circles on the grass.

'I—I——' She didn't know what, she didn't know anything, but felt as if it was all at her finger-tips, and she blundering and sensing into it like the summer moths, knowing nothing, and feeling everything.

'The girl's barmy,' her mother said sharply to her father, shaking the table-cloth out of the back door.

'They all go through it,' Mr. Hollis replied, reading the evening paper.

'It's me that goes through it,' Mrs. Hollis said. 'Oh dear, I can see it all coming——' She ran the hot water into the washing-up bowl and gave it a shot of detergent. 'It's starting all over again, like we had with Ted.'

'Oh, rubbish.'

'You see. You just wait.'

Chapter 2

Ruth was clipping the hedge, her heart shaking her. The van pulled up with a scrunch on the dirt and he got out and went round to the back of the van. Ruth dropped the shears and went down the path, wondering if her voice was going to work. 'I'll take it,' she was going to say, very casual. 'I'll take it,' she practised, her lips moving. She got to the van and stood staring at him, her lips parted, silent.

'One large uncut,' he said, and handed her the loaf. She took it, and one of his fingers brushed hers for a fleeting fraction of a second. She looked at them, withdrawing, and the sticking-plaster, and said:

'How is—you—how——' Oh, God, she wanted to die! She was so hot, she was burning.

'You do anything Sundays?' he said.

'I generally go up McNairs'.' Pure astonishment prompted her. She sounded quite normal.

'Oh, it doesn't matter.' He slammed the van doors shut.

'What?' She must have misunderstood him. She clutched the loaf, wild with fright at her words. 'If—if I've nothing—nothing else—I——' Oh God, again!

'I've got to go to London on Sunday. It's work really, work-cum-pleasure. I thought you could come, but it doesn't matter, if you're doing something else.'

'Oh, no!'

'You won't come?' He was getting back into the driving seat. 'It doesn't——'

'I will come! I will come!' Ruth said, frantic.

'Okay. I'll be on the one-fifteen from Northend. I'll be at the front, and lean out for you at Wickside. Will that suit you?'

'Yes.'

'See you.'

The van leapt into gear and disappeared in a big cloud of

dust down the lane. Ruth clutched the loaf and walked up the garden, seeing nothing, white as a sheet.

'Oh, good heavens, what's the matter?' her mother asked. 'Are you ill?'

Ruth sat down at the kitchen table, and stared at the loaf.

'He's asked me out.'

Her mother's reply was one syllable: 'Oh.' It had more feeling in it than the whole two sentences that had gone before. It jerked Ruth. Cold feelers of apprehension prickled her.

'You can't stop me!'

Her mother gave her a hard look. 'I never said anything, did I?'

'You won't? You can't!'

'I can, Ruth. But I won't. As long as I know what the plans are.'

'He's taking me to London.'

'I beg your pardon?' Her mother looked astounded. 'To London!' London from where they lived was a once-a-year place, for the sales, or Christmas, unless you were a long-suffering commuter with an expensive season ticket.

'He said he's got to go up for his work. "Work-cum-pleasure," he said, and would I go.'

'His work? Delivering bread, you mean? To London?'

'I thought his other work. The student part. The zoology. Perhaps he means the Zoo.' Ruth's face cleared. 'Yes, of course. The Zoo. It's a Sunday sort of thing, isn't it?' And so eminently respectable, full of parents and children, grandparents even, not layabouts and hippy lovers. Ruth smiled, a wide, sweet smile of utter bliss. 'It's all right? It is, isn't it?'

'Yes, it's all right, with reservations. We'll see.' Mrs. Hollis sighed, and went to put the kettle on for a coffee. 'You choose them, not me.' She fetched a bottle of milk, and peeled off the cap. 'Just behave yourself, that's all I ask. You know what I mean. He's a bit different from the boys you're used to, more experienced in the ways of the world, from the look of him. So be careful.'

Later, when she was alone with her husband and Ruth was in in bed, she said, 'What else can you say? If you say no, it's immediately turned into a tragedy on the scale of *Romeo and Juliet*. But if she spends a day with him, he can't possibly live up

to the image she's made of him. He's bound to be a let-down—
so here's hoping.'

Her husband laughed. 'I take it you don't approve of
him?'

'He's a mannerless yob, as far as I can see.'

'We'll have to meet him—the bread-round apart. He's probably all right. It's the way these days.'

'You're a born optimist.'

'Yes. But of course. I'd never have married you otherwise.'

You could see the train coming for a long way, as the line was
straight for a good mile out of the station. Ruth saw it coming
and shut her eyes and prayed to God, 'Please let it be all right!
Please let it be lovely.' She was terrified he might have thought
better of the idea, and gone on an earlier train to avoid her. If
he wasn't looking out of the window she would have to wait for
the next one, or go home. She would die, she thought.

She stood at the top of the platform, and the train grew big
quite suddenly, and there was a head looking out. Seeing him,
the relief was like an explosion. Ruth ran, and he pushed the
door open.

'Hi.'

'Oh, hullo! Hullo.'

Ruth felt as if she had been running for half an hour. The
carriage was a walk-through one, with quite a lot of people in it.
He waited for her to sit down, and sat down opposite her, and
looked out of the window. Ruth looked at him, but didn't say
anything. She was perfectly happy, it didn't need anything else.
And it was so fragile, the start of it, she was so frightened of it
being broken that she would dare nothing. But sit.

He was wearing fawn needlecord jeans and a plain brown
pullover and scuffed suède shoes; he was neither smart nor
scruffy. He combed his hair, which was brown and slightly
curling, long by her mother's standards but not by hers. He was
completely non-committal in his assumed appearance, but his
native expression still had this quality which Ruth found so
compelling. She could not put a name to it, save that it was
quite opposite to any expression she had ever found in Gordon
Hargreaves' face, even at his most animated. It was nothing to
do with being handsome; it was to do, she felt, with some fairly

disturbing emotions; it did not suggest contentment, but an aggressive energy, a dissatisfaction; there was a searching element, something that suggested pressures and difficulties she could not guess at. It was not an easy, amused face, like Ted's (Ted could even see the funny side of Barbara), but a watching, scowling face. Ruth wondered how old he was, and put him at about nineteen, but did not ask.

'I had these tickets. I just thought you might like it,' he said.

'I've never been before. Not there,' she said politely. She had spent three hours wondering what to wear for the Zoo, and was attired much as he was, in cord jeans, a white sweater, and a leather jacket.

'You go up to London often?'

'Hardly ever. I suppose you know it quite well, if you're there all the term time?'

'Mm. Well enough.'

'You—you live at home in the holidays?'

'No. I don't get on with my parents.'

Ruth's heart sank a little, thinking how that would go down with her mother.

'I live with the parents of a friend of mine. A school-friend. He's pushed off now, and I have his room. They're easy. We get on all right.'

'You were at school in Northend?'

'Yeah. I went to the Beehive. Where do you go?'

'Hanningham Comprehensive.'

'I know it. We used to play them at soccer. We always beat 'em by miles.'

'But we're good at soccer. We nearly always win.'

'Well, we were better. We were top in the County three years running. That's when I was captain.' He smiled, tentatively. 'It's the only thing I ever liked at school.'

'D'you still play?'

'No.'

'That's a pity.'

'Well, it doesn't go with what I do now. I can't. I just go swimming, that's all. You can't do much else in London. Are you any good at swimming?'

'Not much.' Ruth, aware of her floundering breast-stroke, felt a qualm. Suppose he asked her? She was too skinny in a bathing costume anyway. 'I ride,' she said. 'I'm not very sporty otherwise.'

'What, a bike? Or do you mean a horse?'

'A horse. A pony anyway. But he's good. He's won lots of rosettes—prizes, I mean.'

'What for? Jumping?'

'Yes.'

'Cripes, I've seen them on the box. The women, I mean. They must be as tough as hell. You one of those?'

'Not as good as them! I don't jump for England! Just the local Pony Club and things. But the pony's not fit at the moment —he's turned out.'

'So you just do the gardening instead? You're always gardening.'

Ruth felt herself go scarlet. But he wasn't teasing; she realized that he didn't know why she was always gardening. She was so relieved that she laughed.

'Well—riding's better. I miss him.'

'The horse? What's it called?'

'Toadhill Flax. Toad.'

'God Almighty, that's unkind.'

'Yes. But that was it, when I had him. He was registered.'

'Sounds like a perennial weed.'

'I suppose it does.'

The conversation closed, nothing else leading from it, and they both looked out of the window. Ruth saw fields and cows and woods, her eyes seeing but her brain registering nothing but a starry, unbelievable confusion, like a drawing in a comic of someone being knocked out. When the train stopped at the next station, he said, 'That bloke in your house the other day— is he your brother?'

'Yes. Ted. He's married but he comes home quite often. He's got a new house in the village, but they're always having rows, him and Barbara. Have you got a brother? Or a sister?'

'No.'

So he was what *Marybelle* called a 'loner', always a particularly romantic figure in *Marybelle*. In fact, Ruth thought, it must be rather horrid, especially if he lived apart from his parents as well.

'What's wrong with your parents? They can't be *that* bad?'

'Oh, can't they?' he said darkly.

A qualm overlaid Ruth's eagerness, half compassion for him, half a jolting apprehension at seeing her mother's unspoken but strongly implied fears being borne out. All her mother's nice boys had exemplary parents, usually good friends of Ruth's mother and father. Satisfactory parents were one of the conditions of her mother's code. Unsatisfactory parents *and* probation . . . Ruth felt the cold breath, and steadfastly ignored it, grasping instead at the hopeful straws she felt might yield more credit.

'You must have done well at school to get to university.' Beehive was a Secondary Modern, only very recently turned Comprehensive. She didn't in fact see how he could have progressed to university without transferring to the Tech. or Grammar first.

'No. I got the sack,' he said. 'I was offered the scholarship the same day I got thrown out. It was a bit of a joke.'

'What did they throw you out for?' Ruth tried to speak quite coolly, as if she knew a lot of people who had been sacked from school. She could see the proper word for it on her mother's lips: '*Expelled!*' and the expression that would accompany it.

'Something I did,' he said, without elaboration. 'But they couldn't take the scholarship away. I was laughing. I packed up school and I packed up my parents at the same time. The County gave me a grant. I hadn't really anything to complain about.'

Ruth looked at him uncertainly. The thought of rejecting such authorities with the abandon he was suggesting awed her.

'Didn't you feel—sort of—on your own?'

'Better than with all that crowd on my back.'

'But now—isn't it better? Isn't there anybody? Your parents——'

'Not my parents. That doesn't change. But it's all right, yes. There's the old friends when I'm down here, and a few at college during term, and my Prof. at college. He's all right. We get on. He bails me out when I'm in trouble.'

'What, literally?'

He laughed. 'If you like.'

Ruth was glad of the laugh, for his eyes were sharp, as if he had guessed she was probing. Ruth, scared by pushing him, resolved to forget it. She had known, just as her mother had known, that he was no Gordon Hargreaves; she would choose to accept the revelations as proving his sincerity in not deceiving her, and his refreshing lack of self-pity, rather than as evidence of a doubtful background. But the starriness had gone; in its place there was something far less fictional, something very solid, in spite of being compounded of tenderness and compassion and all manner of delicate emotions, something that her mother was not going to move, bully as she might. Ruth had discovered Pat wasn't going to let her down. Whether because of or in spite of what he had said—and she didn't know which it was—she admired him even more ardently.

The train journey was over in what felt to Ruth like ten minutes, but was in fact fifty. They walked in silence down into the underground and Pat bought two tickets to Charing Cross. Ruth was puzzled by the destination, thinking that the Zoo was somewhere in Regent's Park, but she got obediently on to the Circle Line train and emerged eight stations later into a daylight that gave on to the Thames embankment. Pat led the way up a flight of steps that led from the pavement and up to the footbridge that crossed the Thames alongside the railway out of Charing Cross. On one side a plane tree reached out its sooty leaves, screening the traffic below, and on the other the electric trains racked towards the Kentish suburbs, uncomfortably close and noisy. Ruth, even more puzzled, saw the Thames glinting below in a doubtful sunlight, and a cruise steamer casting off for Greenwich. Between trains she hesitated.

'Where are we going?'

Pat looked at her in surprise. 'There, of course,' he said, pointing across the river. Ruth looked, and saw a large grey concrete building which she took at first to be something to do with the trains. 'The Festival Hall.'

'The Festival Hall?'

She was completely thrown. 'But you said——' And she remembered that he hadn't said anything at all, only that he had tickets for something to do with his work.

'I thought——' She felt panic seize her, groping for some sort of a connection. For heaven's sake, what was the Festival Hall for? It wasn't a zoo. It was something rarefied and intelligent and serious . . . 'Music, you mean?'

'Yes. Didn't I say?'

'You said it was to do with your work. I thought the Zoo.'

He looked at her for a moment as if she had taken leave of her senses. Then, as if he had remembered, his face cleared and he laughed. He seemed to think it extraordinarily funny.

'Of course! I did say that—and the zoology. I'd forgotten. You thought we were going to the Zoo?'

'Yes, I did. What's so funny?'

'I'm sorry.' But he was still laughing.

'What's this got to do with your work? I don't get it.'

'My Prof. gave me the tickets. Did I say it was to do with my work? How could it possibly be to do with zoology?'

'Well, *you* said. I don't know.' Ruth was put out, trying to adjust. It didn't hang together at all. 'I don't see that music has anything to do with zoology at all. I wasn't expecting music.'

'You don't mind?' he asked rather anxiously.

'No. I'm just surprised. I didn't expect . . .'

It was one of those contradictions again, completely baffling. The Festival Hall was Third Programme sort of stuff surely? She could have understood if it was a pop concert. 'What is it, this concert? An orchestra? That sort of thing?'

'Yes. Rachmaninov and Beethoven. Nothing way-out. You'll like it.'

'But——' She looked at him doubtfully as they walked on, the tide ebbing far below, and the bridge trembling to the trains—'You mean *you* like it? You go often? It's not the first time?'

'No. I go quite often.'

She had to rethink, reshuffle everything. As soon as she thought she knew one thing about him, he said something that undid it all. They were across the river and going down the steps on the other side, crossing the wide-paved concourse in front of the hall. It was the first thing she had learnt about him that she could offer up to her mother proudly. 'He likes classical music. We went to a concert.' It was an impeccable way to spend a Sunday afternoon in London. After the shock had worn off, she felt very happy and pleased, keenly taking in the unfamiliar surroundings as they went up the steps and through the big glass doors. Inside she found that there was, curiously, a slight affinity with the Zoo after all; it was like a giant aviary, seeming to stretch up and out on all sides, with screens of glass and flights of apparently transparent, nebulous stairs, and people wandering everywhere, twittering and bobbing above and below, tropical Sunday finches . . . Ruth was intrigued.

'What a fantastic place! Where does the orchestra play?'

'In the concert hall. Not here. This is all extra, for milling about in beforehand, and afterwards. We've got three-quarters of an hour—we'll go and get something to eat first. There's a café overlooking the river. Okay?'

'Yes. Lovely.'

She had never been taken out like this before. It was like a dream, a *Marybelle* story. She drifted along the self-service counter, taking sandwiches and coffee and a gooey, creamy sort of pie, and Pat paid and they sat at a table looking across towards the river. The café was fairly crowded, and to Ruth everyone looked peculiarly benign and civilized and well-dressed, and she blushed for her Zoo clothes, remembering how she thought she would have been spending the afternoon, looking at camels. And now this . . . and Beethoven, and someone she had never even heard of. She mustn't cough, and clap in the wrong places. She didn't know anything like that.

Pat ate his ham sandwiches and drank his coffee, and offered to fetch another coffee, which she refused. It seemed to Ruth that he had withdrawn somewhat, but she was so happy that she didn't mind. Once a boy about Pat's own age nodded to him as he passed, and Pat said, 'Hey,' without much interest. He did not gaze about him like Ruth, but sat staring into space. His expression did not suggest boredom, but rather preoccupation, almost anxiety, Ruth thought. He was contradicting himself again, the vital, aggressive element quite abruptly withdrawn into this brooding reverie.

Ruth, not wishing to interrupt, was perfectly content watching people going past with their trays. The place was fairly full, but her eye was caught by a striking girl in a long brown velvet coat coming towards where they were sitting, searching for an empty table. She was to Ruth's eyes unusually handsome, with a proud, confident carriage, a face with wide-spaced golden-brown eyes, delicate nervous nostrils and fine cheek-bones like an intellectual French film-star, and a stunning mane of bright chestnut hair. Ruth was not the only one admiring this vision, who was accompanied by an elegant youth in matching brown suède. The girl came down the aisle and to Ruth's astonishment stopped by their table and said, 'Why, Pat!'

Pat looked up with a jerk, his expression reacting slowly, as if he had come from a long way away. Ruth looked jealously for the light of pleasure in his eye, but saw only a cautious surprise.

'Hullo,' he said, very non-committal. And he nodded to the boy. 'Hullo, Bob.'

'Oh, of course!' the girl said. 'We might have guessed you'd be here today! How long until——'

'It's six weeks yet,' Pat said.

'How's it going?'

'Very well, thank you.'

'No problems?'

'Of course. But nothing too bad.'

'Well, I wish you luck. You've got that Hampstead date all right, haven't you? You won't let me down?'

'No.'

The golden-brown eyes came to Ruth and gave her a long, cool look. Ruth felt like a worm. The girl was beyond competing with; Ruth, for all her efforts, felt shabby, spotty, meagre, and worthless.

'See you then,' said the vision, and wafted on her way to an empty table farther down.

Ruth looked at Pat.

'Who's she?'

'Her name's Clarissa.'

'It would be,' Ruth thought bitterly.

'She's at college. We work together sometimes. Come on— we'll go and take our seats. There's not long now.'

He led the way out of the café, not amiable any more, but silent and abstracted. As he had been silent and abstracted before Clarissa had interrupted them, Ruth could not fairly say that it was meeting Clarissa that had put him into this cool humour, but she had a feeling that meeting Clarissa hadn't improved anything for him. The idea of his *working* with Clarissa she would not dwell on; the vision of their two heads bent closely over a dissected monkey aroused qualms she would rather not experience.

But the atmosphere of the Festival Hall was too heady for her to dwell on these doubts, and her spirits rose as they climbed up the centre stairs and threaded their way through the crowd to yet more stairs which appeared to Ruth to be more outside than in, with plane trees familiarly brushing the glass walls. Pat gave their tickets to a man who said, 'Hullo, Pat,' and Ruth said, 'Do you live here or something?' and Pat said, 'No, but I was a waiter for a month or two last year. I got to know people. Look, I'm sorry about these seats, if you've never been here before. You'll only see the violins.'

Ruth saw what he meant when they sat down. They were in the front row, slightly to the left of the centre, and the platform rose up in front of them so that their eye level coincided with the musicians' knees. As yet the platform was empty, and Ruth took in the vast pitch covered with music-stands and chairs, and the tiers of seats behind the platform, and the organ pipes beyond like some giant's toy convoluting into the dim recesses of the so-carefully designed ceiling, and turned round, and saw all the seats fanning away behind in the other direction, filling fast with the brightly plumaged Sunday people, and was excited in a most ridiculous childish fashion, in a most unClarissa-like, uncool bubbling way, which she felt obliged to cover up, with Pat so unimpressed beside her. She didn't have to show what a yokel she was.

Pat showed her the programme. After a Rossini overture, there was the Piano Concerto No. 2 by Rachmaninov and the Symphony No. 8 by Beethoven. It conveyed nothing to her at all. The members of the orchestra were now taking their seats, and getting out their instruments, but Ruth was puzzled by what appeared to be an enormous oversight on the part of the management, and could not restrain herself from inquiring:

'How can there be a piano concerto when there's no piano?'

'They bring it on, just before, and take it away afterwards,' Pat said.

Ruth blushed. Not only was she a yokel, she was a stupid yokel.

She supposed, having seen it on the television, it should have been familiar enough, but to Ruth it was entrancing, listening to 'The Thieving Magpie', and considering the violinists' feet, their socks in various shades of grey and their black shoes, and lifting her eyes to the wonderfully eloquent gestures of their right arms, all flowing together, the little fingers stretched in a way that made her long to be drawing: the black shapes and the white decorations of the fingers, and the golden intricacies of the line of violins, giving out a splendour that was entirely divorced and apart from the complete ordinariness of each individual player, who were the sort of men one saw everywhere, in shops and on the train, doing the crossword, washing the car on Sunday mornings, and taking the dog for a walk. When it was over, dissolved into warm, swelling applause, Ruth remarked on this strange paradox to Pat, and he said, 'But it's only work, to them. To pay their mortgages and buy their cars.'

'There must be more to it than that! Art——'

'Art is eighty-five per cent work,' Pat said. 'Hard work.'

He seemed very sure of this fact, speaking with a vehemence that suggested a personal, somewhat bitter experience.

'Even for him,' he said, when the piano had duly made its appearance and was installed in place, and the soloist had followed the conductor on and was taking a quick introductory bow. 'It's his work.'

Ruth had always rather thought it was a gift. But when the anticipatory hush fell and the soloist wiped his hands nervously on his knees and the conductor raised his baton, she felt a lurch of compassion for his terrible responsibility, before all these people, to hit the right notes—the loneliness of it was appalling. There were surely, she thought, easier ways to pay the mortgage than this? And then his hands came down and played the first broken chords, and it was so fluid and effortless that her anxiety instantly slipped away. Softly at first, and then with an increasing urgency, the chords led the way into a deep turbulent melody. Ruth saw the violinists before her lift their bows, the conductor raise his baton with a tense white expectancy, holding in leash the whole gamut of poised breath and suspended finger until the exact, perfect moment when the solo piano could be resisted no longer, and they were launching on this eager, rhythmic tide which the piano had prepared for them. Ruth, having expected difficulties and incomprehension, was launched along with them, a drowning twig on the breast of flowing waters. Work it might be to them, but to Ruth, completely new to such a happening, it was an overwhelmingly emotional experience which she had no wish nor will to resist. She could not have put into words the effect it had on her; she only knew that in the slow movement she cried, and in the finale she cried again, but she was so happy it was crying for God knew what. Ruth didn't know. But in the crashing uproar of the applause afterwards, she was comforted to see that the soloist, bowing and shaking hands with the conductor, looked almost as shaken as she felt, although what emotion was prompting him she was not qualified to guess at. If it was only work, after all, it could have been pure relief.

She turned to ask Pat, but he was withdrawn in such a way that Ruth had a strange feeling that he was scarcely there at all. But when the appreciation had died down, and everyone had bowed for the last time, he turned to her, and Ruth felt that she was actually seeing him come back from this other world he was inhabiting; it was almost a physical thing, the eyes focusing on her almost with surprise, the mouth easing into the suggestion of a smile, a warming, a softening . . . Ruth was confirmed in her suspicion that Pat was a highly complex animal, a study on his own, well orientated in his zoology school.

'We'll go and get a drink,' he said, very prosaic.

It was the interval, and most people were leaving the hall. They joined the throng, Ruth still not quite sure that her feet were on the ground. Her leaping happiness—all that and Pat too—was dangerous in its intensity. One could only fall from such heights. She tried to temper the mood, but it kept escaping, singing into the firmaments like the Rachmaninov melodies.

'What will you have?' Pat asked.

It was a bar, and Ruth had no idea what to ask for. She had a quick glance round, but everyone had anonymous brown stuff that was no help to her.

'Coke,' she said, and Pat took it without a qualm, and ordered coke and half a pint of bitter. They took their glasses and retreated, guarding them carefully in the crush. Coming towards them, *en route* for the bar and, regrettably, unavoidable, was the magnificent Clarissa.

'Oh, Pat! What did you think of it? I'm sorry to say it wearies me to death. *So* hackneyed. I wonder you can face the prospect at all. If I were you I'd——'

'You're *so* encouraging,' Pat said, without smiling. 'If I were you, I'd stop worrying about what you suppose are other people's difficulties and worry about your own. Your Hampstead date, for instance.'

'Our Hampstead date,' she corrected.

'Well, I'm not worried about my part in that. You should be, from what I last heard.'

Although Ruth had no idea what they were talking about, she could see that Pat was being offensive. Clarissa's eyes went cold.

'You don't change, do you, Pat? I thought at one time we were civilizing you quite nicely. But I was wrong obviously.'

She drifted away into the crowd with impeccable majesty. The suède Bob, following, gave Pat a sympathetic, eye-rolling grimace. Pat grinned.

He said to Ruth, 'She should have been an actress,' and the subject was closed, Ruth could see. She longed to ask questions, but Pat's expression forbade it. It was grim again and Ruth hated Clarissa for her interference.

'That music we heard—is it hackneyed?' she asked nervously. 'I thought it was beautiful.'

'It's both,' Pat said.

'Hackneyed and beautiful?'

'Yes. Hackneyed only means it's played a lot, so that a lot of people know it, and what's wrong with that?'

'I knew it,' she said. 'That beginning—and that slow bit. It was quite familiar to me.'

'Yes. The first time I heard it, I was just little. My mother took me to the pictures to see some crummy film about a housewife who fell in love with a doctor. Every time they were looking into each other's eyes, or thinking about each other on the railway platform—the slow movement came on and all the women in the cinema wept. They all came out looking as if they'd been to a funeral. But my mother said it was lovely. It was Rachmaninov that did it, not the director.'

'Those old films . . . it's only animals dying that make me cry, like *My Friend Flicka*. I think I've seen that film—something about an encounter. The title, I mean. I remember the railway station too, and at the end, she goes home, back to her husband, and leaves the doctor for ever, and she goes in at the door, and the music plays——'

'The coda—and everybody cries——'

'Yes. That's it. I remember. My mother cried too. It was a very sad film, all that parting for ever.'

'Well, I don't remember. Only the music.'

'It must be awful.'

'What?'

'Parting for ever.'

'Oh. Yes. And never coming. Someone you expect never coming.' He said it in a way that suggested he knew. Ruth was silent, caught by a wrenching of her feelings, half compassion, half jealousy, that stopped her voice. Keyed up by the music, moved by a sympathy towards someone stronger than she had ever experienced, she looked at him over the top of her glass, and found him regarding her with equal gravity. The mutual contemplation was undisturbed by the surrounding crush; Ruth felt that they were perfectly alone.

'What's your name?' he asked, never having asked before.

'Ruth.'

'And then we came out and walked across the river and had tea in a place, and then we walked some more, into Trafalgar Square or somewhere, and the church bells were ringing . . .'

Ruth had nothing to hide from her mother. Telling her, it was like saying poetry, savouring the image behind the words, the fountains blown by a cool evening breeze and the starlings' chatter and the gusty din of the bells of St. Martin's pounding off the walls of Duncannon Street, and Pat walking with his hands in his pockets past the Sunday shouters and the American tourists and herself at his elbow in this trance-like state of un-clouded bliss, which had continued right from Rachmaninov to the parting on the railway station.

'So you've got him all wrong,' she said passionately to her mother. 'And he never even touched me either,' she added. 'Not like Gordon Hargreaves.'

Mrs. Hollis laughed, in spite of herself. 'Well, I must say, I'm flabbergasted. A classical concert! You mean Beethoven sort of thing?'

'Yes. It was Beethoven actually. And that piano thing by Rachmaninov that was in that film where the housewife fell in love with the doctor, and went back to her husband and you cried——'

'*Brief Encounter*? Oh, that was a beautiful film! They don't make films like that now! Really, is that what you heard? That was beautiful!'

Her husband said darkly, 'Why did you cry, if the housewife went back to her husband?'

'It was so real,' said Mrs. Hollis dreamily. 'She was just an ordinary housewife, not young and pretty, but just ordinary and dull, and she met this doctor, and he wasn't dazzlingly handsome either, just nice and kind, and they fell in love—fantastically in love, not just a passing thing—but she went back to her husband . . . she went in at the door and he was just sitting there, homely and ordinary. She couldn't leave him, you see. He had never done anything wrong, or hurt her, and she went back, and that was the end of the film.'

'It sounds fantastically old-fashioned,' Ruth said.

'Oh, yes, I've no doubt. Nowadays she'd have moved in with the doctor, and two families would have been knocked for six in order that she could fulfil herself, or whatever. There's a lot to be said for being old-fashioned, my girl.'

'Yes,' said Ruth, and dreamed her way up to bed.

'That's a good old-fashioned thing that's afflicting Ruth now,' Mr. Hollis said to his wife when she had gone. 'Even I'm not so homely and ordinary as to remain unaware of the fact that the girl has got it very badly. Your plan miscarried, my dear.'

'What plan?'

'You said that if she got to know him a little better, he was bound to prove that he had feet of clay. Not so, obviously. He's the Angel Gabriel as far as she's concerned.'

'Well, I must say—again—you could knock me down with a feather. I just put him down as a typical lout. I've never seen him smile, or say thank you, or say anything at all, come to that. He flings the loaf at you and drives off like a maniac. He's a strapping great lad, built like a navvy, hair all over his collar. Although he's got nice hands, come to think of it. The only thing that looks even faintly artistic about him. Long fingers and well-kept nails. But the Festival Hall! No, quite the last thing I would have imagined.'

'Encouraging, I would have said.'

'Possibly. But I'm not convinced. I'd like to know a little more about him.'

'In a place like this,' her husband said, 'I wouldn't think that would take you long.'

Chapter 3

Pat glowered at Mrs. Hollis, handing in a large uncut. 'Five uncut. Forty-eight pence,' he said.

Mrs. Hollis handed him a note, and he scooped about in his money-bag for the change. Mrs. Hollis decided that his neck and his hair were clean, and it was only the clothes that made him look scruffy. And he was working after all. She hadn't the nerve to ask him any questions; there was this block, that Ruth presumably had overcome, this aggressive reserve, as if he was behind a barbed-wire fence.

'Fifty, a hundred.' He counted out her change, hesitated. 'Tell Ruth—tell her I'll be in the Big Top tomorrow night at seven.'

'Where and what is the Big Top, might I ask?'

'It's a coffee-bar on the front. She'll know it.'

'I take it that's an invitation?'

'I'm working. I can't take her out. I just want to see her.'

'Very well. I'll tell her. I don't know what her plans are.' She paused. 'You seem to work very hard.'

'I work in a pub Saturday nights. But I can see her first.'

'All right.'

He slouched off down the drive, whistling. Mrs. Hollis smiled to herself. Ruth, back at school for the last fortnight of term, had not seen Pat since her day out with him but had inquired after him every day, with an increasing despair. It was for her sake that Mrs. Hollis smiled, against her better judgement. She thought, if she saw Mrs. Pargeter, she would ask her a few more questions, although it wasn't really something she cared to do. But if this friendship was on . . . the probation thing worried her.

'I don't know if you can call it taking you out,' she said to Ruth when she came home. 'Pretty casual, I call it.'

But Ruth, after the agony of the past week, glowed like a spark in the wind.

'Oh, it's lovely! I thought——' But it had been only too plain what she had been thinking. It had been a week like a year, bereft of her gardening sessions, and the daily blessing of merely seeing Pat. She had dreamed of him all day and all night.

'Well, if you think it's worth going all that way for half an hour in a coffee-bar . . .' But it could as well have been Cornwall, or twice as far. Mrs. Hollis decided to save her breath.

Ruth went on the bus, which was supposed to get into the bus station at seven o'clock exactly. Running, she would be at the Big Top at three minutes past seven. It was a terrible risk, in her eyes, but her whole family, Ted included, had derided the idea of her going on the bus before—the three o'clock—merely in order to be there punctually. 'He'll wait three minutes, dear, if he loves yer,' Ted said. But Ruth kept remembering what he had said, about someone not coming. And then, sternly, 'But he doesn't think of me like that—not yet. That was someone who mattered.' Mattered terribly, she thought. And she went into another of her dreams, about him being crossed in love, which lasted her all the way to Northend. She got off the bus, feeling sick and unreal, and ran all the way to the coffee-bar, only stopping three yards short of the door. It was no good trying to look as if it didn't matter. She had no breath, not just through running, but through everything. She had bursting stitch, and an agony of mind that was a hundred times sharper than anything physical. She went in, white and shaking.

He was sitting at a table in the window. He had a tie on and a white shirt, and looked quite normal. She went over to him and sat down and stared at him.

'Pat.'

'Hullo,' he said. He gave a very slight smile. 'I thought your mother might not pass the message on.'

'Oh, she's not that bad.'

'No. I wondered if you'd think it was worth it. I have to go to work in half an hour. I thought you might be in Northend anyway, so I mentioned it.'

'She said that. Yes, of course I thought it was worth it.'

'Oh, well.' He smiled. 'That's all right.'

Ruth smiled, all the pains dissolving. It was worth it already. 'What'll you have?'

'Just a coffee.' She didn't want to be interrupted by food.

He ordered two coffees from the waitress, and considered her again.

'Why do you have to work so hard?' she said.

'I do just now. Later it will be all right. I'm sorry, because—well, the other things have to go. Like tonight. We could have gone down the pier or something.'

Out of the window the sea was bathed in a calm pink evening light. The tide was out and the pier marched out over the shining mud on spidery legs; the fairy lights were on and summer couples were walking hand in hand; Ruth could feel the echoing boards under her feet and smell the sea and hear the hollow slapping of it far below. Her longing to walk there with Pat made her quiver.

'I wish we could!' And then, hastily, 'But it's all right. I mean if the work's important——'

'It's five quid tonight in the pub, and I can't pass it up any-way—he'd go raving. Tomorrow I work all day—study, that is—and then it's the bread again. The bread's only part-time, but all the same I'm going to pack it in soon. I'd rather have an evening job, and do my own work in the morning. I must have more time for it.'

'How long have you got to do at university? Aren't you nearly finished?'

'I've got another year. I've only told you this to explain—about not going out. I'm not complaining or anything. But if it's a waste of time for you——' He shrugged. 'You live so far out.'

'Where do you live?'

'Fiddler's End.'

'That's just as far out.'

'We've arranged things badly. Or if I had some transport . . . Well, that's how it is.'

'I don't mind.'

'Hey, mind if I butt in?' Somebody stopped by the table. Ruth looked up and saw a sharply-dressed boy with a cheerful quick face. 'How's things, Penn? Long time no see.'

'Cripes, Maxwell, get lost,' Pat said, but quite amiably, so that Maxwell sat down, and looked with unconcealed interest at Ruth.

'That's Ruth,' Pat said. 'Maxwell.'

'Pleased to meet you,' said Maxwell.

Ruth tried to look more gracious than she felt. 'Hullo.'

'Hul*lo*.' Maxwell gave her a dazzling smile, and said to Pat, 'How's the old——'

'Very well, thank you,' Pat said. 'How's the car trade?'

'It isn't, unfortunately. I've lost my licence for twelve months —the old breath, you know. A hundred and God knows how many milli-whatsits. Green as a cucumber. So I'm working in the stores until I get it back. Dead boring. You on the old stint tonight?'

'Yeah, half past seven.'

'Don't you ever let up?'

'It's a good job, this one.'

'All those sweaty trippers in their cups. What's Ruth going to do then. Come out with Uncle Maxwell?'

'No fear,' Ruth said.

'We could take a stroll, and then call on Penn and see him at work, and take a noggin with him between "Nellie Dean" and "Home Sweet Home". Not agreeable?'

The thought of seeing Pat again later attracted Ruth.

Pat said, 'I'd trust you with him, I think.'

'Where is this pub then?'

'Just down the road a bit. "The Jolly Sailor".'

Ruth knew 'The Jolly Sailor'. It was a huge modern pub which attracted the Saturday night trippers and was always cramful and very rowdy. It was quite a different proposition from the Royal Festival Hall, something she would definitely not want to tell her mother about. Pat glanced at his watch.

'I ought to be going. Shall I see you later?'

'Yes,' said Ruth.

'That's my girl,' said Maxwell.

Ruth looked anxiously at Pat, and he gave her a reassuring wink. 'He's okay. Aren't you, Maxwell?' he added, ominously.

'Straight as a die,' said Maxwell.

Pat got up. 'See you later then.'

Ruth watched him depart, anxious and excited. She had no feelings either for or against Maxwell; he was of interest entirely for what light he could throw on Pat.

'Why do you call him Penn?' she asked.

36

'It's what we called him at school. Pennington.'

'Is that his name? Pennington? You were at school together?'

'Yes.'

The waitress came, and Maxwell ordered sausage and chips, and asked her what she wanted. Now that there was time to waste, she asked for a coffee and a chocolate éclair. Maxwell, she thought, knew all the reasons why Pat was as he was, all the things she wanted to know, but—because of Pat's own reserve— she was wary of asking. It was going down to Mrs. Pargeter's level, prying and nosing. If Pat wanted her to know the story of his life, he would tell her, no doubt, in his own good time. But, having made this noble resolution, her curiosity was too much for her.

'What was he like at school?'

'What was he like?' Maxwell looked slightly baffled. 'The same as all the rest of us, I suppose, pretty blooming awful. He was always in trouble, probably worse than anybody else. He asked for it, mind you. He never did a stroke of work. Soccer was the only thing he was keen on. Soccer and swimming. He was a wizard on the field. We were hardly ever beaten—In fact never, the last year. I was in the team too—we had some good times. I still play, but he's packed it in. Had to, I suppose. Pity.'

'How come he got a scholarship, if he never worked?'

'Oh, he worked in that. He was superb, a natural—nobody was a bit surprised that Prof. bloke taking him up. And since then he's never stopped working. I don't know how he keeps it up. The only holiday he's ever had in three years—we all told him this but I don't think he appreciated the joke—was when he was in the nick for three months last summer.'

Ruth felt as if he had hit her. It was fate's own reward for prying, a cold, sick turning over in her stomach.

Maxwell looked at her and said, 'Oh, cripes, have I said too much? Forget it, for God's sake. I wasn't thinking. It wasn't anything much.'

'What was it?'

'Look, I'm not getting on the wrong side of Penn. You ask him if you want to know. Let's forget it. A slip of the tongue. I'll just get outside the old sausage and chips and then we'll take the air. I take it you're very much struck? I don't know how he does it, without even trying. The last bird he had—oh, cripes, something else we'd better not talk about. That's old history. Don't you worry. He's all right—had a lot to contend with, you know. You haven't met his parents? No, well, try not to. Although I don't think he has anything to do with them now. Tell me about you. Penn's terribly lucky in lots of ways, having a girl like you, mainly. How did you meet him?'

Ruth told him. She was as glad to be talking about herself as Maxwell was for the subject to be changed. After the shock, Ruth found that she just wanted to forget it. She didn't want to know. Her curiosity was cured. She talked eagerly, covering up the abyss that had yawned beneath her feet for that awful moment: therapeutic small talk that was as necessary as air. When Maxwell had finished they went out and walked along the prom, and Maxwell told her all about the car trade, and the night he had got caught out with the breathalyzer and, although it was all so boring, she latched on to it gratefully and made all the right encouraging remarks, while the sun went down over the sea like a great red flower and the sharpness of dusk nipped bare arms and legs. The arcades and cafés and pubs on the other side of the road were filling up fast. Maxwell glanced at his watch.

'Old Penn's been going a couple of hours. We'll go and pay a visit. Not that he's allowed much let-up till closing time, mind you . . .'

They crossed the road. Ruth knew that her last bus home went in ten minutes' time, and she knew equally well that she wasn't going to be on it. Beyond that she would not think. There was a terrible noise of drunken singing coming out of 'The Jolly Sailor'. She steeled herself against her upbringing, and followed closely on Maxwell's heels, passing from the coolness of the sea air into a hot, sweating riot of humanity. The crush at the bar was appalling.

'Hey, don't get lost,' Maxwell said. 'Stay with me. What'll you have. A Martini? What do you like?'

'Coke,' Ruth said.

'What, are you sure?'

'Yes.' She was looking for Pat, but could not see him. The bar was the longest she had ever seen, and there were about a dozen barmen, but no Pat.

'Where is he?'

'Over there, of course,' Maxwell said. He jerked his head towards the noisiest and most crowded end of the room, where a great rowdy phalanx of maudlin, middle-aged men and women were singing 'Red Sails in the Sunset' to an accomplished but invisible piano accompaniment. Ruth, shoved and trodden on, backed out, not wanting beer all over her best dress. She didn't understand, but had to wait for Maxwell. He came, holding the glasses above his head.

'Can you get through?' he bawled at her, nodding once more in the direction of the singing. 'We might get a seat if anyone's moving out.'

Ruth went unwillingly.

'We haven't got to sing, have we? What a terrible place! Where is Pat?'

'He's playing the piano.'

'He's what?' Ruth thought she was hearing things.

'At the piano, of course. What else do you think he's doing?'

Ruth stared at Maxwell's surprised face, pressed willy-nilly about six inches from her own. He had three glasses clutched under his chin.

'I've got him a bitter, if he can get away for five minutes.'

'Did you say he was playing the piano?'

'Yes. What's wrong? Shove on a bit and we'll tell him we've arrived.'

But Ruth was rooted to the ground. The piano, unlike most pub pianos, was being played with a finesse that even she recognized. The knowledge that this was Pat at work was the biggest contradiction yet, like being hit on the head with the keyboard. She stared at Maxwell.

He said, 'Don't tell me he hasn't even told you that? What he does? When did you two meet? Tonight?'

'What does he do?'

'He's a student at the something college—can't remember which one—of music. Playing the old pianner.'

'He said zoology,' Ruth said faintly.

'He said what?' yelled Maxwell.

'Zoology,' she shouted back.

'You mean I've put my foot in it again? Zoology? Where did he dream that up? All this work he does then—what did you think it was? Looking at elephants under a microscope?'

'Yes. Sort of—I thought——'

'Cripes, he's been having you on! I'll tell him, the old fraud! You haven't even heard him play before? Well, I can tell you, make the most of this, because it's usually the old Beethoven touch, dead gloomy, not decent stuff like this. He only does this for bread and butter. Shove on, girl. Let's go and tip this bitter down his neck.'

Ruth shoved on, in a daze. She put her shoulder between two fat men immediately in front of her, and wedged them apart. 'Steady on, ducks,' said one of them, yielding, and she fell through and found herself at Pat's shoulder.

'Give 'm some room, darling,' said a face in hers.

'We've brought you a bitter, Penn,' Maxwell said, arriving with force, the drinks miraculously intact.

'Thanks,' said Pat, 'I'm ready for one.'

He had launched into a current sentimental ballad which his admirers were taking up with deafening fervour. Ruth, resisting the crush behind her to give him room, gazed down at his fingers on the keyboard, mesmerized by this turn of events. She saw the scab on the side of his right forefinger, and the episode of the sticking-plaster suddenly made sense. How dim she was not to have guessed! After the Festival Hall—only an imbecile would have failed to see a connection.

'She thought you studied elephants for a living,' Maxwell was saying cheerfully. Ruth felt herself going crimson. 'What have you been telling her?'

'Just move your solar plexus out of the way, you fool,' Pat said.

'You're a fraud, Penn. Always were. She's far too good for you. I'll take you on, Ruth—I'll give you a break. I'm worth six of this long-haired, tinkling virtuoso——'

'I'll take *you* on when I get to the end of this,' Pat said.

The fervent, beer-washed voice of the singing crowd rose up in maudlin crescendo, and Ruth watched his fingers go up the keys in a running scale so fast that she could hardly follow them, then down in a complicated progression of chords to a thunderous conclusion.

'A touch of the old Rachmaninovs,' he said, reaching for his beer. 'That's to please the old man here,' he added. 'If I just strum he gives me three quid, but if I give the old master touch, he gives me a fiver. He considers it adds class to the place.'

He got up. 'Let's get a breath of air.'

'Don't be long, darling,' said an anxious woman.

'Five minutes,' he said.

They pushed their way out to a place near the open door, and Pat leaned against the wall and wiped his face with a handkerchief. He had pulled his tie loose and Ruth could see the trickles of sweat down his neck.

'I don't think this was a very good idea,' he said to her. 'You coming to this place.'

'It was a lovely idea,' Maxwell said. 'Speak for yourself.'

'I don't mind,' Ruth said. 'Why did you tell me zoology?'

Pat grinned.

Maxwell said, 'He's afraid of his image. Doesn't want to be thought a pansy. That's it, isn't it, Penn?'

Pat said to him, 'Go and get me another pint. It's on the house. Get rid of him for five minutes,' he said to Ruth.

Maxwell went, quite cheerful.

'People have funny ideas about pianists,' Pat said. 'Think you're just a layabout or something.'

'I think it's marvellous,' Ruth said. Jostled from behind, she squeezed in beside Pat, against the wall. His shoulder was hard against hers. 'I thought, last week—well, I should have guessed. I'm a bit slow. You said it was for your work.'

'Yes. I'm working on that concerto now.'

'Is that what you do, after the bread round?'

'Practise. Yes.'

'You've got a piano where you live?'

'No. There's one in the village hall they let me use. It's quite a good one.'

'What, you have the place to yourself?'

'Except clinic afternoons, and the chiropody and things.'

'Then what happens?'

'I just carry on. They don't mind, only if I'm on scales or just working on a few phrases they keep interrupting and asking for "a proper piece", which is a bit annoying. It's like "Open House". The old ladies always want "Abide with Me".'

He turned and smiled at her. The top of her head was on a level with his upper lip. She noticed he had a scar on his lip, and nice teeth, and she realized that he didn't smile very often, which was why she had never noticed his teeth before.

'They're not keen on Rachmaninov cadenzas.'

He finished off his pint, and Maxwell came back with another.

'Your blonde girl-friend wants you back,' Maxwell said. 'She wants you to play "Smoke Gets in your Eyes". Just about her vintage, I should have said.'

'Never 'eard of it,' Pat said. Maxwell offered him a cigarette which he refused. He offered Ruth one and she shook her head.

'How are you going to get home?' Pat said to her. 'What time's your last bus?'

'It's gone.'

'I'll walk her home,' Maxwell said with an optimistic leer.

'It's twelve miles,' Pat said.

'I was joking, of course!'

'If you stay till I've finished, I can get the bread van,' Pat said. 'I can't think of anything else. Can you?'

'No,' Ruth said. 'Only hitch-hike.'

'On a Saturday night, out of this place! That'd be asking for it. I must get back—there's the boss wondering why the lovely silence. He wants blood, that man.'

He straightened up and looked rather anxiously at Ruth.

'I won't be away till half-past eleven. That all right?'

'Yes. Of course.'

When he had gone Maxwell said, 'He's getting terribly civilized in his old age. Not the fellow he was at all. Shall we take a toddle outside? Bit of fresh air and all that?'

'Why, what was he like before?'

'He wasn't so polite. He said more. You get the feeling now he's being very careful. What's it to be then? A turn down the pier? It's a bit late for a film. Or another noggin farther down?'

Ruth chose the pier, but there was no magic in it with Maxwell. The magic was in her head; she was trying to sort it all out again, turning Pat into a pianist. She wanted Maxwell to talk about Pat, but was sensitive enough to appreciate that Maxwell would rather talk about himself. While he talked, she disentangled fragments that had to be rethought: Clarissa, for example, did not study monkeys under a microscope, but played duets with Pat, an enviably intimate association that Ruth preferred not to dwell on. There was only one point about the revelation that she felt moved to offer to Maxwell:

'I would never have thought . . . you know, you think musicians are sort of—different. Frightfully intellectual and—and superior——' But then she remembered the grey socks of the orchestra in the Festival Hall, and Pat saying it was all for paying their mortgages, making that celestial noise. 'He treats it just like an ordinary job.'

Maxwell said, 'But it is, to him. What else would he have done? If he hadn't taken it up he would have had to go and work in some dead-end job like the rest of us—like the bread round. Who wants to do that every day? He might work very hard practising now, but he knows that, with luck, he might get somewhere—he'll earn a lot of money, and travel, and meet people, and people will admire him. Well, that's not bad, is it? Worth trying. More than most of us will ever aspire to. He's got it all worked out pretty carefully, and he thinks it's worth the effort. It was either that, or just get a job down here, earning the old pittance for your forty-hour week. He never put on airs about it that I remember. At school, it was just something he did, like other people did metalwork or the girls did typing. And he hasn't changed in that, at all.'

They went back to 'The Jolly Sailor' at closing time, and waited for Pat, braced among the extremely cheerful streams of departing guests. He came gratefully, looking very hot and tired.

'Thank God that's over for another week.'

They went outside and Maxwell said, 'If you're getting the van, Penn, you could drop me off too.'

'Yeah, if you like.'

They walked up the street, Ruth in the middle. Maxwell was talking to Pat about someone she didn't know, and Pat walked along saying, 'Yes' at intervals, and yawning. They turned off the Parade down the side street to the bakery, and it was quiet and cool. Pat stopped under a street lamp and pulled some keys out of his pocket.

'There's a couple of coppers coming this way,' Maxwell said quietly. 'Is this okay with——'

'Oh, cripes, of course,' Pat said.

Ruth looked at him, the sharp memory recurring. She felt herself shiver involuntarily. They came up to the gates of the bakery yard and Pat got out the key. The two policemen crossed the road and came towards them. Maxwell said something that Ruth didn't catch and Pat swore, softly but forcefully.

'You live here?'

The policemen had stopped behind them. Pat opened the door and turned round.

'I work here.'

Ruth, watching him, saw him stiffen into an attitude of belligerent defiance that was a shock to her law-abiding soul. He stood in the gateway, the contempt so apparent on his face that it was almost an assault in itself. Ruth was frightened, more by Pat than by the police.

'What's your name?' asked one of the policemen.

'Ask Mitchell. He knows it,' Pat said curtly, jerking his head at the speaker's colleague.

'I asked you,' said the policeman.

Pat hesitated.

Maxwell said, 'His name is Patrick Pennington.'

'That correct?' the policeman asked Pat.

'Yes.'

'Funny time to start work, isn't it?'

Pat said, 'We're getting a van out, if you want to know, to drive home in.' He opened the palm of his hand and showed a car-key lying in it. 'It's the van I drive every day. It's allowed. It's one of the perks of the job. Ask Mr. Simmonds, the manager.'

'Show me your driving licence,' said the policeman.

Pat groped in his back pocket and pulled it out. The policeman took it and studied it intently, and passed it to Mitchell. He glanced at Mitchell and raised an eyebrow.

'All right?'

'Seems in order.' He sounded reluctant.

'It *is* in order,' Pat said.

'Watch it,' said the first policeman.

Ruth saw Maxwell touch Pat's shoulder, an urgent needling of the forefinger. Pat stood rigid, waiting for his licence. Mitchell, a sharp-featured man with a close haircut and hard eyes, leafed it through again and handed it back, unsmiling.

'All right.'

'Thank *you*,' Pat said.

The two policemen walked on. Pat flung open the door of the bakery yard.

'Oh, cripes!' he said. 'Mitchell—the swine——!' His voice shook, the self-control he had evidently exercised during the brief questioning spilling into sharp and lurid epithets to describe Mitchell. The underlying violence frightened Ruth; it was a far stronger passion than she had ever met in her own polite circle.

Maxwell was grinning. 'I thought you were going to get yourself nicked again. That's why I told them your name. You want a keeper, Penn, asking for it like that! You know with Mitchell you've only got to lift your hand to scratch your nose and he's got you for threatening behaviour——'

'Oh, don't tell me!' Pat turned away towards the row of vans. 'I know all about that beggar——'

'Who's Mitchell?' Ruth asked Maxwell, when Pat was out of earshot.

'He's the copper that had it in for Penn when he was still at school. He's one of those—you get to know 'em—they go by the book. They'll get you for anything. And Penn's allergic to policemen anyway, even the uncle types, let alone the baskets like Mitchell. It's his upbringing.' He grinned again, as if it was all quite funny.

Pat drove the van through the gates and they closed them and locked them behind him, and climbed into the van. Ruth felt scrambled and cold, the fear still swinging in her stomach.

'It's all right?' she said to Pat. 'They——'

'It's all right now,' he said. 'We're not supposed to use the vans, but if they'd knocked up Simmonds he'd have said it was all right. Then afterwards he'd have given me the sack. Might still, if they check on it. Not that I care.'

His face by the street-lamps was taut and angry.

'Don't get into trouble for me,' Ruth said. 'I can still get a bus as far as——'

'It's all right.' His voice was sharp. Ruth sat back, silenced.

'Have a bun,' Maxwell said affably, from the back of the van. He passed over a brick-like doughnut.

'Thank you, I'm not that hungry,' Ruth said.

They came out on to the arterial, and Pat put his foot down.

'How are your milligrammes?' Maxwell murmured from the back. 'Speaking from experience, of course.'

'Seeing Mitchell's ugly face like that is shock enough to sober anybody.'

'Yeah, but use your loaf, Penn. He'd love to run you in. You jolly nearly gave him the chance just now.'

'Cripes, I'd like to give *him* three months!'

He pulled out and overtook a row of saloon cars, the speedometer flickering on sixty. Ruth watched the road ahead and the stab of the headlights, remembering that Pat did it every day and knew it well, and presumably knew what was beyond the limit of the lights. The emotions now were painful and mixed, the early sweetness trampled. Having learned so much about Pat in the last few hours, she decided she could well have done without the last episode. She did not like Pat's present bitterness. It fitted in too vividly with the picture of him which she wanted to forget, the picture Maxwell had raised over the cup of coffee. The bit she wouldn't mention to her mother.

As they bumped down the lane to the Hollis cottage, with Maxwell still eating doughnuts in the back, Pat's profile softened slightly, and he turned to Ruth and said, 'I'm sorry about this. It wasn't much of an evening for you.'

'It's all right,' Ruth said. 'Honestly.'

'I hope you're not too late.'

'No.' Ruth hoped so too. The light was still on downstairs.

'I'll see you again.'

But he didn't say when. He turned into her drive and braked, and leaned over and opened the door for her. His hair brushed her cheek.

'I'm sorry,' he said again.

'It's all right,' she repeated.

Maxwell, climbing into her vacated seat, said, 'Good night, Ruth.'

'Good night. And thank you.'

She walked up the long drive, very slowly, listening to the van drive away up the lane. Now, the moment he had gone, she felt an agony of longing for him to be there again. It was so sharp she had to stop in the middle of the drive, unable to face her parents with this empty, demented feeling draining all the sense out of her. She stood and looked up at the sky through the pear-trees, lifting her face and feeling the coolness of the breeze that came off the river. It occurred to her, quite inappropriately, that once these strange feelings had been to do with ponies and winning something very special, the times when she had looked at the sky and been filled with inexplicable longings. It was the only thing she had to compare this present ache with. And now, remembering, every inexplicable longing she had ever experienced in the past was as nothing at all compared to this crushing sense of desolation at Pat's going.

'Ruth, are you there?'

Her mother was standing at the kitchen door. Ruth heard her voice and started walking again.

'Are you mad?' her mother said. 'I heard the car go off ages ago. How can you take so long to walk up the drive? Some of us want to go to bed tonight.'

'I'm not stopping you,' Ruth said.

'Dear Ruth,' her mother said ominously, 'you are stopping me.'

'Oh, I'm sorry, but he didn't finish till half-past eleven. We came straight home then. You aren't cross?'

'We—ll. Not now, I suppose.' She sighed. 'One worries—the Saturday night roads ... Do you want a cup of tea?' She yawned.

'No. It doesn't matter. Do you know, he's a pianist!'

'Zoology, you said. What do you mean? He plays for a hobby?'

'No. It's what he's a student of. The zoology was just a joke. He plays the piano *fantastically*.'

'Good gracious, you do surprise me! He doesn't look—well, what do pianists look like? I don't really know. Not like that, I'm sure. Really? Yes, that *is* a surprise, I must say.'

Ruth was gratified to notice that the surprise was a pleasant one, judging by her mother's face. Pianists were, she supposed, eminently respectable—but, even in this generalization, Pat was a contradiction. The other things she had found out she did not mention.

'Are you seeing him again?' Mrs. Hollis asked, almost as if she was quite keen.

'Yes,' Ruth said quietly. 'Oh yes.'

And she went to bed and prayed that she had spoken the truth.

Chapter 4

Ruth did not see Pat all the next week, and he left no message. When, having broken up for the summer holidays, she arrived home on Friday, she missed him by five minutes. It was a hot, cloudless day. Having run all the way from the bus-stop, she could have wept when her mother said:

'He was early today.'

Ruth ate her lunch in silence. Her mother watched her without saying anything. When she had finished, Ruth went upstairs and changed into her old jeans and pink gingham shirt, did her eyes with great care, tied her hair back with a pink scarf and went out to the shed to fetch her bicycle.

'I'm just going for a ride,' she said.

Her nonchalance was not lost on Mrs. Hollis. 'Bit hot, isn't it?'

But Ruth had gone.

It was eight miles across country lanes to Fiddler's End, far enough for Ruth to have terrible pangs of doubt about what she was doing.

'But it can't be worse,' she said to herself firmly, 'than not knowing whether he bothers or whether he doesn't. If he chucks me out, I can forget him.' She wouldn't, but she could start trying. She knew very well that there was much to be said for showing a boy one didn't care, and going out with somebody else, but she was too desperately honest to contemplate such a course. Since Gordon Hargreaves had found out that she had gone out with the same boy two Saturdays running he had kept calling, turning round with a great deal of swanky revving in his new car in their narrow drive and suggesting a 'run out', but Ruth could hardly bear to be civil to him. Peter McNair came down from the stables in his father's car to tell her that Toad was doing very well, and he looked at her as if he had heard the news, with a reflective light in his normally brotherly eye which she had never seen before, and had asked her if she'd fancy going to see a film. But Ruth had laughed, and he hadn't minded a bit. So it worked that way round.

'I'm doing all the wrong things,' she told herself, pedalling hard. But nothing would have turned her back. Her only panic was that it was too hot to work, surely? He would be somewhere else, gone swimming, or at home, and she wouldn't find him. Her sweaty pilgrimage would be in vain.

'Oh no!' she said out loud to the green elm-tops over her head, and they nodded at her passing, impassive, untroubled by her little human passion. 'I love him,' she said out loud again, and a passing car hooted at her and she shouted back, 'Hog!'

The village hall at Fiddler's End had been built by the villagers themselves in 1929, and looked it. Ruth, approaching, saw that it was surrounded by empty prams, and realized that she had chosen clinic day. But the sight was comforting rather than disappointing, for it was the awful, actual moment of Pat's turning round and seeing her in the empty hall that she had dreaded most and now, with lots of mothers and babies to blur the confrontation, she did not feel quite so frightened.

Not quite. It was still bad enough. She laid her bike against the wall and stood outside the door, her heart thudding. He was there, because she could hear the piano. The sound petrified her. She could not bring herself to open the door.

Someone else opened it from the inside and a child walked into her knees.

'Oh, Trevor, look where you're going!' said its mother.

Ruth disentangled herself, smiled like an idiot, and went in, because the woman was holding the door. She felt almost faint, and leaned against the wall, telling herself it was the eight miles, not Pat. But she knew it was Pat. She could not take another step.

The piano was on the stage, along with a pile of rickety card-tables, sagging screens, and ancient wooden folding chairs. Pat had his back to her, and was playing what sounded like some sort of a scale. He had on a faded blue shirt, pulled out over his jeans, the sleeves rolled up. His eyes on the music in front of him, he seemed oblivious of several toddlers who were climbing on to the stage and jumping off with shouts of glee right behind him, the whistling of a boiling kettle somewhere in the wings and the general hubbub of about thirty babies, half of them crying, and thirty mothers, most of them talking, several helpers in white coats giving orders and a group of tea-makers putting out cups and saucers. Ruth stared, her mental image of lonely genius at work shattered.

A woman in a white coat bustled up to her and said, 'Look, dear, just go and tell the doctor I've got the umbilical hernia waiting, if he doesn't mind. It's very crochety in this heat and its mother wants to get home. He's through the door at the bottom.'

Ruth went, knocked at the door and put her head in. A doctor was poised over a baby, who was screwing up its face ready to yell. He looked up, and the baby, reprieved, paused in its intake of angry breath. Ruth got her message in quickly, and the doctor said, 'Very well. Tell her I'm through with this now. I'll have it next.'

Ruth took the news back to the nurse.

'Take him a cup of tea, dear,' she said. 'Go and tell the ladies. They forget him if I don't watch. No sugar.'

Ruth went over to the tea-urn, and said, 'Can I have one for the doctor?'

'Oh, yes. Give him the cup with the roses on, Maud. It isn't cracked. He doesn't take sugar. Here you are, dear.'

Ruth took it. The doctor said, 'Marvellous. Tell nurse there's a box of cotton-wool in the back of my car, will you? I shall want it before I'm through. Here's the key.'

Ruth took the message back and the nurse said, 'It's the red Cortina, dear, round the back. Thank you ever so much.'

Ruth fetched the cotton-wool and delivered it and heard one of the tea-ladies shrill down the hall, 'Do you want a cup of tea, Pat? How many sugars?'

'Two,' he called back.

Ruth went back to the tea-urn and said firmly, 'I'll take it.'

'Oh, thank you, dear. I'll stir it first. We're short of spoons.'

Ruth took the cup of tea down the hall, her hands shaking slightly. She climbed up on to the platform and put it on the top of the piano.

'Your tea.'

'Thanks,' Pat said. He did not stop playing, or even look up.

Ruth did not move, watching his hands doing something extraordinarily complex, and the back of his head, the neck slightly bent, the hair looking damp with the heat. And as she didn't go away, he looked up and, although he did not stop playing, he hit two wrong notes which even Ruth recognized. She tried desperately to divine his reaction, not expecting—from him—anything as extreme as joy, but dreading a veiled exasperation. And in her anxiety, she saw both: his eyes widened with what was surely pleasure, only to be immediately tempered by . . . she was not sure. Doubt possibly. A withdrawal. But even then he smiled, still playing.

'You made me play two wrong notes,' he said, and stopped. 'That's very bad.'

'Of me?' she asked hesitantly.

'No, of me.'

'You don't mind?' she said. 'It was so hot, I thought you might—well, it's too hot to play, I thought . . . I just missed you at lunchtime . . .'

'Cripes, yes, it is hot.' He shoved his chair back and leaned backwards, making it creak dangerously.

'I thought you might be swimming or something. But I hadn't anything to do.'

'The tide's high at six. I might go then.' He took a watch out of his back pocket and looked at it. 'I've only been going an hour.' He looked at her reflectively, and she saw beads of sweat on his upper lip, and the scar. She remembered the policeman, and pushed the memory away. She met his eyes, and neither of them looked away. Pat sighed. Ruth felt terrible, drowned by his displeasure.

'I'm sorry,' she whispered.

'No,' he said. 'You've got it all wrong.' He put up a hand and pushed his hair off his forehead with an irritated gesture. 'It's what I've *got* to do,' he said. 'Not what I want.'

'All the time?'

'Yes. Now. I've got to play in a concert. Until after the concert.'

'When is the concert?'

'Three weeks tomorrow.'

'It's very important?'

'Yes. It's not just me making a fool of myself on my own, but playing with an orchestra. That concerto we heard at the Festival Hall.'

Ruth was awed. 'You!'

'It doesn't just happen,' he said. 'It takes hours and hours for months. I've packed in the bread, as from tomorrow, to give myself more time.'

'Oh, I'm sorry. I do see! I'm sorry I came. I didn't realize it was like that!'

'I'm not sorry you came,' he said. 'I just have to explain why I can't take you out or anything. It's not because——' He hesitated. 'Oh, God, you distract me!'

Ruth did not say anything, her inside expanding with a glory that left no breath for words. She told herself that he used the word 'distract' strictly in the sense of distraction from his work, not in the sense of going out of his mind like an Elizabethan poet, but it was enough. It was a perfect word, and described her own feelings for him utterly.

He glanced at the watch again.

'Look, give me till—say—half-past five. Then we'll go for a walk down the river. If the hall was free tonight I'd stop now and work tonight instead, but it's the Youth Club Fridays. Would that be okay by you? Would you mind hanging around?'

'No.'

'All right.' He smiled, and pulled his chair up to the piano again. 'It's a date.'

'I'll come back at half-past five.'

Ruth went out of the hall, not seeing anything. There was a playing-field outside, and a clump of elm trees, and a man mowing the cricket-pitch with a tractor-mower. Ruth lay in the shade of the elms, and through the open windows of the hall she could hear Pat playing again. Every time the man mowing came down the field the noise of the mower drowned the piano, but when he moved away in the opposite direction she could hear Pat again. They were complementary, the two aural evidences of man's hard work, ebbing and flowing, and Ruth lay curled, feeling the sun on her back and the coolness of the shade just covering her head, and basked in the sensation of being utterly, fantastically content. Even just lying there, smelling the new-mown grass and listening to the work and the fretful babies, she was aware of her privilege, even apart from the other incredible and magical knowledge that she had just received from Pat's very own lips: it was happiness strong enough to hurt. 'Being me,' she thought . . . 'I would not be anyone, anyone, *anyone* else in the whole of the world, in the whole of outer space right to the farthest, farthest invisible star.' And the music came down the keyboard like a waterfall finding its way over tumbled rocks, and the mower approached inexorably, throwing up its fountains of cropped green, spreading its aura of summer on the lightest of July zephyrs. Ruth turned on to her back and thought, 'It is impossible to be happier than this. If only you could bottle it, like plums, for afterwards . . .' And the time was suspended, and everything was rolled into this exquisite essence of perfect content, until the prams started to move away and the noisy toddlers were guided to their teas, and the doctor came out and slammed the doors of his red Cortina, and the sun had taken on the richness of late afternoon, the heaviness of its warmth hinting of over-ripeness, like a Mediterranean peach. Ruth felt herself sticky and lax with the heat. The mowing man finished. Ruth asked him the time, and he said, 'Quarter to five.'

She had the piano all to herself. It was playing the same thing over and over again, very deliberately. Some little boys came and started playing with the drinking-fountain, squirting it in all directions. Two of them went over to the hall and hung through the open windows, shouting, 'Pat, play us "Instant Love"!' But the music did not falter in its stride.

At twenty past five, Ruth went into the hall again and sat on one of the rickety chairs by the door. She thought she would make no noise at all, but the ancient chair betrayed her with its complaint. Pat turned round and she said hastily, 'I'm ten minutes early. Don't stop!'

'It's all right, I'm through,' he said.

She went over to the platform and stepped up beside the piano. 'I've been listening, outside. Lying in the sun.'

'Poor you! Did it send you to sleep?'

'No.' She hesitated. He was closing the lid. 'Will you play me something? Before we go. Just short.'

' "Red Sails in the Sunset"?' He grinned.

'No.'

He opened the lid again. 'The scale of C major?'

'No.'

He considered for a moment, then started to play a piece that was very familiar to Ruth, although she had no idea what it was. It was lilting and wistful, and she could have sung the melody if she had wished.

'All right?' He raised his eyebrows inquiringly.

'Yes. Exactly.'

It was effortless and perfect, and he played it through to the end, closing with the softest and most delicate chords which hung and faded in the quiet hall like the grains of dust raining through the evening sunlight. Ruth was touched. It was all that she had wanted. He did not move until there was complete silence again, then he closed the lid without saying anything, and stood up, shoving back the chair. He looked moved too, but to gloom, Ruth thought, with a touch of anxiety.

'We'll go.' He jumped down from the platform, and she followed. They went out of the door into the heat, and he locked it behind him.

'What was that piece?'

'A Brahms waltz.'

'Hasn't it got a name?' She wanted it to remember.

'Number fifteen. Opus thirty-nine.'

It hadn't sounded like numbers, to Ruth. She walked by his side, and he changed again, the gloom dispersing.

'We'll go down the river, and afterwards you can come back and have tea. Mrs. Bates won't mind.'

The village street was short; a few cottages and council houses, a post-office, a grocer's, and a church, and a lot of elm trees petered out in a gravel lane with high hedges on either side. Midges swarmed and bit in the shade, and skylarks rose up from the grass behind the hedge, shrilling and hovering.

'It's a dead-end, this place,' Pat said. 'Doesn't go anywhere. Nothing happens.'

'It's your home? You've always lived here?'

'Yes. I was born here.'

'I like these sort of places.'

'It's all right, compared with some. Change from London, anyway.'

The lane opened out, giving on to pastures and a sea-wall, with some boatsheds and boats pulled out. When they climbed the wall, the river was at their feet, lipping over half-submerged acres of sea-lavender, shining and tranquil in the fullness of the tide. A few boats swung at moorings, quiet as swans. A man came out of the boatshed and said, 'Hullo, Pat.' He looked at Ruth as if considering the lines of a boat.

'Hi, Jim,' Pat said.

He turned and led the way along the sea-wall, away from the boatshed. There was nothing, only the flatness of reclaimed pasture, and the line of the wall, curving, with withies to mark the mud, and the swamps of sea-lavender bathing in the tide. The sky was cloudless, the skylarks invisible, only the shrillness falling. Pat flung himself down in the long grass where the wall changed direction and the sun beat straight across on to the slope.

'Fiddler's End Riviera,' he said. 'Welcome.'

He shut his eyes, stretched out on his back, his hands clasped behind his head. Ruth slipped down beside him, rested her chin on her knees, and looked out over the water. 'It's better than Northend,' she said. 'Why do they go there?'

'To leave this for us,' Pat said. He turned his head and looked at her, squinting against the sun. 'I'm going to swim. I suppose you're too well brought-up to swim in your underwear?'

'Yes. Besides, I can't. I'd drown.' The warnings her mother had given her swam into her head as she watched Pat undress, and drowned too. He was all prepared, with swimming-trunks on under his jeans.

'There's no bath at Bates',' he said. 'We have to make the best of days like this.'

He flung his clothes up on the wall and stretched his legs out down the slope into the water. He had long straight toes to match his fingers, and brown hairy legs. Ruth remembered Gordon Hargreaves' girlish white legs at the Northend Lido, and giggled. Round his neck Pat wore a gold chain with a small medallion hanging on it. It was old and worn, like a rubbed coin, with what looked like a man's head in relief. Ruth was curious, wondering whether any sentimental associations were attached. The thought disturbed her.

Pat flicked some water at her.

'Go on,' Ruth said. 'Chicken!'

'I'll take you with me if you don't watch out.'

He got up and waded out across a narrow stretch of salting

56

to where a line of stakes showed where the steep bank was, groped for a moment for a foothold hidden under the surface, and dived in. Ruth pulled his discarded shirt towards her, and lay back, using it to keep the scratchy grass off her neck and face. She watched Pat swim away against the tide, not taking her eyes off him, until it was hard to see him against the brilliance of the sun on the water. He swam like he played the piano, not just an idle dabble, but properly, like the life-savers on Northend beach. She had known it would be like that; she had known that he would not let her down: that he would not be flabby and white and feeble. Nothing he could do now would be wrong in her eyes. She was perfectly safe.

About fifteen minutes later he came back and lay on his front in the grass beside her to dry.

'Better than work,' he said, and sighed.

'You're a very good swimmer.'

'Yeah. I'm good at useless things. Swimming and soccer and playing the piano. Where do they get you?'

'The piano's getting you somewhere surely?'

'It's such ruddy hard work. And how do I know if anything'll come of it?'

'What about this concert then? Someone must think you're good enough. Won't all the critics come, and shout bravo, and give you rave notices? And you'll be famous overnight?'

'No. The critics will write, "As yet his technique lacks the reserves required by an aspiring virtuoso in this demanding part." And you know they can't play a flaming scale themselves. And all the fat aldermen of Northend will come to see if I'm worth my grant.'

'It's going to be in Northend then?'

'Yes. At the Pavilion.'

'Is it to do with this German exchange, with the town Northend is twinned with, or whatever they call it? "A cultural exchange" . . . I've read about it in the paper.'

'Yes. That's it. We've sent them a load of hammy song-and-dancers off the end of the pier, and they're sending us one of the best orchestras in Europe. It's stopping off here on its way to America. And our egg-headed town council thought it would be nice to have a local boy as soloist. And if I don't feel like it, they might not feel like continuing my grant.'

'Is that what they said!'

'It's what they meant. They wrapped it up with a lot of hot air.'

'What did they say about it at college? Your Professor?'

'Oh, he thinks it's the chance of a lifetime.'

Ruth picked a blade of grass. 'I see why you have to work. I didn't know all this.' The whole idea of what he was up against was very sobering. She imagined most music students had cultured backgrounds with encouraging parents, not Mrs. Bates with no bathroom. She felt sure Clarissa had a bathroom.

'Can I come to the concert?'

'If you want. They've graciously given me six free tickets. You can have them all.'

She turned her head and considered him, concerned and frowning. He turned at the same time and pressed down the grass that blurred his view of her face, and looked at her in the same way as the man outside the boatshed had looked at her.

'Are you sure you won't come for a swim?'

She shook her head, aware now that he had good reason to think her an easy girl, since she had cycled eight miles without an invitation merely to see him. A cold doubt squeezed her, and her mother's words, nebulous as the rising heat that quivered over the horizon, touched her and were forgotten. She thought she knew everything, and she knew that she knew nothing. She just went on sitting there, watching how the water ran off his hair and in sliding, hesitant drops down over the muscles of his back. He didn't say any more, but laid his cheek on his hand and shut his eyes. His face was cold and angry.

'Why did you come?' he said. 'It doesn't help anything at all.'

Ruth felt sick. She got up and stood for a moment, breaking a stalk of grass over and over in her hand.

'It's not all me . . . you asked me before . . .'

But there wasn't anything to say that would put the moment right. The river and the setting sun were still so lovely that it hurt. She started walking back along the sea-wall, the heat striking her back, the midges in a cloud round her head. The tide had turned and the sea-lavender was uncovering in hazy blue profusion to meet the mud. Ruth felt nothing. She came to

58

the boatshed and the man who had said hullo was just locking up. He had secured the padlock, and came to the top of the wall where the steps were just as Ruth arrived at the same spot. It was necessary to say something and he said, 'After you.'

'Thank you.'

She went down the steps and he followed her.

'What've you done with Pat?' he said.

She shook her head, not trusting herself to say anything, and the man said, 'Tch, tch, tch,' with his tongue against his teeth. He fetched a bicycle that leaned against a store of timber, and put his leg over the saddle.

'He's a funny lad,' he said. 'Always was.'

He cycled away. Ruth supposed she should follow, and find her own bicycle, but she had no will to walk any farther. She told herself it was the heat, and sat on the pile of timber, looking back the way she had come. She remembered earlier and the feelings she had wanted to bottle for future use. She had not thought she would need them so soon. The fall from such heights was like being hanged, breaking one's neck. 'Dramatizing!' she mocked at herself. It was happening all the time; the incident was described by a simple, paltry little word: tiff. Like sniff and piffle. Infinitesimal. She picked at a splinter of wood, pulling a long string out of the grain, hurting her finger-nails.

In the distance, Pat got up and pulled on his jeans and shirt. He started walking back along the sea-wall, hands in pockets, staring at the ground, kicking the grass. Ruth pulled at another splinter. He must have seen her, pink against the store-shed, but he took no avoiding action, and Ruth went on sitting there, the blood thudding. He came down the steps and looked at her, his face still dark.

'Come on. Let's go and get some tea.'

Ruth slipped off the timber and they walked up the lane. Everything seemed much more real to Ruth this time, than when they had walked down. She was suspended, her feelings put away. Pat did not say anything at all, until they had walked through the village and came to the gate of the end cottage, a nineteen-twenties semi with a privet hedge in front.

'This is Bates',' He pushed open the gate and waited for her.

'I'll go home,' she said. 'It doesn't matter.'

'No. She won't mind. Come on.'

Ruth went up the path and Pat followed. 'Go on in,' he said.

The kitchen door was open and a fat grey-haired woman was buttering bread at a table. She was comfortable and motherly-looking in a way Ruth thought of as old-fashioned.

'My, it's hot,' she said. 'Come through, dear. I know I take up a lot of room, but you're little enough.'

'This is Ruth,' Pat said.

'Pleased to meet you, dear.'

'I said she could stay to tea.'

'All right, dear. It's just salad, but there's plenty of ham and tomatoes. I've laid the table in the other room. It won't be a minute. Take her through, Pat.'

Ruth thought, in spite of her easy way, Mrs. Bates' eyes didn't miss much, taking her in, and resting reflectively on Pat's closed-up face. She was shrewd, as well as pleasant in her manner.

'Can I take something?' Ruth asked her.

'Yes, the tomatoes. And the sugar. There you are. The kettle's on already. It won't be a minute. You look as if you could do with a cup of tea.'

'Yes. Thank you. I could.'

Ruth took the things and went through into the other room, which was very small, with french windows opening on to a strip of garden. The table was covered with a chenille cloth, and a white damask one, and there was a vase of plastic roses pushed against the wall. There were two fireside chairs in green moquette and a tiled fire-place with photographs on the mantel-piece, and a television set. Pat turned on the television and sat down in the chair facing it. Ruth put down the tomatoes and the sugar and went back for more. It was almost as if Pat wasn't there at all, but she felt strangely at home.

'There's just the two of you, dear. Dad'll be late tonight. There's a darts' match and they're going in the coach. Here's the tea. I think that's everything. I'll just do a spot of ironing and leave you in peace. Shout if you want anything.'

'Yes. Thank you. That's lovely.'

She went back with the tea. There was soccer on the television and Pat came to the table watching it, and sat with his back to the window where he could see it.

'I thought soccer was a winter thing,' Ruth said.

Pat grunted. He reached for the tomatoes, and Ruth poured

him a cup of tea and pushed it over. 'It's just as if we're married,' she thought, 'me with the teapot and him with the telly and nothing to say.'

'Thanks,' he said. Ruth felt she had scored a point.

She did not venture anything else, but ate in silence. Pat ate and watched the television. When she had finished, Ruth got up and took her cup of tea and sat on the step of the french windows, looking down the garden. It was so stupid, she thought. But the way things happened. And afterwards you knew you should have said this or that, or made just one gesture, and it would have been all right. But now there wasn't anything that presented itself. The whole day was a horrible failure, and then afterwards, when she would start thinking about it, she could not bear to contemplate.

There was a sound of voices in the kitchen, Mrs. Bates' and a man's. The man's was loud and impatient, although Ruth could not catch the words. The kitchen door was round the corner from where she sat.

'Pat!' Mrs. Bates' voice called. 'It's your father.'

'What's he want?' Pat shouted back, still watching the screen.

'He wants you to help him move a wardrobe.'

'Oh, go to hell,' Pat said. Raising his voice he shouted, 'I'm not going to lift things, you know that!' But he got up, all the same, and went to the door. 'I won't be long,' he said to Ruth, and went out. Ruth nearly said, 'It won't make any difference,' but didn't. She heard him go out through the kitchen, and his father's voice, and then the two voices receded down the garden path.

Mrs. Bates came in. 'All right, dear?'

'Yes, thank you.'

'Sorry about that. I told him Pat had someone with him, but you can't tell him anything, I'm afraid. He's like that. Whatever he wants, that's it.'

Ruth was wondering whether she should go. She got up and put her cup and saucer on the table.

'Perhaps I ought to be getting along. I've got quite a way to go.'

'Oh, you can't go before Pat comes back, dear!'

'I don't think he'll be much bothered,' she said. She meant it to sound light, but it sounded bitter and shaky, the way she felt. She regretted it instantly.

'Pat's a very moody boy. Don't be upset,' Mrs. Bates said. She looked at Ruth anxiously. 'Here, have another cup of tea.' She started pouring one out, before Ruth could say anything. 'He could do with a nice girl like you. He works too hard.'

'I don't think he wants to be—distracted.'

'That's a matter of opinion. You stay with him, lovey. You're the sort. The one he had last year did him no good at all—a right nasty piece she was. And when they split up I was glad, I can tell you. But you're different. I can see you're a nice girl. Just what he needs.'

'Interfering old busybody,' Ruth thought. But the woman was kindly, and obviously spoke with concern for Pat, which warmed Ruth to her.

'That's my boy, on the mantelpiece.' Mrs. Bates waved her hand to a photograph of a bearded young man with long hair. 'He looks better without all that face fungus, but that's the way it is these days. He's a folk-singer. Done very well for himself. Funny, isn't it, the things they make a living at these days? There's the dad, worked on the farm all his life since he was fourteen, and not a penny saved, and there's John travelling all over the country, his own car, name in the *Radio Times* . . . makes me wonder sometimes.'

'He must be good, to have got on like that. There's lots of competition.'

'Yes, he always had a nice voice. Can't say as I like the stuff he sings though.'

'He and Pat were at school together?'

'Yes. Pat lived over the road, but he was always in here. He set John off really—John was always very shy, and he wouldn't sing in public, but Pat used to bully him something terrible. He played the harmonica with him, it really did sound very nice. But there were times I used to worry—I used to think Pat was a bad influence on our boy. John's very quiet, you see. And Pat was—well—he got into a lot of trouble, put it that way. Pranks really, but he was wild compared with John. His parents were no help to him, that was at the bottom of it. The only good thing his mother ever did for him was make him keep on with his music. She used to nag him something awful. We used to think it funny, really, a rough lad like that, but it turned out she was right after all. It's amazing how well he's got on. Did he tell you about the concert he's playing in next month?'

Ruth nodded.

'I know he's played in lots of concerts before, but this one is a bit special—to us anyway. Being as it's in Northend and the mayor and the corporation and all that will be there, and this orchestra's very famous, I believe. We're all going—not as we care much for that sort of thing as a rule, but when it's in the family, so to speak . . .'

Ruth drank her third cup of tea, aware of a pang of regret for the uncomplicated baker's boy she had first set eyes on. Or was it sensing the complications that had been the attraction in the first place? If Pat had been a carefree roundsman, chatting her up and happy to stop for cups of tea in the kitchen, she would probably have been bored by him. The way it had turned out, she knew that a good part of Pat's attraction to her was this difficult core so amply explained by Mrs. Bates. She had always been attracted by difficulties. Both her ponies had been difficult, not ready-schooled, well-mannered animals like Gordon Hargreaves, but prickly, uncertain creatures with wild pasts . . . it all fitted in . . . she had only herself to blame.

She put the teacup on the table. 'I really must go.' The sun had gone, and she had no lights on her bike. 'It's been very kind of you——'

'Oh, dear, you must see Pat before you're off. He's only across the road—go and shout him good-bye, dear. It's a bit awkward, you know—they don't like his preferring it here. Only natural, I suppose, but they can be nasty when they choose.'

'I'm all right,' Ruth said firmly. 'I'll go and fetch my bicycle from the village hall, and I'll probably see him on my way back. Thank you very much for the tea.'

She left as firmly as she had spoken, feeling stifled by all the currents that had flowed over her afternoon happiness. She wanted cool air and her own company, and the comfort of a few private tears. She fetched her bicycle, and got on it, and was coming back past the Bates' house when Pat came down the path of the house opposite. She saw him, wobbled, and called out, 'Good-bye. I've got to go—I've got no lights.'

'Hey, wait a minute!' he shouted.

She knew she should have kept on going, but she didn't. She stopped with one foot on the kerb, and he came across the road.

'You've got time yet,' he said.

'I'm going.'

'I'll walk up to the main road with you.'

She got off and started to push the bike, and he walked beside her. She wasn't going to say anything, but leave it to him, but he didn't say anything either, and they walked in silence. When they got to the main road she got on again, angry and miserable.

'Good-bye then.'

'Look, I——' He paused, looked at her, and looked away. 'Oh, blast! It's no good. Leave it. Forget it. I'm sorry if I messed anything up for you.'

And he turned and walked back the way he had come. Ruth shoved off from the grass verge, and set off for home.

Chapter 5

'Well, I'm glad, and won't pretend otherwise,' her mother said. 'Don't expect me to. All the piano playing in the world doesn't alter the fact that he's got a very dubious past. I've heard that he's recently done time for "causing grievous bodily harm". I was going to ask you about it. Has he told you anything about it?'

'No!'

'Did you know?'

'No! I heard something—Maxwell said something, but not what it was for . . . I didn't ask.'

'You don't want to know, do you?'

'No!'

'Oh, Ruth, see sense! You're well out of it.'

'You think I can just switch it off! Like—like knocking off potatoes because you're slimming or something! He's not like anybody else!'

'It's only a crush. You'll go through it lots of times before you're married.' The complacency of the remark goaded Ruth more than anything else her mother could have chosen to say.

'All right, you tell *me* how I feel! You don't know anything about it! You never did, else how could you say a thing like that? The way you—you and Daddy—you've forgotten—forgotten what it's all about——'

She gave a great hiccup, the tears spurting up.

'Oh, Ruth,' her mother said. 'You just don't know.' She wasn't angry. Ruth picked up her empty teacup and flung it with all her force across the kitchen. It hit the wall above the kitchen door, just as Ted appeared in the doorway.

'Ruth!' Her mother sprang up, furious.

'Hey! It's just like home!' Ted said. 'I come here for a bit of peace and quiet——'

'If I was Barbara I'd throw things at you too,' Ruth shouted. 'Always running back to mummy! You're all horrible!'

'Get out!' her mother said. 'Go up to your room.'

Ruth flounced round and slammed the door behind her.

'Good heavens!' Ted said. 'What's up with her?'

'It's her love life,' Mrs. Hollis said tightly, filling the kettle.

'Obviously not running smooth. It must be true.'

'She thinks it's never happened to anyone else. She's so naïve.'

'Everybody thinks nobody's ever suffered like they have. The only thing with me is, I don't just think, I know.' He slumped down in the chair Ruth had so recently leapt out of. 'Do you think there was some truth in what she said?'

'Probably. Oh, my children! Why are they so much more trouble than everyone else's——!'

'It's their upbringing,' Ted said. 'Don't you start suffering too. Let's all throw cups. It must relieve something.'

'She's never done anything like that before. We've had ten days of utter misery, but no violence up till now.'

'He's thrown her over, I take it?'

'Yes, but I don't know what happened exactly. I never asked her. What sparked this little incident off was my telling her I was pleased.'

'The soul of tact.'

'But he's done time, Ted! For assault. "Grievous bodily harm", or whatever they call it. I mean, I think I'm very tolerant, but it would be a funny mother who approved of that.'

'I wouldn't like to tangle with him. I thought that the first time I set eyes on him. She does choose 'em, doesn't she?'

'Well, when there's Gordon, and Peter . . . I know this one's got a very romantic profession, but——'

'Yes, but she fell for him when she thought he was just a baker's roundsman. It's the old black magic, Ma, you can't deny it. You don't understand——'

'Oh, don't you start!'

The kettle started to boil, and she turned to it automatically. At the same time there was a knock on the open door and someone said, 'Is Ruth around?'

66

Ted, turning round abruptly, had the grace to blush. Mrs. Hollis thumped the teapot down with a crash that nearly sent it the same way as Ruth's cup, and said grimly, 'Very much so.'

'Come in,' Ted said.

Pat stepped over the threshold and said, 'I'd like to have a word with her.' He looked neither embarrassed nor particularly friendly, but much as if he had come for the bread money.

'I thought——' Mrs. Hollis said, annoyed. Then she stopped herself, and poured the water into the teapot. 'It's none of my business, I suppose. Call her, Ted.'

Ted opened the door and roared up the stairs, 'Ruth, Pat's here! He wants a word with you!'

There was a long silence, and then, distantly, 'If you think that's funny——'

'Oh, heavens,' Ted said, and went out, shutting the door behind him.

Mrs. Hollis got out the teacups, including one for Pat, and the teaspoons and the sugar and the milk, all with great concentration. She could think of nothing to say to him, and he obviously wasn't going to volunteer a word. He stood leaning against the door-post, gazing into space, his hands in his pockets. He was wearing the usual jeans and a navy-blue tee-shirt, and the ominous physique was only too apparent. The words 'grievous bodily harm' went through Mrs. Hollis's head again, the quaintness of the phrase accentuating its essential gravity rather than adding any touch of charm. The coldness of his face did not invite her to question him. She lacked the required insolence, she told herself, and decided that the whole problem was man's work. If the friendship was on again, Ruth's father would have to have a chat with the boy. She poured the tea.

'You'll have one?'

'Thanks.'

Gordon Hargreaves would have said, 'Thank you very much, Mrs. Hollis. It's very kind of you.'

Ted came in, grinning all over his face, and said, 'She's on her way. Which is mine?'

'That one's got one sugar. How many do you have, Pat?'

'Two.'

He moved off the door-post and came to the table. Ted kicked out a chair for him, and he sat down.

'You packed in the bread then?'

'Yeah. I had enough.'

'You're not working now?'

'No. I'll get something else in a week or two. You can get jobs easy in Northend this time of year.'

The door opened and Ruth came in. Pat turned and looked at her, and said, 'Hullo.'

She nodded at him, her white face flushing up. She took the cup of tea her mother passed to her, and carried it to the draining-board, and looked out across the garden. Mrs. Hollis approved her nonchalance, but knew her well enough to realize that she did not trust showing her face to the room.

'I just came to see if you wanted to come up to London on Saturday. Make it a day,' Pat said, equally nonchalant.

'What to do?'

'I've got to play in a concert. But afterwards I thought we could come back and meet Maxwell and his girl and have a meal and go to a disco or something. Whatever you'd like.'

Ruth went on contemplating the garden, trying to stop the glory showing in her face.

'Yes, I don't mind.'

'Where's the concert?' Mrs. Hollis asked. 'The Festival Hall?'

Pat smiled faintly: 'Not yet. This one's Hampstead. Somebody's church restoration fund.'

The word Hampstead stung Ruth like a hypodermic needle. She turned round and looked keenly at Pat, but he showed neither cunning nor embarrassment. She opened her mouth to inquire further, but he smiled at her, and he was brown with swimming and his hair had grown and curled over his ears and she was lost. She felt herself plummeting, helpless.

'Yes,' she said.

'It sounds frightfully respectable,' Ted said.

'Yes, it is.'

'And you'll bring her home, I take it, after the disco?' Mrs. Hollis put in. Ruth glared at her.

'Yes,' Pat said.

He got up, and said to Ruth, 'I'll meet you on the train, like we did before. Okay? Ten-forty from Northend.'

'Yes. All right.'

He moved over to the door. Ruth made to follow him but her

mother said, 'Wash up the cups, Ruth. Come along. I've got to start getting a meal together and I want the table.' She fixed Ruth with an eye that was impossible to ignore. Ruth glowered at her again. Pat went out and down the drive and Mrs. Hollis said sharply, 'You don't have to show you're *besotted*! Yes, yes, yes . . . I don't know!'

'No,' said Ruth.

She was in a dream, and broke a cup.

'Any more today?' Mrs. Hollis asked, her voice edgy with despair.

'What did you say?' Ruth asked.

They met on the train, according to plan. Ruth, having considered the implications of the invitation very carefully since it was offered, had a good many suspicions in the back of her mind but resolved to say nothing. She did not want to nag. Nor did she want the worst of the suspicions confirmed. She would please her mother and not be besotted, and live in hopes that the day would turn out all right. She had dressed very carefully in a slightly hippyish dress of a peculiar reddish-brownish-purplish design which she considered suited her dark colouring and was the best she could muster against Clarissa. Her mother had groaned when she saw it, but Pat raised his eyebrows and said, 'That's nice.' Ruth felt herself purring inside. Pat had had a slight haircut, but otherwise looked as casual as usual; he had a tatty grip with his 'other gear' in it.

The strongest of Ruth's suspicions was that Clarissa was the 'right nasty piece' who had done Pat no good at all, according to Mrs. Bates. She had no real evidence for this, apart from the veiled, mutual bitterness that she had witnessed the day at the Festival Hall. She also had a very strong feeling that Pat was taking her merely to show her off to Clarissa.

'You're playing in this concert with Clarissa?' she asked him, just to get the basic facts straight.

He looked surprised. 'Yes.'

'I remember she said something about a Hampstead date when we met her at the Festival Hall.'

'Oh, did she? I don't remember.'

'You're playing a duet with her?'

'A Beethoven violin sonata.'

'Violin?'

'She plays the violin. I play the piano.'

'Oh.' Ruth blushed, knowing that Pat knew she had thought he played the violin as well. Her ignorance was abysmal.

'Why are we going so early?'

'We've got to go to her house and run through it once or twice beforehand. The concert's at three. We won't have all that much time.'

'Oh.' So that was made clear. Ruth considered Pat, and decided that that was as much as she wanted to know, for the time being, on that precise subject.

'Don't you feel nervous,' she asked, 'playing in a concert?'

'Yes. Generally.'

She was almost surprised that he admitted this.

'I won't be sorry when next Saturday's over,' he said.

'When are you going to rehearse for that?'

'The Saturday morning, as far as I know.'

'Is that all?'

'Yes. With them, that is. They aren't due to arrive till Friday night.'

Ruth remembered her feelings, considering the lonely pianist at the Festival Hall, and the burden of his responsibility. Pat surprised her by saying, 'It's only the same as this show-jumping thing. You practise, and hope for the best when the time comes. Don't you ever feel nervous?'

'But it's not the same! If I make a mistake, it's part of the fun for the spectators. But if you make a mistake——'

'If I thought I was going to make a mistake, I wouldn't be there,' Pat said. 'But I can do it well or do it badly—afterwards I know, the same as you.'

'I suppose so. Even if you don't exactly have a score.'

She considered him again.

'You look very tidy with your hair cut.'

'That's for the Prof. He says if you look like a student they'll think you play like a student.'

'Will he be there?'

'I shouldn't think so.'

'Will he be there next Saturday?'

'Yes.' He groped around in his back pocket and brought out some tickets. 'These are what they gave me. Did you want one?'

'Can I have more than one? My mother would like it, and my father. We'll pay for them.' It would be a marvellous opportunity, she thought, to show Pat off to her parents at his best. She was sure they would come, out of curiosity.

'No, I don't want them. Here.' He gave her six, then took one back. 'I'd better keep one for Mrs. Bates.'

'What about your parents?'

'They can buy theirs,' he said.

'And the Prof?'

'Oh, he'll have his own. There'll be a few of them coming from London, I imagine. I'll be seeing him on Monday anyway. I'm going up to work with him next week.'

'In London?'

'Yes.'

'You'll stay in town?'

'I expect so.'

Ruth told herself there was no future in it. Not to expect anything. He had his reasons for asking her today, and they were not her reasons for wanting to be with him. She looked out of the window, too frightened to look forward to anything, frightened for how much it mattered.

The journey to Hampstead was complicated. There was a tube, and a bus, and then they were walking down a quiet tree-lined street with gigantic mansions on either side with gravelled drives and opulent cars in waiting. Ruth felt a quiet horror stealing over her.

'Does Clarissa live down here?'

'Yes.'

Her essentially conformist, narrow upbringing had never prepared Ruth for the extremes that Pat seemed to take in his stride: she was going to be as out of her depth here as in 'The Jolly Sailor' on a Saturday night. She had nothing to flaunt at Clarissa, not her looks, her intelligence, or even Pat's regard. She was silent. The houses were the sort Prime Ministers lived in, she thought. Opposition Prime Ministers. Pat, apparently, had none of her diffidence; he turned in at Clarissa's drive as if he were delivering two large uncut. The house was all gabled windows and wistaria and an oak-studded door fit for a castle; a gardener was pruning roses, and a maid answered the door.

'Come in,' she said.

They went in. Pat did not wait for the maid, but crossed the hall, an expanse of parquet and Persian carpets, and opened one of the doors that opened off it. Ruth scurried after him and Pat turned and said to the maid, 'Tell her we've arrived, will you?'

'Yes, sir,' the maid said.

'Golly, have you got a lot of friends like this?' Ruth asked, as Pat unceremoniously slammed the door behind them. They were in what was presumably the music room; it was white and gold, with french doors giving on to a lawn mown in velvet strips like an advertisement for fertilizer, and furnished with an enormous grand piano, several music-stands, and some Victorian button-backed chairs in gold velvet to match the curtains. Ruth leaned against the door, taking it in. She had only seen its like before in magazines. It was the epitome of gracious living, spoiled only by Pat in his jeans and jersey dropping his bag on the fitted carpet.

He grinned.

'Yeah, smart, isn't it? And what a piano! Only the tuner ever plays it, and the odd accompanist once in a blue moon.' His face went serious and he added, 'It doesn't make any difference. She doesn't play any the better for it.'

The honest sense of his scale of values made Ruth ashamed.

'I'm such a snob,' she said. 'This sort of thing impresses me terribly.'

'I used to think that. But it doesn't mean a thing in any way that matters. Only that it makes you jealous—this piano—nothing else . . .' He opened the piano and sat down and played some chords. 'It's beautiful. I used to play here quite a lot. I've never played on a better piano than this one. It's an old one, a family heirloom . . .'

Ruth sat down in one of the velvet chairs, watching him, trying to reconcile the old jeans and the baker's round and the concert pianist. He had as many sides as an old threepenny bit, and as many moods to match. She could not follow him. And why did he used to play here quite a lot? Presumably before the three months in prison . . .? She glowered at him, painfully trying to fathom the maze he was forever presenting. At least with dullness one knew where one was.

'You look good,' he said from the piano.

She resisted, not smiling, resenting bitterly the emotions he evoked in her, and did nothing to comfort. If he had had the mentality of Gordon Hargreaves he would have played her the Brahms waltz to woo her, but he only grinned in a mocking way, and started to play an intricate passage which she suspected was out of his concerto.

Clarissa came in. Ruth was satisfied to note the startled expression that overcame her composure when she saw her sitting in the chair.

'Oh!' She shot Pat a furious glance, which Ruth did not miss. Then she recovered herself and said with a fair amount of grace, 'Hullo. Ruth, isn't it?'

'Yes. Hullo.'

'She's going to turn the pages for me,' Pat said.

Ruth felt her stomach give a jump of surprise.

Clarissa said coldly, 'You turned the pages yourself the last time.'

'Yes, well, I hadn't got Ruth to help me then.'

Clarissa said, 'While I remember, they asked me if you can play the Moonlight Sonata, because some pillar of the church has requested it, and they think she's good for fifty pounds if she's treated properly. I said yes.'

'Very considerate of you.'

'I've got the music if you want it. Have you got a copy of the "Spring"? Or do you want mine?'

'I've brought my own.' He went to his bag and opened it. Clarissa said, 'If that's your suit in there, it ought to go on a hanger. Give it to me.'

Pat took out the music and gave the bag to Clarissa, who went to the door and shouted for the maid. Ruth went over to the piano and said softly, anxiously, 'I can't read music. You know I can't. Why did you say that?'

Pat sat down and pulled a chair up close to the stool.

'Sit down,' he said.

Ruth hesitated. She felt angry, being forced into a role she had no desire for. But Pat turned and smiled at her, very easy, and said, 'There's nothing to it. I'll show you what to do. Sit down.'

She sat down, angry because she was too feeble to remonstrate. Yes, yes, yes, as her mother had pointed out so scornfully. The

73

chair was so close that her knee touched his thigh. She shifted it back. He smiled at her again. She felt lost and hopeless. She transferred her gaze to the music, which appalled her. Even the writing at the top was in a foreign language.

She knew nothing. Clarissa came back to the piano with her violin, her glance very cool. Pat gave her an A, and she started to tune her instrument.

'I'll tell you when,' he said to Ruth. 'And don't worry. I won't come to a full stop if you get hung up.'

Ruth sat back, deciding to be as cool as Clarissa. Clarissa looked very noble, poised with her bow; Ruth could not help but be impressed. Pat pushed up his jersey sleeves and said, 'Okay?' and Clarissa gave an imperial nod and launched forth with a bold, high note into a jaunty little tune, while Pat made a soft rippling accompaniment underneath. Very secondary for him, Ruth decided: how satisfactory for bossy Clarissa, keeping him in his place, but then Clarissa stopped, and the piano ran rapidly up from underneath and took the tune over, very gay and delicate, with Clarissa doing the donkey-work underneath. Ruth stared at the printed page, and supposed that the close-together notes making black slopes were the rapid scales; of the rest, the pencilled numbers and the hieroglyphics that looked like the sign for pylons on an ordnance survey map, she could make nothing. But Pat, his fingers moving very fast, said, 'Ruth, now,' and she stood up and turned as neatly and delicately as befitted a third member of this gifted group. Pat played a very loud and decisive chord, and launched off alone over another very black and mountainous track. Clarissa waited for him, putting in her piece like a teasing wife, and then went skipping very frivolously over a lot of dark close-together notes for Pat until she came to a little questioning melody, which Pat repeated, so that the two instruments, it seemed to Ruth, were having a conversation. Ruth stopped being confused, and became fascinated instead, eavesdropping on the complex pattern of the argument. She realized, very dimly, that—whatever Pat might have said about doing it to pay for the mortgage—there was a good deal more to it than that. Pay for the mortgage it might, but it was not what either of them was thinking as they wove the intricate web of the sonata. There was an absorption and a *rapport* which Ruth could feel as she sat on the edge of her chair; it communicated, as if she were the whole audience of the supporters of the crumbling church, so that the dying, echoing tune at the end of the adagio, delicate and soft as a far-away pigeon's call, repeated on both the violin and the piano and dying with a last scarcely perceptible chord, had her moved almost to tears. The last murmur faded, Pat moved his hands off the keys and rested them on his knees. His expression was so distant, so tender, that Ruth scarcely knew him. There was a long, perfect silence, then he turned the page of the music and started to play the scherzo, which was as light and joky as a new-born lamb trying out its legs. Ruth had never thought it of Beethoven. She watched Clarissa watching Pat, and saw his eyes flick to hers, his hands waiting, and then they went racing up a long scale together, and Ruth found her place in the music again, and thought, 'They've done it together lots of times before.' It was something Clarissa had over her that she could not touch, this professional thing between them that was quite outside her experience. She concentrated on watching for the page-turning, seeing where Pat's eyes had got to. Once he swore and said something to Clarissa she did not catch, but without interrupting his playing; Ruth thought suddenly of 'The Jolly Sailor' and the blonde woman saying, 'Don't be long, darling,' and she thought that Pat didn't have a pigeon-hole anywhere. She turned a page and found that there weren't any more to turn, and she relaxed and watched Pat, his stern profile and the underlip jutting slightly in the deep seriousness of his concentration.

When it was finished, he discussed several points with Clarissa and they went back and played different sections over again. Ruth found that she could pick up a few landmarks out of the maze, like 'tr' for trills, which were recognizable even to her, and dots for staccato passages, and her page-turning improved, accomplished after a mere nod from Pat.

'We haven't forgotten much,' Pat said to Clarissa. 'It should sound all right.'

'*I'm* happy,' Clarissa said, putting her violin away. 'Lunch will be ready, I should imagine. Do you want to come up to the bathroom, Ruth? I'll show you.'

'Have you got the other music? The Moonlight?' Pat asked. 'I'd like to go through it.'

'It's in that cupboard.'

Ruth followed Clarissa out of the room and up the curving, close-carpeted staircase. The bathroom was close-carpeted too, with enormous mirrors and gold rings for the towels, which each had a monogrammed C-S in the corner. Ruth tried not to be impressed; at least, not to show it. She washed her hands and Clarissa combed her gorgeous hair. Faintly downstairs the piano could be heard, the gentle air mingling in a soothing summer manner with the occasional snip of the gardener's secateurs among the fading roses. The hot sun came through the wistaria leaves on to the white porcelain, and Ruth felt one of her familiar, strange longings for something quite out of her reach, out of her experience. With everything unresolved, not really happy, yet strangely content to be just so, with life's possibilities spread out this way and that way. Ruth was suspended in that little moment, with the smell of soap and roses and the sound of the piano.

'Is Pat good?' she asked Clarissa, wanting to know.

Clarissa pushed a towel back through the ring.

'Oh, yes. He's Professor Hampton's darling boy. In spite of everything.'

Ruth looked at Clarissa steadily. 'What do you mean? In spite of everything?'

Clarissa looked at her curiously, almost suspiciously. 'Don't you know?' She shrugged. Downstairs in the hall a gong rang out and a feminine voice called out, 'Clarissa!'

'Oh, it doesn't matter,' Clarissa said. She opened the door and shouted, 'Coming!'

A *Vogue*-like woman was waiting in the hall—for the fashion photographer, Ruth thought, rather than for lunch.

'This is my mother, Mrs. Cargill-Smith,' Clarissa said. 'Ruth.'

'How do you do,' said Mrs. Cargill-Smith, looking rather puzzled. 'Do you play——?'

'She turns over,' Clarissa said. 'She's a friend of Pat's.'

'Oh.' Two very elegant eyebrows arched in surprise. Ruth, with a dart of perception, saw in Mrs. Cargill-Smith her own mother, trying to divine relationships, not wanting to ask, but avidly curious. It was just the same, in spite of the setting and the money. 'It doesn't make any difference,' Pat had said. 'Oh,

76

he is right!' Ruth thought. 'He isn't taken in like me.' Whatever did Mrs. Cargill-Smith think of Pat?' she wondered, her eyes widening with a delicious curiosity every bit as avid as that of Mrs. Cargill-Smith.

'Tell Pat it's waiting,' the woman said to Clarissa. 'So you're a friend of Pat's,' she added to Ruth, leading the way into the dining-room. 'At the college?'

'No, at home.'

'Really? You'll be at the concert next Saturday then?'

'Yes.'

'What a splendid opportunity for him! He is so fantastically talented. We shall all feel so proud, seeing him play under Backhaus. Sit here, dear.'

Ruth sat. The Cargill-Smith eyes, mother's and daughter's, had a devastating coldness, counting all the pros and cons, hawks over stubble. Ruth wanted desperately to know what had happened between Pat and Clarissa. He was perfectly at home in this house, coming in for lunch when the rest of them were half-way through and departing without waiting for coffee, and without apology. The conversation was of music, nothing of any personal interest at all, very safe ground, and Ruth saw Mrs. Cargill-Smith trying to draw conclusions, and failing. She was a conventionally smart and good-looking woman, but her features were hard and Ruth guessed that her perfect upper-class manners, hiding everything, hid a good deal of unpleasantness. Clarissa would be like that when she was forty. Ruth wondered if she would grow like her own mother when she was forty. She hoped not; she did not think she could ever become so insensitive and dull.

Ruth was bothered by whether she was doing the right things with all the cutlery, the bread rolls, the napkins and thanking the maid, but Pat obviously had no such qualms, reaching for what he wanted and scooping up some more potatoes without waiting to be asked. After the peach melba he pushed back his chair and got up.

'You haven't got to play the Moonlight,' Clarissa said. 'I didn't promise them anything. Not if you can't manage it.'

She was not a gracious girl, Ruth thought, the way she spoke. There was an acidity, getting at Pat. It occurred to Ruth then, seeing Clarissa's expression suddenly as Pat moved towards the door, that the ungraciousness covered resentment, that Clarissa was not immune to Pat at all, for all her imperious manner. And Ruth knew that her guess as to why Pat had asked her to come along was perfectly correct: she was his armour, stopping any advance on Clarissa's part.

'I don't mind,' Pat said, and went out.

They drank coffee and Ruth was questioned about her future plans and her A-levels. The piano behind two closed doors raged furiously.

Mrs. Cargill-Smith looked at her watch and said, 'Two o'clock. You'd better get changed, Clarissa. Tell Pat he can use the green bathroom. We ought to leave at half-past.'

They got up from the table and went out into the hall.

'Whatever's he playing?' Ruth asked. 'I thought——'

'The third movement,' said Clarissa's mother. 'The thunder-clouds come up, you know. Nothing is pure moonlight all the way.'

'Very philosophical,' said Clarissa bitterly.

'Don't be silly, dear. Run along. I'll see to Pat. Perhaps you'd like to wait in the sitting-room, Ruth.'

Ruth waited, having plenty to think about.

Ruth thought she would die, walking on to the stage behind Clarissa and Pat, across acres of polished parquet to the insular piano, taking her hard chair while they bowed. If she had known Pat was going to do this to her, she would never have come. Her hands were trembling. She clasped them tightly, and looked at Pat's, which were perfectly composed. She supposed he was nervous, but he didn't appear to be. He looked a complete stranger in a formal dark suit and tie, and Ruth had the feeling that she had wandered into an alien world: the unfamiliarity of both the situation and the feelings unnerved her completely. And all the time there was this great uncertainty, that he was using her. Mrs. Cargill-Smith could have turned for him far more usefully than she could. She felt as far away from him as when she had left him the evening at Fiddler's Creek, and yet her knee was touching his piano stool. He had scarcely spoken a word since they had left the house, but now he turned to her, while Clarissa was tuning her violin, and said, 'All right?'

'No,' Ruth whispered, not letting him have it all his own way. 'I'm distracted.'

He gave her a startled glance, looking very much the old Pat, and Ruth was comforted by shaking him. It wasn't kind at such a moment, but nor was he. Clarissa turned, her bow lifted, and fixed him with her eye. He recovered himself immediately. Ruth saw his lower lip go out, very grim; he gave Clarissa a little nod, and they were away. Ruth turned in exemplary fashion, every crumpled corner gained like a triple-bar cleared without a fault. 'Yes,' she thought, softened by Beethoven running through her blood-stream, watching Pat's face moved by what he was doing, 'I love you, I love you, you beast.' He nodded and she got up and turned two pages at once, completely demoralizing herself, although Pat went on playing as if nothing had gone wrong. 'He knows it,' she thought. 'He's got me here completely under false pretences.' And then it was the last page, and her reluctant part was over. The audience clapped and roared and bravoed, and Pat and Clarissa did very correct bows to the front and both sides while Ruth stood up, not knowing what to do at all. Pat, guessing her plight, turned round and said, 'Follow me,' and they made an exit in single file, Clarissa first. The dark openings of the wings of the stage were like going to earth, private and quiet and blessed. When they got there Clarissa turned to Pat, looking white and ravaged, and said, 'Oh, I'm glad it's over! I made a mess of the scherzo.'

'It was all right,' Pat said.

They went back again for two more bows, then when the audience had quietened down, Pat went back again alone to do the requested sonata, which Ruth was overwhelmingly relieved to see he was going to play without music. Clarissa disappeared but Ruth went on leaning against the wings, soothed by the moonlight and thinking of the remark, 'Nothing is pure moonlight all the way.' 'Why not?' she wondered. 'Why can't it be?' She looked at Pat, and he appeared to be looking back at her, although she knew he wasn't. She thought, 'After today I shall know where I am with him. Whether it's finished or just starting.' And then she remembered that she had thought that the last time. Perhaps she would never know, as Ted never really knew with Barbara, although he was married to her. 'People,' she thought, 'are much more difficult than horses.' And God

79

knew, she had found them hard enough. But, like the moment in the bathroom, she was satisfied, watching Pat, lapped by the gentle melody and knowing that afterwards he was going to come to her and take her home. Not Clarissa. Clarissa would have to say good-bye, pretending she didn't care. Ruth felt a terrible pang for Clarissa. The music skipped into a very innocent, charming little tune, much gayer than the first movement, but Ruth kept hearing the warnings underneath, as if it was talking to her, telling her to watch out, a falling of low wistful notes from the skipping of the right hand. Getting ready for the thunderstorm. In her emotional state, overwrought from the page-turning, she thought of it as an omen. She shut her eyes, and the thunder came, a torrent of arpeggios, scaring all the old ladies in the hall into startled attention. 'Oh, God,' Ruth prayed, 'don't let it go wrong again. Let it be moonlight.' She had an awful feeling that something terrible was going to happen; it was a very clear and certain feeling, and took all the strength out of her knees.

Pat came off, looking absent and hot, wiping his face with a disreputable handkerchief that spoiled his professional image.

'What's the matter?' he said to her. 'You look as if you've seen a ghost.'

She shook her head. The feeling had gone but she felt drained, as if she had been doing all the work, not Pat. It was the heat, she thought. The hall was very hot. Perhaps the thunder was real. Pat had to go back twice more to bow, and afterwards, while the church choir was forming up on stage for the next item, he had to shake some reverend hands back-stage, and be polite. But at last he came to her and said, 'Did you put my Spring Sonata back in the bag?' and she nodded and he said, 'Let's get the hell out of here.'

And they were out in the sunshine and the traffic, and Ruth felt that it was going to be all right after all.

Chapter 6

They went back to Liverpool Street and caught the train home. Ruth felt she had grown up during the day. She was not prepared to be a doormat any more; she realized that her dog-like devotion was not enough, either for Pat or for herself; the relationship needed more nourishment, or it was going to die. And it was for Pat to decide. She thought he would. She felt cool, and optimistic, and about five years older than the day before. She didn't say anything at all. Pat didn't seem to notice, being in a cloud himself, but when they were on the train, and she had merely gazed out of the window for three stations, she became aware that he was conscious of the situation. He was watching her, and glowering slightly. Five stations later the man sitting next to Ruth got out, which left an old man asleep in the far corner, and Pat leaned forward and said, 'Ruth.'

Ruth looked at him.

He said, 'I'm sorry if you didn't like it—if you thought——' He hesitated. 'It was work, you see. I didn't want it to be anything else. And with Clarissa it's very difficult now. But that engagement to play was arranged by my Prof. I couldn't cancel it.'

Ruth thought that it was a greater effort for him to say this to her than to go out on to the stage and play the Moonlight Sonata to five hundred people. He looked far more nervous. She could scarcely believe that he had apologized.

'Clarissa is no more to me than the noise she gets out of her catgut. I don't want you to think anything else, that's all.' He looked better, having cleared this terrible hurdle.

'She was more once? I got that impression.' She was so curious, wondering what had happened, as bad as her mother.

'Well, yes. You've only seen her being bitchy, but she's not always like that. She wasn't. Not last summer. Oh, cripes, let's not talk about that. People like that—and her mother—her mother——'

He looked harrowed, his eyes dark and scowling.

'I'm sorry, I don't want to know,' Ruth said quickly. She wanted to know desperately, but not at the cost of such obvious pain to him. 'It doesn't matter. Not now you've explained.'

'I'm no good at explaining, that's the trouble. I can't talk. They—most of them—at college, they can talk, they know all the words. It doesn't mean they're any ruddy good. But if you listen to them you think they must be. You—you must think I'm a pig, the way I am, but I can't tell you . . . I can't, how difficult it is, I mean. I don't want to—to—I don't want you to think I don't—I don't care. I——'

He paused, looking at her very earnestly, scowling. Then he gave a sort of groan and dropped his head and rubbed his hands through his hair.

'Cripes, it's hot. I must change out of this ruddy suit when we get to Northend.'

Ruth was touched almost to tears. 'It's all right,' she said.

He gave her a very uncertain smile, and said, 'Well, if you think so.'

'The only thing is, I——' Ruth wanted to get it over, now that Pat was in an explaining mood. If this one thing could be cleared up, it would be moonlight indeed. 'If it's not to do with Clarissa—I'm not being nosy, but I want to know why you got sent to . . .' She faltered, suddenly scared to death. 'Oh, God,' she thought, 'why ever did I start?' She looked at him, appalled. 'The three months . . . ?' It came out in a whisper.

'I hit someone,' he said. 'I broke his jaw and his parents got me hauled up for it. His father was a barrister—I didn't know that when I hit him.'

Ruth did not ask any more, but after a pause Pat said, 'He was one of the talkers, like I just said. He could talk about it—you'd think he'd sat there and told Johann Sebastian just what to put, the way he carried on. But when it came to doing, he was pathetic. He never did any work and he had the technique of a Grade One schoolgirl. He didn't like me, because I was going with Clarissa and he had an eye for her. He used to make remarks—he was very witty, he could always get a laugh, and it was easy for him—the way I talk, and when I was a waiter for

82

a bit—he could take me off. I didn't mind about that part, but there was a competition, and I came top and he came bottom, and one day he was talking like *The Times* critic and I said if a piano was played with the tongue he'd got so much practice in he'd have come top—it was the only clever thing I'd ever said in my life, and he didn't like it. He said I put so many hours in because technique was the only thing I had to offer, my working-class brain being incapable of understanding what the whole thing was about. So I hit him. He was in hospital for a fortnight, and his father made sure I paid for it. So they got the last laugh after all.'

Ruth thought it was a marvellous story. She said, 'The satisfaction at the time ... it must have been gorgeous! Even if afterwards——'

'Afterwards was different,' Pat said. 'It wasn't worth it. Not for all sorts of reasons. But at the time you don't think. All you think is, 'I'll smash that beggar,' and it's done. Even my hands —it didn't make any difference that time, although it's stopped me a few other times when I've been tempted. I couldn't play for a week afterwards. The old Prof. was more wild about that than anything. And old Bigmouth—he couldn't talk either. That part was okay.'

Pat's mood changed as if, having put both work and explanations behind him, he was all clear to enjoy himself. When they got off at Northend, he went and changed out of his suit back into his jeans and sweater, handed the bag in at the Left Luggage office, and came back to Ruth more cheerful than she had ever seen him.

'Now, what is it? A meal? Are you hungry? Maxwell said he was going to the Big Top and on to the Black Cat disco afterwards—would you like that? Cripes, it's hot! Let's have a drink first! You fancy that programme?'

'Yes, oh yes!'

He took her in the station bar and bought a pint of bitter and a shandy, then they went out and walked down the High Street to the front. The air was very close, although the sun was low; there was no breeze, and the tide was out, a mile away across the wet, puckered mud. The front was crowded with people, fat bare arms and peeling shoulders, tired babies bawling in their push-chairs, and queues for ice-cream. Ruth,

83

who hated it usually, preferring it in the winter when it had a peculiar gaunt fascination all of its own, loved it tonight because Pat took her hand and said, 'You're okay, Ruth. You don't nag. I don't like naggers.'

'You like doormats?' she said.

'That's right.' He grinned. 'All the females I've ever known have been naggers. Except Mrs. Bates. And you.'

'I'm quite a good nagger, if I put my mind to it.'

'You don't practise enough. I don't believe you. The only thing was when you said this afternoon, "I'm distracted." You threw me. I nearly started on the old concerto instead.'

'Yes, well, getting me up there—I could have died!'

He laughed. 'I didn't think you would do it. But you never said anything. You never complained.'

'You could have turned the pages yourself!'

'Yes, of course. But it was lovely having you there.'

She laughed. 'Catch me again! Not next Saturday——'

'Oh, cripes, next Saturday! It's all in the brain-box for next Saturday.'

They turned in at the Big Top, into a steaming atmosphere of fish and chips and defeated salads under plastic covers.

'We should have had it in Hampstead,' Pat muttered. 'Let's collect Maxwell and find somewhere else.'

Maxwell was at a table in the window, drinking coke with a girl who was introduced as Rita. Pat obviously knew her well. She looked at Ruth curiously. She was older, Ruth thought, as old as the boys, and she had a sophisticated command of the situation which Ruth envied, very casual and friendly, but sharp with it. She was not particularly attractive, but she certainly knew how to enhance what charms she possessed. Ruth felt cautious towards her, not wanting to reveal how unsure she was herself, her unsureness emphasized by the comparison.

'God, it's hot,' Pat said. 'And the ruddy tide half-way to France. I'd rather have a swim than fish and chips.'

'Have a coke,' said Maxwell equably.

'Let's go for a drink and get some cockles,' Pat said. 'Hey, wait a minute.' He got up suddenly, threaded his way through some tables, and started talking to a youth who was sitting alone with a cup of coffee.

'He's very cheerful tonight,' Maxwell remarked. 'What've you been doing to him?'

Ruth smiled. 'I don't know.' 'Not nagging' wasn't a very good answer.

'He must be in lerve,' Maxwell said, winking. 'Who's he talking to? Who's that bloke, Rita?'

'Len,' said Rita.

'Who's Len?'

'Works at the baker's, where Penn used to.'

'Oh. You going to this concert next Saturday, by the way? I know it's Penn and all that, but is the nervous system capable of standing a couple of hours of that sort of stuff? Mine—I doubt it.'

'Oh, yes,' Rita said. 'We're all going. We're going to talk about him in loud voices and impress people. Our friend and all that. I saw Mr. Crocker last week, and he was babbling on about it. He said if you see Pennington, tell him Mr. Marsh has bought a ticket.'

'Cripes, with real money? For old Penn!' Maxwell, for some reason unknown to Ruth, was convulsed.

Rita said to Ruth, 'Mr. Crocker was the music-master at school. He's a decent old beggar, but Marsh—cripes, we all hated his guts. Penn most of all. He was always pitching in to Penn, but Penn got his own back in the end——'

'He got expelled for the pleasure, mind you,' Maxwell put in.

'It was worth it,' Rita said.

'Old Marsh'll be sitting there willing Penn to play wrong notes. You'll feel all the old hate-waves on the back of your neck,' Rita giggled.

Pat came back with Len in tow, and Rita said, 'Hullo, Len. I say, Penn, old Marsh has bought a ticket for your concert.'

Pat scowled and said, 'I hope they only had expensive seats left!' Then his expression went back to normal and he said, 'Len's just taking me up to the bake-house and I'll get my old van. Then we'll have transport for the evening. Simmonds is on holiday so we're in the clear. Len's lending me his key. I'll be back in ten minutes.'

'Good oh,' said Maxwell.

'When d'you get your licence back, Maxwell?' Rita asked him.

'Another couple of months.'

He ordered another round of cokes, and Pat was back before they had finished, honking outside because there was nowhere to park. They all went out and piled in.

'Let's go and have a beer,' Pat said. 'Then we'll go down to the Lido and have a swim and then we'll go to the disco.'

'The Lido'll be shut,' Rita said. 'It shuts at eight.'

'It doesn't matter,' Pat said. 'We know how to get in, don't we, Maxwell? It's better when it's shut. You're game aren't you, Maxwell?'

'Yes. Suits me.'

'You girls can sit it out. We won't be long.'

'Catch me swimming,' Rita said. 'When are you going to grow up?'

'Next Saturday'll put ten years on me.'

'High time,' Rita said.

They stopped at a pub and the boys had beer, Rita had a Martini, and Ruth had another shandy, leaving most of it. She wasn't used to drinking, and couldn't stomach any more. The day was very strange already, without the help of alcohol. They drove along the front to the Lido, and Pat parked the van in the first gap he could find, some way beyond. The pool was boarded up from the promenade, in order that prospective spectators should pay for admittance instead of getting free entertainment by leaning over the railings, but Pat and Maxwell led the way round to the side, ducked beneath a big hoarding advertising an aqua show and, nicely screened by it from the people walking along the front, Pat climbed very nimbly on to the roof of the changing-rooms.

'Come on, you girls. Give them a bunk up, Maxwell.'

Rita made a lot of fuss, but was hauled up without ceremony, very concerned for her tights. Ruth managed more easily, but was happy enough to have Pat's hand to help her. They slid down the roof the other side and dropped down on the concrete sun-deck. Maxwell pulled out two deck-chairs from beneath a pile shrouded with a tarpaulin, and set them out for Rita and Ruth.

'There, what more can you ask?' He offered Rita a cigarette and lit it for her, the match showing suddenly how dark it was, the warm sky close and thick with cloud, no stars showing. Ruth sat down, hearing the scrape of her chair echo round the blank façades of the changing-rooms. The big pool lay very still below, rank with chlorine. It didn't attract her with its chill breath, its occasional blink of stray reflected light a crocodile's eye in the darkness.

'Nut-cases,' Rita said. 'Keep your pants on in case you have to run for it.'

Ruth couldn't reconcile it with the afternoon, the formality of the Hampstead fund-raising, and now the horseplay on the side of the bath, the two figures wrestling, overbalancing, Pat's fall turned by a twist into a smooth dive and the stillness splintered, the crocodile's eye fractured . . . She leaned her chin on the cold balustrade, wondering about the strangeness of the way things happened, the waywardness of one's feelings, so that there was no knowing . . . not anything . . . she was as dependent now for her happiness on Pat's whim, as he was dependent on the buoyancy of the water for keeping him afloat. It wasn't at all a desirable state of affairs but—conversely—the newfound fragility of everything that mattered was the sweetest thing that had ever happened to her. She saw the glow of Rita's cigarette-end, and wondered if Rita had such feelings.

But Rita only said, 'That should cool 'em off. They really are nuts.' Her eyes kept going, somewhat nervously, to the promenade above. Maxwell came back, and lit a cigarette from Rita's and sat on the top of the steps smoking, until he had dried off. Then he stood up and bawled, 'Come on, Pat! You going to be all night?'

He started to pull his trousers on.

Suddenly a strong beam of light flashed down from the promenade, transfixing Pat where he lay floating on his back in the middle of the pool. Ruth saw the startled expression on his face; he turned over and swam smartly for the side, the light following him.

'Oh, cripes,' said Rita. 'Here we go. Get Pat's clothes, Ruth. Where are they, for heaven's sake?'

The light swung round, and focused on Maxwell hopping about half-in his trousers, and Rita scrambling for her handbag. Someone shouted, the voice resounding like a trumpet in a cave.

'What is it?' Ruth jerked out of her dreams.

'The coppers,' Rita said. 'We have to run for it.'

Pat came running up the steps, half-laughing, half in earnest.

'I've got your things,' Ruth called. She was petrified, not knowing which way to turn. But Pat caught her by the wrist and said, 'Come on. Down here.' Maxwell and Rita were already away. There was a flight of steps at the end of the terrace, and at the bottom a door which Maxwell had already unbolted. Pat was laughing.

'Is it all right?' Ruth asked him.

'Yes, of course. Watch it—the steps are rotten.'

The door gave on to a wooden flight of steps that ran down to the beach. Ruth stumbled down behind Rita, and Pat jumped over the rails and was waiting at the bottom, taking the bundle of clothes off her. They ran up the sand, Rita floundering as she lost a shoe, Maxwell shrugging into his shirt. The light picked them up again and a voice bellowed, 'I'll have the law on you!'

'I thought it *was* the law,' Ruth said.

'It must be the pool man. They say he does a patrol on hot nights.'

'There was a copper,' Maxwell said. 'Let's keep moving. I saw him.'

They climbed on to the promenade, the boys bunking the girls up first. Ruth rolled over the railings, getting tangled up with a pram and two children eating candy-floss. Rita had a fit of the giggles, hopping about trying to put her shoe on. The pool man gave another roar, mostly swearing, and everyone on the promenade stopped and stared, amused by the diversion. A policeman, not running but walking very briskly, was coming down the promenade from the direction of the pool's pay-box.

'Okay. Sharpish,' Pat said, and ran for the van. They all piled in, and Pat had it out neatly nosing into the stream of traffic while Maxwell was still slamming the door.

'Ruddy spoil-sports,' Pat said.

'Lucky you had your pants on,' Maxwell said, grinning.

Ruth, pressed hard against Pat in the front seat and feeling herself growing rapidly cold and damp, was calmed by the collective indifference of the other three to their brush with authority. They were amused, sorting themselves out, Rita cursing because she had left her cigarettes behind. They stopped at some traffic-lights, and Pat reached for a cloth in the glove-locker and towelled his hair. A man in the car alongside gave him a hard, curious stare.

'What now?' Rita said.

'Eat,' Pat said. 'That's given me a nice appetite.'

'I suggest you get dressed, before we all pile out in the High Street,' Maxwell said.

'Yeah. Who's sitting on my clothes?'

They all were, and dragged them out with difficulty. Pat turned off down a quiet residential road and pulled into the kerb. He got out, pulling his jeans behind him. A woman came out of the door of the house opposite and came down the garden path, dressed to go out. She gave Pat a horrified look and said, 'Really! I've a good mind to call the police!'

Pat cursed, turning his back on her, and Maxwell leaned out and said, 'Yes, I would, madam. It's worse than the television. He's on the stage, and stage people are given to running around with no clothes on. If you want to see him, next Saturday at the Pavilion he's got his own show——' Rita hit him with her handbag, nearly knocking him under the dashboard. Pat zipped up his jeans and leapt back into the van.

'You raving twit, Maxwell!' The van shot off down the street. Rita was helpless with laughter, shaking against Ruth's shoulder. Pat could not find the gear-lever for knees, and swore again. At the next red traffic-light he struggled into his sweater, and at the next one he combed his hair, peering into the driving mirror.

'Where are we going then?' he said to Maxwell when he had put the comb away. 'I fancy joint and two veg.'

' "The Golden Cockerel" is all right,' Maxwell said.

'Okay.'

'The Golden Cockerel' was smart and cheerful, with pop music and a wine waiter. They ordered chicken, and the boys ordered beer, and lagers for Rita and Ruth. Pat's knee came up against Ruth's under the table, and stayed there, hard and comforting. She did not move away.

After the meal they drove down to the disco. Ruth had been there several times before but never with anyone that mattered. Pat parked the van in the street outside, and went to buy some cockles because he said he was still hungry. Maxwell and Rita disappeared inside, and Ruth waited for Pat while he ate, leaning against the wall outside the disco.

'You all right?' he asked her. 'Want some?'

'No, thank you. Of course I'm all right.'

'I don't know what you're thinking half the time. You just look and don't say anything.'

'I'm thinking I'm very happy. I'm sorry—shall I nag you?'

He threw away the cockle bag and reached for her hand.

'So am I,' he said. 'And even if you nag me it won't make any difference. I wish it was like this every day.'

They went into the hallway through the bright lights and into the vibrant gloom beyond, into a cavern of noise, of intimate anonymity, body to body shifting and weaving through the slowly revolving beams of coloured light. It was hot and the noise hurt, the rhythm seizing the knees, urgent and primitive, impossible—in the willing mood of pure happiness—to resist. They started to dance, laughing, very easy. Ruth had thought that Pat, steeped in classical music, would not be much of a dancer, but she saw that the argument was ridiculous: he had more rhythm and movement in one foot than most of the boys had in all their sweating, flailing bodies. For all his size, he was lithe and agile: Ruth's past partners paled into a limbo; she laughed, and Pat sang the pop words, the rubbish that now was as right as the sonata had been earlier, carefree in a way she had never seen him before, taking her, pulling her close, his hand on the back of her neck among her hair, singing in her ear and laughing and, as the pulse of the music quickened, turning away, pushed into movement by the compulsion of the noise— Ruth, too, getting breathless—and their eyes linked all the time, changing colour in the revolving lights. Ruth saw Pat's eyes green as emeralds and diamonds of sweat sparkling; she saw his purple hair and the psychedelic lobe of an ear showing beneath, orange locks curling on the nape of his neck as he turned away to give the gaze a rest, the blood growing restless. Ruth felt the restlessness too.

The music changed, and the lights went half-down, the weaving slowed to a nebulous, hazy interchange, and the mood was changed. Ruth felt the heat, and the stirrings of her own instincts, charged and suddenly very painful. She looked at Pat, dazed and wanting, lost suddenly, and he pulled her close against him, one arm round her back and the other over her shoulder, the hand stroking her hair. She put her face in the hollow of his neck and touched his skin with her lips, and he moved her head back with the caressing hand and kissed her eyebrow and her temple and said in her ear, very softly, 'Oh, Ruth, Ruth!'

'Pat,' she said, stupidly. He was like a tower for her need; whatever it was she had wanted she had it in his arm holding her, and his body hard and warm against hers. She put her arms up and touched his neck and pushed the hair away from his ear, and heard the amplified voice singing out of the warmth and the bliss of love and pain and despair and comfort.

'You hear what he says,' she whispered, and he kissed her hair and her cheek and said, 'Yes,' and kissed her lips, and smiled, looking at her, so close that she thought his eyelashes were almost touching hers. Her skin felt as if it were quivering all over. It was so strange, the other shoulders and hip-bones brushing them and swaying and shifting them about and they, a little cocoon, dancing very slowly and the sad voice washing them. The first shock of it past, Ruth was overcome with happiness. She dropped her head, seeing the glint of the gold medal he wore and feeling the warm roughness of the chain on her cheek where it ran over the ridge of his collarbone.

She thought she saw Maxwell grinning. Pat's fingers ran down her jawbone, lifting her head up.

'Ruth, I want——'

And then there was something else, an intrusion.

'I want a word with you.' Another voice, not Pat's. Ruth came up off Pat's breast, blinking. A policeman stood there. She thought she was dreaming.

'If you'll just step off the floor a moment——'

'What for?'

'You'll find out.'

Ruth, still in Pat's arms, looked up and saw his face unbelieving. His arms loosed her, and his hand took hers, very tight so that it almost hurt. Everyone was looking now, still dancing, grinning.

'Come on. We haven't all night,' the policeman said.

He was an older man, very sure of himself. Pat hesitated, then shrugged, and moved away, glowering, still holding Ruth. They went out to the side of the floor, by the doorway, where another policeman was standing, an unsmiling, hard-faced man. Ruth recognized him as the one who had stopped Pat the night outside the bakery. She felt a strong fear grip her, so strong that she shivered.

'This him?' the policeman asked Mitchell.

'Yes. That's him. Pennington,' Mitchell said.

'I want you to step down to the station with me, Mr. Pennington,' the policeman said.

'What for?'

'I'm charging you with taking and driving away the vehicle KRW 618E, the property of the Parade Bakery, without lawful authority.'

Ruth saw the young policeman smile. Pat loosed her hand and hit him, with such velocity that she wasn't aware of its happening, except for the expression changing on Mitchell's face, his eyes glazing and his jaw sagging. The older policeman put out an arm, but Pat evaded it with a flick of his body and was out past him into the hallway. The policeman bawled something and was after him, and Ruth found she was there too, although she had no conscious awareness of moving at all. She found she was standing on the top of the steps, looking out into the street, and screaming. The hall bouncer had tackled Pat outside, and two policemen who had been waiting in a patrol car had jumped out and run for the scuffle. Ruth saw Pat break out and run again, but one of the policemen made a dive and caught him by the arm.

'He's knocked Mitchell out!'

Pat was swung against the wall, the three policemen converging on him. Ruth heard his head hit the bricks from where she stood, and then the thud of a blow, and another one . . . She started to run down the steps, but could not move. Someone held her, and she turned round, pulling and sobbing.

'Shut up, you fool! *Shut up!*'

It was Maxwell, shaking her silly. 'I'll slap you!' he hissed, furious. 'Do you want them to take you too?'

'They're killing him!' She jerked at his hand, but he tightened his grip, wrenching her towards him. His other hand came up with a sharp slap across her cheek.

'They'll take you as well! You were in the van too! We'll all get done if you don't shut up——'

She gasped for breath, shaking. 'I want to go——'

'For God's sake,' Maxwell said. 'Are you daft?'

A crowd had gathered, craning and muttering. Ruth could see the policemen bending over Pat on the ground, and the crowd pushing in. She wanted to shut her eyes, but they stayed resolutely open; she wanted to turn away, but she could not move. She saw the crowd part, and the dark figures straighten up. They had Pat between them, supporting him and holding his arms twisted up behind his back at the same time. He appeared to Ruth to be barely conscious, his legs dragging, stumbling across the width of the pavement, dark threads of blood running down his shoulder where his jersey was torn. One of the policemen opened the back of the van; they pitched him in bodily, head-first, and slammed the doors on him. The crowd broke away, and the policeman who had apprehended Pat in the first place came back up the steps of the disco, smiling and slapping his hands together. The two patrolmen got back in the van and drove off.

'Maxwell!' Ruth turned to him, all the strength drained out of her. Her voice was a whisper.

'Count yourself lucky,' Maxwell said. 'Me too. Let's get out of the way for a bit. Mitchell's lying in there, out cold—he saw us at the pool—it was him, you know, I saw his face under the street-lamp. He'll have recognized me, I'm sure. Let's go before he wakes up.'

He put an arm round Ruth's shoulders and held out a large handkerchief, propelling her into the street at the same time, walking briskly.

'Cheer up, sweetheart. Here, mop up. Pat'll be all right. Don't worry.'

'He isn't all right,' she wept. 'Didn't you see what they did to him? I thought—I thought—policemen weren't like that——' she hiccuped into Maxwell's handkerchief, shaking with sobs—'Not British policemen——'

'For God's sake, Ruth, what d'you expect them to do? He'd just laid one of 'em out cold, and was making a bunk for it, wasn't he? He wasn't going to stop if they'd said, "I say, hang on a minute, old boy." Pat's got a punch like dynamite. They weren't risking any more.'

'What'll happen to him? Can't we go and see?'

'I can tell you without going to see. He'll be locked up and charged with stealing and assault.'

93

'Stealing!' Ruth stopped in her tracks and stared at Maxwell in amazement. 'That wasn't stealing!'

'It is to them. What we call borrowing they call theft.'

'But he's not a thief!'

'No? You tell them that.'

'But that's terrible!'

'Yeah, and knocking out a policeman doesn't endear anyone to the beaks either. I can't see him getting away with it, not with his record.'

'Oh, Maxwell, you mean——' Ruth could not say any more for crying. It was the moment in the wings on the Hampstead stage, when she had been afraid: it had caught her up and over-whelmed her. She heard the thunder of the arpeggios and saw Pat's face again, fierce with concentration, remembering how the fright had twisted her, and he had asked if she felt all right. The tears streamed down her face.

'There,' said Maxwell, embarrassed but strangely tender, giving her shoulder a comforting shake, 'don't cry. It'll be all right. He always gets by. He's used to trouble.'

'I love him.'

'Yeah, well, what's he got to worry about then? He's lucky.'

'What will they do with him? Now, I mean? When he gets to the police-station?'

'They'll charge him, and get him to make a statement, or whatever they call it, then they'll put him in a cell for the night.'

'Then what? Tomorrow?'

'Well, you're either let out on bail or remanded in custody.'

'What's that? Remanded in custody?'

'They send you to a prison, until your court case comes up. I think they send 'em to Brixton from here.'

'Oh, God! How awful.'

Maxwell didn't say anything, but steered her into a little café, sat her down in a corner and brought her a cup of strong coffee. Ruth didn't say any more. It was still so close, she could feel Pat's hand on her hair and his eyelashes brushing her skin. She saw his hands, very strong and agile as she had watched them all morning, and his expression changing with the music, his involvement making this invisible barrier that kept her from following, that kept her apart, waiting for him to come back. She would never follow him there, and he had made it his whole-time occupation. It was all very useless. And the part of him left over for her was this difficult, tangled, lonely and undisciplined nature which by its crying need for support endeared him so much to her; and so uselessly, because she was in no position to help him, being as tangled herself and immature in her emotions as a fledgling caught against a window-pane. The coffee stopped her crying, but did nothing more to help; her feelings were too anguished and confused to cope with.

'Can't we do anything to help him?' she asked.

Maxwell said, 'No,' very firmly.

'What about next Saturday? They won't keep him for that?'

'I don't know.'

Maxwell got up. 'Come on. We'll go back and find someone to drive you home.'

Ruth followed him. There was a boy called Crombie he knew, who was persuaded by circumstances to leave the disco on this errand of mercy. He had an old, rattling Morris Minor with a top speed of thirty miles an hour. Ruth sat in the back and half-heard them discussing Pat, laughing and amused. She kept thinking of him loving her, and his arms holding her, and him smiling and his lips touching her, and then hearing the thuds of the police hitting him, and his head against the wall. She was past crying, feeling that her own particular world had stopped, although everyone else was carrying on as if nothing had happened at all.

'Cripes, old Mitchell getting his desserts like that! I bet he's sorry now!'

And they laughed, and turned off the arterial down a side road, seeing a rabbit's eyes like green lamps in the road.

'If you had a gun, you could pot 'em easy as anything,' Crombie said. 'They just stand there.'

'Yes,' said Maxwell. 'We ought to try it. My brother's got an airgun.'

Chapter 7

She slept very late, having taken until dawn to fall asleep, and was woken by her mother calling, 'Ruth! Guess who's here? A nice surprise for you!'

She sat up very suddenly, and the black memory hit her like a physical blow between the eyes, so that she lay back again and groaned. By daylight the confusion was cleared; the story was merely stark and sordid, and Pat a thief and a thug to be punished by the perfectly correct machinery of the law. Yet the sun was shining and there was a smell of coffee and warm grass. It was a perfect Sunday morning. And Pat would be stiff and sore and in despair and no one to help him. She remembered the words of the song they had been dancing to with perfect clarity. And she was lying in bed and shortly to take her breakfast, and her father was oiling the lawn-mower, and her mother singing. They didn't know anything of what had happened and she had no intention of telling them. Was it really as bad as she had thought it was last night? She dressed very slowly, pulling on her old jeans. Yes, she thought, it was. She didn't know what to do. The only thing she knew without any doubt at all was that her mother must not know what had happened.

Ruth looked at her face in the mirror as she combed her hair. She had a splitting headache and she was very pale, but at least she did not look as if she had been crying. She must be very clever, and aloof. Her mother would think they had had a row.

She washed and went downstairs and into the kitchen. The room was full of sunlight, making her blink, and in the doorway stood Peter McNair, holding her own gorgeous Toad. The pony had both front feet inside the kitchen, and stood there looking like something out of a legend, the sun turning his coat to pure gold, his friendly familiar eyes taking everything in. When Ruth came in, he gave a little snort and a flutter of his nostrils and Peter laughed and said, 'You old flirt!'

'Oh!'

Ruth was quite overcome. Why, she had no idea, except that Toad and everything he stood for was so dear and familiar, and now seemed so far-distant and impossible—it was a terrible pang like homesickness.

She went up to him and buried her face in his lovely flaxen mane, quite overwhelmed. Her parents were laughing at her. The smell of Toad was as comfortable and kind and desirable as anything she could think of in the world. And so remote from everything that beset her. He was no good to her any more. It was terrible, now, trying not to cry.

'The vet's given him a clean bill of health, and it was such a super morning I thought I'd bring him down,' Peter said. 'He goes just like he ever did. Shall we turn him out?'

'Yes. Put him away and then come back and I'll give you some breakfast,' said Mrs. Hollis.

Ruth walked down the back orchard with Peter, ducking for the old pear branches, watching Toad snatching at the grass. The grass was all wet with dew and full of buttercups. It was like a hundred years ago, Ruth thought.

'Is something wrong?' Peter said.

'Yes.'

She told him, while they took off Toad's tack and opened the gate and let him loose in the big flat field that gave on to the marshes. The sky was full of skylarks. They hung over the gate, Peter chewing a stalk of grass, just as dear and familiar as Toad. She could tell him everything. They had been through all sort of dire confrontations since the age of eleven, both on and off horses, and she knew Peter. He had his troubles too, but he wasn't a hysterical twit like herself; no one ever knew when Peter was troubled. He was very quiet and shrewd. He leaned on the gate, watching Toad move away through the wet grass, the animal's long early shadow undulating from the round white hoofs.

'You've really got it for this Pat, haven't you?' he remarked gravely.

'Yes. I love him terribly. And I know you're only being polite not making any remarks about how unsuitable he is for me and all that. I know you think that, but you must understand it doesn't make any difference. And that's why I must help him, because he hasn't got parents who are going to bother, like most people. In fact, I bet nobody but me and Maxwell know where he is at the moment. And nobody will care—even Mrs. Bates will just think he's stayed in London.'

'But what can you do to help him? The police just do it all according to the book. You can't change it. Anyway, quite likely he'll be out this morning. They don't keep everyone, surely? They charge them, and then you appear in court later. And in between times you carry on just as usual.'

'You mean he might be out by now?'

'Yes. I think they just keep you long enough to cool off, and then let you out. Unless it's something really bad.'

'Oh, heavens, I must find out!'

'Ring up the police-station.'

'Yes, of course. Oh, golly, it helps, just talking about it. I feel better already. Let's go and ring up the police-station. We'll go up to Ted's and use his phone.'

'Have breakfast, or your mother will suspect something.'

'Oh, yes. She mustn't know. She disapproves frightfully of Pat as it is, and this would finish it.'

'Why doesn't she like him?'

'Because he doesn't say please and thank you and his hair's too long and his parents aren't nice and he's been in prison before.'

'Has he?'

'Yes. But only for hitting someone.'

Peter grinned.

'My mother wants me to go out with Gordon Hargreaves,' Ruth said.

'Cripes!'

'Somebody nice. Or you.'

'I resent being put in the same category as Gordon Hargreaves. Very much.'

'Golly, yes. I didn't mean that. I'm sorry.'

Peter smiled, and they went and had breakfast. Ruth took two aspirins when her mother wasn't looking. She felt very nervous and on edge, and the toast stuck in her throat. They walked up to Ted's house, a neat new semi on the estate, and hammered at the door. Ted put his head out of the window, very tousled, and came down.

98

'It's Sunday,' he said. 'S—U—N—D—A—Y. The day of the long lie-in. Or didn't you know?'

'Please can I use your phone?'

'Yes.' Ted was on the telephone for his work, as sometimes he was called out at night to take a breakdown truck to an accident. Ruth envied him his telephone, but her father wouldn't have one. 'Who wants to pay for being disturbed?' he said.

Ruth looked up the police-station number in the book, and told Ted what had happened.

'Oh, cripes, your lover's a nutter,' he said. He looked serious. 'That's bad, Ruthie. Do the parents know?'

'Of course not.'

The phone was ringing at the police-station, and she felt ill. Her fingers were shaking. Ted went into the kitchen and put the kettle on, and Peter picked up the newspaper off the mat and sat on the stairs reading it. Someone said, 'Northend Police-station.'

'I want to know—I—I'm asking about someone called Patrick Pennington.'

'A missing person?'

'No. You've got him. I want to know what's going to happen to him.'

'Patrick Pennington?' The voice went dim, talking to some-one else. She heard it laugh and she caught the word Mitchell, and someone said, 'Your coffee, George.' A typewriter clacked in the background. Then the voice came back and said, 'He's being remanded in custody. He'll be going to Brixton tomorrow. Who is that inquiring?'

'Ruth,' Ruth said.

She put the receiver down, and sat looking at Barbara's wall-paper, green and gold squiggles on a lumpy fawn background. She saw Pat's face, and the way it had looked in the colours from the disco ceiling, very close to hers. And her inside felt as if it was turning over with the pain of what George had said.

'They're taking him to Brixton,' she said.

Neither Ted nor Peter smiled. They went into the kitchen and Ted poured out the tea and Ruth tried not to cry.

'Now what?' she said to Peter bitterly.

Peter shrugged. 'I'm sorry,' he said. 'It didn't help at all, did it?'

'I suppose, if they're keeping him,' Ted said, 'someone ought to tell these music people, who think he's going to play in this concert of theirs. They might get him out, if they've got a bit of authority on their side.'

'The Professor,' Ruth said. 'He would help him. Pat was going up to his place on Monday—tomorrow. Perhaps we could ring him up?'

She thought furiously. The Professor was the man to take charge. She didn't even know his name, let alone his address. Clarissa would know. She must ring up Clarissa and find out. Clarissa was in the London telephone directory, which Ted hadn't got.

'What do you do?' she said.

'You ring inquiries and asked for the number,' Ted said.

Ruth went back to the telephone with her cup of tea. She sat on the floor, which was where Ted kept the telephone, and found out Clarissa's number. She rang it. They were a long time answering and she supposed they were all in bed. Perhaps it was the maid's day off.

Clarissa's mother answered.

'Pat's professor? It's Professor Hampton, dear. He lives in Chelsea somewhere. I don't know where exactly, but I could find out from Clarissa. She's been to his place. Wait a moment.' There was a long, long pause, interrupted by the pips. Ruth hoped Ted didn't pay his own telephone bill. But Mrs. Cargill-Smith came back with both the address and the telephone number. Ruth wrote it down. 'Is anything wrong, dear?' Mrs. Cargill-Smith asked, but Ruth was already ringing off.

She rang Professor Hampton's number, her heart beating very hard and making her breathless. Another long, long wait. Then a woman's voice.

'Professor Hampton?'

'Professor Hampton won't be back until late tonight. He's in Paris just now.'

'Oh.'

She rang off. He would be back in time to meet Pat in the morning, but Pat wouldn't be there. She would go instead, and tell him what had happened. She put his address in the pocket of her jeans.

'You do choose 'em, Ruth,' Ted said.

'I can't help it.' She could have added, 'Hark who's talking!' but didn't, being under Barbara's own roof. She told them what she was going to do, and Ted said, looking worried, 'Ruth, are you sure he's worth——' and stopped, seeing her expression. Peter said, 'If that's all we can do today then, how about coming home and you can try the new hunter Dad's got? She's super.' And Ruth, to keep out of the way of her parents and have her mind distracted, said, 'Yes. Very well.' And for the rest of the day she felt that she was operating as two distinct persons, the Ruth that galloped Painted Lady through the McNair pastures, the sun hot in her face and her physical self gorgeously content, and the Ruth that was a little white ghost of the night before, terrified by what had happened and her inability to cope, and anguished by the thought of what Pat was going through. The contrast was so stark it was hard to believe that it was real, the emotions so torn that she came back feeling drained, as if she had had a whole day's hunting. Peter was kind, as Maxwell had been kind, but the whole thing was her own, and they couldn't make it any different.

The next morning she went to London, telling her mother she was going to Northend for the day. The journey was a night-mare with her anxieties and not knowing the way: she arrived at the Professor's front door and rang the bell with the feeling that she was a desert nomad arriving at an oasis. The house was in a Chelsea square, Georgian and pretty and immaculate; the area had a local, almost a village feel, with women shop-ping at the top of the street and an old lady walking her dog.

The door opened. A tall, middle-aged man with a stern, handsome face regarded her without smiling.

'Professor Hampton?'

'That's right,' he said.

'If you're expecting Pat,' she said, 'he's not coming. Please may I speak to you? Something awful has happened.'

'Oh, no!' said the Professor, closing his eyes and clutching his forehead. 'Don't tell me . . .' The concern, although dramatic, was no act. There was no glimmer of a smile. Ruth saw a stiffen-ing, a pulling-together in preparation for bad news, from what had been initially a cordial enough attitude.

'You'd better come in,' he said. 'I shall need a drink, if it's as bad as you say. Where is he?'

'In Brixton.'

'Oh, my God, not again! Oh——!' The man groaned out loud. He gestured her inside, and Ruth stepped over the doormat, feeling that at last she was with someone who was going to suffer as acutely as herself, if for different reasons. The Professor shut the door behind her and said flatly, 'Walk on—the door on the right. Oh, my God, the fool . . .'

The room on the right was large, and mostly filled by two pianos. Shelves crowded with books and piles of music lined each wall and there was a tape-recorder on the floor and a tangle of wires, and one armchair pulled up beside the fire-place.

'Sit down,' the Professor said, gesturing to the chair. 'Tell me all. He hit someone again? Who are you? A girl-friend?'

He gave her a stern, close look, and poured himself a whisky from a bottle on the mantelpiece.

'Do you want one? No? Some coffee?' He went to the door and shouted to the nether regions for some coffee, and came back and stood with his whisky, looking down at Ruth. 'Tell me.'

She told him, briefly, mentioning the concert, and Clarissa, and taking the van, leaving out the swimming and how Pat had kissed her.

'Assaulting a policeman . . . Is the boy mad?' The Professor was moved almost to incoherence. Ruth could see that he was a somewhat forbidding character, and sensed that his nature was austere and reserved, not easily given to the sort of despairing rage she was now a witness of. An elderly housekeeper brought in a tray of coffee and biscuits, and Ruth saw her surprise at the Professor's expression.

The Professor said to her, 'It's Patrick, Clemmie. He's in trouble again. Can you believe it? After all we went through before——'

'Oh lor,' said Clemmie. 'Never! Oh, dear me, the poor boy! And him coming along so—oh, dear me, sir, what a blow!' Her face was all genuine concern. Ruth felt strangely comforted, that there were other people, after all, to whom Pat mattered. All her panicky feelings faded, and Pat took on a new dimension, another facet showing itself through the Professor's concern. This Patrick was not the boy eating cockles, saying he wished it was like it every day; this Patrick was the stranger in the dark suit at the keyboard, the one who went where she could not follow. And yet, in this room, he seemed unaccountably close. She felt very much better.

'You can do something?' she said. 'You can get him out for next Saturday?'

'Well, God knows. I couldn't stop it before, could I? Three months he got, and all I could do was send a piano down there in a furniture van and they let him do two hours before lights out, after a day spent mixing concrete or something. If that was the sum total we could achieve last time——' He shrugged. His face was tight with anger. He walked up and down the room, jingling some money in his pocket. 'I have never, in all my years of teaching, come up against such a paradox as this boy. In some things, musically, he is quite astonishingly civilized—are you musical?' His glance snapped at Ruth and she shook her head. 'Do you know anything of——? No. Well, I won't bore you with what you won't understand. In music he has an intuitive grace, in the very best sense, and in his behaviour he can be so graceless that it is hard to credit. Do you understand me? Do you know him well? How long have you known him?'

'Not very long. But I know what you mean.'

'You do?' He gave her another very searching look. 'Do you find him such a mass of contradictions as I do?'

'Yes.'

'I have always thought that his life here—his musical life— was smoothing his natural aggression. I must have been wrong. The very first time I met him he was on his way to the police-station to be charged for something—I forget what. It seems we have progressed no farther. He disappoints me bitterly.'

His face was so stern that Ruth began to wonder whether Pat would find much joy in a visit from his tutor, even if it was in order to secure his deliverance. She began to understand something of the pressure Pat worked under; she did not think the Professor was an easy man to please. She tried to explain the personal element in Pat's brush with the law, his long-standing acquaintance with Mitchell, in order to put his sins in a slightly better light, but the Professor was not mollified.

'To hit someone at all, considering his vocation, is imbecile. To choose a policeman is wanton. And to do it a week before a concert of the importance of this one on Saturday is——' He broke off with a gesture of complete disgust. 'There are no words to describe it.' He glanced at his watch. 'I must go down to Brixton and see how things stand . . . get hold of my lawyer . . . there must be no question of his being unable to play next Saturday.' He gave Ruth another of his keen glances. Ruth sensed that he wanted to know the relationship, how much of a competitor she was for Pat's attention.

She said, 'He's been working very hard for this concert. All day. Every day.'

'Not, I hope, with you in the vicinity?'

Ruth was cut by the man's meaning, and coloured up with indignation, but was too nervous of him to say anything back. She shook her head. She saw Pat lying on the sea-wall, the water glittering on his face, the Professor's influence binding his desire, darkening his expression . . . or was she being fanciful? She hated the Professor.

The Professor said, 'It is essential that he works hard at this stage. Don't you understand that?'

Ruth lifted her chin stubbornly. 'Yes, I do understand it. And he does work hard. I've never met anyone who works so hard. If you think I get in the way, you are wrong. The only times he has ever taken me out, it has been to concerts. Even on Saturday—it was to a concert, and practising all morning first.'

The Professor looked surprised at her tartness, and softened slightly.

'Good. Very good. I'm told he played very well on Saturday. I'll put it down to your influence.'

Ruth could not tell whether the remark was meant kindly or sarcastically. The Professor continued, 'Occasionally, in this job, we get a student who makes everything worth while. Patrick is one of those. Unfortunately, he has personality problems that are apt to overwhelm us at times, as you can see. I knew this when I took him on. I considered the risk and have not, until now, regretted it. I tell you this because I want you to understand that I do not take this trouble with all my students. With quite a lot of them, I feel six months sewing mail-bags would make very little difference to either them or me. But for Pat, it is another matter entirely. For example, I would not presume to give advice to the girl-friends of any of my other students, but to Pat's I would say, "Do not waste his time." Do you understand me?'

Ruth understood him very well. She did not reply, feeling too bitter to trust her voice. Her lips very tight, she stared into her coffee-cup. So much for her journey, she thought; she had accomplished a good deal more than she had bargained for. She saw her own fingers tighten on the cup-handle, and remembered hurling one of her mother's cups at the wall at home only a week or two earlier. She could well have done the same with the Professor's, the way the anger caught her, the indignation swelling like a physical pain. She put the cup down and stood up and went to the door.

'If I hadn't come, no one else would have told you what had happened to him. There isn't anyone else,' she said. Her voice shook dangerously, and she knew she would cry if she said any more, so she went blindly out to the front door. Unfortunately, the latch had an automatic lock on it, and she could not get it to open, and had the humiliation of being forced to wait for the Professor to do it for her. He came out and put his hand on it, and she waited, back to the wall, her face stony with trying to hide the rampaging of her thoughts. But the Professor gave a bleak smile and said, 'Yes, I'm very grateful. Thank you very much.' He opened the door a few inches, and held it.

'Are you coming to the concert on Saturday?'

She was forced to look at him.

'Yes,' she said.

'Then you will see him there. Don't worry, my dear. Things have to be said. The situation understood. Then we all know where we are. Don't be angry.'

He let the door go and she went out, stumbling down the steps into the street. He was sympathetic, but she did not look back, the resentment too strong, shaking her. She thought he was inhuman, ruthless . . . *unkind*. He cared very much about the Pat that produced music, not the Pat that was a human being. 'Personality problems!' Ruth muttered furiously . . . all Pat's frustrations and difficulties and deprivations rolled into social-worker's jargon, getting in the way of his career . . . the phrase speared her. And then, souring and confusing still further, she remembered that Pat liked the Professor, respected him. He had said so. He was prepared to accept the Professor's standards; he had turned away from her on the sea-wall because of the Professor. But on Saturday night he had forgotten.

Ruth had no idea where she was, hurrying along a crowded street, muttering and scowling, all bound up in such a confusion of thoughts that she saw nothing. Her thoughts got her nowhere; there were no conclusions, they were so wild and undisciplined and prejudiced. Her anger left her, and she was hungry and her head ached.

And then, staring unseeing at her own reflection frowning back from a boutique full of black leather dresses, she wondered if Pat had meant what she had thought he meant on Saturday night. The doubt came like a jolt out of the blue, fixing her to the pavement. Or was it the beer and the dancing and what all boys did, moved by the moment, quite meaninglessly? In Brixton, moved by a very different atmosphere, he might well not have given her a thought at all. How did she know? Why had she taken it for granted so glibly, that he might love her as she loved him?

'Oh, God,' she said, staring at the straw eyelashes on the shop model, hypnotized by the horror of this revelation. 'He wants it to be like the Professor wants it. He's as good as said so. Even Saturday—the disco—was only a reward to pay me back, for protecting him from Clarissa. And kissing me like that . . . Was she so old-fashioned, so naïve, so antediluvian, that she thought it meant anything? Had he ever shown that he cared tuppence, sought her out, been jealous of her, even held her hand with the damp, trembling passion of Gordon Hargreaves? No, not any of those things. Only the offhand affection for not nagging, the routine pressure of a knee under the table. There was nothing. 'Oh, God,' she thought, the tears bursting up, the shop-window dissolving, 'I am so infantile, so stupid, so dumb, so *feeble*!' Even the crying, a wet rag, not knowing anything, where she was, what to do . . . she was so *pathetic* . . . no wonder she did not move him. Everybody kissed everybody all the time without the sky falling. She was a nineteen-ten girl, straight out of the nursery.

She did not remember getting home. She remembered, at Northend station, that Pat had left his suit there, and she got it back, after a lot of argument and the intervention of the station-master and a phone call to the police-station.

'Whatever have you got there?' her mother asked.

Ruth said, 'Pat's suit.'

She remembered all the things that her mother mustn't know, surfacing from her stupor.

'He left it at the station on Saturday night. Then we forgot it.'

'I'm surprised to hear he possesses one,' Mrs. Hollis said.

'He doesn't wear jeans for concerts,' Ruth said scathingly.

'Are you all right?' her mother asked. 'You look peaky. All washed out.'

'Yes, I'm all right.' She went upstairs and hung Pat's suit on a hanger. It was a beautiful suit with a Simpson's label. There was nothing in the pockets save a handkerchief and a diary. She looked doubtfully at the diary, and riffled through the pages very rapidly, to see if there was anything in it. She knew that if there was, she mustn't read it, but did not know whether her frame was up to such restraint. She very much doubted it. But the diary was empty except for, every few weeks, the name or names of some pieces of music and the name of a place. She assumed they were concert engagements, and confirmed it by looking up the following Saturday. It said, 'Northend. Rachmaninov C Minor under Backhaus. God save us.' There were no girls' names, no girls' addresses, neither her own nor anyone else's.

Ruth lay on her bed and looked at the ceiling.

The week passed. The posters for the concert, both in the local newspaper and in Northend remained uncorrected as to the soloist for the concerto, and Ruth assumed the Professor had achieved Pat's freedom. She heard nothing, and could not bring herself to ring up the Professor. She did not exist, she thought, not for them nor for herself. She was just a walking, eating thing, mooching down the field, going for long slow rides on Toad and lying in the grass looking at the sky, going shopping and forgetting what she had gone for. She thought of Pat the whole time.

Her mother, with magnificent restraint, asked her no questions. Only, 'I take it we're all going to this concert on Saturday?'

'Of course. He gave us the tickets, didn't he?'

'Yes. I just thought you'd dropped out with him or something.'

'He's in London all this week.'

'Oh, I see.'

On the Saturday morning Ruth got up early and went to Northend, with the suit. It was an excuse, if she needed one. Her mother had washed the white shirt, which had been scrumpled, and ironed it, and it lay on the top of the suit which her mother had expertly folded. Her mother's part in it made it seem that Pat was accepted—now, when there were more reasons for her to reject him than ever before, did she but know them. The homeliness of the washed shirt touched Ruth, so that she had quickly to think about something else, to keep herself from buckling again.

The Pavilion was on the top of the cliffs, set among the corporation gardens that were terraced down to the sea. It was a perfect September morning, very still and bright, and everyone about their Saturday business, brisk and unconcerned. Ruth walked between the ranks of geranium and cineraria, along the gravel, swinging the bag, praying. The Pavilion appeared deserted, gazing out to sea with its glass frontage aflame, its posters making a mess of the architect's intentions; a dust-cart was parked outside. Ruth went in the front door. A woman was washing a vast expanse of rubber-tiled floor, down on her hands and knees.

'Is there a rehearsal here this morning?' Ruth asked her.

'I think so, dear. Coffee for ninety-three, they said.'

'Can I go in?'

'As far as I'm concerned you can.'

She heard it, opening the swing door, a great sigh of strings. Thick carpet hushed her feet. She pushed open another door, and the music lapped her, embracing the whole theatre. The stage was brightly lit but the auditorium was in semi-darkness. Ruth had expected it to be empty but there were quite a lot of people listening, several of the middle rows being almost filled up. Whatever they were playing, it was not Pat's Rachmaninov for there was no one at the piano. Ruth walked down the gangway and sat down close to where everyone else was, and saw immediately that there was a group of about a dozen people sitting to one side down in the front. The conductor, a small man in shirt-sleeves, turned round while he was still conducting and called out something to this group, and one of them said something back. The conductor put down his baton and the orchestra stopped playing, apart from a flute that wanted to finish its own particular bit. Ruth saw someone stand up and recognized the Professor; he went forward and the conductor came to him and they started talking. The members of the orchestra shuffled their chairs, changed their music, and started to chat, some of the strings tuning, and the people in the audience murmured among themselves.

'Now,' thought Ruth, 'I get up and walk down to the front and give Pat his suit.'

But it was quite impossible.

Pat was with the Professor. The Professor turned and said something to him and he got up and went to join the discussion with the conductor. Then they all went up on to the stage, and stood talking for some time, leafing through some music on the top of the piano. Then the Professor went back to his seat and Pat sat down at the piano and everyone stopped talking. Ruth went cold and sick, as if she was going to play it herself, and shut her eyes. There was a long, long silence. Then, quietly, the chords she remembered, not nervous and stumbling at all, but rich and urgent, unrolling towards the waiting strings and the raised baton as eloquently as Ruth remembered it in the Festival Hall, surging into the great tide of melody, so that Ruth forgot that she was nervous and in despair, only marvelling that this was Pat, who had written 'God save us' in his diary, who was no doubt in as deep a despair as herself, but yet was capable in his playing of making everything else but the music completely irrelevant. 'It doesn't just happen,' she remembered him saying, but now it did, or to Ruth it seemed so, sweeping her up on such confident waves of pure and beautiful noise that nothing else mattered any more. What had she expected? She didn't know. What had he been worried about? She didn't know, the music taking her, wrapping her about with such tenderness that it was as if the whole past week of anguished uncertainty had never happened. She wanted to laugh and cry at once, like the ladies in the cinema that had watched the film. Oh, how she loved him! There wasn't anything else but this, and the music was all her feelings distilled and swelling the corporation dome, escaping into the lovely morning and the hazy September sky. Her heart filled her, pressing everything else into insignificance.

When it was finished, the little audience broke into a

spontaneous outburst of cheering and clapping. The conductor turned round, smiling and holding his hand out to Pat, and called down something to the group of people in the front row. Ruth saw the Professor get up and go up to the platform, and the first violin got up and went and said something to Pat. Everyone started buzzing. Ruth got up and started to walk down the gangway, propelled by some force quite outside herself, and quite undeniable. She could not even feel her feet touching the ground. She went up to the edge of the platform, slipped between a pair of fat, solemn men talking in German, and called out, 'Pat!'

He was still sitting at the piano, and the conductor was saying, '. . . We do this part again . . . where the clarinet comes in, or from the beginning of the movement if you prefer it. I feel we take it too slow from what you want. You say.'

Pat turned his head and saw Ruth. His face, very taut and grim, seemed to Ruth to flower, the smile coming as she had never seen it before. He got up, leaving the conductor in mid-sentence, and came to the edge of the platform, and leaned down to her, holding out his hand.

'Ruth!'

Another hand, hard as a vice, clamped itself round Ruth's elbow, and a clipped angry voice, directed at Pat, said, 'Will you kindly remember what you are doing!' and Ruth felt herself moved off across the space in front of the seats and up the carpeted gangway as much by an implacable will as by the physical force on her arm. She went in a dream, Pat's smile lighting her, her feet feeling several inches above the ground. The Professor directed her through the swing doors and swung her round to face him.

'Go away!' he said.

Ruth smiled at him.

'When I said you would see him today, I meant *after* the concert. Never before. Do you understand?'

'I brought his suit.'

'I beg your pardon?'

'His best suit. He'll need it tonight. It's in a bag on seat H ten.'

'Oh.' The Professor looked at her very closely, and Ruth saw him visibly soften. He almost smiled. Not that she cared.

'Don't you dare put your face through these doors again. Not until tonight. You will see him *afterwards*. I promise you. Now run along.'

'But now, when he's finished . . . ?'

'He hasn't finished. He has only just started.'

'But it was perfect.'

'It was very far from perfect.'

'Afterwards then?'

'He will be at my hotel, resting . . . having a bath, keeping his mind in order. Nothing you can help him with, thank you very much. Good-bye.'

Ruth sighed.

But it was all right. She went, drifting past the geraniums and the cineraria, not seeing anything at all.

Chapter 8

Sitting squashed in the back of her father's car with Ted and Barbara, on the way to the concert, Ruth didn't think that even Pat could feel more nervous that she did herself.

'They've given him bail then?' Ted asked her, out of earshot of everyone else.

'They must have. I don't know.'

She should have asked the Professor what had happened but in her dream this morning she had never thought.

'You haven't told them? They don't know?' he asked, nodding towards their parents.

She shook her head.

In the car, she kept wondering if thoughts of her had intruded upon his thoughts of Rachmaninov that afternoon. She was in competition with the Professor's ideals. It was still for Pat to decide, for she had neither the wish nor the will to stand down. She was done for.

'Barbara's going to have a baby,' Ted said suddenly.

Mr. Hollis nearly drove into a telegraph pole. Mrs. Hollis. gave a little shriek and turned round, clutching her seat, her face flushing up with strained pleasure.

'*Darling*! How lovely! Oh, how lovely!'

'Well, well, well,' said Mr. Hollis.

Ruth looked at Barbara and saw that she was genuinely happy. Her usual peevish expression was changed to a self-satisfied glow. Ruth wondered if motherhood could work such a far-reaching miracle that Barbara would stay looking like this, that her character would be changed. Perhaps it was what she had wanted all the time she had worked and come home tired and had to cook the supper and nagged at Ted because he didn't wash up. It was what it was all about, after all. She thought of Pat and wanted to cry. The Professor didn't want it, not at all.

112

'Auntie Ruth,' her father said, and laughed.

She tried to smile.

'Grandad,' said Barbara. They all laughed like mad.

'This is a celebration then,' Mrs. Hollis said. 'How lovely! It really is the first time we have all gone out together since you two were married! That was very considerate of Pat, Ruth. He's going up in my estimation all the time.'

Ted winked at Ruth, but with a gleam of sympathy. He recognized her feelings in the dark uncertainty of her eyes and the pale cheeks. Pat would go down in their mother's estimation a lot quicker than he had come up, they were both thinking, when she knew. Ruth stared out of the window.

Outside the Pavilion was a notice saying, 'All seats sold.' There was a crush of cars and people greeting each other, streaming in along the geranium walks, their best evening clothes rudely tossed by the breeze coming off the sea. They waited for Mr. Hollis to come back from parking the car, Ruth keeping apart, not wanting to have to talk. She was nervous of seeing Maxwell or Rita, and them saying something that her mother might overhear. But her father joined them and they went inside and took their seats. They were in the middle beside the gangway about five rows from the front. 'Too close, if it's loud stuff,' said Mr. Hollis, but Ruth thought, 'It's close enough to see what he's thinking.' Much closer than she had been in the morning. She could not believe that it was going to happen, in spite of all the evidence. There was a man on the stage putting music on all the stands. Members of the orchestra started to take their places, tending their instruments, blowing their noses and chatting quietly.

'Pity it's not Duke Ellington,' Barbara was saying to Ted.

'What a gorgeous girl,' Mrs. Hollis whispered to Ruth, and Ruth turned and saw Clarissa coming down the gangway with her mother. She turned back quickly, shrinking in her seat, and said, 'That's Pat's ex-girl-friend. The one whose house we went to last week. She plays the violin.'

'My word, but she's beautiful.'

'She's horrible,' Ruth said.

Her mother smiled. The chestnut hair floated away into some seats safely out of range, and Ruth relaxed. Clarissa still loved Pat, Ruth remembered; she saw Clarissa's expression across the lunch table, and heard the bitterness in her voice. What had happened between them? She wished——

'Good evening, my dear.'

She turned round, and found the Professor easing himself into the seat immediately behind her own. She gaped at him, the colour flaring.

'If you want to have a word with Pat afterwards,' he said, 'I'm warning you we shall have to leave as soon as he's finished. Like Cinderella, he has to be back at the gates of his other world on the stroke of midnight.'

He smiled, all sweetness.

'But——' Ruth was panic-stricken. 'I must see——'

'Yes, dear girl. You can come with me when it's over.'

'Oh, thank you.'

'Whoever's that?' her mother whispered.

'His Professor. His teacher.'

'Whatever did he mean about Cinderella?'

'Oh, it's the way he talks. In riddles.' 'Oh, good lord,' she thought, 'suppose he talks to his companion about Pat being sent to Brixton!' Her mother was obviously going to listen to anything he might say.

But he was saying, safely, in reply to a question, 'Yes, of course he's nervous, very nervous. But it would be amazing if he wasn't.'

'Quite. Playing under Backhaus doesn't happen to many students. How did the rehearsal go?'

'Very well.' They launched into technicalities and Mrs. Hollis said to Ruth, 'What a distinguished-looking man! When did you meet him?'

'Last week.'

'I must have got Pat all wrong,' her mother said. 'I just didn't realize . . . He didn't give me the impression that he was anything other than the typical offhand, mannerless teenager. I still can't quite believe this is going to be the same person that used to deliver our bread.'

Ruth found it impossible to reply. Her feelings, assailed from all directions, were beaten to a numb, flickering mess of contradictory emotions, jumping like the nerves in a bad tooth.

She had expected Pat first, forgetting the overture. The eminent conductor received an enthusiastic reception which he acknowledged with smiles and waves more Gallic than Teutonic and launched immediately into something very soothing and lyrical. Ruth sat back and shut her eyes, wanting to be soothed, but the piece came to an end before she noticed any change in her feelings.

Backhaus left the stage to a storm of applause and Mrs. Hollis said to Ruth, 'I don't know about you, but I'm quite nervous.'

Ruth watched the members of the orchestra chatting again, and putting the Rachmaninov music ready. Somebody opened the piano up. The second violin turned up the corners of his music to make them easy to turn over, and Ruth remembered that they only did it for their wages; they did it nearly every night, year in, year out, and it meant nothing to them at all. She didn't believe it.

The applause started again, and the conductor came out from the wings with Pat. Pat was in evening-dress, which shook Ruth—and evidently her mother too, for she gave an audible gasp—but walked to the piano with a scowl on his face that was familiar enough to counteract the unfamiliarity of the appearance. He gave the briefest of nods to the audience, an uncertain smile to the first violin, and sat down with a professional flick of his tails over the back of the stool. If he was nervous it didn't show, apart from the grimness of his expression. Backhaus said something to him and he nodded, and the violins all got ready to go with a communal movement that made Ruth think of the archers in some medieval battle. Pat rubbed his palms down his thighs, glanced at the conductor, who nodded, and Ruth leaned back, feeling all her tensions slipping away as the piano sounded out of the waiting silence. She could watch, feast herself on Pat, knowing that—whatever the Professor's opinion—his playing was flawless. He gave the impression of utter and complete involvement, without any anxieties at all, only a tenderness that Ruth had never seen except when he was at the piano; he was away, over her boundaries again, where she could not touch him, although he was physically so close that she could follow his every movement, almost as if she were turning the pages again. How could he remember it, she wondered? It was so complex and rich in its great profusion of sound, not clean and linear like the sonata last week, but a thing of eddies and surges with cascades of notes all sounding off to drown her again, as she had been drowned in the Festival Hall. It surely wasn't *easy* to do—it was 'hours and hours for months and months'—and when the solo instrument threw in its lot with the whole orchestra and flung out the magnificent theme in virtuoso abandon against the soaring strings and brass, it looked to Ruth like very hard physical work, but the acceptance of it was effortless and total: it was wings lifting all the sour old pains into limbo. Ruth could have laughed out loud.

'My word, I would never have believed——!'

Between movements, Mrs. Hollis couldn't find words. Pat wiped his face and his hands with a pristine handkerchief and shifted the stool a fraction, and scratched his nose. Ruth remembered that at the same time last week they had been climbing over the roofs of the bathing-huts at the Lido. She sat there idiotically smiling, and the melody of the slow movement reached out and caught her off guard, very quiet and simple, a soft rippling of the piano over which the clarinet lifted the sighing tune. Pat played as if he was dreaming, very still and upright, taking the tune himself and meandering with it through a background of strings. It grew more urgent, the current taking it, swelling and falling over smooth stones, until, through flurries and long lilting waves of melody he took it all alone to its conclusion, very grave and soft, with Herr Backhaus watching, sad and still. Closing, it left the listeners in suspension, not a murmur, not a squeak. Backhaus smiled. Pat dropped his hands and glanced at the conductor, not showing anything. He rubbed his hands over his forehead and pushed at his hair, then sat scowling, biting the side of his thumb-nail, waiting for the orchestra to gather itself to the raised baton.

Ruth heard the Professor say, 'Biting his nails, my God!' but his voice was full of satisfaction.

Ruth thought she guessed why Pat was biting his nails, led by the orchestra into an altogether more restless involvement, his dream given over to a very businesslike concentration. The now familiar melodies were leafed about with a fresh urgency; Ruth sat back, pushed, enslaved by the noise. 'Hackneyed,' she remembered. Clarissa would be wearying across the gangway, unless the fact that it was Pat playing had the power to unweary her. But the climax building up between the piano and orchestra stopped the silly wandering of her brain, shaking her, stopping her from everything but a pulsing participation. It was impossible to be detached as the piano climbed the scale and ran down again in spectacular figures that Ruth could put no name to, while the orchestra soared up on the last outpouring of the marvellous tune, the piano crying out underneath until, faster and faster, it cascaded to the final thudding halt with chords delivered by Pat with the whole of his very considerable strength in exact accord with Backhaus's cutting-off gesture with the baton. That it might have been any otherwise would have been disaster, but that it happened with such breathtaking perfection left Ruth limp with a sense of utter completion, gorged in every one of the faculties which had earlier been in such dire need of refreshment.

The applause was immediate, almost a carrying on of the music's thunder. There were shouts and stampings and a storm of clapping. Pat got up, looking stricken, and the conductor came round and put his arm round him and shook his hands, and Pat remembered the procedure and smiled, and went and shook hands with the first violin, and then he stepped forward and bowed very correctly to the audience, dropping his head so that Ruth noticed the gash among the hair which he must have got in hitting the wall last Saturday.

Mrs. Hollis fortunately noticed nothing but his elegance in the formal black suit, for she said to Ruth, 'Magnificent! Gorgeous! I still can't quite believe it!'

The Professor leaned over to Ruth and said, 'Are you coming my dear?'

They walked out together through the noise, shutting it out through a padded door. They climbed some steps and went up on to the side of the stage, seeing it all from a fresh angle, the backs of the double-bass players and the cellos, and the piano far away, its lid yawning. The Professor was smiling.

, Ruth said, 'It was perfect, wasn't it?'

'It was all right,' he said, and smiled again. 'Promising,' he said.

Pat come off with the conductor, his face quite expressionless. Whether it was Brixton or whether it was Rachmaninov, he looked to Ruth a good ten years older than when she had last seen him, exactly as he had promised Rita. Perhaps it was the suit. The Professor went up to him and Ruth knew that it was only his public school upbringing that stopped him embracing him. As it was he put an arm round him, and said something Ruth did not hear. Ruth, watching, felt a small pang of jealousy. Whatever the Professor said, Pat would take. Whether it was about Rachmaninov or about girls.

The applause was still tumultuous. Backhaus was shaking the Professor's hand and laughing, and Pat took a comb out of an inner pocket and combed his hair very carefully, and wiped his face and his neck with his handkerchief, and Backhaus did the same and they went back together to take another bow.

The Professor turned to Ruth and said, 'Pat has the very precious gift of being able to produce more, the bigger the occasion. The more it matters, the more nervous he is, the better he plays. There are many unfortunate, and equally gifted musicians, who would give almost anything to have this particular— well, what is it?—quirk of nature, perhaps? Showmanship, if you like. It is terribly necessary to a concert pianist.'

'Oh,' Ruth said. She didn't want a concert pianist. She wanted Pat.

After the second bow he came to her, while the Professor talked to Backhaus. He put his arm round her shoulders and gave her a little squeeze, but did not say anything. In a strange way it was as if he wasn't there at all; it was as if a current of electricity had brushed her. His eyes had seen her, but his brain was not connected; it was away where she could not move it. Curiously, she was not upset. It seemed perfectly in accord with the occasion; even she was not immune to the vibrations, shaken by the fading trail of Rachmaninov's glory through the dusky, gold-lit haze of the auditorium. So how could Pat, who had made it, come down so soon? Backhaus, more practised, took him by the elbow and said, 'And again, my friend. Again.' And they went out to take another bow, and Ruth thought how strange it was that there was nothing there, once it was done. Nothing at all. Like being a medium. And yet, even more strangely, it was just a job, born of long hours at a village-hall piano and lessons paid for by the Northend corporation. The enigma she had first sensed in the Festival Hall. The Professor was smiling, his austere face lit with what Ruth guessed was a rare excitement.

After the fourth bow there seemed to be a whole lot of people who wanted to see Pat. The members of the orchestra streamed off for the interval and Ruth almost got carried away in a black stream of German chat. When she had fought her way back to the Professor, she found both he and Pat talking to a little old grey-haired man who looked to Ruth as if he was close to tears. Pat called him sir, and seemed to be coming back to earth in his company, a faint smile breaking. The Professor introduced several very cheerful, well-dressed men, and then Mrs. Cargill-Smith and Clarissa and two or three boys who looked like students broke in, but Pat, Ruth noted, did not put his arm round Clarissa, but merely nodded and muttered something, and Ruth was content to have them say their piece and go.

At last, by dint of moving further in when someone else moved out, she found herself next to Pat. He turned away from a rather fulsome woman in black who seemed to be a friend of the Professor's, and looked at her very gravely.

'I don't know what I'd have done if you hadn't come,' he said. 'I've been thinking about it all the week—that you would be finished, after last Saturday. You haven't come to—to—say that . . .?' His voice was soft and uncertain, his face drawn and tired.

'No,' Ruth said. 'I couldn't stay away. I've been thinking about you all the week too.'

He smiled as tenderly as if she were a little dreamy piece of Rachmaninov. Ruth, strangely, remembered the Brahms waltz in the village-hall. Her own smile was out of control, all over her face.

'It's what happened before,' Pat said. 'And I was so scared it was going to be the same. This last week has been awful—not knowing about you. Not the other things. I——'

'If you're going to hear the rest of the concert, you'd better go and take your seat,' the Professor said to Ruth. Everyone else had vanished and the orchestra was all ready and waiting again, and Backhaus emerging out of the doorway to the dressing-rooms.

'She's not,' Pat said. 'She's coming with us.'

He took her by the arm and marched her through the door-way the conductor had just come out of. The Professor followed them. They heard the applause breaking out, like waves on a beach, and they were in a quiet corridor, the door closing behind them, the concert shut away. Pat opened another door and they were in a dressing-room; Ruth saw Pat's jeans and sweater flung over a chair, and the Professor's expression in the mirror, not angry, but amused and complacent. He was glancing at his watch.

'We've time,' he said. 'It's all right. You get changed, and we'll go and have a little drink. Sit down, Ruth.' He pulled out a chair. 'A little celebration, before we set off. I think we can consider we've plenty to celebrate just now, in spite of all the other problems that beset us. We'll forget them for the time being. He played very well, eh Ruth? Don't you think I'm a very good teacher?'

Ruth smiled cautiously, taking the offered seat. Pat took off his tailcoat and waistcoat, and his white tie and shirt and washed very splashily. Ruth seeing the drops of water running down his back, remembered the sea-wall and the shadow of the Professor; she knew the Professor would not leave them alone together. Just as he had been there on the sea-wall. She got up and handed Pat a towel that was hanging over a rail, and he blinked at her through the water and smiled. She saw the little gold medal hanging round his neck and wondered if Clarissa had given it to him. He put his old clothes on and the Professor gathered up the suit and the odds and ends that were lying around, and they went out to put the things in the Professor's car. The breeze came up from the sea, sharp with the smell of the mud-flats and the seaweed under the pier, hinting at old wet timber and crushed crab-shells and whitened sticks and blobs of tar on the smooth pebbles. A ship was moving down on the ebb, its lights passing the pier, the soft thud of its engines like an animal breathing in the dusk. The water was calm, brimming beneath the first stars to the far shadow of the Kentish shore.

Pat watched the ship, and said softly, 'Oh, God!' He kicked the wheel of the Professor's car, his hands thrust into his pockets. 'What a ruddy mess! What a——' He shrugged, turning away.

'Come on,' the Professor said sharply. 'There's a pub across the road. We can spare ten minutes.'

Pat took Ruth's hand, and they crossed the road and went into a cosy, dimly-lit pub with an oak-beamed ceiling and candles in bottles, and soft canned music, all very comforting and suitable. The Professor bought two double whiskies and a sherry, handing the sherry to Ruth. He pushed one of the whiskies to Pat and said, 'We'll take you back happy. There's nothing in the rules against it, as far as I know.'

Pat gave a faint smile.

'What's going to happen?' Ruth asked. 'When will you know?'

'The case comes up before the magistrates on Tuesday,' the Professor said. 'It appears that it is almost certain that it will be adjourned to the Quarter Sessions, to be tried before a jury, and there is very little we can do save plead not guilty and try and get bail. We have hired a very high-powered lawyer who thinks he might manage this, as he managed—against all the rules in the book—to get Pat the day off today. If he doesn't manage, the next Quarter Sessions aren't for another month, so that Pat will disappear from human ken as soon as the case is over. And there will be nothing at all we can do about it. These minions of the law—they are quite immovable. The whole thing is completely out of our hands. British justice, unfortunately, is utterly irrevocable, absolutely implacable, quite ungiven to accepting the odd bribe, yielding to the sly hint! I have considered everything, even to putting in a plea of insanity.'

'Thank you,' Pat said gravely.

Ruth could not tell whether the Professor was really joking or not. She could not divine the Professor, the meaning of the gleam in his cold grey-blue eyes. Although he cared so much for Pat, it was not a fatherly care; it was a driving, implacable—his own word for British justice—care; it was something very stern, although it had love in it. To Ruth it explained a great deal of Pat, and she now felt that it was this cold, caring pressure that made her own love for Pat by comparison so mushily, defensively emotional. Pat seemed so vulnerable suddenly, in spite of every apparent physical indication to the contrary—just another of the innumerable contradictions that so entangled him—that she felt of her own love now as entirely a giving, protective thing, to help him. She wanted nothing from him for her own comfort, but only to give it to him. Perhaps it was the sherry, but the feeling was so strong she could not have said anything sensible at that moment. Pat did not say anything either, staring into his whisky, turning the glass round in his fingers.

There was a long, thoughtful, sad silence.

Then the Professor said, 'This was supposed to be a little celebration. For tonight. A very successful day, Pat, whatever else might or might not happen. Backhaus was very happy. Let's drink to that.'

They drank, and the Professor started to speak to Pat about his performance. Pat, although he said very little, listened attentively and Ruth stood close beside him in a warm haze of her sherry, thinking that the Professor would carry on like this right to the gates of Brixton prison, dissecting, analysing, shredding into little technical facts the whole fabric of what to Ruth had been a thing which words could not touch. Did he never let up at all? Ruth felt her expression hardening, impatient, and angry.

He glanced at his watch again, put down his glass and started to walk towards the door, still talking to Pat. They crossed the road back to the car-park and went to the car. The Professor unlocked it, got in and pushed the other door open for Pat.

'Get in,' he said.

He started talking about the restatement of the second subject in the first movement. Ruth put her hand on Pat's arm. The Professor started the engine.

'Pat,' Ruth said.

Pat looked at her, letting the door swing to.

'Ruth,' he said, 'you must come back, afterwards. I can't— I can't——' He reached for her, pulling her hard against him. 'Don't go away.' She put her arms round him, frantic, lifting up her face. 'No! Oh, no! I won't ever——' He kissed her, stroking back her blowing hair, then, with what was almost a groan, pressing her head closer, kissing her again. His strength almost hurt, yet there was a tenderness, an asking not a demanding. Ruth felt herself lost, holding on to the hardness of the back of his neck, brushed by the softness of his hair.

'It's all right,' he said. 'It's all right as long as you don't go away.' He kissed her again, very gentle.

'Pat!'

Ruth wanted to laugh, but she thought she was crying. The Professor was furious, revving up his engine. He pushed the door open. Pat straightened up. Ruth saw his eyes, lit by the electric street-lights, full of her own reflection, not thinking about the

Professor at all. She laughed then, almost like crying, and said, 'I love you.'

'I love you too,' he said.

'Do you mind?' said the Professor acidly.

Pat got into the car. Ruth saw the Professor's face, green in the street-light, filled with unstarry thoughts, lined, and grim. He let in the clutch and the car went away with a well-bred roar, very fast. Ruth walked across the car-park to her father's car, and sat on the wing, staring into the warm darkness. She was not real. She was away with the stars and the breeze off the water, holding Pat's kisses, filled with the sad urgency of his voice. Pat, oh, *Pat*! It was a pain and an agony and a happiness beyond words. She had never been kissed by anyone who mattered before Pat, and it occurred to her then that he was as accomplished in his loving as he was in his playing; he had practised, she thought, with a sad diversion of her mind, recalling the puppy fumblings of the other boys, the clumsy advances, the unsubtle grabs. Never had she felt so right, so filled, so piercingly sure of anything as when Pat had held her, and she wanted to convince herself that the conviction of his caresses was prompted by love, not merely by plenty of practice. But he had said so. He had been torn and shaken, not teasing and amused. His face in the lamplight had been stark, almost fierce. 'It is true,' Ruth thought. 'He loves me. He said so.' She could not move herself from this fact, shivering on the wing of the car, held by glory of what had happened.

The car-park, suddenly, was no longer deserted. People started to filter through from the park, spilling out of the Pavilion, talking and laughing. Ruth tried to come back to earth, and couldn't.

'Oh, there you are!' her mother said. 'We thought you were with Pat. Whatever are you doing, all on your own?'

'He's gone. He had to go. It wasn't worth my coming back.'

Mr. Hollis unlocked the car, and they all piled in.

'Whatever else he isn't, according to your mother, he's a very fine pianist. I must say, I thoroughly enjoyed that.' Mr. Hollis put the ignition key in. 'Okay at the back?'

'I think he's dishy,' Barbara said. 'Why was I always out when he brought the bread?'

'I shouldn't imagine he'll have to do those sort of jobs much longer. What's his programme now? Has he left College?'

'Not yet.'

'Why did he have to rush off then?' Mrs. Hollis asked. 'He's not had to go back to London, has he? I would like to have told him how much we enjoyed it.'

Ruth did not reply. Ted started to talk about something else, tactfully, and Mr. Hollis nosed the car out into the traffic. They cruised along the top of the Upper Promenade, looking at the lights below, and the great calm darkness beyond, which was the sea.

'You ought to invite Pat home one evening, Ruth. We ought to get to know him,' Mrs. Hollis said. 'He obviously isn't what I thought he was.'

'He is what you thought he was,' Ruth said.

'How do you mean?'

'He had to rush off because he has to be back in prison before twelve. Brixton. They just let him out for the concert.'

She was past subterfuge now; she was not even afraid of saying it. It would be public knowledge on Tuesday, and what her parents might say, then or now, would not move her in the slightest degree.

Her mother gave a sort of groan and turned round, her face green and tight in the neon-lighting, with much the same expression on it as the Professor had revealed when he had driven away. Mr. Hollis changed gears with a crash and said, 'Any more surprises tonight? Let's have them all while we're on the subject.'

'There aren't any more.'

'What did he do?' Mrs. Hollis demanded. 'Why is he in prison?'

'He borrowed a car and when a policeman came and asked him about it, he hit him and ran away.'

'When did this happen?'

'Last Saturday.'

'You mean, when you were with him?'

'Yes.'

'Oh, my God, Ruth, you mean you were involved in it? You might have landed up in the police-station too?'

'I might have, but I didn't.'

'How dare he! How dare he put you——'

'He didn't! It just happened. He didn't plan it! He was sweet to me. It was the loveliest evening in all my life.'

'It sounds like it! Dragging you into——'

'He didn't drag me——'

'Please,' said Mr. Hollis. 'Not tonight. Not after he gave us so much pleasure. Can't we talk about it tomorrow?'

'Yes,' Ruth said. 'I don't want to talk about it again. That's all there is. I've told you now. There's nothing else to say.'

'Oh, isn't there?' said her mother, grim as the Professor. 'That's your opinion, Ruth, believe me.'

'Later,' said Mr. Hollis.

'Yes,' said Ruth's mother. 'Very well, we'll talk about it later.' And she stared out of the window, her face as black as the darkness over the sea.

Chapter 9

Ruth, as always, it felt to her, knew nothing, not even who to ask or where to go. She had had nothing to do with the law all her life; the village policeman was a friend, the only policeman she knew. This was Pat's side of it, this gaunt hall of echoing footsteps and brown doors, of worried people conferring, a woman crying, policemen everywhere . . . the smell of cold swabbed floors and brass polish. Every day, she had discovered: six courts sat every day, and she had passed the imposing civic building hundreds of times in her life with never an inkling of what it was all about. 'So this is where I find out,' she thought. She felt sick with nerves.

She went up to a policeman standing at the bottom of the flight of stairs that led up out of the entrance hall.

'Where do I go for—for—to hear my friend—er—tried?'

'Magistrates' court?' the policeman asked. 'Or is it trial by jury? The magistrates' courts are upstairs. These two down here are Quarter Sessions. Each court has got the agenda pinned up outside.'

'Oh.' She thought back to the Professor, and decided that it was the magistrates' court. The Quarter Sessions were to come later.

'Upstairs . . . thank you. Will he be—be up there now?'

'Is he on bail or in custody?'

'In custody.'

'He'll be downstairs in the cells then, till the case is called.'

She climbed slowly up the stairs, not wanting to see Pat in a cell, even if it was allowed. The only cells she knew about were the big barred cells in Westerns, where the man inside got hold of the jailor through the bars and half-throttled him with one hand while relieving him of the keys with the other, and the pictures in the newspapers of new prisons, with flowers and pin-ups and the occupant with his face blanked out. Neither seemed

126

relevant to Pat at all, yet he was in custody, and that's what it meant, bars and locks. She found it very hard to accept this fact, the whole experience of being outside the law completely beyond her narrow privileged world, where meals were always punctual, arguments were just grumbles, and crises no more than a pound note in the washing-machine by mistake. 'I don't know anything about anything,' she thought. Pat had done all this before; he knew the procedure, he knew what it was like to be in prison, to be pushed around by the screws. To her 'screw' was a book word, in quotes, but to him it was perfectly familiar vocabulary. She supposed that, by the end of the day, she would be able to accept this alien experience; it would be part of her experience through Pat. Pat had caused her to grow up more quickly during the last few weeks than in all the other years of her life. Just for an instant, hesitating on the top of the stairs, she realized that all this had happened because of the instant's decision she had taken that day in the lane, to turn round and stop his van, and ask for a lift. 'Suppose I hadn't?' she wondered. And the thought was exploded by scorn into instant fragments.

She was on another floor of brown doors and policemen chatting, and men in dark suits going in and out.

'Patrick Pennington,' she said to a policeman. 'Is this where he comes up?'

'I'll have a look, Miss.'

It was there in writing, pinned on a board, half-way down a long list, 'Regina v. Patrick Edward Pennington. Taking and driving away a motor vehicle without lawful authority. Assaulting a constable in the execution of his duty, thereby causing actual bodily harm.'

'This room, Miss. Number two.'

'How long will it be?' There seemed to be an awful lot of people in front of him.

'Can't say exactly, Miss. But a lot of these are very quick— parking offences and such like. He'll be in before lunchtime.'

'Can I go in?'

'Are you a witness?'

'No. Just a friend.'

'You can sit anywhere at the back. Wherever you like.'

Friendly and obliging, he waved her through the open door into an impressive wood-panelled room. There was a raised platform facing the door, with a long desk and three chairs pulled up to it with the town's coat-of-arms in gold on the dark leather backs. Below it was a long table with several of the dark-suited men chatting and setting out papers, all quite affable and normal. Several of the chairs round the room were taken by policemen and various nondescript people whom Ruth supposed were friends and interested parties like herself. There was nobody she knew. The sun shone into the room through long windows overlooking a cemetery. It was another kind of September morning like the morning of the rehearsal, a day for lying on the sea-wall in the thick yellowing grass. Ruth saw Pat's brown naked back and his eyes watching her, the grass crushed down, his blue shirt flung like a patch of the summer sky. She felt crushed inside.

Someone bellowed, 'Stand!' and everyone stood up, abruptly silent. The magistrates came in from a door at the back and took their places at the bench. The room seemed to fill up, and someone was shouting through the door into the corridor outside, 'Call Peter James Anstruther! Peter James Anstruther!' Peter James Anstruther, a stocky man with long sideburns, came in and was directed to a chair just in front of Ruth, where he was charged with driving a car with defective brakes, treadless tyres, and no tax.

'Do you plead guilty or not guilty?'

'Guilty, sir.'

Ruth was watching the magistrates. The middle one of the three, who seemed to be the one that mattered, was a woman. She was elderly, with a strong, lined face, an angular figure, and strong brown hands. 'If I were her,' Ruth thought, 'what would I think of Pat?' But she could only think of the woman thinking, like herself, that Pat was marvellous. She gave Peter James Anstruther a fine of twenty-five pounds. The next man, for stealing a leg of lamb out of the supermarket, she fined fifteen pounds. Parking over the stipulated time, parking for fifty minutes on a yellow line, driving a motor vehicle with defective lights, using threatening behaviour likely to cause a breach of the peace, drunk and disorderly in a public place . . . the men at the long table came and went, shuffling papers . . .

'The beer was dripping from the ceiling, and the mirrors were shattered. Damage was estimated at thirty-eight pounds . . .'

The man just in front of Ruth was a little, vague-eyed news-paper-seller.

'He's very sorry . . .'

A man came in and took a seat against the back wall. By his build and the way he walked, Ruth guessed he was Pat's father. He had the same thrust of the lower lip and the aggressive frown, the same cautious eyes. Ruth watched him, the nervous-ness thudding inside her.

'Relationships in this family are not entirely satisfactory. Mrs. Wilde's son said, "I'll smash you with a bloody chair." To which the accused replied . . .'

'Oh, God,' thought Ruth, 'how many people are there in trouble?' Pat was only one of countless thousands. Surely his case was no worse, no better . . . couldn't she say to Pat, the woman with the strong, intelligent face, as she was saying to the miser-able man facing her now, 'I have every sympathy with your situation, but it is no excuse for this sort of behaviour . . .' A fine wouldn't hurt Pat, but to shut him away when the sun was shining and the sea was coming up the beach over the warm sand and the trees on the crumbling sandy cliffs were yellow and gold in the still air . . . Ruth caught herself up in her mawkishness and shook her head.

'Fifteen pounds and five pounds costs.'

The door opened again and the Professor came in with a man in a dark professional suit and a file of papers. Two policemen came and sat down next to Ruth.

'Call Patrick Edward Pennington!' the voice bawled at the door.

Ruth felt as if she couldn't breathe.

One of the policemen said to the other, 'This is the young beggar that broke Mitchell's ribs.'

'If it had to happen, he couldn't have picked a better bloke.'

'No. It won't do him any good though. Not with the new directives come through about tightening up on police assault.'

'Not before time.'

Ruth looked anxiously towards the door and saw Pat come in with a policeman. He was wearing his best suit, the one Ruth had rescued from the railway station, and looked more like one of the lawyers than the accused, very serious, his face expression-less, the lower lip pushed out slightly. He came across the room to the chair by Ruth, saw her, but made no acknowledgement. He turned and faced the bench, and the policeman stood beside him. The woman magistrate looked at him, and did not remove her eyes, while the man at the table, who seemed to do most of the talking, picked up his papers and found the right page.

'You are Patrick Edward Pennington?'

'Yes, sir.'

'You live at 4, Church Cottages, Fiddler's End?'

'Yes, sir.'

'Your date of birth——' He fumbled again, coughed, and found the correct place. 'Your profession—I understand you are a music student?'

'Yes, sir.'

He turned to one of the other men at the table, who Ruth had gathered was some sort of public prosecutor, and this man picked up his sheaf of literature and intoned in a parsonage voice:

'Patrick Edward Pennington is charged that on September the third this year he did take and drive away a motor vehicle belonging to the Parade Bakery without lawful authority, and secondly that when apprehended by a police constable he did assault him thereby causing actual bodily harm.'

He then said something to the man who had come in with the Professor, and turned to the bench and said in a normal voice, 'I would formally ask you, madam, to take this case to trial at the Quarter Sessions.'

The magistrate nodded.

'Is he on bail or in custody?'

'He is in custody, madam.'

The Professor's lawyer stood up and said, 'I would make a very earnest application, madam, for Mr. Pennington to be released on bail until the Quarter Sessions.'

The magistrate looked at the prosecuting counsel, and he said, 'The police oppose bail, madam.'

A frown passed over the magistrate's face and she studied Pat thoughtfully. She then studied the sheaf of papers that had been handed up to her, presumably, Ruth guessed, describing Pat's offence, and the Professor's lawyer said, 'His own Professor, Professor John Hampton, a director on the board of the College of Music, will stand bail for him, and will have Mr. Pennington to live in his own home until the trial comes up. I would add, madam, that Professor Hampton's interest in this student's circumstances is by no means trivial. It is an extremely unusual and tragic case, in that this trouble has come into this young man's life just when every opportunity is opening up for him in his career—as you would understand, madam, if you were present at the concert at the Pavilion on Saturday night when he played as soloist under the visiting German conductor, Otto Backhaus.'

'I was present,' said the magistrate.

'On the strength of that performance Backhaus has invited Mr. Pennington to play with him again when he returns to this country at the end of the month, and there is also an invitation for him to play in a concert at the Albert Hall at the end of the week, in place of the original soloist who has been taken ill. You will understand, in these circumstances, how very strongly I would advise that bail should be granted.'

'This is not entirely to the point,' the magistrate said. 'He is no doubt not the first person to time his appearance in court at a very inconvenient moment for himself.'

She turned and muttered something to the magistrate beside her, and the three of them had a short confabulation. Ruth looked at Pat, who was almost near enough for her to touch him, standing very still, his hands clasped behind his back. The magistrate stopped muttering and said to the prosecuting lawyer, 'Who is the police officer in charge of this case?'

'Inspector Griffiths.'

'And he opposes bail?'

'He does, madam.'

The magistrate frowned again, and appeared to sigh. She stared at Pat, as if she would read his intentions, but there were no intentions written there. Pat looked back at her, his face congenitally defiant, the brows drawn down as they always were, the jaw set. But Ruth could see a pulse ticking in his neck, and his fingers moving restlessly, and the dampness of apprehension on the cheek-bone. 'So would I feel,' Ruth thought, 'and the sun shining and the sea warm outside and everyone going for their lunch in shirt-sleeves, and the old ladies paddling . . . So do I feel.' She found she was holding her breath, and

131

it hurt, and she wanted to reach out for Pat. *Pat*. She shivered.

'Is Professor Hampton in court?'

The Professor stood up.

'You are willing to have this young man live with you until his trial at Quarter Sessions?'

'I am.'

'Very well. Patrick Edward Pennington, I will remand you on bail in the sum of one hundred pounds, and you are to appear here to be committed to trial at the Quarter Sessions on the twenty-seventh of September . . .'

Ruth got up, because everyone else was moving and the constable at the door was shouting, 'Call Arthur Percy Macintosh! Arthur Percy Macintosh!' Pat turned round, white as a sheet. He looked at Ruth and said nothing, but Ruth saw him in that instant as if laid bare—it was as if, in one fragment of a second, he had no defences at all. He looked at her and it seemed to her that he was at an end, against a brick wall, quite alone. She saw immediately that, for all the lawyer and the Professor and his father and Mrs. Bates and herself, when it came to the thing that mattered there was no help at all: nor ever could be. What one did was one's own. It was a thought like a hammer-blow. And as quickly, it was gone, because his expression came back, his human shell covering up his soul, and Ruth thought that her own emotions had run away with her. Pat wasn't like that. She looked at him, walking beside him out of the room, and he smiled at her. She was mistaken, she thought. Pat could take anything.

'Clear the landing, please.'

'Pat,' she said.

He took her hand. His own was as cold as ice. They walked down the stairs, and the man Ruth thought was Pat's father put his hand on Pat's shoulder and said:

'Good on you, Pat! I'd have kicked up a ruddy fuss about being kept inside until today. Where've you been?'

'Brixton.'

'What's it all about then? Mrs. Bates told us, and your mother wanted to come but I talked her out of it. Thought she might stand up and make a scene. What's the bodily harm charge? That's what they'll get you on.'

'They say I broke one of his ribs.'

'Should've broken the whole ruddy lot!'

'Yeah, well, it's nothing to what they did to me——'

'Well, you got a good lawyer on it, haven't you? And if you've got marks to show—you're slow, Pat! You ought——'

'Oh, cripes, Dad, you know they just stand up there and say you fell down the steps to the cells, or you walked into the door. You say they pushed you into the door and who's going to believe it? It's not worth the trouble.'

'No, you can't win, that's the pinch . . . Good luck all the same. I'll drop in and see how you get on on the twenty-seventh. You'll get sent down again, I suppose!' He shrugged, and his gaze turned on Ruth. 'You're not alone, I see. You got someone to hold your hand.'

'This is Ruth,' Pat said. 'This is my father.' The introduction was cold. Mr. Pennington said, 'Pleased to meet you,' and Ruth dropped Pat's hand to shake his father's.

'Very nice,' said Mr. Pennington. 'What happened to that gorgeous red-headed bird you——'

'For cripes' sake!' Pat glowered at his father.

His father glowered back. 'Whether you're stewing in Brixton or doing a Paderewski in the Albert Hall, you're still my boy. I got a right to know things. You remember that. And you might remember us when the big money starts coming your way. You didn't learn to play that ruddy piano out of thin air, you know. Your mother——'

'If I ever have a ruddy penny to my name I'll come and stuff it down your——'

'Pat, Mr. Merriman wants a word with you.'

The Professor edged in, his voice sharp. 'If you'll excuse us,' he said very politely to Pat's father, 'Mr. Merriman has to get back to London.'

Pat turned away to talk to the lawyer and Ruth was left with Pat's two father figures, eyeing each other cautiously, as dissimilar a pair as were ever likely to meet, pointing the contradictions in Pat's nature.

Mr. Pennington said, grudgingly, 'I'm sorry he let you down.'

The remark surprised the Professor. He said, 'He's never let me down in his playing. It's what makes all this other business so sad.'

'Oh, well, he's young. He'll learn sense. It's too late for me,

133

but he'll make it, I dare say. I'll be seeing you.' He dipped his head to the Professor, and then to Ruth, and hurried away.

The Professor looked at Ruth and shook his head. 'An extraordinary gentleman. He goes a long way towards explaining Pat.'

'Like you,' Ruth thought.

The Professor smiled. 'You're still faithful, I see?'

'Yes,' she said stubbornly.

'You realize, don't you, that next time he won't get off? Mr. Merriman thinks the very least he can expect will be nine months and a pretty steep fine. I can pay the fine, but I can't do the nine months. Will you still be faithful then?'

'If he wants it.'

'You're a sweet girl,' the Professor said, very smooth. 'You're too good for Pat. What do your parents say about it?'

She did not answer. She suddenly felt that of all the influences on Pat's life, it was the Professor's that was the most baleful. The feckless unsubtle father seemed like a great draught of fresh air beside the Professor and his guile, the grinding pressure he brought to bear, his possessiveness.

She turned to Pat who had come back to them with the lawyer at his side.

The Professor said, 'How about lunch, Merriman, then we can see about getting back to London? We can leave the two young people to their own devices, if you've finished with Pat. I've no doubt they can entertain themselves for a couple of hours.' He smiled his polished smile. 'All right, Pat?'

Pat nodded.

'You'll be coming back to London with me, of course. Suppose you meet me at the "White Hart", say, in two hours' time? Will that suit you?'

'Yes,' Pat said.

'Very well.'

They went out of the court-house into the sun, and the two men walked off towards the car-park.

'Does he own you?' Ruth asked bitterly.

Pat grinned. 'He does at the moment, I suppose. I'm his hundred quids' worth.'

'No. I don't mean that. I hate him.'

'What's he been saying?'

'He keeps warning me off. As if I'm trespassing. As if you belong to him.'

Pat frowned. 'You don't want to take any notice.'

'Well, I——' She shrugged.

'Look,' Pat said. 'It doesn't matter. It's just how he is. He wants everything his own way. He's a bully. If he wasn't I'd never have got so far as playing with Backhaus on Saturday. Well, with my playing, that's all right, I don't mind, but in this it's different. He's no claim on my personal life at all. What *we* want now, he's just got to take. So don't you worry. You stand up to him, and you'll find he's all right.'

Ruth considered this and felt better.

'Is it true, what the lawyer said, that you've got to play in the Albert Hall or something?'

'Yes. At the Proms. On Friday. Whoever it was who was doing it has got mumps or something stupid, and they asked me. The Rachmaninov again.'

'Do you mind?'

'Mind?' He looked at her curiously. 'It's marvellous. Why should I mind? I'll be scared as hell, but that's something you just have to get used to.'

'You said, after the last concert, that you wouldn't have to work so hard.'

'Yes, I did. But I see now, there's always something else ahead, and if there isn't it means you're no good. Backhaus asked me if I wanted to play one of the Beethoven concertos with him next year—the end of next year. He's coming over for a sort of Beethoven marathon—Edinburgh and London. So— well, I suppose that's how it works——' He looked at her, not quite sure of himself. 'You—look, in spite of what the Professor said, there will always be time for you. You haven't changed your mind? What you said on Saturday—it's true? You wouldn't have come today if——'

'No, it's true.'

He put his arm round her shoulder and she felt his fingers touch her neck and her ear, and caress a lock of hair. She didn't say anything. They were walking down the High Street towards the sea, the shoppers and the trippers jostling them.

'We'll go down the pier,' he said. 'I'll buy you an ice-cream. I love you.'

'Yes,' she said.

'I'm going to buy a pair of jeans first. I can't walk down the pier in this suit.'

He let her go and went into a shop and she leaned against the window, facing the sun, waiting. It was very hot and she could smell the sea mixed up with the buses, and the perspiration and the fish and chips, and the smell of new corduroy out of the shop. 'It's impossible,' she thought. But it was true. He came out of the shop in blue denim jeans and a red cotton tee-shirt, with his suit in a carrier-bag. The jeans had a label on the back pocket saying, 'Genuine Hee-Man Denims. 30 waist. 34 inside leg,' and the tee-shirt said 'Made in Portugal.' Ruth removed the labels and Pat took her hand and they crossed the road where it fell away down to the lower promenade, and the sea took over from the High Street, blue and calm and shining.

'I must have a swim,' Pat said, looking at it.

Ruth laughed. 'You've got a fixation on swimming, a thing about it.'

He shrugged. 'Compared with all the other things, it's the only one that doesn't matter, where you're free. After concerts, and Brixton, and the Prof. and the fuzz—cripes, sometimes I just wish I'd been a farmer like old Bates' dad.'

'You didn't think that when you just finished on Saturday night. You won't think it on Friday.'

'No. If you've done it as well as you can—it's pretty good afterwards. The best thing of all, I suppose. Only you know that it's never good enough, and as soon as it's over you want to start work again. It can't ever be perfect, even if you live to be a hundred. I'm hooked on it now.'

They walked down the pier, out over the acres of wet mud to where the sea started and the fishermen clustered on the rail. The pier splayed out, sideways and up and down, left to the lifeboat and right to the restaurant, straight on for the amusement arcade, and the sun-deck where the deck-chairs were out in soldierly rows and the couples sat with newspapers over their heads, gently dozing. The air was crinkled with the heat, distorting the distance. Pat bought two ice-creams, and led the way down some iron stairs into a dark echoing landing, where, once, the paddle-steamers had tied up and the passengers had landed or embarked. They walked through the clammy shadow and came out at the end on to a lonely wooden jetty with steps down into the water, where people came for speedboat rides. But the speedboat had engine trouble, and was on its mooring beyond the lifeboat shed, the engineers working on it with their shirts off and cans of beer on the foredeck, and Pat and Ruth had the little private jetty to themselves. The boards were almost too hot to sit on. Faint canned music drifted down from above and occasionally someone threw down a sandwich paper, or orange peel, and the sea-gulls wheeled round, waiting, eyeing Pat and Ruth with beady, greedy eyes.

'I think we'll be late for the Prof.,' Pat said. 'I feel it in my bones.'

They sat side by side, eating their ice-creams.

'You can't believe it, after this morning,' Pat said.

'Life is very peculiar,' Ruth agreed.

'If I'd had to go back, today,' Pat said, 'I think——' He looked at the water, scowling. 'I think I'd have hit somebody else. That prosecuting bastard.'

'The one who said the police opposed bail?'

'Yes.'

'Why did the police oppose bail?'

'Because they've got my past history. I absconded last year, and once before I—well, they don't like you, anyway, when you take a swing at them. They just want to make it as bad as possible for you. The magistrate didn't know all this, of course, but she guessed it.'

'She doesn't know what you've done before?'

'No. If you plead not guilty, it's not made known until—unless—you're proved guilty. Then it's all read out, so the magistrate can decide what sort of a ruddy sentence to give you in light of all you've done before. It's all very *fair*.'

'But the police know all along?'

'Yes, of course.'

'Why did you abscond?'

'Oh, cripes, there's enough to bother about without digging up last year's performance. That lawyer buddy of the Prof.'s thinks I'll get nine months. Did they tell you that?'

'Yes.'

'Do you mind?'

'Do *I* mind! What about you?'

'Yeah, well, by the twenty-seventh I shall have got myself in the frame of mind to go back. There's nothing else you can ruddy well do. But today I wanted to talk to you. Today was worse, in a way. I want to know, when it happens, what you'll do?'

He was staring into the water, not looking at her.

'I'll just wait till you come out.'

'What'll your parents say?'

'They've said it already. It doesn't make any difference. I haven't noticed, the way you talked to your father, that *you* take much notice what *he* says.'

'No, well, he's just a bum. But your parents are probably right, what they say.'

'Are you talking me out of it too?' She looked at him, shaken.

'Cripes, no! Can't you see? I'm just weighing up my chances —I mean, whether you'll be around when I'm back in circulation again, or whether this finishes it. You must see, it'll make a difference to what it'll be like when I'm shut up—cripes, Ruth!—can't you see what it means——'

'I've told you!'

'And when I come out I'll have—according to this Merriman bloke—about a hundred quids' worth of fine to pay back to the Prof. and I'll have so much ruddy work to make up—I won't be fit to earn anything for months. And I'll be all seized up. I've got to tell you this, Ruth—you must know all this—I mean, even when you've waited all that time, what good is it—for you——'

'Look, I'll wait. There's nobody else. There's only you. And when you come out, whatever happens—happens. I don't see that it's at all complicated. I thought you were going to have a swim?'

He was silent. She looked at him, and he turned his head and smiled. The reflection of the water lapped on his cheek, moving gently, a weaving pattern of light across his jawbone, touching his mouth.

'You're all right,' he said.

The brightness of the water made her blink. She screwed up her eyes. He moved very close, twisting sideways, pressing her back against the steps, his face dark as it turned away from the sun.

'You make everything sound very simple. I hope to God it

will be how you say. I do love you.' He kissed her, his weight suddenly hurting, his arms holding her very hard. She could not move. She groaned, laughed, dazzled by the sun in her eyes and his loving her, and he groaned too, not laughing at all, and dropped his lips into the hollow of her neck, so that her face was full of his hair, soft and smelling of institution soap. She freed an arm, and brought up her hand, holding his head against her, feeling his eyebrow under her finger-tips, and his skull and his cheek, smooth one way and rough the other. A little piece of orange-peel fell on his hair.

'Hey, mister! The tide's coming up!'

A rolled-up sandwich paper fell on Ruth's head and bounced into the sea. She opened her eyes and saw a trio of giggling heads peering over the rail above.

'Oh, *Ruth*! If only——' His voice stuck, incapable. He lifted his head and stared at her. His expression twisted her.

'It's all right,' she said. 'It'll be all right.'

'Will it?'

A large piece of orange-peel fell on her nose.

'Spit on them! Spit on them!'

'Oh, *cripes*!' Pat twisted round and let fly a stream of language. The boards thudded to flying feet. Ruth lay back and heard the water swilling round the wooden piles in the dark shadows behind them. Two little boys were walking down the landing towards them with fishing-rods. The water slapped to a passing wash, hollow and cold, and splashed idly up over the steps, and the little boys danced over the grating, chasing crabs. Their voices echoed and flitted among the saturated piles. Pat stood up and pulled off his new shirt and his shoes and socks, and dived in off the steps. Ruth saw him disappear, and sat up. He did not come up for what seemed to her a hundred years, long after she had pictured him drowned, and brought in by the motor-boat men, blue and still, and all the people clustered silent on the sun-deck, watching . . . She stood up, her eyes full of tears, and he surfaced some fifty yards away, very leisurely. She sat down, and he swam back to her, very easy and strong, and came up to the steps and lay there, holding the step where the tide had reached. Ruth took off her shoes and sat with her feet in the water.

'I thought you had drowned.'

'What would you have done?'

'Oh, got some lunch, I suppose, done a bit of shopping, caught the bus home.'

'You little——' He was smiling.

And, as if because he smiled, it was her turn now to be twisted, the self-control sliding away.

'Oh, why——!' She had to catch herself up, nearly choking, turn away, look into the dark shadows under the pier. He shoved off again, turning over, floating, watching her. With a considerable effort, she said, 'That's no way to treat new jeans,' and he said, 'Yes, it is. It shrinks them.' He was dissected, half dark blue, merging with the water, half golden brown, arms stretched out, all hard muscles. Ruth smiled.

'Do you do weight-lifting or something?'

'No. Only piano-playing. It's very good for the physique.'

'It's what grew the hair on your chest?'

'Of course.' He smiled back, his eyes screwed up against the sun.

Ruth felt she was back where she had started from, admiring the physical Pennington, the baker's boy with the scowl and the aggressive presence. It was only mere weeks since that was all he was. And now, what she had got into was altogether the most demanding situation she had ever encountered, stretching her from bliss to despair in moment, sweet and hard, funny and tragic, to extremes she had never known existed. But not dull. She felt stiffened, accepting it. Better, after all, however much it was going to hurt, that it had *happened*. It was what she had wanted, wasn't it? Watching him, she felt a fierce, jealous sense of possessiveness. The gold medallion lay on his chest awash in the furrow of his breastbone, catching the sun.

She said, 'Who gave you that? Clarissa?'

He put his head up, the hair falling sleek and smooth. 'What, this?' He reached for the steps, turning over, hitching himself on the one where Ruth's feet were. 'Are you jealous?' He sat up, shaking back his hair, grinning. 'Yes, she gave it to me, and swore eternal love until the day she died.'

'Honestly?'

'No. I bought it in the Portobello Road. It's Beethoven. Look. He makes me play all the right notes when I'm wearing him.'

She took it in her hand and looked at it. Beethoven had

140

slightly the same expression as Pat, a truculent scowl. The medal was old and worn and delicate.

'It's my good luck.'

'Were you wearing it that Saturday, the night you——?'

'I always wear it. I never take it off. I played well at Hampstead. What happened afterwards wasn't *his* fault. He's only for my work, not for when I'm out with my bird. That's not his department.'

'What happened with you and Clarissa?' She let the medallion drop, glad that it had no female connections. She had no compunction in asking this question now.

He frowned. 'I've forgotten Clarissa. It doesn't matter.'

'She hasn't forgotten you, judging from the way she looks at you.'

He hesitated, the expression darkening. His voice was angry.

'She should have thought of that when *I* wanted *her*, in that case. She took me up because I was the best student in our year, and she was in a position to choose. Let's face it, anyone Clarissa fancied had to be very strong-minded to say no. Those looks, and that home, and their piano, and Mrs. Cargill-Smith buttering you up, and her father one of the directors of the Royal Symphonia Orchestra . . .'

He paused, and Ruth tried to imagine Pat's initiation into the Cargill-Smith home: had Mrs. Cargill-Smith's reaction been anything like her own mother's?

'I wasn't their sort, but because I was good they wanted to know me. I think they sort of like to think of themselves as being patrons of struggling young artists, and if the struggling young artists are a bit off when it comes to saying "How do you do?" with the right accent and using a knife for peas they think it's eccentric and amusing. Not like the ruddy Prof. who bawls you out for behaviour the same as he does for wrong notes. You know where you are with him. But with Mrs. Cargill-Smith when you're so eccentric that you land up in a detention centre, then that's going too far—she isn't amused any more. She doesn't want to know. You're not a person to her, you're just a status symbol in the musical rat-race. And when that happened to me, I wanted Clarissa pretty badly, but she retired, along with her mother.'

'You loved her?'

'Yes. I thought I couldn't live without her at the time. When I got nicked, she promised she'd come and visit, and that's all I thought about, day and night—shows how green I was! But when the day came she didn't turn up. She said afterwards she came as far as the gates and then she said it was so depressing she couldn't face it. She turned round and went home again. So I waited and waited, and she didn't come. Afterwards she told me she thought I'd understand how she'd felt. Well, she never knew what *I* felt. I never told her. I've never told anyone. Only that's the night I cleared out—I went to the nearest town and got blind drunk and in the morning they picked me up and carted me back—I didn't care whether I lived or died. But it cured me. I didn't want to know any more, afterwards.'

Ruth, appalled, said, 'But did she want it how it was before? Or was she ashamed?'

'She was friendly enough, but I wasn't. It was pretty difficult because we had a lot of work to do together—she had a whole lot of engagements, and I wanted the money. We used to have the most tremendous rows—musical rows—sometimes we'd go on the platform not even on speaking terms. God, it was terrible —the poor music. So it all folded up. I don't know how it is with her now, but I've no feelings for her at all. We do the occasional concert if it's forced on us. That's all. And you saw how it is . . .' He shrugged.

'But her mother seemed quite well-disposed towards you. Has she forgotten?'

'If she has, it's only because I got myself some good notices, and things like that concert with Backhaus—that's why she's friendly again. She's a musical snob. It suits her now to forget last year, but she'll never make me forget last year, not if I live to be a hundred. I didn't know much then. I know now that there's people like her who want to be friendly for what you do, not what you are.'

Ruth, considering the implications of this story, felt the weight of her responsibilities settle and take hold. It was almost an ageing process, She looked at Pat, sprawled in the sun, contemplative, the eyes bitter . . . His stubborn streak of social irresponsibility, so out of keeping with the almost painful responsibilities he was prepared to accept in his work, exasperated her.

'You ought to have learnt—if it hurt so much!' She could not stop herself. She heard the nagging tone of her own voice and put her hand on his shoulder, not wanting to hurt him. 'I'm sorry, but—oh, it's such a waste—if you go away! Why didn't you *think*?'

He looked at her sharply. 'I thought enough to hit him in the belly instead of on his beaky nose, which I would like to have flattened all over his face. I thought that much, not to hurt myself for the concert.' He frowned, the expression hardening, almost challenging. 'I'm not sorry,' he said. 'I don't regret what happened, if that's what you're thinking. I'm glad I hit him, and, if I'm sorry about anything, it's only that I didn't do more damage.'

'But——'

'Yes, I know what you're thinking—I'm going to pay for it, but it still doesn't make me sorry.'

'It doesn't make sense.'

'It does to me. They put the old psychiatrist bloke on you, and the social what-nots, the busybodies, and they try to tell you all this, and it's meaningless. You do it because——' He shrugged. 'They just don't know. There's a lot of things—you can't explain. *You* don't know what it's been like for me—my parents—*cripes*, when I took Clarissa home! She *wanted* to, she insisted. You can't imagine—you can't tell these people how some things feel—any more than you could make them know how it feels in the middle of the Rachmaninov on Saturday night—it's not something you can explain. And sometimes I feel —oh, God, there's just some things you can't take. It wouldn't be any different, if it could all happen again. I can't tell you— I can't explain. Oh, hell . . . we'd better go, the Prof. will be raving.'

He got up, gathering his things together, shoving everything in the parcel with his suit. They walked back into the damp, echoing shadow of the landing, Pat scowling and unhappy.

'It's going to be ruddy awful, I know. I shan't get any remission, I don't suppose—I'll never get through it without getting into some sort of trouble. As soon as you get in court—oh, God, the feeling . . . next time, it'll be a proper court with a dock and the blokes in wigs, and the jury in their best suits, and they'll stand up and do their ruddy spouting—it's all such a farce, the stuff they talk, it's nothing to do with what really happened. They don't know anything about what it was like, kissing you, and then that copper—for nothing at all—all so senseless, but they expect you to take it, yes sir, no sir. They can't go wrong, with their uniforms and God save the Queen and the other claptrap—Well, you can't expect—oh, cripes, it's useless . . .'

His voice echoed and faded into the slapping of the water under the grating, and they came out into the sunshine and walked in silence up the steps. Ruth felt cold.

'I—oh, well, that's how it is. But it's no good telling you I'm sorry. You might as well know.'

Ruth remembered his look in court, against the brick wall.

'Have you got a comb?' he said.

'Yes.'

She found him one and handed it over. How could you tell what somebody else really felt, or how they saw, out of their own eyes? The innermost part was always one's own. She could not reach Pat there. She could only grope through his words, and try.

'I never talked to Clarissa the way I've said all this to you,' he said.

He gave her back the comb. 'Thanks.' He padded along beside her over the hot boards, the wet jeans leaving a trail behind him. His face was closed up, scowling, as if he had departed. Ruth felt suspended, nothing, a dust mote floating on his moods, unable to make her own progress at all. Where did this thing lead to? It was as unsubstantial as the shimmering air over the cliffs. It was nothing like the beautiful sure perspective of the pier running straight and true to the shore. She wished it was.

'You can keep my Beethoven medal,' he said.

She was startled.

'I shan't need it in the nick,' he said. 'They take your things away. I don't want them to have him. I shall need him on Friday, then after that you can have him, until I come out. Then you will have to come and see me, to give him back.'

'I would love to have it, but I will come anyway, not just to give it back to you.'

'You say that now.'

'I'll wear it all the time. I will come. I promise.'

144

'We'll see,' he said.

'All right. As you like. I can't say any more, can I?'

'No.' He smiled at last, just. The medal caught the sun, and Beethoven scowled. Ruth wanted to have it, there and then, as if by holding it in her own hands safely she could make Pat's life perfectly secure to match.

'Can I come on Friday?'

'Yes. Of course.'

She remembered the last concert, and the Professor saying the more nervous Pat was the better he played, and herself wanting just Pat alone, without the musical overtones.

'This nine months,' she said, seeing Pat as the Professor saw him, 'it won't be very good for you—musically, I mean . . .'

'No. It could finish anyone.'

She was startled.

'It won't! Not after all you've achieved!'

'No, it won't,' he said. 'I've thought about it. I think about it all the time. They won't take that off me, not after all I've put in.'

'What will you do? How can you, without a piano——?'

'Oh, there's some things obviously you can't do, but quite a lot you can. I'll have no excuse for not knowing the concerto for Backhaus, for example, with all that time to get it into my head. I shall take the music of everything I want in my repertory during the next few years and read it and read it and read it. And I'll keep my arms and my hands from rusting up, even if it means playing on the ruddy bedstead all night.'

Ruth did not smile. His stubbornness did not surprise her, but the stark determination in his voice was daunting. It was useless—she saw it now quite clearly—to think that Pat existed apart from his music, because he didn't. She could not, any more, want him without it. She remembered the feeling that Pat's playing had created in her . . . Surely to be jealous of that part of him, and even of the Professor, was to deny what Pat actually was?

'Pat——'

The sun caught the medal and she thought Beethoven smiled.

'It will be all right,' she said. 'I know it will.'

He put his hand on her shoulder.

'You think so?'

145

'It will be.'

'You can make it all right,' he said. 'That's all there is to it. I can cope with the other.'

'Yes. We've nothing to worry about.'

'Not if you say so.'

He smiled then, in the way that came so rarely. He took his arm away and undid the medal and put it round her own neck, doing it up under the warmth of her hair.

'It's like a ring,' he said.

'But what about Friday?'

'He'll be there, just the same. He can watch me just as easily, can't he?'

'Yes,' she said happily. 'We won't let you go wrong.'

Chapter 10

Sitting in the bus, waiting for it to go, she felt strangely happy. It was as if she was afloat on the sea of Rachmaninov again. She had a feeling that she was not on the seat at all, but drifting up against the ceiling, disintegrating like a dandelion clock, her mind scattered to the warm breeze. She tried to take a hold on herself, to stop smiling, aware of the suspicious glance of the Gas Board man on the seat opposite, but it was no good. She told herself that she was going to be very unhappy, but for this moment it had no meaning. The gold medal was warm on her breast, and Pat loved her.

The Gas Board man was blotted suddenly from her view by the totally unexpected figure of her mother, laden with shopping baskets. Ruth jumped.

Her mother said tartly, 'I told you I was coming into Northend. You didn't hear me, any more than you've heard anything anybody's been saying for the last few days, but I did tell you. So don't look so surprised.'

'No.'

Ruth tried to gather the drifting seeds of her mind. She smiled at her mother.

'I saw you,' her mother said tightly.

'Where?'

'Coming up the High Street about half an hour ago.'

Ruth went on smiling, remembering the way Pat had smiled, and the hardness of his thigh against hers as they had walked up the street with their arms round each other. Her mother wasn't smiling.

'I take it he did have a shirt on when he appeared in court?' Her mother's voice was acid.

'Yes, of course. He wore his suit.' He was wearing it again now, driving the Professor's Lotus back to London because the

Professor had eaten too well and was sleepy. The Professor had said good-bye to her, as if he had meant it, but Ruth knew that he was far from being rid of her. She was sorry for him now. She almost loved him.

'What happened? Did he get off?'

'No. He's out on bail. He comes up again on the twenty-seventh.'

'Oh, and then what?'

'He'll get nine months they think.'

Her mother's expression changed, the sharpness fading. She looked old, and sad, as she had when Ted and Barbara had started to go wrong.

'You wouldn't be told, would you?' she said. 'You just didn't want to know, right from the start. The let-down wouldn't have been so hard if you'd taken it then. Now, well . . . I'm glad it's over.'

'It isn't over.'

'It will be when he's back in prison.'

'No.'

Ruth wasn't dandelion fluff any longer. She could feel the sap returning, the roots going down. Her mother did not reply. This was real, Ruth thought. Why had she thought she could just idiotically smile? She looked out of the window. The bus was leaving the bus station, heading for the sprawling amorphous belt of summer suburban concrete and prunus trees. Ruth did not feel she belonged anywhere.

Her mother said, 'You've told him this? That you're going to—wait for him, I suppose is the phrase?'

'Yes.'

'When are you going to see him again?'

'On Friday. He's playing in the Proms on Friday.'

There was a long silence. Ruth was suspended again, the happiness balanced by fear of what her mother was going to say. Whatever, in fact, her mother was going to say would make no difference to what she had decided, but it could be nasty. She felt herself hardening, a core of resolution.

Then her mother said, 'Would he find time, before the twenty-seventh, to come and have tea and meet your father?'

Ruth looked at her mother, astounded.

'*Why?*'

For one disbelieving moment she thought it was a Mrs. Cargill-Smith reason, because he was playing in the Proms, but she realized that her mother's reasons were far more profound. So profound that Ruth couldn't follow them.

'Why?' her mother repeated, as if she was hurt. 'It's quite normal, Ruth. A quite normal invitation. Just to meet him.'

'You—not to—not to warn him off?'

'Invitations to tea are generally issued with cordial intentions. This one is perfectly straightforward. Just to meet him.'

'But I thought—I thought——'

'You thought I would forbid you to see him again? You were all geared up for a fight?'

'No. I wasn't thinking about it at all,' Ruth said tightly. 'Only about him.'

'I'm tired of fighting,' her mother said. 'I've decided you're old enough to know what you're doing. If you want to go through with the difficulties and the hurt of the situation you've got yourself into, that's up to you. And I've decided I ought to know Pat a bit better before I pass judgement. When I heard him play on Saturday, God knows, I thought there must be more to him than the bit I've seen. That sort of thing must grow out of good intentions somewhere, whatever happens off-stage.'

'You won't—you won't nag him?'

'No. Look, I'm not condoning it. Don't think that. I want you to be happy, and I don't think he'll make you happy. But it's your choice. That's all there is to it.'

'But it's the other way round too. That he should be happy.'

'Yes. I agree. But don't be so naïve as to think you can make him so. He's his own worst enemy. You think that the love of a good woman is going to cure him—well, believe me, you won't be the first innocent girl to have this dream. I just want you to be realistic. If you want him, you must want him as he is now. Don't expect him to change. I'm not saying you can't help, but you can't change the nineteen years that happened before you met him. As long as you know this, Ruth. You understand what I'm saying?'

'Yes.'

'I won't say this again.'

Ruth looked at her mother and thought that she looked about sixty. 'It will be all right,' she said to her, as she had said to Pat. She knew it would.

'Yes, it might be. I just want you to know the other side though. And the nine months, remember. You——'

'Yes. Really. I've thought.'

'It will be very hard.'

'Yes. You won't say anything like this when he comes to tea?'

'No. Oh, no.'

Her mother groped for her handkerchief and blew her nose. Ruth thought of Pat coming to tea, and her mother offering cake and Pat saying, 'Thank you, Mrs. Hollis,' like Gordon and Peter. Perhaps, if her parents were to take him without criticism, he might be glad of their friendship? Just a dull, modest home and perhaps Ted, even Peter, as a friend, and nobody to press and nag? It could give him a touch of the ordinariness that he so conspicuously lacked. It was an intriguing thought. Ruth was full of tenderness towards her mother. She was sorry for her.

She smiled at her and said, 'Perhaps he could come on Saturday, after the concert's out of the way?'

'Yes.' Her mother was fishing for something in her handbag. 'Look. You might be interested. It was in the local paper.'

She handed Ruth a cutting.

The cutting was headed, 'Local pianist plays with Backhaus.'

Ruth read, 'To local musicians the most fascinating part of the evening came when the young Northend pianist, Patrick Pennington, took on the demanding part of soloist in the performance of Rachmaninov's Concerto No. 2 in C minor. Let it be said at once that this young artist has the technical equipment to go far indeed. Whether he will do so, pursuing the exacting path of truth and integrity in all that he attempts, or whether the aggressive element in his temperament will adversely affect the balance of his playing, remains to be seen.

'Given the evidence we were offered last night, the omens are good. There is beneath the brilliance of the attack a deep sensitivity. This was particularly evident in the thoughtful account of the slow movement which by its complete freedom from sentimentality was more deeply-moving than many a more extrovert performance aimed at the heart-strings. The case against, a tendency to lose this restraint in the more powerful bravura passages, resulted in an occasional harshness that was the only flaw in a very fine performance. Let us put this down to the exuberance of youth, and look forward to the further development of this very promising young player.'

Ruth looked for the author's credit and found the initials E.C. She connected these with the grey-haired man who had been so moved backstage after the performance, whom she guessed was Pat's old teacher at school, but whether she was right she had no way of knowing.

She re-read the words, taking in the message. Whoever had written it, surely *knew* Pat? It fitted the situation perfectly. It was Pat.

'Here's another one,' her mother said. 'Out of *The Times*.'

Ruth took it. It was very brief, from another initialled power. It set the scene in a few sentences and for Pat's part stated, 'This was playing of extraordinary promise. If this boy can during the next few formative years control the many surging facets of this flowering talent, a player of exceptional stature should emerge.'

This distant, uninvolved critic satisfied her even more. To both the critics Pat and the music were one, and what the newspapers were predicting about his musical future, so it would be with Pat himself. He might have declared that he had no regrets for what he had done but he had also revealed that, musically, he was preparing to get through the wilderness with the same thoroughness with which he had rehearsed his concerto. Given all that had happened, one could not hope for more.

She fingered the Beethoven medal, staring out of the window. Committed to the nine months herself, it occurred to her that she too might do a little homework, find out a little of what it was all about, even if merely enough to make herself useful in turning over. If Pat planned to commit a whole concerto to heart, she at least could learn when he had come to the bottom of a page. With Beethoven himself to encourage her ... She smiled. She did not know why, primed with dire maternal pessimism, but the smile kept coming.

The Gas Board man, getting heavily to his feet, gave her a wink and said, 'It's great to be young.'

'Yes, God help us,' said Mrs. Hollis, and put her handkerchief away.

And Pat, travelling down the fast lane of the clearway to London at seventy-five miles an hour, the Professor dozing in the passenger seat beside him, felt oddly optimistic, considering what lay before him. He started to whistle the Brahms waltz.

Pennington's Heir

Chapter 1

Ruth didn't know what was going to happen when Pat came out of prison. To her, that is. Pat's future was arranged. He was going to live with the Professor. But the Professor didn't approve of Ruth. She distracted Pat from his work and to the Professor Pat's work was all that mattered.

She wanted to discuss it with him during one of her monthly half-hour visits, when they confronted each other through a sheet of glass like zoo animals and stared hopelessly at each other under a warder's bored supervision, but Pat seemed disinclined to talk about the future. Or the present, come to that.

'Are you all right?'
'Yes, of course.'
'Are they nice to you?'

'If they feel like it.'

He had got nine months for knocking out a policeman and didn't look as if he would think twice about doing the same thing again if he got half a chance, sitting there scowling and restless. She hadn't expected to find Pat resigned and philosophic and smiling; she had expected his characteristic attitude of contained, aggressive energy to be exacerbated by the frustrations and humiliations of his new way of life, and she wasn't wrong. It didn't seem tactful to mention her own worries about the future. She didn't even know if she was really engaged to him at all, from the oblique way he had put it before the trial, but she was only too well aware that she loved him desperately whatever his humour. She just stared and stared at him and the half-hour was gone. But when she got up to go, he leaned forward and said urgently, 'You will come next time? Promise?'

'Of course. I'll always come.'

But next time they said she couldn't see him. No reason. She went to Chelsea and called on the Professor, who opened the door to her, forbidding as usual, impeccably correct. He frowned when he saw her.

'Please,' Ruth said.

'Come in.' He was resigned. 'What's wrong?'

She only ever saw him when anything was wrong. He taught Pat. Pat was his star pupil, the only one of his pupils, as he had told Ruth at their first meeting, to whom nine months sewing mail-bags could be considered a complete disaster. But in fact he had arranged with the authorities for Pat to go on studying in prison, and he visited him once a week to give him a lesson.

'Have you seen Pat this week?' Ruth asked. 'They said I couldn't. Why?'

'Poor child, come and sit down, and I will tell you why.'

He led the way into his marvellous music-room with its two pianos and book-lined walls and gave her the elegant armchair before the fire-place. Although he didn't approve of her, because she distracted Pat from his single-minded devotion to his job, he was kinder to her since their joint troubles. Their concern for Pat was a mutual bond.

'He has been in trouble, I'm afraid. He has lost his remission. Did they tell you that?'

'No!'

2

'He has also lost his "privileges" for two weeks, which include apparently your visit, my lessons and his practising. I saw him for five minutes and he said they were locked up all over the week-end and he got fed up and there was an argument . . . He doesn't remember much about it now. A perfectly logical sequence of events knowing Pat, but—' The Professor clutched at his intellectual forehead in a rare state of emotion. 'For heaven's sake, with so much to lose, you would have thought . . .' He shrugged, calming himself with an effort. Ruth could see the anger in his eyes. 'Well, that's why he's in there, I suppose, for his lack of self-control. What a waste of time and talent! I can never understand what moves that boy, that he is capable of such remarkable control and application where his playing is concerned, and yet his behaviour—we've covered all this ground before, haven't we?'

'Yes.' They had indeed. Ruth had covered it many times with her parents too. 'He's had to fight to get where he has with his music,' she said. 'Nothing's ever been easy for him.'

'He's never had to fight *physically*! Good God, it's criminal for him to use his hands to such an end, apart from the ethics of the thing! He couldn't play for the next two weeks, the state he's in, even if they were to allow him. He's got a splendid black eye as well—what does he gain by it? You tell me!'

A release of a kind, Ruth supposed. Not the one he wanted, though.

'The sooner we get him back here into a civilized atmosphere, with a routine of hard work, the better for all concerned. He's costing the country heaven knows how much a week in that damned place, and it's of absolutely no use to anyone at all. Least of all to him. Fantastic material going to waste here, all for want of a little restraint, a quite normal modicum of common-sense.'

Ruth noted that the Professor considered Pat as 'fantastic material'. He wasn't a person; he wasn't Patrick Pennington, twenty years old, six-foot two and fourteen stone, mixed-up, aggressive, gentle, thoughtful, violent, extraordinarily sensitive in some ways and thick as a mule in others. The product of a useless pair of parents and a devoted music-master at an otherwise lousy school, he was to Ruth the light of her world—to the Professor an incipient concert-pianist of such remarkable promise that

3

anything which deflected his mind from his work was to be deprecated with vehemence. And although the stumbling-block at the moment was Pat's incarceration for nine months in Pentonville, Ruth knew that when that was over, the stumbling-block, in the Professor's eyes, would be herself. He had told her so quite bluntly, at their very first meeting. Pat was not to waste his time on girls. Pentonville had been unavoidably prescribed by the law, but girls were another matter. After Pentonville, the Professor would be the law. The Professor had great influence over Pat. Ruth foresaw an almost impossible situation for herself.

'The best thing you could do is forget him and get on with your studies,' her mother told her sharply. 'If he chooses to spend more time in prison just because he can't keep his temper, what sort of a husband is he going to make?'

Nobody transgressed society's rules in Ruth's family, which lived calmly and without ambition in a small Essex village. It occurred to Ruth that if her mother was in prison, no harm would be done; she had no soul to struggle with; she would not go berserk being shut in a little room all through an April week-end with the blackbirds trilling on the roof of Pentonville itself. Pat was *human*, that was his trouble.

'And if he marries you, what are you going to live on?'

'He plays in concerts and gets paid for it,' Ruth said.

'Not as soon as he comes out, surely?'

'No, but as soon as he gets going again. Everyone's got to start, haven't they? You know he can, you saw him with your own eyes. It's not just my imagination, you know. I don't make it all up. When he comes out he's got an audition with Backhaus to play a Beethoven concerto.'

'Hmm.' Her mother pursed her lips.

It did seem a far cry from his present situation, she had to admit when she saw him again. It was hard to remember him in white tie and tails on the concert platform, this morose figure with the awful haircut and the fading remains of a black eye darkening his face, hunched into the drab prison clothes.

'Don't say anything about it,' he warned her. 'I can't change anything. It happened. I got a lecture from the Prof but why does he think I can change? I can't change myself.' For Pat, this was bordering on the philosophical.

'What did you do?'

4

'Oh, there's no point—you wouldn't understand. I told you right from the start I'd lose my remission, so you can't say you're surprised.'

'No. Only disappointed.'

'Yes. Well, I'm good at disappointing people. Ask the Professor.'

'He can't wait to have you under his thumb!'

'No.'

'I wish you weren't going there afterwards. He disapproves of me so.'

'Well, that's his bad luck. Clarissa's mother offered me a room. Would you prefer that?'

Ruth was stung. 'No! She hasn't—she hasn't been to see you?'

'No. She wrote.'

'You wouldn't—'

'God, no!'

Pat's scorn was a comfort. Clarissa had been at College with him. Although she was an *ex*-girl-friend, Ruth was deeply suspicious of Clarissa, who was both talented and gorgeous. She also, for good measure, had musical parents who could be extremely useful to Pat in his career, her mother being a self-confessed Lady Bountiful to struggling talent and her father a concert impresario. Pat couldn't stand them.

'Oh, Pat—'

It always came round to this, for Ruth: an agony of what her mother called her adolescent passion, just looking at him. She knew that in bed tonight she would just cry and cry, remembering him, but now, while she was with him for these incredibly mean thirty minutes, there was no way of expressing anything at all, not even his hand to touch. They were neither of them talkers, and the confrontation, controlled and supervised, stifled their natural reticence into a hopeless failure at communication. She always went away feeling far worse than at any other time during the intervening months.

When, eventually, the day of his release came, she went to meet him outside the prison. She was trembling like a leaf. The Professor's car was parked by the gate.

'It's lucky I'm thick,' she thought, acknowledging him. Otherwise the frost in his eyes would have withered her.

'Wait in my car,' he said. 'The wind is cold.' He had perfect manners. But she knew better than to believe that he was pleased

5

to see her. When Pat came, she was too shattered to say anything. He smiled at her, then past her at the Professor, very equal. He looked shattered too.

'I thought it would never come,' he said. 'I can't believe it.'

The Lotus was a two-seater, so Ruth got in the back, which was almost non-existent, and Pat got in the front, next to the Professor.

'I thought we'd go straight back and talk things over. Clemmie's making a special lunch to celebrate, and I've nothing on until this evening.' The Professor spoke to Pat, and Ruth wondered for a moment if he would dare to exclude her from the gathering. No, she was being too sensitive. Her heart was thumping like a steam-hammer, her cheeks burning. But Pat was pale and cool, his eyes watching the walls outside, past the Professor's head. He half-turned in the seat and looked back at her, not smiling. He shifted his elbow over the back of the seat and his hand came down and rested on her knee. She put her own hand over his and their fingers caressed. She could feel his bones. After all the time apart it was almost too much to take in, that in the space of a minute—after all the agony of the nine months—he had come out of the gate and got into the car and was there in the flesh, holding her; the very expression that she had sought so desperately to recall during the intervals of not seeing him through the long shady months of the sentence was there before her eyes to drink in: the delinquent scowl and the restless eyes, the untrusting, untranquil, nervous energy in the quite normal features that had the power to transfix her. She was like a camel come to an oasis. And, drinking him in, she knew she was as dotty as a camel too, dotty enough to burst, and she was shivering with the excitement of it, holding his hand while he talked to the Professor, and his hand stroked her knee, and her other hand came up quite without her willing it and touched his wrist and felt the pulse beating through his artery, soft underneath and on the other side bony and hairy. She could hardly stop the idiotic happiness bursting out, especially after her doubt, and the Professor right there talking about some old concert he wanted Pat to go to at the week-end—God, what a vulture the man was! Driving and pecking. No wonder Pat blew up at intervals.

'Funny to see it from the outside,' Pat said.

The sun was shining and the road smelt of tar, blown newspaper, and a whiff of chips frying. The Pentonville walls were ugly to the point of obscenity. Ruth, always early for visits, had tramped all round them on several occasions, and was familiar now with the decaying streets, the boarded windows, the thud of demolition machinery. And the walls, and walls within walls, so high and blind as to suggest some secret religion, some monastic order, even the plane-trees lopped and tonsured to conform . . she never wanted to come here again. The car slid away down the Caledonian Road.

'Never again,' said the Professor, feeling the same. The Royal Borough of Kensington was his province. Pat grinned.

'No. It's like being *born*, getting out of there.'

Ruth felt born too. Everything was sharper, more positive; there was a purpose again. She did not know where they were going, but life had flowered suddenly like a cherry-tree in April.

'My God, but you've got some work ahead of you,' the Professor said to Pat. Ruth's cherry-blossom felt the frost, contracting. But Pat nodded affably, as if the prospect quite pleased him.

The car nosed through the traffic, deft with its expensive acceleration, jousting and thrusting. Ruth, anticipating the formal lunch with the Professor, had a twist of longing to be making for her home-ground with Pat, out on the marshes along the sea-wall with the tide flopping against the stones, the track dried into its clay cracks and warm underfoot. But for Pat, with his most civilized of professions to pursue, it had to be the city and all its contacts. But better Kensington than Pentonville. The Professor's house, for the time being Pat's home, was a stucco Regency villa in a quiet road. He had recently moved, and Ruth could see the attraction: the village atmosphere, the pink roses over the porch, the shade of pollarded lime-trees, yet all within a stone's throw of Knightsbridge. She thought, 'It stinks of money.' She saw Pat's expression and knew that he was not keen on this patronage. He looked uneasy, taking it in. The Professor parked the Lotus neatly in its allotted resident's bay.

'You've gone up in the world,' Pat said to him.

'You like it? It's fantastically handy.'

'A bit of a change for me. I—' He shrugged, frowning. Ruth could sense the struggle already, the Professor's pressure taking hold. It had taken less than half an hour. The Professor led the way up the steps, groping for his key, and Pat followed. He put his hand on Ruth's shoulder, pulling her with him, a quick hug. Ruth felt rather than saw Hampton's expression, cool, quick. She could feel herself rejected, even while she was stepping over the doorstep. But stubbornness was one of her characteristics; she had been told so all her life by her mother. It would support her now.

The atmosphere was improved by Clemmie, the Professor's housekeeper, an elderly, motherly, entirely uncomplicated soul whose joy at seeing Pat again swamped the nuances among the three of them.

'My word, you look as if you could do with a bit of fresh air and a square meal—I'll bring some coffee, and then in an hour when you've had a bit of a chat, I'll serve the lunch.'

'I'll help you,' Ruth said. She was always more at home in kitchens. Clemmie, she sensed, was sympathetic. By lunchtime she knew she would have had her fill of being excluded from the Professor's conversation with Pat, which would be all about work. All he ever thought about. He was a maniac, Ruth thought. She remembered then what Maxwell had said about Pat's first sentence: 'Three months—the first holiday he's had in years.' It was a bit funny really, to think that Pat might be returning refreshed from his nine months in Pentonville, to resume his studies at full bore again. Only the Professor could provoke such an idea.

'Doesn't he ever think about anything else but music?'

In the small kitchen the coffee was already percolating with a comfortable, expensive aroma. Clemmie reached the cups down from their hooks.

'No, dear. Music and chess, that's all.'

Clemmie had a sort of brisk, nannyish demeanour that emanated good sense and comfort. It occurred to Ruth that she could, in fact, very likely have been Hampton's nanny when he was a little precocious Kensington boy. She would have liked to ask, but didn't dare. It fitted.

'He doesn't like me getting in the way.'

'No, dear. He's very single-minded. But he can't expect a boy like Pat not to have a bit of fun. It would be unnatural. Pat's not one of those droopy, dreamy sort like some we get, like dish-cloths wrung out. He will work ten times harder than any of them, and then be ready for the next thing. I suppose it's all this energy that gets him into trouble.'

'He doesn't think.'

'Reckless. He'll grow out of it . . . a boy of twenty. A steady girl like you, just what he wants.'

Ruth smiled. 'Will you tell Professor Hampton that?'

Clemmie smiled too. 'I'm not paid to give him advice. Only meals.' She was watching the milk, its surface just starting to crinkle. She warmed a jug with hot water, ready.

'Did Clarissa come here?'

Clemmie's smile faded. 'Yes, she did.' From her expression she might have added, 'The hussy!' Or was she imagining it? Ruth wondered. Clarissa was so fantastically attractive one could not easily get her out of mind. Why had Clarissa's mother invited Pat to make his home with them? Ruth had tried to bury this bit of knowledge like a dog with a bone, but—like the dog's bone—it kept reappearing, unearthed by the uncontrollable, jealous, despicable streak in her nature.

This uncontrollable bit of her now pressed Clemmie, pouring out the hot milk. 'Did Professor Hampton object to Clarissa in the same way that he objects to me?'

'Professor Hampton is a great friend of Clarissa's father. It was a bit different, you see. Clarissa came here to play duets with Pat, for lessons.'

But a lot more than lessons had passed between Pat and Clarissa. Pat had told her so.

'But she *distracted* him too!' Clarissa had been suitable, herself unsuitable. What a hurtful thing it was to discover! She was quite surprised at the feeling. She had gone too far and it served her right.

Clemmie said, 'Settling down would be good for Pat, in my opinion. A man will work all the better for a bit of home comfort.'

Ruth followed her out of the kitchen door into the garden, with this vision of carpet-slippers, sleeping cats and hearth-rugs all mixed up with her Clarissa complex. The garden was small but perfect, the high walls hung with roses, shaded by next door's acacias and cherries. The garden furniture was arranged on the stone terrace where Pat and the Professor sat talking.

Pat looked up and smiled at her, and Ruth's heart gave its great uncontrolled leap of adoration, seeing him face on, receiving his whole attention, like the sun bursting out of cloud. He didn't move or get up—gentlemanly manners being one of the attributes he conspicuously lacked, as Ruth's mother had pointed out often —but sprawled comfortably, his physical presence, even in repose, very positive, very active—('Or is it just me?' Ruth wondered uncertainly. 'Like a poor moth to a candle?').

There was a garden chair for her, she was relieved to see. Clemmie put the tray on the table.

'Would you like to pour it, dear? The Professor takes his black, no sugar.' She gave Ruth a sense of belonging, which was a relief.

'We've got the top bedroom ready for you, Pat, the one that gets the sun. It's only small, but there's a big cupboard for your things.'

'I haven't got any things,' Pat said. 'They're still at Mrs. Bates'. I'll have to go and collect them.' He was wearing his concert suit, the one he had appeared in court in, to look as respectable as possible. 'If I take Ruth home this afternoon, I could collect them then.'

'You're working this afternoon,' the Professor said.

Ruth saw Pat's face harden. He opened his mouth to say something, and shut it again.

'The water's hot if you want a bath,' Clemmie said. 'There'll be time before lunch, if you like.'

'Thanks, yes. I would like one. It would be marvellous. And the coffee—the smell—you can't imagine—'

Ruth thought she could imagine. Civilized living breathed here, from the very flagstones of the patio. To have come from breakfast in Pentonville to morning coffee here was as big a step as one could take in atmospheres. Ruth, aware that Pat set little store by his surroundings, could see that this time it was too much to take, and Clemmie's bath idea was far more practical than Hampton's programme.

Pat departed; Clemmie brought out a colander of peas for Ruth to shell; and the Professor put some Mozart on in the music-room, so that the sound wafted up out of the windows into the pale pink roses, a perfect affinity, an underlining of the exquisite surroundings to which the Professor had attuned himself. 'Life isn't like this,' Ruth thought. Life was the Caledonian road, or her mother vacuuming the carpet with the Jimmy Young show on the transistor and the milk boiling over. Beautiful music was apt to bring out a reaction in Ruth, so that sometimes it made her very sad and angry, thinking of starvation and Calcutta and South Africa, because the music was a perquisite of people who had the education, the leisure and the opportunity to listen to it and enjoy it. And yet a great deal of the greatest music had been born out of poverty and war and distress: her argument was full of holes. She was always getting moved and vehement about the injustices of life, and having great rows with her mother (her father didn't have rows, ever) but at the same time she was aware that she herself was completely powerless to change anything. She couldn't even win the arguments. Her mother's dogma enraged her, all the indisputable facts brought to bear like battle-ships on Ruth's poor little explosions against capitalism and Tories and inequality, the arguments levelled with all the same familiar tags . . . 'You'll find out when you're older that . . .' and 'Human nature being what it is, I'm afraid that . . .' Ruth got all tied up in her refutations, but amongst her frustrations her rage and her ideals burned all the harder. This was the effect her mother had on her. She wished she were calm and poised and terribly intelligent (like Clarissa). She had no confidence at all.

Clemmie duly served lunch, and afterwards the Professor, ever-anxious to remove Ruth, said, 'Perhaps you would like to go out for the afternoon while we work, and come back at tea-time?' How smoothly rude he was! Ruth said stubbornly, 'I would like to listen. I'll sit on the sofa. I won't say a word.' The sofa was under the front window, a carved chaise-longue heaped with cushions and looking most inviting after the lunch and the day's emotions.

The Professor said to Pat, 'Sit down and think about the C Major study. And I mean think.' He sounded cross, and was taking it out of Pat instead of her. 'I want total concentration, not automatic fingerwork.'

'Pig,' Ruth thought. 'Bullying pig.' But during the lesson they argued quite a lot. She had often wondered what Pat's lessons with the Professor were like; she now felt that the master-pupil relationship was fairly gruelling. It wasn't just a matter of playing pretty pieces through, punctuated by exclamations of encourage-ment and congratulation; it seemed to consist of agonized appraisals over a few bars, discussion and argument, and then great surging passages played with great power, broken off abruptly, restarted . . . Not at all restful, Ruth decided. All the same, she dozed off, and came to later, intuitively, to hear Pat playing in quite a different mood, something soft and lilting, very delicate, caressing. All her senses came awake at once, with a rush of joy and gratitude. The Professor had gone, and Pat was playing the Brahms waltz that he had once played especially for her. It was for her now, she knew. She got up and went over to him and put her arms round his neck, burying her face in his hair.

'Where's the Professor?'

'The phone rang. He's gone to answer it.'

She could see his hands moving over the keys like large spiders, very smooth and supple. They played the last notes and came up to take hers.

'What will the Prof say?' he whispered, smiling, moving his face against hers.

'He'll say I'm bad for you.'

'Good for me. I need you.'

'I love you.'

'Yes.'

They heard the ting of the receiver being put down. Ruth leapt back to the sofa and buried her face in the cushions. She heard the Professor come back into the room, and the voices talking again, and then Pat was playing what she thought of as 'properly', on and on; it was beautiful, all mixed up with the warmth of the sun on her back and the smell of the velvet cushions. She dozed again, and when she awoke, someone was offering her a cup of tea.

'I'm going to take you home,' Pat said. 'The rest of the day is our own.'

The Professor wasn't there. Pat put her cup of tea on a small table and sat on the sofa. He looked very tired.

'He says I can borrow the car. We'll go and look at the sea. I need it.'

Pat's home was near the sea, like hers. He had been born there. But he lived with a landlady called Mrs. Bates, the mother of an old schoolfriend, because he could not get on with his own parents. Mrs. Bates lived just across the road from his own home. 'We can call on Mrs. Bates and collect my things.'

'I've got your medal for you. Here.' She fished it out of her shirt collar, the little gold relief of Beethoven on a gold chain that he had given her before he went into prison. 'I never took it off.'

Pat smiled.

'You'll need it,' Ruth said. 'To play the right notes.' That was what he had said it was for, his luck.

'Cripes, I'll need it all right, if I've got to make my playing pay for my keep.' The smile faded. He had never been one for smiling much. Ruth hoped that things would change now. There was nothing to worry about any more.

'Come on,' he said. 'I can't wait.'

She drank half the tea, and they went out into the hall. The Professor came down the stairs.

'Here are the car keys. And a door-key. I don't have to tell you to drive as befits one so out of practice.'

'Thank you for having me. Thank you very much for the lunch.' Ruth felt very affable.

'A pleasure, my dear,' lied the Professor charmingly.

Pat and Ruth went outside, and got into the Lotus. 'At last,' Ruth thought. And yet there wasn't anything that needed saying; it was just to be free, at last, together. Pat didn't say anything either, only, 'It's so strange.' He drove very carefully down the road, watching everything. It was very hot, the shadows just beginning to draw out, the rush-hour traffic throbbing at the top of the road. It occurred to Ruth that it was very generous of the Professor to lend Pat his expensive car. Riding in it with Pat, just the two of them, was altogether more than she had allowed in her dreams—not that Pat had many moments through all the rigours of Hyde Park circus, Oxford Street, Holborn and the City in all their going-home chaos, to remove his concentration to her, but she was content. She felt like a girl in an advertisement.

'I've forgotten,' Pat was saying. 'I've forgotten everything.'

He was not carefree and laughing, as she had imagined it, even when they were out to the arterial with all the snarl-ups behind them and the Lotus zooming down the outside lane. The advertisement analogy faded from Ruth's mind. Pat's arm was not round her shoulders and her hair wasn't flying out in the wind. Pat was saying, 'It's as hard to come out of prison as it is to go in.'

'You can't mean that!'

'No . . . But you think when you get out all your troubles will be over, and then when it's happened, you see that they're only just starting.'

'Not *troubles*.'

'Difficulties.'

'You've got to adjust. You can't expect to take up exactly where you left off.'

'I didn't expect anything. What happened last summer—that concert and the notices—was too good to be true. Then the other happened to even things out. Now we're back to square one. Only worse off, because in spite of being able to work in the nick, it wasn't the same as being at college. I can't play as well as I should be playing. It's like climbing this ladder up the side of a skyscraper, and half-way up about six rungs break, and you drop back.'

'But you still have the Professor to help you, and a home—' She would have liked to add, 'and me,' but she was still very uncertain of how much she meant to him. There had been so little time before, and in prison he hadn't had anything much else to think about, but now—now she was back in competition with the piano and his ambition, and his musical friends and the Clarissas of the world.

'Yes, it's true, but to be dependent on Hampton is the worst thing of all. You must see that. It's being a prisoner in another way. Look at today.'

'Yes.'

'I don't want to live there. But he's not charging me anything. How can I afford not to? And I must have his lessons. He's not charging me for those either. But he virtually owns me in exchange.'

Ruth considered. 'You're looking at the worst side of it. You've got a home and food and lessons. Suppose you'd come out and there was no one who would help you? You might have had to give up altogether.'

'It might not have been a bad thing.'

'You wouldn't have said that before. Not after that concert. And that Backhaus man saying you were marvellous.'

'He didn't.'

'He wanted you to play with him again, didn't he?'

'He did. Two months from now. Beethoven's Third Piano Concerto. If he'd heard me this afternoon—cripes, he'd be a worried man! I can't see it happening.'

'Oh, Pat, stop it! How do you expect to feel, the first day out?

Only the Professor would have made you work, instead of letting you go out and wander around and look at the buses and the shops and go into a pub or a Wimpy bar or something. You couldn't possibly have felt like it.'

'No.' But she had merely gone round in a circle and caught up with the beginning of the argument, the Professor's possessive pressure.

'Don't,' she said. 'Don't think about it now.'

They turned off the arterial and headed for the lanes that went down to the marshes. Everyone else was roaring on for Northend. The sun was burnishing the fields, the flowering grass rippling in dusty pink waves, ready for hay, roses in the hedges. The elms cast long shadows across the road. Ruth thought of Pat locked away for all those months. And yet he had said he was glad he had done it and wouldn't have changed anything. How could he think that? The Professor had said he couldn't understand him, with so much to lose. 'You don't know how it feels,' Pat had said. 'There are some things you can't take.' She couldn't have taken what he had chosen. Would she ever understand how his mind worked?

They came to the village where he lived, and went straight through, past Mrs. Bates' and his parents' and the church, and down the dusty cart-track to the creek. This is where they had come before, and everything had been spoilt. 'It can't be like that this time,' Ruth thought. But she expected nothing. Pat was silent, looking across the fields. He parked the car by the boatshed and they got out and climbed up on to the sea-wall, scrambling up through the long grass. The sun was behind them and their shadows went right across the creek to the opposite side. The tide was almost gone, threads of gold water trickling out through channels in the mud. The yachts in the centre of the creek lay perfectly still; silence, save for a curlew. Pat stood looking, saying nothing. Then he turned and started to walk along the sea-wall, upstream, his hands in his pockets. Ruth followed. Three hours from the Royal Borough of Kensington and Oxford Street. Ten hours from Pentonville. The grass flowers powdered her thighs and the smell of seaweed and mud came like a draught.

Pat walked as far as the bend in the creek, and sat down, looking at the half-tide and the uncovered mud. He took off his jacket and sat chewing a blade of grass. Ruth sat down beside him.

Because of his mood, which she could not quite place, she felt that her own feelings were suspended, waiting for Pat. She was that much dependent on him.

But he turned and smiled, at last, and slipped down the bank so that he was lying facing her, his head propped on his hand. It seemed to Ruth that this was the very first time they had ever been alone, with nothing between them, the physical presence being enough to blot out all other thoughts. No problems, no past, no future. The feeling grew between them, surging so quickly, so passionately, so perfectly, that there was never any question of Ruth withdrawing, doubting. Afterwards, because she knew she always doubted, was always knotted by her suburban hang-ups, her groundings—grinding—of conventional morality, she could not understand her own release. It was something she had never known was in her, this power to unlock herself from every minute of the seventeen years of careful upbringing that had gone before. It would have terrified her, if she had been in the mood to think about it in everyday blood. But the evening was unique; it was not everyday. It would not happen again in just this same way, this coming together after all the time apart, this very first time. It could never be the same again. Ruth, aching, crying, 'undone'—and the word was in her own head, with its truly Victorian associations—and yet powerfully, fiercely happy, lay clutching Pat on the cold bank, not thinking of anything but her love for him, not—for once—thinking of what might happen, what might have happened. The sun had gone, and the familiar dank smell of the evening marshes, a lacing of hay with mud, and pollen with oyster-shells and crabs' remains and the stalks of tide-washed marsh-grass, came with the soft rising of the on-shore breeze. They lay feeling the dampness of the grass all round them, and their own warmth a cocoon, a private world. Pat was smiling. Ruth had never seen him, ever since she had known him, smile in quite the same way he was smiling now. She looked into his eyes, three inches away, with her own shadow in them, and at his eye-lashes and his eye-brows and the faint scar through his upper lip, and at his hair growing down in front of his ears and then shaved suddenly, the cheek pale in the dusk. Impossible. True. But not to analyse it: just to let it exist, to have him, to be perfectly happy. And she didn't think she had ever been happy before.

When it had got cold, and almost dark, they sat up, and Pat put his jacket on, and they walked back along the sea-wall to the car. It was too narrow to walk together, to hold hands. They walked separately. Back to normal, Ruth thought. Two people. Had it really made any difference? To her, the whole world was changed, but to Pat—she couldn't tell. That was what he was like. But at the steps he took her hand and put his arm round her, and when they got back into the car, he kissed her again, very gently.

Then he started the car. 'Mrs. Bates,' he said.

'Oh, God,' Ruth said. She didn't want to see anyone else. She looked in the car mirror and saw herself all white and dishevelled, grass in her hair. She combed it. It was too dark to do anything to her face. She had to go home, look her mother in the eye! Impossible. Inevitable.

'I wish I could come back with you.'

'Yes.'

'I wish—oh, Pat! I—'

He put his arm round her and she laid her face against his smooth concert suit. They drove into the village slowly, and he parked outside Mrs. Bates'. Ruth sat up. She didn't want to share the moment with anyone. But before they could get out of the car, there was a sharp tap on the window on Pat's side, and a face peered in. Ruth heard Pat's soft blasphemy, then the door was flung open.

'It is you then! God Almighty, let's have a look at you! Jim Purvis said it was you in a smart car and I said he was dreaming. And then I saw the car come back and I said to Bill, "There, I reckon it could be—the nine months is just about up." Well, now, what a surprise! Come out now and give your mum a kiss! Let's all have a cup of tea. Bring your girl-friend. Clarissa, is it? Do you remember me, dear? Come on, both of you.'

Ruth felt Pat's hand give her a quick, regretful squeeze, then he was climbing out, giving his mother a brief peck on the cheek, turning for Ruth.

'This is *Ruth*, Mother.' His voice was fierce. 'I just came to get my things from Mrs. Bates. I haven't much time. I've got to go back to London.'

'If you haven't time to come into your own home for five minutes to drink a cup of tea, after all we've had to put up with—' The voice had changed key, swerving into indignation. 'It's nearly eighteen months since I've seen you! D'you realize that? Come and say how-do-you-do to your father and have a drink in your own home. Then you can go off for another eighteen months. We don't ask much!'

'All right!'

Pat turned round for Ruth, scowling. She could see the apology in his expression, the mute gesture of despair. Ruth went with him, following his mother across the road and up the garden path of an unkempt council house. She had been warned about Pat's mother, but had never met her before, only the father.

'Come in then. Ruth, d'you say? Come in, Ruth. I'm pleased to see any lady-friend of Pat's, you know. Not that he brings his friends here very often. Not now. Ashamed of the place he is, now he's got so high in the world.'

'Pentonville,' Pat said.

'When did you come out then?'

'This morning.'

'This morning, eh? I thought you looked peaky. You did the full term then? No remission? You're just like your father. Can't keep out of trouble. What d'you think of him then, Ruth? Not much good to a girl if he's always getting put away. You'll have to see if you can keep him on the primrose path as they say. Here, I'll put the kettle on. You're looking very smart, Pat, I'll say that for you. Never a one for suits—mind up, let me get to the sink. At least you got a good haircut for once—never thought I'd ever have anything to thank one of Her Majesty's prisons for! What d'you think of him, Ruth? You missed him last year? You never brought her to see me before, Pat? Ashamed of us, I know. You don't have to tell me. We both know, your father and I—'

She went on and on, banging around the poky, dirty kitchen with a tin tea-pot and a bottle of milk. Ruth stood by the door, realizing gradually that, for all the questions put to her, she wasn't required to answer any of them. She remembered Maxwell's saying once, 'Have you met his parents? Try not to.' She could see that Mrs. Pennington was one of those fiftyish, embittered, hard-working, shrewish little women; she was lean and quick and bony, with frizzled brown-grey hair and sharp, evil eyes. She was horrible. Ruth, watching her, thought of the long afternoon in Kensington on the velvet sofa, listening to Pat playing the piano. The contrast was so sharp it was hard to believe. Pentonville to the sea-wall, the Professor's town house to this. No wonder Pat was mixed-up. It was all a part of him, what had made him. And she most of all, his own mother who had raised him, she was awful.

'We don't expect gratitude,' she said to Ruth. 'We don't ask much. We never said anything, not even when he moved his things across the road to the Bates'. But you can imagine it gave the village something to talk about—when a boy moves out like that—not *away*, mind you, but just across the road—'

'Pack it in, for heaven's sake,' Pat said. 'Let's just have the cup of tea.'

'And all those lessons we paid for, year after year. And him staying on at school when by rights he should've gone out to work—'

At this point the tirade was interrupted by the appearance of Mr. Pennington, a grizzled, burly man with Pat's scowl. Having sampled the mother, Ruth felt she now understood the family scowl. She thought that Pat might look like this when he was old if everything went wrong, but if everything went right he would be quite different, his truculence and his aggression smoothed, the charm that he now revealed on very rare occasions far more apparent, the smile more ready. Hard to imagine, glancing at him now. Back-to-the-wall, he looked like his police-record photograph.

'So it was you!' His father clapped him on the shoulder in welcome. 'The bad penny turned up again! How's things then? How long you been out?'

'Only today.'

'Cripes, today! How was it then? How is the old place these days? Better than in my day, I bet—they make it all easy now. I read all about it in the papers. Piece of cake today. Rest-home. I would've come to see you but I didn't seem to get round to it. I see you still got a lady-friend. How do you do, my dear. I think I saw you once before—in court, was it? I don't know, Pat, you always seem to have someone waiting for you! I don't know how you do it, always falling on your feet. That Professor bloke keeping you on, is he?'

'Yes.'

'You still at that College?'

'No. They stopped my grant. I've got to get a job.'

'Yeah, well, not before time. Playing in concerts and suchlike, you mean?'

'Oh, anything.' Pat wouldn't make the slightest effort to talk shop to his father. His mother poured out the tea and while Mr. Pennington questioned Pat about 'the old school' (Pentonville), Mrs. Pennington fastened herself on Ruth and asked her a lot of nosy questions about where she came from and how she met Pat and what she did and what she was going to do. And all the time Ruth was picturing Pat growing up with these two unsympathetic people in this untidy, depressing little house, meeting aggression with aggression, scolding with truculence, until the day he was inspired enough to move across the road to Mrs. Bates'. It explained a whole lot about him which she had only guessed at before. Mrs. Pennington embarrassed her acutely; she had no idea how to parry the prying, the self-pity, the veiled accusations. She was infinitely relieved when Pat, having finished his cup of tea, moved purposefully to the door.

'I've got to go back to London tonight, I can't stay. Come on, Ruth.'

'I was lucky to see you,' his mother said. 'Only because you didn't see me first—'

'Oh, stop beefing, Norah!' said Pennington senior. 'You don't expect him to care about an old bag like you when he's got a lady-friend with him. It's not his mother he want now, it's a—'

'For God's sake!' Pat shoved Ruth bodily out of the door. 'Why do you expect me to come back when you always carry on like a bloody tap dripping? It's always the same—'

Ruth scurried down the path, cold, harassed. She began to feel that the day had gone on for ever. Pat obviously felt the same, for he got into the car, slammed the door and drove off immediately.

'I thought we were going to Mrs. Bates'?'

'I can't stand any more people. Enough has happened today.'

'Yes.'

'I can't stand them.'

'No.'

'I didn't want—I'm sorry, sorry you got caught up.'

'It's not your fault, what they're like. I didn't mind meeting them.'

'I'll take you home and then I'll shove off back to London. I'll come down again at the week-end and we'll go to Mrs. Bates' then.'

The car sped down the dark lanes, rabbits' eyes gleaming, farm cats jumping into hedges. Pat did not speak again. Ruth sensed that he was very tired. She tried to feel just what the day had been like for him, after the nine months inside, but her brain could not stretch to it. It was impossible. Even in her mind it was a jumble now, only the time on the sea-wall sharp and warm and close, all the other things blurring together. Other places, other people. They didn't matter. She had no sense of guilt or shock or fear. She thought she ought to have, but she didn't. They drove through her home village and down the lane to her house. Pat turned into the drive and stopped the engine. 'You're sure you don't want to come in?' Her parents had promised that they would be pleased to see him, although she knew that it might cost them an effort.

'No.'

She was relieved, although she wanted the time with him to be stretched out.

'You'll come on Saturday?'

'Yes.'

He made no move to touch her, embrace her, but only said, 'I'm sorry about my parents.'

'It didn't matter.'

He shrugged, reaching for the ignition. It was very dark; she could not see his expression, but could feel the withdrawal. He had always been like this, retreating without warning into this slightly hostile silence. It always left her doubting, uncertain, although she was used to it. If he felt he wanted to withdraw in this way, he would not concede the smallest sign or gesture to alleviate the other person's uncertainty. Ruth put it down to his musical side, the side she could not approach, the part of him she had no hand in. It was part of what her mother called his bad manners. She thought of it more as artistic temperament. She didn't suppose he thought of it at all himself.

'Good-bye then.'

'Good-bye.'

'Saturday?'

'Yes. In the afternoon some time.'

'Be careful going back.' She thought he might fall asleep.

The car slipped out of the gate. Ruth watched the lights sweep round in a bright arc and head up the lane. What was he thinking? How could she tell?

She walked very slowly up the drive, not wanting to go in.

Chapter 2

Pat, w .n three hours to go before his audition with Backhaus, had never faced any ordeal he felt less confident about, and—God only knew—he had played enough times now with plenty at stake: auditions and competitions and examinations and all the other heart-stopping, stomach-turning occasions that went to make up this masochistic profession. He was quite used to being sick before a concert, although everyone told him that he looked as if he had no nerves at all, but he wasn't familiar with not feeling pretty well on top of what he intended to do, which was how he felt now. The nine months had left their mark; he felt sapped of some vital ingredient in his previous make-up. Confidence, presumably. The prison life wasn't designed for improving one's self-confidence. Quite the opposite.

'Patrick!'

He opened the door cautiously. Clemmie's voice floated up the winding Georgian staircase:

'Telephone for you!'

Perhaps Herr Backhaus had been run over by a bus and wasn't coming? The audition was to be in the Professor's music-room, with the Professor playing the orchestra's part on the second piano. He went hopefully down the stairs.

'Hullo?'

'Pat, is that you?'

It was Ruth. Pat felt pleasantly ready to be distracted from his gloom and said, 'Yes, it's me. How's things?'

'Pat, I must see you! I'm in London. I've got to talk to you before I go home. It's terribly urgent.'

Pat had never heard Ruth speak in this vein before. She sounded upset, almost as if she was crying.

'Whatever's the matter?'

'I can't tell you on the phone. I must see you!'

'Cripes, but I'm playing for the Herr conductor tonight. Where are you?'

'Kensington tube-station.'

Pat glanced at his watch. Five past five. The Prof was due back from the College at half past six. Pat knew that it was more than his life was worth if he was discovered chatting up Ruth when his mind was supposed to be on higher things.

'How about the "Birdcage" then? If we both start walking now? Say, in ten minutes. I've got to be back here at a quarter past six, though. Will that be O.K.?'

'Yes. Ten minutes.' She rang off abruptly. Pat put the receiver down more thoughtfully. Peculiar. Not like Ruth at all. He felt slightly uneasy. Ruth never demanded things of him, least of all his time when he was bound up with work. She had a touching reverence for his work which sometimes annoyed him. He went out of the front door and down the steps, feeling in his jeans pocket for any hopeful signs of money. Three tenpence bits and a button. She'd be unlucky if she was hungry. But she didn't look hungry. She looked white and fragile, all eyes and hair. She was waiting for him outside the small café they sometimes used, not smiling at all. Usually, because they didn't manage to meet very often, she was laughing and eager and flatteringly pleased to see him. She didn't use the cool sophisticated ploy, which was a relief, and he didn't think she was putting anything on now. But cripes, whatever it was, he hoped it wouldn't take too long. Her timing was unfortunate.

'Oh, Pat!' It was close to a sob.

She came up to him and he put his arm round her, his heart sinking heavily.

'What's up? What's wrong?'

'I'm going to have a baby.'

Pat, having asked the question in the same way as one might comment on the weather, hadn't expected a straight answer, and certainly not the one he got. It was so completely unexpected that he could not take it in. He could not believe that he had heard her right. There was a long silence, and Pat realized that he was holding his breath, and let it out very carefully. He looked at Ruth closely. She was looking at him with an expression he could not make out, something beyond the obvious distress.

'Look,' he said. 'You *are* joking?'

'About a thing like this!' She blazed suddenly and pulled herself away. 'Some joke!'

'But we never—we *haven't*—'

'Only the once.'

'On the sea-wall?'

'Yes.'

'But you can't—not just the once—'

'I thought that too. Well, it's not true.' The tears came welling up and ran down her cheeks.

'Oh, Lord! Stop it!' They were standing in the middle of a swarming pavement, dusk just coming and the sharpness of autumn pinching, the buses flaring past in a haze of diesel fumes. He could not believe it. He felt furiously angry.

'Oh, come on,' he muttered. 'Not here, for God's sake.' He took her arm and steered her along the pavement, walking with the rush-hour mob. He felt so angry and confused. He could not say anything, because his brain wasn't coping. He wasn't sure if he believed it.

'How do you know?'

'Oh, don't say you don't know how it works! I came up today for a test, to find out. You read those advertisements and go to an address and they do a test and tell you if it's positive or negative. Well, it's positive. I knew anyway.'

Pat wanted to ask if it mightn't be somebody else's, but he daren't. If it was true, it was the biggest bloody disaster he could conceive of (and *there* was a good pun, he registered viciously)—worse than Pentonville.

'Cripes, but *once*!'

It was beginning to sink in. He was appalled. He couldn't find anything to say to improve the situation. He walked along staring at the pavement, and Ruth wept beside him.

'Does anybody know? Your parents?'

'Not yet.'

He pictured himself telling the Professor. It was impossible. He felt sick again—the prospect of playing Beethoven to Herr Backhaus was roses beside this. Cripes, Ruth must be *potty*—he glanced at her, and was smitten for the first time with a pang for her. She looked about ten, thin as a twig, crying in a silent, painless sort of way that made his heart lurch uncomfortably. He put his arm round her and gave her a squeeze. He couldn't think of anything to say at all.

There was a Wimpy bar, and he steered her in because people were staring. He ordered two coffees, and Ruth sat with her elbows on the table, her head in her hands, staring out of the window between the leaves of a large rubber plant. The tears were easing off; the expression remained difficult to define. Pat felt uneasy. The idea had sunk in; it only remained to discuss it. But he didn't know how to start. The waiter brought the coffees and wrote the price down on his little slip of paper. Pat glanced at his watch. It was twenty to six.

Ruth said, 'It's all right now I've told you. I've got to go home.'

'And tell your parents?'

She shrugged. 'If I *dare*—'

'And then?'

'Whatever you decide.'

'Me?' He heard the shock in his own voice. He hated being manoeuvred, and was angry, at a loss.

She said, 'It can't be decided in a hurry. Only one thing: I'm not going to get rid of it, whatever you decide. I only wanted you to *know*. I didn't know there was anything special on tonight. I'm sorry if I've put you off. I just couldn't go home without telling you.'

From anyone else one would have suspected sarcasm behind these sentiments, but not Ruth.

'No,' he said.

'What are you doing tonight?'

'Playing for Backhaus—Beethoven's Third. He's coming to dinner.'

'I'm sorry. It's important, isn't it? I didn't time it very well, coming today.'

'No. But your thing matters—God, it's more than—' It was *somebody*! His! Heavens, he was a daddy-oh! He pushed his coffee away, feeling sick. But it was the females who were supposed to feel sick. The jumping pre-concert feeling was knotting his stomach. But there was no running away from this one, just like a concert. They would soon all be gathering to pontificate: Ruth's parents, his parents, the Professor . . . the Professor! Even Clemmie, and Mrs. Bates, Clarissa. The prospect was dreadful. But, God—his mind lurched off again, it wasn't anything to ruddy well do with *any* of them!

'Look, whatever *they* say—' He spoke quickly, before he could change his mind. 'It doesn't matter. It's all right.'

'What do you mean?'

Pat could see the Professor's face, the charm wiped out, flint showing, the anger pinging like hailstones. It had happened before. He didn't have to let it matter again. Say it quickly, while the vision gave courage.

'We can get married. Get by—we don't need anybody to tell us what to do. Find a room somewhere.' Cripes, what was he saying?

'We needn't decide now,' Ruth said, but now her expression made sense. She was glowing; she could not hide it. She was like a thirsty white daisy given rain. He could not believe that she could want him so much. But his big foot was well in it now.

Ruth said, 'Listen, you don't have to say that!'

'No, but—'

'Honestly. You can't spoil your work. You must think about it properly.'

'It's no good the way it is now anyway, just being a parasite on the Prof.' This could be the shove he wanted. He'd just have to get by now on his own efforts. But the prospect was daunting. He leaned on the table, drawing a pattern in spilt sugar with his teaspoon. He felt strangely excited. To live with Ruth was a far nicer idea than living with the Professor. While he had been in prison he had thought about marrying her, but when he came out the idea hadn't seemed so bright; the flesh had been more than willing, but the resources non-existent. They still were. He looked at her, scowling thoughtfully. He didn't quite know what he felt about Ruth sometimes. He thought that he loved her as much as he was capable of loving anyone, but he did not rate himself highly at loving—properly loving, in the sense of caring for and looking after, not the sex thing which he had learnt with Clarissa and found very easy, much to his surprise, having worried about it considerably beforehand. (Clarissa had knocked the whole thing for six, but he did not ever think of Clarissa now.) He knew that he had worked so hard because work had mattered more than people. In fact, work had come as a sort of relief, in a funny way.

'You look terribly miserable,' Ruth said, all closed up again. Very earnestly she said, 'I couldn't bear for you to do anything you don't want to do, because you feel it's the right thing. It would be far worse than if you were just to say, "Oh, bad luck. Good-bye."'

'Did you think I would say that?'

'How can I tell?'

'No. I won't.' He didn't know what the hell he was going to do, though. Had he proposed marriage a few minutes ago? The desperate feeling came back. He tried not to let it show.

'We—look, we'll have to work it out.' It was ten past six! God in heaven, he'd have to gallop. 'The week-end—I'll see you. I'll come down. I'll meet you in Northend.'

'All right.'

'The station, about eleven?'

'Yes.' Ruth got up, following him. 'Will you—I mean, you'll have to, whatever you decide—come and see my parents?'

'Cripes, yes!' He heard the toughness in his voice—plain funk at the thought. The classic encounter. Not to think about it now! Think himself back into Beethoven where he belonged. But the evening was a dead duck already. He didn't want to say anything else, frightened to commit himself again. Having already done so, he was shattered by his impetuosity. He wasn't in a fit state to decide anything.

They went out of the café and Pat walked Ruth to the tube-station in silence. Ruth seemed composed, withdrawn. Pat was grateful for this restraint, having a strong suspicion that it was rare in such circumstances. For the first time, he felt her strength; he admired her. It steadied him. He had never been so thrown, he realized, not ever—even during his worst moments on the wrong side of the law. But at the tube-station when they got to the ticket barrier, she kissed him good-bye with a desperation that he could sense, although she didn't say a word. It was an electric current of emotion—compounded of God only knew what powerful, urgent ingredients . . . it left him mindless, drifting back to the Professor's in a state of numb shock, head down against the jostling pavement. Ruth's face, tightly not saying anything, yet with all those powerful feelings buttoned away behind the dark, silent eyes, would not go away from his vision. He had never felt so bewildered, so deeply involved.

It was a quarter to seven when he got back. The Professor was in the hall, cold and business-like.

'Where have you been?' Pat shook his head and went on up the stairs, quite incapable of speaking one word of sense. The Professor must have taken his trance as a sign of communication with Beethoven, for he merely stared after him curiously, and then went away into the music-room, and Pat was free to moan and groan about his bedroom, his mind freeing itself from Ruth's spell to concentrate with startling clarity and vision on his own plight. Away from Ruth, secure in his own pad, this was now taking on its true and awful proportions. He was being pulled into matrimony by the ears—a month away from the altar, and he had no money, no job, no home, not even a ruddy piano of his own . . . Was he dreaming? A *child*—!

He heard the doorbell ring. He changed quickly, and combed his hair and went downstairs. He had to go down. He didn't know what he was going to do. Not about Ruth, nor even with the Beethoven. He kept thinking that he must think of Beethoven, but all through dinner he could only think of Ruth's electric-current feelings and the seed inside her that had perversely chosen to grow into a human being, quite heedless of the train of chaos it thereby set in motion. Every time he looked at the Professor he knew that the Professor was thinking that his abstraction was due to his normal state of nervous tension before a performance. The Professor was benign, fatherly (*fatherly*, a very relevant word!). Pat could imagine him when he knew, the anger, the scorn, the white fury—he had experienced it all before. All his life he had had the knack of inspiring this emotion in his elders and betters: his parents, teachers, and various elements of the law. It was nothing new, nothing he did not know how to accept. But getting married was new. Clemmie leaned over from behind and took his empty plate away. He hadn't noticed he had eaten anything, or what it was. It wasn't nerves for what might or might not happen during his performance, but nerves about what had already happened and what was surely going to happen in a very short time over and above what he was presently going to do to Beethoven's Third. He pushed the plate away and stood up.

'You may leave us if you wish,' the Professor said smoothly, smiling.

Pat went out. He heard Backhaus chuckle in fatherly (fatherly!)

29

manner and caught his words, 'I know so well the feeling . . .'

How many bastards had the old buffer put into the world then? Pat wondered bitterly. Clemmie followed him out into the hall and said, 'Come into the kitchen and I'll give you something. They'll be chatting a while yet.'

He followed her and sat down at the kitchen table, amongst the pile of dirty dishes.

'What's the matter with you?' she said.

'Ruth's going to have a baby.'

'Oh, my Gawd!'

Clemmie set down her tray abruptly and gave Pat a shocked glance.

'That's a pretty kettle of fish! My word, Pat, you—' She could not think of the words, and stood shaking her head. 'The poor little thing! Poor little Ruth! She's just a child. Oh, dear me. And me thinking it was only the nerves. Oh, my word, Pat, but that's bad. Very bad.'

He could not disagree. Clemmie started laying out the coffee-cups, her plump face all puckered up and twitching with disapproval. Pat knew she wanted to rate him, but was held back—such was her years of grounding in such things—by knowing that in a few minutes he had to play for Herr Backhaus.

'You'd better have some strong coffee,' she said severely, as if it had the power to purge both mind and body. 'What a time to have this broken to us! Dear me! I don't know why you children don't *realize*—oh dear.' She pulled herself up short, clicking her tongue. 'Really, Pat, you . . .' She stopped herself by a great effort. But it was all in her pursed-up mouth and her censorious expression. Pat, taking his coffee, remembered Ruth's arms about him and the smell of the cold evening grass all bound up in their brief and beautiful and solitary moment of loving six weeks ago on the sea-wall, and wanted to shout at Clemmie, '*Poor* Ruth! *Poor* Ruth!' There had been nothing poor about Ruth then, and she would be the first to acknowledge it. But he said nothing and took his coffee into the music-room and sat down at the piano. The doors were closed, and he shook his wrists and his arms and his shoulders into a playing disposition and laid his fingers on the keys. Soon the Professor would come in and sit down at the other piano to play at being a sixty-strong orchestra, and the other man, the sharpest critic of any he was ever likely to meet in all his life, would lie back in his armchair and light up his cigar and roll his brandy in the Professor's expensive crystal brandy glass and say, 'Very well then, shall we start?' and he would have to do this thing, whether his life's course was shattered or not. The only thing he could think of, sitting there, was to remember Ruth as she had been, loving him, and would be again, God willing, when this monumental muddle was a thing of the past and then, with that to power him, hope that there was some remote and ailing chance that his soul might grope its way in Beethoven's direction and his fingers do its bidding.

Chapter 3

Ruth's mother looked nervously out of the window for the umpteenth time and said to her husband, 'If they caught the four-fifteen bus they ought to be here any minute now.'

'Hmm.'

Mr. Hollis was reading the newspaper but was not concentrating very hard.

'It's they who ought to feel nervous,' he pointed out. 'Not us.'

'Yes. I know. But I feel awful. The whole thing is horrible.'

'Have I got to play the heavy father. I mean, get angry?'

'Of course! You're not pleased, are you?'

'I don't mind if they get married.'

'I'm not at all sure whether that's the best course. It would be if he were a decent, stable character. But he's a jail-bird. He hasn't even got a job—oh, we've been through all this! I wish they'd hurry up and we could get the wretched business over! I never dreamt I'd have to go through all this with Ruth! Ruth of all people—she's never been the slightest bit interested in boys. I still can't really believe it's happened.'

'Hmm.'

'I keep thinking I'll wake up and find out it's just a nightmare.'

'It's not the end of the world.'

'But such a mess! At that age, seventeen! And what's he—just twenty? He had his birthday in prison, I believe. What sort of a start is it? The coming of a child should be a lovely thing, not a great ghastly mistake with ructions all round.'

'Fifty per cent of the population are great ghastly mistakes, and always have been, all through history.'

'Oh!' Mrs. Hollis gave a great sniff of exasperation. The calm reasonableness of her husband had always exasperated her. He had always taken Ruth's part, ever since she was little. She was shattered by what had happened: he was philosophical. Mrs. Hollis knew that Ruth was quite aware of her basic security. In spite of what had happened, Ruth knew that she wouldn't be thrown out, and her mother was annoyed by the girl's acceptance of this fact. She could not stop voicing her own bitterness. She had been voicing it every day since she had found out. It had the effect of making Mr. Hollis stick up for Ruth. The whole family had talked itself round in circles, airing opinions but deciding nothing.

'Because it's not for us to decide,' Mr. Hollis had pointed out firmly to his wife. 'It's for the pair of them.'

'And if the lad decides he doesn't want to be involved, and Ruth is left with the baby, who is going to be lumbered with the job of looking after it? Tell me that! It will be me, of course! The universal doormat—'

'You like babies.'

'I won't *have* it! I don't want to start all that again at my age!'

The voice had verged on hysteria. It had railed spasmodically through all the grades from horror and grief to indignation for the last four days, and now, faced with the actual confrontation, to make the decision, it was taut with nervousness. Mrs. Hollis could hear her own voice, querulous and agitated, and was annoyed with herself. It was not for *her* to be nervous! It was for her to dictate, to take command, to make it go her way. But she felt defeated before it even started.

'The young today—they do just what they want,' she muttered. 'No morals, no standards . . .'

If the boy had been more suitable, she supposed she might have felt more optimistic. But what little she did know of him was daunting. The only opportunities she had had to observe him at length were during his playing of the Rachmaninov Piano Concerto in the Northend Pavilion a year ago, when he had appeared to her to be extraordinarily controlled, refined, and gifted; and during his appearance in the dock at the Northend Quarter Sessions a few weeks later when he had struck her as equally uncontrolled, unrefined and downright undesirable. Her last sight of him was of his being bundled into the back of a Black Maria, en route for Pentonville, handcuffed to a young man with long hair who had knocked out an old woman and stolen her handbag—while she coped with a weeping Ruth and her own

33

mangled feelings, having aged another year or so during the day. It was not entirely surprising that she felt apprehensive about meeting him in the present circumstances, not knowing which of his Jekyll and Hyde faces to expect. Nobody she had ever come across was quite such a paradox. And Ruth not only in love with him, but irrevocably pregnant . . . 'Oh!' Mrs. Hollis could not suppress another groan at the prospect.

'Here they are now,' said Mr. Hollis from his armchair.

Mrs. Hollis flounced round, tight-lipped. 'Huh!' She went to the door, her hands shaking.

It was going dusk, the smell of frost in the air, the elms gold and baring across the lawn. Ruth was in front, almost running, laughing, her face bright with cold. Her mother had never seen her look so healthy and happy, so *unsuitably* carefree—it made her almost snort with rage. Pat was behind, not looking nearly so carefree, Mrs. Hollis was gratified to note, but not particularly apprehensive either. It was his old expression, the look he always wore when he had been the baker's boy, and which had annoyed her then, not polite and helpful and how-are-you-today, but slightly hostile and impatient—his normal expression, she supposed. She had thought of him in the past as ominous, and had no reason now to change her opinion; his movements were not politely contained in a nice public-school manner, but brought to her mind the ridiculous simile of a tiger in a cage. He had always given her this unease, she realized, even when he had been a mere baker's boy. There was this feeling of restrained energy about him, a total lack of the normal human conditions of boredom, indifference and relaxation: he was large and taut and disturbing, even when he was just standing there doing nothing, and Mrs. Hollis had always wanted a *nice* boy for a son-in-law, a kind, well-bred, soft-voiced, *normal* boy. Pat was none of these things. She suppressed another groan, looking up at him, and said in a tight voice, 'Do come in. We guessed you would be on that bus.'

He came in. He was wearing, Mrs. Hollis noticed with distaste, patched jeans and a black polo-necked jersey, and his hair was fast losing its neat government appearance. She nodded to him curtly, and he nodded coldly back. It was not an auspicious start to what was likely to be a long, intimate relationship. 'Son-in-law,' Mrs. Hollis thought; the title stuck in her brain, meaningless. More like out-of-law—there was nothing lawful about what he had done to Ruth. Mr. Hollis got out of his armchair and advanced slowly, holding out his hand.

'How do you do.' He was perfectly right, his wife thought with surprise, cordial but rather aloof, only the faintest smile. Very civilized. Pat shook hands and muttered something under his breath. Mrs. Hollis realized then that he certainly must feel worse than she did, whatever sort of a face he was putting on it, and immediately she felt better.

Ruth, flinging off her coat, her face positively beaming light and joy, said, 'It's all right, we're going to be married!'

Her father turned to her, as flinty as Mrs. Hollis had ever seen him, and said, 'Surely the decision has still to be made? Isn't this what we are all meeting for?'

Ruth's mouth dropped open in astonishment.

'But—'

'Old-fashioned as it may seem to you,' Mr. Hollis continued, 'your mother and I are still the ones to decide on your future.'

Mrs. Hollis was almost as amazed as Ruth at the unprecedented sternness in the voice of this carpet-slipper man whose mildness they had taken for granted all their lives. She saw Ruth's face, white and blasted, and felt a most unusual stab of triumph go through her. '*Yes*,' she thought, 'why must it always be *we* who are the manipulated, the pitied, the derided?' The arrogance of the young was so total that their elders could be quite unkeeled by it, their own scraps of wisdom, garnered by hard experience, quite tossed away by sheer, bursting confidence. What, for heaven's sake, had Ruth to be laughing about, shackling herself for life to a jobless young jail-bird, with the child to tie her freedom right from the very first moment? And yet, apart from her momentary surprise at her father's attitude, she was obviously over the moon with excitement and pure joy. Her confidence was, to her mother's eyes, quite maniacal. And yet, of course, to the young quite normal.

'I'll put the kettle on,' she said flatly. She could not help noticing that Pat did not appear to be sharing quite the same confidence. Or if he was, it wasn't quite so evident. 'Poor young devil,' she thought, with a quite irrelevant and completely out of place pang of sympathy. He was going to pay for his seduction with a vengeance! Ruth had assured her that they had only made love on the one occasion. There was, if you were dispassionate enough to stand back and appreciate it, a distinctly ironic and funny side to most of the common human dilemmas. With all this philosophy swilling unusually and somewhat disjointedly through her mind, Mrs. Hollis went to make a pot of tea.

'Go and sit in the other room,' she said. 'I'll bring it in.'

Mr. Hollis led the way and sat in his usual chair opposite the television set, wondering if Pat was as acutely aware as he was that Arsenal were playing Spurs and they only had to turn the knob to enjoy themselves, instead of ploughing through the agenda before them.

'Interested in soccer?' he said.

'Yeah, I played a lot once.' Pat then looked at the blank television set in such a way that Mr. Hollis knew that he knew very well what was on.

'Years since I played it,' Mr. Hollis said. 'I still follow Ipswich, though. That's still the home team, as far as I'm concerned. It's had its moments.'

'Yes, it has. I used to train evenings sometimes with some of the Northend United reserves. Before I left school. I thought of doing it sometimes, but then so did a lot of others.'

'Easier than what you *are* doing, I'd have thought.'

Pat shrugged. 'I got the opportunity.'

'Ever regretted it?'

'Not yet.'

'It's very competitive, as jobs go.'

'Yes. Like soccer.'

'How did it come about?'

'Professor Hampton heard me, when I was still at school. It was a coincidence, really—that he heard me, I mean. And he offered me a scholarship, talked me into it.'

'Is he the man whose place you're at now?'

'Yes.'

'Does he know—about—what's happened?'

'Not yet.'

'Your parents?'

'No. I don't see them much.'

'You've no brothers and sisters?'

'No.'

'Not really any family life at all?'

Pat shook his head, frowning. Mr. Hollis could see that he

hated being questioned, yet knew that he had put himself in a position that made it inevitable. For his own money he preferred Pat to the boys that his wife would have considered suitable as son-in-laws, but he could not help agreeing with her doubts as to whether this taciturn lad was actually going to make Ruth happy. He could see the romance part of it, yes . . . the physical desirability of the boy he could acknowledge without any difficulty; his particular talent was impressive and persuasive and by its very nature far more attractive than bank-clerkery, motor-car selling or hod-carrying . . . but when it came to the brass facts, shorn of romance, the boy was insecure, aggressive, penniless, jobless, temperamental, irresponsible and without prospects—except possibly long-term prospects. Mr. Hollis sighed. His glance went again to the blank screen of the television set. Mrs. Hollis brought the tea in on a tray and Ruth pulled up a small table.

'You must be cold,' Mrs. Hollis said to her. 'Out all day in just that thin jacket. It's turned quite sharp.'

'I wasn't cold.'

'There's a meal in the oven we can have a little later. I didn't know what time you'd be back.'

She sat down and poured out the tea. They all took their cups, passed round the sugar, stirred, and sat back in the easy chairs. Nobody said anything. Mrs. Hollis sent an angry, impatient glance in her husband's direction. He intercepted it, resisted.

'Put the box on, Ruth. We'll just get the end of that match, I'd like to know—'

Ruth grinned, and got up and switched on the television. She dared not look at her mother. The commentator's voice came through, taut, clipped, and the picture followed slowly, the ant-like figures running across the screen. Pat's eyes flicked up.

'Three minutes to go, and two minutes' injury time . . . Spurs will really have to pull something out of the bag if they're to equalize now!'

'Arsenal. That means they'll be playing the winner of the Ipswich—Colchester match next.' Mr. Hollis looked deeply contented.

'Ipswich,' Pat said.

'You reckon? Five minutes to play . . .'

They all watched the television until the match was over and spectators spilled out over the screen, making faces and waving.

Mrs. Hollis got up and turned off the set pointedly and Mr. Hollis said, 'Any more tea?'

She took his cup and refilled it, her face grim. He got up and sugared it and took it back to his chair again.

'Well?' Mrs. Hollis put the tea-pot down firmly. 'What—'

'Yes,' said Mr. Hollis. 'Let's see what these two have got to say for yourselves. The object of the exercise.'

'We're going to get married,' Ruth said.

'You mean you would like to get married?'

'Yes.'

'Pat would like to get married too?' Mr. Hollis turned and looked at him.

'Yes.' Pat was still looking at the blank television screen.

'Because you've got to?'

Pat's head jerked up. 'No. I didn't say that.'

'You don't feel you've got to, then? You don't feel any responsibility for what's happened?' Mrs. Hollis cut in.

Pat glared at her. 'I am responsible. I never said I wasn't.'

'And what can you offer her, if you get married? Are you in a position to offer to marry her?'

'I will be soon enough if I put my mind to it. I'll get a job, and we'll find a room somewhere, and then we'll get married.'

'A room!' Mrs. Hollis snorted.

'It's all we want,' Ruth said.

'What, with a baby and the washing and nappies and—'

'Oh, Mother! It will be all right!'

'Oh!' Mrs. Hollis positively snorted. 'When will you ever, *ever*, come down to earth! I—' She choked, her face working. She turned to Pat. 'And you! You've nothing! Nothing to offer! And yet you take her, and you do this to her without any thought for the consequences, and then you have the arrogance to—'

'Mary, don't—it doesn't—'

'Oh, she is such a child! She's no idea—'

Pat was looking white, stricken. 'After a slow start,' Mr. Hollis was thinking, 'we're in with a vengeance.'

'Mother, we're not stupid,' Ruth said. 'Of course we'll manage! You're making it sound as if we're imbeciles.'

'Well, sometimes I wonder—'

'Let's be practical,' said Mr. Hollis. 'What will you do, Pat? What sort of a job will you get? You mean with your music?'

'No. Any job to start off with. Just anything, to pay for some-where to live.'

'And the music will—'

'It will fit in. I've done it before. I've often had to get jobs. You do the job, and then when you've finished you get the practice in. And then I'll start getting engagements and eventually I shall make money that way and then I can give up the other.'

'Have you any money of your own, now?'

'No.'

'Well, I suggest the first thing you do is get this job and some wages and find somewhere to live and then we'll talk about your getting married. How does that strike you?'

'That's all right.'

'You're quite prepared to do that? I understand that you'll be giving up a good deal if you part ways with this teacher of yours?'

'Yes. But it's time I got by on my own.'

'He's been very good to you, I understand?'

'Well, yes. He has.'

'And you've yet to tell him about these present developments?'

'I haven't told him yet. I will now.'

'I don't know how much influence he has over you. I imagine he won't want you to get married—he might try very hard to talk you out of this course. You're prepared for that?'

'Yes. He'll go berserk. I've had it before.'

Mrs. Hollis said tautly, 'You repay him well for all he's done!'

'He knew what he was taking on. I've never asked him for anything, ever.' Pat was looking at the carpet, as if trying to memorize the pattern.

'Why I'm saying this,' Mr. Hollis went on rapidly, 'is so that we all know exactly what the situation is. You might have decided a certain course now, but when all parties are brought into it—your parents as well—you might well be prevailed upon to take some other action. I don't think you ought to feel bound to go ahead with this marriage, until you've talked to these other people concerned. Ruth's mother and I are not forcing you to marry Ruth, you understand. In fact we aren't sure whether it is the best solution at all. For all we know, you might have said you'll do it because you thought you had no alternative. But you're still a free agent. You understand this?'

Pat was silent, the carpet absorbing him. Ruth said nothing, looking petrified.

'You understand?'

'Yes.'

'Well, shall we leave it at that for the time being? You can come back when you've had more time to consider your situation and we'll talk again.'

'In other words, he can get off scot-free if he so wishes, as men always have done and always will do!' Mrs. Hollis's voice shook.

'We both agreed on this, Mary,' Mr. Hollis reminded her.

'Oh!' It was an explosion of despair and disgust, choked with hopeless anger. Ruth looked from her father to her mother and said, 'One thing, I'm not giving up the baby, whatever happens.'

'We can talk about that later,' her mother said.

'No,' Ruth said.

Her mother turned to her, eyes flashing, but Mr. Hollis said sharply, 'How about that meal, Mary?'

Mrs. Hollis slumped, the tears coming up into her eyes.

'I'll help you,' Ruth said, aghast.

'I can manage by myself, thank you!' She got up and walked out to the kitchen, slamming the door behind her. Mr. Hollis leaned back in his chair, gazing at the ceiling, silent. The atmosphere was lacerated, the clock's ticking unfamiliarly loud in the sudden strained silence of shock and embarrassment. In the Hollis household emotional upsets were rare: it was as if the very house was surprised. Ruth could feel it painfully, and wondered if it was as sharp to Pat, who was well-grounded in emotional upsets in a great variety of situations, and might consider this a very minor example. He looked heavily, angrily miserable, not at all like a lover looking forward to marriage. Ruth did not know now where she stood. She could feel the tears rising up from so deep inside her that it was almost a physical pain. She looked desperately at her father, who had gone half-way to rejecting Pat, and he, as if feeling her pain, half got up from his chair and said to Pat:

'How about playing something for us? It's time our piano knew what it was all about.'

Ruth said, 'Oh, Father, really! He surely doesn't feel like—'

'Well, if he's a professional, that's where the difference lies.

Isn't that right, Pat? You play to order, not when the muse stirs?'

Pat sighed. 'I suppose so.'

'I feel that something soothing could be very beneficial just at the moment. Come on now! Did you know that Ruth has acquired a piano and is trying to teach herself to play?

'No, I didn't.' Pat got slowly to his feet.

'Only to learn turning over,' Ruth said hurriedly. 'Pottering. I can't do it at all. I'm useless.'

'She made us get a piano. An old lady down the road was throwing it out, and she got Ted to bring it down here on his breakdown lorry. It's only done hymns all its life, and then Ruth's efforts—'

'Bobby Shafto with one finger.'

'Come on. Give it a surprise.'

Pat smiled, looking as if it was an effort. He crossed over to the piano, sat down and looked at the keys, not saying anything. He played some chords and arpeggios to see what it sounded like, then stared into space some more, bit his thumb-nail thoughtfully —presumably adjusting from thoughts of a shotgun marriage to consideration of a work in suitable mood—then launched into a piece so melting and poignant that Ruth's painful efforts to cool her feelings were sabotaged in the first ten bars. If only it had been brisk and knotty and extrovert like some of the pieces she had heard him play! But it was quiet and flowing, a quite heart-stopping piece, familiar enough to know what was coming and to anticipate the exquisite, hanging crescendoes of the melody, almost held back, to savour the poignancy to the full, then falling down soft and fast to catch up, in such a way that Ruth had consciously to steel herself against it, not to be drowned. She almost hated him, for making it so hard—one had no defence against music, this great mainspring of pure emotion—and she was in emotional disarray already, without Chopin to add to it. She was torn, the music shredding her, and she resisting manfully, because she still did not know where she was with him; she could not allow herself to give in. She watched him angrily, the absorbed tenderness of his expression which she had noted long ago when he played, inspired by his work, needling her with such a mixture of jealousy, despair and downright adoration that she felt quite overwhelmed. She lay back in the armchair and shut her eyes so that she couldn't see him any more, but the music—it seemed to her—got in under her very eyelids, crumbling all her defences.

When it stopped, there was a long silence.

'Ah.' Mr. Hollis broke it with a satisfied sigh. 'The very thing. Very soothing. What was it?'

'Chopin.'

'What's its name?'

'Nocturne in B-flat Minor.'

'Oh.' He sounded disappointed. Ruth remembered she had asked, long ago, the same thing about the Brahms, and found that it was only a waltz, with numbers. It was very precise, the cataloguing of music: there was no clue in the title 'Nocturne in B-flat Minor, Opus 9, number one' to suggest what a passion it had the power to evoke in a susceptible breast. Ruth sniffed.

Mrs. Hollis put her head round the door and said, 'If you've done, the macaroni-cheese is on the table.'

Pat's thoughts after the interview were in equal disarray. They were unworthy, self-centred and completely materialistic, and he knew it. His heart kept whizzing up with relief that the old man had given him *carte blanche* to scarper, but, ironically, the release had come too late, for he had spent the last week forcing himself to think of all the advantages of marrying Ruth, instead of the whole calamity of the situation which had been his earlier reaction. And he had talked himself into a very real readiness to leave the Professor, so much so that the sudden thought of not leaving him made him feel incredibly restricted again, like a child.

And now the piano! During the very first bars of the Chopin piece he knew he would be happy to marry Ruth for her piano. It was only an upright, but quite the nicest upright he had ever come across. His lack of a piano, if he moved out of the Professor's, had been something of a stopper to his plans. At least if he got Ruth's as a dowry, it was something to keep going on. The unworthiness of this sentiment made him feel somewhat guilty, but he could not quell it. It wasn't, in any case, as unworthy as that instinctive surge of utter relief that had shaken him when Ruth's old man had told him he needn't marry her. This door suddenly opening again, restoring the status quo, knocked all his planning for six. Cripes, there was nothing to stop him, if he really wanted, to get shot of the lot of them, ship himself off somewhere

where no one had ever set eyes on him, get a job and start again from scratch!

He sat in the train going back staring out at the racing lights that were the back bedrooms of all the tens of thousands of married couples in the suburbs of London, and tried to think of himself as one of them, and then he thought of himself playing a pub piano in St. Ives, hitching to Afghanistan or Tangier, or even stealing a car and going to Birmingham or Manchester or Clacton-on-Sea. He had only to *choose*. There was no one to stop him. But freedom on such a scale was as frightening as all the other prospects, and he knew himself so well—he had had the opportunity to do all this before, when he had been in equally tight corners, and he had never taken advantage of it. The possibilities had flowered in his head, as they were doing now, but they were as insubstantial as candy-floss. He had no faith. He had learned from an early age that, for him, nothing was easy.

And then, the nub of the whole thing, which ought to provide the answer, did he truly love Ruth? He ought to know, after Clarissa, what love was, but sometimes he thought that she had merely taught him what it wasn't. What he felt for Ruth was such a tangle of affection, guilt, desire, resentment, tenderness, anger and pure confusion that there was no knowing what the real answer was. He peered out of the window, scowling. The bright windows were still flashing past, miles and miles of evidence of married life. One more window, what difference did it make? What a drop in the ocean! He couldn't draw any conclusions at all.

The old man had been all right, but her mother—there was an old cow if you like. . . .

Chapter 4

'What did he say when you told him?'

'Don't talk about it! I don't want to discuss it—I want to *forget*—'

'Do you, Patrick Edward, take this woman, Ruth Margaret, to be your lawfully wedded wife . . .'

'I want to forget—'

'He plays the C Minor as if his mind is elsewhere . . .'

Forget!

Pat opened his eyes, as if aware in semi-consciousness that present reality must be better than what he was dreaming about. He had this feeling of panic which was now almost familiar, and the feeling of having to struggle up to some mythical surface, as if he were in very deep water, swimming up, and the panic to be kept down, drowned, under his feet. He was in a sweat, and groaned as he awoke. The sun fell across the pillow, a pigeon crooned on the window-sill outside.

He shifted, stretching under the sheet, putting his arms up and linking his fingers under his head. The sun dazzled him, making a live spark of the little gold medal of Beethoven round his neck which was all he wore. Morning sun had been the chief attraction of the small room—its only attraction, a cynic might have said, but Pat, his eyes roving round slowly, found comfort in it. He liked it. 'You'll feel at home here, after Pentonville.' Ruth's mother hadn't actually said those words, but Pat had sensed them in her look. He smiled at the ceiling. It was yellow and homely; the wallpaper was so old that the walls were just a pink blur; Ruth, looking very closely, said it wasn't William Morris reproduction, which was the 'in' thing, but original William Morris if they wanted something to boast about. There was actually a jug and basin too, that antique shops sold to smart people.

The water tap was four floors down in the café kitchen and the jug and basin were for real, not ornaments. 'I suppose that's for bathing the baby in,' Ruth's mother had said in her scathing voice. Afterwards they had rolled about laughing. There were times when they couldn't stop laughing and Pat, who wasn't used to laughing, had found himself wondering sometimes what it was all about. Everything had gone wrong; all the events that he had just been dreaming about had actually happened, and each one had been exceedingly painful at the time, but lumped together, put behind him, they had liberated him to a degree that was still a pure astonishment every time he thought about it. It had its panics, the deep-water feeling—he could scare the living daylights out of himself if he thought about it hard enough—but on the surface it was a magical relief, a rebirth. He was answerable to no one for the first time in his life, and Ruth didn't count, for weren't they, in the extraordinarily quaint words that had been used by the Northend registrar to marry them, now 'one person'? On their tod together. And he loved Ruth dearly now for being so happy with the absolute nil he had to offer her. They were at rock-bottom. They could only rise up. Awake he liked it, but asleep he got the panics sometimes, the underwater feeling, which was because he knew it couldn't last long, the status quo—he would in fact, *have* to rise up, for the arrangement was strictly for the moment. It didn't include his work, nor the baby. When he started thinking about that, he stopped laughing.

His work . . . that was the crunch, that was what really gave him bad dreams, not the baby, which must take pot-luck like all human beings. But the baby decided the time-factor. By the time it was born he must have got somewhere. This was where, if he was wise, he stopped thinking, and turned his mind back to the ceiling, blank and warm above his head. He did so now, scowling. He concentrated on the ceiling. It was completely unmusical, flat and abstract. 'A cup of tea,' he thought. That meant going down four floors to fill the jug, which had been empty last night and was no doubt still empty now. The thought put him off. 'Ruth,' he thought. That was much better. He turned and looked at her, still asleep. 'Ruth, Ruth . . .' Better than ceilings. Better than work, and better than thinking.

'I love you.' He had put her before his work so it must be true. He could say it now. His new freedom had released all sorts of inhibitions, including his tongue. He felt the flowering of this strange, lovely happiness which was the antidote to the darker thoughts, the ceiling thoughts, the drowning panics . . . it was what made sense of the whole thing. . . .

It was Sunday. Nothing to get up for. Pat had got the room through a Pentonville connection: the brother-in-law of its owner had been in the next cell, was still there in fact. 'The old-boy network,' Pat had called it. Luigi, the owner of the cafe, had remembered Pat from visiting day, and had offered him the room in exchange for a 'spot of washing-up and the little wife as a waitress, eh?' Pat had put the proposition to Ruth somewhat doubtfully, but she had been thrilled at the idea of being a waitress. (Pat could not help thinking of Clarissa at this juncture, although he thought of her very rarely now. The thought made him laugh.) Luigi considered Pat's prison-record a commendation for the job. 'You in ze keetchen, very 'andy if we 'ave ze drunk man in ze café. We 'ave ze bouncer then. Me not beeg enough.' Pat washed up from eight in the evening until two in the morning, and all the rest of the time he was free to pursue his musical career. His musical career, it seemed to him, was now centred on a small landing half-way up the stairs, which was as high as they had managed to get Ruth's piano without getting stuck. Ruth's brother, Ted, had brought the instrument up to London on a borrowed lorry, but the combined efforts of Pat, Ted, Luigi, Luigi's father and Luigi's brother, could not get it past a particular part of the banisters three floors up. It was Luigi's idea to leave it on the landing.

'You play it 'ere. There is room for ze seat. And you 'ave ze electric light. Mama is deaf, she do not worry.'

'Cripes,' Pat thought, when he had extended the light-flex and got the bulb hanging in the right spot over the music-rack— if the Professor could see him at work! If anyone came up the stairs he had to get up and move his seat out of the way. From below, warm smells of spaghetti and risotto and coffee came up to tickle his nostrils, and above him the sagging, fly-spotted ceiling rained gentle flakes of distemper during forte passages. The sound of the ancient plumbing and the flushing of the lavatory pipes punctuated his pianissimos. Carmen, Luigi's wife, brought him cups of coffee at hourly intervals but, otherwise, surrounded by the bare damp-stained walls, threadbare lino underfoot (the acoustics were unnerving at times, after the Professor's music-room) there was absolutely nothing to distract. Not even a window to look out of. His exercises resounded up and down the stairs in both directions and amongst the crashing of china, the explosions of the espresso-coffee machine and the loud Italian conversation from below, he could play unremarked. He missed his lessons with the Professor desperately but kept telling himself that—if he was the musician he hoped he was—it was high time he managed without his mentor and started to work it all out his own way. When it sounded terrible he told himself it was the conditions. Sometimes the panics would get him and he thought he was useless, but he had had those feelings at times ever since he had started studying. It was just a part of the whole business. But now there was no one to get him on a level keel again, only himself. He had to do it all by himself. It was terribly hard.

'What are you thinking about?' Ruth asked him.

He had got up and was shaving, scowling into the mirror over the marble wash-stand with such ferocity that Ruth was prompted to ask the question. She was in bed, watching him. She could watch him by the hour, still trying to convince herself that it was true that she was married to him. Sometimes she thought it was just a dream.

'Growing a beard,' he said. Actually he had been thinking about trying to get some engagements and where to start knocking on doors. He had a repertory that was good enough, a proper mixture of the fashionables with the warhorses and enough to suit it to most audiences—it was just a matter of finding an agent, the right person . . . Now the Liszt sonata was coming together—if anyone wanted that it could be ready, God willing and the stars kindly, not to mention quite a lot of Schumann, the Beethoven sonatas that mattered, three of Prokofiev's and two of Scriabin's, and if it was Tory ladies in Kingston-on-Thames or a musical evening in Steeple Bumstead, he had all the right Chopin and the Moonlight and the Golliwog's Cakewalk, not to mention the Air on a G-string and several Hungarian rhapsodies to boot. 'Blast!'

'You've cut yourself,' Ruth said.

'Blunt blade.'

But Pat had to admit that he was happier shaving with blunt blades over a chipped china basin with roses round the rim than he had been borrowing the Professor's expensive machine in the plushy bathroom in S.W.1. With the kettle boiling on the ring in the hearth, the gas-fire popping in homely fashion and Ruth, decorative as well as useful, groping herself into her dressing-gown and preparing to make toast, there was a good deal to be said for the squalor of bed-sit life. If some agent could only be persuaded to think he could play half as well as Ruth assured him he did, life would be pretty well perfect.

'Do you think a beard would make me look a better pianist? Older, more impressive?'

'Oh, you impress me no end as you are, and who wants to look old before their time?'

She did say some extraordinary things at times, Pat thought. He thought that, considering they were a married couple, they didn't really know each other very well. There had been a bare three months before Pentonville, with not very frequent meetings, then nine months of seeing each other for half an hour once a month, then bang: they were married. He liked it. It was interesting, finding her out.

'What are we going to do today?' She fetched the loaf from its bin on the landing and started to cut some slices for toast. 'I like Sundays. I like every day. But Sundays best.'

'I must do an hour or so on the Liszt first.'

'I'll do the housework then, with the door open, and tell you when you go wrong. Is that the one full of great swooning bits, and then all maniacal? Starts as if he's dropped something and is looking for it in the dark?'

'Yes.'

'I like that. I wish I could play a bit. Couldn't you teach me?'

'Only for money.'

'All I have is yours!'

They had fourteen pounds and sixty-four pence exactly. Ruth sat down on the hearth with the bread stuck out to the gas-fire on the end of a fork.

'Isn't giving lessons a quite easy way to earn money?' she asked.

'It might be for some people.'

'You could practise on me.'

'Yes. But I don't want to be a teacher.'

'Oh.' That seemed fair. Nor did she. 'What a pity I can't do something frightfully lucrative.' One year at an art school had

48

taught her how lovely life was, but nothing about earning money. Her only qualification, after seventeen years, was her Pony Club B test.

'How do you like your toast? Striped?'

'Of course. Shall I make the tea?' He reached for the tea-packet on the mantelpiece and shook some into the tea-pot. He poured water from the kettle into it, put it in the hearth, and sat down in front of the fire beside Ruth.

'It's nice, isn't it?'

'Yes.'

'You know, Pat, you ought to tell your parents you've got married. It's three weeks now.'

'Why? They won't mind.'

'They ought to know.'

'Why?'

'Parents like to know things like that. You could write to them. You haven't got to actually see them.'

'Well, I might do that.'

'It would be thoughtful.'

Pat grinned. He took the buttered toast she was offering him, and poured out the tea. 'After breakfast I'll practise the Liszt. Then I'll write a letter and tell my parents that a scheming little bitch got her claws into me and I had to marry her, then we'll go for a walk up to Hyde Park and post the letter. Then we'll go to Luigi's cousin's place and get some chips for lunch, and then we'll go to the South Bank and see if we can get a couple of seats for John Ogdon; we'll have some tea and come back here and work the rest of the day. Then tomorrow I'm going to put my best suit on and go and call on all the people I can think of who might get me an engagement. Every morning next week I'll go out looking for work—I mean music, not more washing-up.'

'Concerts?'

'Anything. Don't expect me to come back with a recital at the Q.E. hall in the bag . . . don't expect anything at all. There are thousands of pianists as good as me, all looking for work.'

'Oh, rubbish. You're by far the best.'

'Backhaus didn't think so.'

'He didn't say you were no good! He said you needed more time.'

'Who doesn't? He couldn't very well say I was out-and-out lousy after the meal Hampton gave him, could he?'

'It was my fault, telling you all that just before!'

'No, it was my fault.'

'Oh, that time—' It had been dreadful—Ruth's face went stark. They had had their bad bits, more than their share, right up to getting married, facing up to the Professor . . . but the bits her mother had prophesied would be bad, having no money and living in squalor, had not turned out bad at all. She loved this funny little room, with its battered window looking out over a yardful of dustbins, walls, roofs and—if one nearly broke one's neck craning—the corner of the church in Hanover Square where all the best people got married—and she loved sitting on the floor (the only chair was down on the next landing with the piano) with Pat beside her, drinking tea and making toast. When the baby came . . . well, they would have to have got a bit by then, she supposed, but she didn't think ahead. She had implicit faith in Pat to provide. Thinking about providing had caused Pat to lapse into a heavy silence, staring into the puttering, expensive flame. He was given to long periods of silence; after telling the Professor, one had lasted for three days. He had gone down to stay with Mrs. Bates, and had taken Ruth out, but he had scarcely spoken at all, except for necessities, and Ruth, aware that she was the whole cause of this dreadful condition, had been steeped in such reciprocal despair that the memory of it could still freeze her in her tracks. She had never heard exactly what had taken place. It was like Pentonville: some things Pat would not discuss.

'Oh, well.' Pat got up, slowly. 'This won't get us anywhere. I'll get started.'

'Leave the door open.'

'You can go back to bed,' Pat said, looking down at her. He wished he could too. There were times when he wished he didn't have to be a pianist. He could have been a waiter, like Luigi, with no worries.

Ruth went back to bed, and lay curled in the hollow left by Pat's weight on the sagging springs. Luigi and his family had gone to mass, and the house was unfamiliarly quiet. Somewhere in a technical magazine Pat had left lying about she had read that Liszt's B Minor sonata was 'one of the most technically daunting in the repertoire', so when its great tirades started flooding up the staircase she could lie in her warm hollow in this strange state of complete relaxation, basking in the marvellous noise that was as taxing to make, presumably, as the hardest work one could care to think of, and which by its very essence was relaxing and entrancing to the listener in a way that was the very antithesis of hard work. Not for the first time Ruth was drawn to ponder on the strange case of music, what it was and why. And how it drove Pat, stretching him with all this effort and worry, when he could quite easily have earned enough money by being a bus-driver. It possessed him completely. She knew perfectly well that, with the house to himself and no distractions, he wouldn't be ready in an hour—more likely three—but she was quite happy to lie and wait, listening, the music driving her thoughts, the content inside her so strong, so impregnable that it was almost frightening. She loved living with Pat.

The music broke off and Pat came back, scowling.

'Where did I leave the music—the Liszt? I had it by the bed.'

'It's on top of the wardrobe, on the top of the pile. I dusted them all yesterday. The brown one—is that it?'

Pat groped about, muttering, 'It's not right, that ruddy bit right near the end, just when you think you're nearly there, home and dry—it's *unkind* . . . this is it . . .'

He retreated and after a long silence from below, as if gathering strength, the wild climax broke out again, funnelling up the staircase and into the room almost like a physical presence, culminating in a torrent of double octaves—then cut off in mid-bar and repeated again, and again . . . and again . . . Ruth opened her eyes and looked at the clock. It was one o'clock, the letter to write . . . 'Dear Mother and Father, Just to let you know I got married a week or two back. Hope you are well . . .'

'Oh, cripes,' Pat was saying. 'Is that the time?'

He got back into bed beside her and put his arms round her. He was all hot and sweaty and Ruth laughed.

'Do you like my lovely sonata? Would you pay a whole pound to hear me play it, if you were a proper connoisseur of good music?'

'Not when I can have it free, in bed, with cups of coffee. I thought sonatas were little after-tea sort of things, not to make you all sweaty and smelly . . .'

'No, no. You don't know anything.'

'Oh, I do! I do know! I do know I love you—'

'Tomorrow,' Pat said, 'I shall start looking for a job. It'll work out. It'll have to.'

'Of course,' Ruth said. And laughed.

Chapter 5

There was a man who knew a girl whose mother ran a music club in South London who said they were looking for a pianist. 'We won't be having another audition until March, but if you want to give us your name . . .'

'That big fat contralto with the teeth—what's her name?— Ingrid something—she was looking for an accompanist a week or so back—'

'Where does she live?'

'You've got me there, mate . . .'

'Haven't I seen you playing somewhere? I know your face.'

Pat lost track of faces. It was impossible, dunning all these people and bashing on all these doors, to get the practice in *and* wash up. The big fat contralto offered him a pound a morning which he turned down; he could have played for a ballroom-dancing class in Croydon if he could have had the evenings off. But the evening spent washing up was their home. He went to all the agents and they were very polite. They had heard of him. They would take his name. There was a stocky, brooding young man with a pock-marked face and a foreign complexion and a lot of golden-brown hair who followed him out of one of the agencies and said, 'Didn't you used to play with a violinist, a girl?'

'Yes.'

'What was her name?'

'Clarissa Cargill-Smith.'

'That's it. I remember you. You were a lot better than she was, but she looked good. Very striking looking. A striking looking pair, people said.'

'You don't get engagements by what you look like.'

'You'd be surprised. Why not a pleasure to the eye as well as to the ear? After all, people come to see you. They could stay at home with their records if they preferred it that way.'

'Well, girls perhaps.'

'Her father, I take it, is *the* Cargill-Smith?'

'Yes.'

'Why are you looking for work, if you know him?'

'I fell out with them.'

'Unwise.'

Pat shrugged.

The young man followed up: 'Are you the guy that played that concert with Backhaus and then went to prison?'

Pat looked at the man curiously. He seemed to know a lot about him.

'What if I am?'

'Just for the record, I might be able to help you some time. Where are you living?'

Pat wrote it down for him and the young man put the piece of paper in his wallet.

'Cheers then.'

Pat did not reply, and the man walked off. The agent's place was in a narrow street off the Strand, heavy with the smells of the market. Pat stood, indeterminate, shrugged down into the collar of his hairy jacket. He had known what it was going to be like, but to feel optimistic was asking too much. He had the address of a woman in Hammersmith who wanted a pianist for a ballet class. What a haul, after the life's blood he had expended on his craft! Being ruddy good just didn't come into it. He kicked an orange viciously into the gutter.

'That bloke you were talking to—'

He looked up, and saw someone he had known vaguely at College, a woodwind man. He had been in the agent's, talking engagements.

'What about him?'

'He's useful to know. I mean, if you're looking so suicidal, take heart.'

'Thank you very much.' Pat was sarcastic, unconvinced. The woodwind man looked very affluent. Pat remembered that his name was Wilfred.

'Don't mention it. They're open. Fancy a beer?' Wilfred was a friendly youth, and Pat needed a friend.

'Okay.'

They drifted towards the nearest pub. 'That bloke, Mick he's called, Mick Something Unpronounceable, from Bulgaria or Armenia or the Ural mountains or somewhere, he's supposed to be branching out on his own as an agent. They say he's got a nose for new talent. Like a terrier for rats. Instinct.'

'Who says?'

'Well, the old boys who do the job nicely. They don't like him. They've just given him the sack.'

'That's typical. If he's good, don't promote him, give him the sack.'

'Yes.'

'He seemed to know what I've been doing.'

'I tell you, he knows everything.'

Pat tried to feel a bit more cheerful.

Wilfred said, 'I thought you'd have got by with Hampton behind you. You always seemed to impress the right people.'

'Not any longer. I fall out with all the right people as fast as I impress them. What are you doing?'

'I play with an Early English consort. That keeps me pretty busy. Teach the recorder in an infants' school. And play sax in a rock group.'

Wilfred's indelible aura of success depressed Pat. Wilfred was one of the world's favoured; even without his full time-table of desirable work, he had well-off parents and that cheerful insouciance that Pat always envied, grown of confidence and a good education. He was successful by birth. His woodwind playing was competent and workmanlike, but he could just as well have been a good bank-manager.

'Drink up! You'll soon be dead.' Wilfred ordered two more pints.

'Do you know a piano anywhere—needs playing—?'

'Got one myself.'

'Yeh, but I couldn't practise in your place. Not with you fluting.'

'I flute upstairs. The piano's downstairs.'

'Just standing there doing nothing?'

'That's right.'

'What is it?'

'Steinway grand. Came from my mother's place.'

Pat couldn't believe it was going to happen.

'Your mother—would she mind—if no one's using it—?'

'She's past playing now. She's harping. If you want to use it for practising, you go ahead. Move in if you like. There's room. Have to pay rent, mind you.'

'Where is it?'

'Off Finchley Road, Hampstead way.'

Pat stared into his beer. It was the opportunity of a lifetime. A Steinway! Just lying around. Rent.

'I'm married,' he said.

'Oh.' Wilfred was surprised. 'Well, it's a big house.'

'What would the rent be?'

'Last chap paid twelve quid.'

He couldn't afford twelve quid. He'd *have* to afford twelve quid.

'Twelve pounds!' Ruth said, frightened. 'But if we leave here we won't have any money at all!'

'There'll never be a chance like this again!'

'Did you go there? What's it like?'

'It's a Steinway, I told you. A grand—'

'Yes, but the rest of the place. Is it a flat?'

'I don't know. It was a big room, downstairs. Great big house. There was a garden too.'

'It would be all right when the baby comes? Did you ask him?'

'No. But it would be all right. Bound to be.'

'Why? He might hate babies. Crying and all that. If he plays the flute. Does he live there all alone?'

'No. There was a female. His sister, I think.'

'What was she like?'

'I don't know. I didn't notice. The piano is perfect. I *must* find a job—nights perhaps. I'll go and see him again.'

Wilfred said he could play the piano whenever he liked, and move into the room when he could afford it.

Ruth went to see it. It was raining. Ruth had a strange impression that she had been there before; the atmosphere of the road was familiar. She was trying to place it without success as she walked along, sniffing the odours that the rain brought out of the worn pavements, the earth smells crushed by drains and car exhausts and oil and cats. But she hadn't been to this exact place before—

there was nothing evocative about the house itself, an ugly early Victorian house standing back, shabby, hung about by a lot of dripping overgrown trees. The path to the front door was made of patterned tiles. On one side there were similar houses, on the other a high wall blanking it in, garages and a workshop, a few shops and then the main road going by at the bottom with a ceaseless hum and swish of wet tyres, the tired acceleration of buses from the bus-stop. There was a front door filled with stained-glass panes and a note hanging on the knocker saying 'Two pints please'. Wilfred had said his sister was usually in, so Ruth rang the bell and after a while someone shouted from inside, 'Half a mo!' There was a long wait and then the door opened.

'Wilfred said I could come and see the room.' Ruth spoke nervously. She was nervous. It all meant so much, that Pat should have his piano, and that they could have the baby here. It was a baby place—she could see that already, with a garden and room in the hall for a pram.

'Oh, yes, come in. I'm Rosemary. Are you the wife of the fellow who's got his eye on the piano?'

'Yes.'

'Plays Liszt? That piano's not met Liszt before. I hope it's man enough. I'm on the top floor luckily so it won't worry me. I paint for a living. You have a look round, just as you please— I'll go back to work. There's some friends of Wilf's staying—I think they've been sleeping in there, but they're only temporary.'

The hall was dark and Rosemary disappeared before Ruth got more than an impression of her looks, but she seemed cheerful enough, rather plump and blonde and about twenty, Ruth supposed. She wore a black smock and smelt of linseed oil. Encouraging, Ruth thought. Not at all snooty and smart. Ruth didn't like smart girls.

The hall was as big as a room in itself, with mahogany stairs going out of it and doors opening off. The doors were painted a deep purple. Ruth opened the nearest one and found a curtained bedroom with two men asleep in the beds. She shut the door hurriedly and tried the next one. This was the room with the piano: it was very large, shabby, gracious and cold, with a high corniced ceiling, faded rugs on the parquet and faded curtains at the windows. It had a double divan in it, and the enormous piano which was parked like a car across the French windows. Ruth stood looking, feeling. It was quite quiet, save for the sound of the rain outside, trickling in the gutters and dripping off the bare winter trees. She could see the small square of garden outside, bowed down by the rain, dark and secret, feel the damp and the dust in the big room, sense all the questions, all the possibilities harboured: she knew that if they had this room it could see them happy and successful, or it could see them in debt, or ill, or in despair; it could be warm and kind and happy, or it could tax them beyond their means. It could see Pat to the concert platform, applauded and smiling, or it could watch him work and sweat in vain. The piano, silent, dusty and neglected, was like a key to their future, to let them in or shut them out. Ruth did not want to be aware of all this, but it was as if, standing there, the realization came at her, cobwebs of feelings, half-sensed, touching her. It was not like Luigi's, smelly and cheerful and temporary: this place was serious, where it must all be worked out, for better or for worse as it said in the marriage service. Ruth had no idea why she felt so solemn about just looking at a room, but she could not help herself. She thought it must be the weather and her condition, and yet, far inside herself, she knew that the feelings were the real truth. It wasn't just a great coincidence that she had married Pat; it was all part of something that had a pattern yet to be worked out. For the first time, it seemed, she was aware of the dangers. She was frightened. She could have ruined Pat, if it didn't work out right. His path with the Professor would have been smooth and clear and inevitable. With her it had obstacles as big as double-decker buses.

'Oh God,' she said to the piano. 'Make it be all right! Make it work!'

If she had had an abortion she could have married him just the same and gone out to work and kept him while he got started, and there would have been no worries. He never mentioned the baby; he had no interest in it at all.

'But I couldn't have done that . . .' She could never have done it. She started to cry, standing there, and all the time she knew she was being absolutely stupid. She had only come to look at a room.

'I say, it's not as bad as all that, is it?'

Ruth almost choked, jumped round and found Rosemary looking at her curiously.

'Oh, heavens, no! I'm— I'm sorry—' She wanted to die. She felt terrible.

'It's a devil to keep warm, it's so big. But much nicer in the summer. Are you all right?'

'Yes, I am. Really! It—it's just things—I was thinking of—'

'Oh, don't. It all comes out in the wash. Come and have a cup of coffee. You must be frozen. Come up to my department.'

Ruth followed her up flights and flights of stairs, feeling sick and awful and demoralized. She didn't know what had come over her. It was the thought of Pat not making it . . . looking at the piano . . . and all the things her mother had said rising up to haunt her. She felt very tired. She had to go and be a waitress in less than an hour.

'I have to go to work—'

'It's all ready. Don't worry. Sit by the fire for a minute or two. Are you going to have a baby?'

'Yes.'

Rosemary's room was a riotous jumble of painting things, large cardboard boxes of bits of material, an unmade bed and piles of books. It was brightly lit by neon strips, and a large gas-fire roared in the hearth. It was so different from the silent room downstairs that it did not seem to Ruth she could be in the same house. It was cheerful, lived-in chaos. It occurred to Ruth that, should she and Pat ever move in downstairs, that room too could easily become as chaotic, Liszt and a baby's bawling contributing.

'He didn't say you were pregnant.'

'No.'

Ruth tried to pull herself together, sensing that Rosemary's remark was perhaps a rebuke. Perhaps they didn't want a baby in the house. Wilfred's invitation, after all, had only been for Pat to play the piano.

'I'm sorry. I only came—to see. I—I don't suppose we could— I don't know. If we move from our present place, Pat would have to get a job first. I don't know if we can afford it. And you probably wouldn't want people with a baby.'

'It would be ideal for a baby, with the garden,' Rosemary said. 'We wouldn't mind. We can't make the rent any less, though.

The house belongs to our father and he says it has to be economic. He lives in the next road—'

She mentioned the address, and Ruth then realized why the area had seemed familiar. Clarissa lived there, in the same road as Rosemary's father; they had walked this way the day Pat had come to practise with Clarissa, the awful day that had ended with his being taken into custody. If they came to live here now, Clarissa would be just up the road.

She shivered, huddled over the gas-fire.

'Are you sure you're all right?'

'Yes.'

Rosemary was kind, but Ruth had got herself into such a state that she couldn't really take Rosemary in. Their situation was so difficult now: why ever hadn't she realized before! The baby was only three months away and Luigi's place was no home for three. She hurried away from Rosemary, excusing herself awkwardly, and ran to the tube-station. Rosemary had noticed her condition, and when she ran she was uncomfortably aware of it herself; she couldn't manage far, lumbering and out of breath. When she sat in the train, she could feel the child moving inside her. Usually she loved to feel this movement, but now it only emphasized the problems she had suddenly awoken to. She went back to Luigi's and found Pat just in himself after a 'visit to the ballet class in Hammersmith. He was in the kitchen, helping himself to a plateful of chips. Ruth tried not to go hysterical on him, but felt shaky and queer.

'What's the matter?' he said. 'Did you go up to Wilfred's place?'

'Yes.'

'What do you think of it?'

'It's—it's nice. It would be marvellous—'

'There'll never be another piano like that again,' Pat said. 'Even finding a place where we could take yours—it would take a lifetime. We must go there—'

'But the rent?'

'I can have this job in Hammersmith if I want it. I told her I'd let her know. It's real hack—just thumping away for a dancing class, but it's something. Then if I can get something else near home—any ruddy thing—I'll go and have a nose round this afternoon—we might be able to manage the rent. I doubt if we'll eat—have some chips, make the most of it. You all right? You look funny.'

'Worried.'

'Here, sit down. That makes two of us. It'll be all right. Nobody actually starves these days.'

They were in a corner of the café kitchen, with Carmen and Luigi and Carmella jostling and shrieking through the hatch and the sizzle of beefburgers and chips drowning their conversation. The smell of the food made Ruth feel sick.

'You look awful,' Pat said. 'Why don't you go up and get into bed? I'll do the waiting.'

'But you've got enough to do.'

'No, not this minute. Go on. I'll bring you a cup of tea. I'll do the lunch stretch, then I'll go and look for a job Finchley Road way.'

Ruth gave in. She had never really suspected Pat of being kind, in a solicitous sense, but there were times when he surprised her.

She lay on the bed and Pat put the eiderdown over her and put the cup of tea where she could reach it.

'It's all right?' he said, frowning down at her. 'Nothing's going—going wrong?'

'I don't think so.' She had no idea really, knowing very little about the process.

'I wouldn't like—now—' He hesitated, and turned away. 'I wouldn't like it not to happen, in spite of everything.'

After he had gone Ruth wondered if she had heard him right. She thought she had, and wept a little more, but not for despair and fear, only for relief.

Five days later he came home at tea-time and said he thought he'd got a job which would see them through.

'Doing what?'

'Driving. Car-hire firm, mostly weddings.'

'Good heavens!'

'The big advantage is that most people get married between lunchtime and about four o'clock, which is the time of day that I can spare best.'

'You mean a big smart car with white ribbons on the bonnet?'

'Yeh, a Rolls, like the Queen's.' Pat grinned.

'You've really got the job?'

'I've got to see the boss's partner tomorrow, but it sounds hopeful. It's right near Wilf's place too. If I get it, I'll go and tell Wilf we'll move in.'

'What about the ballet class?'

'With luck, I'm hoping I can do that as well. She starts at eight-thirty. Depends what time I have to start driving. I'm supposed to start the ballet class on Monday.'

'When will you practise?'

'I'll get up early and do it, and when I get home.'

'Suppose—' Ruth hesitated. Suppose anything. It was all fluid and tricky and nothing to make real plans on, only hope. She was frightened of leaving the security of Luigi's. But she was nearly past waitressing as it was, getting more cumbersome day by day.

That evening she was clearing tables when a man touched her shoulder and said, 'Someone called Patrick Pennington work here?'

'Yes,' she said. The man looked foreign, dark-skinned, although his mane of hair was curiously fair, a reddish-gold colour. 'He's in the kitchen.'

They were very busy and she hesitated to say that she would ask Pat to come out, but this man was obviously a man of action for he took the laden tray from her with a charming continental courtesy and said, 'Lead on.' The kitchen was such an inferno of activity that she didn't think anyone would notice an extra waiter, so she took him across to the sink where he could unload the tray and talk to Pat at the same time. Judging from the state of the draining-boards, there was not much prospect of Pat taking time off for a chat.

'This man was asking for you.'

Pat looked up and saw the visitor. A nervous suspicion came into his eyes. He straightened up slowly.

'We can talk here?'

What was his name? Pat was trying to remember. Mick Something-Unpronounceable from points East of Europe. 'Yes, if it's okay by you. I can't knock off for a couple of hours yet.'

'I'll wipe,' Mick said.

He unloaded his tray into Pat's washing-up water and Ruth took it off him. She had no idea who he was and could not spare the time to listen-in. When she came back with the next load, he was diligently drying plates, and Pat, reaching for the wire wool with one of Carmen's pie-dishes in his hand, was saying, 'The

Scriabin four is all right. I can do that now. I'd need at least a week to work up the Handel Variations.'

'The Chopin sonatas?'

'Yes, but I'd rather do the Liszt.'

Ruth thought it must all be coming true and went off with one Spanish omelette and chips and two egg, sausage, and bacon, feeling so agitated that she gave them to the wrong people. She did not dare believe it, but the temptation was so strong that it was hard to stop her imagination from running away with her. At these times it was nothing less than the Festival Hall, and everyone standing up shouting 'Bravo!' and clapping with their hands held out to the platform where Pat would be taking his bows, and the orchestra would be clapping as well and one of the most eminent conductors in the world would be smiling, and she would be standing in the wings in a long elegant dress, and talking to a member of the Royal Family. She took another pile of plates back and Pat was aiming a squirt of detergent absently into a fresh sinkful of water and saying, 'I'll get the music tomorrow and go through it. How often do they rehearse?'

'They'd probably step it up a bit for this. Usually they do two or three evenings at Albert's house. I'll give you his phone number and when you're ready you can give him a ring.'

Pat was wearing denims and plimsolls and Carmella's apron with roses all over it, but the stranger was in a soft suède jacket and a silk tie and had a rich but shabby look which Ruth had always thought the ideal to aim at, as if you didn't care but it wasn't money that was stopping you. She wished they had enough money for Pat to look like that. He only had his concert suit and his evening dress wrapped up in plastic bags in the wardrobe, which were tools of the trade and never to be worn for ordinary life, and otherwise the uniform old rubbish that most students wore, only the patches on his were not merely for decoration. The stranger appeared to have finished his interview, for he hung the tea-towel on the rack and said, 'I can find you here then? In case anything crops up—'

'No,' Pat said. 'We're moving tomorrow.' He gave the man Wilfred's address.

'You know where to find me,' the man said. 'I'll see you on Wednesday afternoon.'

'Okay.'

He gave Ruth a charming smile. He had gold stoppings, she noticed. He was attractive in a very peculiar, slightly sinister way. Luigi was shouting at her, waving a plate of risotto in the air, and she had to hurry back to the dining-room. When it was time for her to finish, she went straight up to her room to bed; she wanted to talk to Pat in bed, not in the kitchen. Something had happened; the man in the suède jacket had come to talk business. Tomorrow they were going to live in that great cold room with the acacia trees tapping at the windows. She knew she ought to feel pleased, but she felt terrified.

'What was it then? Who was that man?'

'I thought you'd be asleep.' Pat put the light on and came and sat on the bed. 'He was an agent. He's got me a recital.'

'Oh, Pat, that's marvellous!'

'It might be.'

He started undressing, dropping his clothes in a heap on the floor. Ruth could see that he was excited, but trying not to be.

'What do you mean? "Might be"? It must be!'

'Yes—well—if I do it all right. Someone else was going to do it, but now he wants to do something else that night. They want mostly the same programme, because they've gone to a lot of trouble doing programme notes. I'm just a stand-in, playing someone else's programme. Like an understudy.'

'Is it your sort of stuff?'

'Yes, fairly. I wouldn't have accepted otherwise. The Scriabin four and the Brahms Variations and the Liszt sonata—the other bloke was going to do Chopin, but Mick said the Liszt would be all right.'

'Mick?'

'His name's Mick Zawad—something—don't know how you say it—ends in ski, all ks and zs—he gave me his card—Wilfred knows him, said he was useful to know. This recital—don't get excited. It's only a music club in the outer suburbs—some school hall and an old beat-up piano and an audience of old ladies. You'll have to come and be polite. I hate that part, before. You can do it now—it's what wives are for.'

'To talk to old ladies?'

'To help their husbands. Have you seen Brahms' Handel Variations?'

'Brahms is on top of the wardrobe.'

'And Schubert?'

'Schubert's under the bed. Up to M is on the wardrobe and M to Z under the bed.'

'I'll look in the morning.' He put the light off and got into bed. 'Cripes, I can't believe it's really happened!'

'But it has.'

'And yet it's nothing really. To play to people like that—they're only there for the coffee. Ninety per cent of them don't know Brahms from Liszt anyway, whatever you were to play. And yet it matters terribly when you're sat up there. To yourself.'

Pat rarely spoke about feelings, and most of what he thought about his work Ruth had gathered merely from his silences, which were at times almost impregnable—she knew how much it meant by how much it occupied his mind, and that was as near totally as the particular exigencies of their way of living allowed. Whether he was really good or not she had no way of knowing. She had heard him play so often now that she knew when he was playing well by his own standards, or badly, but how these standards compared to the general standard she had no idea. He had told her that the general standard got higher and higher every year—she supposed like the time for running a mile and the record for the single-handed Trans-Atlantic yacht race and how many sausages could be eaten at one sitting—and that to prove you were merely capable at your craft it was necessary to be able to perform pieces that once had been considered too taxing for all but the supreme virtuoso to manage. And even when one could perform these incredible technical feats, one could still be damned as 'a mere pianist' and not a real musician, which apparently still mattered even more. And how Pat stood in the hierarchy she had no idea.

'Are you good?'

He was lying beside her in his characteristic attitude, hands linked behind his head, staring at the ceiling. The back alley lamp through the window gave their little room the perfect Bohemian touch, softening its dereliction into a desirable homeliness, and Pat's face in the same improving light was grave and thoughtful and turned in Ruth such a turmoil of passion for him that she was almost afraid.

'Yes,' he said in answer to her question. 'If I didn't think so, I wouldn't go on.'

'Mick must think you're good.'

'I've got to go and play for him on Wednesday.'

'But this engagement is for sure?'

'Yes. But there are other things as well. Enough to go and live in the other place. I'll tell Luigi tomorrow.'

In the other room the rain ran down the windows like Chopin's prelude, full of a great sadness of spirit. Ruth remembered her panic, and wondered why she didn't think of what a good place it was to have a baby in—how big, and how jolly with Rosemary upstairs and the shops just round the corner and a clinic nearby with orange-juice and advice, but all she thought of was how happy they had been in this little room with the William Morris wallpaper. She had never been a great optimist in her life, always fearing the worst, even when it had just been riding ponies, and now she could not learn to look ahead with great confidence and gusto, even when Mick had come with all his promises. Real happiness, when it depended on other people, was very vulnerable, she thought.

'What are the other things?' she asked.

Pat did not reply at once. He was frowning, still watching the ceiling. Then he turned over towards her and put his hand over her shoulder, caressing her long hair.

'You mustn't mind,' he said. 'You've never exactly said, but I've always thought—you minded—'

'Minded what?'

'Clarissa.'

'What do you mean?'

'This Mick wants me to play with her. She's in a quartet, and they want a pianist to do "The Trout" with them. He asked me if I'd like to try it.'

'It's not Clarissa alone?'

'Not this time.'

'Would it ever be?'

'I doubt it. She's not good enough.'

What could she say? Clarissa just up the road, Clarissa in the quartet . . . It was inevitable that she should crop up again some time, but *already*—Ruth turned her head, touching Pat's cheek with her own.

'I hate Clarissa.'

'Yes.'

But how could she tell him why? Because Clarissa could approach him through his work, which she never could; because he had loved her 'desperately' (his own word) and she had let him down when he most needed her; and, mostly, because she still wanted him, and she was clever and beautiful and fantastically well placed to help him in his career, while she herself was an encumbrance, a liability, with an ever-thickening figure, soon to be housebound by the child.

'I'll tell you what,' he said softly.

'What?'

'You can come too. To turn the pages. Like you did before.'

'To warn her off.'

'That's right.'

'Transfix her with dagger-like glances.'

'Yes. Exactly.'

'I hate her.'

'Yes. But don't mind about it. Because we want the money. And I would love to play Schubert with a string quartet.'

She supposed, if she had to be jealous, it was his work that ought to spear her: even now, it was Schubert before Clarissa. But Schubert was dead and buried and Clarissa was still queening it in West Hampstead, and Ruth knew that she was jealous, even without cause. She could not help herself. If Clarissa had grown indifferent towards Pat—then it would be all right. Perhaps Clarissa was infatuated with a new lover and when she saw Pat she would just shrug and be perfectly normal, and nice to his new wife—that would be all right. But Ruth, with such an infatuation for Pat herself, could not imagine Clarissa having fallen out of love with him.

Chapter 6

It was hard to tell, when they met again, what Clarissa was thinking. Ruth, all geared up to hate her, was considerably shaken when Clarissa came up to her and kissed her and said without any discernible trace of malice, 'How lovely about the baby! I'm so pleased for you!' And to Pat, 'It's lovely to see you again! What are you doing now? I hear you've left old Hampton?' She made no attempt to kiss *him*, Ruth was pleased to note.

She looked rather plumper and less imperious than Ruth remembered her, but she was still eligible for the description 'gorgeous', with a natural elegance and flair for clothes in addition to the handsome, sensuous features and gold-and-tawny colouring already endowed by nature. Nobody, male or female, could help but look at her twice. And she had this fantastic poise and confidence of the extrovert, attractive girl which Ruth always felt that she herself conspicuously lacked, being quiet by nature. And now, not only quiet but tired and heavy and lumbersome—a state she was perfectly happy to accept except when faced with Clarissa's lissom grace. But Clarissa's warmth towards her, as well as to Pat, rather disarmed her.

They were introduced to Albert, Pongo and Richard, the other players of the Schubert quintet. Albert, the leader of the group, was an affable middle-aged man, bald on top and wearing a fawn cardigan like a man in a knitting pattern. It was his house they were rehearsing in, a comfortably casual, rambling old house but with the blessing of central heating, Ruth was quick to notice, unlike Wilfred's (one thing about being pregnant, one did keep warmer than usual, and at Wilfred's that was now a great advantage). Pongo and Richard were younger and hairier, Pongo rather earnest-looking with spectacles which he kept pushing at, and Richard more dashing and forthcoming in a bright orange shirt and black cords falling to bits. They played the cello and double bass respectively; Clarissa was playing the viola part. There was a transistor playing pop-music in the room next door and the sounds of small children doing evil to each other.

'The wife is bringing coffee in a moment,' Albert said. 'Get you warmed up! We've been playing for an hour already. If you want to try the piano . . . Here's a chair for Ruth.' Albert moved his violin off it and put it at the piano.

There were aspects of Pat's work, Ruth decided as the evening progressed, that were very nice; this was one of them. She could see that it was very hard work, but it was lovely hard work, and practising with a group seemed to Ruth far more fun than the hours of grinding practice alone with no one to discuss and joke with, which was Pat's normal lot. Her mother had come to visit for the day to see what she thought of the new abode, and Pat had played nearly the entire day, not whole pieces, but endless repetitions of furious passages full of diabolical fingerwork, and her mother had retired into the kitchen in a rage and said, 'I don't know how you can stand it! In one room—it's enough to drive any ordinary mortal crazy! And what when the baby comes and it has to live with it and sleep through it—!' The kitchen was minute and Wilfred's two friends wanted to make breakfast (at three o'clock in the afternoon) so her mother was driven back into the living-room again, and sat crouched by the gas-fire, knitting baby clothes that were a whole generation out of date. Ruth had been very hurt by her disapproval—'So cold! And so un-healthy doing everything in one room. I admit it's a big room, but with that monstrous piano taking up three-quarters of it there's not much room for—' Ruth hadn't listened, but she had been bitterly angry. If Pat had played Schubert, things might have been a bit better, but, as if for spite, he had played nothing but Scriabin and Liszt in his darker moments. Even her mother, Ruth thought, would have been melted by 'The Trout' music, which was like sunshine after Scriabin; it was like coming back to earth from some outer, mystic and terrifying firmament, and finding fields and cows and streams and stones and the fish in the cool shadows and lovely simple things—'Schubert for sunshine,' Ruth thought, and she taxed Pat with his dark choices, and he had smiled and played her a melting 'Impromptu'. This was after her mother had gone, and when he had finished, he got up from the piano and flung himself down on the bed. The room still bathed in Schubert, Ruth had gone over to him and put her arms round him and he had grinned and said, '—to your mother!' very rudely, and pulled her down beside him. They had then laughed themselves stupid, and toasted some buns at the gas-fire, still lying on the bed, and Pat had said, 'Living in one room is full of advantages, like cooking in bed. Your mother doesn't know anything!'

According to how 'The Trout' went, Pat might get himself another engagement. Ruth, turning the pages, thought he was acquitting himself very well. She had only heard the piano bits, on their own, and threading them into all the other parts seemed to her a very complex task, but Pat made no mistakes. Mick had said he thought he could get him an engagement in Manchester playing the Rachmaninov two with a newly formed orchestra, and there was the recital in the outer suburbs to take place the following day, which would pay the rent for a week or two. They had so little behind them that the engagements were essential, to keep them in bread. If she ever stopped to think about it really seriously, Ruth thought she would run screaming back to her parents. The driving job started the following week but it remained to find out how that would suit; Pat had accepted it in preference to the ballet class, which he had only done for two weeks. He would have liked to do them both, but the timings had overlapped. The driving job would be a certain security, if it worked out all right, but it wouldn't keep them entirely. Ruth preferred not to dwell too closely on the situation. There was a chance she could do some work at the garage too, but Pat hadn't sorted it out yet.

'Wait till I start. I might drive into a brick wall the first day. How do we know?'

The first hurdle was the music-club engagement, which was a demanding programme and, in spite of the total insignificance of the occasion, important because it was Pat's first real solo recital— solo in a complete sense, apart from his erstwhile musical mentors —also because Mick was going to be there 'to assess his impact'. Ruth didn't like the sound of that, but apparently Pat was used to having his impact assessed.

His impact on Albert, the leader of the group, seemed satisfactory, for they finished the rehearsal in very good spirits and Albert made a date for another meeting.

70

'We—I mean the regular quartet—generally have two or three engagements a month, at a hundred pounds a time. If you're interested, we share it equally—expenses on top. We all have other jobs—in the profession, of course. This doesn't pay much, considering the rehearsal time, but we like doing it, so nothing's lost. How are you fixed?'

'I want everything I can get,' Pat said. 'I'll play with you any time. Through Mick—I have to do it through him. He's my agent.'

When they went out, Clarissa said, 'I'll walk with you. I go your way.'

Pat said nothing. It was raining slightly, but not cold, a few stars coming and going faintly beyond the radiance of the street lights. Ruth thought of her old home and the lane thick and muddy underfoot, sludgy with dead leaves—the quick, instant pain of homesickness, and her father's face, kind and content; it would come without warning, and tear her. She had last been home on Christmas Day, with Pat—a day of dreadful tensions mixed with a strange traditional bonhomie, saved by the normality of Ted and Barbara and the antics of their eight-month-old daughter. She rarely thought of home consciously, only when this unaccountable nostalgia came at her without warning.

Clarissa said to Pat, carefully, 'If I get any engagements, would you play with me again?'

Pat said, 'Surely you've found someone else after all this time?'

'I've been playing with Arnold Patience, but he's not as good as you, and he's moving to Southampton shortly.'

'How many engagements do you get? I thought it was just a hobby for you?'

'Yes—but Daddy gets me recitals. He likes me to do it. I get quite a lot.'

'For money?'

'Oh, yes. Unless it's a charity.'

'I'm not playing for charity. We're our own charity at the moment.'

'You'd play with me if you got enough money out of it?'

'I'd play with Felix the cat if I got enough money.'

'You will then?'

'You'll have to see Mick about it.'

'Would you like to come over and go through a few pieces

71

some time? Ruth too, of course. Mummy would like to see you again. Would you like to come for dinner?'

Pat shrugged.

Clarissa said smoothly, 'Or would you have to ask Mick first?'

Ruth looked across at her, and saw the way she was watching Pat. Her malice was provoked by his rudeness; because he did not respond, she had to try and needle him. Ruth was not sure whether his extreme coldness expressed his genuine feeling for her, or whether it was because he had a wife listening to the conversation. After Clarissa had left them, without an answer to her invitation, Ruth asked him: 'Would you play with her?'

He shrugged again.

'She's improved a lot. I would for money.'

Ruth was silent, unhappy with the answer, but acknowledging its sentiment. Pat went on, 'She knows all the right people. It would help to keep in with her—her father and all that . . . But in this business—I mean, I don't approve of it, but it helps—it helps to know somebody like her father. If we didn't *need* it—but for God's sake, we do—'

He sounded angry and pressed, and Ruth did not say any more. They did need it. But the thought of his playing with Clarissa disturbed her considerably.

The next day he hardly spoke at all; he looked white and gloomy, and wouldn't eat anything. He played all morning and went out in the afternoon to get his hair cut while Ruth brushed his evening suit and tried to fold it up to fit into the disreputable old grip which was all they had in the way of a suitcase. She brushed his one and only pair of black shoes and wrapped them up in newspaper. Outside it was foggy and drizzling and almost dark by half-past three, and the gas-fire had no pressure, puttering feebly in the great hearth designed for an uneconomic Victorian blaze, to be fed by the footman and polished every morning by the kitchen-maid. Ruth crouched by it with a mug of tea, worried and miserable. Pat came back but the tea was cold; she went to make another pot, and Pat lay on the bed staring at the ceiling, silent.

'Your hair looks nice,' Ruth said, bringing a fresh pot and another mug.

'Should do, what it cost.'

She poured out the tea and put it by him, but he just lay there and it went cold too. She didn't like to say anything.

'Did you put the music in the bag?' he asked.

'But you don't use it. No, I didn't.'

'I want it in. I like to know it's there.'

Ruth wondered what possible use it could be in the tatty old bag, if he was out on the stage playing and forgot what came next, but she pulled the books out of the piles on the floor under the piano and obediently put them in the bag. The Liszt was twenty-five pages long, the Brahms not much better. 'Heavens, why does he do it?' she wondered. How to *remember*, let alone get ten fingers on the right notes at the right moment . . . when you could be a farmer, or a mechanic in a garage with a transistor going and blokes to lark about with. It didn't make sense sometimes. She sat crouched on the hearth-rug in the dark, listening to the wind in the bare trees outside, the twigs scraping on the windows.

They went in plenty of time, the journey awkward on the underground and two buses. Everyone else was going home, squashed together in wet mackintoshes reading the evening papers, bound for lamb chops and chips and a nice evening watching the telly in their warm, bright houses. 'Why do we have to be so different?' Ruth wondered. 'Going the other way.' She had to carry the bag because Pat had to keep his hands unused, unstretched, warm in his pockets. When they arrived at the school they were met by a little posse of well-dressed ladies and two teacher-looking men. Ruth remembered that this is what she was for, to deflect them from Pat, who had not said a word since setting off and didn't look as if he was going to say anything now, apart from, 'How do you do,' at introductions. They stood in the school hallway where it was warm and bright and smelt of new polish and plimsolls, the eternal smell of school, and Ruth had to make her great effort, taking on the members of the Committee unaided.

'. . . so pleased you could come, so pleased you managed to get here nice and early—'

'Do come in—mind the step . . . we'll take you to the staff-room . . . a cup of tea?'

'We are very keen, you know—we have a very enthusiastic group . . . meet here every Friday evening . . .'

'. . . try to have four or five recitals each winter—as many as we can afford . . .'

'. . . generally a full hall. You would be surprised. People do like the *real* thing, don't they, after records . . .'

They were so kind, and fussing—Ruth could see how Pat could not possibly cope with such attention in his present mood; he had known what it would be like. How useful that she had a part in the performance—she was pleased to be so important to him, saying the right things and smiling and doing all the conversation, while he quickly drank his tea and went out to try the piano before any of the audience turned up. When the early-comers started to dribble into the hall he retired to a piano in the gymnasium where he did five-finger exercises until it was time to change. Ruth went to fetch him. The gym gave her an extraordinary sensation, as if she had never left school at all. 'Ten minutes,' she said. 'Are you ready?'

He changed and came and stood beside her in the wings of the stage, while the chairman of the music committee gave out the month's notices and the last comers settled into their seats. The greetings, coat-shifting, umbrella-shaking, laughing and talking had settled into an expectant tension which Ruth, in her sharpened awareness, could feel reaching out from the corners of the hall. She found she was sweating and trembling, yet all she had to do was listen. Pat was silent, so far removed both in spirit and appearance that he might have been someone she had never even met. She had no idea at all what he was thinking. He might have been the man in the moon.

Pat had not realized, until the few hours before the concert, how much he had lost during the last year. Until it happened, he had persuaded himself that nothing was any different from the last time he had played in public. He had always felt bad beforehand, that was nothing new, but it was quite new to feel so utterly *alone* as he did this time, walking across to the piano. The feeling was quite terrifying. His *own* concert, the pieces entirely his own concern, worked over entirely without advice from anybody, the interpretation his own, the success or failure his alone, credit to no one. He had thought himself ready for it, kicked out of the Professor's nest but the wings ready, the feathers formed; sitting down at the piano, he was not sure at all. The isolation was terrible. In his misplaced arrogance, he had set himself a formidable programme; he had never supposed that he might lack confidence, given an audience and a platform to himself. Afterwards it occurred to him that the whole of his nine months in Pentonville had been designed to flatten the aggressive ego that had got him in there in the first place, and the aggressive ego was exactly what he now felt the need of, the stiffening of mere confidence, to do justice to his composers. Their stuff could not be played by a flattened man.

It was always the worst moment, starting, the sound of the first bars reacting on unknown acoustics, the unfamiliarity of the instrument surprising his own ear, but, 'Cripes!' he thought. 'If I'm not *into* it by the time I start Scriabin, I might as well pack it in!' The introductory Schumann pieces were the only charming works of the evening, and it was upon himself that the charm must work. It was like an examination: if he didn't pass tonight, he wouldn't be able to go on with it. There were no excuses allowed: that the piano had a sticky A flat in the lower registers, that the hall smelt of damp tweed, that he felt constricted in these ridiculous clothes . . . but the first fragment was finished: he had played no wrong notes, muffed no runs, no one was booing—indeed, he felt a cordiality in the atmosphere, a sense that—although they knew it was not the place to clap—they would have liked to. He edged the stool back a fraction. Ruth was standing behind the curtains watching him, monumental in her seven months' shape, but delicate about the face and neck, her ears showing where she had pushed her hair back, giving her the look of a child. He had heard people say about her, 'But she's only a child,' which he always took as an accusation towards himself, but he knew that in her strength she was no child. Seeing her there helped. She smiled at him. He played the Schumann for her, deceptively simple stuff with a warm, sad melody, feeling it now, the hands growing happier. By the third piece, more glittery, he was enjoying it, beginning to look forward to the hard work to come—even, fleetingly, mischievously sorry for wooing them with Schumann only to prepare them for the metallic shocks of Scriabin—God, he must have been a fool to say he would do that thing! Just to impress Mick the Unpronounceable, and merely as an *hors-d'oeuvres* for the mountains beyond . . . But now he *wanted* to—he was all wound up and raring to go, bowing to the applause and having to walk off and on again twice because they were so easily pleased . . . Oh, come on! There is so much to do and we must get out before closing time . . .

Ruth sat down. It was no good standing there like a piece of furniture all the evening because she was too nervous to relax. Pat had smiled at her when he came off, the first smile for twenty-four hours, and it was still all to come, so something must have defused the tensions that had wound him up all day: he must have realized that he really could play the piano without the Professor to hold his hand. She sat down and let herself unwind too, letting the first spooky bars of the Scriabin, deceptively muted, flicker through her brain. He was all right if he was smiling, she didn't have to worry; he could do the worrying, flinging all those peculiar jazzy rhythms and nervous staccato hammerings into the warm receptive hall, to make the comfortable ladies frown and raise their eyebrows and think how advanced they were, paying to listen to such stuff. He was away, she could see now; she could lean back and shut her eyes and think of all the lovely money, resisting the music because she didn't like it very much, but still able to appreciate that it was shaping as well as she had ever heard it. Its splitting climax was irresistible, through sheer force, and the applause came with it in great waves of appreciation. How lovely the afterwards was, compared with the before!

After that it was all right. She knew he was playing well. Did they know? she wondered. All the tricky bits which she had heard practised to distraction now took their rightful place so smoothly that, even to her, who had sat in on the labour, the illusion of the whole thing being easily within his compass was complete. And not only the technical side—there was no sense of the Brahms fugue being merely well practised: it was compelling in a way which she, who had not come in any sense to receive the music as an experience like the people in the audience, found moving beyond her expectations. It was monumental, inexorable, a performance so intense that Ruth herself was knocked out of all her petty preoccupations by its sheer power.

It was the first time she had heard Pat play in public since she had become so familiar with the music, and it reminded her of the Professor's remark that Pat had the luck—was that the word he had used?—to possess the rare and valuable temperament that rose to the occasion. She had not been prepared, now, to listen in any other than a strictly critical, personal way, to comprehend Pat rather than Brahms, but Pat had compelled her into Brahms. When it was finished, and Pat was making his bow, she felt for

76

the first time since they were married that she need no longer endure her nightmare that Pat might never make it to the concert platform.

Having found his old confidence and concentration, Pat then gave a passionate performance of the Liszt sonata. The Professor, Ruth remembered Pat's saying, had advised him against putting this work in his repertory; Pat had since worked at it more ardently than at any other work. There was nothing half-hearted about the Liszt—it required total emotional involvement. Played badly it could sound a decadent, self-indulgent thing, full of moonlit melodies and manic frenzies; played well it was a compulsive, all-embracing experience. Ruth, not sure whether she was carried away by the music itself or by the pure excitement of having Pat's ability so plainly exhibited in public, went to meet him as he came off the platform, and hugged him rapturously. He was sweating, smiling.

'We made it!'

'Oh, it was lovely! You did it beautifully!'

'It went all right. It all worked. God, I feel pulverised!'

He was normal again, exhausted but human. The audience was clapping with enormous gusto and it sounded to Ruth as if it was for everything, not just the music, but for her being married to Pat, and for the baby and all the hopes and aspirations that kept leaping about in her breast when she was in an excited state— which she was at this moment.

'Oh, Pat, it was *all right!*'

He was wiping his face with a handkerchief. She kissed him again and he laughed and said, 'Go and bow for me—you look marvellous! Like a great big bus.'

'I can't bow. It's in the way.'

'I love you.' He was smiling at her and combing his hair, making himself tidy to go and bow. The audience kept on clapping. He had to go out three times and they wouldn't stop, so he had to sit down again to do an encore.

'Three waltzes from Brahms' Opus 39, numbers thirteen, fourteen and fifteen.' His public speaking was not up to the standard of his playing; Ruth doubted if anyone beyond the first three rows had heard him. But it didn't matter. It was a perfect ending, the dash and vigour of the first two and then the tenderness of number fifteen—'our tune', Ruth thought—and Pat was looking at her as he played, smiling again, and she knew it was for her, as it had been the day he came out of prison. Beneath his thorny hide, a tiny vein of sentiment lurked. Once or twice in a lifetime he had let it show.

Mick Zawadzki met them in the pub afterwards. Ruth had forgotten all about him. He was in a very good mood. Pat bought him a pint.

'I reckon I owe *you* one,' Mick said. 'That was a splendid night's work. I enjoyed it. I wasn't sure what to expect, you know. The public performance isn't always the same thing as the private performance. I don't have to tell you that.'

'No.'

'You come over very strongly, you have a very positive presence. That's the show-biz side of it, and it helps—it helps enormously. There is the excitement and the fire—but as well the playing is terrifically accurate, scrupulous. I like that—the two things together—one cannot ask for more. I feel very optimistic about getting you work.'

'Yes, well—the way we're placed just now—I'd do anything. Solo, accompanying, I don't mind. Just as long as I get paid.'

'How much modern work do you play? After Liszt—do you do any Ravel? Debussy?'

'Some of the Debussy preludes—yes, quite a few . . . Ravel's "Jeux d'eau". I've worked on "Gaspard"—I can play the "Tombeau de Couperin" but I wouldn't want to do them in public yet. A couple of Prokofiev sonatas . . .'

'What do you like?'

'It changes. At the moment, Liszt and Schumann. Before Liszt, Schubert. It's too soon not to want to do everything. I suppose later you find what you're really best at. There just isn't enough time, though.'

'Too much fodder. You've chosen the wrong instrument.'

'Yes. I often think that. Too much competition.'

'I don't think you need fear the competition.'

'Easy to say! You only keep up with it by doing it, thinking it full-time. And yet without the engagements you've got to earn some cash other ways, wasting time. Next week I start being a chauffeur.'

'Hell! Who for?'

'Car-hire firm. Weddings and suchlike. I've been on a dummy run without denting anything, and they start me on Monday. I have to take a bloke to Heathrow before lunch and a bride to church after lunch.'

'God, we must deliver you from that as soon as possible!'

'That's why I said I'd do anything. Hack-work, not just being a virtuoso. I only want the money, not the glory.'

'Accompanying you said?'

'Yes.'

'That girl, what's her name—Vanessa?—'

'Clarissa?'

'Yes. The girl with the father. She came to see me. She said she wanted you to play with her. She could get an engagement but her pianist has left for foreign parts, she said. Southampton or somewhere. Would I instruct you—her word—to do a Brahms sonata with her at Hemel Hempstead on April the tenth. Also give you permission to go to dinner at her house. She said you told her to arrange everything through me.'

'I was giving her the brush-off—I was bloody rude to her. What a nerve! She actually called on you and told you that?'

'This morning!' Mick was grinning. 'I thought she was rather a peach myself. I didn't take her very seriously, but I think *she* was serious. At least about the engagement. She said you could have half the fee and expenses and what she called "practice facilities" whenever you wanted them. I was going to pass it on to you in any case—I told you earlier I thought you made a good pair— musically, of course—' he gave Ruth his small continental bow and his charming smile—'but you said she wasn't good enough. I think she passes muster myself, but it's up to you. Half the fee is fifteen pounds, less my ten per cent, of course.'

'Well, it's a week's rent,' Pat said. He looked at Ruth dubiously. He was glowering characteristically. 'She's got a flaming cheek. About the dinner—'

'I thought it was rather funny,' Mick said. 'I told her I'd like to come myself, and got an invitation straight away. I was a bit bowled over—thought she might think me a bit pushing, so I changed it to a dinner on me, tomorrow night. I'm rather looking forward to it.'

'Good luck, that's all I can say.'

'Shall I tell her you'll accept the engagement?'

'Yes. But the practising will be done at my place, not hers.'
He looked at Ruth, slightly nervous, she thought. 'You don't
really mind? Not for the money?'

'No.' She did mind, but it wouldn't help to say so. She thought
of them going to Hemel Hempstead together. She'd have the
baby by then and have to stay behind. The thought made her feel
quite sick with jealousy. She knew that Pat was reading this in
her expression. She thought that it was genuine that he didn't
want to do it with her. But the money was what mattered. Pat
put his hand up and squeezed her shoulder. She knew too that
Mick wanted to ask Pat about Clarissa, but was polite enough not
to in front of her. He must have guessed—or had Pat told him?—
that they had been lovers. The evening, having run the gamut
through nervous foreboding, dry-mouthed fright, excitement,
joy, triumph and—now—nervous foreboding again—was beginning to pall. Ruth felt very tired.

'Come on,' Pat said to her gently. 'I'll take you home.'

'My pleasure,' Mick said. 'I've got my car.'

'Thank goodness,' Ruth thought.

Chapter 7

Pat duly drove the Iranian oil magnate to Heathrow and Miss Priscilla Mainwaring to St. Martin-in-the-Fields—to get married, with a copy of Brahms' music in the glove locker of the Rolls, and Ruth went to the hospital for an examination and was told that her baby was the wrong way round and if it didn't turn of its own accord they would have to try to do something about it. She didn't ask what, not particularly wanting to know. She didn't like the clinical side of having a baby; the other mothers made her feel as if she was only playing at it, all being so much older, worldlier and worn out than she was. She felt guilty about Pat having to work so hard and having nothing to do herself; she wished desperately that she could play the piano too and be able to talk to him intelligently about it, in the same way that Clarissa could talk music to him. She asked him to teach her, and he sat her down at the piano and sat next to her and showed her how to play the notes of the scale of C major, with her thumb going under to the fourth note, and how to play 'Twinkle, twinkle, little star'.

'Mozart composed a set of variations on it, did you know? No, fourth finger. Lift it up. Holy Moses, you're paralyzed.'

'It won't go on its own.'

'Do this.'

His fingers went up and down quite separately, like pistons.

'Exercises?'

'You've got fingers like duck's feet.'

'You wouldn't make a very good teacher. If I was paying you, I mean. I'd be insulted.'

'I'm no good at teaching. I just can't see how you can be so bad at anything so simple.'

'Well, you've been taught often enough. I don't see how you

can be so stupid as to not understand how hard it is if you don't know how to do it.'

'Come again?'

'I mean, the Professor must have thought you were stupid quite often.'

'He used to get cross. And yet he was a good teacher.'

'How do you know he was?'

'Because I learned so much so fast with him. If I start earning money, I would like to have lessons again—not with him, but with—well, there are one or two, if I could get accepted. It's too soon for me to do without lessons.'

Ruth was amazed. 'But you—'

'I thought it was all right—well, it is, really, but there are things you want to work out. You don't always know if you're doing it the best way—you want someone else to—to just be there, to work it out with, just talk about it. You can't always *hear* what you're doing as well as you ought. You want someone to tell you.'

'If you went to see the Professor, would he—'

'I wouldn't go back to him. Not after what he said.'

'It was my fault.'

'*It's* fault.' He put his hand on her bulge. 'What's this about it being the wrong way up?'

'Feet first.'

'Sounds sensible to me. Landing on your feet.'

'Well, it's wrong apparently.'

'So what are they going to do?'

'Shove the poor little thing round.'

'How?'

'Ugh! I can guess! I didn't ask. I never did like biology.'

'God, I'm glad it's not me.'

'You aren't a very keen father! Lots of them go to classes about it at the hospital, and they're going to be there when it's born. The hospital encourages it. They've already asked about you.'

'Cripes, I'd faint! You're not serious? You don't really want—you didn't tell them—'

'No, I didn't, don't worry! I don't want you there. Only afterwards . . . you have to come with flowers and a box of chocolates, properly, and be nice about what it looks like.'

'That's all right. I can do that. But the other—' He looked worried. 'You don't—'

Ruth was amused. 'No, honestly! I don't.'

'I don't like hospital things.'

'Well, that's not surprising. But having a baby isn't being ill.'

'No, but I'm still glad it's the female department.'

'We're all happy then. I wouldn't want to do what you do.'

'I thought you wanted to learn?'

'Enough to understand.'

'All right. Thumb on C . . . twin - kle, twin - kle, G with the fourth finger and A with the fifth.'

'Where's G?'

'The dominant, five up. There. No, with the fourth finger, else you haven't got a finger left for A.'

The lesson ended with Ruth sitting on Pat's lap concentrating hard on the melody, and having enough fingers required, and Pat playing an accompaniment on either side of her bulk. They were engaged in this when the doorbell rang with three rings, which meant it was for them. Ruth went out to answer it and found Mick and Clarissa standing on the doorstep. Clarissa had her violin with her.

'Okay to come in? We were just passing—'

'Do! Business or pleasure?'

'A bit of both,' Mick said. 'Some good news for Pat—work, I mean, and Clarissa wants to see how the sonata sounds—'

It was dark and raining outside and they both looked wind-tossed and breathless and glowing in a way that made Ruth wonder if they had fallen for each other. Clarissa was in a nature-girl guise, her hair loose, her clothes flowing and billowing in the draught. It occurred to Ruth to wonder if Mick was married. Pat came out into the hall and Clarissa turned to him and said, 'Mick says you've agreed to do the Brahms with me at Hemel Hempstead. I'm so pleased.'

Pat stood looking at her with a strange expression on his face. Ruth had the impression that so many conflicting thoughts were going through his head at the prospect that he was unable to remark on any one of them. In the end he smiled politely and said nothing at all.

'Perhaps we could try it out, if you're not busy?'

'Perhaps we could.'

'Do come in,' Ruth said, wondering if covering up for Pat's bluntness was going to be one of her major roles in life.

'I've come to ask you how are you on the concertos?' Mick asked. 'Could you knock off the Brahms two if requested? Not entirely a hypothetical question. There's a possibility I might get you an engagement—'

'You *are* joking?'

'No.'

'I played it with the College orchestra.'

'Ah! Splendid! Just work on it, in case.'

'In my spare time?' Pat gave him a scornful smile.

Ruth turned the gas-fire up and put the kettle on the ring. She didn't ask them if they had eaten, for there were only two eggs in the pantry and that was their breakfast. They only had two pounds to last until Friday, when Pat got his garage money. She knew, suddenly, that if Clarissa asked Pat to give her piano lessons at fifty pence a time he would agree. Mick sprawled himself on the divan and Clarissa sat down on the hearth-rug. The firelight shone on her coppery hair.

'Apart from the hypothetical Brahms, Mick's really got you a job, Pat. From someone who wants more.'

'He heard you at the recital last Tuesday. Wants the same again —the Liszt sonata, anyway—at an Arts Group in Guildford, end of March. He suggested some Debussy or similar, said they were prepared to be "stretched". I said yes, you would. Then this Oswaldtwistle Philharmonic—Ramsbottom Symphony—or whatever, is all set to play the Rach. two with you if you're game. I suggested a rehearsal the same day—it seems a lot of time if you go up any more. They say they know their way around it so I presume it'll be okay. That's short notice, three weeks. You'll have to get an engagement diary.'

'We'll write the dates on the calendar,' Ruth said, glowing. 'Great red rings round them! I'll get a diary at Boots tomorrow.'

'One of those big ones,' Mick said, 'with lots of room. When is the Music Societies' competition? That's a date in March some time. You told me you'd entered for that.'

'Yes, I have. The London heats—the finals are to be in Scotland.'

'You'll have to get a car at this rate,' Clarissa said.

'I'll tell you what—at the rate we're getting people interested, you might have to pack in your driving job. The Brahms concerto is a definite possibility, probably for the late summer. As your personal manager, I'd like you to be able to play it, put it that way.' He smiled, but not light-heartedly. Ruth recognized that he was as serious about his work as Pat himself. He was one of these people who never relaxed, who always had to be driving, building, achieving.

Pat said, 'There's no question of my packing in the driving job until these engagements are regular. Unless, as my personal manager, you're prepared to advance me some wherewithal to live on.' He smiled too. Another entirely serious smile. 'I imagine it's a bit soon.'

'At the moment, yes. But as soon as I see my way to it, I would agree to that. You've got to have the repertoire. I don't know your rate of learning as yet, but if I go out and get the work, it's no good if you haven't the time to prepare it.'

'Even with the driving job, I do five hours a day. I've done two hours before breakfast.'

It was true. At six o'clock he got out of bed, flung on several layers of clothes, put on the kettle and sat down at the piano. The room was deathly cold and dark, the music-rack illuminated by a lamp with a sinister green shade. Ruth, putting her nose out of the blankets, would watch Pat's green-flushed face scowling over the sheets of music, his new work, which he reckoned 'softened' more easily at the start of the day than at the end. He would warm his hands on the tea-mug, do ten minutes of cascading scales in all directions and then start on the difficult bits, muttering and swearing at the composer and the world in general until brief moments of accomplishment and the first glimmers of daylight mellowed him.

'Yes, it's true,' Ruth said, loyally. 'It's all he does when he's at home.'

Clarissa gave her a strange look, almost sympathetic.

'He learns very fast,' Clarissa said to Mick. 'Prodigious memory.'

'Not for telephone numbers or names or what happened last Saturday,' Pat said.

'For notes. Unfair advantage.'

'My luck,' Pat said.

'Well, I'm glad to hear it,' Mick said happily. 'Carry on with the good work. What are you on now?'

'Schumann mostly. Fantasy in C. Lots of lesser Liszt. Did you say Debussy for Guildford?'

'Yes.'

'Preludes?'

'Very suitable.'

'Three or four? I'd rather just do the ones I'm happy with now, not work up the dicey ones—not by then. It would mean dropping the other things. I can do them a very nice Brahms rhapsody—how about that? Does he want the Scriabin again? A drop of Beethoven to start with?'

'Well, you work it out, and we can let them know. I could ask him to telephone you and you can discuss it with him. Would that be the best thing?'

'Yes, any evening. But not me telephone him, because I can't afford it.'

'Not yet.'

'No. Unless he pays for his concert in advance.'

Mick grinned. Ruth fetched coffee things out of the cupboard and set the mugs out in the hearth, hoping the firelight was doing for her what it was doing for Clarissa. She felt breathless and heavy; she *was* breathless and heavy. On the strength of one recital behind them and one ahead, Mick and Pat were concocting concerto schedules.

'The Brahms two by August. You can have the Rach. two, Liszt one, and Grieg now and the Beethoven three, four or five if you give me a reasonable warning . . .'

'Clarissa's only given me Mendelssohn and Brahms.'

'Are you her personal manager too?'

'Yes. I've finalized Hemel Hempstead. Are you going to go through it tonight? I ought to have a preview.'

'You might cancel it. Better not.'

'No, you must,' Clarissa said. 'It's ages since we played together. I've forgotten—with you—Arnold didn't annoy me half so much. With you it was quite different. Harder.'

'He covered up your mistakes? She makes a lot of mistakes,' Pat said to Mick, 'but the audience is so fascinated watching to see if she'll get her hair caught up in her bow that they don't notice.'

'You're exaggerating!'

'Your time-keeping is eccentric, to put it mildly. She expects the piano to keep up with her, even if it means the pianist having to leave out a few bars here and there, or put some in while he's waiting. Perhaps Arnold was better at it than I was.'

'He didn't get nearly so cross.'

'That's what I mean. He humoured you. I'd rather humour the composer.'

Clarissa said to Mick, 'I told you Pat was appallingly rude. Haven't you got any polite pianists on your books?'

'None as good as him. I don't care what happens in rehearsal as long as the result is okay.'

'I do,' Ruth thought. She hated Pat talking music with Clarissa. The news of the engagements had put him in a good mood and although he was being insulting, his manner was kindly, not spiteful. He was obviously quite prepared now to play in public with Clarissa, in spite of what he had said earlier.

'Coffee?' she said abruptly, looking up from the mugs. Pat was actually smiling and Clarissa was looking up at him with her glowing, inviting expression which made Ruth's fingers on the coffee-mug twitch with irrepressible rage. She knew she was being ridiculous, but she couldn't help it, any more than Clarissa could help being so attractive. Clarissa was in fact being charming, not only to Pat but to herself as well.

'Lovely!' she said, taking her coffee. 'Just a moment—I must go to the loo first! Which direction? No, don't get up—I'll find it—'

'Across the hall, the door on the right,' Ruth said. 'I left the light on.'

'Fine.'

As soon as she had left the room Mick said to Pat, 'You're not being very intelligent if you don't accept an invitation to dinner at her place. You know perfectly well that you and I can work like beavers getting you engagements, and yet one word in the right place from her old man is worth three months of toil on my part. That's why I want you to play this recital with her. For your own good, not hers. She's adequate, but no more. You can't afford to miss chances like this. Not when you're starting. Afterwards, you can snap your fingers at the lot of them, I won't care. But this is my work as much as yours. If you want it that way, that is.'

Pat was frowning.

'You can't afford temperament,' Mick said. 'Not yet.'

'I don't want favours.'

'God, man, I'm not talking about favours! An opening, a way in, isn't a favour!' Mick looked almost angry, his mane of hair standing up in leonine vigour round his bony face. Ruth thought suddenly that he really did look like an impresario. She could see that Pat needed him, and that he was talking sense.

Pat said, slowly, painfully, 'It's not a question of—of work. I've told Ruth this—when I first started in London, I went there a lot, they were kind—to suit themselves. But when I got into trouble, and I really needed some help, they didn't want to know. I suppose I embarrassed them. They went potty, dropped me like a red-hot brick. You can't, afterwards—go to people like that as if nothing's happened. I was so green—now, it wouldn't worry me the same way, but at the time I thought people like that—you know, educated, rich—I suppose I thought they were different. That's when I found out they weren't. Even Clarissa . . .' His voice trailed off and he shrugged.

Even Clarissa what? Ruth wanted to ask. But didn't.

'Yes, well,' Mick said, all fatherly. 'That's past history now. You're in no danger of repeating the antics that got you into trouble, surely? You can forget all the differences.'

'Yes, I can forget all that happened but I can't change how it made me feel about certain people. That's all I'm saying.'

What he really meant, Ruth was thinking, was that when he landed in court the first time, Clarissa's mother decided that he was unsuitable for her daughter, and Clarissa, dominated by mother, gave him the brush-off. Afterwards she was sorry. The second time it happened, Ruth, defying *her* mother, visited him every visiting day and was rewarded for her fidelity by getting him as a husband. The only cloud in this lovely sky was the fact that he had married her out of a surprising kindness, because of what he had done to her, and not at all out of the consuming passion which he had once, on his own admission, felt for Clarissa. Ruth minded this very much when faced with Clarissa, although she had felt secure enough before.

Mick said, 'No, that's reasonable. But don't throw away opportunities when they arise except for fantastically convincing reasons—which you haven't got now. Or I'll go and find someone else to personally manage.'

'If you say so.'

Ruth handed Pat his coffee. He looked quite amiable, and Clarissa returned to a conversation on the bugbears of Brahms in general and the concerto in particular, on which Pat could wax quite eloquently.

'The sonata Clarissa has chosen, of course, being one of those in which the piano is definitely the inferior instrument,' he pointed out.

'Of course,' Clarissa said. 'It's my recital, after all. I don't want to be outplayed.'

'This time last year you wouldn't have admitted the possibility,' Pat said.

'I don't work hard enough,' Clarissa admitted.

'Ah, that's very unwise admission to make in front of your personal manager,' Mick said. 'If you worked as hard as Pat then—'

'I'd be playing Brahms' violin concerto by now, instead of having to sweat over a mere sonata.'

'It's not all that mere.'

'Come and sweat then. Ruth will turn over—you don't want me music-less for this recital, I hope?'

'Not necessary, no.'

'I'm not turning over at any concerts,' Ruth said hastily. 'I don't mind now, but—'

She followed Pat to the piano to take up her lowly role, while Clarissa tuned her violin and flung her long hair back out of the way.

'Which one?' Ruth asked, hunting through the dog-eared heaps.

'A Major,' Pat said.

He sat down and started to play Brahms' piano concerto while Ruth hunted out the music.

'*Do* you mind?' Clarissa shouted at him. Ruth hastily opened the sonata on the rack and Pat switched to a gentle introductory melody. 'Allegro am-a-a-a-bile,' he said to Clarissa.

'What does that mean?' Ruth asked.

'Amiably fast. Smile as you quickly play. Come, Clarissa, you've missed the gun. And again.' He started again. Clarissa said something rude and played a few notes. Pat's face became absorbed, eyes on the music. Ruth, watching him, thought painfully of 'Twinkle, twinkle, little star'. He was taken up totally with Clarissa, through playing the music, committed entirely to her efforts. When Ruth turned over two pages by mistake and he had to come to a halt, she got sworn at, but when Clarissa went wrong he laughed, and when she repeated the tricky bit nicely he said, 'Good girl!' and smiled as if she had done him a favour. Afterwards they worked at the harder bits, with lots of repetitions, and she didn't have to turn over any more, but sat staring into the fire. Mick was lying on the bed. Once she looked up and found him staring at her, and was distracted. She thought his eyes were for Clarissa. She heard Pat say, 'God, you can't even *read* it. It's not—' demonstration on the piano—'it's—' — another demonstration. She was pleased. Clarissa called him a big-headed anti-feminist pig, and they started to play a fast bit together, full of spite, but then, into their stride, it started to come together—even Ruth could feel the difference—and they were entirely serious and tender, and Brahms in his grave could rest in peace, it was all as he intended. Ruth hated Clarissa then more than ever, basking in Pat's approval.

'But listen to this,' he said when she laid down her violin. 'This is lovely. Are you going to let me do a piece on my own at your recital? I'll play them this.' He started to play the Schumann Fantasy, which at six o'clock every morning Ruth had never heard him describe as lovely.

'No. It's much too long,' Clarissa said. 'You can play a little short piece.'

'You can't have enough of this.'

'Oh, the conceit—' Clarissa shook her head and sat down beside Ruth on the hearth-rug, and Pat went on playing. It was true, Ruth thought, when he played it properly, that one couldn't have enough. It was the flowing, romantic music that she loved, and now, played to friends, uninterrupted by repetitions, curses, one monotonous phrase done sixty times to the metronome and coffee between movements, it was magical. This, in the firelight, playing for pure pleasure for friends, was the rare essence of music, better than concerts, far better than lonely practice, with all the warts showing. The conditions exactly right, Pat played superbly, and no one tried to stop him.

At the end Mick said, 'We ought to have had a tape going. How about that for the Guildford recital?'

'It's not ready yet,' Pat said. 'Not the second movement. And anyway not with the Liszt. You can't give them two king-sized romantics in one evening. I'd like to try the "Waldstein" on them, but that's a bit hefty with the Liszt as well. It's just that I'd like to try it out in public. "Les Adieux" is shorter, might be better.'

'See what the bloke says when you ring him—he rings you, I mean. Often they have ideas of their own—they don't always know much about programme balance. I wouldn't bother so much about balance at the moment as playing what you want to try out on them. You want the experience.'

'You mean it's me that wants stretching, not this audience you mentioned earlier?'

'You get all you can out of it. Keep the niceties for when you appear on the South Bank.'

'Thank *you*,' Pat said drily.

'With me,' Clarissa said, smiling.

After they had gone, Pat said to Ruth, 'Her father is on the administration of the Royal Festival Hall.'

'That's what Mick meant about keeping in with them?'

Pat shrugged.

'I take it. He's as bad as the Professor, keeping me up to the mark. I must say, though, he doesn't let the grass grow. It all sounds quite hopeful.' He yawned, stretching in front of the fire. 'We might even make some money.' He smiled. He looked tired. 'Brahms' two is worth more than peanuts.'

He didn't say anything about Clarissa.

Chapter 8

'Well, look, are you sure?' Rosemary's face was crumpled with anxiety. 'How long have you been like it?'

'No, I'm not sure, that's the trouble,' Ruth said. 'I've been like it for two days. Not really pains, but a sort of—ugh—low-down, heavy feeling. It's not really enough to go to hospital on.'

'No, but going to Guildford with Pat tonight is a bit potty. Have you told him?'

'I mentioned it but he—oh, you know what he's like when it's a concert—at least, he was like it before. He just said, "Oh, you must come", as if it was nothing. The baby's not due for a fortnight so I suppose it's all right. And if I tell him it's coming, it's not very good for his playing tonight, is it? I mean, it might put him off and we can't afford that.'

'Yes, but you can't let that stand in your way. Heavens, it'll put him off if you have it on the train on the way to Guildford.'

'Oh, I'm sure it's not as close as that. I'm a bit worried, that doesn't help. I only came up to see you because I've got the fidgets. Pat should have been home half an hour ago. If he doesn't buck up we'll be cutting it pretty fine. The concert starts at eight.'

'Is he out driving?'

'Yes. He had a wedding at half past three. I thought he'd have been home by now. I've put all his things together. We shall have to hurry.'

'I still don't see why you have to go.'

'I want to go, and he likes me there. It saves him having to make polite conversation.'

'You spoil him!'

'Yes, but he works terribly hard and I don't do anything.'

'You will soon. Have you got everything ready you want? Nappies and things? A pram? A cot?'

'No, not yet. Until Pat gets paid for tonight we haven't any money. I've tried to save but it always has to go on something. And the Rachmaninov people haven't paid yet as apparently they've got to have a committee meeting or something. Pat was fed up after hitch-hiking there and back and no actual money to show for it.'

'Yes, that's not good enough. I don't blame him. Here, sit on this box. I'm afraid the place is in a bit of a mess.'

'I must keep an ear out for Pat.'

Ruth sat on the box, pale and anxious.

'If the baby's coming you'll want those things,' Rosemary said. 'Have you looked in the adverts for a pram?'

'Yes, I looked in the paper but every time I said I'd go and look at one, Pat hadn't any money.'

'You can use the pram for a cot as well for a bit. I'll find you one, if you like. I mean, if the baby's really on the way—'

'Oh, don't say that, for heaven's sake! It can't be. I wish Pat would hurry. We're supposed to be at Waterloo at half past six. What's the time now?'

'Half past six.'

'Oh, God! Whatever's happened to him?'

'Don't worry! He might go straight there if he's running late.'

'But his clothes are here. He can't play in his chauffeur's suit.'

'Oh, no. Well, he'll be here in a minute. I think you ought to stop worrying about him and think about yourself. He only thinks about *himself*. I don't think you ought to go.'

'I *want* to go. It won't come yet, I'm sure. Don't say anything to him, for goodness' sake. The time I told him about it in the first place, he played so badly afterwards that he missed the chance of a lifetime doing Beethoven's Third in Edinburgh.'

'Poor lad—I'd love to have seen his face! At least he can't say he's not expecting it this time.'

'No, but all the same, don't say anything.'

'All right. We'll all be nice to him. Because you need the money for the pram. Talk about cutting it fine!'

'He's been ever so bad-tempered the last week or so. Too much work to do—he hates the driving, because it takes up so much time. I'm hoping I'll be able to go out and earn something—somewhere I can take the baby with me. Golly, I wish he'd come!'

'I'll make a cup of tea. Have you eaten? There are some crumpets in a bag. If we do something, it's much better than just waiting.'

He came at ten past seven. Ruth heard the front door go, and thundered downstairs.

'For God's sake, where's my suit? I'll change here. Get it out! We're going in the Rolls—Paddy's given me permission. Otherwise we'll never make it. That ruddy bride—changed her mind—I had to wait while they all talked her into it—an hour and a half—'

He was flinging off his clothes, while Ruth feverishly unpacked the suitcase, shaking out the folds that had taken her such agony to get right earlier.

'Here you are—'

'Cripes, I ought to shave—Wilf's got an electric razor—go and nab it—'

'I'll get it!' Rosemary, hovering on the stairs, galloped back up.

'Shirt! Where are the braces? This flaming clobber, for God's sake—'

It was made for more leisurely times, for a man with a valet to do up the studs, tie the tie. Ruth didn't know how it went.

'This coat *smells*!' she discovered, horrified. 'I should have taken it to the cleaner's.'

'Yeh, what do you expect? You sweat like a pig—should play in a track-suit. Are you ready? Only the first few rows will smell it. Where's the other cuff-link?'

Rosemary came down with the razor; Ruth scrambled for her coat, gathered up the music.

'Have I got the right ones? I don't know why on earth you take it—'

' "Les Adieux" ', Debussy's preludes . . .'

Rosemary saw them to the door. The Rolls-Royce stood outside, white satin ribbons on its bonnet, the inside a mass of confetti.

Rosemary shrieked with laughter.

'Can I be a bridesmaid? Have a lovely honeymoon!'

Pat was scowling furiously.

'Forty minutes! Jesus!'

Ruth didn't dare say, 'Do drive carefully.' She felt fragile, although she couldn't honestly say she was experiencing pains. It was quite impossible to say anything to Pat about her condition. The Rolls was beautiful, a warm palace purring through the dusk. Ruth looked out of the window at the drivers of old vans and

Minis, her long hair picking up the glittery confetti. They gave strange looks back, trying to beat them away from the lights and failing. A lot of people smiled at them, presumably because of the white ribbons. Ruth thought of the bride who changed her mind, and was 'persuaded' into it, while Pat sat outside drumming his fingers. What was she thinking now? How terrible not to be sure; how terrible for her now, wondering if she had done the right thing! 'I have done the right thing,' Ruth thought, even if it had only been her father's old Anglia and the Northend registry office, and Maxwell popping out of the motor showroom for ten minutes to be best man. No Rolls, no white ribbons, not even any confetti. If anyone had doubted, it had been Pat, although he had not actually said so, only looked—rather as he did now—pale and screwed-up and silent. There was a lot of traffic, and he kept swearing dreadfully. When they got out on to wider, more business-like roads, the Rolls swept along, its needle obediently on seventy, no more, no less. The last time Pat had 'borrowed' a car he had landed in prison for it; this time Ruth presumed it was all right. He said Paddy had given him permission. One day, when Pat was a famous concert pianist, perhaps they would have their own Rolls and going to recitals would always be like this, only without the white ribbons. Pat did not say a word, concentrating hard. Ruth knew better than to disturb him. They reached the hall where the concert was to take place at seven minutes past eight. Ruth knew it was for her to do the explaining, the apologizing, the gushing, for Pat had to think himself into Beethoven's Opus 81, the first piece on his programme and concerned with far higher things than traffic difficulties and brides who changed their minds at the last moment. He was already in his withdrawn, absent state when they stepped out of the car; Ruth thought he looked positively ill, but she didn't feel very marvellous herself.

The welcoming posse this time received them with exclamations of relief and delight. Ruth did all the explaining very rapidly and excitedly while Pat locked himself away in the lavatory in order to think himself into Beethoven.

'I'll go and explain to the audience. They'll wait another five minutes while he composes himself, as long as they know he's here. Far better than if he rushes straight on immediately.' The committee-man understood the situation, and was sympathetic.

His wife said to Ruth, 'Do have a chair, my dear. I do hope the rush didn't upset you. It's very difficult for a performer when things like this happen. But he'll find it's a very appreciative audience, a fairly knowledgeable one too, as these club meetings go. He should find it worth while. We were very impressed when we heard him last month. He has such a range for one so young—he gets you right *into* the music, such an involvement, besides the technique—'

Ruth was hoping that it was money she meant when she said he would find it worth while. She went to root him out of the lavatory, not sure whether he was being sick or merely thinking. He looked like she felt. When does a "feeling" become a pain? she wondered. It was a pain now, holding her, and relaxing. 'God in heaven, it can't happen here!' she thought. Pat walked straight past her, not even looking at her, down the corridor and on to the stage. She heard the applause break out, and stopped bothering about him. He was there; it was his pigeon now, her part done, and she had her own plight to cope with, her own act of creation to control. There was no doubt now that the baby was on the way. She must have been daft, coming, so wrapped up in Pat's artistic temperament! If she were just to sit down, quietly, and think about something else, it would surely not bother her for an hour or two . . . first babies never came very fast. Did they? She suddenly felt the sweat breaking out—pure fright! Whatever was it going to be like? She had heard such stories . . . oh heavens, and no pram, no nappies, no money . . . Pat! She wanted him, sitting on her hard chair alone. The whole building was wrapped in silence, save for the distant piano going like the clappers, and a scuffle of starlings in the chimney above her head. Rosemary . . . she wished Rosemary was there; she could have come. She wanted her mother. The pain came again, far off in a curious way, but quite adamant. She got up and walked about slowly. She mustn't let Pat see it, whatever happened, which meant not letting anyone know, not for just the hour and a half of his recital. Nobody had a first baby that fast. They could be back in London in an hour, straight to the hospital, and everything would be all right. Barbara, her sister-in-law, had been fourteen hours from the first pain. Time enough for Pat to go through his Beethoven and his Scriabin and his Debussy and his Liszt . . . they needed the money, for heaven's sake!

She walked down the corridor towards the back of the stage. Beethoven, having lamented the departure of his friend, had just received him back with a forte of joy, and Pat had embarked on the frantic bit marked 'vivacissimamente'. Ruth was so familiar with all Pat's concert work that—knowing nothing of music—she yet knew these particular pieces bar by bar. If he were to go wrong, she would know instantly, even if he covered it up. She thought, 'The baby will know them too, living in one room.' It already knew them. She sat down on another handy chair, where she could see Pat through the wings, and thought about the baby. It seemed quite extraordinary that in a few hours it would be *there*, a boy or a girl, a human being on its own. It was a quite terrifying thought, what they had done: created another human being. Not even meaning to. A whole, living, breathing human being with its life entirely in their hands, to make happy or to make sad. And yet it was the most common-place incident in the world, a birth. The thought of actually holding the baby, having to look after it, was quite terrifying to her. She supposed a sort of instinct might tell her what to do, or a magazine. She thought there was a Penguin book, Dr. Spock or somebody . . . or had she got muddled up with 'Star Trek' on the television? The man with pointed ears. Everything was in books, if you knew where to look. But mares knew what to do with their foals, even the first one . . . she had seen one of the hunters at MacNairs, doing everything right the first time, and no one to tell her.

There was suddenly a most tremendous crashing of applause. Ruth came to with a jerk, and the ridiculous footnote out of the sonata book concerning the last seven bars came into her mind, quite unbidden: 'In case the player is technically incapable of mastering the difficulty of this passage with the requisite rapidity, the following facilitation is allowable, or at least preferable to an involuntary dragging . . .' Why ever should she remember that? Pat was standing beside her, presumably having managed the requisite rapidity—and she had never even heard him. She stumbled to her feet.

'All right?'

He looked anguished. Who was asking who? She wasn't sure.

'It ought to have been better,' he said.

'Well—' The applause didn't suggest so. '*They* aren't complaining.'

'They're just relieved they got anything at all,' he said.

He went out to bow again and came back. Ruth stood there wondering if he had *learned* bowing as a student. She imagined a whole class of them with a teacher, bowing. He came back and combed his hair, which she suddenly noticed was rather long. It looked longer, somehow, with a suit, than with his usual scruffy rags.

'What now?'

'The two Debussy. Then Scriabin . . .' He was what she thought of as 'going into' the first Debussy even while he spoke, his mind disengaging from her presence almost before the words faded away. He just stood there, and she thought that, if a pain came *now*, badly, he wouldn't notice. He could be looking at her and not notice. But fortunately the next pain didn't come until three-quarters of the way through the Scriabin four, when the music was becoming so violent that she could let out a small moan of apprehension undetected. When he came off the stage she was all right. She kept telling herself it was nothing to worry about, only the very beginning; she had to hold out through the interval, and then after that they would be on the home run. She thought perhaps it was her imagination, and not really birth-pangs at all, just a sort of cramp, because of being nervous about Pat. The committee-man and his wife came back-stage bringing a coffee for Ruth, very kind and tactful, understanding about not bothering Pat, who was staring out of the window on to an asphalt car-park.

'We kept a seat for you in the front. If you want to come out after the interval . . . or do you prefer it here? I should have brought a more comfortable chair. Do sit down. You must be having your baby quite soon? How lovely—'

Ruth wondered what would happen if she said, 'Yes, now actually.' But she smiled hopefully, and the man said, glancing at his watch, 'We'll keep the interval as short as we can. He's obviously wanting to get on.' He nodded in Pat's direction. 'Afterwards you must come for a drink, and meet some of our friends . . .'

To Ruth's intense relief she got through the interval without giving anything away, and Pat played the Brahms Rhapsody and was half-way through the Liszt before another pain came. It wasn't her imagination at all. She felt quite sick with fright. She got up and walked about and hung over the hot pipes. The Liszt was nearly through, coming up to the wild octave bit before it all went quiet for the end. Something was wrong with it. Ruth straightened up with a jerk, the shock as bad as the last pain. Wrong notes in the left hand and then, not a smooth professional cover-up as if no mistakes had sounded, but a sudden ringing silence, abrupt and awful. Ruth couldn't believe it. No applause, like a proper ending, but a murmuring in the hall, a buzz of speculation and surprise. Pat was still sitting there, looking at the keys without any expression. He lifted his hands, then gave a slight shrug, got up and came off the stage. Ruth stood and stared at him. She thought if she hadn't got the radiator to hold on to she would have fallen over. The murmur in the hall was a frenzy of excitement, as if a physical accident had occurred.

'Pat! Whatever—!'

'I couldn't do it.'

'You forgot it?'

'No.'

'But you can do it. You've done it hundreds of times.'

'I couldn't do it then. I just couldn't. That's why I came off. If I'd forgotten, I'd have stopped and gone back.'

Ruth couldn't believe it had happened. It was even worse than having the baby here in the hall. Pat was standing there looking white and stunned, his arms hanging loosely down and his wrists turning, his fingers playing against his thighs.

'You've got to,' Ruth said. 'You can't just leave it. You've got to do it.'

He didn't answer.

The committee-man came out from the hall, his face all screwed up with anxiety.

'Are you all right? A lapse of memory? Don't let it throw you. It happens to the best people. Can I get you a drink?'

'He's all right,' Ruth said. She felt suddenly as hard as nails, thinking of the money. 'I'll get the music,' she said. 'You can have it with you. There's no law about it.' She wanted to say, 'Get on with it. I'm having the baby.' She wasn't in the mood to pander to temperament. Pat had always said it was a job like any other. She fetched the sonata and opened it where he had stopped. It looked terrible. No wonder he had lost heart.

'There.' She thrust it at him. 'Take it with you. It's your memory at fault, your concentration. Not that you can't do it.

For heaven's sake, go back and play it. You can't leave them in the middle of it. They've *paid* to hear it.'

The committee-man was shocked at her nagging.

'There's no hurry,' he said. 'Have a few minutes to collect yourself.'

'There is, there is,' Ruth thought. She felt quite desperate. 'Don't be so damned stupid!' she said sharply to Pat. 'Go back and get on with it! You know you've got to. The longer you leave it the worse you'll feel.'

What he actually felt like just at that moment she had no way of knowing, but he turned round and went back on to the stage. The committee-man, throwing Ruth a hurt and disapproving look, hurried after him. The audience started clapping madly as if he had done something marvellous instead of miserably failing. Pat sat down and said something to the committee-man, and the hall went suddenly silent. Ruth felt sick again, and slightly hysterical. The committee-man came tiptoeing off, still with the music, and Pat said into the hush, 'I shall start at the fugue, half-way through,' and started to play. It sounded perfectly all right. Ruth felt another pain coming, a great eager, awful pain.

The committee-man stared at her.

'It's all right,' she said. 'The baby,' she added, by way of explanation, when she got her breath back.

He looked horrified, terrified.

'Oh, my dear!'

Through all the alarms and excursions of the evening, Ruth—seeing the man's face—saw, faintly, a very funny side to it. She hadn't time to pursue the thought, but she thought, afterwards, when she told Rosemary, Rosemary would appreciate it. The man was not knowing whether to give his whole attention to her or to Pat.

'It's all right,' she reassured him. 'Plenty of time.'

'Does your husband know?' he whispered. 'Is that why—?'

Ruth, with a flash of inspiration, nodded her head. What a marvellous let-out for Pat's lapse! No one, in those circumstances, could possibly hold the breakdown against him. The man looked pale, obviously convinced she was going to give birth before the end of the sonata.

'Don't worry,' she whispered. 'Truly, it's all right. Only just started.'

Even she, in her predicament, was now more intent upon Pat's safe delivery of the B Minor sonata than of her own child. There was a tenseness in the atmosphere that suggested that everyone in the audience was feeling the same. Because he had stopped before, the same place was going to be his testing-ground. Ruth knew that he was playing very well now; she thought it would be all right, but she could feel her skin pricking with nervousness when he came to the great majestic theme which heralded the finale and all its rigours. The committee-man was nervously rubbing the side of his nose with a forefinger. Was everybody in the audience, Ruth wondered, feeling the same? It was all wrong, to be tensed up for the middleman instead of drowning in the composer's glorious imagination. Pat would be furious when he came to, however well he might play it the second time. Ruth could picture his self-disgust, and was thankful that she could give him the baby for distraction, and keep safely out of his way in hospital. If he failed a second time, she did not dare . . . she couldn't contemplate it. Whatever had happened to him? Was it the upset at the start, being late, his state of mind? No proper concert pianist ever did it, did they? Did they? She didn't know. His playing now was completely assured. He went through the crisis part without a falter, both hands thundering up and down the octaves without a single blurring, boldly up to tempo, magnificently controlled: Ruth had never heard it played better. The relief was so great she wanted to lie down on the floor; her knees were trembling. She felt terrible. The sonata drew to its strange, breathless close, with a pulsating silence after the final bottom single note which Ruth felt she was interrupting by her very breathing. Then the applause broke out, clapping and cheering, and the committee-man was beaming. 'Splendid! Splendid!'

Pat came off looking exhausted and nervous. Ruth went to intercept him. She put an arm round his neck and said into his ear, 'The baby's on its way. We ought to go home.' She didn't want him not to know, when the committee-man opened the conversation. He looked at her as if she had gone out of her mind. He looked terrified, just like the committee-man. The audience was going mad, cheering and stamping and shouting. Pat said, 'Cripes, *now*? It's coming now?'

'Yes.'

'God Almighty.'

He looked completely demolished. He groaned. The audience went on shouting and clapping. Ruth said briskly, 'Go and bow, for heaven's sake. Wake up, you look ghastly!' Nag, nag, nag. She wanted him to look after her, and it was all the other way round: she wanted to scream. She gave him a handkerchief to wipe his face, and a push to get him back on to the stage, and the audience went on with its cheering and stamping. Pat came back.

'They *like* it when you fail. It's ridiculous.' He was looking angry, which was an improvement. He looked closely at Ruth. 'We'd better go. I'm dropping. I suppose we can't.'

The audience wouldn't stop clapping. The committee-man came over and shook Pat's hand. He had to shout to make himself heard. 'You'll have to go back!' He looked dubiously at Ruth and said, 'They want an encore. If you could possibly—? Something very short? I don't want to hold you up in the circumstances. Oh dear, it's very difficult.'

Pat shrugged. He looked at Ruth.

'Oh, go on. You'll have to. I'll go and wait in the car.' She was past making polite conversation. She could see that Pat couldn't just walk out. He had created a situation, and had to see it through. The committee-man escorted her anxiously outside. When he saw the Rolls with its white ribbons, his eyes opened wide and he gave Ruth a strange look. Ruth felt sorry for him, his evening being full of shocks, right from the start when they hadn't turned up in time. But she didn't want to talk any more. She wanted the lovely elegant peace of the silent car. But Pat had the key in his pocket. She had to lean against the Rolls in the cool darkness.

'I'm quite all right. You must go back. I'd rather stay here until he comes.'

'I'll get him away as soon as possible.' He started to walk back and Ruth remembered something terribly important, that she was sure was going to get forgotten. She hurried after him.

'Please—'

He turned back, anxious to please.

'Please don't—' —the embarrassment caught her, flushing her face—'Don't let him come away without the—without the cheque.' They were going to want the pram, and the nappies, and whatever else it was Rosemary had said. It was no good being polite and waiting for the money. The committee-man gave her yet another surprised look. 'No, of course not.'

By the time Pat came, at last, she felt close to tears. He opened the car up and she got in, curling up in the roomy seat. She wanted to be looked after.

'Have you got the money?'

'Yes. He gave it to me.' Pat got in and started the engine. 'Are you okay? Have I got to hurry, I mean? Blue light flashing?'

'No. Just ordinary.'

'You're sure it's coming?'

'Yes.' He heard the note of panic which she could not prevent, and started the engine immediately.

'It's all happening tonight.' His voice sounded quite normal. Ruth had expected him to be in a terrible mood because of the mistake.

'Franz Ludwig von Pennington,' she said. It's what they called the baby, after Liszt and Beethoven. 'He's ready. Sending messages.'

'Did you know, when we set out?'

'No. I felt peculiar, but no pains. It started when you were playing.'

'Enough to give anyone pains, how I played tonight. It might not be the baby at all.'

'*They* liked it.'

'Huh.'

He drove in silence for a bit and then said, 'It's like your show-jumping thing. The horse that knocks everything down—they clap like mad.'

'It's not like that at all, but after you went back, and did the Liszt again, you played it as well as you've ever played it. If you'd made a hash of it then—*then* you'd have something to worry about.'

He didn't answer. Ruth could see that he was going to go through an agonizing post-mortem on why he couldn't complete the Liszt, but she would have her own problems, and he would have to work it out on his own. She had timed things worse than she knew. But she was too far gone now to carry his troubles. She couldn't help feeling frightened about what was happening to her; she couldn't really think about anything else.

He drove fast, in silence, concentrating. Whether he was

thinking about her or about the concert she had no way of knowing. She had to make herself be very calm, holding her breath,
terrified for the next pain. They weren't very close together; she
wasn't afraid of not getting there in time, only for the pain itself,
which threatened this precarious calm. She could feel the sweat
gathering. You had to relax, she remembered. They said that
part of the pain was because of being tensed up and frightened.
Take deep relaxing breaths.

'Are you all right?' Pat asked suspiciously.

'Yes.'

The deep relaxing breaths were frightening him. She stopped,
and felt a bit giggly.

'It's not going to—?'

'No. It's all right.'

'We'll go straight to the hospital? Or have you got to go home
for anything?'

'I think straight there. You can bring my nightdress and things
when you come.'

It was strange, but she wanted to get there now, to be looked
after. She wanted people who knew about these things; she
wanted to be told it was all right. She wanted her mother. She
started to cry. She couldn't help it.

'Cripes!' Pat was pale as a ghost. He jumped the lights on
amber and the Rolls went down the Bayswater Road at sixty miles
an hour.

Chapter 9

Pat couldn't get the page of the sonata out of his mind, where he had faltered. The feeling of his fingers actually stopping, the numbness of his mind, not actually forgetting—which would have been forgivable—but seeing the notes in his mind and somehow not being able to make them happen. It was inexplicable, a kind of spastic refusal of the nerves to work the fingers. It appalled him. Just to recall the moment made him come out in a cold sweat. It had been a great weariness, as if, when it got very difficult, he just hadn't the pure energy of spirit to see it through. Trying to think of it logically, he supposed it was in fact caused by fatigue, by the day's frustrations, the lateness, the lack of opportunity to concentrate beforehand. And yet he had been so sure that he was professional enough now to surmount those sort of obstacles—not play well, perhaps, under adverse circumstances, but at least to see it through in such a way that an undemanding audience would accept it as a reasonable performance. But he hadn't. Even a moronic audience could not have failed to see that something had gone wrong, that he wasn't capable. The fact that he had played well afterwards, which he knew he had, and given a stunning performance of a taxing Chopin étude for an encore—to prove to himself, not only to *them*, that he was good, in spite of such a bungle—could not erase the awfulness of the moment. He needed confidence, he needed to know that he was good, to make all the incredible difficulties of the whole business worth persevering with. And to do this—fall flat on your face in public—was enough to undermine anybody's ego, let alone as nervous a one as his.

He wasn't in a state of mind to accept it and forget it, as in normal circumstances—with Ruth and his friends to reassure him and a good stiff whisky to drown his sorrows in, he would have managed. By the time he got home, having walked from the garage up a cold, midnight Finchley Road clutching his useless music, he felt abandoned, gibbering, suicidal. He knew he ought to be thinking about Ruth, but all he could think about was the damned music. He felt that Ruth had left him just when he most needed her, and in fact from henceforth would be taken up with the wretched brat that he had no money to support. The cheque in his pocket would just about pay last week's rent, next week's rent, and buy the list of baby equipment that he could put off no longer, and then they were back to normal—penniless. And if he made another mistake like the one he had made tonight, there wouldn't be any more cheques to come either.

He now felt very restless, not at all tired. Walking up the road, some drunken youths jeered at him and his evening clothes, and he could easily have waded in and banged their heads together. He wanted to do it, and had consciously to stop himself, keep his hands in his pockets. He felt aggressive and angry. It was how he had felt many times in the past, when things had gone wrong, but since marrying Ruth he realized that the feeling had become quite rare. It came as quite a surprise, realizing this. 'An old married man,' he thought. And he felt abandoned again. And angry because he wasn't thinking of Ruth. Angry with himself. He had delivered her to the hospital, followed her down some antiseptic corridors, heard a woman somewhere screaming, and departed at a rate of knots, sweating and sick. The car-parking attendant and the maternity receptionist gave him extraordinary looks, which he could not fathom until his mind had surfaced farther down the road, and he was able to picture Ruth's arrival as they had actually seen it, getting out of the Rolls with its white ribbons and confetti, straight into the door marked 'Maternity'.

Ordinarily this would have been good for a laugh, but nothing was funny tonight. When he got home, he wanted to talk to Wilf or Rosemary, but the house was deserted. They had gone away for the week-end; even Wilf's two friends had gone. He rang up Mick, but there was no reply. He stood in the hall, having banged down the receiver, and the whole house seemed to him balefully empty, spiting him. There were draughts under the door, the net curtains bulging, the laburnum eternally tapping, a soft March wind outside with the smell of spring in it, but rain in the air and the clouds dark as hell. The dim electric light was hostile. Their big room was cold and untidy, his clothes strewn about, a mat askew in their haste, tea-mugs in the hearth. It was nothing without Ruth in it. Just a sort of barn. It was shabby and poor-looking, not a penny spent for comfort. Normally he never noticed, but without Ruth it somehow all showed. Apart from his night away playing the Rachmaninov it was the first night he had been without Ruth. He resented it bitterly. It was the first time the baby was putting itself in the way, deflecting her from his needs, and he had a strong feeling that it was not the last. He didn't like it. He could feel himself being petty and ridiculous, and it didn't make any difference. He ought to be feeling tender and excited and full of sympathy for Ruth, but he was angry with her, and full of a pig-headed self-pity. He didn't care a damn about the baby.

He flung off his clothes and pulled on his old ones, decided to have a bath, and went to start running it. The condition of the pipes made this a long-drawn-out business, and the water-heater, eating coins, was unreliable. He left it mulishly spluttering and spewing and went to raid the house for a drink which he badly needed and which he doubted whether he would find. Wilf had two gallon cans of beer, unopened, which he was dubious about broaching, Rosemary a sour bottle of milk and two bottles of tonic water. There was nothing in the kitchen, but the room of Wilf's two dubious friends yielded six half-pints of bitter. He took two of the cans back to the bathroom. This was the sort of occasion when a joint wouldn't have been out of place; to go clean out of his mind for a few hours would have been no bad thing. But he knew from past experience that it solved nothing. It was all just that much worse coming back. No friend of ambition. Just an emotional procrastination. A pint of beer would cool his physical thirst; the bath would clean the stale sweat of pure funk from his body, but the old brain would be at square one, on the straight and narrow, with a fresh disaster to chew over. He had never stopped in public before. He had made mistakes; he had forgotten once or twice, but covered up quickly enough to bluff an amateur into thinking nothing had happened at all, but he had never experienced this quite shattering blank before. Remembering the feel of it, sitting there, made the flesh creep. Suppose . . . He had the competition next week, and the Liszt sonata was his centre-piece, the one he had asked to be judged on. The way he felt now, this minute, it wasn't possible to contemplate . . .

He plunged out of the bath, wrapped himself in a towel and went back to his room. The house was like a great ghoul, empty and cold and heartless, creaking and tapping and gurgling, unconcerned, an asthmatic old pile, home of lost causes, dead ambitions. The gas-fire flickered blue and hopeless. He pulled on his old clothes. The dress-shirt was lying on the floor, in disgrace; he made no move to put it away. He wanted to go to bed but he didn't feel tired. It was a quarter to one. Was it too late to change his choice for the competition? He could ring them up on Monday, see what they said. Get a job as a bricklayer.

He walked about the room, kicking at the rugs, the patch where coffee had been spilt, noticing the chipped paint, the flaky walls, the sagging armchair. He had never really noticed them before. His poverty depressed him utterly. There was only the piano, the lovely, ruddy piano, like fate itself, a confection of strings and hammers, a meaningless piece of furniture. He walked up and down, the damp bath-towel draped round his neck, looking at the piano, hating it. Paddy would take him on full-time, if he wanted. Driving to Heathrow every day, a sort of drugged existence, bound up in the traffic, learning patience, cunning, deceit and more patience. Being polite. A nice wedding every afternoon. He sat down at the piano and stared at its grubby yellow keys. It was nothing, without the person to play it. And the person to play it was nothing without the person who had written the music. He started to play the music that came into his head, the first variation of Beethoven's Opus 109, and whether it had come into his head because it suited the moment, or whether, having come into his head, it changed the moment, he did not know, only that it was suddenly very desirable to be a piano-player, impossible not to be one, Beethoven in the soul, to be his medium, his ghost, realizing his incredibly perfect, hesitant, melancholy, haunting tune, so that one was moved all by oneself to a rare and ecstatic state of communication. All the labour was for this, the distillation of the composer's genius delivered as intended, no more, no less. For Beethoven to nod his head and say, 'Yes, that's what I meant.' Nothing else. For Liszt, from the shades of his life's tempest, to say, 'Yes, that's what I meant.' Not retch with frustration in his afterlife. Not to have people clap because *you* were good, but because you showed them the composer's intention. Not to be big-headed, self-opinionated, a jumped-up finger-gymnast. 'Oh, God,' Pat said to the piano. 'If only it was easier.'

After all he had done, to *stop*! . . . He ought to play the Liszt, but it was impossible. He kept to Beethoven, the daddy of them all, to calm, to inspire. After three-quarters of an hour he felt very cold. It was getting on for two o'clock and he remembered Ruth was having a baby. The bath-towel was clammy and heavy. He flung it off and marched out into the hall and rang the hospital.

'Maternity.'

A wait of ages. They were all in bed. Surely women had babies all night?

'Yes?' Slightly breathless and cross.

'Has she got a baby yet? Ruth Pennington?'

'Good grief, it's two o'clock in the morning. Take some aspirins and go to bed.'

'I'm entitled to know, aren't I?' He wanted to crash the silly woman's head against the wall.

'What, at this time of night? Yes, I suppose you are, but you'd be far better off in bed. What's the name?'

'Pennington.'

Long, long silence. Distant voices, clatter of tin things. Feet coming back.

'Pennington? Are you Mr. John Pennington? Twin boys, six pounds each.'

Pat felt sick. 'I'm *Patrick*. Patrick Pennington! She's Ruth.'

Cripes, it was a common enough name! She wasn't—she couldn't have—

'Hang on a minute. When did she come in?'

'Tonight. Elevenish.'

'You're sure you're not John? I haven't got her name. I'd better go and . . .' The voice faded. Feet going away.

Pat found he was shaking. He was freezing cold and his teeth were chattering. The stupid, silly b—

'Ruth Pennington?'

'Yes.'

'Oh, you'll have to ring in the morning. Nothing to report.'

'You mean—she—isn't she having it?'

'Yes, but you're too soon. Ring in the morning.'

He put the receiver down. The shock of John Pennington's twins had made him feel disintegrated. He stumbled back to their room and crawled into bed. It was freezing cold without Ruth. He had got accustomed to her big hummock against his hip and her mass of hair on the pillow getting in his face, making him sneeze. He felt abandoned again. What on earth were they doing to her in that awful incompetent place where they got all the names mixed up? Suppose, with two Penningtons, they got the babies mixed up and he got one of John Pennington's twins instead of his own? A woman like that could easily get them muddled up. The panic he felt was akin to the Liszt panic; he was trembling. It was that woman saying twins. He threshed about, trying to get comfortable, longing for Ruth. How long would she be? He couldn't do without her. Baby or no baby, he wanted her back. He wanted her hair in his face and her arms round his neck. He couldn't sleep without her.

He dreamt he was back in Pentonville. He dreamt he was in his cell and three screws came in to beat him up; he was up against the wall and he was all tied up, he couldn't get his arms out to protect himself. Struggling frantically, he started to shout for help. He woke himself up, and found that he was all wrapped up in the sheet like a mummy, with the eiderdown on the floor and his bare feet sticking out in the cold. It was seven o'clock, icy cold and grey. He could still smell Pentonville in his dream; it was so vivid. It made him feel deathly, remembering it. It was so awful, as if he really had been back. He lay still, remembering slowly about being alone, and Ruth, and Liszt, and having no money. None of it seemed very awful after the dream. It was extraordinary how he had gone through all that, known it was going to happen from the very minute he had hit Mitchell, and yet not been in any way sorry that he had brought it on himself. Even the night in the police-station, like something out of 'Z-Cars', only far more real and painful and elemental, refusing to admit that he had stolen the car, not making it any easier in spite of knowing he was quite defeated . . . he could not believe it now. The dream had reminded him more fiercely than anything he could have conjured up in consciousness. He must have changed since then. He could not imagine being so bloody-minded any more. He unwound himself from the sheet, chastened, shivering. It had been terrible, the dip back into his past. He felt he could face anything now, knowing that all that had been only a dream. He wrapped the eiderdown round him and went out to the telephone.

'Ruth Pennington? Just a moment. I'll go and see.'

Long, long wait. Prickling with excitement. Was he a father— had he got a son, a daughter? It didn't seem to make sense. He felt quite faint at the thought of a child looking like himself. He had never really thought about it before, that it was a real person coming. He just hadn't thought about it as anything but a worry and a nuisance, because of the money—the lack of it—

'Ring up at lunchtime, dear. Nothing to report.'

'Nothing? But—' He didn't understand. 'Is she having it?'

'Yes. She's in the labour ward now.'

'Well—' Cripes, how long did it take, for goodness' sake? He had no idea. He thought it was just . . . well, he hadn't ever thought what it was like. Was she still having pains like those she had in the car? Had she been having them all night?

'Is she all right?'

'Yes, quite all right.'

He couldn't understand it. The woman rang off. He went back to the room. How could she be quite all right? He wished there were someone he could ask. He wished Rosemary had been there. But she hadn't ever had a baby. God, it was only seven o'clock. Ring up at lunchtime, she had said. That was *hours* away. Whatever was he going to do all that time? He put the kettle on and when it was hot took it into the bathroom so he could shave. The bathroom was freezing, with bits of mould clinging to the damp walls and hairs in the wash-basin. Ruth's one pathetic tin of talcum powder, a Christmas present, sat on the cracked glass shelf, and made him feel bereft. He smelt it, to be reminded of her smell. Whatever was happening to her now? He didn't trust those confused people in the hospital. Perhaps he ought to go and see. But he didn't want to see. He was a coward. He wanted her to have it without bothering him. Woman's work. And thank God for it. He shaved, scowling into the mirror. He had long sideburns and his hair was down to his shoulders again. It grew very fast; he didn't want it any longer, but not much shorter either. It was thick and handsome and reminded him of the Professor who hadn't liked it and who had given him money for haircuts at regular intervals. But there was no joy in remembering the Professor, he knew from past experience; it was all pain in that department. He tried to sheer his mind away, wondering if he was getting too heavy—not fat, because it was all hard muscle. His shoulders, thanks to Liszt and co, could have belonged to a coal-heaver. Who was it who had worked out that playing Rachmaninov's Third required as much effort as moving ten tons of coal?—and that in forty minutes was going some. He had read it somewhere. It felt like it, no argument there. But however hard his muscles he doubted whether he could *run* far, not like in the old soccer school days. Soccer reminded him of the hospital again. Ugh. Driving there with that funny young sports master, Matthews, the one who had stuck up for him . . . He had waited for him in Casualty, taken him home again afterwards with a broken arm and been amazed because the house was empty— 'What time will your mother be home? I can't leave you like this in an empty house—' His mother had come home at midnight, and Matthews had been asleep on the sofa. He needn't have stayed. But he had. Asking him questions. 'Why are you so bloody-minded all the time?' There had been nothing to eat in the house save half a stale sliced loaf and three rashers of bacon. No butter, no milk. Matthews had gone out to the pub and come back with some cheese rolls for him, but he had felt too sick to eat anything. His mother was drunk when she came home. When he had gone back to school, a few days later, Matthews had said to him, 'I know why you're bloody-minded now. I shouldn't have asked.' That had been worse, he remembered, than anything else, Matthews saying that. And yet it had been his way of saying that he would still stick up for him. And Matthews, that time after the swimming gala . . . thinking of that, an idea came.

'I'll go to the swimming-baths.' Sunday morning early, it was the best time. He got dressed and found his trunks and a towel and let himself out. It was warmer out than in, grey and greasy and still raining. Funny how, being alone, you thought about all these things. No one to talk to. He missed Ruth dreadfully. He didn't really feel all there without her. And yet when she was there he often didn't say anything to her for days. He wasn't always very nice to her. It was rough, not having any money, but she never complained. 'God,' he thought, 'I'll work like a maniac and make her some money. We'll have a good time, it'll come right.' He'd win that ruddy competition next week. If he won that, and the finals in Scotland, he would be assured of a dozen recitals—it was part of the prize. Tomorrow he'd ring up the organizers and see if he could get his entry-form changed, not to play the Liszt. He'd do the Schumann Fantasy, and if it wasn't quite ready—well, it might be all the better for not being over-worked. He'd have to get stuck into the Brahms too, for Mick. That was weeks of solid work.

He swam countless lengths of the municipal baths, imagining that he was successful and what sort of a house they'd have, and a car, one each, and a Steinway of his own. It was a good way of killing time, and proved he was still fit enough. On the scales he weighed in at fourteen stone. No more, no less than he had been for years. 'I ought to walk more, that's all.' Get a dog. They could have two dogs, and a great big garden. And a gardener. Somewhere in Hampstead proper. Walk on the Heath. The baths were filling up with paunchy fathers bringing their young. He was dressed, going for a cup of tea. He'd never let himself get paunchy. A girl coming in stared at him, He could tell, from the way she looked, that she was wishing she had been a bit earlier, and seen him undressed, swimming. His instinct told him; he had no conceit. He got his cup of tea and sat where he could see her when she came out of the dressing-rooms. He had worked as a life-guard in the evenings for some months when he had been a student, and had always tried to see what a girl looked like dressed, after he had admired her swimming. It had nearly always been a disappointment. He still looked at girls, in spite of having Ruth. It was just a habit. This one was nothing special. He finished his tea and went out into the rain again.

He could not face going home to the empty, tatty, cold house. He could not work. He walked, not much caring where he was going. He was starving hungry, but daren't go anywhere to eat. There was only Paddy's money to last for the week, if the recital money was to get the baby gear and do the rent. The next recital bonanza was not for another fortnight, when he was playing with Clarissa, and that wouldn't be much. He must ring Mick up and see if he could get him anything else, playing for auditions or singers or something. Or any old music club, even for ten quid. Or he'd have to start giving lessons, God help him. He didn't notice much where he walked, but by opening time a pub loomed up and he decided to have a quick bitter, then go home and telephone again. Or telephone in the pub. He went in and went up to the bar. He was standing there, gazing into space, when a familiar voice brought him back to earth.

'Why, Pat, what are you doing here?'

It was Clarissa, with a smart-looking Guards officer type in tow. Pat came out of his trance, and realized that he was, in fact, quite close to Clarissa's home and that this was her local. He had been there before, in the old Clarissa days. It was full of glass fishermen's-floats and phoney fishing-nets and its clients were smart young executives and upper-class hairies like Clarissa. He hadn't noticed it was familiar, only that it had a telephone in the bar, which was what he wanted.

'Oh, hullo.' He should have asked her what she wanted to drink but was too poverty-stricken, knowing her expensive tastes.

'It's lovely to see you! This is Jeremy, Pat. Pat, Jeremy. Where's Ruth? What are you doing up here all on your own? Are you coming up to practise? I thought you spent all your time practising? Especially with the competition on Wednesday. I see you've entered.'

'Yes.'

'You're joint favourite with James Dupont, according to my information. Masses of entries.'

'How do you know?'

'Daddy's on the executive.'

Cripes, he might have known. 'Who's judging?'

'Oh, some Russian bod, and a French lady virtuoso, and Sir What's-his-name—' She mentioned an eminent conductor—the one Mick had told him to learn the Brahms concerto for. He ought to go home and do some work. Wasting time mooching around!

'Why are you on your own?'

He told her. She was full of female gush and concern.

'Oh, Pat, you poor thing! Why don't you come home and have lunch at our place, and you can ring up from there? Then we can drive over to the hospital this afternoon. You don't want to be on your own—do come! Mummy and Daddy would love to see you again.'

It occurred to Pat that Daddy, if he was on the executive, could probably smooth over his changing his programme for the competition. Also he was very hungry.

'Okay, I wouldn't mind.'

'Jeremy will drop us, won't you, darling? What a good thing we met you! If you're all on your own you can stay at our place, Pat. We could get some work in on the sonata—it's only the week-end after next, you know.'

Her effusiveness, and the thought of her plushy home and the traditional Sunday dinner groaning on the polished mahogany, was too much for Pat's scruples. He allowed himself to be swept back to her place in Jeremy's Mercedes, where Mummy and Daddy Cargill-Smith welcomed him with surprise and beautifully controlled curiosity.

'Why, Patrick!' Mrs. Cargill-Smith's elegant eyebrows shot up in the air. 'Well, fancy . . . and I'd been thinking you were avoiding us.' Her eyes took him all in in one practised swoop, from the scuffed toes of his shoes to the hair still drying from the baths. He gave her a cold stare in return. 'Still the same old Pat! What have you done with that charming girl Ruth?'

'That's the point, Mummy—she is actually at this moment producing *the heir*! Pat, do ring up.' Clarissa pushed him towards the telephone.

'Really? How very exciting . . .' Mrs. Cargill-Smith's voice was dry, with an edge of sarcasm. Pat could see her mind turning it over: out of prison end of June, sudden marriage end of September, birth of child end of March . . . he had seen his own mother at it, and even kindly Mrs. Bates on occasion. Did he think it was all he had married Ruth for, merely to do the right thing? Did she think? . . . And he knew she did. Standing there with the telephone receiver in his hand, he knew she thought that Ruth had caught him, and she was amused, sorry for him. Clarissa thought so too; Clarissa thought Ruth didn't count, that she was just his duty. Clarissa standing there, smiling at him, confident that she was highly desirable, as indeed she undeniably was, if one discounted all past experience. If one took her at face value, on the winning side, when she was generous and amusing and talented and pleased with herself, she was more desirable than anyone he had ever met. Close to her, the warmth of her personality was as positive as the smell of the scent she wore; the invitation in her golden-brown eyes was no figment of his imagination. Fixed to the telephone, while it burred nonsensically in his ear, he was aware of having fallen into a terrible temptation, coming back here to be fed and flattered and reminded what it was like to be comfortable and rich and in a position to claim attention for one's talents . . . It would do him no good to be seduced by the easy path, let alone by Clarissa. And he had a very uncomfortable feeling that that was what Clarissa was about; he knew her too well to mistake her intentions. All these thoughts ran through his head in the time it took for the hospital switchboard to put him through to Maternity; they were interrupted by the now familiar voice answering, 'Maternity. Can I help you?'

'Maternity' never seemed to know what was going on, without making the long journey into the hospital hinterland to inquire.

'You said Mrs. *Ruth* Pennington? Nothing as yet, dear. You're too early.'

'But—' Again, this feeling of complete helplessness. What on earth were they doing? 'It's—I mean—it's all right? She's—she's all right?'

'Yes, as well as can be expected. Ring up this evening and we might have some news for you.'

Might have! 'But—' But what? He didn't know what to ask. The woman had rung off. He appealed to Mrs. Cargill-Smith— after all the old hag had been in the same position as Ruth some twenty years ago, although one could not imagine her losing her mascara over the event.

'Why does it take so long? That's just what they said before— "You're too early." They keep *telling* me to ring and then all I get is, "You're too early." I don't think they know what they're doing—'

'Oh, Pat, don't worry! It's often pretty slow. She's in very good hands. Come and have a drink. We'll take you up there this evening and see what's happening. This is a classic situation, you know—nervous young father waiting for news.' She smiled, put a hand on his shoulder and pushed him gently towards the sitting-room where her husband was already pouring out the pre-luncheon sherry. Cripes, what a creep, what an evil smoothie she was—she had eyes like stones and yet a smile like royalty. Clarissa was sweetness and light beside her mother. The old man was a crisp, autocratic figure who had turned music into a business. He made money out of it; he couldn't play a note of any instru-ment, yet his knowledge was very deep and wide. He always had the effect on Pat of making him feel that his feet were smelling or he had a tidemark round his neck. Seeing him standing there, holding out the sherry and smiling quite amiably, Pat saw what enormous advantages lay in being friends with this family, just as Mick had pointedly reminded him, yet the whole set-up gave him the belly-ache. He knew perfectly well that Mrs. Cargill-Smith's patronage was offered purely on the gounds of his talent: she was laying her money on him to make the grade, and she wanted to be in on the ground floor when he made good. This was her hobby. He supposed it gave her a sense of power; there was no doubt that a lot of aspiring concert-players did in fact go out of their way to be very polite to her. She promoted a good many recitals, mostly for charity, but usually to discerning audiences, and to play for her was a good way of getting one's face known. Mick knew this perfectly well, also how the old boy had the power to promote anyone he favoured with one of the big orchestras—it could well be him, indirectly, that Mick was pushing the Brahms for: no wonder Mick had been so sharp over missed opportunities!

'Well, here's to your heir, Patrick!' Mr. Cargill-Smith lifted his glass. 'Very nice to see you again. Although I was expecting to see you on Wednesday in any case. I shall be listening, although I've no say in the voting.'

'Perhaps we might go along, Clarissa?' his wife put in, 'I'm free after lunch. You're looking tired, Pat. Are you working too hard? Or is it your present state of anxiety? What do you want, both of you—a boy or a girl?'

God, he only wanted Ruth! Clarissa's gold eyes were needling him. Why ever had he come?

'Lunch is served, madam,' said the maid at the door.

That is why he had come, of course. The great polished table, all laid with a mass of glass and silver, and the lovely roast beef breathing on a vast carving dish . . . he needn't tell Ruth. What was happening to her now, in that vague, complacent hospital, down the long white corridors? 'As well as might be expected . . .' What did that mean? As well as might be expected with those awful pains to contend with.

'Isn't it taking a long time?' he asked Mrs. Cargill-Smith. 'If she started last night—?'

'It's quite normal, for a first baby. And she's only a little thing.'

'Does that make it—?' He didn't really feel very hungry. 'Is it worse then?'

'It might be a bit longer. But I'm sure she's being very well looked after. When have you got to ring again?'

'This evening.'

'We'll distract you until then. You can play for us after lunch. It's a long time since we heard you. It will be most interesting to hear how you're progressing.'

'I came out because I didn't feel like doing any work.'

'Ah, well, I think you should sing for your supper, so to speak—play for your dinner—don't you think so, Julian? You'd like to hear him, darling, wouldn't you?' Ice-cold stare and stunning smile. 'You haven't changed a bit, Patrick. You really haven't.' Just as rude as ever, Pat knew she was thinking. He remembered that he wanted to change his piece for the competition. No good saying what he really thought.

'I meant to tell Mick,' Mr. Cargill-Smith said, 'there's an invitation in the office—a film company auditioning for someone to play Chopin. It might suit you, Pat. You might try it.'

'You mean play Chopin's music, or be Chopin?' Clarissa asked.

'I think they have a scene set in a Paris salon, and they want whoever they choose playing in the background—as Chopin. They stipulated the "Winter Wind" study, so I didn't think they'd get very many takers.'

'How far in the background?' Pat asked.

'Behind a pillar, if they choose you,' Clarissa said. 'Chopin was only six stone something.'

'Yes. You'll have to stop eating, Pat. The pay would be pretty good, though. The audition is at the end of April.'

Pat felt himself sinking under the load of his commitments. 'You could spend the whole month working it up, and then be thrown out for not looking like Chopin.'

'True, but all the young men who look like Chopin and can't play the "Winter Wind" study are just as likely to get thrown out too.'

'It's amazing what these make-up people can do these days,' Mrs. Cargill-Smith said.

'Dissolving seven stone or so might prove fatal, of course, but the money's good.' Clarissa, across the table, was giggling into her apple-pie.

'If I were you, I'd give it a try. Two hundred quid.'

Two hundred quid! He felt like work immediately. A few windfalls like that and life would take on a different complexion.

'You'll look lovely,' Clarissa said. 'Shrunk by the make-up department, dressed in knee-breeches and lace ruffles.'

He ignored her. For two hundred quid he'd do it in his underwear.

'More cream, Pat? You needn't start shrinking yet.'

After lunch they sat around in the music-room drinking coffee and liqueurs. Clarissa lay on the floor reading *The News of the World*. Mr. Cargill-Smith suggested that Pat should play some Schumann. 'Can you play "Carnaval"? Get the music, Clarissa. Do you need it?' Pat obliged. Clarissa turned the pages for the bits he wasn't sure of, leaning very close so that he got a faceful of her red hair and couldn't quite be unaware of her white breasts exposed by a low-cut blouse just below his eye-level . . . He played one or two wrong notes and heard her giggle softly. God, she was unscrupulous! He remembered that she always had been. He kicked her, accurately and hard, on the ankle and she sat down abruptly and left him to turn the next page himself. He was only flesh and blood and Clarissa knew him. He began to feel ill-used, very tired, the Schumann difficult to do justice to at the best of times, but the Cargill-Smiths needed to be shown. No good slacking. He was as sycophantic as all the rest of them, playing for a kindly pat on the head from the impresario-man. He shouldn't have come.

'What are you playing on Wednesday?' the great man asked, when he had finished.

This was his chance. This is what he had come for. Not to mention the reason why. . . . 'I think now I'll stand a better chance with the Fantasy . . .' It was worth it, for Cargill-Smith said, 'No great difficulty there, I think. In any case you might not be asked for your preferred piece. I'll see what I can do. What is your programme exactly?'

He told him, and Cargill-Smith asked to hear the Scriabin. Afterwards they went through the violin sonata. The grey afternoon darkened and the lamps were lit on the low tables; a maid brought tea. A blackbird was singing outside the window with the poignant urge of early spring that made Pat feel suicidal and optimistic at the same time, stirred up by his peculiar day in a very uneasy fashion; he didn't know if everything was starting for him with the birth of this child, or merely progressing into a deeper slough of debt, struggle and unremitting work. Walking up and down the deep-piled carpet listening to the blackbird, he ached for Ruth's ordeal. Evening, they had said, ring up in the evening. It was evening now, with cups of tea and the blackbird on the lawn. She might be dead.

'Can I ring up again?' His voice sounded quite desperate, even to himself. Mrs. Cargill-Smith looked up, startled.

'Of course, dear, but—'

He wasn't listening, on his way already.

'No news yet—'

'There *must* be! What are you *doing*? Can I come and see her?' He wanted to be with her quite desperately.

'Yes, well, I suggest you come and wait here, if you're worried. It shouldn't be long, and then you can see her straight away. Not much point before—she wouldn't know you from Father Christmas at the moment. Unless you want to see the baby born. She said you didn't.'

'Oh, heavens, no! I just want to see her.'

'We'll see what we can do then.' She rang off.

'What is it?' Clarissa asked.

'Will you take me to the hospital?'

'Yes, of course. What's happening?'

'Oh, that damned woman—she doesn't tell you a thing! I want to go. She said it shouldn't be long.'

'I'll fetch my coat. Mummy, have you got the keys of the Capri?'

'On the hall table, darling. Do let us know the news afterwards, Patrick. It's terribly thrilling for you. Do let us see you over here again, too. We've missed you.'

He must have played to her satisfaction, at least. He followed Clarissa out to the garage, and watched her shoot the bright yellow car out on to the driveway. He got in. She was a flashy driver; he didn't like driving with her. He sat slumped, staring into the dusk, feeling about ten years older in the space of twenty-four hours. Clarissa was silent, for which he was grateful, and delivered him promptly to the Maternity door.

'Would you like me to come with you?'

'No.'

'Shall I wait?'

'No. I might be ages.' He slammed the door and hurried up the steps. The building reared up into the sky, ablaze with lights against the singular electric blue of the spring dusk, a hive of living and dying in which he had a part whether he wanted it or not. Brisk, kindly nurses. 'This way.' Miles of corridors and stairs and baby-wailing, a sour-faced sister looking him up and down, needling out the patches on his denim knees.

'Mr. Pennington?'

'Yes.'

'You've got a son.'

'Ruth—Ruth's all right? Can I see her?'

'You may see her shortly. She's very tired. Just for a minute. It was a breech birth and she's had a hard time.'

He stared angrily at the disapproving sister. She thought it was all his fault. It *was* all his fault. He hated her.

'You can wait here and Nurse will call you when we're ready.' She walked tartly away. He leaned against the wall, feeling himself quivering. The younger nurse who had brought him up said, 'Don't mind her. She doesn't like fathers with long hair. Do you want to see the baby?'

He didn't particularly but the nurse obviously didn't expect him to say no, and said, 'I'll fetch him.' She went away and came back with a bundle. He tried to feel excited, but he felt numb. It was screaming furiously, and Pat's only emotion was sympathy— all these ruddy women—he could well have opened his mouth and screamed too; he would have felt a lot better for it. It was all red and bolshie, screwed-up, with black hair and squinting, scowling black eyes. 'Give 'em hell, mate, well done,' Pat thought.

'He's like you,' the nurse said, giggling. 'He hasn't been cleaned up yet. Five minutes old.'

It was just a noise, the cause of their trouble, Ruth's pain. He didn't feel like a father.

'What are you going to call him?'

'Ludwig.'

She rocked the baby kindly in her arms. 'Poor little darling. Poor little Ludwig.' She took it away, then came back.

'D'you want a cup of tea? There's one in the pot. Here, you can wait in the office.'

He went in and sat down. She poured him a cup of tea, then

sat at Sister's desk and wrote out 'Ludwig Pennington' on a piece of tape to tie round the baby's wrist. Pat hadn't the energy to say it wasn't true. At least it would distinguish it from John Pennington's six-pound twins.

'When can I see Ruth?'

'In a minute.'

It was nearly an hour before the nurse came back.

'You can see her just for five minutes. Come with me.'

Ruth was parked all by herself in what looked like a laundry room, lying on her back in a high white bed, her face as white as the sheets, her eyes shut. Pat thought she was dead. The nurse gave her shoulder a little shake and said, 'He's here, dear. Your hubby's here.' Ruth's eyes opened. Pat stood staring at her, transfixed. She smiled. Pat felt terrible, almost faint. She looked ghastly.

'*Ruth!*'

He didn't dare touch her, she looked so fragile. And that beastly baby, how it had screamed, all that energy at Ruth's expense, all that bawling rude male health.

'Have you seen him?' He had to strain to hear what she said.

'Yes. He's lovely,' he lied.

'Looks like you.'

'Poor little devil.'

'You—all right? Last night . . .'

'*I'm* all right. It's you—cripes, Ruth, I—I—' He wanted to say that she mustn't die because he couldn't do without her, and she looked so nearly dead, but the nurse didn't seem to be much worried. He felt quite desperate to tell her how important it was that she got better.

'You *must*—Ruth—Ruth, you *are* all right? It's awful without you.'

'Yes,' she whispered. She tried to say something else. He couldn't hear her.

'What? What is it?'

'My parents.'

'What about them?'

'Tell them.'

'Yes, yes, of course I will.'

Her eyes shut. He thought she had died. He touched her, put his hand on her cheek, and it was warm. He could feel her breath. She was breathing.

'Have you finished, Mr. Pennington?' It was the horrible sister.

'Is she all right?'

'Of course she's all right.' She sniffed, as if to add, no thanks to you. 'Very tired. Only to be expected. Come along now, we've work to do.'

He glowered at her, shrugging away. Bossy old bitch. She might know all about how babies arrived, but he doubted if she knew much about how they started.

'When can I see her again?'

'Tomorrow. Seven thirty.'

He went away, back down the endless corridors, in a trance. He felt battered, worse than Ruth. He needed a blood-transfusion. He let himself out into the cool darkness. Above the London roofs the sky was full of stars.

'Hullo. I waited.'

It was Clarissa. He glared at her.

'I'll run you home.'

His legs felt like water, so he nodded and followed her to the car-park. Past caring. What was she after?

'What have you got? A boy or a girl?'

'Boy.'

'Congratulations! How lovely! How's Ruth?'

She didn't really care how Ruth was, he thought. She was thinking it might have been her. Only she was cleverer than Ruth, on the pill. They'd have to think about all that now, not to have another. He couldn't stand another. Ask old boot-face, the sister, for advice. Old boot-face didn't believe they were married at all, from the look in her eyes. Clarissa ran him home and stopped outside the dark house.

He opened the door and she leaned forward and put a hand on his arm.

'May I come in with you?'

He remembered the awful empty room with the tea-mugs in the hearth and his clothes and the bath-towel lying on the floor and the piano waiting for the onslaught of the 'Winter Wind' study on its aristocratic keys. Clarissa was looking earnest and warm and comfortable and homely and incredibly beautiful.

'No,' he said. 'You can't,' and slammed the door.

She waited while he went up the steps and fumbled for the key. He let himself in and shut the door without looking back.

'Oh, heavens, what have I let myself in for? Picking up with her again, getting jobs off her old man, doing the duet in Hemel Hempstead. Don't think about it. It won't happen, only if you allow it to.' Let Ruth's parents know they were granny and grandpa. They weren't on the phone. Ring Ted, he could tell them. His mother-in-law would be over in a flash, organizing them, telling them what to do, cleaning everything madly, scouring the bath and pouring germ-killer down the lavatory pan. He wouldn't tell his own parents until the excitement was over. They didn't want them over as well, the grandparents clashing on their own hearth. They had enough to bear, without that ultimate horror.

Chapter 10

'I don't know how you can bear it! It's enough to drive anyone demented. And heaven knows how it affects the baby!'

'I like it,' Ruth said.

'You must be mad.'

Pat couldn't hear, through the wild storms he was making at the piano, and would only have grinned if he had heard.

'Two hundred pounds,' Ruth said to her mother.

'Day and night! It's enough to turn the brain.'

'You're exaggerating. He's out half the day driving.' Ruth suspected that Pat was using the 'Winter Wind' study as a great cloak to shut himself away from his mother-in-law, a barrier of sound to shelter behind. True, the fiendish piece needed hours of practice, but when her mother pushed the baby out in the pram to do the shopping, Pat would stop and talk and come and sit on the bed. Ruth had to stay in bed for a week.

'I thought you'd died,' Pat said.

'Worried you'd have to cook your own meals.'

'Yes, I was.'

'I wish I hadn't missed the competition on Wednesday. I would have loved to have heard you!'

'Winning.'

'Yes, it's fantastic.'

'Except its only a semi-final. Three good ones still to beat.'

'I don't know why the final has to be in Scotland.'

'No. But I shall get expenses.'

'Enough to buy a white shirt?'

Pat smiled, then frowned. The financial situation was not at all funny. On the morning of the competition he had discovered he had no shirt to wear with his concert suit; the dress-shirt was no good, apart from which it had still been lying on the floor where he had left it the night after the Guildford concert. He had had to borrow one from Wilfred, and Rosemary had painted his heels with Indian ink where they showed through the holes in his black socks. Wilf had produced a tie which he reckoned would get him first prize and he had set off for the ordeal feeling disturbed and in the wrong frame of mind. One look at his fellow competitors in the hall, and the awful memory of his last performance in public, and he had gone to the lavatory to be sick. If he had had to play the Liszt, he thought that he would have packed up and gone home again.

'You should have played the Liszt, all the same,' Ruth had said. 'All that work you've put into learning it, and to be put off by such a little thing.'

'It wasn't a little thing to me.'

'If you'd played it, everything would be straight again. But by not playing it, you've been beaten.'

'You're exaggerating.'

'No. You're exaggerating—thinking the Saturday night thing was such a disgrace, letting it stop you from playing the sonata in the competition.'

'Oh, don't be stupid. I shall play it again soon enough.'

'In public?'

'Of course.'

'You can play it for the final.'

Pat did not reply. Ruth was right, in a way. It had been an admission of failure to change his programme. If he had played the Liszt sonata and still won, the incident would be closed. As it was, he knew he was now very reluctant to play it again in public.

'It's a waste, for no good reason, if you don't play it. You play it beautifully—and it's a terribly impressive piece, you know it is.'

'I can't help how I feel. When it matters very much, it's useless if you don't feel confident when you sit down to start. It's bad enough when you do.'

'Will you play it for the final?'

Pat didn't reply.

He was saved by his mother-in-law reappearing at this point and demanding some money.

'We really can't get by on only two dozen nappies, not without somewhere to dry them—this weather's hopeless, and you've nowhere to air them. You'll really have to get a spin-drier,

Ruth, and one of those electric airers. I don't see how you can possibly manage without.'

'She'll have to manage without,' Pat said shortly.

Mrs. Hollis rounded on him. 'If you'd get out and *earn* something—do some work for a change, instead of sitting there playing that wretched piano all day long, she might have—'

'Mother!' Ruth's voice was appalled.

'I've been doing the housekeeping out of my own money ever since I came here! I'm sure I don't want to starve, even if you're used to it! And cooking in that poky little kitchen with all the greasy washing-up dumped in the sink by those two lay-abouts next door—'

Mrs. Hollis, after three days of living in what were for her completely uncongenial conditions, knew perfectly well that she shouldn't speak to her son-in-law like that, but she was past caring. She disapproved strenuously of her daughter's living arrangements and, having cleaned the whole place out madly 'to make it fit for a baby to be brought up in', done the shopping, the washing, the cooking and everything else that needed to be done non-stop since she arrived, she was past caring about being tactful. She disapproved of the house and all its inmates, and longed to be back home in her clean, orderly box where everything was sane and tidy and as it should be. She was tired and desperate and the piano-playing was driving her mad.

'You can go home,' Pat said shortly. 'We don't need you. I didn't ask you to come.'

'And I suppose *you'll* look after Ruth and do all the baby-washing and the shopping and the cooking!' Mrs. Hollis rounded on him furiously. 'God help them, that's all I can say! You— you can't even pick your own clothes up off the floor and put them away. You can't even wash up your own teacup! You're totally and completely irresponsible—'

'Mother, stop it!' Ruth screamed from the bed, bolt upright and white-faced. 'You don't understand! It's not—'

'I understand your condition, my girl, which is more than he does!' her mother screamed back. 'It's not him I'm bothered with—it's you! If I go home now it's you that will suffer, not him. He won't lift a finger—I know his sort. He might be a genius at the piano but as a help about the house he's a pain in the neck—take, take, take—'

127

'Shut up!' Ruth sobbed. 'Shut up!'

Pat was sitting at the piano, rapidly considering which was the loudest and most violent piece in his repertoire. He started on some Brahms, and his mother-in-law gave a choking shriek and slammed out of the room. In his second-hand pram, the baby started to cry. Ruth wept. The doorbell rang, three rings for them. Pat swore violently, got up and crossed over to the bed.

'Don't cry,' he said to Ruth.

'I'm sorry! I'm sorry for what she said—'

'Well, it's true. But don't cry about it.'

'She—she said—"Do some work"—to *you*! I—' she knew that working on the 'Winter Wind' left him exhausted.

'Too tired to carry a teacup,' he said.

'Oh, *Pat!*'

'She's lucky I have to go out driving. Else I'd do ten hours, like Liszt.'

'Did he?'

'Yes. For years. She doesn't know anything.'

Their doorbell rang again.

'Mop up,' he said. 'We've got visitors. It might be Mick.'

'Give me Ludwig. He's hungry. Oh, I feel so dreary! So hideous. Don't expect me to make polite conversation.'

'You're beautiful. Get under the quilt and snore. He'll take the hint.'

'I've got to feed the noise. Push him over.'

Pat lifted the baby gingerly out of the pram. It never ceased to amaze him, every time he looked at it. Screaming with rage.

'Don't let his head roll about!' Ruth said anxiously.

'It won't fall off.'

'You're supposed to support it. Oh, poor Lud—give him to me!'

The baby was officially called Daniel, but seemed to have got stuck with Ludwig. Pat handed him over and went to answer the door. It was Clarissa.

'Oh, God,' he said, staring at her.

'I've come to make the arrangements for Saturday,' she said. 'The recital at Hemel Hempstead,' she added, to illumine Pat's blankness. 'They want to know what you're going to play for your solo.'

'Come in.'

A loud crashing of washing-up was coming from the small kitchen across the hall.

'How's Ruth?' Clarissa asked. 'If there's anything I can do to help . . . I meant to come down and offer earlier, but I've been so tied up.'

Pat looked at her dubiously. 'There is, as a matter of fact. Go and do the washing-up for my mother-in-law. Smooth her over. Go and show her what nice friends we've got.'

He pushed Clarissa bodily towards the kitchen. He didn't want her bursting in on Ruth without any warning; in fact he didn't want her bursting in at all. But if she wanted to be useful, charming people was the one thing she was quite phenomenal at. She looked surprised and amused, but unruffled.

'Mother-in-law trouble?'

'Yes.'

'My sympathy is all with her.'

'Go and tell her that then.'

He went back into the living-room, ignoring any meaningful looks Clarissa might be sending him under her chestnut eyelashes, cursing his luck. Anyone would think that the A Minor study was quite enough on its own, without weeping wives, irate mothers-in-law and tactless old flames to cope with. It demanded a great deal technically, as well as all the feeling that was being wasted on his domestic problems, and the fire of pure inspiration to boot. For the last item to make itself available, one needed to live a monastic, dedicated, untroubled and beautiful life, from which one could easily lift oneself into the required sphere of communication. At the moment, this last vision seemed to Pat as distant as a Himalayan peak in all its rare and impregnable beauty.

'Who is it?' Ruth asked. She was feeding the baby at her breast, an act that had a markedly pacifying effect on them both. Pat sat heavily on the bed.

'Clarissa.'

Ruth frowned. 'What have you done with her?'

'She's helping your mother.'

'Good heavens.'

'She's come to make the arrangements for Saturday.'

'That recital? If you get paid we could get those nappies.'

He shrugged. Brahms for nappies. 'Yes.' But Beethoven had written his heavenly sonatas and dispatched them with crochety letters to his publishers, complaining about money. Pat knew he was in good company. He went back to the piano.

'Does this practising worry you?' he asked. 'Really?'

'No. I'm used to it. I don't mind it.'

He wondered what he would have done if she had said yes, it did. The piano needed tuning. That was more important than nappies. The man was supposed to be coming tomorrow. The piano had a hard life too. Keeping back the money for the tuner was the reason he hadn't given any to his mother-in-law for food. It wasn't that he had forgotten. The tuner wouldn't do it until he actually got the money; he was wise to Victorian bed-sitters and student pianists. Pat shut his eyes and thought himself into starting on the Chopin study again. He felt very tired. It was like starting on a marathon race after a day's work. If he played it through just once, up to tempo, as well as he could, it took his whole day's strength. How could you begin to explain to anyone as thick as Ruth's mother? It was impossible. He started to play some gentle, soothing Schumann.

'That's nice,' Ruth said.

Feeding Ludwig at her breast and listening to Pat play gentle music was as rounded and restful a way to feel happy as Ruth knew she would ever experience. Even after the fireworks of ten minutes before. She had never dreamed how she would become so possessed by pure animal mother-love; it amazed her. She had instincts she had never guessed at; she was irrational, even hysterical, at times, and then cowlike, entranced, as she was at this moment, steeped in the fantastic content of regarding this astonishing child. By the time Clarissa made her appearance, carrying a tray of tea, she was no longer in a mood to resent her.

'Your mother's bringing poached eggs,' Clarissa said. 'Is there a table?'

Ruth and Pat had always eaten on the floor, but Ruth's mother had imported a table from the room next-door, appropriating it when the 'lay-abouts' were away, and even conjuring up a tablecloth from Ruth knew not where. It was all very civilized. Clarissa admired Ludwig, and Mrs. Hollis came in, obviously much soothed.

'Push it near the bed. I can sit by Ruth.' There were only two chairs. Pat brought his over from the piano and they all sat down.

'Clarissa tells me she's playing in a concert with you on

Saturday,' Mrs. Hollis said to Pat. Ruth suspected an effort to mollify him for what she had said earlier, this polite opening of the conversation. Pat muttered something incomprehensible through a mouthful of toast.

'They rang up to ask what you were playing for your solo,' Clarissa said to Pat.

'Play the Liszt,' Ruth said.

'No. The Schumann Fantasy. Or is it a very thick audience?'

'No. Apparently not. It's the distillation of culture from all Herts., Bucks. and Berks. from what I gather.'

'Why have they asked you then?'

'Because Daddy's on the committee.'

'Oh, God yes, I'd forgotten.'

Clarissa took Pat's rudeness in perfectly good part. Ruth could never guess whether she was so used to it from the past that she just didn't notice, or whether she was very coolly hiding what was surely a justified indignation. She was very good at it, if so. Ruth was full of a nervous suspicion where Clarissa was concerned. She didn't want to think about their day together in Hemel Hempstead.

'Or I can play some Chopin, if they'd prefer it. Or some pretty Schumann. Or a Beethoven sonata.'

'I'll try and sell him the Fantasy. Or why don't you ring him now? I've got his number.'

'Can't afford it.'

'I'll ring him tonight then, and let you know. Write down what you're offering. Mick says you're to be impressive because he's going to try to get you some club bookings for next season on the strength of it. There'll be a lot of music-club people there. It's a conference, and we're just for light relief, with the coffee.'

'If there are people worth impressing, I'll play the Fantasy.'

'Very well. Will you go through the sonata again after tea?'

'If you like.'

'There's something else I wanted to ask you. I've been talking it over with Daddy.'

Pat gave her a discouraging scowl and reached for another piece of toast. 'What's that?'

'I wondered if you'd give me piano lessons?'

'I don't teach.'

'Why not?'

Pat stared at her crossly. 'I've got enough to do.'

'I would have thought it a far less wearing way of making money than driving that taxi. You know I've been going to old Zippy-Thumbs? Do you know what I pay him?'

She mentioned a most impressive sum.

'But he's a renowned teacher,' Pat pointed out. 'He's got a waiting-list. He's like God.'

'Well, he bores me to tears. I said I wanted to give up, and Daddy said why didn't I try somebody else. Somebody with a completely different approach. He said ask you.'

'*He* said? Daddy said? He didn't say he'd pay me the same money?'

'Yes.'

Pat looked at Clarissa with scathing disbelief. 'Is your daddy a registered charity?'

Clarissa smiled. 'No.'

'Is there a catch in this?'

'No.'

'I don't believe you. You know I can't teach?'

'Do *you* know you can't teach? You might learn, if you try. You've never tried, have you?'

Pat shrugged. 'I can't—communicate, I suppose is the word—'

'In words, perhaps. But in music—surely that's what you can do superbly?'

'But you can't tell someone else how to do it. *I* can't. The best teachers very often aren't public performers at all. You know that. I suppose I could teach how to play notes.'

'Why don't you try? It's an opportunity you ought to take. Practise on me. If you *are* useless, I'll soon give up. And if you find you aren't, think how much easier life would be. You could take pupils instead of driving. It would pay as well.'

'At the rates your daddy pays it might. I don't know how many other people would think me worth it. Precious few.'

'But you don't know, do you? Unless you try.'

'You could certainly do with some extra money,' Mrs. Hollis put in pointedly.

Clarissa smiled at her sweetly, and Ruth saw Pat retract, almost like a tortoise, closing up. Ruth was wise enough not to say a word. She could not trust herself.

Clarissa said, 'Well, think about it. It's a perfectly genuine offer, and it would suit me down to the ground. Twice a week here. Save me trailing all the way over to Chelsea. Can we go through the sonata?'

Pat looked stunned, manoeuvered, frowning anxiously.

'Just once,' Clarissa said. 'I'd feel happier.'

'Mmm.' Pat looked at Ruth. She didn't say anything.

'Will you turn over for me?' he said to Ruth.

'If you want.'

Ruth reached for her dressing-gown and took Ludwig over to the piano with her. Pat brought the two chairs over.

'You can't do it with him.'

'Of course I can.'

Mrs. Hollis started banging the plates together with a lot of noise, her lips pursed together. Clarissa said, 'Let me help you carry them out,' and put her violin down and went to help. When she had disappeared briefly into the kitchen, Ruth said to Pat, 'Are you going to?' and Pat replied, 'She's mad. And so's Daddy.' It wasn't an answer. Ruth opened the Brahms music on the rack and sat waiting, holding the baby on her lap. He was asleep, frowning just like his father. Ruth looked out of the window beyond the faded velour curtain and saw the scraggy daffodils flowering at the foot of the laburnum and a thrush pecking about in the damp spring earth. There were leaves on the trees and the sun-shot speck of an air-liner high in the fading sky, very pure and distant. Ruth could sense all sorts of things stirring, looking at the garden, cradling the baby, waiting for Clarissa. It was that sort of moment when one had an intimation of the whole of life lying in wait, inscrutable, full of tricks and surprises and ecstasies: Ruth would not let her thoughts take charge, only fix her eyes on the music, the 'Allegro amabile' and feel the atmosphere, hold it in her mind, feel herself absorbing it, like a sponge, thinking nothing. She felt quite weak, not through anything post-natal, but through her possessive love of Pat.

'Are we ready then?'

Clarissa was back, standing in her boastful violinist's stance, head up and back, arm outstretched.

'Pat?'

Ruth looked up at her warily. It was the way she looked at Pat, warm, intimate, as if she was sharing with him all the memories of what happened long before she, Ruth, had come on the scene. Ruth dreaded Saturday, their going to Hemel Hempstead together. It wasn't that she didn't trust Pat, but it was hard to imagine that he was completely immune to Clarissa's scheming. And Ruth felt sure that the lesson idea was pure scheming. To sit at the piano with Pat as close to her as she was to Pat now; their thighs were touching . . . Pat would lean forward and put his hands on the keys by Clarissa's, and his face would be full of her mass of red hair . . . Ruth turned the page for him. She wanted to put her head on his shoulder while he played. She loved sitting by him while he played, watching his incredible hands, sensing the power of his concentration which was total and which sometimes almost frightened her. In his more taxing pieces, like the Schumann Fantasy, he finished with his mind exhausted. It was the only way she could think of to describe it. He didn't seem to be there at all for some minutes afterwards. If only her mother could appreciate a small part of the peculiar strains he endured, she wouldn't go on about electric airers. But nobody could know, who did not live with it. She had had no idea before. She didn't, even now, really understand quite how Pat worked, what drove him. It wasn't just for buying nappies, because he had been like it when she first met him. She wasn't sure if he knew himself.

Near the end of the Brahms sonata the doorbell rang again, three times for them. Nobody bothered. When the sonata was finished, Mrs. Hollis came in looking cross and said, 'There's a visitor for you. He says he's called John Bates.'

Pat said, 'God, did you say *Bates*?'

He got up from the piano and leapt across the room with rare animation. Ruth, having heard of Bates through hearsay, looked up curiously. She remembered the photograph that Mrs. Bates had shown her—a photograph that had been in the *Radio Times*—of a thin, bearded folk-singer; raising her eyes, she saw him, dressed in an old fur coat, with a bulging bead-embroidered satchel-bag in one hand and a guitar in the other, nervously expectant, smiling.

'Bates, you old fool! Fancy you turning up here. How did you find us? Where've you been all this while? Come in, don't stand there.'

Pat dragged him into the room. Bates looked round, blinking.

'This is Ruth,' Pat said, dragging him towards her. 'I'm married to her. This is Clarissa. This is my mother-in-law. Bates,' he added to them all. 'This is Bates.'

'And who is Bates?' Clarissa asked.

'We were at school together,' Pat said. 'He sings.'

'Sings what?'

'Oh, he'll show you, won't you, Bates? Have some tea. Are you hungry? Have you eaten?'

'There are no eggs left,' Mrs. Hollis said coldly.

'Cup of tea then?' Pat said. 'You'd like a cup of tea. Take your coat off. You can stay, can't you? You're not dashing off. How did you know where we are?'

'My mother's got your address.'

'Go and get him a cup of tea,' Pat said to Clarissa.

'Is this yours then?' Bates asked, looking at Ludwig. He gave Ruth a shy smile. He had a white, bony face underneath his beard, and dark tangled hair down to his shoulders. He moved in a clumsy apologetic way, as if unsure of his welcome; his eyes were dark and anxious, nervous.

'Yes, he is.' He answered his own question. 'He's just like you, Penn. How funny, you—' He grinned. 'He's lovely,' he added to Ruth politely.

'Take your coat off. Sit down,' Pat ordered.

Ruth went back to bed with Ludwig, and lay with the baby asleep beside her, while Pat and Bates talked, sitting on the hearthrug in front of the fire. Clarissa brought some more tea and put the lamps on and sat in the best chair, and Mrs. Hollis came and sat on Ruth's bed with her knitting. Ruth lay propped on one elbow, looking at Ludwig. He was scowling just like Pat, his fists clenched up over his face. He had an aggressive underlip, and a lot of curly black hair.

'Ron called on Ted last week, did I tell you?' Mrs. Hollis said to Ruth. 'He's set up his own, you know, car-bodies—respraying, that sort of thing. I think he wants Ted to join him.'

'Good idea,' Ruth said.

'Ron's got a nice girl he's going steady with. I think he'll marry her, but no hurry. He's not a one for hurrying anything, not Ron.'

'No.' She had liked Ron. 'What's Peter doing?'

'Peter McNair? He's gone to work for a trainer in Berkshire somewhere. National Hunt—he wants to be a jockey. He's too heavy for flat-racing. He always asks after you when he's home.'

The horses had got him. She had always guessed they would. He was a beautiful rider, better than any of the others. She might have gone out with him, if she hadn't met Pat. She might have become the wife of a National Hunt jockey. As bad—worse—than being married to a concert pianist. Funny how the only two boys she had ever liked had such spectacular careers. She had known Peter better than anyone, almost better than she knew Pat. He was easier to know than Pat. Pat and John Bates were reminiscing about what they had done at school.

'. . . the time we took those bits left over from dissecting in the biology lab down to the incinerator, and Maxwell got that sheep's eye, with all the bits and tubes hanging off it, and it was the day the inspectors were there—'

'And he put it in his stew at dinner, and left it on the side of the plate, and the inspector came along—'

'And he didn't say anything, just looked, and Maxwell was chatting away as if it was all quite normal—'

'And that concert where I had to turn the pages for you, and I was dead drunk—'

'And you kept turning them three at a time until all the music fell to bits and I didn't know what I was playing, and that old geezer singing away, deaf as a post.'

'I had to get drunk to sing, do you remember? It still helps, I must say.'

'I'll get you some beer. Wilf's probably got some upstairs. Do you still sing the "Butcher Boy"?'

'Sometimes. Do you still play the harmonica?'

'I've got it somewhere. I haven't for years. Have you seen it around, Ruth?'

'Seen what?'

'My harmonica?'

'It's in your drawer with your socks and pants and things.'

'God help us,' Clarissa said.

'He's jolly good,' Bates said to her. 'He got me started.'

'Started on what? What do you do exactly? Where do you sing?'

'Folk clubs mostly. There's a few of us. I've got a bloke plays banjo with me. I play the guitar but only just enough to sing to. I'm not much good with instruments. Penn—Pat—ought to join us. We could do with a harmonica.'

'Do you make a lot of money?' Clarissa asked.

'Enough for all I want. We made a record and that's made us a bit, and a few stints on the BBC, and last summer we played holiday resorts, and we made a lot doing that. I've never been short of cash.'

'Hmm.' Pat, having found his harmonica, blew an exploratory run. 'Perhaps I ought to join you, in that case. Go and see if Wilf's got any beer,' he said to Clarissa. 'Tell him to bring his blowpipe down. He can play some nice tunes.'

Ruth looked at her mother, and saw that she was concentrating on her knitting, all screwed up with disapproval. Ruth knew she couldn't do anything to make it any better for her, and curled up in the bed, cradling Ludwig. Wilf was out but Rosemary came down with a gallon can of beer and Clarissa got some tea-mugs and set them all out in the hearth.

'Beer, Mrs. Hollis?' she asked politely.

'No, thank you very much.'

There wasn't anywhere else for her to go, unless she sat out in the kitchen. Bates was shedding his fur coat, revealing an incredibly thin body in a curious T-shirt with embroidered lions all over it and faded pink trousers. He got his guitar out of his case.

'How many pints do you need to sing the "Butcher Boy"?' Pat asked him.

'I work up to it,' Bates said. 'Start with something happy.'

'You never used to sing anything happy at all. All deaths, drownings, murder and suicide.'

'I've mellowed,' Bates said. 'Is that the same old harmonica? What key's it in? G, wasn't it?'

'Yes.'

He started to play something. Ruth wasn't very up on folk, although she recognized the tunes. She had never heard Pat play the harmonica, and was amazed to see him so animated after his hard day at the piano; it was as if Bates had tapped a fresh source of energy—or was it that this particular music was in fact easy enough to be a release, a relaxation? They certainly weren't taking it very seriously, larking about and breaking in on each other. Rosemary and Clarissa were talking. Ruth curled herself round Ludwig and lay admiring him, half listening, half dreaming, trying not to think about Saturday and Pat linked in that intense, musical effort with Clarissa, in the marriage of their two instruments. She supposed she was being a bit ridiculous about it, but she knew Clarissa wanted Pat. It wasn't her own jealousy that made her think it. She wondered if her mother had noticed anything. She was very astute about things like that. She would ask her afterwards 'Do you think Clarissa is in love with Pat?' She hadn't known Pat could play the harmonica; it was quite different, his playing the strange, sad accompaniment to Bates' voice, decorating the plain melody with a descant high above it; it gave Ruth a feeling of quite piercing nostalgia, unexpected and wrenching. Bates' voice was very unusual, a clear, high tenor with an in-built sadness. In the jolly songs it was competent and unremarkable, but in the softer, quieter songs it was moving in a way that surprised her. It had a sad, lonely quality of its own.

'I told you he was good, didn't I?' Pat said, as if he was responsible. 'Have another beer, Bates.'

'You ought to play harmonica with us, Penn,' Bates said. 'We could just do with you. I've never had a good harmonica since you used to do it with me. I mean, I've met them, but they were always tied up in another group. Some songs need a harmonica, or a penny whistle—it suits them.'

'Funny, I can remember all your songs, all the words and everything,' Pat said. 'We must have belted them out a few times, I suppose. Do you still do "Lowlands Away"? "Down by the Royal Albion"?'

They were off again. Clarissa was watching Pat. Ruth tried to read her eyes. She looked very happy, tender—but it could have been the music.

'How odd,' she said. 'Your being friends together at school. And both so talented.'

'I like your friend,' Bates said to Pat. He looked at Ruth and gave her a sympathetic smile. Ruth wondered if he had noticed the way Clarissa looked at Pat. Then she wondered if she was getting a fixation about it. Bates had a very sensitive face, nervous, sad—almost too gentle for a man. By comparison Pat didn't look like any sort of an artist at all, more like a soccer player.

'She says all the right things,' Pat said, not at all kindly. Clarissa only smiled. She was as hard as nails, Ruth thought.

'It's a coincidence, all the same,' Clarissa said. 'You could go to a hundred schools and not find two talents as good. And you both in the same form in the same school.'

'I'd be working on the farm with my dad if it hadn't been for your coincidence,' Bates said. 'Penn—Pat forced me. Bloody cruel he was.'

'Yeh, well, you needed it. You were so wet. Admit it. You only sang in public when you were blind drunk. And then we couldn't stop you.'

'That concert—and you poured that brandy down me. I nearly passed out, and you only trying to impress that girl—what was she called? She sang folk at that club.'

'Sylvia. I went home with her. And her mother made me play the flaming piano all night, and I got mad and went on and on, and they all went to bed, and I went on playing—her old man fast asleep in the armchair.'

'That's what started you off with that Professor bloke. So what are you beefing about?'

'Why did it?' Clarissa asked. 'You mean Hampton?'

'Yes. He was trying to sleep in the flat above. He heard me. Couldn't help it.'

They started on another song. Ruth wished she knew Pat as well as Bates did, since he was eleven. Pat hardly ever spoke about past things, only present and future. She had known that he had always been in trouble at school and with the police, been expelled from school, escaped Borstal by the skin of his teeth, and the Professor's timely intervention—but he had never told her any details. Bates had been in nearly everything with him, including the police-station. Bates could no doubt elucidate on the reasons for Pat's long history of argument with authority, and his hatred of the police which had so unnerved her when she first met him and which, though mellowed, was still apparent enough to unnerve her now when she thought about it.

Wilfred came home and heard the row, and brought his flute in. Rosemary went for some more beer and some chips. Clarissa made coffee in the hearth, and walked up and down with Ludwig when he awoke and cried. Ruth watched her with a confusion of feelings.

'Bring him to me,' Pat said. 'We'll play him a lullaby. Lullaby, Bates. Instant hush. Lud, are you listening?'

They played a sad, peculiar love-song, and Lud tried to focus his eyes on the gleam of firelight on Pat's harmonica, flatteringly silent in Clarissa's arms. Ruth wanted him back. Her mother said to her, resigned, 'Does this go on all night?'

'Very likely,' Ruth said.

'There,' Pat said when they had finished. 'You can tell he's musical. He appreciates it. He wants some more, Bates. How about the "Butcher Boy"? You've had enough to drink.'

He started to play again and Clarissa sat with the baby, watching him. The song was about a girl's suicide, for getting herself with child, and Bates sung it with such compassion that Ruth felt herself stricken, sitting there, almost to tears. Her similar predicament, made so much less awful by the contemporary outlook, made her feel the girl's agony, so extraordinarily communicated by Bates, as a chillingly personal grief. Whether anyone else felt it or not she didn't know, but there was a long silence at the end of the song which she felt obliged to break by a great clatter with her coffee cup, to cover up her emotional embarrassment. Bates sent her a kind glance, smiling.

'Give me Lud,' Ruth whispered to Clarissa, and took him back in her arms with a great surge of her hysterical post-natal dottiness, that no doubt the doctors had a long name for, so that she had to hide her face in his woolly middle to cover up.

'Good, isn't he?' Pat said to her.

She nodded.

'I'd forgotten,' Bates said to Pat. 'What you did to that tune with the harmonica. It's far better than guitar accompaniment. If you were in with us I would sing that more often. Do you want a job?'

'That's the second you've been offered tonight,' Clarissa said.

'Yeh, I'm popular. I've got too big a job already, trying to play the bloody piano.'

'What's that thing you drove the whole school potty with, for that competition? Something by Mendelssohn?'

'Opus 14.'

'Something and something capriccioso. Play it. Go on, for old times' sake. I liked that.'

'If I can find the music.' Pat went to scrounge through the piles under the piano, and came up with a particularly dog-eared piece. He put it on the rack and started to play. Clarissa got up to go and turn over for him, but Bates politely insisted on doing the job, and when the piece was finished he gave a demonstration of how he had turned the pages for Pat the day he was drunk, for the song 'Cherry Ripe', which put everyone into a state of helpless laughter, except Ruth's mother.

'I want to go to bed,' she hissed at Ruth.

'Get in with me,' Ruth said. 'Pat can sleep in the camp-bed.'

'Don't be so ridiculous! I'm not going to bed in public. Give me Lud, and let me get him ready for the night, then I'll go and find a hotel somewhere.'

To Ruth's intense relief, by the time Lud was washed and changed and fed for the last time, the party had broken up. Bates was offered a bed on Wilf's floor; Clarissa made her parting arrangements with Pat and the upstairs trio departed. Pat then went upstairs with Wilf and Bates to give his mother-in-law a chance to get into bed, and stayed talking another hour; by the time he came down again Mrs. Hollis was fast asleep.

'Fancy old Bates turning up,' he said to Ruth, scrambling out of his clothes. 'That was nice. Are you still awake?'

'Yes.'

He put out the light on the piano and slid into bed beside her. 'He's doing well, isn't he? You'd never have guessed—if you'd known him earlier—you'd never have guessed he would ever do anything at all.' A long pause. 'Better than me.'

'Moneywise. But not for long. You're a better long-term bet.'

'Have you told your mother that?'

'She'll find out.'

Back to money again. The proposition Clarissa had put forward lay heavily in the ensuing silence. Ruth waited for Pat to say something, but he was silent, lying on his back with his hands behind his head, staring at the ceiling. Eventually she had to ask.

'Are you going to teach Clarissa?'

'It's five quid a time.'

'She's after you.'

He didn't say anything.

'It's not my imagination,' Ruth said. 'At least, I don't think it is.'

'If we do it here, you could sit in on it. You know, knitting or something,' he said. 'If it worries you.'

'Hmm.' He was treating her like a child. It annoyed her. But justified, she supposed.

'I thought you said you couldn't teach?'

'For that money I will try. We need the money. Ask your mother.'

'Don't be horrible. I'm jealous.'

'It's purely work.' His voice sounded angry. 'Holy cow, you don't think I *want* to do it, do you? The prospect's bad enough without you getting temperamental! What else is there? If I win that competition, things might start looking up, and there's the Chopin audition. They're both in May—two big chances. And there's a recital with Alfred and co in June. After that—what? Damn all. No music-club work through the summer, and the only thing Mick thinks he might get me before next winter is the Brahms concerto, which isn't exactly a walk-over and will take all my practice time and more right up until the day. Some prospect! Clarissa's lessons will be a godsend, if I can do it.'

Ruth didn't reply. There was no answer. They lay side by side in the darkness in silence.

Eventually Pat said, 'If I work up the Brahms and it seems like a possibility, I might start working for Moscow. I'll talk to Mick about it.'

'Moscow?'

'The competition. The biggest of the lot. It's the year after next. You only have to raise your fare there. The Russians pay everything else.'

'God,' Ruth thought, and she was fed up with the thought of his going to Scotland . . . She buried her face against him, agonized. Proper pianists travelled all over the world, all the time. Sometimes she thought she didn't want him to succeed.

'Play the harmonica with Bates,' she whispered.

'It would pay me better.'

'No, I'm only joking. Go to Moscow. I shall be able to go out to work soon.'

He didn't say anything.

Chapter 11

In actual fact, although he wouldn't admit it to Ruth, Pat suspected Clarissa's motives himself, and was nervous of being alone with her. He knew her pretty well; he knew she was very experienced at getting her own way and he wasn't too sure of his own strength of character, given certain conditions. It was nothing to do with not loving Ruth, which he now knew very well that he did; it was only to do with his own temperament, which he had never pretended to Ruth was anything that it wasn't, and which he had no great opinion of himself. There were times in the past when he had behaved with great irresponsibility and he had no reason to be sure that anything had changed. They might have, but, until faced with a sufficiently taxing situation, how could he tell? And he had a feeling that Clarissa might tax him, given the chance.

Going to Hemel Hempstead with her in her yellow Capri, he sat beside her in total silence. This was through no wish to repulse her, but merely because of the usual pre-concert absorption in what he was going to play, which came across to uninvolved people as a condition of irritable gloom. But as Clarissa too was involved, and in much the same state herself, the silence was reciprocal and without tension. They arrived at the school where the conference was being held an hour before they were due to play, while the conference was still in session, and one of the women preparing tea showed them the hall where they were to play, and the staff-room where they could change. Clarissa was able to practise, but Pat wasn't, as the hall was full of the conference. He lay stretched out in one of the staff-room chairs, feeling sick and cold and utterly miserable, oblivious of Clarissa's fiddling.

'Just like old times,' Clarissa said, when she had finished. 'You look like death.'

'Thank you.'

'They're having tea. I think it's time we changed.'

Pat had decided that six o'clock, the time of the concert, was too early to be deigned evening and to wear evening dress, but Clarissa had insisted on wearing a long dress, so he had been obliged to match her. This made him hate her bitterly. She had a dress of dark green-blue silk which showed off her creamy skin and chestnut hair to perfection; it was cut low enough to provoke Pat to remark, 'You'd better be careful when you bow.'

'I've practised,' she said. 'It's quite all right.'

They went downstairs and on to the platform at the required moment. There was a slight hiatus while someone asked for a volunteer to turn the pages for Pat, and he sat scowling at his music, desperate to start, while Clarissa tuned her violin with a great show of hair-tossing and furrowed concentration, which brought all their past performances back to him in an unnerving flash of memory, just when he least wanted to be distracted. An old girl of about eighty-five perched herself on the chair beside him and said, 'I'm ready, dear, when you want.' He wished suddenly, with a positive surge of longing, that it was Bates—sober. He lifted his hands off his knees and glanced at Clarissa, the intense, expectant silence of the hall engulfing him with the familiar panic to get moving, to galvanize the petrified fingers. Once away, things improved. It was never any different, time after time, the misery beforehand.

Clarissa stunned them with her visual performance, if not the musical one, only missing out three bars in the first movement and adding a few in the second. Her timing was far from impeccable, but Pat was grateful that they finished each movement at the same time. The Schumann, by comparison, held only known complexities. The piano was quite nice. Pat gathered his concentration fiercely. Failing in the Liszt had left its mark; he had not been aware of it till now. It was a spur of the most painful proportion, goading him to superb effort. It was not until he had finished that the enormity of the effort made itself felt; he could scarcely get up off the piano stool. The applause was more an affliction than gratification. He bowed, holding on to the piano and feeling the sweat running down his back between his shoulder-blades. He did not want to talk to anyone. He was stirred up, in a state unknown to anyone who had not done the same thing themselves, not quite sane. Clarissa knew. He wanted to lie down somewhere, in a quiet, dark place, but there were people everywhere, all wanting to talk, and when Clarissa said suddenly, 'Do you want to go?' he knew that he did. The place was unbearable. They gathered up their things and went out to the car, not stopping to change. Clarissa drove, turning the heater on, and the mechanical soft purring of the engine and the smooth road was a comfort, the womb feeling of the insulated travelling box, sealed from all outside pressures. Pat curled up in the front seat, resting his head against Clarissa's shoulder. She did not say anything, and he dozed, quite spent.

It was a warm spring Saturday and the traffic was heavy. About half-way Clarissa pulled into a lay-by and said to Pat, 'Will you drive? I've got a headache.'

He came to, feeling a lot better, and they changed places.

'I'm sorry it's not the Rolls you're used to,' she said.

He smiled. He liked driving, finding it restful after piano-playing.

'Do you feel better?' Clarissa asked.

'Yes.'

'You played beautifully. You are very good, you know.'

'I don't know. I wish I did.'

'Daddy says you are.'

'Good for Daddy.'

She pulled her legs up, curling herself round so that her head rested on his shoulder. As he in his exhausted state had used her in exactly the same way a short time before, he could not find any cause for complaint, but he felt himself instinctively retracting. She moved her head about, finding the most comfortable position, which proved to be with her eyelashes brushing his ear in a fairly suspicious fashion. He didn't say anything, concentrating on the driving. She rested there in silence for some time. He could not help being very conscious of the warmth of her body against him, and the shape of her thighs under the silk of her skirt pulled tight by the way she was sitting. Her hand fell on to his knee in a very easy, natural fashion, but she still didn't say anything. He concentrated on the road, which needed it, but it could not be said that his mind was wholly on his driving. This was the very situation he had wanted to avoid.

'You look very worried,' she said, slightly taunting. Her eyelashes moved up and her eyes were looking at his, distractingly close.

'I thought you were tired,' he said abruptly.

She smiled.

'Relax,' she said. 'You're over it now. You scowl too much. You've got lines where you scowl. You'll be a hideous old man if you go on taking everything too seriously.'

'It won't worry you.'

'Ruth won't like it.'

He would not be tempted to discuss Ruth. He moved his knee away, but had to move it back almost immediately to change gear. Clarissa shifted slightly, and brought her other arm up across the seat back behind his neck. She did not touch him, but he was aware of it there, waiting its chance. He was furious. He pulled out to overtake a week-end car in front, but had to nip back in face of an oncoming lorry.

'Lay off,' he said. 'I can't drive with you breathing down my neck.'

'I told you, relax. You're exaggerating—I'm not breathing down your neck. I'm soothing you. You'll drive better if you're soothed. It's a scientific fact. You have a terribly bad temper, you know, Pat. You always had. I think you are mistaking my intentions, flattering yourself.'

He was pretty sure he wasn't. Clarissa's other hand was touching his hair, caressing it.

'I've always been very fond of you, Pat.'

If he did relax, he supposed he could enjoy it. He had to stop at some traffic lights, and the man alone in the car alongside sent him a glance that was quite clearly envious. It was true that he had a bad temper. He found Clarissa extraordinarily unnerving, which was a sign of something; he was very worried. He tried to put it right.

'Look, I'm quite fond of you too, but I'm not free to mess about any longer. I'm not interested. I don't want you to get any ideas.'

'It's you that has the ideas. I haven't any at all. I've told you, you flatter yourself. I just want you to stop worrying.'

'God, woman!' he thought. He shook himself free of her, but could not move far enough away to make it effective. He decided to drive into the next café or lay-by and get out; the road was too busy to stop by the kerb. But no sanctuary was forthcoming. He put his foot down and overtook three cars in front of him. Clarissa laughed, and kissed his neck, just under his ear.

'I love you when you're angry,' she said.

There was no defence at all. She had her hand in his hair, twisting it round her fingers. He only had to glance at her, to see the way her eyes were looking, and the way her white throat and chin were lifted up, her mouth mocking him, for all the old memories of her to come hitting at him—all the good memories, just to be perverse, not the quarrels and the bitchiness and remembering her eyes like stones with hate, but the early days when it was all new and fantastic and laughing and magical, which he had quite forgotten and buried and never even *wanted* to remember. It was so bloody unfair. He knocked her hand away angrily and she laughed. He put his foot down and overtook another car, saw a café forefront open up suddenly on his left, and zoomed in across the overtaken car to get into it. Another car was coming out. He heard the blare of the overtaken car's horn, wildly indignant, and missed the oncoming car by swerving on to a proudly mown strip of lawn and ploughing through a rose-bed. The car he had just missed was a police-car. Clarissa was laughing her head off.

Pat switched off the engine and saw the two policemen get out of the car and start walking towards him. Clarissa stopped laughing and looked at him.

'Pat, don't—'

He could feel it all mustering inside, as if he had been saving it up for all the past months—the fantastic indignation with his lot, the *injustice* of it, the great swelling rage with Clarissa, baiting him off his so carefully, painfully built holy path, and those bloody policemen sitting there waiting for him, as if they *knew*—

One of the policemen opened the door and stood looking down at him. Clarissa put her hand on his arm, not caressingly at all.

'Pat, don't!' she said very sharply.

But he couldn't help it.

'Because of Ruth,' Clarissa said. 'Ruth!' She almost bawled it in his ear.

'Get out,' said the policeman. 'Stand up.'

He got out. The policeman looked him up and down.

'Drinking *before* the party isn't wise. Come over to our car and oblige us by blowing into our breathalyzer.'

Pat stayed where he was, holding on to the door-handle. He needed to, to keep his hands down, to stop them doing what they wanted to with such passion that it was almost beyond his power to control them. He was shaking like a leaf. Clarissa got out and ran round and put her hand on his arm again.

'He's not well,' she said to the policeman. 'He hasn't been drinking.'

'We'll test him all the same.' The policeman gave her a hostile look. 'Step along,' he said to Pat. 'We haven't all night.'

Pat took his hands off the door-handle. Clarissa took one and held it tightly. Pat was glad of it. He remembered Ruth taking those shuddering breaths the night in the Rolls when the baby was coming, and he found he was doing the same. Only it was better. It was working. If only that cold-fish, pea-brained, stinking bastard of a policeman was civil to him, he might make it. He walked over to the police-car, and the two policemen fiddled about with their stupid apparatus. Pat was pretty sure that one pint of Wilf's beer last Wednesday, the last drink he had had, wouldn't register, and was proved right. The policemen were obviously surprised.

'Let's have a look at your licence.'

It was in his jeans pocket in the back of the car. They went back to the car and Clarissa got it out. Pat dared not open his mouth to speak, afraid of what might come out. One of the policemen copied all the particulars down into his notebook.

'It's my car,' Clarissa said. The policeman stared at her and she batted her eyelashes at him and smiled. 'It was all my fault,' she said. 'We were having a row. I started it. He told me to pack it in while he was driving, but I didn't and he lost his temper and told me I could damned well walk, and that's why he came in here.' She smiled again.

'Hmm,' said the policeman. He was a young man, and Clarissa's face was all warmth and admiration and innocence, held up to him with the expression in the eyes that Pat knew only too well.

'He's very tired—he's been playing in a recital, for the National Society of Music Groups. Schumann, Opus 17. Do you know anything about music? It's a very taxing piece. It was all my fault—I should have known better than to carry on at him.'

'You were quarrelling? About his driving, no doubt.'

'About his wife.'

'Hmm.' The policeman made a doodle on the edge of the pad, and looked carefully at Pat.

'You're a professional musician?'

'Yes.'

'My father will be along very soon,' Clarissa said. 'He drives a Silver Ghost—you ought to be able to spot him quite easily. He'll vouch for Pat. He's very reliable. He's on the board of the—' She reeled off a whole list of weighty establishment interests. 'Julian Cargill-Smith, O.B.E. You can check up. He was presiding at this conference where Pat was playing.'

The policeman wilted visibly.

'I've got a very bad temper,' Clarissa said. 'He'll vouch for that too. Enough to make anyone drive through a rose-bed when I'm on form.' She obligingly tendered up her address, which was as impressive as her father's directorships.

The policeman wrote it down and Clarissa smiled and spelt the name of the house for him, and the policeman smiled back and said, 'I suggest you drive the rest of the way, miss, and no quarrelling.'

'All right. I promise.'

They got back into the car, and Clarissa reversed out of the rose-bed and drove out of the forecourt with a cheeky pip on the horn. Pat sat slumped in the passenger seat, trembling. His past police grillings had come up out of his subconsciousness with the same uncanny vividness as his Pentonville dream a couple of weeks back. All the things he most wanted to forget, even his old relationship with Clarissa, shifted through his brain-box with an appalling reality, all the things he thought he had overcome and buried. And the near-mania he had just experienced, faced with a fresh encounter with the law, had left his whole physical body feeling shocked, as if an electric current had gone through it. The agonizing longing to explode, choked back with such phenomenal difficulty, felt as if it had detonated inside him instead.

'I think we could do with a drink—I don't know about their thinking we'd had one,' Clarissa remarked. She now looked shaken herself.

'For God's sake, you don't want to park this car outside a pub now.'

'A bit farther into London then—I'm shaking like a leaf. It was you—I thought—I thought you were—going to get yourself put back inside again—'

He couldn't bring himself to talk about it. He felt shivering cold and sick and as if he wanted to black out, sleep for ever. He put the heater on full blast, and dozed, but the dreams kept spiking him; the half-consciousness was like lying on the edge of a nightmare. He realized he was suffering from nerves, like a neurotic housewife. He longed for a black, drugged unconsciousness.

'Are you all right?'

Clarissa had parked outside his house, and was peering at him anxiously.

'Shall I come in with you?'

'Heavens, no.' He remembered Ruth's taut jealousy, his cow of a mother-in-law with her tight, disapproving mouth . . .

He moved himself cautiously, and climbed out. Clarissa gathered up his clothes for him and pushed the bundle after him.

'Okay?'

'Yes. It's all right. I think.' There were all sorts of things he ought to say, he knew, but he hadn't the strength.

'Good-bye then.'

'Good-bye.'

He let himself in and went into their room. Ruth was out of bed and sitting in front of the fire with Lud in her arms; her mother was sitting on the bed, and in the other chair across the hearth was Clemmie, the Professor's housekeeper. They were all obviously very cheerful, with cups of tea going and lots of gossip, cosy and feminine . . . Pat stared at them blankly, wishing them all in purgatory.

'Oh, God.'

He dropped his clothes on the floor and turned around and went out again. It was more than flesh and blood could cope with. He went upstairs and into Wilf's room. Wilf was writing letters, sitting in the hearth by his gas-fire. His bed was empty.

'Do you mind?' Pat gestured towards the bed. 'I'm knackered—room full of ruddy women—'

'Go ahead,' Wilf said cheerfully.

'Got any aspirins?'

Wilf got some out of a drawer and threw the bottle over. Pat took four, took off his shoes and got into bed. He was freezing cold. He pulled the eiderdown over his head and sank into a black pit of dreamless sleep. Ruth came up a few minutes later and looked at him doubtfully.

'Is he all right?' she asked Wilfred.

'Yeh. Post-concert blues. Quite normal. Felt like it myself sometimes.'

'He was terribly rude.'

'Not his fault really. Reaction.'

Ruth frowned. 'Tell him, when he wakes—' She shrugged. 'It doesn't matter, I suppose.' She paused. 'Did he say how it went?'

'No.'

Ruth went away.

Pat woke up at six o'clock. He had a splitting headache, but otherwise felt quite normal. Wilf was asleep on the floor, with some cushions underneath him and the hearth-rug for a blanket. Pat stirred him with his toe and said, 'Thanks, you can have it now. It's still warm.'

He went downstairs, carrying his shoes, and into the kitchen to make a cup of tea. He could remember everything quite sanely now, even to the point of being sorry for being so rude to Clemmie. He thought he could ring her up to apologize, then realized that he would probably get the Professor, and that would be impossible. But, standing over the kettle, waiting for it to boil, he realized that he had left a great deal unsaid to Clarissa. It seemed so urgent that he went straight out into the hall and dialled her number. Her father answered, and sounded reasonably cross.

'For God's sake, Pat—at six o'clock! Can't it wait?'

'No.'

'Wait a minute.'

Long, long pause. Then Clarissa, a bit slurry, 'Pat?'

'Clarissa, I ought to have said—'

'Do you feel okay now?'

'Yes. I've come round. That's why I rang.' In the kitchen the kettle started to shrill.

'What's the matter?'

'Nothing. It's just that I wanted to thank you for what you did. You were marvellous. You got me out of it.'

'All those lies!'

'You were inspired.'

'Well, I thought—I got you into it really, so I was obliged to do my best, wasn't I? I'm sorry about it. I shouldn't think you'd get a summons, though. You might, but doubtful.'

'Only an endorsement if I do. Better than another nine months for assault. Thank you for holding me down. That's all I wanted to say.'

'Any time, Pat. Anything for you.'

'No wrong ideas—'

'Yes. I'm full of them.' She rang off, and he put the receiver down, a bit disturbed by the last innuendo. Perhaps his impulsive telephone call hadn't been such a bright idea. But she had been fantastic, working on the fuzz; he couldn't not have told her so.

He went back into the kitchen and found Ruth taking the kettle off, silencing its row. She gave him a deeply suspicious look.

'Who on earth were you talking to?'

He considered telling a lie, but couldn't think of anything convincing. 'Clarissa.'

She gave him a very funny look.

'Was it all right? Nothing went wrong?'

'No.'

'Were you ill last night?'

'I felt terrible. I'm sorry if I was rude.'

'You were terribly rude. Clemmie nearly burst into tears.'

'Oh, God.' He didn't feel so good any more.

Ruth said, 'You could have taken your suit off.' He looked in the kitchen mirror and realized that he did look very odd for a Sunday morning, still in white tie and tails, covered with Wilf's leaky eiderdown feathers, a new beard struggling through. Then, out of the gloom, he remembered that he had played the Schumann Fantasy pretty well, all things considered, and he had stopped himself from exploding in the face of the law, which was a considerable feat. With Clarissa's help. The way she had physically held his arm—he had been right to thank her. She was a bitch, but a useful one.

'I think I'll have a bath,' he said.

'Tell me what happened,' Ruth said.

'I'll have a bath first, then I'll tell you what happened.' He could think up a good doctored version of the story in the bath.

'All right. I'll bring you a cup of tea. Give me your suit, you treat it dreadfully.'

'Okay.' He gave her the jacket and trousers and went to run the bath.

Chapter 12

When Ruth had regained her strength and her mother left them, the atmosphere improved considerably.

'Summer's come!' Pat said, flinging open the French windows and taking big sniffs of an indubitably warm April morning. Ruth had Lud in bed with her, feeding him.

'I think it's time I went out to work,' she said. 'Can you fix something at the garage?'

'Oh, must you?' Pat said.

'You're a fine one to ask! Surely it will make it a lot easier all round? Just while you get started.' She was wondering if she had offended him.

'I like having you around. Anyway, what about Lud?'

'Well, I'd have to take him, wouldn't I?'

Pat scowled, coming back to the piano. 'I'll see. Perhaps with Clarissa's lessons it'll be okay. We can scrape through till next winter.'

'What does Mick say?'

'Oh, Mick's got this fixation about the Brahms concerto. For August. In Bournemouth. I think it's fairly definite now. He keeps asking me if I can play it. I told him I can play most of the notes, but whether I can actually perform it . . .' He shrugged.

'I thought you said you *had* played it.'

'After a fashion. My standards are getting higher in my old age. You should play it when you're forty really—spend twenty years of hard thinking on it, get it into your hands . . . after forty you'd be getting too feeble physically. It takes fifty minutes to play and it's mostly flat out for the soloist. But if Mick commits me I've no choice. I'll just have to do it well enough. I'll be pleased, in a way. It'll give me a clue as to whether it's worth preparing for Moscow.'

They were on a higher plane now than electric airers and nappies. Ruth had put up a washing-line between the lilac and the laburnum and the sun did the job.

'If I go to work, perhaps you could pack in the driving and have more time.'

'Wait till this competition comes off. If I win that, things will start looking up.'

There was a recital with Alfred and co, to play Schubert in Exeter; two letters from music clubs in Nottingham and Whitby asking what his fees were, which he had passed on to Mick; the competition in Scotland; and now Moscow . . . Ruth was beginning to realize that success was not wholly to her advantage.

'Anyway, we have Clarissa's five-quids' worth this afternoon. That'll keep us in bread till Friday.'

Pat, after four lessons with Clarissa, was now sure that she had an ulterior motive for her piano-playing, but the money was a godsend. It had taken the edge off their desperate poverty. Ruth had taken his dress-suit to the cleaner's, and he had been able to buy his own music for the Brahms, instead of borrowing it from the library, also a white shirt. For that sort of luxury he was prepared to work very hard at teaching Clarissa, and to summon unaccustomed reserves of tact to turn her off him without offence. Ruth had strict instructions not to leave the room.

'She *has* got an eye for you still! I knew she had.' Ruth was glad Pat had had to admit it. It made her seem less neurotic. Pat was clearly embarrassed.

'Well, I'm not saying she—she—Oh, with Clarissa, anything in trousers—she can't help it.'

'Don't be so modest. It's your fantastic, intrinsic charm, your exquisite manners, your impeccable grooming—quite irresistible —'

Ruth had good cause for amusement, for Pat's distaste for getting involved with Clarissa again was quite evident. He had told Ruth a fairly unvarnished version of the day of their joint recital, and she had accepted—even been grateful—that Clarissa had come out of it with credit. No one had to remind Ruth of Pat's dangerous potential when faced with minions of the law, for she remembered her own experience only too vividly, which had parted them far more decisively than any trips to Whitby or Moscow that threatened. If Clarissa had prevented a repetition of that disaster, one could only be grateful.

'When I told Clemmie you were out for the day with Clarissa, her eyes came out on stalks. "Clarissa!" she sort of snorted. I told her it was only work, but I'm sure she didn't believe me. It was nice of her to call. She'd heard about the baby—indirectly, via Clarissa, I suppose. She's ever so nice. I told her how hard you were working and what a good husband you were and how charming you'd become with being a family man, and then you came in at the door and ruined it all. I might have saved my breath.'

'Serves you right for telling lies.'

The early-morning work was now devoted to Brahms. The Chopin for the audition was well in hand, and the programme for the competition was as well learned and considered as Pat reckoned he was capable of, needing only the awful tension of the competition atmosphere itself to spark it into what Pat hoped would be a winning performance. He had stepped up his practice hours to eight hours a day and the driving interlude he had come to consider as a rest in the middle. One day he overdid it and fell asleep while he was waiting for the bride. The best man had to come and root him out of his parking bay several hundred yards from the church, and Paddy the boss was justifiably annoyed.

Clarissa came for her lessons at four o'clock on Tuesdays and Fridays, the two days that Pat got home from work earlier. Ruth liked to take Lud out in the afternoons; by the time she had given him his two o'clock feed and got him ready, it was a bit of a push to get back again by four. Once or twice she was late and came in in the middle of the lesson. In each case Pat and Clarissa were working with impeccable rectitude, the first time discussing how to play a cross rhythm of three in the left hand against seven in the right, and the second time Pat was standing leaning against the mantelpiece while Clarissa played. The situation was on the point of settling into routine, and Clarissa evidently thought that she was getting her money's-worth. 'I don't find your lessons a bit boring,' she told Pat. 'I got bored before.' Ruth wasn't sure whether this was because the teacher was Pat, as opposed to old Zippy-Thumbs, who had known Elgar in 1910, or whether it was because, contrary to all expectations, Pat really could teach.

'Can you?' she asked him.

'Well, it's okay with Clarissa. I don't know about anyone else. I mean, I can say what I like to her. She doesn't mind. Tact isn't my strong point.'

'I've noticed.' Ruth remembered something. 'Next Tuesday I've got to go to the hospital for a check-up. Four o'clock. So you'll be all on your own. Is that all right?'

'I suppose so.'

'You're big enough to fend her off if she attacks.'

'I can't knock her under the piano and still expect to get the five quid.'

'No. Well—I'll put garlic in your sandwiches or something. That'll put her off. I shall have to leave Lud with you. Will that be all right? If he cries you can put him down the bottom of the garden.'

She left him in the garden before she went. The garden in spring had proved a heartening addition to their ground-floor room, the windows opening out on to a positive jungle of over-grown lilac and laurel and laburnum. The lawn in the middle was like a glade amidst the old-fashioned profusion of damp ferns growing against the smoky brick walls and the knotted sprouts of a mass of peony shoots. It was small and hemmed in, over-hung, and smelt of cats, but Ruth loved it. It was marvellous for Lud, and would be a godsend next summer when he was mobile. She was getting very domestic-minded. A cabbage. But it was hard to raise the mind above the immediate economics of the situation. Time enough to start advancing her thought-processes when Pat was able to supply enough money to stop her pre-occupation about the cheapest way to keep alive and healthy.

As soon as Pat came home from the garage, Ruth departed. Pat put the kettle on and went and sat on the doorstep in the sun. He was tired, but that was nothing new. It was always an effort to get started on the last hours of practice in the evening, the concentration growing more sporadic as the day progressed. All right once he was started, but so many reasons presented them-selves as to why he should delay the moment—sitting talking to Ruth, sitting in the sun now that it so obligingly shone into their room from the west in the late afternoon, drinking tea, doing anything but sit down at the piano. If he hadn't got a definite schedule to work to: the competition next week, Chopin the

157

week after, and Brahms in August, he wondered sometimes if he would have the willpower to get on with it at all. Rather, drift off with Bates and play harmonica in a folk group. Bates made more money than he did. Bates had asked him to. There were times when he was almost tempted. Sitting in front of the Brahms score, considering its problems, he was inclined to think that it was made for a greater mind than his would ever be, however well his fingers learned to scamper; he could get deeply depressed sometimes, when he was tired.

'Oh, just in time!' Clarissa had come in round the back, and the kettle was boiling. 'I'll make it,' she said. 'Isn't Ruth here?'

'She's got an appointment at the hospital.'

'Is she due back?'

'No. She's only just gone.'

That was his first mistake. He realized it immediately. 'We'll get started,' he said, getting to his feet.

'Oh, for heaven's sake, let's have the tea. Have you only just come home?'

'Yes.'

'Well, you need it. Sit down. I'll bring it over.'

He sat again. It was part of his weakness, to be tempted by idle chat and cups of tea. Earning his five pounds—and he was very conscientious about it—wasn't all that easy. It needed considerable effort to articulate when it came to criticizing somebody else's playing; comparatively simple to know what was wrong, not so easy to put the helpful, constructive criticism into the proper five-pounds-worth of words—not for him anyway, who had always preferred to keep silent rather than expose too painfully his lack of a polished education. He did sincerely want Clarissa to improve (there was plenty of room for it) and it was as much effort on his part to effect this as it was on hers. More, he thought sometimes. He had learned quite a lot about teaching since he had started. He would no longer have described it as 'money for old rope', which is how he had thought of it before. His thoughts had even flitted uneasily now and then to the Professor, who had been doing it for thirty years. But he still could not bring himself to think of the Professor without reopening painful scars . . .

'I've sugared it. Two. Here you are.' Clarissa brought the tea, and one for herself, and sat down on the step beside him.

158

'Oh, it's gorgeous—' She tossed back her hair and held her face up to the sun. It was very warm. The noise of the Finchley Road traffic, the distant throaty hum that accentuated their own lax content on the doorstep, was no match for the trilling of a blackbird in one of the lilacs. Lud slept blissfully. The big room behind them was bathed in sunshine; even the piano looked mild and harmless, like a basking cat stretched out, resting, across the doorway. Stupid, Pat thought, not to unwind when the moment suggested itself . . . five minutes. He leaned against the doorpost and felt the sun on his neck and face. Clarissa watched him reflectively. His eyes were shut. She sat holding her tea-mug, watching him. His skin was pale, indoors-looking; even relaxed, the lines of intense concentration showed on his face. He looked older than twenty. She put her tea-mug down, and put her hand out, resting it on his knee. His eyes opened abruptly.

In that second, Pat knew he should react with great decision. But he didn't. It was his second mistake. He knew perfectly well that he was being very stupid, but when he saw Clarissa smiling at him in the sunshine, he smiled back—not because he had any feelings for her at all, but just because he was comfortable and the sun was shining and she had made him a cup of tea . . . and it was so nice to stop, not to bother, not to think, and not, for the moment, to have any pressing anxieties: everything was going along quite nicely. With his eyes shut he had been thinking he would win the competition—and he knew he stood a good chance of winning—and then he would get quite a lot of work, and, all being well, their hard times would be over. His whole body was relaxed, soaking up the sunshine, optimistic, hopeful. These moments were rare, and it was unkind not to enjoy them when they came. So he smiled at Clarissa and Clarissa smiled back. And when she smiled, he remembered all the things as they had been once, long ago, before anything had gone wrong at all, when he had discovered for the first time his real talent under the Professor's discipline, after the years of groping, and Clarissa had blessed *him* with her favours when there was a queue of smoothies all avid for her smiles . . . He noticed, again, her quite undeniable attractions, and he knew at the same time that she knew he was noticing them, and that the whole situation was highly dangerous, but he still didn't move away.

'Pat,' she said softly. She moved against him and laid her head on his shoulder. Her arm slipped behind his back. She smelt delicious. He knew he didn't love her at all, but it was nice.

'You've no principles at all,' he said. 'I'm a married man.'

'Why does that change anything for me? Not my feelings. I've never been anything but potty about you, you know that.'

'Oh, come off it! Go and find some other poor fish. You had a funny way of showing it—am I supposed to have forgotten?'

'It was my mother,' Clarissa said. 'She wouldn't let me have anything to do with you after that spot of bother.'

'Well, it was all to my advantage in the end.' He felt almost paternal. She was like a purring, golden-eyed cat nestling against him. She had claws too. He was aware of them, almost tempting them. 'If I'd got hooked with you I'd never have had Ruth.'

'Do you love Ruth?'

'Yes.'

'But you only married her because—' Her voice dropped. 'Did you love her then, when you married her?'

'I think we'd better start the lesson.' She wasn't purring any more, and Pat didn't want to get embarked on any soul-searching. He had let it go too far already.

'No, answer me.' Her voice was sharp. 'I really want to know.'

He didn't know what the answer was himself. 'I don't know. I was scared, I suppose. But I know now.'

'What?'

He didn't reply. He went to get up, but Clarissa moved to stop him, burying her head against his neck and putting her arms round him. He remembered Ruth's saying he was big enough to fend her off, but Clarissa was a big, determined girl and her emotions were aroused.

'For God's sake, Clarissa—' He moved her hair out of his mouth, and remembered the five pounds at the same time. 'Please,' (more gently) 'we can't—'

'Don't be so old-fashioned! You weren't once!'

'For crying out loud—' Five pounds or no five pounds, he'd had enough. He heaved himself urgently to his feet, dragging Clarissa with him. She was crying, but beautifully.

'I do love you so!'

'Yes, well—' He couldn't disentangle himself, and tried to back indoors towards the piano. She had both her arms round his neck, pressing herself to him, her face buried against his neck so that he was blinded by her hair. It was useless trying to be tactful.

'For heaven's sake!' He put his arms up to release her grip round the back of his neck and she started to sob in earnest. He got hold of her wrists and pulled her hands away by brute force, pulling them back in front of them and forcing her off him. She resisted like a tiger.

'Grow up,' he said. 'You're just a spoilt child, wanting what you can't have.'

He was fast losing patience, worried about the strain on his hands, for it was like holding dynamite. She was writhing and struggling to get free, and kicking as well. He had always known she had an uncontrollable temper, for he had seen it in action before, but he had never had it directed against him physically.

'You wanted me once, when it suited you!' she screamed at him. She wasn't beautiful any more, her face screwed up with rage.

'Well, I don't want you now and you might as well know it once and for all!' He was getting angry too. 'I've got all I want, and I'm not having you trying to break it up, pretending you want to learn the piano. I'm not hurting Ruth. God, you bitch—'

She aimed a kick at him which caught him painfully on the shin. He flung her away from him with considerable force, and she went staggering backwards over the doorstep, sprawling. He turned away, intending to beat a hasty retreat up to Wilf's room.

'I hate you! I hate you!' she screamed after him.

He half-turned, to see that she hadn't killed herself, and as he did so she snatched up one of the tea-mugs that was still on the doorstep and hurled it at him with all her might. He put his hand up instinctively and ducked, but her aim, stiffened by pure malevolence, was true. It was a heavy stoneware mug, part of a wedding-present set from Maxwell, and it caught him on the back of the hand.

'I wish I could kill you!' she said viciously. 'I wish—I wish—'

The tears were choking her. She snatched her handbag from the chair and ran to the door. The hurricane of her departure echoed through the house, door-panes and skirling mats, a frightened cat running for its life. Pat stood still, listening, still holding his hand up, too scared to move. He could not bring himself to look at the damage. He lowered his arm slowly and cradled his hand with the other one, trying to pretend that the pain was purely emotional.

'She can't—' he said out loud. 'It can't—'

But it was, he knew it was. He looked down very slowly and the hand lay there, held by the other one, looking perfectly all right. He dared not move. Perhaps it was his imagination—because he dreaded it so much. It was always at the back of his mind, that it might happen. While he stood quite still, like a stone, he could be comforted.

'It's my imagination. A mug couldn't—'

He then lifted the hand up out of the other one, and the awful, thick pain flooded up from the knuckle, through his wrist and right up his arm. It was so patently not the product of his imagination, that he had no possible doubt about its meaning at all. It was a fracture.

He could scarcely believe it. He just went on standing there, trying to pretend it hadn't happened. After Clarissa's skirmishing, the house was as quiet as the grave. The sun still shone in at the window, the kettle was still steaming on the ring in the hearth. While he kept his hand very still, supported, it felt all right. He didn't think that the mug, and a girl's strength, could possibly have done such harm, but he only had to try to move his forefinger and it was quite apparent that it had. He had to accept it; it was useless trying to pretend.

He could easily have cried. An awful stifled feeling like crying felt as if it was throttling him; an amalgam of rage and grief and a piercing shaft of helpless, hopeless indignation at the *injustice* of it—a familiar feeling to Pat, mostly suffered in the arms of the law. But *this*—this was a new one, the eternal fear having come to realization and in such an unexpected fashion, when one spent one's whole life being particularly careful of car doors and bread-knives and not carrying anything heavy, and then this, of all things, a mere argument with Clarissa. But then arguments with Clarissa had never been mere—he should have bloody well known, when she started—instead of sitting there like a mental case, smiling at her. The fault was obviously all his, giving away an opening . . .

He would have to get down to the Casualty. The sooner the better. He couldn't wait for Ruth. He'd have to leave her a note. Holy cow, it was his right hand—he couldn't even write a note.

He started hunting around for what he wanted, something for a sling, a piece of paper, a pencil. Once he started moving, the hand hurt like hell. He found a scarf of Ruth's and knotted it round his neck, using his teeth, and laid the hand in it, then he wrote her a note with his left hand and left it on the piano. It said, 'Hurt hand. Gone to hospital.' All the music for his competition was on the rack, staring at him, and the Chopin study which was at last beginning to sound like something—it was like being fractured in the brain-box, thinking what had happened to him. It was really beginning to sink in now, along with the numbed suspended pain in his hand, what this injury meant. The choking feeling spread up his gullet again. He groped for some money in his back pocket—cripes, everything was geared to his right hand, he couldn't get at it without agonizing contortions—twenty pence— but he couldn't face the underground; it was nearly rush-hour and the thought of his hand in the rush-hour made him feel ill, There were some five-pence pieces for the gas-meter; he took them, enough for a taxi, and went out. He never gave a thought to the baby in the garden.

When Ruth got home, the baby in the garden was yelling blue murder, and there was no sign of Pat at all. She went out and brought the pram in, indignant at Pat, for the sun had gone in and Lud was cold and hungry.

'He's a rotten father, Ludwig. Useless. I wonder where he's gone?'

She didn't find the note until after she had changed and fed Lud and laid him on the bed. She saw the tea-mug on the floor under the piano, went to pick it up and saw the note. She could barely decipher it at first, but when she had, her reaction was one of cold, bitter despair. She sat down on the piano stool, staring at the note. His right hand, obviously. There was no blood any-where, only the mug on the floor, which seemed odd. What hospital? The nearest. The quickest to get to was probably the one she had just come home from. He knew it too. She must go and find out what had happened.

At that moment, just as she was wondering whether to take Lud with her or not, Rosemary let herself in at the front door. Ruth deposited Lud into her surprised care and set off for the tube-station, running. She realized that she was shaking with fright; she could not sit down but stood by the door in a fever of impatience. When the train stopped she leapt out and ran all the way to the hospital, elbowing her way through the rush-hour crowds, shoving and pushing. The Casualty department had long rows of people sitting waiting, and lots more milling about, but there was no sign of Pat. She wandered up and down a few corridors and then went to ask at the desk. She had to wait for several people in front of her, filling in forms and being awkward, all the time getting more agitated herself. The girl had to look through all the admissions.

'What was wrong with him?'

'I don't know.'

The girl gave her a curious look. 'An accident?'

'Yes, to his hand.'

'Here it is.'

'He's here then?'

'Yes. You'd better go and ask Sister.'

Ruth wasn't sure which one was Sister. Nobody seemed to want to stop and chat. She asked a passing nurse who said, 'Try X-ray,' which struck Ruth as quite a bright idea. She followed the signs and came to a wide corridor full of people waiting. Pat was sitting there, hunched up and white.

'What is it? What's happened?'

He showed her his hand, which was now all swollen up and a peculiar colour.

'It's fractured. The doctor said it was—a fractured metacarpal —but I knew anyway. Only I've been here nearly a flaming hour and this queue just doesn't move. I told him I was a pianist but it didn't make any difference. They've got two radiologists off sick or something. Some of these people have been here two hours.'

'But with you—you ought to have a specialist see it, surely? It's not just any hand.'

'Yeh, I was thinking that. The Professor knows a bloke—I went to him before—he was marvellous. He knew it from the piano-playing end, as well as being a doctor. I don't think some doctors know what a piano is.'

'Can't we go to him? Do you know his name?'

'No. I know his address, though—Harley Street. We haven't any money and now we're not likely to earn any, are we? Not even the driving.'

164

'Whatever happened? What did you—'

'Clarissa heaved a tea-mug at me. I had to fight her off—I told her what I thought of her and she upped and started throwing things.'

'You mean it's *her* fault?' Ruth heard her own voice shake with pure venom. 'Clarissa's?' And all that money Clarissa was surrounded with! 'She ought to pay! Go to a specialist and send her the bill! What did she say? What did she do about it?'

'Nothing. She didn't know what happened. She just threw and ran.'

'Her father would pay—'

'No.'

'But you need help. It's no time to be proud. Not for a thing like this.'

'Not them.'

'But, Pat.' Ruth felt desperate. A baby was crying incessantly, and some women were voicing their complaints loudly and monotonously beside them. The queue hadn't moved at all.

'Two and a half ruddy hours,' one of the women said. 'I was here at half past three. The kids'll be home and nobody there.'

'I'll go and see someone,' Ruth said. 'I'll go and make a fuss.'

She got up and went searching for someone to complain to. It was only because she felt so desperate—she wasn't brave enough to complain as a rule. She broached a woman fierce enough to be someone in command, and got passed on to an Indian doctor who couldn't understand what she was saying. She gave up and cornered a very young student-looking doctor in a white jacket and explained the situation, but he only said, 'I honestly can't do anything about it. We're understaffed—everyone's off with 'flu. There's only one man working in X-ray and he's due off in half an hour.'

The system appeared to have broken down. Ruth thought of Clarissa with almost maniacal hatred, then took a conscious hold of herself. It was no good appealing to Pat. He would not ask the Cargill-Smiths for help, but there was another possibility. She went to the phone-box in the hall and groped about for a coin. The number was in her head and she dialled it quickly.

'Clemmie? It's Ruth. Is the Professor in?'

'Why, Ruth! Yes, he is, dear. Just this minute. Do you want to speak to him?' She was plainly surprised.

'Yes. It's urgent.'

'Just a moment then.'

The Professor came to the phone, also surprised. His voice was very cautious. 'Is that Ruth?'

'Yes. I'm very sorry to bother you, but Pat has had an accident to his hand. He's broken it and there's no one here who's got time to look at it—'

'No one where? Where are you?'

She told him. 'He's waiting in the X-ray queue but it's miles long.'

'I'll be over immediately. Wait for me outside the door. Don't let them touch him, whatever you do.'

He rang off without another word, and Ruth put the receiver down. Her feeling of relief was tempered by the thought of breaking the news to Pat.

'It's all right,' she told him. 'Someone's coming for you. We've got to go back again, to the reception.'

He got up and came without a word. They walked along the corridors and down the stairs. Ruth was trying to pluck up courage.

'It's—' She realized she was terrified. She couldn't tell him. She looked at him sideways. He looked drawn and morose, in his very worst temper.

'It hurts,' he said, as if he was six years old. It made her feel strong and maternal.

'It's all right. The Professor's coming. He's on his way.'

Pat stopped walking.

'The Professor?'

'Yes. I telephoned him.'

'You telephoned the *Professor*?'

'What else can we do? You tell me!' She was angry. It was like the night he had stopped playing in the middle of the Liszt sonata—he had to be goaded, nagged. 'You can't afford not to see to it—*I* can't afford! It's not a question of people or anything. It's only that—' She gestured angrily to his cradled hand.

He just stood there, looking stricken.

'All right, go back then, if you want to!' she hissed at him. 'If you're so stupid, and proud! Go and sit in that queue for the next hour and a half. You're not finished then, remember, only X-rayed. I'm going home. I've got Lud to see to.'

He was furious, she could see, but reason prevailed. He had no option. She began walking and he started to trail along behind. They went down through the Casualty reception and out through the swing doors into the car-park. Pat leaned against a waiting ambulance, silent, looking cold and mutinous. He had no coat, only a faded corduroy shirt and threadbare jeans. When the Professor came, he brought with him this aura of privilege: his sleek car and his gold cuff-links and impeccable suit, like a banker; his faint soap and cigar smell; it all struck Ruth with incredible force, the desirability of this privilege through money—that it was Harley Street, instead of the overworked Casualty, but only if you had money, not because you were a fantastic pianist with an injured hand . . . She felt as fraught and manoeuvred as Pat.

The Professor leaned over and opened the door.

'I'd better go back to Lud,' Ruth said. The car was only a two-seater. But Pat said urgently, 'No, you've got to come. You've got to.' He gave her no choice.

They got in, moving very carefully in the cramped space.

'Well, Pat, what have you done?' The Professor spoke, not looking at them, turning to see if the road was clear. It struck Ruth that he found the situation as difficult as Pat did; only the smoothness of his manners covered embarrassment. Pat would not say anything. It was not entirely temperament, Ruth supposed; he was having a very painful afternoon, both mentally and physically.

'It's broken,' Ruth said. 'Clarissa threw something at him.'

'I beg your pardon?' The Professor was startled.

'A tea-mug—a stoneware one.'

'Good God! Why are you children all so violent?' He looked shaken. 'You're sure it's a fracture? Have you had it X-rayed?'

'No, but it is,' Pat said.

'I rang Harper. He said he'd see you straight away. We'll go straight to the clinic, not to Harley Street. I don't think you need worry too much if he takes care of it. It's straightforward, as far as you can tell? Show me.'

Pat showed him.

'Tragic for you, all the same.'

Nobody disagreed. Now that everything was in hand, Ruth was beginning to feel shaky herself. Past making polite conversation, Pat looked awful. Whatever was he thinking? Ruth wondered. She could not guess at the depths of his despair. He had retracted as he usually did at moments of stress, so that he seemed not to be there at all. The Professor drove fast, without saying any more, and delivered them to a very smart, secluded Edwardian house near Regent's Park. He parked on the gravel drive and got out. Pat and Ruth followed him, not very eagerly. They went inside to an impressive reception, radiating calm and efficiency, as expensive-looking as was compatible with germ-combat. It reminded Ruth more of a beauty parlour than a hospital. She could not imagine anyone being admitted if they were vomiting or bloody, or not ill in good taste.

'Dr. Harper?' the Professor said to the smooth beauty at the desk. 'John Hampton. He's expecting me.'

Dr. Harper duly arrived, very charming and handsome, and after a short chat about nothing to the Professor, he looked at Pat's hand and said, 'We'll go and do something about this then. How about if I ring you later,' he added to the Professor, 'and let you know what's happening? All right?'

'Perfect.'

'If you'll come this way, Mr. Pennington . . .'

Pat hesitated and looked at Ruth, and the Professor said, 'Don't worry, I'll look after Ruth.' When Pat had disappeared, Ruth had a feeling that he had wanted her there, to hold the good hand, and she had this extraordinary feeling of surprise, which she had experienced once or twice before, that in some things her Patrick, whose strength she trusted and rested against like God Almighty, was very vulnerable.

'Well, young lady'—the Professor was looking at her with his old expression of tempered suspicion—'I'll run you home, shall I?'

'Yes. Thank you.'

She wondered if he was going to dump her, and then take over the reins again for Pat. She knew he would like to.

'He won't be staying here, will he?' she asked. 'He'll be home tonight?'

'Oh, I should think so.'

'Pat didn't know I rang you up.' She thought she had better make the situation plain. 'I did it because I thought it was very important. How much do you think it will cost?'

'I wouldn't worry about that,' the Professor said. He opened the car door for her, and held it while she got in.

'I'd rather know.'

'Dr. Harper is a good friend of mine.'

'I wanted your help, to get the treatment, but not for you to pay. You will tell Dr. Harper to send the bill to our address?'

The Professor was smiling. 'Of course.'

How they were going to pay it was not something she was prepared to think about. Later. Their prospects were now so bleak they didn't bear thinking about.

'How long will it be, an injury like that?'

'Hard to tell. About five weeks to mend, but rather longer, I suspect, to get back its agility. Bad enough, I'm afraid.'

Ruth didn't want to think about it. She couldn't bring herself to ask any more. Perhaps Mick would be able to help? She would have to go out to work. She would have to get Lud weaned on to a bottle. Her thoughts were zooming all over the place.

'Don't worry about Pat tonight. I'll bring him home when he's ready, or I'll ring and let you know what they're up to. What's your telephone number?'

The Professor delivered Ruth to the door, and wrote the number in his diary. Ruth thanked him.

He said, 'I'll do all I can to help. Don't be afraid to ask.'

Ruth hesitated, standing on the pavement looking down at the Professor. 'You are very kind,' she said spontaneously. She had honestly never thought so before, but now she did. He shook his head and smiled, and drove off without saying anything else. Ruth let herself in. She felt very tired.

Pat came home a couple of hours later in a private car belonging to the clinic. His hand was in plaster from the knuckles to half-way up his arm.

'Have you rung Paddy?' he asked. 'He'll have to find another driver for tomorrow.'

'No. I haven't rung him.'

'I'll do it.'

That was the only thing he said for the rest of the evening. Ruth decided that it would be better to save all the questions she was dying to ask until a less charged time. She got herself something to eat but Pat wouldn't have anything. He just lay on the bed staring at the ceiling. Lud, as if sensing the atmosphere, wouldn't stop crying. Ruth fed him early, in desperation. She sat down on the hearth in front of the gas-fire, leaning against the bed, and held him against her, smelling his lovely clean-washing smell and stroking his funny black hair. The thought of leaving him all day and going out to work was terrible. He was the cause of all the difficulties they faced; he had been the reason for their getting married at all; he had a lot to answer for. It was strangely quiet, with the pianist out of order, only the muttering of the gas-fire and the spring wind fluting round the windows. Ruth felt charged, nervous and shaky, as if it was she who had had the accident.

'Poor Ruth.' Pat put out his good hand and touched her hair. 'You shouldn't have married me.'

She didn't answer.

She fed Lud and soothed him and put him to bed in his pram, then fished out her nightdress and got undressed, and turned out the fire. Pat lay watching her.

'Am I supposed to be sorry?' she asked.

'You married me? Yes, of course.'

The look on his face was quite different now. She was smiling. 'No,' she said. 'We shouldn't ever have got married.'

She lay down beside him and put her arms round him. 'The worst thing we ever did.'

'The very worst,' he agreed. 'I'd never do it again.'

'No, not to anybody else.'

They started to laugh. They should have been crying. But this was what it was all about, Ruth remembered thinking—that nothing, not anything at all, really mattered, as long as . . . God, life was too stupid . . . he could have gone to bed with Clarissa and not broken his hand at all and what would she have to laugh about then?

Chapter 13

They were awoken in the morning by the doorbell ringing. Ruth had already got up once and changed and fed Lud—he was in bed with them; she had been dozing, but Pat was still sound asleep.

'What's that?' he said, jerking awake. The sudden movement hurt him and he remembered what had happened. 'Oh, God. Oh, hell . . .'

'It might be Mick,' Ruth said. But nobody had told him. She pulled her dressing-gown on and shook back her hair. 'I'll go.'

It was the Professor.

'Oh, heavens,' Ruth said involuntarily.

'Am I too early? It's nine o'clock.'

Pat was usually up before six, but today was different.

'There wasn't anything to get up for. I'm so sorry,' Ruth explained. 'Do come in.'

'How's Pat?'

'I don't know. All right, I think.'

The sunlight shone through the stained-glass window-panes, making the hall look like a cathedral. It was a bounding spring day, when even the blown newspapers were the urban equivalent of gambolling lambs, and the Hampstead cherry-trees were being lured into flower. Their own room, facing west, was dark and cold in the morning. Ruth, remembering everything, felt with a sudden shiver that this sunlight was not for them; it was right that she should lead the retreat to their cold lair. Pat was still lying in bed, hunched up with Lud under the blankets.

'It's Professor Hampton, Pat.'

'Oh, cripes.' He sat up, groaned, and lay down again.

'How's your arm?' the Professor asked.

'It hurts.'

After the first shock of the meeting, Pat must have reconsidered his manners, for he slowly sat up again, combing his hair back with his fingers, and looked at the Professor.

'I'm sorry.'

'No, please. I'm rather early. I had a reason, though, something I wanted to mention.'

'Do sit down,' Ruth said, bringing up the chair. 'I'll make a pot of tea. Pat, give me Lud—he'll suffocate.'

Pat groped under the blankets. 'I can't—he's all right. He can stay here.' He heaved the baby up a bit and Lud lay beside him, frowning with his black eyes at the bright plaster arm lying on the blanket before him.

'That baby is extraordinarily like you, Pat,' the Professor said, intrigued. 'Clemmie told me, but I wouldn't have believed.'

Pat looked at Lud, as if expecting to see his own face staring back. Lud squinted at him, hiccuping gently.

'I'm not cross-eyed.'

'Don't be so horrible,' Ruth said. 'It's the focus, not a squint. They're all like it. Aren't you going to get up?'

'No. I'm ill.'

'What did Dr. Harper say about it?' the Professor asked. 'No complications?'

'No.. Five weeks, he said. Then when the plaster comes off he'll treat it to get it moving as quickly as possible. He wasn't very optimistic about my being back to normal before next winter.'

'Next winter!' Ruth was horrified.

'Well, back to standard. Brahms' number two standard.'

'Is that what you're working on?'

'I've got a date for it, in Bournemouth in August. I must ring up Mick and break the news to him. It will be another year now.'

'What are you going to do—now this has happened?' the Professor asked. 'This is what I came to see you about. Have you any idea? Have you talked it over?'

'Not yet.'

'No—well, I did think—it's just an idea—' The Professor hesitated, looking embarrassed. 'I don't want to interfere, you understand, but I did think—if you want a little breathing-space, a short rest, there's a nice flat in Brighton you can borrow—have a bit of a holiday. I understand you've been working very hard. It wouldn't cost you anything. A few of us use it whenever we feel like it, and there's no one there now.'

Pat looked at him suspiciously. The Professor smiled. 'No strings attached, Pat, I assure you. If you are financially embarrassed—to put it nicely—I suggest you have a talk with Mr. Zawadzki. It would be quite in order, you know. He is likely to make a lot of money out of you in time to come, and it's only right that he helps you now. He is a very astute young man. He won't risk offending you.'

'I don't want to lose this room, and the piano,' Pat said. 'It's not very cheap.'

'No. A place like this is hard to come by.' Hampton glanced at his watch. 'You needn't decide anything now. I'm on my way out to Winchester, and I thought I'd just drop by and suggest this flat business. It would do you both a world of good, this time of year. And afterwards, if you want any help—well, I won't say ask for it, because I know you won't, but there are a few of us who want to see you get on, Pat—a purely selfish interest, if you like, and if you want to drop round, any time, you will be more than welcome. Just to talk.'

Pat, propped on his elbow, was examining Lud. He didn't say anything. Ruth was glad of the kettle noises, and made a clatter of the cups and tea-jar to cover up his silence, but the Professor didn't seem put out. The thought of a holiday in Brighton appealed to her enormously. Such was the pace of Pat's normal working-day that she realized they had never had any time off since they were married, apart from Christmas Day and Boxing Day. They had never been home except then or to Pat's parents; in fact Pat's parents only knew about the baby because Ruth had prodded Pat into writing them a postcard, and Pat's mother had rung up one evening and delivered some rather sarcastic congratulations. Two days later she had called with her husband and spent the evening arguing with Pat and rocking Lud in her arms until he was sick. She had promised to call again, but hadn't, fortunately.

Ruth made the tea and offered the Professor a cup, wishing that they had a table and that everything wasn't quite so squalid, and the Professor talked to Pat about left-handed compositions and promised to bring over what music he'd got.

'I could learn the Ravel concerto, perhaps,' Pat said. Then he

173

changed his mind. 'No, I can play the Brahms left-hand for five weeks.' It will be a good chance.'

'Try it in Brighton. There's a piano there too.' The Professor smiled, and shortly afterwards took his leave for Winchester.

It was as if they always did what the Professor wanted, Ruth thought—in the end. But this time she had no regrets at all. People were unexpectedly kind. Paddy the car-boss agreed to pay Pat half his usual wages until he was fit again; Mick agreed to pay the rent, but Wilf said, 'Oh, let it go for a week or two. No one will say anything,' so Mick gave it them in cash and they had something to go to Brighton with. The flat was luxurious, and the refrigerator and pantry were freshly stocked with food by the woman who 'kept an eye on it' when it was unoccupied, presumably on the Professor's orders. Ruth's parents wrote and invited them to come and live at home for a few weeks, and Bates followed them to Brighton and left six five-pound notes under a milk-bottle on top of the refrigerator, saying, 'Pay me back when you do a gig in the Festival Hall.' They prevailed upon him to stay, and he persuaded Pat that he could play the harmonica, plaster or no plaster.

'Can't get the effects,' Pat said.

'Play the ruddy melody, man,' Bates said. 'I'll do the effects.'

He took Pat out to a pub with him the following evening, and came back with five pounds.

'Two pounds fifty for me, two pounds fifty for you,' Bates said.

'How come you can make five quid just ruddy enjoying yourself?' Pat was confounded.

'Because we enjoy ourselves so ruddy well,' Bates said.

It was all a bit too good to be true, considering what had happened. Ruth was a cautious optimist. She knew there was a long time to go yet, and they spent as little as possible. Pat played left-handed Brahms all morning, and after lunch they would go crunching down the beach for a couple of hours, sometimes taking Lud and sometimes leaving him with Bates. The weather was soft and warm, remarkably well-disposed.

He was more relaxed, more ready to laugh. It really was a holiday, in spite of the way it had been forced on them. Ruth didn't want to go back. Bates came and went, a gentle, congenial presence. Once he said to Ruth, when Pat wasn't there, 'I will help you—moneywise, I mean—until Pat gets going again. I don't need much, the way I live. I give most of it away anyway. And it's true, you know, if it hadn't been for Pat early on, I wouldn't have ever done anything. Only worked on the farm. I'd have been quite happy, I daresay, but—' He shrugged. 'There's something about Pat.'

Ruth had always thought so too, but had supposed she was biased. But it was curious, now, to find how many people were so well·disposed towards him, enough to offer very real help although he had never put himself out to be kind to them, or even polite.

Bates said, 'It's because you feel, with him, that he won't ever give in. He was like that at school. They just couldn't win, whatever they did. And now with this, there's this colossal will-power —single-mindedness. It drives him. And when you think what it's for—although he knows it's got to make him money, he's playing for money, if you like, it's only got to make him money so that it justifies his going on playing, which is the only thing that means anything at all to him. And most people, I think most people feel like me—you feel you want to have a hand in it, somehow—you admire it, you know you could never do it yourself, so the best you can do is tag along and want to be his friend.'

'I thought it was just me who felt like that.'

'No, I don't think so. It's something he generates. The only people who can't stand him are the ones who are jealous. As long as you aren't jealous, you think he's marvellous.'

'I don't think he thinks of it like that himself.'

'No. I'm sure he doesn't. He doesn't think about it at all. He doesn't think he's anything exceptional.'

'He thinks he plays well enough for it to be worth going on with. That's all. He thinks about playing all the time. Even when he's driving, he takes music to read while he's waiting about. He doesn't talk about it, but I'm sure it's all he thinks about. He doesn't talk to me, anyway—he might to people who know about it, like Mick.'

Mick came down at the beginning of the second week, and they talked about it all night. Ruth sat curled up in one of the elegant armchairs and listened. Some of it she understood, and a whole lot she didn't, but the atmosphere was so charged with dynamic, intentions that it was impossible not to be involved. 'I have received as many inquiries about possible dates for you to play, since your recital at the Society conference, as you would have got anyway if you had won that competition,' Mick told Pat.

'I would have got them *as well*,' Pat pointed out.

'Yes, but this is so encouraging—these are the people who actually heard you play, and want you to play in their clubs. I want to get out some literature on you—it's fairly urgent. We shall want a decent photo. Perhaps we can get one taken tomorrow —unless you've got one?'

'No.' The only ones he had ever had taken were for police records, and he wasn't going to admit this.

'We'll do that then. And make out some recital programmes. That's the important thing.'

'This is for next winter, I take it? We can't think about much earlier.'

'It depends, of course, on everything going smoothly with your hand. I've seen Harper.'

'Oh?'

'He's got your convalescent programme all laid on, exercises and what you can play and what you can't play until something or other gets its strength back—all highly technical and involved. I should think, talking to him, that whatever we have to pay him will be well worth it.'

Ruth noted the use of the plural in the last sentence and felt a bit happier. Pat looked surprised. 'You mean we have to submit the programmes to him first and he marks them up: "suitable sixth week post-plaster-removal, seventh week, eighth week," etc.? How about Brahms' number two?'

Mick laughed. 'I didn't mention that. We'll work up to it. But you don't think it's too optimistic to offer it for next year?'

'Hand permitting, no. If we make it definite, then I know I've got to do it. I would rather work to deadlines, if you like. Otherwise you would give yourself ten or fifteen years. If you had any sense you would. I can do the Rachmaninov two and Liszt one. The Beethovens I want to do more work on, especially the G Major. But nothing else now. Not with the Brahms.'

'No. And for solo recital—your main works would be—?'
'The Schumann Fantasy. Brahms' Handel Variations. Of the Beethoven sonatas I would prefer "Les Adieux", the "Waldstein", and the 109, but most of them if necessary. The Scriabin four. Chopin's sonatas—B Minor preferably.'
'The Liszt sonata.'
'No.'
'Why not? I thought that was your best piece.'
Pat hesitated. 'I stopped—you remember.'
'So?'
'I'd like to forget it for a bit. It shook me.'
'But your playing of that sonata is one of the best things you have to offer. The best, if you ask me. Just because on one occasion you stopped—' Mick shrugged. 'It can happen to anybody.'
Ruth said, 'I think you should play it.'
'It scares me now, the thought of playing it in public.' Pat looked worried at the thought.
'If you played it successfully, just once,' Ruth said, 'it would be all right again. You've got to do it. It's like throwing away all that time you've worked on it, to drop it now. Anyway, it's marvellous. Your best.'
'It is,' Mick agreed.
'It might be. But if you were me, sitting there—'
'I thought the Professor said,' Ruth said, 'that the more it mattered, the more you rose to the occasion. So if the occasion matters very much—'
'He said that, did he?'
'Yes.'
'I agree with Ruth,' Mick said. 'It's a terrible waste to drop it. As far as I'm concerned I would like you to play it at every recital you do. It's a splendid showpiece.'
'Played in one piece,' Pat said.
'Next time,' Ruth said.
Pat shrugged. 'Ruination to my metacarpal. It's not that I haven't given it a great deal of thought—'
'No. Well, think again,' Mick said. 'If you're considering Moscow, you can't afford to be put off by a minor lapse. We'll put it on the list.'
Pat did not protest but his expression aged two or three years.

177

Ruth wasn't sure how serious he was about Moscow: the fare was a major stumbling-block, but if Mick wanted it—and if the Professor had come back into their circle. . . . Mick had a list of the music clubs who had inquired about Pat's playing for them, and they were from all over the country, not just the London suburbs. The more his career succeeded, the less she would see of him. It was the lot of the twentieth-century musician, to be a high-powered travelling man. Sitting there, watching the two of them, it occurred to her that in this point in Pat's career, fractured metacarpal or no, *she* was as likely to be as happy as she ever would be. If the engagements flowed in, she could not see Pat turning them down to stay at home with her. And even if he wanted to, there was no longer the choice, for his career was in Mick's hands. And Ruth could see that it was in very capable hands, but equally Mick was successful because he was a pressure man. He had the same nervous energy as Pat, but his nervous energy was channelled into making money out of Pat. He had been to Dr. Harper, chafing at the delay, because the engagements were coming in. Watching him, Ruth recognized that there was an aggressive streak in his nature. He was one of life's pushers and shovers, for all the charm; he was shrewd and sharp and demanding—exactly as a good agent should be. Ruth wasn't sure if she liked him now. She was a romantic at heart, and Pat's music had wrapped her love-affair in a pink cloud, like a bad film. She wanted her life with Pat to be sentimentally happy, with him playing the piano and the sun shining and the children running in from a big garden full of flowers and birds singing, but now she saw that—however dedicated his own approach—to exploit his art for money was as business-like and commercial an undertaking as stockbroking. She could see it in Mick's attitude. No doubt Pat knew it too. The music would remain inviolable, but their way of life would of necessity be tautly organized and full of stress, for to tie the temperament of the artist to a commercial schedule was surely an incompatible task? Or was Pat already trained, through his scrupulous years of practice, to perform according to schedule? She supposed he was—to play gentle, introspective Schumann straight out of the rush-hour on a wet night in Ilford was already part of the job, or all-consuming Liszt when your wife was having a baby—but the training was not infallible, because this was why he went to the lavatory to be sick, or stopped in mid-movement, and wouldn't talk to anybody. It didn't just come out of the soul, born of joy and passion, as her romantic dreams would have it. It was tempered to time-tables and cold Town Halls as it always had been, even for the dying Chopin playing in Glasgow for sixty pounds so that he could pay his doctor's bills, so who was she to want it any different for Pat? She watched him talking to Mick, very practical and matter-of-fact, about the hardest problems of the Brahms concerto, demonstrating with his good hand in the air, the plastered one lying on his knee, and she felt something very like affection towards Clarissa for being the cause of this respite, this nice holiday, this breathing-space. To be happy for the day was what mattered, and she was happy now.

Mick wanted to watch something on the television. Lud was asleep and Pat said to Ruth, 'Let's go out for a drink. It's nearly closing time,' so they went out and walked along the sea-front. It was too nice to go into a pub; the air was warm and the sea calm and not many people were about. They walked in silence for some time. Ruth thought Pat was thinking about his music, but after a while he put his arm round her and said, 'Like old times.'

'Yes. I was thinking that. Thanks to Clarissa.'

'Old married couple. Nearly a year.'

'A lot has happened.'

'This time last year I was still in Pentonville.'

'Seems ages ago.'

'We haven't done enough of this.'

'Nothing, you mean?'

'Yes. We haven't done nothing ever since we've been married.'

'Well, I have. It's you.'

'I can't. Later I shall.'

Ruth doubted it. She said, 'Funny, that it was Clarissa—giving us a sort of honeymoon.' They hadn't had one before. 'Does she know what's happened?'

'Yes, of course. Mick called on them, but she knew already through the grapevine. Mick said the old boy was very upset. I don't suppose Clarissa was, mind you.'

'Perhaps he'll pay the doctor's bill.'

'Mick said we needn't bother about it.'

'Really? Is he paying it?'

'I'm not sure. I didn't ask.'

'Perhaps the doctor will do it free, being a friend of the Professor's. When he takes the plaster off, can you start playing straight away?'

'I don't know. I suppose so. I hope so. There's an awful lot to do if Moscow is going to come off. If I can afford to enter for it.'

Ruth didn't want Pat to go to Moscow, or work for it either, but she wanted him to be happy, and one was dependent on the other. She couldn't win. It was what her mother had said way back. But she didn't want to change anything. They walked back. They went home the following week and Pat started his driving job again, and Dr. Harper removed the plaster from his hand. The hand was stiff as a board. When Pat tried to play the piano with it he became acutely depressed and went out and got drunk. Ruth was angry, appalled. Pat wouldn't speak for several days. He did the exercises that Dr. Harper prescribed, but for too long, and suffered severe pains which depressed him still further, and tried Ruth's philosophy to its limits. She knew now that she was only happy if Pat was happy, and during the weeks of his recuperation she was sorely tried. For normal usage the hand was acceptably cured, but for the extremes to which Pat wanted to drive it, it was sadly out of condition. Dr. Harper's therapy was highly skilled, but he hadn't the power to alleviate Pat's frustration at the slow rate of progress. The doctor wouldn't agree that progress was slow, but Pat, finely aware of the hand's former capabilities, found it almost impossible to accept its present limitations.

'Cripes, it'll be as long as Pentonville all over again! He never told me this early on! He calls this "a most satisfactory improvement"—and we're still on ruddy grade three stuff. How long does he want?'

'Don't be ridiculous! He can't work miracles. He's not God! You've got plenty of time. It's only July.'

'I shall have the best bloody left hand in the business, at this rate, while the right hand messes up everything it's put at. Nobody ever wrote music like I can play—it wasn't intended that way round.'

Mick came and listened anxiously, while Ruth lay on the last patch of evening sun at the end of the garden with Lud beside her, trying to pretend it didn't matter, and knowing very well that their very lives depended on it coming right. She had a job as dogsbody to a solicitor's family in Hampstead, where she could take Lud with her, and with her money and Pat's driving wages they made just enough to pay the rent and barely live on. The job exhausted her, the solicitor's wife being an exacting woman and the mother of four spoilt small children, and Ruth came home with little appetite for Pat's moods. She tried very hard to be patient and sympathetic, but being so tired herself made her inevitably short-tempered. The weather was hot, and the end of the garden was the best place when Pat was practising, and Lud her dearest joy and comfort in what she euphemistically thought of as 'a bad patch'. It wasn't that she didn't understand how Pat felt, for she understood only too desperately well, remembering how the 'Winter Wind's' right hand had stormed through the keys the days before the accident, but she hadn't the strength to be patient and constructive in the face of Pat's bad humour: she merely felt mangled and at the end of her tether. Her money was essential, otherwise she would have saved her energy to pander to him. He hated her being away all the time. He was hopeless at feeding himself, even at getting something out when he had finished driving, and when she came home tired and with the baby-washing to do and Lud to see to, he was always ravenously hungry and demanding a meal. After supper he would go on practising, left hand only after the right had given out. Ruth couldn't decide whether he was a male chauvinist pig or a genius. 'Both,' Pat said, and went on practising. His right hand hurt him nearly all the time. Ruth wished she had the energy to make an effigy of Clarissa, so that she would have the satisfaction of sticking pins in it.

'It's improving fast,' Mick said, one evening. He dropped in fairly often, anxious about the programmes that were booked for the coming winter. 'Watching his bread and butter,' Pat called it. 'When you feel you're ready to play something to an audience, let me know. Old Cargill-Smith was asking.'

'He doesn't want me to accompany Clarissa, I hope?'

'No. She's in Vienna at the moment. He's got something up his sleeve—"Ask young Pennington to dinner," he said, "and we'll have a few people in. He can play." From anyone else it wouldn't mean much, but from him—it's different. I might find out more for you later. Just thought I'd drop you the hint, though. When do you think you might be able to manage it?'

'Autumn some time.'

'He feels he owes you something. We must make the most of it.'

'He doesn't owe me anything at all.'

'As you like. Clarissa owes you six months' working time—put it that way. He must feel responsible.'

Pat growled something.

'And your old professor, Mr. Hampton—he keeps inquiring about you. Doesn't want to interfere, but you might go and see him. Wouldn't do any harm.'

'It would do *me* harm,' Pat said angrily. 'I don't want to get involved. I've learned to do without him, because I had to. I don't want anything from him now. I have a bad conscience—I want to forget it.'

'Relax! Just be friends! Conscience needn't come into it at all. You don't have to be so prickly.'

'Well—it's the time factor. I've no time.'

'He said to tell you if you want to use his tape-recorder, or if you want him on the second piano, to practise the concerto—entirely friendly and well disposed.'

'That gives me an even worse conscience,' Pat said.

'It's up to you. Useful bloke, though.'

'Yes.'

'And you still want to go to Moscow?'

'Want to—yes. I've been going through some stuff—Stravinsky, Rachmaninov—reading it. But I don't want to make up my mind to go unless—well, there's so many ifs and buts at the moment. It's no good getting excited about it. Money, for one. And being good enough so it's not just a waste of time.'

Ruth noted that he put money as the first problem, and being good enough the second. She didn't think he lacked confidence, in spite of his hand. It was true that it was improving fast, but in his gigantic appetite for work Pat couldn't accept that it was fast enough.

For Ruth, the summer passed under the cloud of the solicitor's wife and the endless chores in the large, smart house. At least she had Lud with her. Even if she had been a highly efficient secretary by training, instead of a useless nonentity, she would hardly have been able to find a job where Lud would have been welcome alongside the typewriter, so she counted her blessings, trudging to and fro morning and evening with her pram from the seedy environs of the Finchley Road to the more elevated residences where such as she were welcome in the kitchen. Lud enjoyed every minute of it, and Ruth supposed she was happy. At least there was Pat to go home to every night, hungry or no. He wasn't yet in Moscow, or doing a recital in Ashton-under-Lyne or Swindon or Clacton-on-Sea. When he was, presumably, they would have enough money for her not to work. 'I don't know what I want!' She had to scold herself for the perversity of her feelings. But she was too tired to be objective.

'Look.'

Pat got up from the piano and showed her the card on the mantelpiece.

'Mr. and Mrs. Julian Cargill-Smith request the pleasure of the company of Mr. and Mrs. Patrick Pennington to dinner . . .' Underneath, scrawled in pen, 'Would you be prepared to play something after dinner? We should be so delighted if you would.'

'I've nothing to wear,' Ruth said.

'No. Nor have I. At least, only the trousers.'

'Go like that. Black trousers and red braces and your Beethoven medal.'

They got giggly. Ruth opened a tin of spaghetti, and Pat lay on the hearth-rug with Lud sitting on his chest, trying to pick up his shirt-buttons.

'What will you play?'

'Something to go with the coffee and liqueurs. Not to give them indigestion. I'll think about it. To be accompanied by the tinkling of teaspoons and the clicking of false teeth on wine-glasses. Performing monkey—free.'

'Mick said—'

'Oh, Mick wants to believe all sorts of things. What does Julian C. Smith care who plays at his dinner-party? I'm near, in need of a square meal and likely to be grateful. We'll go for the dinner. I'll borrow Wilf's dinner-jacket and perhaps Rosemary could find you something.'

'I'll ask her. It'll swamp me. She'll have to look after Lud too—unless we take him. We can take him in the pram, I should think.'

Lud pulled off a button and put it in his mouth. Pat scooped for it. 'I need that. Give it here. Hey, he's got a tooth. He bit me! Did you know he's got teeth?'

'Yes, of course. I told you in bed the other night and you said, quote, "I wonder if I could get the Petruschka Suite out of the library? Or perhaps the Professor's got a copy."'

'Did I? The Professor *has* got a copy. I remember now. I might go and see him. No, he'll be at this dinner, I daresay. I can ask him then. Do you think Lud still looks like me?'

'It's going off a bit, luckily.'

'He's wet.'

'He'll curl the hair on your chest. Give him to me. I'll change him. What have you been playing today?'

'Liszt. Chopin. All fireworks, and my hand doesn't hurt.'

'Splendid.'

They duly borrowed some clothes, and Rosemary agreed to have Lud for the evening. Ruth cut Pat's hair to coincide with the collar of the dinner-jacket and Mick picked them up in his car. Mick had just come back from Germany, and was talking about the possibilities of playing in Europe. Ruth was tired after her day with the solicitor's wife, and was looking forward to a good dinner, and hoping that the safety-pins that were holding her dress together didn't show at the back. Pat had a recital in Coventry in a fortnight's time, the first since the night Lud was born, and it sounded from the way that Mick was talking that things might be getting rosier.

'Thank God your hand has made it in time,' Mick was saying. 'That's the main problem solved. What are you playing tonight?'

'I'll sound out the old boy. I thought the Chopin preludes, or some quiet Brahms—whatever seems best.'

Mick opened his mouth to say something, but thought better of it and drove on in silence. The Hampstead house was all lights and smart cars outside. Mick parked and turned off the engine, and they sat for a moment, looking. Ruth realized, hungry as she was, that it was work, when all was said and done. Pat had gone quiet. It did seem a very long time since he had played in front of an audience.

'Is there a catch in this?' he said suddenly to Mick.

'If there is, it's entirely to your advantage, if you want to make use of it.'

They got out and went up to the front door, which was opened by Mrs. Cargill-Smith herself in a cloud of yellow chiffon.

'My dears, how lovely to see you again!' She kissed Ruth and shook hands with Mick and Pat. Ruth wondered if she had any qualms about taking Pat's hand, but she never then, or afterwards, made any reference to what had happened. 'Do let's go and find my husband. There are several people he wants you to meet tonight. Do you want the cloakroom, Ruth? It's over there, the last door.'

They had no coats to give the hovering maid, not having been able to produce a respectable garment, male or female, in the whole household, so Ruth went to comb her hair and gather up courage, feeling terrified of the first glimpse of what was in store, and Pat and Mick went into the sitting-room with their hostess. Ruth could not find anybody apparently under the age of forty, and was quite relieved to be nobbled by a comparatively harmless-looking old dear just inside the door who said to her, 'Are you a friend of Clarissa's? I understand Clarissa is in Vienna?'

'Yes, she is, and I'm not a friend of hers,' Ruth said, not even for the sake of politeness being able to admit to liking Clarissa.

'Such a relief, I have to admit,' the old lady said, confidentially. 'We won't have to listen to her play.'

Ruth felt apprehensive. A waiter offered her a drink and she took one nervously, and the woman continued, 'Such is parenthood, that our charming hosts, quite the most astute judges of instrumental playing that I know, are completely blind to how well below their own standards dear Clarissa falls. She is impossibly spoilt, I'm afraid.'

'Yes,' Ruth agreed.

'I understand there is to be some music tonight, that's why I wanted to be sure about Clarissa. Now I can look forward to the after-dinner interlude with real enjoyment. Clarissa apart, one is never bored by music in this house. Judging by who is here, I suspect that whoever plays tonight will be very well worth listening to; Julian won't want to lose his reputation in such company.'

'What do you mean?' Ruth asked nervously. She looked into the room, to see if there was anybody she recognized, but the company looked to her extremely sober and dull, mostly rather quiet elderly men and very well-dressed women. Pat, standing by his host, stood out by reason of his hair and his youth, but looked more sober than anyone in the room, in fact positively miserable. Ruth recognized his pre-recital withdrawal symptoms and realized that the situation was a bit tricky for him, having to be polite because the circumstances demanded it; it wasn't a job for money tonight, but a . . . Ruth felt her stomach give a nasty lurch.

'Who is here?' she asked the woman.

'Some extremely discerning people, my dear. The man with his back to us, talking to Julian, is Ernest Brunow from New York, the conductor of—' She proceeded to list several names, some of which even Ruth had heard of, all in the musical world. She remembered Mick's saying, it seemed a long·time ago, something about Cargill-Smith's saying he would have 'a few people in' when Pat was ready to play, but she hadn't somehow connected it with this invitation and Mrs. Cargill-Smith's scrawled 'we should be so delighted . . .' It was a bit different from playing to a lot of wet mackintoshes in Wembley. Had Pat had any idea? He probably had by now. He was looking desperately serious, being introduced to a man with white hair and a white moustache. Ruth excused herself from the elderly woman and sought out Mick, who was talking to Professor Hampton.

'Did you know? You didn't tell Pat—' she started.

'Tell him what?' Mick was looking amused.

'What important people would be here—to hear him play.'

'Isn't it lovely!' Mick said. 'I guessed. I thought there might be one or two, but Julian has surpassed himself.'

He was obviously delighted, and not at all worried.

'You could have warned him!'

'Dear Ruth, I did all I could. But he is so spiky—you know it— if there had been any suggestion of Julian's doing him a favour, he would have gone communist on us. You know how he is.'

'Julian is very conscience-stricken about what Clarissa did,' the Professor said. 'For my own part I'm surprised no one has physically attacked Pat before now, the way he treats people, but—' he shrugged and smiled. 'He brings the most fearful consequences upon himself, and somehow, for him, it all comes right. It wouldn't for anybody else, but for Pat life is like a game of snakes and ladders. Down to the depths, and then the struggle back. I wouldn't say that he thrives on it, but it appears to do him no harm. I suspect that his upbringing has something to do with it, and it taught him this *tenacity* . . . one can only admire, in spite of everything. And his work has this extraordinary strength and feeling, out of such difficulties—no one else I have taught has possessed this elemental quality to such a degree. Allied, of course,

186

to the impeccable musicianship which I taught him.' The Professor smiled. 'What have we to worry about? Dear Ruth, stop looking so worried.'

Ruth was amazed at the Professor's speech. Neither he nor Mick was in the slightest way anxious about the evening's work for Pat—they who cared more for his progress than anyone else apart from herself. Had she got it wrong, all this time, that she worried so for Pat? She only took it from Pat himself, and how she knew he felt. And yet his mentors here had such confidence that they were laughing at her doubts. The Professor put his arm round her.

'Come, it will be a lovely evening. You have nothing to worry about. Didn't I once tell you about Pat rising to important occasions? It's the greatest talent of the lot. You are a very lucky girl, Ruth. You are looking very charming. Pat is a very lucky man too.'

Ruth thought the Professor had had too much to drink. But he did not appear to be drunk in any other way. Perhaps it was herself. Mick said to her softly, 'You see that man Pat is talking to now?'

She looked and nodded.

'That man is prepared to finance any young pianist he feels worth encouraging to go to Moscow. He told me so himself.'

Ruth looked more closely. Pat was staring at the man's shoes, scowling.

'Fortunately his judgement will be based on Pat's playing, not on his drawing-room manners,' the Professor said.

He and Mick both laughed.

Ruth looked round, still feeling far from serene about the evening's eventualities. The way both Mick and the Professor appeared to see Pat diverged sharply from her own experience of living with him. This bland optimism overlooked entirely Pat's own day-by-day worries: they only saw the result. Although they knew it happened, they did not actually live with the exacting concentration that Pat brought to bear on his work every day. They did not sit in on his dawn starts and listen to his hardest current problems being given the treatment, as she did, and know intimately the parts that had caused him the hardest thinking; they did not witness the fraught allocations of their two wage-packets to the most pressing of their debts, her deliberations over the most economical ingredients with which to assuage Pat's healthy appetite, their ridiculous borrowing of acceptable clothes for any out-of-the-way events, like tonight's, the constant 'borrowing' of gas-meter coins and shunning of the occasional temptations, like a good film, or a drink at the local with Wilf and Rosemary, even her having to cut Pat's hair tonight—it was miles away from the Professor's avuncular comments about having nothing to worry about, and being lucky. They both got so tired and so screwed-up and Pat wouldn't talk and Lud cried all through some punctilious pianissimos so that Pat threw the music across the room and went up to see Wilf . . . What did the Professor know?

They went in to dinner and the Professor took her arm and said, 'Perhaps you could both spare the time to come and see me one day next week? I would like to feel that any differences we had in the past are quite forgotten now.'

'Yes, of course.'

But she couldn't think about next week, only now. Pat was next to her at the dinner-table, and Mick on her other side. Pat had Mrs. Cargill-Smith on his left, and presumably she understood about his not feeling talkative, so Ruth was relieved. The Professor was opposite, next to the Moscow financier's wife. Were they really lucky? She couldn't stop trying to work it out. Only that she wouldn't change anything. And so terrifyingly precarious to think that good fortune or bad depended only on what Pat was able to do within the next hour or so. She could only see it like that, not as the Professor saw it; she didn't have his confidence. And whether Pat had it or not she couldn't tell. Pat wasn't giving anything away. He wasn't eating a thing, nor drinking.

'Do you feel all right?' she asked him.

He didn't answer. He sat crumbling his bread roll into little pellets and piling them round the edges of his plate. His fingers were moving all the time. Ruth realized that she felt as sick as he did, although she was so hungry and the food was delicious. Mick was saying to her, 'Of course, everybody comes here for the food. It's renowned throughout London. And what with all the wine, whoever plays afterwards can only be a roaring success. So don't waste your opportunities.' It was true, Ruth thought, she had never seen anything like it out of a film, with candles all down the table and the food served by waiters from silver dishes and a different wine with every course. Just like an Edwardian dinner.

She began to wonder if it was all quite real. It took ages, and Pat's mounds of pellets grew like fortifications, and Ruth began to think she had drunk too much, she felt so tensed up. She tried to think what she would feel like if it was only a dinner-party and no piano-playing to think about, and she realized that she would be laughing and gorging just like Mick, and enjoying the Professor's compliments. But linked so closely to Pat, she could only feel with him, and this time it was agonizing. Would it always be? Was that part of the luck? Yes, she thought. If it all came right, and the luck saw them through, it would one day be like this waiting in the wings of the Royal Festival Hall. It would be like this the first time he played the Brahms concerto. But perhaps by then the confidence would have grown, and feeling sick would no longer be part of the job.

'Coffee and liqueurs will be served in the music-room,' Mrs. Cargill-Smith announced at last. The table was a sea of crumpled napkins, the silver candelabra sailing serenely above. Everyone got up and began to drift out across the hall to the music-room, but Pat went up the stairs on his own. Ruth followed him. He went into the bathroom on the first floor and shut himself in the lavatory, where she could hear him being sick. She went and opened the window and leaned out, looking out on the garden. There was the scent of late roses; she could see the beds of them below, immaculately tended, the pale, opened blooms gleaming in the light that flooded from the house. She had been here before, the first time she had met Clarissa, and Pat had been playing Beethoven downstairs. She had looked out of the window at these same roses, and not known then what was going to happen at all. It was the same day that Pat had been taken to prison. It seemed a very long time ago. The night outside the house was calm, with the smell of autumn that reminded her of home. It was very comforting. She suddenly felt that the confidence that had so surprised her before dinner was not so misplaced after all.

Pat came out and ran the taps into the wash-basin and leaned on them, dangling his hands in the water. Ruth took a Cargill-Smith face-cloth from its elegant gold ring and handed it to him.

'It's all right,' she said. 'I know it is. The last time I was here, in this bathroom, do you remember?' No, she supposed he didn't, for he had been downstairs.

'Pat.' She put her arm across his shoulders. 'It will be all right. I know it will.'

He said, 'Don't worry about me. I can't help it.'

'There isn't anything to worry about.'

He straightened up and dried himself. Ruth found him a comb in her handbag and he combed his hair and she did hers. They looked at each other and Ruth smiled. Pat's expression reminded her of the day in the clinic when he had gone away with Dr. Harper, as if he had wanted her to go with him and hold his hand. But then, as now, there was absolutely nothing she could do to help in the thing that mattered. Only on the sidelines. That was her job for life. She was beginning to get the hang of it.

'Come on. The old girl will think you've run out on her.'

He gave her a faint smile, and they went downstairs. Mrs. Cargill-Smith was just coming out of the music-room door. Her face beamed at them.

'There you are. Splendid! We're all ready for you. Everyone knows who you are—I don't think you need any introduction. Go straight over to the piano and tell them what you're going to play. Then it's all yours.'

They went into the room. Ruth could not get any farther than inside the door, where there was a convenient chair, but Pat threaded his way through the semi-circle of chairs and coffee-tables and went to the piano. Ruth knew he would waste no time at all.

He turned to the audience and said, 'Liszt's sonata in B Minor.'

Ruth bit her tongue with shock. Then she remembered what the Professor had said about 'the greatest talent of all', remembered that there wasn't anything to be afraid of, and sank back in her chair. The first quiet staccato notes sounded across the room. He could have gone on being a chauffeur, after all. It was only what he had chosen.